DARKENED SKIES BOOK FIVE

TOWARD DAWNING LIGHT

H.E. BAUMAN

This is a work of fiction. Names, characters, places, and incidents either are the product of the author's imagination or are used fictitiously. Any resemblance to actual persons, living or dead, events, or locales is entirely coincidental.

First paperback edition October 2024

Cover design by MiblArt

Map by Cartographybird Maps

Jeanine Harrell of Indie Edits with Jeanine

ISBN 979-8-9888024-9-5 (paperback)

ISBN 978-1-965479-00-1 (hardcover)

ISBN 979-8-9888024-8-8 (ebook)

www.hebauman.com

Content Warnings

Thank you for picking up *Toward Dawning Light*, the final book in the Darkened Skies series. If you have not read the previous four books, you will need to do that before you read this book. The series must be read in order.

The story includes themes and events that may not be suitable for some readers:

- Fantasy and magical violence, including artillery and other "modern" weaponry, used both in war scenarios and against civilians

- Blood and injuries

- Stalking and threats

- Nightmares, anxiety, and PTSD

- References to torture, hypothetical sexual assault, parental death, mild alcohol consumption, current war, historical wars, and rebellion

Please take care of yourself as you read.

THE NORTH SEA
TALMARIS
GRAND DUCHY OF NOVARIA
ZINDIR
THE ZAIKUD EMPIRE
MACADIAN MOUNTAINS
POSAN
FORT AVALON
NARIZON
FORT BLACKROCK
CORSYCA
FORT IRONWING
KINGDOM OF DELIA
SAPOI
THE WESTERN SEA
CAPITAL CITIES
CITIES
NOTABLE TOWNS
FORTS
MEMATOS
ILESOURIA

THE LOST ISLES
IRVINA
MANTARES MOUNTAINS
THE HELOSIAN EMPIRE
THE BADLANDS
RING OF FIRE
TINALE BAY
KALAMA
SEZIA
REPUBLIC OF TORNAMA
THASIA
KATAVENA
TAIPOLI ISLANDS
THE EASTERN SEA
THE SOUTHERN OCEAN

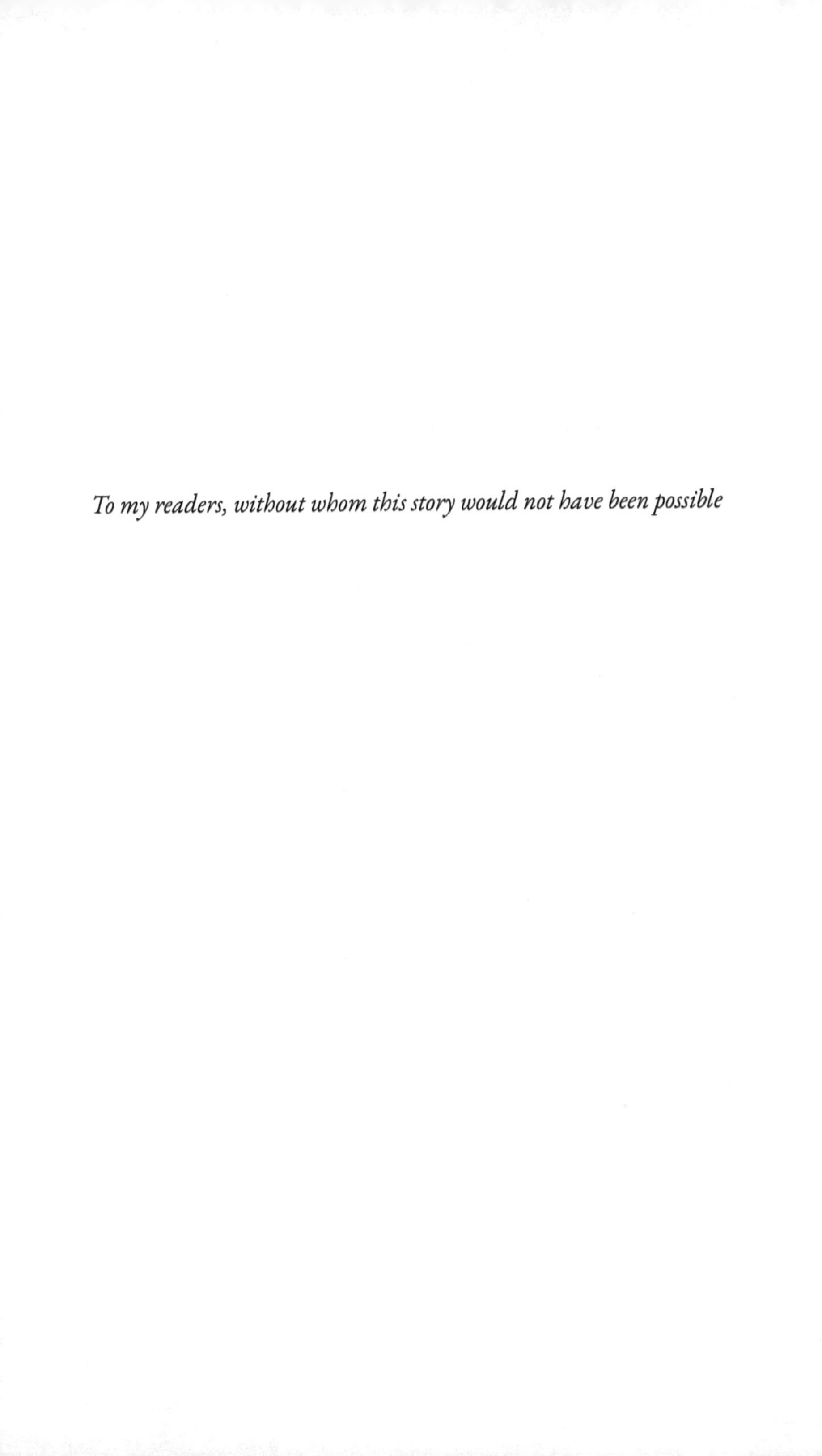

To my readers, without whom this story would not have been possible

Chapter 1

There, in a prison cell just a few feet away from Astrea, was the man she never—not once—expected to meet.

Her father.

His face was so foreign but familiar. They had the same round chin. Their hair, too, was the same black-brown. Even their pale skin had the same rosy undertones.

But those eyes, the iciest of blues, like the ones she'd only ever seen behind The One's mask.

Astrea's breath caught in her chest, a painful stab right to her lungs.

Her father. Her father. Her father.

The only consolation was that he was no void mage.

No, his emotions were open to her now. Curiosity and relief tangled around him in shades of green, stark against the dark stone walls of the cell.

And those eyes. They were trained on her even as Lucian interrogated him. Even as Marko stood to one side, ever watchful. Even as Jin, prince of Helosia and Novaria, stood right next to her. Valen hadn't looked away from Astrea.

"Why are you really here?" Lucian asked.

"I already told you," said Valen. "I'm here to see my daughter. I heard she was looking for me."

"How did you hear that?"

"Whispers spread eventually," replied Valen. "Surely you know that as a military man."

"Do you have a contact in Irvina?"

"Not directly, but word got back to me."

"Could you be any more vague, Mister . . . ?"

"Ramkas," Valen said. "Valen Ramkas."

Astrea's chest tightened again. Jin reached for her hand and laced their fingers together. She didn't dare move a muscle.

"Mister Ramkas." The words rolled off Lucian's tongue with disdain. "Can you prove your identity?"

"No, unfortunately. I've been living away from most of society for a while now."

"How convenient," Marko drawled. "You show up now, after all these years, with no identification, no witnesses, no one to corroborate your story."

Valen's stare, while intense and uncomfortable, didn't suggest to Astrea that he meant any harm. But what did she know? Her head was so fuzzy from exhaustion and grief that she didn't trust herself to be a good judge of anything.

As she stalked toward the door tucked away in one corner, Jin's heavy concern followed her. He said her name, but Astrea ignored him and swept past the Novarian guards lining the hall outside. She headed straight for the next door, taking in the cool morning air as it drifted over her skin.

"Az." Jin's large hand settled on her shoulder as he caught up to her.

"I can't do this," she whispered. "I just buried Saros. I can't do this."

"Then you don't have to."

Astrea's body begged her to run away, yet she was so weak she thought she might collapse onto the very ground in front of Jin. Her body and mind were at war, one begging for release and the other begging for rest.

"I have to," she whispered again. "I don't have a choice. He's my father."

"We don't *know* he's your father," Jin said.

"We have the same chin. The same skin, the same hair. He has the same eyes as The One." Though Astrea wasn't sure of anything anymore, that much was clear. That man in that cell was most certainly her father.

"Alright, well, you still don't have to deal with this right now." Jin slung his arm around her shoulders. "Let Lucian do his work. Come on."

She let out a weak sound of protest, then said, "I have to speak with him eventually."

"And you will, but right now, let's get some coffee. Maybe he'll actually give Lucian his full attention if we aren't in there."

"Yeah, maybe," Astrea mumbled. "I feel like I can't even think straight."

"Understandably."

With Jin's arm still around her shoulders, Astrea started for the officers' lodgings. They made their way straight to the dining room. Some of the fort's officers were taking their breakfast there, chatting away in low voices. A radio was even playing, broadcasting pro mage sports news from Talmaris.

And three very important people were huddled at a table in the corner: Adi, Sarsali, and Balthazar. Jin steered Astrea that way. She tried and failed to muster up a smile as they approached the table, then tried and failed again when Jin snagged one of the empty chairs from a nearby table for her to sit next to Sarsali. She plopped down onto it and slumped forward.

"He wasn't giving Lucian much," Astrea said before anyone else could speak. "I can't believe . . ."

"Nor can I," said Sarsali, placing a gentle hand on Astrea's forearm. "The timing feels off."

"First Theo's offer, then Nazarov showing up in Helosia, now your father . . ." Balthazar shook his head. "Either we're incredibly lucky he's shown up, or things are about to get worse."

Adi drummed his fingers on the table. "I hate to be the one to ask, but could he be working with the Paragon?"

Astrea had wondered that, too. "He's not a void mage as far as I can tell. Not that it means anything." No, plenty of non-void mages worked for the Paragon, too. "Oh, skies, what if he's here to try to make me help him overthrow Nazarov?"

Part of Astrea was relieved that her father was alive. After all, that meant *he* was technically the next leader of the Paragon, void mage or not. And although Nazarov would surely still target Astrea . . . Well, at least Nazarov would have to contend with Valen, too, whether he was on Astrea's side or not.

Grabbing the copper pot in the middle of the table, Jin poured Astrea a cup of steaming coffee. He nudged it to her, then poured a second for himself. "Hopefully Lucian can find that out."

"Why show up now, though?" Balthazar leaned back into his chair and folded his arms loosely over his abdomen.

"He claims he lives far away from society and only just heard whispers that I was looking for him." Astrea pinched the bridge of her nose. All she wanted was a few more days to try to recover from the shock of what had happened in Helosia. A few more days to try to mend her heart enough to carry on with the mission.

"Maybe . . ." Adi's lips pursed. "Maybe it's not a bad thing he's here. Maybe he knows something about the Paragon that will help us figure out Nazarov's next move. Assuming he's not working with Nazarov, of course."

"Maybe," Jin said absently. He held his coffee in one hand, the other settled on Astrea's thigh as he drew tiny circles with his thumb.

"I think you all should get some rest." Blue sadness tangled around Sarsali as she added, "Some real rest, now that everything's settled."

How was Astrea supposed to do that with her father so close? After twenty-four years of wondering who he was, how was she supposed to go take a nap?

But her body yearned for that rest. She could barely keep her eyes open. Maybe, if she got a little sleep, she'd be able to help Lucian get some answers. Besides, Cressida would need her.

"I should go check on Cress," Astrea said.

"Don't." Balthazar shook his head. "She doesn't want anyone around while she's with the healers."

"But I'm a healer."

"And she asked that everyone stay away for now," Sarsali said.

Astrea frowned. Not go check on Cressida? She'd gotten plenty of medical intervention in Thasia after the initial surgery to repair what they could of her arm, but Cressida was going to need healing for a while. Losing her hand like that . . .

"Are you sure?" Astrea asked.

"She's alright," Sarsali said gently, though yellow worry trickled into her aura. "Or so she insists, and I must take her at her word." She smiled, but it didn't reach her green eyes. "Now please, go get some sleep, sweetheart. I need both of you to actually listen to me."

"I always listen to you," Astrea said, earning her a look. "Fine, but only for an hour."

"I'll come wake you, don't worry," she said. "Go on. All of you. Balthazar and I will make sure you're up in an hour."

After draining the last of their coffee, Astrea, Jin, and Adi all left the dining room. Rather than going upstairs, they went to the royal airship, the one that had been meant to bring them all back to Talmaris that very morning.

Until Valen had shown up.

When they reached the empty airship's second level and Adi started to go his separate way, Jin said, "Wait." Adi paused, a sheen of gray confusion coating his limbs. "Are you really going to sleep?"

"I planned to," Adi said.

"Then follow me."

"Why?" he asked. "My things are in my room—"

"Adi." Jin's voice left little room for argument.

Astrea was confused now, too, especially when Jin walked right past their room and headed for the final door at the end of the hall. The room Eliana and Nicos had been sharing.

"What are we doing in here?" Adi asked as Jin pushed the door open.

Inside was tidy, neater than Eliana usually kept her space. Maybe that was Nicos's doing. But other than that, the room was relatively unremarkable aside from the large bed and nicer bed linens.

"I don't want any Novarians around right now," Jin said. "And I don't want any of us to have to stand guard. We'll just sleep in Ellie's bed."

"I can stand guard," Adi said.

"No." Again, Jin's tone left little room for argument, though it wasn't mean. Sighing, Jin rubbed the back of his neck. "I don't trust Nazarov not to show up, but we *need* some sleep, and—"

"And more of us means better odds if he does pop in," Adi said. "Yeah, I get it. I'm not going to argue." With a yawn, he strode toward the bed. "But I'm taking an end. I'm not getting between the two of you," he said, motioning to Astrea and Jin.

It was surely meant to be a joke, but Astrea couldn't even muster a fake smile. She crawled into bed, which was softer than the one she'd been sharing with Jin and certainly bigger. Maybe not perfectly large enough for the three of them, but if Jin held her close, they could make it work.

He settled down behind her, curling his body around hers. The mattress dipped as Adi slid in behind Jin.

"Not so bad," Adi said with a groan.

Jin mumbled something in return, but Astrea couldn't even make it out as her exhaustion finally took her under.

Too many limbs tangled with Astrea's. Not just Jin's but Adi's, too, somehow reaching Astrea as he spooned Jin. Cold air prickled her skin, but both men were warm, too warm.

"Astrea," Sarsali whispered, shaking Astrea's ankle.

Blinking against the daylight streaming in through the windows near the ceiling, Astrea pushed up on her elbow as best she could. Sarsali stood at the edge of the bed, wringing her hands together.

As Astrea started to speak, Sarsali shook her head and brought a finger to her lips. She tilted her head toward the door, an invitation. With great effort, Astrea managed to pry Jin's arms from around her waist. She slipped out of bed, leaving him and Adi to rest for a bit longer. Her sleepy mind called forth a memory of their time at the ruins out west so many months ago, Adi's jokes about loving to cuddle. It seemed to be true.

Shaking herself mentally, she joined Sarsali in the hall and closed the door halfway. Her mind was static, just a slow, sludge-like mess as she tried to focus on the energy around her. Sarsali's grief and anxiety. The heavy sleep behind her. The curiosity, boredom, and fear of whoever was patrolling around outside the ship.

Astrea scrubbed her face. "What time is it?"

"Half past one."

"Half past one? No, we were only supposed to sleep for an hour."

"I couldn't wake you." Sarsali pressed her lips together. "The three of you looked so tired. It didn't seem right."

Astrea scrubbed at her face again; there was nothing to be done about that now. Besides, she hadn't slept at all the night before, having spent hours and hours on the beach by the lake as she watched Saros's pyre burn. The few hours she'd napped clearly hadn't helped much. "Any news from Lucian?" she asked.

"None. And since nothing else important seemed to be going on, I thought it best to let you be. Cressida's resting in her own room, too. Told me to tell you not to worry about her."

Yawning, Astrea nodded. She hadn't had a chance to see Sarsali much in the last few days. As soon as they'd gotten back from Thasia, Astrea had made whatever small plans she'd been able to for Saros's funeral, and outside of those decisions, she hadn't been receptive to much conversation from anyone.

Now, as she stared at the woman who had helped Saros raise her, and as sleep receded from her mind, Astrea really took Sarsali in. The growing bags under her eyes. The pallor to her deep bronze skin. That midnight blue grief clinging to her like a storm cloud.

"I'm sorry," Astrea whispered. "I'm sorry I couldn't help Cress or save him."

"Oh, my sweet, sweet girl." Sarsali pulled Astrea into a tight hug, like she had many times over the years when Astrea had been just a child. "You have nothing to apologize for."

Astrea buried her face in Sarsali's shoulder. She was all cried out, but maybe she could ignore the world for a second longer.

"Balthazar told me it was Kaius's doing," Sarsali whispered. "You can't blame yourself for that."

"It was more than that," Astrea croaked. "It was his vision, Sarsali. The one from that day at the train station in Kalama fourteen years ago. I was trying to save Jin, and Kaius was aiming for *me*. Saros intervened, to save me, but he . . ." She sucked in a shaky breath. "He took his own life so I couldn't even try to heal him. He kept telling me to save Jin."

Cold anger and sharp gratitude pierced Astrea's gut, a confusing and nauseating mix as the blue surrounding Sarsali brightened. She pushed away from Astrea enough to cup her cheek.

"That is not your fault," Sarsali said, voice both firm and achingly gentle. "Saros was many things, and he always had a bit of a martyr complex."

"But if I'd just tried *harder*—"

"Knowing you, my dear, you had already done everything you could."

"I felt him slit his own throat," Astrea choked out. "I felt it."

She shook her head. "I know he was trying to spare you, but . . . I can't help but be a little angry with him, even now."

Astrea was angry with Saros, too. Angry for taking the choice away from her again, even if she *couldn't* have saved him. And perhaps grateful, too, that he didn't have to suffer the effects of aetherium for longer than necessary.

It still hurt. It was still confusing and painful and gut wrenching. He was gone. She would never see him again. She would never share another meal with him, walk Kalama's streets in search of cinnamon pancakes with him, or even find him up late in his observatory. He was gone, forever.

"But no matter what, Balthazar and I will always be here for you," Sarsali said. "No matter what. We're still family."

Still family. The Nikaphoroses would always be her family. So would Jin and Eliana. Adi. Nicos. And the rest of the team were becoming family, too. She wasn't alone, even if it felt like her entire world had been torn apart again and again and again these last months.

"There's so much I didn't get to say to him before he left," Astrea whispered. She'd never told him about what Nazarov and the Paragon had done to her. She'd never told him most of what had happened before they reunited. "And I didn't even get to tell him I loved him."

"He knew you loved him, sweetheart."

"I was so angry with him all summer . . ."

"And he still knew," Sarsali said. "Before you came back to Kalama, we were still having dinners as often as we could. And he always talked about how much he missed you and hoped you were safe . . . and all that he regretted. He hated that he'd caused you pain."

Astrea wiped at her dry eyes. "Thank you for always taking care of both of us."

"You never have to thank me for that."

"Still, I can't thank you and Balthazar enough," Astrea said. "Look what being friends with our family has dragged you into."

"There's no way any of us could ever have predicted this," Sarsali said. "Even Saros asking us to keep your secret . . . well, I never would have imagined it spiraling like this. Some things are beyond our control, and I would never change knowing you just so this hadn't come to pass."

Would Astrea give up knowing the Nikaphoroses—and everyone else from Kalama—to avoid all of this? It didn't matter. She couldn't change all that had happened, not in recent months nor centuries before when her ancestors had led the Paragon in the Great Wars.

"I should go wake the others," Astrea said quietly. Jin would probably need to talk to Eliana about when they were going to go back to the capital.

Sarsali patted Astrea's shoulder, then headed for the stairs. "I'll make sure there's coffee for the three of you. Take all the time you need."

CHAPTER 2

After her talk with Sarsali and after waking the others up, Astrea had decided it was time to check in with Commander Lucian. Besides, Jin *had* needed to speak with Eliana, and Adi had gone to check on the rest of the team.

Astrea needed to just deal with her father—Valen—and figure out what he wanted.

Pushing her shoulders back, she smoothed the front of her dark blue dress and exited the empty airship. It was already midday, and crisp—almost cold—autumn temperatures had settled over the Novarian forest. The breeze tickled her skin, making Astrea shiver.

She was halfway across the courtyard when she spotted the very people she was looking for: Commander Lucian and Marko. Lucian's features were pinched, but Marko seemed almost relaxed as he folded his arms loosely over his abdomen.

As she crossed the distance to them, Lucian motioned for her to move in closer. He kept his voice low as he said, "We're making very little progress with him."

"And?" Astrea asked.

"We've handed the situation over to Vernie for the time being," Lucian said.

"Why Vernie?" Astrea asked. Vernie, the other Souleater at Fort Silverpine, was a talented mage, but they were not whom Astrea would've assumed would take over the interrogation. If anything, she figured Lucian would've had Jin or Zephyrine step in. Certainly Zephyrine. Maybe even the fort's commander.

"Vernie will get the answers we need," Lucian said.

Marko shifted his weight from one foot to the other. His wall was tight. So was Lucian's.

"What do you mean they'll get the answers we need?" she asked, her stomach constricting into a painful knot. "What does that mean?"

Lucian shrugged. "Vernie is good at their job."

Astrea didn't like the implication in Lucian's words. "I don't doubt that," she said, "but I would like to speak to my father alone."

"Are you sure?" Lucian asked. "We still don't know anything about him."

"He doesn't seem dangerous," Marko said. When Lucian glared at him, he added, "What? He doesn't."

"We don't know that for sure." Turning to Astrea, Lucian said, "It's dangerous. He's still entirely unknown to us."

"And I'm strong enough to fight him off," she argued. Hopefully it wouldn't come to that. "And he's behind bars, right?"

"He is, but—"

"But nothing," Astrea said, trying to command the same tone Jin had earlier, in charge but not unkind. "Let me speak with him. I'll see if I can get any information out of him before Vernie tries their own methods." Methods Astrea was sure she wouldn't want to hear about.

"Fine," Lucian said. "But all three of us will be right outside the door, and you are not to go near the cell."

"Fine," Astrea said. "Lead the way."

With an exaggerated sigh, Lucian spun on his heel and started back for the building he'd just left. As Astrea followed, Marko fell into step beside her.

"Don't mind the commander," he murmured. "He gets exceptionally grumpy when he hasn't had enough sleep."

"I didn't think that it was possible for his mood to be any worse," Astrea replied, earning her a smirk.

Inside, all of the guards stood at attention as Lucian swept past, his boots barely making a sound on the wood floors. When they finally reached the door that would lead into the brig, Lucian turned to Astrea.

"Remember, no going near him. We'll be right outside," the commander said.

Astrea nodded.

With that, Lucian stepped into the room. "Vernie," he said, "that will be all for now."

Vernie, near the bars but not inside the cell, fixed their attention on the door. With one raised eyebrow, they took several steps back. "Very well."

"Good luck," Marko said to Astrea as he closed the door after him and his two colleagues.

When the door clicked shut, Astrea sucked in a deep breath and pivoted toward the cell. The room was small, and the single cell was even smaller. And there, sitting on a cot in one corner, was her father.

His dark, floppy hair was a bit mussed, and fatigue rolled off him in waves, but Valen looked no worse for the wear despite suffering Lucian's questions for hours. There was even an empty tray on the floor, clearly once used to give him food, water, and even a cup of coffee. The narrowest of windows was nestled right near the ceiling and let in a little sunlight. The overhead light was on, too.

It was certainly better than the cell *she'd* had while with the Paragon.

"You came back," Valen said, pushing himself to his feet. His voice was deep, rumbly almost.

Crossing her arms over her chest, Astrea leaned on the wall across from the cell. She stayed there, several feet away despite her father moving toward the bars. "I wanted to speak with you."

"I want to speak with you, too." He gave her the smallest smile as he asked, "How's your mother?"

"Dead."

Gray confusion and deep blue grief swirled around Valen. His thick, dark eyebrows furrowed. "What?"

"She's dead," Astrea snapped. "She died fourteen years ago, and it seems your brother had something to do with it."

"My brother?"

"Yes, The One, the leader of the Paragon."

"You know about that?" Valen asked.

"My mother's brother is dead, too," Astrea said. "Not at the Paragon's hand but thanks to aetherium. Do *you* know about *that*?"

He shook his head. "No . . ."

"No, you don't know?" Her own anger singed her skin, all the way from her toes to the tips of her ears.

"No, I mean it wasn't supposed to happen this way," Valen whispered.

"What, are you a Stargazer or something?"

Valen's eyes narrowed. "You're angry with me."

"You show up after twenty-four years and suddenly want to ask how my mother is?" Astrea's voice cracked. "Well, your brother seems to have killed her, poisoned her maybe. Oh, and your brother's dead, too."

"What?" Valen straightened a little. "When? How?"

"A while ago, not far from here. In a fight. With me and a man named Victor Nazarov."

"Who?"

The gray confusion undulating around Valen seemed genuine enough. And besides, Nazarov wasn't that much older than Astrea. He would've been a child when Valen left Roxana. Maybe Valen really didn't know him.

"He's the new leader of the Paragon."

"But it's a hereditary role," Valen said.

"Yes."

"He's not . . ." Valen blinked rapidly. "My brother didn't finally procreate, did he?"

"Not to my knowledge," Astrea said. Nazarov wouldn't need her to legitimize his rule if he were The One's blood. "Where have you been for the last twenty-four years?"

"Me?" Valen almost balked at the question. "Far away from here."

"Why'd you leave?"

The corners of Valen's lips twitched, almost like he was fighting off a frown. "It's a complicated story."

"Good thing we have time."

Valen swallowed hard. "I loved your mother, Astrea. I hope you know I'm being truthful when I say that. Tell me, are you gifted with magic like she was?"

Astrea couldn't determine if he was telling the truth about loving her mother. But she didn't see the harm in telling him about her magic. He would surely find out one way or another. "I'm a Souleater."

He scoffed. "Skies, no you're not."

"Yes, I am. Would you like me to show you?"

"That wasn't supposed to happen . . ."

"Like you can control what type of magic I inherited? If I would inherit it at all?" Astrea snapped.

"I hoped you wouldn't," he said.

Hope. He *hoped* she wouldn't inherit souleating. *Ridiculous.*

"Well, I did." She met his gaze, that same ice cold blue as The One's. But where The One's eyes had been hard, Valen's were softer around the edges, kinder and surrounded by tiny wrinkles, almost like he must have laughed a lot over the course of his life. "You don't seem to be a void mage."

"I am not," Valen said. "A disappointment to my family."

"Is that why you impregnated my mother? To force the Paragon's so-called prophecy about the sun and moon to come true?"

"What?" Gray confusion and steel pain undulated around his pale skin, and hot anger blazed across Astrea's cheeks and arms. "Is that what you think?"

"Seems reasonable to me," she said. "You found a Lightbringer, got her pregnant, and come from a line of void mages. And then out I came, a Souleater. Your brother was the leader of the Paragon, and you just said you were a disappointment. Maybe you tried to create the moon to bring some kind of honor back to yourself."

"Skies, no, I loved your mother!" Valen exclaimed. "I'll tell you everything if you give me a moment."

Astrea sank back against the wall opposite his cell, exhausted just by the effort of standing there. But she couldn't let him see that. She pushed her shoulders back.

Valen ran a hand through his dark hair, then shook his head. "My not being a mage was a disappointment to our family legacy, but I was the younger brother. I left home when I could and tried to make a life for myself. Cato—The One, as you know him—took over from our mother when she died. I was about your age when she passed."

Astrea hadn't even considered that she might have grandparents out there. Her maternal grandparents had passed before Astrea was born.

"He let me leave and said I would drain the Paragon's resources by staying around since I couldn't contribute to his reign. I left and settled in northern Helosia, then took on a role at a modest business as the bookkeeper. That turned into more, and I soon found myself traveling between Helosia and Novaria. Irvina, mostly, but some other small towns as well."

Astrea swallowed hard. That was what she and Saros had learned from her mother's old colleague, that Valen had been a merchant of some kind.

"One day, I twisted my ankle very badly while in Irvina. One of the people I was doing business with called for a healer, and your mother showed up. That was how we met." He glanced up at Astrea, his expression softening even more. "I did not seek her out, I swear to you."

"And?" she asked.

"And things progressed quickly from there. I'd thought I was stable enough to take care of her *and* you when she got pregnant early in the relationship. I was going to move to Irvina, but I had to settle a few things back in Helosia first. And when I returned to my apartment there, I had a letter waiting for me from my brother. I hadn't heard from him in several years.

"He wanted to see me. So I went. He wanted to bring me back into the fold as an advisor, and he was especially pleased with the wealth I was building for myself."

"He was following you?" Astrea asked.

"I couldn't be sure, but as soon as I took that meeting with him, I knew I'd messed everything up, Astrea. I couldn't bring your mother into that mess that was my family."

Right. The "mess" that was his family. Not the mess that was the Paragon and its plans for destruction and anarchy.

Valen's fingers dipped below the collar of his shirt. He removed a gold chain, and on the very end was a small pendant. He slid the necklace off and offered it to Astrea through the bars. "Open it." When she hesitated, he said, "Please, open it."

Reluctantly, Astrea took a step forward and snatched the necklace—a locket—from him. Inside was a sepia-tone photograph, clearly worn with age. And there was Roxana.

She looked so young, younger than Astrea was now. Her round face, plump figure, and short stature. The way her eyes and nose crinkled when she smiled. And next to her was a much younger Valen, grinning as wide as she was.

A knot tightened around Astrea's heart. She couldn't breathe.

"It was the only thing I allowed myself to keep of her," Valen said. "She gifted it to me the day she told me she was pregnant. And after that meeting with my brother, I knew I couldn't go back to her."

"Did you go back to work for your brother?" Astrea asked, still staring at the photograph. Her parents looked so happy.

"No. I could not make myself go back to that. I promised him I would, that I just needed to wrap some things up for my business partner and cash out all my accounts. I told him I'd bring the money to him when I was done. I told him it would be for the Paragon to use. And so he let me go.

"After that, I rushed to cash out everything I could. I returned to Irvina under the guise of doing business, but I deposited the money into an account for your mother and then went to see her again. She didn't know it was goodbye."

The young, smiling Roxana stared up at Astrea, unaware of all the terrible things that had come to pass. Astrea could almost see the happiness and love radiating off her mother, the pink and gold. She snapped the locket shut.

"After that day, I faked my own death. Crashed my car on the road back to my home in Helosia and left no trace of your mother or my movements in Irvina. It took some time, but my brother eventually returned to look for me, and the police told him about my death."

If Valen really had faked his death like that, why had her mother never told Astrea her father was dead? Surely Roxana had known. Maybe she hadn't wanted to burden young Astrea with that.

She sighed. "He believed them?"

"He did. That was all I wanted, for him to not go looking for your mother. And he didn't seem to. I kept watch on Irvina for over a year and never, ever saw him."

"How do you know what the police told him?"

"It wasn't hard to get information from town if I greased the right palms."

He almost sounded like Rami, talking like that.

"Why tell me all of this and not the commander?" Astrea asked.

"It was not his story to know. It is our story, our family story," Valen said. "You may tell who you wish."

"We've been up against the Paragon for months now," Astrea said. "It's my understanding that your brother knew about me from child-hood. He found me somehow and was sure I was the moon in the prophecy his people follow. He waited until I was an adult to try to snatch me."

"I'm glad to see you unharmed," Valen said.

"I'm not unharmed," she spat, her breathing shallow and painful. "He got me, and he tortured me with dreamwalking, and Nazarov tortured me physically in the name of the Paragon. So no, I'm not unharmed." The words poured from her mouth before she could think better of it. The things she'd wanted to tell Saros but now never could. "And they're still coming after me."

He looked down at the ground. "I didn't know . . ."

"I guess I can't expect you to," Astrea muttered. No, if Valen really had been hiding away from the world and the Paragon for all these years, he probably didn't know about any of that. And she doubted Lucian would've told him much.

"I'm sorry about your mother and your uncle," Valen said quietly. "This is the future I was trying to avoid."

A future he'd been trying to avoid, just like Saros had been trying to avoid so many futures, too.

Astrea passed the locket back to Valen. "Thank you for showing me this."

As he took the necklace from her, he gestured at her hands. "You're married?"

Her face heated. "Yes."

"To whom?"

She didn't see the point in hiding that from her father, either. The Paragon already knew. The emperor already knew. The only people in the world who would somehow use it against them already knew.

"Prince Varojin Auris," Astrea said.

Valen chuckled quietly. "I'm sorry, did you say Prince Varojin Auris?"

Forcing her expression to stay neutral, Astrea said, "We got married about a month ago. I've known him since I was ten years old. Saros took me to Kalama after my mother died, and I grew up on palace grounds there. We had some years apart, but he's been helping me survive all of this."

Valen's face softened as he tucked the locket back under his shirt. "I'd like to meet him."

"You sort of did already. He was with me earlier."

"The tall one?" Valen asked, and she nodded. "I didn't recognize him. I'm not exactly up to date on continental politics."

"Well, regardless," Astrea said, "he's going to have questions for you."

"I'll answer whatever I can. If you're really up against the Paragon, you're going to need all the help you can get."

Could she trust him to provide that help? Desperation filled his eyes, and a sheen of midnight blue grief clung to his skin.

Jin was usually good at reading people, so Astrea said, "I'll see what I can do."

"Your father said all of that?" It was the first time Lucian had spoken since Astrea had asked him to meet with her and the rest of the team.

Adi and Marko were there, as were Eliana, Nicos, and Zephyrine. The twins had volunteered to help the Nikaphoroses finish checking on the airship.

And Jin was there too, of course. He watched Astrea closely, like he wasn't sure what to make of all the information she'd relayed. She didn't blame him. It was a lot, and yet it also wasn't very specific. There was so much Valen surely hadn't said, so many details he'd left out.

"Can we trust him?" Eliana asked. "Do we even believe him?"

Astrea shrugged. "As far as I can tell, he's being honest. I could be misreading him, but nothing suggests he's actually trying to deceive me."

"Do you think he's working with the Paragon?" Nicos asked.

"I would hope not after the story he told me," she said. "He had a picture of himself with my mother. They looked so happy."

"A lot of people can *look* happy in photographs," Nicos said.

"I know, but something in my gut says he's telling the truth, or at least mostly the truth," Astrea said as Jin's hand brushed the small of her back. "He wants to meet you, Jin."

"Me?" he asked. "Why?"

"He asked who my spouse was, and I didn't see a reason not to tell him."

"Does he know the Paragon think I'm the sun?"

"I didn't tell him that, no."

"I think we need to go back to Talmaris," Lucian said. "We will take Valen with us but keep him under heavy guard. Hopefully he'll be willing and able to give us more information. I'll send some people to Irvina, too, to look for these old police reports."

"He said he would help, that we would need it if we're going against the Paragon," Astrea said.

"Then let's keep trying to figure out what he really wants and see if we can learn anything useful," Lucian said.

"When do we leave?" Marko asked.

"I'll need a couple more hours to make arrangements, but if we leave by then, we can still make it to the capital before midnight."

Astrea was so tired. Too tired. The thought of more preparation, more travel, weighed her down. But she had to keep going, and so she would, until she finally had the answers she needed.

CHAPTER 3

Being back in the Novarian capital was almost foreign. The halls seemed bigger, emptier. Even the room Astrea and Jin had been sharing for weeks felt different.

They'd arrived the night before, Valen in tow. As soon as they'd landed, Lucian, Marko, and a retinue of palace guards had escorted him—in chains—to the jail in downtown Talmaris. Astrea wasn't so sure it was the best place to keep Valen, but Lucian was staying there until everything was settled.

She splashed water on her face, then reached for the soft white towel on the bathroom counter. They were supposed to meet with not just Grand Duke Veiko but his council, the Tornamian president, and the ambassadors from Delia, Tornama, and the Taipoli Islands. It was something. And it felt like a lot . . . and not enough. Too much, yet so little.

Patting her skin dry, Astrea pulled the towel away and found Jin leaning against the bathroom doorframe, arms crossed over his chest.

"How are you?" he asked gently.

She shrugged. "I just hope this meeting yields something positive."

One side of his mouth quirked up in a pathetic half smile. "I'm sorry we have to go at all."

Astrea shrugged again. "We need to stop your father and find Nazarov."

She went to move past him, but Jin grabbed her by her forearm. "Az."

"What?"

"Please, don't shut me out." His wall was solid, impenetrable.

"You're shutting *me* out."

"I don't mean to. I'm trying to focus."

"So am I."

The faintest hint of blue sadness floated above his skin. "I want to know how you are after everything. Not about the mission. *You.*"

"I'm sorry," she whispered, focusing on the buttons trailing up his silky black shirt. "I don't mean to be sharp with you."

"It's alright."

"I'm tired, Jin. I'm so tired." Astrea closed her eyes. "All I want to do is cry, but I don't think my body has anything left to give."

Slinking his arms around her waist, he pulled her closer. Astrea wrapped her arms around his neck, burying her face there. She breathed him in, that faint hint of eucalyptus.

"I know," he whispered as he stroked the back of her hair. "I'm sorry that we have to keep going."

And it was that simple. They had to. Even if they never stepped foot on the battlefield again, they'd still have to be involved. Coordinate from the palace. Guide the armies and teach them about void magic. And it wasn't like Nazarov or the emperor would let them off the hook. It didn't matter. They had to keep going.

"It's fine." Astrea pulled away from the embrace and pushed her shoulders back.

"It's not fine."

"Well, I have to pretend it is, otherwise I'm never going to be able to function again."

He nodded. "Pretending it is, at least for now. How about after the meeting, if there's still time in the day, we go visit Lucian? I can try talking to Valen."

"I think that would be good." Astrea slipped out of his grasp and headed for the wardrobe, pulling out a dark blue skirt and black sweater. "The sooner we get more answers, the better," she said as she finished changing.

"I'll try to get a read on him, but I would think you and Lucian would do that best," Jin said as he joined her. He passed her both her wedding and engagement rings.

"I'd still like your opinion." After slipping on the rings, Astrea fluffed her hair. "And he seems to want to meet you, so maybe he has something he feels he needs to tell you."

"I guess we'll find out soon enough."

"I just hope he's not some kind of monster like his brother was," Astrea said, shaking out the pleats in her skirt. "Maybe it's naive to hope that."

"It's not naive. It'd be really fucking nice, actually."

Nice, sure, but could they really count on a total stranger? Valen had claimed he was going to help them with their Paragon problem, but it still seemed entirely possible to Astrea that he might be working with Nazarov or maybe even some third faction of void mages.

"Let's just get to this meeting," Astrea said. "We can worry about my father later."

She would need to check on Cressida, too. But first, she had to put on a brave face and try to convince the continental leaders to throw themselves into this two-front war.

Walking into a room full of politicians never seemed to get any easier despite the number of times Astrea had done this the last few months.

She walked beside Jin as Marko escorted them into Grand Duke Veiko's war room. The Grand Novarian Council filled in their spots around the table. Next to them were Tornamian ambassadors and President Sikori. There were Delian ambassadors, too, one of whom Astrea recognized from their meetings in Thasia. Novarian military leaders, judging by their uniforms. Taipoli officials, too. So many more people than at the meetings they'd had right after the grand duchess's death.

Princess Delfine, her wife, Katerina, and Grand Duchess Letizia were also at the table. Eliana, Nicos, and Zephyrine, of course.

And then there was Grand Duke Veiko, seated at the head of the table and looking as imperious as ever. It was still strange, seeing him in that position. Astrea's heart ached.

"Prince Varojin," Veiko said. "Princess Astrea."

Astrea balked. She couldn't help it. *Princess* Astrea? No, that most certainly would not do.

Jin squeezed her hand, as if he knew exactly why she'd gone rigid. As if to say, "Don't worry, we'll deal with it later." But he simply smiled at his cousin as he and Astrea took their seats next to Eliana and Nicos. "Apologies for the delay."

"No matter," Veiko said. "Shall we begin?"

Astrea hadn't realized everyone would be waiting for them. Had they been that late? Why hadn't Veiko sent someone to fetch them? Her cheeks burned as the whole room seemed to appraise her and Jin.

Veiko made introductions for the new ambassadors, Novarian generals, and councillors, but Astrea was never going to remember all of their names. Not when her mind was already so distracted and torn.

"Well," Veiko said unceremoniously, "I know all of us in this room have been briefed on what has recently been happening in Helosia and even in Novaria, but there are things you must understand about the situation."

"Things?" asked one Taipoli official. His thick hair was styled into rows of braids, which he'd piled on top of his head in a fashionable bun. Yellow worry seemed to stick to his dark brown skin. "Princess Delfine mentioned something about a magical problem here on the continent? Something to do with Emperor Aelius?"

"Oh, it's more than just our father, Ambassador Pavares," Eliana said. "Though he must be stopped, too."

"More than your father?" The man chuckled, but his hazel eyes held no amusement. "What more could there be?"

"As mentioned in earlier meetings," Veiko said, "it is void magic, and it is worse than we anticipated. Emperor Aelius has begun developing weapons with a material called aetherium, which contains some properties similar to void magic. It almost sucks the life energy out of anyone whose skin it pierces."

Memories of that hot and cold pain flickered in Astrea's abdomen, her shoulder, her neck. All the places Jin and Saros had been hit. Nausea crept up her throat. Under the table, she grabbed Jin's hand. He drew smooth circles across the top with his thumb.

Several people gasped while heavy disbelief pressed into Astrea's bones. As Veiko began explaining what they'd found at that camp and additional information certain spies had uncovered, gray confusion spiked around a couple of the dignitaries.

When it was laid out like that . . .

It sounded bleak.

It *was* bleak.

As shouts of annoyance and disbelief crowded the room, President Sikori brought her fingers to her mouth and whistled loudly. The chatter stopped. "I sanctioned a representative of Tornama to join Prince Varojin, the commander of the grand duke's guard, and other allies on a mission into Helosia. It's true, what they say, this void magic. I have even seen it for myself."

"Void magic in Thasia?" asked one of the Tornamians, a woman with silky black hair and bronze skin. Her narrow nose wrinkled. "Why is this the first I'm hearing of this, Madam President?"

"It was need to know until today," she replied coolly. "Our military has been on high alert for the last several weeks."

"Were you attacked?" the woman asked.

"No, Delegate Marosikis, I was not," President Sikori said. "Void mages helped Prince Varojin and the rest of the team get back to Thasia safely after the mission went sideways."

More confusion filtered around the room, dancing over Astrea's skin like little bolts of electricity.

"And what is this of so-called Princess Astrea?" asked the Taipoli Ambassador Pavares. "Princess of what?"

"Of Helosia, by marriage," Veiko said. "She is Prince Varojin's wife."

"I did not know you had married, Your Imperial Highness," Delegate Marosikis said almost snidely. "We hardly know anything about you."

This was what this woman was going to get caught up on? Jin randomly showing up married after years outside of the political landscape?

"I don't see why that's any of your business, Delegate," Jin said, and the woman shrugged.

"Why should we trust what you have to say about this mission?" Ambassador Pavares charged. "What right do you have to lead a mission?"

Irritation boiled up inside Astrea, but she didn't have it in her to fight with these people. She slumped back in her chair.

"I've spent the last eight years fighting in my father's wars," Jin said coldly.

"Eight? But you're twenty-six. Helosians don't enlist until they're twenty," said the ambassador. "Besides, princes don't *fight*."

Jin shrugged. "Explain that to my father." The man's thick eyebrows furrowed as Jin continued, "Eight years at war, most of them serving under General Kanakos." He gestured to her. "I know a thing or two not just about my father's military but the lengths he's willing to go to get what he wants. And what the grand duke said is true. My father has weaponized void magic, and this cult he speaks of is not only after my wife but me *and* the power my father now has."

Gasps rippled around the table.

"That power in anyone's hands will be devastating," Jin said.

"What is this power?" asked one of the Delian officials. Like Nicos, he had auburn hair and pale skin dappled with freckles. His eyes, though, were blue.

They took turns explaining the situation to the politicians in the room, from Caliban to the confrontation with Kaius, everything that had happened with Nazarov and the Paragon. Of course, they left out the part about Astrea's father being alive, and they also left out Saros's death. But by the time they were done with the tale, the only thing left in the room was ice cold horror. It was as if the reality of what the emperor was now capable of had finally set in.

"In short, we found test logs," Jin said. "He's been testing these aetherium weapons on his own military, and I got shot with an aetherium bullet while on this mission."

"Was it your father who tried to kill you?" asked one of the Novarian generals, an elderly woman with white hair and skin.

"I don't know, nor do I care," Jin said.

"I thought the material was instantly deadly," said a Taipoli official.

"Not instant, but close to it," Jin said. "I wouldn't have survived if not for my wife."

At the confused looks, Astrea mumbled, "I'm a Lightbringer."

"So it's healable?" asked Ambassador Pavares. "These aetherium effects?"

Astrea shifted awkwardly in her seat. "It . . . it took everything I had to save him. Both of us nearly died in the process."

"So what you're saying, Your Imperial Highness," he said to Astrea, "is that this isn't something we can fight by sending extra healers onto the battlefield?"

The tiniest wisp of peach amusement flickered around Eliana, no doubt at Astrea receiving the title of *Your Imperial Highness*. Any other day, Astrea would laugh. She'd have to tell Cressida; she would find it hilarious.

"I don't think so," Astrea said. "I'm a particularly strong healer and barely managed."

"It sounds like we must take out the emperor's war machine in a different way," said one Novarian councillor. "Not by sending in foot soldiers."

"I agree," said Zephyrine. "Targeted strikes, especially air strikes on where we know he's building weapons and mining the ore. Then we can begin to figure out how to force him to abdicate and put an end to this."

"What about the Paragon?" asked Princess Delfine. She'd been surprisingly quiet the entire meeting, only shooting Astrea a knowing glance when anyone brought up Jin's marriage. "It sounds like they won't stop, even if we destroy the emperor's weaponry."

"They won't," Jin said. "No, Victor Nazarov, a Helosian noble, is leading the Paragon now. He won't stop until he's dead. Taking him out must be one of our top priorities."

"I still believe pooling our resources and setting up a task force is the best way to move forward," Eliana said. "A joint effort by all of our nations, land, air, and sea, to find and stop not just the Paragon but my father. It's going to take everyone working together to put an end to this. It's not something any of us can do alone."

"With all due respect, Your Imperial Highness," said the red-haired Delian ambassador, "but if you intend to depose your father, will you take the throne? Or will Prince Varojin?"

"I won't be taking any thrones," Jin said quickly.

Eliana sat up even straighter in her chair as she said, "I would step in, yes, Ambassador."

"What of Prince Apelo?" the man asked.

"We've reached out to him but haven't heard back," Eliana said. "But I doubt he's aware of our father's movements or plans. If he is, he's apathetic about it all at best. If we could evacuate him and his family from Helosia, I would feel most comfortable with that. I fear my father won't let him leave easily, though."

"Indeed," the man replied. "But I wonder what your policy will be toward Delia when you are on the throne? I cannot, in good conscience, continue supporting the Auris dynasty with this kind of aggression running rampant in your government. Emperor Aelius on one side, this Lord Nazarov on the other."

A tight smile pulled at Eliana's mouth. "I don't blame you for that, Ambassador," she said. "I would gladly meet with any of you to go over my plans for a new government, if you share the ambassador's concerns."

Several of those around the table immediately voiced their acceptance of Eliana's offer, and she promised to meet with them later that day.

"Let us reconvene in the morning, then," Veiko said. "We'll begin discussing these strikes on the emperor, as well as how to find the Paragon."

"Actually, Your Highness," Jin said to his cousin, "I think I know a way we might be able to get a jump on the Paragon."

"You do?" Veiko asked.

"It's not exactly how I wanted to broach the subject . . ." He gazed down at Astrea, asking silent permission. She nodded. She didn't see the point in hiding this next part. "While we were in Helosia, we were approached by Theo Kadis. You remember him?"

"I do," Veiko said. The rest of the table remained quiet.

"He revealed that he and a group of followers have split off from the Paragon. He was previously Nazarov's right-hand man, but Nazarov has gone too far even for him. And they believe Astrea is their rightful hereditary ruler—"

"She's Paragon?" called someone, a foreign, heavily accented voice Astrea couldn't pinpoint. Anger singed her skin, and red clouded her vision.

"She's not Paragon," Jin said sharply.

"I'm not," Astrea said. "But I've recently learned that I'm descended from one of their prominent leaders from during the Great Wars. The Paragon believe that because of this connection, *I* am their next leader."

"How can we trust you?" called that same voice.

Maybe that was a fair question. Astrea imagined, if she was only now learning all of this information in the span of a couple hours, she would also be wary of someone with hereditary ties to the Paragon.

"They have done terrible things to me," Astrea said. "They have hunted me, tortured me, and tried to force me to work for them. I want nothing to do with them, but I understand your concerns."

"I know none of you know Astrea personally," Eliana said, "but I do. I've known her since we were children. So has Varojin. And maybe that doesn't mean much coming from two Aurises, but please, try to give my promise some weight."

"I've known Miss Sovna for several months now," Veiko said, "and I do not believe her to be a threat. She wants this to end as much as we all do."

Astrea's lungs tightened. But finally, the anger in the room receded. Confusion and uncertainty prickled her skin, like those foreign politicians couldn't decide whether they were going to trust her or not. But Astrea would take that. Maybe they would with time. Or maybe not. She didn't really care so long as they played their role in ending Nazarov and Emperor Aelius.

"As I was saying," Jin said, "Theo's revealed this to us. He helped us get out of Helosia. I think they'd be willing to fight for us. For Astrea, I mean. They don't trust the governments, but they're now looking to her for guidance."

"And you, as her husband, I would assume," said President Sikori carefully.

Jin shrugged. "They implied that, yes."

"Then we must get in contact with this Theo," Veiko said. "As soon as you can."

"We don't have a way to contact him," Jin said. "So far, he's shown up randomly."

"Does he know you're back in Novaria?" asked the president.

"I assume so. He seems to be able to track us somehow and promised to get in touch."

"If we haven't heard from him in a couple of days, then we'll begin searching for him," Veiko said. "Anything else?" When nobody said anything, he said, "Very well. Thank you all for coming. I'll see you tomorrow."

Astrea didn't know how they were going to find Theo, much less Nazarov. But with the backing of these other governments and militaries, maybe they would stand a chance.

Chapter 4

The meeting with the politicians continued on for another fifteen minutes after Veiko adjourned everything. It had mostly been talks about logistics and who else the representatives could speak with about the problem, plus ensuring they all had accommodations.

Now, Astrea was on her way to the palace infirmary. She wished Cressida would've gone to the hospital downtown, but she'd insisted she only needed Ivy's help and that the Tornamian doctors and healers had already done what could be done.

Jin, Adi, and Marko trailed after her; they were all going to go to the police station after this so that Jin could talk to Astrea's father. Astrea didn't mind their company, but she wasn't sure Cress would want any more fussing, and Astrea was definitely going to fuss.

As she paused at the closed infirmary door, Astrea turned to face the men. "I need to do this alone," she said.

Adi frowned. "Cress won't want to see us?"

"She needs some space, alright?" Astrea said. "I'll meet you all by the garage in fifteen minutes."

"I'll wait right out here," Jin said. "I'd prefer you aren't entirely left alone."

Astrea wasn't going to argue that with him. She left the men in the hall and slipped into the quiet infirmary.

Cressida was tucked on a bed in the far back corner. Ivy stood in front of her, water swirling around her palms and glowing blue. Her hands rested on Cressida's forearm, which was missing the sling and bandage that had become commonplace in recent days.

"Hey, Az," Cressida said, focusing not on Ivy's work but where Astrea stood at the foot of the bed. "How was the meeting?"

"Politicians being politicians," Astrea said. "But they seem to want to work together."

"A small blessing," Ivy murmured, her brows furrowing together in concentration.

"At least our work in the Badlands wasn't for nothing," Cressida said.

"Yeah." Astrea's rings clinked against the metal bed frame as she wrapped her fingers around the footboard. "Ellie can give you the details if you want them. I wanted to stop by to see how you're feeling."

"Oh, enough hovering, Mother," Cressida replied wryly. "Tell her I'm fine, Ivy."

Ivy's cornflower blue eyes met Astrea's. "All things considered? I'd say Cressida's recovery is coming along very well."

"Lucian can be helpful when he wants to be," Cressida said, making Ivy chuckle.

It was good to see Cressida make a joke. Seeing her smile just a little bit.

"You know, Astrea saved Prince Varojin from an aetherium bullet that struck him," Cressida said, cutting off what Astrea had been about to say.

"I thought that was impossible," Ivy replied.

Astrea's cheeks burned.

"Not for Az," Cressida said.

"A strong healer, indeed," mused Ivy. She straightened and pulled her hands away from Cressida's arm. "Let me get you some fresh bandages," she said, shuffling toward a large armoire filled with vials and medical supplies.

Where Cressida should've had her left hand, there was nothing. Her copper skin was smooth, except for the scar, the only sign of the trauma her body had endured. No blood. No leaking wound. No redness or swelling.

"Does this mean I can start building my prosthetic?" Cressida called. "Am I clear?"

"If you feel up to it, I don't see why not." Ivy pushed up on her toes and pulled down a spool of white gauze bandages. As she neared the bed again, she offered the material to Cressida. "Here. I'll let you do it. You should keep it wrapped for a while yet to prevent any swelling from coming back, and you may need to keep wrapping it as your body adjusts to the prosthetic. Come see me when you start wearing it."

"Will do," Cressida said, taking the bandages with her right hand. She began unspooling them with practiced ease. When she caught sight of Astrea's furrowed eyebrows, Cressida said, "I used to unwind a lot of wires with one hand in the workshop."

Astrea sat on the edge of her cot and took the bandages from her. "Listen, Cress," Astrea said as she began winding the gauze around Cressida's forearm. "I know Ivy says you're healed up, but are you sure you feel up to this?"

"I feel fine."

"No, you don't." The tightness in Cressida's voice was enough to give her away. Astrea didn't even have to look up to see if any colors spiked in her aura. Ivy had made herself scarce. "What can I do to help?"

Cressida was silent for so long Astrea wasn't sure she'd answer. She finished wrapping up Cressida's arm, then tied off the bandages. And maybe she couldn't make Cressida talk about it, but even with everything else going on, Astrea was not going to let Cressida deal with this alone.

Swallowing hard, Cressida said. "I don't want my parents worrying about me. Ma's so upset."

"I know she is."

"And . . . I know this isn't going to be easy." Cressida lifted up both arms, one with her hand intact and the other without, its fresh bandages bright in the light. "I mean, fuck."

"I know," Astrea said. "I know it's not. But I'll be here. Jin and Ellie will be here. So will everyone else. However you need help, however you *want* help. Just tell us."

"Yeah." Cressida sucked in a shaky breath.

"Maybe you can take a few more days," Astrea said.

"I'd rather not. I think doing something is what's going to help me keep moving forward."

She couldn't blame Cressida for that. Moving forward—not slowing down—was the only way Astrea felt like she wasn't completely drowning.

"Promise me you won't push yourself too hard?" Astrea asked.

"I promise. Ma won't let me, anyway. Dad's going to help me build the prosthetic." She sighed. "What's everyone else getting up to? Assignments for the next meeting?"

"That," Astrea said, "and Jin's going to talk to my father."

"No shit?" Cressida asked. "What do you think he'll say?"

Astrea shrugged. "I don't know. But Jin's going to try to figure out if Valen was telling me the truth. Maybe get some more information out of him."

"Good luck."

"Thanks, we'll need it." Astrea patted Cressida's knee. "We'll be back in a few hours. Stay out of trouble until then."

Despite the heavy military presence in Talmaris, the city was operating at its normal pace. At least, that was how it seemed as Astrea stared out the car window as they drove toward the police station downtown. Cars and trolleys filled the street, and pedestrians roamed the sidewalks in droves.

The grand duke had not yet announced they were going to war, Astrea knew that much. But that announcement would surely come soon, especially with the other countries signing on to join the fight. It was only a matter of time until some of these people inevitably got dragged more into this mess than they already had been.

She tried to stamp down her guilt and focused instead on what they had to do next: try to get her father to give them more information to work with. If nothing else, maybe Jin could get a good read on him, and then they could start trying to get said information.

"You'd think early afternoon wouldn't be the worst time for traffic," Adi muttered from the front passenger seat. "Don't these people have jobs?"

"People are on many different schedules in Talmaris," Marko replied as he hit the brakes. They all jerked forward in their seats, and Jin held Astrea back to keep her from completely falling over. Marko swore at the driver in front of him, who had stopped short.

"Let's just focus on getting there in one piece instead of quickly," Jin said. He curled his hand tightly around hers.

Jin had been prone to touching her ever since they began their relationship, and that had only escalated with Nazarov's constant stalking and threats. But he'd taken it to a new level after what happened in the Badlands. He was always finding the smallest ways to touch her—more so than he did before. She didn't mind. Not really, anyway. Knowing he was right there was a comfort even when her senses were overwhelmed. And she knew he'd stop if she asked. But she didn't want to ask that of him.

"Was Cress doing alright?" Adi asked.

Marko turned the car right down another wide, busy road. The buildings grew taller the closer they got to downtown.

"As alright as I can expect her to be right now," Astrea said. "She's going to start working on a prosthetic with her dad."

"You think it'll be all metal?" Adi asked.

"Probably." Astrea hadn't talked Cressida's plans over with her, but back in Kalama, before all this started, Cressida and her father had started supplying metal prosthetics to Metalli hurt during the war. Ones they could control with their magic. They'd wanted to find more materials to use for other mages—and non-mages—but had never had the chance.

Marko switched lanes, cursing out another driver.

"Should've let me drive," Adi said.

"Why, so you could get mad at them instead?" Marko asked.

"I don't get mad."

Jin smirked. "Oh, I've seen you get mad, Adi."

"Like when?"

"Do you really want me to list all the times?"

Adi huffed and thunked his head against the headrest. "No."

"We're here anyway," Marko said. "Talmaran police headquarters."

He pulled the car into a half-circle drive, which separated a tall gray and white building from the main road. Several of the trees near the building were brilliant orange and red, something Astrea never saw in Kalama.

After parking the car, they all climbed out and headed inside the building. Shiny black and white tile floors spread out across the lobby and down several hallways. Several people waited on benches lining the wall to Astrea's right; they were dressed like civilians. Two officers in midnight blue sat behind the sleek mahogany front desk.

One of the officers, a woman with short spiral curls and umber skin, perked up when she made eye contact with Marko.

"Hi, Kaya," Marko said with more friendliness to his voice than Astrea expected. He was rarely friendly. "Here to talk to a prisoner. Where's the commander?"

"Fourth floor in interrogation room seven." The officer glanced at Astrea, Jin, and Adi, offering them a tight smile. "Go on up."

Marko led them down one of the hallways shooting off the lobby. He stopped again in front of two elevators, then pressed the button to go up.

"So . . ." Adi nudged Marko's shoulder. "How'd you know her?"

"Oh, Kaya?" Marko shrugged. "We go back a ways."

"Back how?"

"We went to school together."

"Ah."

Marko's eyes narrowed. "What does that mean? *Ah*?"

"Nothing. I was just curious."

Astrea couldn't place Adi's question, either. No jealousy flared in his aura; the anxiety and curiosity that had been there all morning remained.

The elevator chimed, then the doors slid open. An older man strode out, and behind him came another civilian, a woman who had to be close to Sarsali's age. Her cane thunked against the tile floors as she headed for the front of the building.

Their group loaded into the elevator, then Marko pressed the button for the fourth floor. Up and up they went, the bell above the doors pinging with each floor they passed. Jin's hand brushed the spot between Astrea's shoulders.

Once on the fourth floor, they walked past multiple desks set out in an open office space, then turned down a dimly lit hallway. Closed doors lined each side, numbered starting at one. When they reached the one marked seven, they stepped into a small, nearly pitch-black room. A glass window separated them from what had to be the actual interrogation room, where Lucian sat at a table across from Valen. Bags had formed under Valen's eyes, but he'd clearly cleaned up and changed his clothes.

Marko stepped up to a small intercom next to the window and pressed the button. It buzzed and crackled as he said, "Commander."

On the other side of the glass, Lucian shifted in his seat. Green curiosity floated around Astrea's father, doubling in brightness when the commander stood and moved toward the window. A narrow door opened, then Lucian closed it behind him.

"Good, you're here," he said. "Finally."

"Got caught up at the meeting with the other politicians," Jin said. "Sorry."

Lucian huffed. "That's alright."

"Get anything from him?" Astrea asked.

"No," Lucian said. "He would tell me even less than he told you, Astrea. I'm just surprised he's not a void mage."

Astrea shrugged. Maybe a surprise in some ways but not in others. If Astrea's mother had felt that strange cold that seemed to surround all void mages, surely she either would've investigated or not engaged with Valen at all.

"Are you ready to talk to him, Varojin?" Lucian asked.

"Ready." Jin took Astrea's hand in his, then moved for the door.

The interrogation room itself was brighter than the one Lucian and Marko were staying in. Astrea peeked at the window, but all she saw was her reflection. She turned back to her father.

Valen studied the two of them, his expression unreadable.

"I'm told you want to speak with me?" Jin asked. He made no move to sit, though he did drop Astrea's hand and cross his arms over his chest. The way he towered over the interrogation table was nothing less than intimidating.

"Prince Varojin Auris," said Valen. "An honor to meet my daughter's husband. And to learn she married royalty, too."

"I'd hardly be thrilled about her marrying into my family," Jin said. "And I can't say I'm particularly thrilled to be marrying into yours."

That was going to be Jin's approach? Entirely aggressive?

"Don't blame you there," Valen said coolly. "My family is atrocious."

"At least we can agree on that." Jin huffed. "Astrea's already told you that your brother is dead, and she says you claim to know nothing of Victor Nazarov. So tell me, Valen Ramkas, what *can* you tell us that will help us stop the Paragon?"

"Well . . ." Valen let the word hang heavy in the air. "If we're going to exchange information, I'd like to learn a little, too."

"You're hardly in the position to be asking anything of us."

"Am I not?" Valen's jaw tightened. "Because it seems my only crime was siring my daughter despite my family's legacy. I've done nothing illegal."

"Maybe not illegal, but you've shown up at quite the convenient time," Jin said.

Valen shrugged.

The two men stared at each other, unyielding. This was not the side her father had shown the day before when Astrea had spoken to him alone.

She set a hand on Jin's forearm. He looked down at her, eyebrows raised in a silent question. She tilted her head toward her father, hoping Jin understood.

With a sigh, Jin said, "What would you like to know?"

"Is it so wrong to want to get to know my daughter and her husband?" Valen asked.

"When there's a multi-pronged war on the horizon? Yes," Jin replied.

"Well, that's my price. If you want to know what I know, you'll let me ask a few questions."

"Go ahead," Astrea said before Jin could deny the request. She didn't see the point in trying to strong-arm Valen into speaking. Maybe if they tried to give him a little, he'd give back. "But then you talk."

Valen's expression softened. "You told me you lived in Kalama for many years. Why are you not on the Helosian front lines? I've seen the reports of the wars when I dare venture into any town for supplies."

"My uncle had a vision of me dying on the battlefield and had me hide my magic," Astrea said.

He nodded. "And what were you doing while you were hiding?"

"I got two degrees at Kalama's university and had started a career as a librarian before everything went to shit."

Valen nodded again. "Impressive."

She shrugged.

"Were you ever curious about me?" he asked.

"Of course I was." She didn't see the point in lying, sad as the truth sounded coming out of her mouth. "I was a little girl who wanted to know who her father was."

"I thought about you every day, Astrea," Valen said. "I am truly sorry for not being there. I thought it was for the best."

Astrea shrugged again. It probably had been.

"And you, Prince Varojin." Valen tilted his head. "What has your life been like?"

It seemed like the strangest of things for Valen to be asking. Nothing in his aura changed. That calm curiosity remained.

"I served in the Helosian military for the last eight years," Jin said. "Trained to kill in unimaginable ways."

"Point taken," Valen said. "What made you want to marry my daughter?"

Astrea balked, but Jin said, "She's one of the kindest and smartest people I've ever had the honor of knowing. She's gentle, resilient, and beautiful. I've loved her for a long time. There's no one else I'd rather have as my partner."

At that, Valen's expression softened again. "Just like her mother," he murmured as deep blue regret pulsed around him. "Alright. What do you want to know about me, Prince Varojin?"

"First, I'd like to know why you actually showed up when you did."

"It's as I told Astrea," Valen said. "I heard she was looking for me."

"But how did you hear?" Jin pressed. "You claim to live outside of society, yet you heard *that*, of all things? There's got to be more to it than that."

Valen hesitated as his gaze darted between the two of them. "True that I live away from society," he said slowly. "But there are others like me, those who do not follow the Paragon's creed despite being raised in the organization. We keep in quiet contact. One such person lives near Irvina and heard it from someone else in town. That's how I found out about the attack on the fort, too."

"Are those the Wanderers?" Astrea asked. "The ones who don't follow the true path?"

"No, no," Valen said. "No, we were never called such. Wanderers were those who disagreed with The One's way of doing things. Although . . . I suppose we might fall into that group."

Astrea frowned.

"How many people have left the Paragon?" Jin asked.

"I know of little more than a dozen, spread out around southern Novaria, northern Helosia, and northwestern Tornama. I'm sure there are others, but as you can imagine, they're not easy to find without putting yourself at risk. We mostly live alone, though some have grouped up."

"Sure," Jin said so evenly Astrea couldn't tell if he believed Valen or not. "We were recently in the Badlands, and the Paragon's new leader, Victor Nazarov, showed up. He's allied with at least some people in the Zaikudi government. Has the Paragon always had that connection?"

"Not that I'm aware of," Valen said. "Neither my brother nor mother were keen on outside alliances."

"Do you know where Nazarov might be hiding out? Or if there's some Paragon location he might use as his base of operations?"

"There is a safe house just outside of Talmaris, as well as several locations in the mountains," Valen said. "There may be more, though. It's been over two decades since I left."

"If I got you a map, could you pinpoint those locations for me?" Jin asked.

"I can."

"What do you know of aetherium?"

"Only that it was spoken of with reverence by our historians," Valen said. "Why?"

"Because my father's found an enormous deposit in the Badlands and is making extensive weaponry with it."

"What?" Cold horror snaked over Astrea's skin as Valen said, "No, that's impossible, one of our earliest leaders hid away the remaining aetherium weapons in Paragonian control—"

"Even if that's true, my father's found some out in nature, so if you know anything that might help us stop him or weaken the aetherium, you'd be saving thousands—hundreds of thousands—of lives."

"Is this something my brother knew of?" Valen asked. "I didn't think he would ever go to such lengths . . ."

"Did you think he'd kidnap and torture his own niece?" Astrea asked.

Valen's thin lips pressed into an even thinner line, and blue sadness coated his skin. "I feared he might try to take you into the organization but no, nothing like that."

"He spoke of the sun and moon helping him restore balance by taking down the continental governments," she said. "He believed me to be the moon and Jin to be the sun. How were we supposed to help him?"

"I don't know, truly," Valen said. "I may be a Ramkas, but I was never given much information." When Astrea huffed, he asked, "Could it be something with the aetherium? Does it enhance your magic?"

"Not that we're aware of," Jin said. "Is it supposed to?"

"I do not know."

It seemed Valen didn't know much at all.

Forcing her jaw to unclench, Astrea asked, "Do you know how to read the void language?"

"Void language?" Valen's eyebrows furrowed.

"There's an alphabet we've found at several Paragonian sites," Astrea said. "We didn't know what else to call it."

Teal understanding flashed around him. "Oh, that. Only a little, and that was many, many years ago, but I may be able to read some of it."

Astrea glanced up at Jin and murmured, "The manuscript back at the palace, the one with the notes in the margins . . ." She didn't know if Noemi had made much progress with Tomas and the linguist, but it might be worth seeing if Valen could tell them anything about it.

"Alright, Mister Ramkas," Jin said. "Here's what's going to happen. You're going to go back to your cell for the night, and in the morning, we're going to come back with maps and some documents we need you to look at. If the information you provide helps us, we might consider letting you out of prison.”

“Whatever I need to do,” Valen said. “Anything to help.”

As if that were some sort of cue, the door behind Astrea opened. Lucian stepped in, followed by two Novarian police officers.

“You heard Prince Varojin,” the commander said. “Back to your cell for the night.”

Valen stood up with little fanfare and let the two officers place him in handcuffs. He offered Astrea a tight-lipped smile as he walked past, disappearing into the dark room beyond as the officers led him away.

“Well?” Lucian asked as Marko and Adi stepped into the interrogation room with the rest of them. “What did you think, Varojin?”

“I’m not sure,” Jin said. “He didn’t *seem* to be lying, but who can ever truly be sure?”

“Nothing in his aura suggested he was lying,” Lucian said. “Although I found his questions for the two of you odd.”

“Was it that or a father who wants to get to know his child and child’s partner?” Marko asked. “Not to be optimistic, but he looked almost . . . sad. Like he had many regrets.”

“Regrets that he’s going to betray us or regrets that he abandoned Az when she was a baby?” Adi asked.

And that was what Astrea didn’t know for sure.

“It’s like Jin said. If he provides us information and intelligence that checks out, then maybe we consider trusting him further,” she said. “And if not, then we’ll know for certain that we can’t trust anything he says.”

“I fear that’s the best we can do,” Lucian said. “Alright, back to the palace with you four. I’ll see you back here first thing in the morning. We’ve got work to do.”

CHAPTER 5

Pencil scratched against paper, grating on Astrea's nerves as she carefully transcribed the looping void letters onto blank sheets of paper.

They may have been going to the police station the next morning to have her father try to translate some of the void language for them, but Astrea didn't trust anyone enough to let the book leave the safety of the palace. Instead, she would take a few of the transcriptions to her father to see if he could even tell them anything. Maybe he couldn't. Maybe he *wouldn't*. And besides, Noemi, Tomas, and the linguist were still working on building out a way to translate everything, so even if Valen was ultimately useless, they had options.

Marko yawned, making Astrea glance up. He was seated on the armchair across from her, one leg crossed over the other. She was on the floor of the sitting room she shared with Jin, supplies spread in front of her on the coffee table.

"Don't yawn," she murmured, going back to her work.

"Why not?"

"Because then I'll yawn."

"Maybe you should go to bed."

"Not until I'm done," she said.

Astrea *could* stop whenever she felt the need. She'd already copied enough to use as a test on her father. But she didn't want to go to bed without Jin. Ever since that day in the Badlands, it felt like Nazarov might appear out of thin air. Like he was lurking nearby in the shadows, waiting for an opportunity.

And Jin was down the hall, speaking with Eliana, Nicos, and Zephyrine about potential next political moves. They'd invited Astrea to join, but she didn't want to think about politics. She just wanted to figure this out.

"I thought you were only bringing him a sample," Marko drawled. "That's more than a sample."

"Well, if he ends up being useful and can translate more, it'll be ready to go."

Marko harrumphed.

"You're grumpier than usual."

He harrumphed again. "I'm not grumpy."

"My magic disagrees," she said as bright rusty annoyance flared around him. Setting her pencil down, she leaned back against the sofa. "What's wrong?"

"You and I wanted to have someone translate this weeks ago, and yet here we are, finally getting it done."

"It is what it is."

"Is that really how you feel?"

Astrea shrugged one shoulder. "It's not like we can change it." There were so many things Astrea wished she could change, this included. But that simply wasn't possible. "We're here now."

"Do you think Theo will help us if we can find him?"

"Probably," Astrea said. "If we can locate him soon, maybe we can have him translate the same thing my father does, then compare."

"Try to figure out if one of them is lying," Marko mused.

"Well, my father did say it's been a long time since he's read the language. Maybe he'll just get something wrong."

"He could," Marko said. "Best to have both translations regardless."

Astrea went back to copying a few of the void letters, also making a couple of notes on the back of the page about the Novarian contents of the book in that section. Maybe, if her father needed context, she could at least give him something. But . . .

"How do you think we can find Theo?" Astrea asked, glancing back up at Marko. His attention was focused on the ceiling.

"Being patient?"

"When have you ever wanted to be patient?" she replied. "We need to find him as soon as possible."

"I doubt he's at any of the known Paragon sites." Marko folded his arms over his abdomen. "Do you think he'd come back to Talmaris?"

"And hide his void mages where, exactly?"

"Maybe they're not with him."

"Wouldn't he contact us if he was here?" Astrea asked. "If I'm supposed to be his new queen or whatever?"

Marko chuckled. "Queen Astrea Sovna."

"Shut up." She bit her lip. "It's not funny."

"It's a little funny. No offense, but you? Queen?"

She set her pencil on the table. "Now what's wrong with that idea?"

"Do you have the right temperament?" He gestured at her. "You're so quiet."

"As if you're not?" Astrea arched an eyebrow.

"I certainly am. I'm not saying it's a bad thing. But queens and monarchs tend to be a little more . . . forward. Which is not a word I'd use to describe either of us."

Marko wasn't wrong, and Astrea certainly didn't want to be a Paragonian queen or princess or lady or anything of the sort, but the fact that he couldn't imagine it at all was a *little* offensive.

"*Anyway*," she said, "why would he hide out in Talmaris if he needs my help? Jin's help?"

"Maybe he doesn't even know we're back."

"So do we go to his store to look for him? It seems like Nazarov would check there, too."

"It might be worth looking into," Marko said. "We can see if he has any aliases he's registered other shops or businesses under. It seems to me that there's more to Theo than meets the eye."

"Yeah, a lot of nothing good," Astrea muttered.

"If he wants to be our ally, I won't say no, Astrea," Marko said. "A queen would know to take that deal."

"I think a queen would know that it's a gamble to trust people who once imprisoned her," Astrea retorted. Theo and his group had helped them in the last couple of weeks, but that didn't mean she fully trusted them yet. "Could you look into that? Any other businesses he might have, I mean." It seemed like something they should've done as soon as they'd realized Theo owned one shop in Talmaris, but it was too late to go back. They just had to try to course correct now.

"I can certainly make the effort."

"Please do."

"Giving out orders now, my queen?" Marko chuckled again.

"Don't make me throw this pencil at you."

Marko grinned, peach amusement flashing brightly in the air. The knot around Astrea's heart loosened for a moment, returning a beat later as she looked down at the book open in front of her. The book Saros had helped her deconstruct.

The door creaked open, and Adi called, "Aw, Marko, you're not upsetting Az, are you?"

"Of course I'm not upsetting Az."

"She sure looks upset," Adi said as he joined them and plopped on the floor next to Astrea.

She swallowed hard and blinked away the tears threatening to form in her eyes. "Just a little overwhelmed," she said to Adi. "That's not Marko's fault"—she forced a smile—"though apparently he doesn't think I'd make a very good Paragonian queen."

Adi threw his arm around Astrea's shoulders. "You'd make a great queen as far as I'm concerned. You're kind, smart, and determined. All good traits in a leader."

"At least someone believes in me."

"We were discussing how to find Theo," Marko said, then explained their idea about Theo having other business ventures in the city.

"Would he risk coming here with Nazarov still on the run?" Adi asked.

"I don't know, but there's no other logical place to start as far as I'm concerned," Marko said. "We could go to city hall tomorrow and see if they have any business licenses. Ask the police, too, if they have any known aliases or even anyone involved in antiquities trading on their radar."

The door opened again, and this time, Jin walked in. He smiled tightly at their trio.

"Hey, Jin," Adi said. "Get everything sorted?"

Shoving his hands in his pockets, Jin shrugged. "Define 'sorted.'"

"A master plan to get all these countries on the same page?"

"I wish," he said. "But Ellie's going to cover for me tomorrow while we go to the police station. I'd rather split our attention based on our strengths, and she's certainly the better diplomat than me."

"And you're the . . . detective?" Marko asked.

"Astrea's father seems open to talking to me, so I thought being there was important," Jin said.

"We want to go to city hall, too," Astrea said, then explained their idea of checking into Theo's business dealings, possible aliases, and the translations.

Faint teal understanding wavered around Jin. "Maybe we'll get lucky." When Astrea yawned, he added, "But maybe it's time to call it a night."

"Sounds good to me," Adi said. He helped Astrea to her feet, then followed Marko toward the door. But before he stepped into the hall, he turned and bowed with a flourish. "Good night, Your Majesty," he said, winking at Astrea.

"Adi?" Jin said with a sigh.

"Oh, right." Adi bowed again. "And of course you, too, Your Majesty."

"Adi," Jin said.

Peach amusement flared bright around the Earthmover. "Yeah?"

"Shut up."

Astrea couldn't help but laugh with Adi. He grinned, vermilion pride bright in the air as he waved to Astrea and hurried after Marko.

Jin closed the distance between himself and Astrea, then wrapped his arm around her waist. "I was serious before," he said, then kissed the top of her head. "About going to bed."

"I was mostly waiting for you to get back anyway," Astrea said.

"Well, I'm here now." He kissed the top of her head again. "Come on, Your Majesty. Let's get you to bed."

"Skies," Astrea muttered. "Now look at what Adi started."

Jin chuckled. "I'm just teasing."

She tried to force a smile. "I know."

Astrea was still so bone-deep tired she couldn't tell where her fatigue ended and Jin's began. It didn't matter anyway. There was nothing she could do to help Jin tonight; he needed some rest.

After cleaning up, Astrea finally changed into her pajamas and slipped into bed. The sheets were cold, but as soon as Jin joined her, the bed warmed. She laid her head on his chest, ready to ask him more about the meeting with Eliana. But as she peeked at him, she realized he was already asleep.

So Astrea curled into him and let her fatigue win, too. They could talk more in the morning.

The police station was even emptier the next morning they arrived. Astrea adjusted the strap of her satchel as she walked, trying to ease her nerves. As planned, they'd only brought some examples of the void language as well as the maps Jin had wanted.

And now, they were quickly approaching the same interrogation room as the day before. Number seven. Jin carried three coffees in to-go cups. One was for Jin himself, another for Lucian, and they'd decided to bring a third for her father as a gesture of goodwill. Astrea had her own coffee, of course.

Marko and Adi had opted to stay downstairs and look more into any information they could find about underground antiquities dealers and records of anything pertaining to Theo's business activities. Once they were done with Astrea's father upstairs, Astrea and Jin would join the other two to venture to city hall across the street.

"Good morning," Lucian said as soon as he opened the door to that small, dark room with the two-way mirror. He accepted one of the coffees from Jin. "Thanks."

"Is he ready for us?" Jin asked.

Beyond the window, Valen sat at the table again, all calm nonchalance.

"Ready," Lucian said. "Do you need my help?"

"Stay here and watch?" Astrea half asked, half suggested. "I'd like to know if you catch anything in his aura that I don't."

"Of course," Lucian said. "Good luck."

Jin opened the door to the actual interrogation room, then motioned for Astrea to go in first. She did, taking measured steps toward the table in the middle of the space. Valen perked up.

"Good morning," he said.

"Coffee, if you want it." Jin set one of the cups down in front of Valen. "We didn't know how you took it."

Valen watched them carefully, though nothing flared in his aura nor touched Astrea's skin. He smiled after a moment. "Typically with extra sugar, but I'll take anything this morning. Thank you."

Astrea set her satchel down in the empty chair across from Valen and dug out the pieces of void language to be translated, as well as a blue colored pencil and the map Jin had brought. "Here," she said, sliding the materials to him.

"Let's start with the map," Jin said. "If you can mark off any Paragonian sites you know of, whether they might be ancient or in current use."

Valen unrolled one of the maps, humming quietly to himself as he began examining the terrain and marking off spots with the pencil. He continued on like that for several minutes, then set the pencil down. It clinked against the metal table. "There you go."

Passing his coffee to Astrea, Jin took the map from Valen and scanned it over. Astrea leaned around him to get a look. There were the sites marked off in the Macadian and Antare Mountains, as well as the house in Talmaris's suburbs. And then there were several others: another in the Antare Mountains, one in the far reaches of northwestern Novaria, and another in a valley between Zaikud and Novaria.

"Those are the only ones I'm sure of," Valen said. "There may be others. Two and a half decades is a long time, many opportunities for things to evolve."

"Right," Jin murmured, not taking his eyes off the map. "And are these the exact locations?"

"As close as I can recall, but they're probably not fully accurate."

It was something, Astrea supposed.

"This one in the northwest," Jin said. "What's there?"

"An old fortress built into the side of a mountain," Valen said.

"Sounds like someplace Nazarov would go." Jin rolled the map up. "Alright. Az?"

"These are a sample of the language I told you about yesterday," she said, gesturing to the papers in front of her father. "If you could give me even a rough translation, that might prove useful."

"Only a sample?" Valen asked as he examined the four sheets of paper Astrea had passed him. "I was under the impression there was quite a bit you couldn't read."

"There is," she said. "But let's see what you do with this first."

"Very well." After taking a sip of coffee, Valen picked up the pencil again and studied the first sheet. His eyebrows furrowed, a mix of gray confusion and teal understanding swirling around him.

"What does it say?" Astrea asked.

"It speaks of the wars."

"The Great Wars?"

"Yes."

Astrea pressed her lips together. They already knew about that. "Does it say anything specific?"

"Tytas Ramkas dreamed of deposing the Sun King and Novarian Queen."

They already knew that, too. Astrea tried not to grind her teeth together.

"Anything else?" Jin asked.

"As I told you yesterday, I haven't read these letters in many, many years," Valen said. "Could you give me some time?"

"We're kind of short on that," Jin said. "But you can have a few minutes." Then he tilted his head toward the door. "Az?"

She grabbed her bag and coffee, then followed Jin to the exit. He made her go first, and once the door was closed securely behind him, handed the map to Lucian.

"Can you have someone take this to Tomas?" Jin asked. "Have him cross-reference those locations with any known historical sites."

"Are you not going back to the palace after this?" Lucian asked as he took the map.

"No, we're going to city hall to try to find some connections Theo might have," Jin said. "Any head start we can get might be worthwhile if we're serious about connecting with him soon."

"What did you see?" Astrea asked the commander.

"Confusion, understanding." Lucian shrugged. "Though not hard to read, your father isn't very emotional, either. The coffee seemed to throw him off."

"I was just trying to be nice," Jin said.

Lucian arched an eyebrow.

"Seriously," Jin said. "A friendly gesture here and there won't hurt in case he really is on our side."

Through the mirror, movement caught Astrea's eye. Valen was waving and staring right at them. "He can't see us, right?" Astrea asked.

"No, he cannot," Lucian replied.

"Well, let's go see what he has to say," Jin muttered.

He and Astrea joined Valen again in the interrogation room. Valen offered them a small smile.

"Well?" Jin asked.

"I've done what I can," Valen said, sliding the papers and pencil toward Astrea. "I don't remember as much as I'd hoped, but maybe it'll get you started."

With unsteady hands, Astrea picked up the papers and leafed through them. Indeed, he'd written rough translations out, though a few of the sentences had question marks where there should've been words. Still, there was enough that she could understand roughly what was being said.

Or what Valen claimed was being said.

It was a little more about Tytas Ramkas's desire to depose the existing powerhouses on the continent. It sounded a bit like the Paragon's current goals, though back during the Great Wars, there had been many, many other leaders to contend with. Ramkas had, apparently, also had his sights set on a leader from a Zaikudi clan and another from a leader in the western part of modern-day Novaria.

It came as little surprise to Astrea, but if this was the true translation, why wouldn't this have been written down in Novarian? That was what didn't make sense to her. It hardly seemed like a secret given the other information written in the book.

She pulled another sheet out of her satchel and handed it to Valen. "This is from a different part of the book," she said. "Can you tell me what it says?"

This sample was a single sentence she'd found at the bottom of one page in the section about aetherium weapons being hidden away by Silya Ramkas.

"Let's see . . ." Lifting the paper closer to his face, Valen frowned. "Something about Silya."

"What specifically about her?" Jin asked.

He shook his head. "I'm not certain."

"Please translate what you do know, or even what you're mildly confident about," Jin said. With a small sigh, Valen took the pencil back and scribbled down a couple of words, then passed everything to Jin. "Thank you."

"That's all you have for me?" Valen asked.

"That's all for now, yes," Astrea said. There was plenty more they needed help with, but now, she really wanted to find Theo and see if he could explain what this book said. "We appreciate the effort."

"You speak as if we're strangers, Astrea," Valen said.

"We are."

"We're family."

"By blood maybe," she said. "But you're not family."

No, Valen was not her family, and it was bold of him to try to push that idea on her now, after only speaking a few times. Blue sadness flashed in his aura, but what did he have to be sad about? That her mother was dead? That he'd never gotten to know Astrea? Things that were, in some ways, his own fault.

No, the Nikaphoroses were her family. Jin and Eliana were her family. Adi. Nicos. Marko, even. The very people who had supported Astrea for most of her life, or at least in recent months. The people who loved her. Valen might have loved her in the way a parent had affection for their offspring, but as far as Astrea was concerned, that was the extent of it.

"We'll be back if we need any more assistance," she said.

Grabbing the translations, Astrea spun on her heel and headed for the door. Jin followed close behind, so close that she felt his heat.

"Here," Astrea said, pushing the papers toward Lucian once the door was closed again. "Send these to Tomas, too. He might be able to do something with them. Or Mariya."

Lucian hesitated, then nodded. "Very well."

"Come on," Astrea said to Jin. "Let's go find Adi and Marko."

She didn't wait for him, instead heading right for the exit. He hurried after, his worry electric on her skin. When they were in the hall, he grabbed her elbow and said, "Az, wait."

With a huff, she glanced up at him. "What?"

"Hey." His expression softened. "You're upset."

"Of course I'm upset. He doesn't get to call me family. Half of my family is dead and the other half—you and everyone else—is in grave danger because of the life he once led."

"I don't know that he truly understands that."

"Well maybe I should take him to Mom and Saros's graves to get the point across."

Jin closed what little distance there was between them. "Don't torture yourself over this, Az. You don't have to see him again if you don't want to. It seems he'll give me the information."

"I'm pretty sure that if I stop showing up, he'll stop talking," Astrea mumbled. She didn't know why she felt that way, but she did. Something in her gut just told her that Valen was only so interested in being helpful because of the blood they shared.

"Well, if it ever gets to be too much, I'll at least try to deal with him on my own, alright?" Jin said.

"Sure. Can we go find Adi and Marko now?"

With a tight smile, Jin motioned down the corridor and said, "Lead the way."

Chapter 6

Cool air drifted into the car as Astrea cracked the window open. She leaned back into her seat, reveling in the feeling on her skin. She was still burning too hot, still frustrated and exhausted.

They'd found one measly connection at city hall. Theo Kadis had registered his business—of which they already knew the name and address from once visiting that shop—under the names Ren Eklit and Edoard Hestiko. They didn't know who Ren Eklit was, but Astrea had quickly realized Edoard Hestiko was an anagram for Theo's full name.

The business partner, Ren Eklit, had a second business on the northeastern edge of downtown Talmaris. Either that business partner was actually another alias Theo was using or someone who might know where Theo was hiding out. Maybe someone also connected to the void, or someone at least willing to lend Theo a hand now that he was on the run.

"I'm still worried this is just going to be some trap and Nazarov will be waiting," Adi murmured from the front seat. "Doesn't this feel a little easy?"

"I think we could use something easy after what we've been through, don't you?" Marko asked, and Adi grunted. "We'll approach with caution and make sure he's not around."

"Should we have brought more people?" Astrea asked.

"Too many people draw unnecessary attention," Jin said. "If we'd gone back for Civan and Lennor, maybe Balthazar too, and shown up with so many people into what appears to be"—he glanced down at the paperwork in his hand—"a crystal shop, that would be suspicious."

"A crystal shop," Marko muttered. "Of all the pointless things . . ."

"We'll go in and take a look around, and if we don't find anything on Theo within a few minutes, we'll leave," Jin said. "Simple enough."

Right. Simple. Because everything leading up to this moment had been simple.

They continued on through a few more intersections, then turned down a narrow side road with towering trees and pastel storefronts.

"Park here," Jin said to Marko. "It should be several stores down across the road."

Marko pulled to the curb, then shut the engine off. As they all climbed out, Astrea narrowly avoided a pedestrian with an aggressive stride and chip on their shoulder. Red anger flared around the stranger as they continued down the street, briefcase clutched tightly in their hand.

"What was their problem?" Adi murmured as Astrea shook out her skirt.

"I don't really care," she said, watching as the stranger turned the corner at the end of the road. Their energy got farther and farther away until she could no longer sense them. "Let's just see if we can find Theo."

They joined Jin and Marko on the other side of the car, then darted across the road. Several cars in varying colors were parked along the curbs, and a couple of shoppers exited an antique store, but otherwise, the area was quiet.

"That's the shop." Jin pointed at a store a few hundred feet ahead. A sign hung above the door, but the ink was so faded Astrea could barely read it.

"I don't feel much of anything," Astrea said as they moved closer. "Someone's inside, but they're not void."

"Are they scared or angry or anything?" Adi asked.

"No." Just as the area was quiet, the person's emotions were calm and steady. Hints of curiosity that barely tickled the end of Astrea's nose. "They seem to be in fine spirits."

"Then let's go inside," Jin said. "Let's get this over with."

As Marko pushed the door open, a bell tingled, announcing their arrival. Surprise danced over Astrea's skin.

"Hello?" a feminine voice called.

The storefront was mostly open, with display shelves lining the walls and a few tables sitting in the middle of the room. All around them, crystalline dishware and figurines glittered in their cases. Nobody stood behind the counter. Were they in back? Or on the second floor? A narrow staircase was tucked away behind the counter.

"Hello!" Jin exclaimed, nodding to Adi in some silent signal. Adi and Marko split off from where Astrea and Jin stood near the middle of the store, each of them going separate directions. "We're looking for Ren Eklit," Jin added as the other two men crept silently away. "My wife and I are in the market for some new crystal, and we were told this was the place to come."

Rough hesitation scraped against Astrea's cheeks, making her skin itch. "I'll be right out!" the woman yelled as cold fear wafted through the store.

"She's scared," Astrea whispered to Jin, so low she almost didn't hear herself.

He frowned. "That's never a good—"

A loud boom echoed through the shop. A bullet pierced a nearby vase, sending splintered glass through the air and onto the floor. Jin shoved Astrea to the ground so hard she banged her elbow. Adi and Marko sprinted toward the back of the shop as fear and panic overwhelmed the air, a mix of orange and white.

"What was—"

Another shot exploded through the shop, making Astrea's ears ring. More crystalware shattered.

"She's trying to go out the back!" Marko yelled.

Jin hauled Astrea back to her feet. She sprinted after him, past the counter and down the narrow hallway Adi and Marko were in. Panic and fear pressed and pressed into Astrea's chest.

"She's scared!" Astrea called to her friends. None of them responded as they flew out the door one after the other in pursuit of the shooter.

The back of the shop opened onto a dark, narrow alley. Tall buildings rose up on either side of them, obscuring the uneven cobblestone street in shadows. Adi punched out in a quick flurry of motions, not getting anywhere near the shooter. An earthen wall shot up in front of her, blocking her from getting any farther down the alley.

"What was that you said earlier about this being too easy, Adi?" Marko grumbled.

Orange and white undulated around the woman as she turned and aimed a shotgun at the group. "Come any closer to me and I'll blow your heads off," she snarled.

"Will you stop trying to shoot us?" Adi huffed. "Skies."

Astrea wished more than anything Cressida was with them. She'd be able to bend that gun in half with a twitch of her fingers and prevent the woman from firing on them again.

"Why should I?" asked the woman. "I know who you are."

"How could you possibly know that?" Marko asked.

"Because very few people know that name, Ren Eklit, and one of them is dead and the other is an overbearing, narcissistic terrorist." The more this woman spoke, the clearer her slight Zaikudi accent became prominent. Astrea tried to make out her features, but the alley's shadows kept her mostly hidden. "You have ten seconds to tell me why I shouldn't kill all of you."

"Because that overbearing, narcissistic terrorist, Victor Nazarov, wants us dead, too," Astrea said. It was a gamble, assuming Nazarov was who this woman spoke of. But if she knew Theo, and if she was that scared, then there was a good chance that's who she was referring to. "I'm trying to find Theo Kadis. He helped me in the Badlands not that long ago—"

"Theo's dead," the woman spat.

"He's not," Astrea said. "Or, he wasn't the last time I saw him."

Gray confusion spiked in the stranger's aura. "When did you last see him?"

"Very recently in the Badlands," Astrea said. "I'm The One's niece, and my name is—"

"Az," Jin whispered. "What are you doing?"

Astrea took half a step forward, hands held in front of her. The shadowy woman raised her shotgun higher.

"My name's Astrea," she said, trying to hide the tremble in her voice. Staring down the barrel of a gun suddenly seemed like a foolish, foolish gamble. "Theo came to me in the Badlands to warn me about Nazarov. Why do you say he's dead?"

"Because he left me a letter and said he'd probably never come back here," she said. "Because he said there was a slim chance he was coming back from his quest, and he hasn't made contact since. He said if he hadn't contacted me by this week's end, then I should assume he's dead."

"You're assuming he's dead before the deadline?" Marko asked.

"He's got to be if he's crossing Nazarov."

"I don't think he's dead." Astrea lifted her chin a little higher. "I really don't. I think he got sidetracked after what happened in the Badlands and needs to hide out. Please, can you put the gun down? Can we talk?"

"Why the skies should I believe what you say?" asked the woman. "You could be void mages for all I know, sent by Nazarov."

Astrea summoned a tiny ball of light over her hand, illuminating the alleyway. The woman standing before Astrea was tall, with warm tan skin, small eyes, and dark brown hair similar to the twins. Perhaps she was descended from the same region of Zaikud as them.

"I'm not a void mage," Astrea said.

"You're a Lightbringer?" Ren whispered. "Skies . . . look at your eyes."

"Souleater," Astrea corrected. "But yes. I told you, I'm—"

"The next One." Ren lowered her gun. "I'm sorry, I—"

"Can we go back inside and talk?" Astrea asked again. "Please. We need your help if we're going to find Theo and stop Nazarov."

"Fine." Ren jerked her chin back toward her shop. "We can go inside."

Astrea motioned for her to go first. "After you."

With one more skeptical look, Ren started for the building. Fear and worry still clouded her aura, but so did a flicker of green curiosity. That was good. If Ren was curious enough to hear them out, maybe Astrea could convince her to tell them whatever she knew.

The ground rumbled just as Astrea neared the entrance back to Ren's shop. She peeked over her shoulder and found the earthen wall was gone. The alley looked no different than it had originally. Adi's work was solid.

"Follow me," Ren said once they were all back inside.

She headed upstairs, then into a small room with low, slanted ceilings. Jin and Adi both had to stand in the middle of the room, and even then, their heads almost touched the very top, flat part of the ceiling. A couple of small boxes sat in one corner, and there was also a narrow writing desk, but otherwise, the room was empty.

"I take it your name's not Ren Eklit," Jin said, "considering Theo used an anagram for his own name."

"My name's Nezrin Tilke," the woman replied.

"It's nice to meet you, Nezrin," Jin said. "I'm Varojin Auris."

"As in . . ."

"Yes, as in," he said with a tight smile. "This is Adi Kuwat and Marko Livante, and then you've already met my wife."

Nezrin's gaze darted to Astrea. "You're married?"

"Indeed," Jin said.

Nezrin's mouth dropped open, then she shook her head. "The sun and moon . . . the vision was right . . ."

"We don't believe we're this sun and moon," Astrea said. "But it seems your previous organization wants to force us into the roles."

"They are nothing if not persistent," Nezrin said.

"What made you leave?" Marko asked.

Nezrin rolled up the cuffs of her long-sleeved blouse. On both of her wrists were the Paragon symbol, the same four-point star and two concentric circles they'd first seen tattooed on people back in Kalama and Sezia.

"Like many, I wasn't born into the Paragon," Nezrin said, her light brown eyes downcast. "My late husband was, though, and brought me in, too, when I was very young." Nezrin couldn't have been older than forty. "Like me, Theo joined in adulthood. And like me, he began to question the way things were done. Leaving wasn't easy."

"I can imagine," Jin said. "It doesn't seem like a group that will let its members leave voluntarily."

Nezrin shook her head. "My husband and I got out, but only after we paid them huge sums of money. Nearly bankrupted us. He died a few years ago from a sudden-onset illness."

"It couldn't be healed?" Marko asked.

"We had no money left for healers." Nezrin shook her head again and huffed. "Theo and my husband had been good friends, but Theo stayed with the Paragon for longer than we did."

"Why?" Astrea asked.

"He believes in restoring balance one way or another." Nezrin set the butt of her shotgun on the ground. Orange fear spiked above her head as she said, "I never followed Nazarov, but I knew of him. When Theo told me he was breaking off from The One, I thought he meant for good, but . . . apparently not. I warned him that Nazarov was too aggressive, too . . . unhinged, quite frankly."

"Don't disagree with you there," Adi muttered.

"Theo was helping me out financially after my husband died, hence the business license," Nezrin said. "But in the last few months, he's come around more. Always in the dead of night. Always in a rush. And then he told me what I mentioned before, that if he wasn't back by the end of this week, to assume he was dead. I don't want to believe he is, but . . ."

"Nor do I," Astrea said. "As *I* said, Theo came to me recently. He warned me of what Nazarov wanted from me: to either kill me or force me to bear a child so that he had some connection to the Paragonian throne. And then he helped us escape Nazarov and make it to Thasia."

"Thasia?" Nezrin asked, eyebrows furrowing.

"Yes, and we haven't seen him since," Jin said. "We need to find him. We think he can either lead us to Nazarov or get us one step closer to shutting down the Paragon."

"He has some defectors on his side," Astrea said. "Other people who, like you, Nezrin, think Nazarov's gone too far. People who still want balance but not in the way Nazarov is promising it."

"Chaos and destruction," Nezrin mused. Blue sadness twined around her thin body. "War does terrible things to people, you know. My father became a very cruel man after fighting in one of the wars with Delia."

"That's why we want to stop as much of that as we can," Jin said. "There's been enough war and suffering. People deserve a chance at peace and healing."

"Theo was always such a kind soul." Nezrin's shoulders slumped forward. "I never understood why he decided to follow Nazarov. He reminds me a lot of my husband that way . . . being kind, I mean. Theo's the only family I have left."

"Then help us find and protect him," Astrea said. "Please. You'll be protecting your family and many others."

"He told me about you," Nezrin said. "Both of you. When I last spoke to him, he said to help you if you ever came here."

"Does Nazarov know about this place?" Jin asked.

"It probably wouldn't be hard for him to find," Nezrin replied with a shrug. "Our pseudonyms weren't exactly foolproof."

"And Nazarov knew of Theo's antiquities shop on the other side of town," Marko said. "We should assume this location is compromised, too."

"If you help us, Nezrin, we'll protect you," Jin said. "We'll protect you, and we'll do our best to find Theo."

With a shuddering breath, Nezrin said, "I suppose I don't have much of a choice at this point if I want to stay alive." She nodded. "Fine. But let me grab everything important."

"Be quick," Jin said. "We don't want to stick around too long if Nazarov might be looking for you, too." As Nezrin slipped out of the room and went back downstairs, Jin said, "Marko, go watch her?"

With a grunt, Marko headed after Nezrin.

"You think she's telling the truth?" Adi asked.

"I do," Astrea said. "Her aura was full of fear any time she mentioned Nazarov. She was terrified when she thought he'd sent us to kill her."

"Maybe, but does she actually want to help?" Adi asked.

"Even if she only wants to find Theo alive and well, that's good enough for me," Jin said. "We'll keep her under tight security at the palace . . . in the guardhouse. And we'll get to work on finding Theo as soon as we can. Let's go help Marko keep an eye on her."

As Jin followed the first two and returned to the first floor, Adi hesitated. So did Astrea, watching as a flicker of dark green concern lit up the space around the Earthmover.

"Adi?" she asked.

"It's fine," he said. "I don't know. It all feels like a lot lately."

The Badlands, her father, now this Nezrin . . . It *was* a lot.

"If we can just get a lead, maybe we'll be able to straighten it all out," she said.

"Right." He offered her a tight smile. "A lead. One that hopefully doesn't involve any cross-continental travel."

Astrea hoped so, too. Because as much as they all desperately needed a break, there wasn't any time for that. If they could at least stay close to Talmaris for a little while longer, maybe they could regain some of their footing and end the rest of this quickly.

CHAPTER 7

By the time they returned to the palace, the sun was beginning to set and the compound was preparing for its nightly lockdown. Guards and soldiers hustled past the garage, where Vernie met Astrea, Jin, Adi, Marko, and Nezrin. Astrea hadn't expected to see Vernie back in Talmaris anytime soon, but she also felt like she didn't have much of a handle on anything lately.

"Commander Lucian told me to expect you back," Vernie said. "This is our . . . informant?"

"Vernie, this is Nezrin," Jin said. "She's a Paragon defector and close with Theo Kadis."

Vernie nodded. "Very good. This way, please, Nezrin."

Hesitation scraped Astrea's skin. "It's alright, Nezrin," she said. "Vernie is great. They're one of the best guards here and a close supporter of the cause."

"Because that makes me feel better," Nezrin murmured.

"We'll be around if you need us for anything," Astrea said. "Just ask for any of us."

"And until then, am I a prisoner here?"

"Informant in protective custody," Jin corrected. "Not prisoner. You'll be in the guardhouse for safety, but you'll be given meals and access to us. Besides, we'll need your help tomorrow. We've got some information to go over with you as we plan our next steps."

"Right," Nezrin said with a huff. "Finding Theo."

"Get some rest," Jin said. "We'll see you tomorrow."

Once Nezrin followed Vernie into the darkening gardens, Jin wrapped his arms around Astrea's shoulders. "We need to talk to Ellie and Zephyrine," he said.

She leaned into his half embrace. As irresponsible as it was, Astrea wanted to call it a day. Her capacity was low. Not just her mental energy but her social energy. Her ability to even think. It was like she was moving through molasses.

"And eat something," he continued, then glanced at Adi and Marko. "You two want to come?"

"I'd actually like to see what Vernie's planning to do for Nezrin." Marko shifted his weight from foot to foot. "Do you need me?"

"No," Jin said. "We'll be fine. Do whatever you need to do."

With a quick glance and frown at Adi, Marko hurried off in the direction Vernie and Nezrin had gone. Adi huffed.

"Something wrong?" Jin asked.

"No . . ." Adi shook his head. "But that was strange, right?"

Astrea shrugged. Marko was often a bit aloof, especially when on the job.

"Strange how?" Jin asked as they started toward the palace.

"I don't know," Adi said. "He's been acting strange since we got back from Thasia."

"Maybe because you got shot and it scared him," Jin said.

"Well he got that concussion from those Helosian soldiers and I didn't get scared."

"You were a little scared, Adi," Astrea said. She'd hardly seen Adi terrified, but when Rami and Marko had returned to the safe house in southern Helosia and Marko had been injured . . . "More than a bit scared."

"Yeah, well, I didn't pull away," he murmured.

"Be patient with him."

"Yeah. Yeah, you're right."

The palace halls were filled with Delian, Taipoli, and Tornamian guards, all dressed in their countries' colors. Light blue, tan, and green, respectively. They stuck out among the Novarians dressed in midnight blue. Veiko must've invited the delegations to stay in the palace.

As they neared their rooms, Astrea was relieved to find only Novarian guards, as usual. At least they weren't going to suddenly have to share this area.

Jin knocked once on Eliana's door, poised to knock a second time, when Nicos opened it. His long auburn hair hung loosely around his shoulders instead of being in its typically tidy bun, and his beard was freshly trimmed. He wasn't in uniform, either, but a simple gray shirt with black training pants.

"Finally," he said, side stepping so they could enter.

Jin nudged Astrea inside first, then Adi, before he finally followed. "Where's Ellie?" he asked, closing the door behind him. "We've got a lot to talk about."

"I'm here," she said, waltzing out of the bedroom and into the sitting room. Her hair was wet, like she'd just taken a shower. "You're finally back. What took you so long?"

"We ended up with a slight change in plans today." Jin sat down on the small sofa, and Astrea followed him, reveling in the soft cushions as soon as they hugged her body.

"Bad change?" Eliana asked, sitting down across from them in an armchair. Nicos and Adi both remained standing.

"Good change, I think," Jin said. He explained that Valen had given them some locations and at least a few translated phrases, then the debacle that was finding Nezrin.

Eliana's eyes narrowed. "You call getting shot at twice a good change in plans?"

"Obviously that part wasn't ideal," Jin said, "but we found a connection to Theo, Ellie. And we found it quickly. I'm hoping that either she knows where Theo might be hiding out or that one of these old Paragon sights can lead us to either Theo or Nazarov."

"You think Theo would go to an old Paragon site?" Nicos asked. "Even though he's defected?"

"It's not my first guess, but maybe there's one they no longer use or one Nazarov doesn't know about that he'd visit," Jin said. "Or maybe there's someplace he'd go in Talmaris or some kind of coded message Nezrin can leave for him. I don't know. We'll figure it out in the morning."

Eliana's lips pressed together. "I see."

"You don't think it's a good idea?" Jin asked.

"No, it's not that. We need to find Theo and these other void mages and quickly," Eliana said. "Our new allies are eager to meet with them and discuss what options we have to stop Nazarov and Father."

"And we will get that arranged as soon as possible," Jin replied.

Eliana ran a hand through her wet, tousled waves. "I just want to make sure we're being careful and doing our due diligence."

"Vernie and Marko are organizing Nezrin's custody right now," Jin said. "They're skeptically optimistic. So am I. A little hope right now wouldn't hurt."

"Father always used to say hope is a dangerous thing," Eliana said.

"Bleak," Adi muttered.

"As his lessons with us often were. But I'll be skeptically optimistic about the whole thing, too," she said. "Did you three have dinner yet? You must be starving after being out all day."

"I was going to check on Cress before I did anything else," Astrea said. "Has she been by today?"

"No, but I've been trying to give her the space she asked for," Eliana said.

"Well, I'm still going to check on her." Pushing off the sofa, Astrea held back a groan. "Do you need me for anything else?"

"All the delegations want to meet again tomorrow," Eliana said. "And they'd really like to see you both there. They weren't pleased by your absence."

"An absence that got them the lead they need." Jin rolled his eyes. "But yes, we'll be there."

"Good." Eliana turned to Astrea again. "That's all. Tell Cress she's got to see me eventually."

"I will." Astrea managed a weak smile as she said good night and headed into the corridor. She had to make herself not look toward Saros's old room.

Cressida's door was a few dozen feet down the hall. Pausing outside, Astrea sat with the energy pulsing around her. The boredom and curiosity of a few of the nearby guards. Heavy exhaustion farther away—probably Jin's based on the direction. And coming from Cressida's room was a mix of frustration and fatigue.

Astrea knocked. That frustration grew.

She pressed closer to the door and called, "It's me, Cress. I wanted to say good night."

A few heartbeats passed, and Astrea wasn't sure if Cressida would answer. Finally, though, the door swung open.

"Hey, Az." Cressida's left arm was back in its sling, mostly obscured by the white fabric. Her shoulders rolled forward as she sighed. "Sorry."

"No need to apologize."

"You just wanted to say good night?"

"And let you know we have a lead on Theo."

Cressida nodded, but her expression didn't change. "That's good."

"We'll get started on it all tomorrow morning if you want to join us." When all Cressida did was shrug in response, Astrea asked, "Did you get anything done with your dad today?"

"I don't really want to talk about it, Az," Cressida said with a huff. "Nothing against you, just the topic."

Leaning forward, Astrea lowered her voice even more and asked, "Something with your dad?"

"Yeah, he's being overbearing and won't let me do anything on my own. As if I can't. Says I shouldn't while I'm using pain tonics."

Maybe Balthazar had a point with that. Working with metal often meant sharp edges, and pain tonics had side effects like dizziness and sleepiness.

"I see," Astrea said.

Cressida frowned. "You agree with him."

"No!" she said quickly. "No, well . . . a bit. Maybe take it easy for a few more days until you don't need the tonics anymore."

"Great, you're on his side." Annoyance arced out from Cressida in waves of rust red. "Wonderful."

Astrea pressed her lips together. Now probably wasn't the time to have this conversation with Cressida. Still, she said, "You know I think you can do anything, Cress. *Anything*. But tonics limit even the most brilliant and capable people, including you."

Cressida grunted.

"You know where to find me if you need me." Astrea started across the hall for her room, but she paused and peeked over her shoulder. "Night, Cress."

"Good night," Cressida said, already shutting the door.

So much for Cressida's earlier optimism. But Astrea couldn't blame her. The tonics alone would mess with someone's mind, let alone the trauma Cressida had been through.

The trauma all of them had been through.

Astrea had certainly had more than her fair share of moody days. And even now, after losing Saros, all she wanted to do was curl up in a ball and cry.

Let it be, Astrea told herself as she walked into her bedroom. *Try again with her tomorrow.*

CHAPTER 8

Hot and cold fire warred on Astrea's skin. She gasped, her eyes cracking open. The bedroom was dark, quiet.

Dark? Jin had set her nightlight on. Had the bulb burned out?

Her eyes fluttered shut again. Tired. She was so tired.

And cold, now that visions of the Badlands were fading into the back of her sleepy mind.

Astrea patted around her side of the bed in search of covers. There, at her feet maybe?

More goose bumps prickled her exposed skin. Stupid nightgown. Its thin straps and light fabric did nothing for the cold autumn night.

Moving toward the middle of the bed, she bumped into something hard and warm. So warm. As soon as she touched his naked back, Jin rolled over and pulled her close. Astrea settled against him, yawning and burrowing deeper into the bed with him.

Her eyes closed despite how hard she tried to open them. Large, firm hands skimmed her waist. Warm lips pressed against her neck.

"You awake?" Jin murmured, voice thick with fatigue.

"Mhm."

"Can't sleep."

Astrea let out a little sigh. "It's okay."

"Yeah." His head settled right behind hers.

Electric anxiety skittered across Astrea's skin. She rolled over in Jin's arms. She fumbled around in the dark, eventually finding his cheek. His beard had grown in some in recent days, thick under her fingers.

"It's okay," she said again. Orange clung to his skin, faint in the night.

"Can't believe I took you there, Az. Into Helosia. You and Saros and Cress . . ."

"It's okay." She pulled his mouth down to hers and gave him a soft kiss. Jin rested his forehead against hers. "Not your fault."

"I'm sorry." His lips brushed the skin just below her ear. "Sorry I woke you."

"You didn't."

"Really?"

"No . . ."

Chuckling, Jin draped his arm over her. She nuzzled the base of his neck and pressed a gentle kiss there. His pulse thudded under her lips, strong and true.

"Go back to sleep," he whispered.

She slung her leg over his hip and moved in closer. He was so warm. And smelled so good, like eucalyptus and sage.

Jin sucked in a sharp breath and kissed her neck. Something hard pressed against her belly. She wiggled her hips. Need overtook her and battled with her exhaustion, barely winning.

Jin whispered something against her throat, then sucked on the delicate skin there. Astrea's back arched, and he pressed a hand flat against her back, holding her in place.

"Good?" he asked.

"Mhm."

Wet heat pooled in her core. It ached. *She* ached. Jin hadn't touched her like this since the day after their wedding. There'd been no time. No privacy. Too much to try to fix.

But here, safe in the Novarian palace, in the middle of the night . . .

Jin's hand drifted from her waist down toward her hip. He caressed her thigh, bringing his fingers lower and lower. He touched her on top of her bloomers, sucking in a sharp breath.

Astrea reached between them and palmed Jin through his underwear. He was rock hard. She slipped her hand under the waistband and gripped his erection, moving her hand up and down in slow strokes.

Jin cursed, and warm pleasure spread over her limbs. Tart lust exploded on her tongue. He yanked down her bloomers, then pushed her hand away and yanked his underwear off, too. Somehow, he got her rolled over so her ass was pressed into his groin. Then he pulled her leg over his, spreading her wide open. She tried to reach for him again, but he held her in place, fingers caressing every inch of her. She mewled, an embarrassing little sound.

"Fuck, Az," Jin whispered into her hair. His free hand grabbed her chin, turning her head so he could kiss her as his fingers slid inside her. "Fuck, I missed you."

Astrea moaned into his mouth as her whole body came alive.

"I know," he murmured, letting go of her chin and yanking down the top of her nightgown, exposing one breast. He swirled his thumb around her nipple, already hard from the cold air.

His fingers pumped in and out of her, faster and faster, as he pinched her nipple with his other hand. Astrea's hips bucked. He slowed, then pulled out of her.

"Please," she whispered.

He shifted them, rolling Astrea so she was on top of him, on her back. Her head rested on his shoulder. The head of his erection rubbed against her entrance, and Astrea rolled her hips, desperate.

He pushed in. Astrea's eyes fluttered shut as he stretched her.

"Skies," she whispered, head swimming. "Missed you, too."

Astrea's fingers drifted right to her clit, rubbing smooth, quick circles, and Jin thrust into her again and again and again.

"Fuck," he growled. "Fuck, Az."

His fingers joined hers, rubbing the same spot over and over and over again. Her inner walls clenched and clenched. He fucked her right over the edge, until she was a quivering mess on top of him.

He rolled them over again, this time climbing on top of her and pushing right into her. He groaned. "Missed this," he said again. "Need you."

Jin gripped her thighs and pushed her legs back, spreading her wide for him. He slammed into her again and again. Stars danced behind Astrea's eyelids. Her fingers tangled in his hair, the other hand gripping his strong arm. She reveled in the way his muscles flexed, the way he rolled his hips against hers.

He brought her legs all the way to his shoulders, pushing deeper, deeper, deeper into her. Astrea's core tightened. He kissed her calf so gently, but his pace was punishing in the best way. She fumbled her way down to that sensitive spot again, barely pressing into it and climaxing again.

Jin lowered her legs, bracketed his arms around her head, and kissed her hard, slow, deep. Astrea whimpered into his mouth, oversensitive. But skies, she wanted to feel that bliss he felt. Didn't want his warmth to go away. Just wanted to feel good.

A few more thrusts had him tumbling over the edge with a loud swear. Warm bliss spread first into Astrea's chest, then down her arms and torso. So warm she almost wasn't cold anymore.

As Jin pulled out of her and rolled to one side, Astrea forced her eyes open. Raspberry lust, that deep purple reverence, pink love, even orange anxiety and deep blue sadness. The colors danced through the night, bright and true and real.

"I'm sorry if I woke you," Jin whispered, one arm circling her shoulders and pulling her closer toward him. He kissed her forehead.

"You didn't." Astrea sighed contentedly, burying her face in the crook of his neck. A light sheen of sweat covered his skin, but she didn't mind. She *had* missed this. Not just sex but getting to be with him, feeling everything he did. The way her body seemed to relax around him, like it knew she was safe.

As her breathing slowed and her eyelids grew heavy, Jin nudged her. "Gotta clean up."

She groaned.

"I know." He kissed her forehead again. "C'mon."

"Get me an extra blanket?" she asked, then she forced herself out of bed and into the bathroom. The tiles under her bare feet were freezing, jolting her mind back to the realm of the waking. Astrea hurriedly cleaned herself up, then scurried back to bed.

Jin went into the bathroom, too. When he returned a minute later, he had another blanket draped over his arms. He laid it on top of her, then went to the corner of the bedroom where her nightlight sat. He muttered a curse.

"Bulb burned."

"It's alright. Come back to bed."

He circled to his side of the bed and climbed in. "Better?"

"Yes, thank you."

Astrea rolled close to him again, pulling on her light and pressing it to the shoulder where he'd been shot. There it was, that permanent reminder, a gnarly scar with faded shadows swirling out from the center. She pushed that warm light under his skin, searching. Magic swirled in her mind's eye, but it found nothing.

"What are you doing?" Jin whispered, laying his hand on hers.

"Checking on you."

"You did a very good job of healing me the first time."

"Just want to make sure." Dismissing her light, she pulled her hand away. She didn't love the darkness taking over the room, but being tucked into Jin's side, the shadows didn't seem as overwhelming as usual.

Jin smoothed her hair back. "I was thinking . . ."

"Oh, here we go," Astrea whispered. "Thinking."

"Shush." He kissed the end of her nose. "I was thinking more about what Eliana said. About hope."

"In the middle of the night?"

"Yes. And what you said earlier about family," he said quietly. "I don't want you to lose your hope for winning this fight after what happened."

Tears pricked her lash line. "I don't know that I had very much to begin with."

"Maybe not, but I want you to know we're going to do everything we can, alright?"

She nodded, though he probably couldn't tell with the way her head barely moved against his chest. "Cress needs some hope, too."

"We all do. We just have to find a way to hold onto it."

"A problem for the morning," Astrea whispered.

"Yes," he said gently. "Go back to sleep."

"What about you?"

"I'll sleep, too. Once you do."

"Promise?" Astrea yawned. "I can feel how tired you are."

"I promise."

With Jin's word and love settling near her heart, Astrea pushed back against the shadows, hoping not just for better dreams but a better future, even if it was hard to imagine.

Chapter 9

Astrea rubbed at her tired eyes, glad she hadn't yet put on any of the makeup spread before her on the bathroom counter. She wouldn't normally bother, but going to speak with all the delegates from their alliance was important enough to warrant the extra effort.

"Here." Jin strode into the bathroom in his underwear, then set a small mug on the counter. "It's not the good stuff, but it's something."

"Thanks." Astrea picked up the kohl pencil and examined it, trying to decide if it was sharp enough. The mirror was still foggy after their shower a few minutes before.

"You alright?"

"Not really," Astrea admitted. "Cress is upset—understandably—I barely see Lennor or Civan anymore, Sarsali treats me like I'm going to break every time we're in the same room, and I really, truly do not want to go to this meeting."

"You could skip it if you wanted to," Jin said. "Ellie and I can handle it."

Astrea shook her head. "I need to go. They need to see me there. See that I'm serious about stopping Nazarov and finding Theo. I don't want them thinking I'm somehow siding with the enemy."

"You don't think Ellie and I can convince them of that?"

"Honestly, I don't think it matters how convincing you two are. Any missteps on my part will probably look even worse than usual now that they all know I'm connected to the Paragon by blood."

"You're probably right."

Setting the eyeliner down, Astrea reached for the mug instead. She didn't even have to inhale deeply; it was clearly weak. Watery. The bad stuff. "This is really all we have to drink?"

"Working on getting some Tornamian stuff imported," he said with a small smile.

"Thank the skies." Her first test sip made her grimace, but she took another one anyway. "Alright, when do I need to be ready by?"

"Another ten minutes?" Jin shrugged. "Meeting starts at half past the ninth bell, but I figured we should be early this time."

"Good idea."

They continued working in tandem, Astrea dabbing on the lowest acceptable amount of makeup possible and Jin trying to get his wet curls dry with a spare towel. They split the coffee between them.

Finally, they were dressed and nearly ready to go. All she needed were her wedding rings and opal necklace. She crossed the distance to her nightstand and plucked up the delicate jewelry.

"Let me," Jin said as she fumbled while clasping her necklace.

He moved her hair over one shoulder, then took the necklace from her. Jin's quick fingers made it seem so easy, especially when he was fixing her hair again a moment later.

"Thanks," she murmured as his hands came to rest on her shoulders.

Jin pressed a kiss to the back of her head. "Any time."

With that set, they left their room and headed downstairs. The closer they got to the central part of the palace and the war room where the meeting was to take place, the more crowded it became. So long had these halls been either mostly empty or patrolled just by Novarian soldiers that it was still unsettling. Part of Astrea didn't trust these people at all. But based on their auras—many of them readable—she had no reason to find them suspicious. No reason other than Zaikudi betrayals, Paragon attacks, and all manner of deception there might be in these halls.

When they reached the war room, a Novarian guard opened the door. Jin motioned for Astrea to go in first. She did, and much to her surprise, the room was empty.

"Maybe we came a bit too early," Jin murmured as the door shut behind them.

"Better so they see we're serious," Astrea said.

They sat across from the door so they could watch everyone who entered. After a few minutes, a palace staffer swept into the room with a tray of coffee. Two more staffers came after that, rolling in carts laden with pastries, tea, and juice. Astrea hoped that food and drink wouldn't be too much of a distraction for seasoned politicians and diplomats, but she'd also heard enough of Eliana's complaints over the years about how these types of people would take any opportunity they could to delay the process, including tea.

Still, when Jin poured Astrea a cup of coffee, she took it, dumping in an extra spoonful of sugar in hopes of covering up the terrible taste. It helped a little. She was about to ask Jin for a refill when the door opened again, though this time, a knot of orange anxiety filled the air.

"Good, you're here early," Eliana said as she strode in, delicate heels clicking on the wood floor. They perfectly matched her red dress, which featured a full, tea-length skirt and tight bodice that showed off her curves.

Nicos followed her, looking somehow regal despite only wearing a charcoal gray shirt and black slacks. His auburn hair was pulled back in a short braid, though a few loose pieces framed his freckled face.

"Wanted to make a good impression," Jin said.

"Since when do you care about good impressions?" Eliana asked as she swiped a muffin from one of the pastry carts set against the far wall.

"It's not like I ever *want* to make a bad impression."

She shrugged and bit into her muffin. "Just do what we talked about last night, and it should all be fine."

"What did you talk about?" Astrea asked.

"Those who must be persuaded," Eliana said. "Some of these representatives aren't exactly eager to get going."

"Oh, wonderful." Why hadn't Jin told her that, though?

"It shouldn't be an issue," Nicos said. "We have enough support to at least start. If the first few efforts go well, it should sway the others."

"Spoken like a politician," Eliana said, smiling up at him.

He gestured to the empty chairs around the table. "Would you like to take a seat, Your Imperial Highness? Or are you going to shock everyone when they walk in and find you standing eating a muffin like a commoner?"

"Spoken just like my governess, who always thought I had poor manners," Eliana said, winking at Astrea.

All Astrea could muster in return was a tight smile. Despite their teasing, anxiety still swirled around the pair, and next to her, Jin was rigid.

Eliana sat on Jin's other side, and Nicos sat next to her. It put the Auris siblings at the middle of the table, facing the door. Ready to be seen by whoever walked in next.

Zephyrine joined first, then Marko. Princess Delfine, too, then more delegates, councillors, and politicians whose names Astrea couldn't remember. They all studied her and Jin, though whether it was due to surprise or not wasn't exactly clear.

Marko sat down next to Astrea with a small huff, but he didn't say anything. She couldn't get a read on him, either. And she didn't get a chance to ask him what was wrong because Grand Duke Veiko finally arrived.

"Good, everyone's here on time today," he said. "Let's begin."

What followed next was a series of pointless conversations, at least to Astrea. There was much rehashing what they'd apparently discussed the day before, from troop numbers each country could commit to the cause to ideas for reconnaissance to Helosian defectors arriving at the Novarian border. It wasn't *pointless*, exactly, but if it had already been discussed, why argue about it again?

"I think we should also consider sending planes over various Helosian camps and bases to distribute pamphlets," said one Novarian general, a woman with light tan skin and golden hair.

"We've already started doing so in southern Helosia," said Nicos. "We went over that yesterday."

The general raised her pointed chin in the air. "We distribute them over as many Helosian bases as possible, tell them what their emperor is really up to and offer to let them come fight for our side."

"Would that even work?" asked President Sikori. Her wheelchair squeaked as she leaned forward to grab her coffee cup.

"Logistically or converting people?" the general asked.

The president shrugged. "Both."

"I don't know that it would be feasible logistically . . . too much airspace to cover while avoiding the Helosians," said Zephyrine, "but it may convert some troops, especially with the way others are already deserting."

Rusty annoyance flared about the Novarian general. "We can figure out the logistics."

"What do you think, Eliana?" Veiko asked. "Would it work?"

"I don't see why not," Eliana replied carefully. "Especially if we tell them their pay has been cut for my father to fund some kind of . . . super weapon development and testing."

"And what do you think, Varojin?" asked Veiko. "You know the military as well as General Kanakos."

"Well . . ." Jin pursed his lips. "We'll have to be particularly careful flying over Helosian bases, as they have heavy artillery they'll be ordered to use, but if everyone's comfortable with that risk, my sister is right. It can't hurt to try to get information to the soldiers on the ground before we launch real attacks."

"Then it's decided," Veiko said. "Generals, begin work on this immediately."

As the Novarian generals murmured among themselves, one Delian delegate, a man with thick black hair and dark brown skin, said, "We already know Emperor Aelius's approximate location and what we need to do about him. What of the Paragon and Lord Nazarov?"

"Actually . . ." Jin cleared his throat. "We have some new information about that."

Curiosity and annoyance exploded around the table. *Why be annoyed, though?* Astrea frowned.

"Ah, yes, our *prisoner*," said Councillor Reis. He shot Jin and Astrea a withering glare.

"Not prisoner," Jin replied. "Yesterday, we not only received intelligence on several potential Paragon hiding locations, but we also learned more about Theo Kadis, our potential void ally in all this. We found one of his contacts here in Talmaris, and though she believes him to be dead, she's willing to help us try to find him."

Whispers and shock rippled around the table, forcing Astrea back in her seat.

"While we aren't quite sure how to find Theo Kadis yet, there's one site in particular that I'm interested in checking out," Jin said, mostly to Veiko and Zephyrine. "It's in the far northwest of Novaria. Very remote."

"You think Victor Nazarov is working from this location?" Veiko asked.

He shrugged. "I don't know, but my gut is telling me to go there."

"Oh, wonderful," drawled Delegate Marosikis, the Tornamian woman who'd been less than friendly at the last meeting. "Prince Varojin has a gut feeling. Is that really where we need to focus our attention, or should we think about more practical matters? "

Her colleague, a man with dark brown skin, shook his bald head.

"You can't write him off simply because you don't believe in gut feelings, Tei," replied the umber-skinned woman next to Marosikis. "We have enough resources combined that we can get moving on other tasks while we also assign a few people to look into this Paragon site." Her blue eyes slid to President Sikori. "Madam President, it's my formal suggestion that we proceed exactly as previously stated. Focus our attention on Helosia but devote some resources to the Paragon problem."

Before the Tornamian president had a chance to respond, several other delegates around the table jumped in with their own opinions. The words were a jumbled mess, and Astrea cringed as annoyance and anger scraped and singed her skin. What was wrong with them? It seemed like a reasonable request, balance between the two fronts they had to fight a war on.

"It seems to me," Eliana called above the noise, making most of the others quiet down, "that Delegate Lani is correct. I won't pretend Helosia isn't the bigger threat at the moment. They are. And we *are* better able to determine their movements. But to focus solely on them leaves an opening for the Paragon. We must split our resources somehow."

"I'll lead the investigation into the Paragon." Jin's posture stiffened. "My team and I will follow up on these leads, and if they don't go anywhere within a week, we'll redirect our attention however this council sees fit. I'm just asking for time to look into this."

Astrea forced her expression to remain neutral and her body to stay still even as she desperately wanted to move away from the energy flowing around the table. Acceptance, anger, annoyance, curiosity, confusion—it all slammed into her, unwelcome and overwhelming. But she didn't dare pull her barrier back, not even when the delegates all started arguing about Jin being in charge of the Paragon mission with his connection to the Paragon's prophecy.

"Enough!" Veiko called over the noise. They didn't quiet. The grand duke shoved out of his seat and again shouted, "I said *enough*!"

A hush fell over the room.

"Prince Varojin has been nothing but helpful throughout this entire ordeal," Veiko said. "My council has not always agreed with his actions, and frankly, neither did my late aunt. But he has proven time and again that he is trustworthy, and I will *not* have this argument again. If he wanted to side with the Paragon—or with Helosia—he would have long ago." He glanced at Jin and Astrea. "That said, with the current unknowns, I think it best if you wait several days before making the trip to the site. Let another team go ahead of you and establish a perimeter."

"But—" Jin started.

"That is the only action I will authorize," Veiko said. "I am sure the rest of the delegates can agree to this."

At that, the politicians around the table began to murmur their agreement. A few abstained from saying anything, while a couple others still disagreed. But almost everyone was on board, which was as good as it was going to get, Astrea supposed.

"Then it's decided," Veiko said. "Prince Varojin and his team will remain in Talmaris for a few more days to continue their investigation while they await word from an advanced team. The rest of us will begin coordinating the air strikes and information distribution campaign. I'll also need to plan a radio broadcast to tell my people we're headed for war." He looked around the table. "I suggest you all do the same. Tell your people. Prepare them for what's coming. We all have a long road ahead."

After being dismissed by Veiko, Astrea followed her friends down the wide corridor, past the other delegates, and to a small alcove tucked around the corner.

"What's this about, Jin?" Eliana asked

"That Tornamian delegate, the one who didn't like my suggestion—"

"Delegate Marosikis," Eliana said.

"Yes, her," Jin said. "Keep an eye on her, would you?"

"You think she's going to try something?" Nicos asked.

"Other than trying to get some of the others to go against this plan? Maybe recruit Councillor Reis if they're not already working together? No, probably not." Jin folded his arms across his chest and sighed. "Wrangling that many people into one course of action will be nearly impossible. We don't need her derailing the agreements we *do* come to."

"And how am I to stop her from doing that, exactly?" Eliana asked. "She's an independent person and isn't even Helosian, not that I was ever able to sway all of the councillors back home . . ."

"But you swayed some," Jin said. "I just think we should focus a bit of our energy on continuing to sway the majority to our side."

Eliana's eyebrow quirked up. "*Our* energy?"

"Your energy," he said.

"You say you're no good at politics, Jin, but you've obviously got some head for it," Zephyrine said.

"I do not," he muttered.

Rolling her eyes, Eliana said, "Fine. But only because you need to focus on the Paragon, otherwise I'd—"

Astrea shushed them as voices and hot anger drew nearer. Tornamians by the sound of it. She didn't dare risk a glance over her shoulder to see if it was who she thought it was.

"Ah," came the very voice she was expecting. Delegate Marosikis, the woman who didn't like Jin's plan. She was alone, and the heat of her anger warmed Astrea's face. "Prince Varojin, Princess Eliana, General Kanakos." She sniffed as she looked at Nicos and Astrea. "Sidebar?"

Jin loosened his posture and tucked his hands into his pockets. "Just checking in with my people before I get to work on finding the void mages," he said.

Rust red annoyance arced out from the delegate as she peered down her narrow nose at them. "How fortunate that you all work so well together."

"I should think so, Delegate," Eliana replied. "I know personally how hard it is to get people around a table to see eye to eye. A frustrating position to be in."

"Yes, well, my colleagues and I don't always get along." She flashed a smile. "All part of the job, though, isn't it, Your Imperial Highness?"

Eliana smiled back. "Indeed it is. And a fair trade-off considering the privilege we get with such power, wouldn't you say?"

Marosikis's uneasy smile returned as rusty annoyance arced out from her. "Yes, of course." She shook her head once. "Well, I'll leave you to your sidebar. I look forward to hearing more of your findings, Prince Varojin."

Marosikis turned on her heel and stalked off before any of them had a chance to reply.

"She was annoyed," Astrea whispered. "And a bit angry."

"No surprise," Eliana murmured. "Obviously she didn't like the implication."

"And that was?" Jin asked.

"That she's trying to make some kind of power grab. President Sikori's term is up in the spring. Delegate Marosikis could be trying to position herself for election."

"And you said I have a head for politics?" Jin asked Zephyrine. "I didn't even know they had an election coming up."

"Leave this part to me," Eliana said. "You handle the war, I'll handle the rest."

"Oh, great," Jin muttered.

"What?" she asked. "Our specialties, right? Let's play to our strengths."

Astrea set her hand on Jin's forearm and squeezed it gently, trying to ignore the cold, steely pain whispering from behind his wall. It was callous, at best, for Eliana to suggest war was Jin's *strength*. Even if he'd lived it for eight years. Surely Eliana knew he didn't want that to be his strength.

"We should go speak to Nezrin and Tomas," Jin said to Astrea. "I'll fill you in later, Ellie." Then with a nod to Nicos and Zephyrine, Jin grabbed Astrea's hand, and they headed down the hall.

"You're alright?" Astrea asked as the pain floating around Jin receded inch by inch.

"As good as I can be." He kissed the back of her hand. "Come on. Let's get to work."

Chapter 10

The guardhouse, being smaller and less grand than the palace, felt more welcoming. Less drafty, less enormous. But it was more crowded than Astrea remembered seeing it before, with more Novarian soldiers milling about among the palace guards.

"Astrea!" called Marko. "Jin!"

As he pushed through the crowded corridor, he muttered a curse at one of the soldiers, a young man who seemed completely oblivious to what was going on. Behind Marko, Adi murmured polite excuses and even a few apologies.

"We were going to speak with Nezrin," Jin said. "Where is she, exactly?"

"I'll take you to her," Marko said. "This way."

Marko scooted in front of them, then continued on his rampage down the hall.

Adi sighed. "He's been in a sour mood since last night."

"Lover's quarrel?" Jin asked as they followed the blond Tempest.

"I swear I had nothing to do with his mood," Adi said.

"I was just teasing."

"Yeah, well, I wish I *was* the problem," Adi said. "At least then I'd know how to fix it."

Astrea pressed her lips together. She had no idea what to tell Adi. Marko's wall was as tight as could be, shutting her out completely. Other than his obvious annoyance, she couldn't glean what he was really feeling.

"Have you seen Cress this morning?" Astrea asked.

"Yeah, she was going to see her parents," Adi said.

That was good at least. "Has she seen Lennor?"

"I don't think so."

Astrea frowned. Maybe not so good. She'd have to try to check on Cressida again later. But first, they had a former Paragon member to talk to.

Eventually, Marko turned right and began descending a well-lit staircase, and Jin jokingly asked, "You're not keeping her in some dungeon, are you?"

"No," Marko muttered, "we're not keeping her in a *dungeon*. There are additional rooms downstairs."

Even for Marko, this was grumpy. Jin glanced down at Astrea, but all she could do was shrug.

At the bottom of the stairs, they turned left down a plain hallway. The floors and walls were stone, and simple electric lights hung at even intervals overhead. After passing several wood doors, Marko stopped at one and knocked.

"Nezrin, it's Marko!"

A muffled response came, followed by an uncomfortable mix of curiosity and annoyance. Marko opened the door and pushed inside. It was as plain as the hallway, with a simple wooden bed, small table, and wash basin.

"I thought you said this wasn't a dungeon," Jin murmured.

Marko shot him a glare over his shoulder, then turned to Nezrin. "We'd like to speak with you more about where Theo Kadis might be or where the new One might go. Do you have time?"

Nezrin, who was seated on the bed and looked no worse for the wear despite spending the night in this sad little room, grimaced. "What else could I possibly have to do?" she snapped.

Why was everyone so testy? First some of the delegates, then Marko, now Nezrin? All Astrea wanted to do was find answers, not deal with peoples' attitudes. Was that so much to ask?

"I'd actually like to show you some maps up in the library," Jin said. "Maybe you can help us figure out which target to go to next."

"You think I'd be any good at that?" asked Nezrin.

"You've spent more time with the Paragon than us," Jin said. "It's worth a try, right?"

Nezrin's full lips pressed together. "I suppose that was why I came here in the first place."

Without another word, Marko spun around and stalked out of the room again. Astrea was going to have to get him alone for a few minutes to see what was wrong with him. But until then, she would have to try to ignore him.

They wove their way back through the guardhouse in heavy silence, then cut through the gardens before re-entering the palace closer to the library. All the while, Nezrin marveled at the sights, green curiosity lighting up the air around her despite her earlier snippiness. It was no small thing, being at the palace. Astrea briefly wondered if Theo might also be enchanted by it, the same way he'd been eager to see other pieces of art and history back in Kalama.

Inside the palace once again, Marko marched right to the library and opened the doors. Astrea had half expected to find the Tornamian delegate in there just to spite them, or perhaps someone else from the newly formed alliance. But the library was quiet as always. The only difference was that a low fire now burned in the fireplace on the far side of the room.

"Tomas!" Marko called. "I've brought visitors."

The librarian emerged from his office on the second floor and circled the mezzanine. He hurried down the spiral staircase, calling, "Prince Varojin! Adi! Astrea! Perfect." Once on the ground floor, he pushed his round spectacles up his nose with his free hand while his other held several sheets of paper and rolled-up parchment. He appraised Nezrin, then asked, "Who's this?"

"This is Nezrin Tilke," Astrea said, "an associate of a void mage who's offered an alliance with us. We thought it might be helpful for her to review what we gave you yesterday."

Tomas's eyes narrowed. "Is *she* a void mage?"

"No," Nezrin said quickly. "Not a mage at all, actually."

"Good." Tomas gestured to one of the nearby tables. "Shall we sit?"

As they all settled in, Tomas spread out the rough translations Astrea's father had provided as well as the map with the marked Paragon sites. Nezrin immediately reached for the translated pages.

"Where did you get these?" she asked.

Astrea hadn't even thought this woman might be able to read the language. "Do you know what they say?" she asked.

"No, but Theo was always interested in it," she said. "Did he give you these?"

"Not exactly," Jin said. "Another former Paragon member did, though he doesn't read the language fluently, so those are half translations at best."

"My husband was fluent," Nezrin murmured. "So was Theo."

"Yes, he translated something else for us a while back," Astrea said.

"What?" Gray confusion sparkled around Nezrin for a moment, then she shook her head. "Why would he do that?"

"It was an exchange of information, but now I wonder if he was always trying to help us in some way," Jin said.

"He *did* fight to let us keep the original journal . . ." Adi pinched the bridge of his nose. "Was this always his plan? Why not come to us sooner?"

"I don't think so," Astrea said. But even if it had been, what did it matter now? Theo hadn't been *that* helpful during that meeting so long ago in his shop, and he'd only really seemed to turn on Nazarov recently.

Nezrin set the translations down. "I don't understand how this is going to help us."

"Those may not," Jin said, reaching for the rolled-up map, "but this might." He unfurled it and passed it to Nezrin, who held it flat with her palms. "See these spots marked off?" Jin asked, pointing to the site up near the northwestern coast of Novaria and another farther south. "Do you know these places?"

Leaning forward, Nezrin examined the locations. "Yes, the more southern location is one I know. We went there often for meetings, my husband and I."

"And the northern one, near the ocean?" Jin asked.

"No, actually." She frowned. "What's there?"

"We think it might be an ancient Paragon site," he said. "Would Theo know about a place like this?"

Nezrin bit her lower lip. "He might. He was always reading as much as he could on Paragonian history. Always told me and my husband that it was key to understanding our next steps in achieving balance."

"Did you believe him?" Adi asked.

She shrugged. "I never was one for studying or school."

That didn't really answer the question, but Astrea wasn't going to push. It didn't seem like a useful thing to argue about. Instead, she said, "Would other Paragon members know about it?"

Nezrin shrugged again. "Many simply followed what the higher-ups told them. So if the site wasn't disclosed, then no, they probably wouldn't know."

"So the question is still if Nazarov knows about this place," said Marko dryly. He'd remained standing on the far side of the table, broody as he'd watched the whole exchange.

"I think it's safe to assume he does," Astrea said. "He seemed to be The One's right hand, and now he may have access to all sorts of old Paragon documentation. He'd probably want to go someplace remote after what happened . . ."

"So we go and stay prepared if Nazarov does show up," Adi murmured.

Jin nodded, then said to Nezrin, "If there are any other places you know of where Theo might go or might send one of his followers, could you please write them down for us? We'll investigate every one if you think they're worth our time. We really need his help."

"You're still convinced he's alive?" Nezrin asked.

"I have to be," Jin said. "As I said, we need his help. I won't give up until I know for sure he's dead."

Nezrin stared down at the map again, then at Jin and Astrea. "If you're really the sun and moon, I must trust you to bring balance, as promised. I may not belong to the Paragon anymore, but my husband wholly believed the prophecy was true." Red determination wrapped around her small frame. "I'll tell you what I know, even on the off chance you find something you need."

With Jin gone to help plan for the impending trip to the northwestern part of the country, Astrea made her way back upstairs in search of

Cressida. She would not leave her best friend to deal with any of this alone. And besides, Astrea really didn't want to be alone, either. If she stopped moving—stopped doing—the grief became unbearable.

So, she would keep putting one foot in front of the other. Despite wanting to return to her bed and curl up under the blankets, she would instead stay upright and active. Anything to not be crushed by the weight of it all.

Astrea passed by Cressida's room, feeling only emptiness. Cressida wasn't inside. She continued down the hall, passing by the room Saros once occupied. Her throat tightened, but Astrea didn't even let herself look at the door. She kept her eyes forward, trained on her true destination: Sarsali and Balthazar's room.

Almost as soon as she knocked, the door opened, revealing Balthazar's kind, familiar face. He smiled down at her. "Just the person we could use!"

"Really?" Astrea asked, stepping inside as he made room for her.

Sarsali wasn't there, but Cressida was sitting cross-legged by the coffee table and fiddling with several pieces of silver metal. Blue grief, steel pain, orange anxiety, and even red determination swirled around her, obscuring the colors of the scarf wrapped around her hair.

"What's all this?" Astrea asked, trying to make her voice more cheerful.

"Working on plans for my new hand," Cressida said, not taking her attention off the gleaming metal in front of her.

"And why am I the person you could use?" Astrea asked Balthazar. "You know I'm the last person to ask about anything like that."

"We don't have a question about the metal but about her skin," Balthazar said.

"Why . . . is something wrong?" Astrea tried to get a look at Cressida's injured arm, but it was still obscured by her sling.

"We're afraid the metal will irritate it," Cressida said.

"Oh." Astrea may have been a healer, but she didn't actually know all that much about caring for the human body. There were plenty of nurses and doctors—mages and non-mages alike—who would be better suited for that job. "Would Ivy know? I'm not really sure . . ."

"I don't feel like going down to see her."

"I could call her," Astrea said.

Cressida shook her head. "I'd really rather not."

Balthazar huffed.

As Cressida leaned forward, reaching for a piece of silver, she winced. Pain rolled down Astrea's left arm, from her shoulder all the way down to the tips of her fingers. How was that possible, when Cressida no longer had a left hand? Astrea had heard of patients feeling that before, but she hadn't expected to feel the echoes with her magic.

"When was the last time you took a tonic for the pain?" Astrea asked.

"I'm not taking them anymore," Cressida said, making Balthazar huff again. She glared at him. "I don't want to hear a word."

"Cressida, my dear, won't you just—"

"No! They make me feel like shit, and I already feel terrible enough without the side effects. I don't want to take any more tonics."

Astrea's heart ached. She understood. As much as she could, she understood. It wasn't the same, but after being taken by the Paragon and being drugged up with blue lotus, Astrea's mind had taken weeks and weeks to recover. To stop feeling slow like molasses. Some days it still felt that way, worse since Saros had died. The healing tonics would cause a similar effect in Cressida, and if there was one thing Cressida didn't like, it was being inebriated when there was work to be done.

"Balthazar, could you give us a moment?" Astrea asked.

He shot her a confused look, but eventually, he made his way out into the hall. His energy retreated farther and farther until he was gone, too mingled with other energy for Astrea to distinguish his from the crowd. Only then did she cross the distance to where Cressida sat on the floor between the sofa and coffee table.

Astrea dropped down next to her. Cressida kept her gaze trained on the small pieces of metal she still fiddled with.

"Cress."

"What, Az? It's fine if you can't answer the question my dad had."

"I know, but I'm worried about you."

"Don't be."

"Don't be?" Astrea shook her head. "How can I not be? You're in so much pain." The kaleidoscope of colors around Cressida flared brighter, arcing out and stinging Astrea's skin. "I see it. I feel it."

"Sorry."

"Don't be sorry," Astrea said gently. "Tell me what's wrong. Why aren't you taking the tonics if they'll help?"

"I can't do what I need to do if I'm laid up in bed all day, half-delirious." Cressida's jaw clenched as she began aligning the metal pieces into the shape of a finger. "I told you—told Ellie—that aetherium was bad news. And now look where I am. Look where all of us are."

That mission in the Badlands had gone horribly, terribly wrong. But it wasn't like they went in not knowing the risks. Not knowing what aetherium could do. It was nothing short of a miracle that they had not lost more people. That Cressida had been fast enough to prevent the aetherium's poisonous magic from spreading. That Astrea had been strong enough to save Jin. That they proved it was not necessarily a death sentence.

But telling Cressida all of that wasn't going to help. It didn't change what had happened to her. To Jin. To Saros.

"We need to stop these other governments from controlling it," Cressida said. "All it's going to do is get people hurt."

"I don't think that's only up to us."

"Whatever."

"If you don't want a tonic, will you at least let me heal you?" Astrea asked. "Just enough to take the edge off. I know how badly it hurts."

Cressida's fingers stopped playing with the metal. Her eyes fluttered shut. "It's not fair, Az."

"I know." None of it was fair. Not one single bit of this. Not to any of them, not to the civilians now caught in the crossfire, not even to the soldiers forced to serve under the emperor's command. Tears pricked Astrea's lash line. "I know it's not. But please, let me heal you. Until things start feeling better on their own. Then you can do your work, and I know that always makes you feel better."

A tight laugh left Cressida as tears spilled down her cheeks. She let out a shaky breath. "I suppose it does, doesn't it?"

"And let your dad help. He's worried."

"I know. But he and Ma won't stop hovering."

"They love you. We all do."

Resting her head on Astrea's shoulder, Cressida sighed. "I know."

Astrea circled her arm around Cressida, letting her palm rest near her left shoulder. Light trickled out from between Astrea's fingers as energy coursed through her veins. She pushed it deep under Cressida's skin, low and warm and gentle. It surged ahead, down Cressida's arm with Astrea's guidance. And there. So much pain, like a vise cutting off circulation right above Astrea's wrist. Pins and needles and gut-wrenching pain.

She sucked in a deep breath and pushed more healing energy into her best friend. Cressida relaxed against her shoulder. And finally, the pain lessened, though Astrea's arm still ached with such intensity her head began to swim. Though she wouldn't force Cressida to take any drugs she didn't feel comfortable with, Astrea hoped she would at least take something before bed, something to help her get through the night.

"There," Astrea said as her magic faded to a few twinkles of stardust. "That should help for a while."

"Thank you." Cressida's voice was small, tired.

"I'll always be here to help you, Cress."

"I know." She wiped at her wet cheeks and sat up straighter. "I can't stop thinking about how none of this is fair."

"We'll find a way to make it right." Astrea had to believe that. She just had to, otherwise all they'd lost and all they might still lose would be for nothing. And she could not let that happen. "We'll find a way, Cress. I swear."

Chapter 11

When Astrea had gone to see Cressida again the next day, Jin had left to continue trying to find Nazarov and handle the politics of the whole messy situation. Now, with Cressida working on her prosthetic and not wanting any more company, and with Jin busy, Astrea figured the least she could do was see if there were any updates on building a cipher with which to translate the void language.

Strangely, no guards trailed after her as she walked through the palace halls. Astrea was so used to being accompanied by someone that it was almost peculiar to be alone. But, she supposed, there would be no need with guards and soldiers stationed every dozen feet. Should something happen, there would be plenty of people to assist her.

Astrea even managed to make it to the library completely undisturbed. A few minutes to herself was nice, even if she could never truly be alone with her senses spread wide.

Pushing the library door open, Astrea found not just Tomas but Noemi, Adi, and Lennor, too, all gathered around one of the round tables near the fireplace on the far side of the room. She'd expected Noemi might be there, but Adi and Lennor? Astrea had thought they would be helping Jin plan things out.

"Hey, Az," Adi said, smiling brightly.

The closer Astrea got to their table, it was like a ghost appeared. She could practically see Saros sitting there, not all that long ago, trying to puzzle things out.

Would it ever not hurt? Would her heart ever feel whole again? It was like she was a rowboat lost at sea, always at risk of a giant wave crashing into her and upending whatever little bit of stability she managed to find.

She couldn't cry about this, not now. Not when she needed to check on everything, see how she could help. She couldn't give in to her grief yet. Not when there was so much to be done.

"What's all this?" Astrea asked, pushing her shoulders back.

Spread out were all kinds of worksheets, which appeared to be void letters corresponding to the standard alphabet used on the continent. Not everything was filled in, though, and several parts were scratched out. Beyond that were copies of the void language samples they had, plus the notebook Theo had once translated.

"We've been hard at work on this," Noemi said, gesturing to the table, "but it's still not done."

"Looks like you've accomplished a lot," Astrea said.

"Much of it on her own." Tomas grinned. "Our linguist hasn't exactly been the most accessible person but did get us started."

"You did all this?" Astrea asked Noemi.

Magenta embarrassment flared around her as she ducked her head. "Some."

"*Most*," Tomas corrected. "She did most of it."

"Well, it was important," Noemi said, ducking her head again. "It wasn't that hard to figure out once that linguist got me started . . ."

"Nonsense! You're a natural," Tomas said, and the magenta embarrassment surrounding Noemi flared brighter. "Perhaps you should consider becoming a translator."

"Oh, I don't know about that . . ." Noemi smiled shyly.

"Well, regardless, this is really great, Noemi," Astrea said. "Really, really great. Thank you."

Astrea still didn't know Noemi very well, but she was clearly a smart, hardworking young woman. And Astrea imagined that, if they'd met on different terms and not under the threat of war and death, not with Astrea's mind being pulled in twenty different directions a day, they would already be very good friends. She hoped that they'd have that opportunity sooner rather than later.

And thanks to Noemi's hard work, they had a real break in the mystery of those notes. Even if they had a few missing spots and didn't fully know how the language was spoken, the fact that they *could* translate most of what they had made all the difference in the world.

"Can you two"—Astrea nodded to Tomas and Noemi—"work on the markings in the margin of the book we stole from Kalama? Whatever you can translate would be amazing. Same with the bit on the back of the prophecy we stole in Kalama."

"We'll work as quickly as possible," Tomas said.

With any luck, the void language notes would reveal something they could use as they searched for not just Theo but Nazarov, too. Part of Astrea wanted to stay to help, but three people didn't need to be working on that, and besides, she couldn't bear to be at the same table Saros had sat at not long ago, no matter how badly they needed to find answers.

Excusing herself, Astrea left the library in search of someplace that wouldn't make her lungs squeeze so painfully tight. She hadn't gotten more than a few dozen feet down the hall when Adi called her name.

"Az!" he called again.

Slowing, Astrea folded her arms over her chest. Adi was striding toward her, Lennor a few steps behind him. She practically had to run to keep up.

"Noemi didn't think I was being rude leaving like that, did she?" Astrea asked.

His eyebrows furrowed. "No, not at all. But you did run out of there pretty quickly."

She shrugged.

"I was going to ask how Cress is," Adi said.

"Is she alright?" Lennor asked. "I've been trying not to bother her . . ."

Astrea pressed her lips together. How much did she tell them? She didn't think they needed the details of Cressida's emotional state. That was for Cressida and Cressida alone to decide if and when to share.

"She's getting there," Astrea said. "She was working on some kind of prosthetic with her dad earlier. I think she just needs some time."

"It's a big adjustment," Adi said quietly. "A big loss for her. I've seen it before."

"Can we do anything for her?" Lennor asked. She fidgeted with something in one palm. Her pocket stone, the one gifted to her by Cressida, maybe?

As much as she wanted Cressida to recover quickly, Astrea couldn't push her. Not when she had to grieve what she'd lost—not just Saros but literally part of her body, too. It wouldn't be something Cressida could simply get over. She would need to adjust to her new normal, all on her own terms.

"She's resilient," Astrea said. "She needs space, but she also needs to know we're there. Maybe write her a note or send something to her room so she knows you're thinking about her."

Lennor and Cressida's relationship—if one could call it that—was still so fresh, but Astrea didn't think recent events would scare Lennor away. They might spook Cressida, though, especially given how unsure she was about everything a couple of weeks earlier.

"I can do that," Lennor said with a small smile. "Anything I should include or avoid?"

"Keep it light. Anything else you two need from me?"

Again, she felt like she was being rude, but the palace walls pushed closer around her. She needed to leave, to do something.

"We were actually going to go help Jin, if you want to join us," Adi said. "Noemi's got things handled in the library."

Staying in the palace was the last thing Astrea wanted. But what was she going to do? Say no when there was work to do? And so, Astrea forced herself to smile and follow her friends.

Chaos. The war room could only be described as chaos when Astrea trailed Adi and Lennor inside.

Jin stood at the head of the table, arms crossed tightly over his chest. Rusty annoyance snapped out from him in long lashes, as if reaching for the others around the table. There was Zephyrine, of course, and Lucian, as well as Marko and Civan, but then there were also other Novarian officials. Or at least, Astrea guessed they were Novarian based on their midnight blue uniforms.

"Have you lost your skies damned minds?" asked one of the Novarian officials, a woman with pale skin. Her graying hair was pulled back into such a tight bun that it seemed painful. "You really want to go out there now?"

Astrea took up a spot near the door right next to Adi, trying not to focus too much on the colors swirling around the table. Her eyes and head ached, and they'd barely been in the room for a minute.

"We don't have a choice, Colonel," said Lucian. "This is clearly our next target."

"No doubt it's our target, Commander," the woman replied. "But *Prince Varojin* going? Do you have a death wish, Your Highness?"

"Of course I don't have a death wish," Jin said. "But I do wish to finally take out Victor Nazarov, and *your* 'most trusted scouts'"—he made air quotes around the words—"have just reported that there's activity at this exact location."

"But we can go in without you," said another official, a man with a balding head and tan skin. Astrea couldn't see his face; his back was to the door. "Let the Novarian military handle it. It's not like you've been successful so far."

"The grand duke has already authorized Prince Varojin to go," Lucian said. "And besides, he's one of the few people who's gotten close to Nazarov. You expect him—us—to sit this out?"

"We expect you to heed our advice," said the original woman. A few others nodded. "Let us take care of it."

"I won't," Jin said. "No. My team has the most experience fighting him. He may have gotten away before, but if this is him, then we stand the best chance of taking him down. Inexperienced soldiers won't last more than a few minutes."

"You doubt us?" asked the balding man, voice cold.

"I doubt anyone who hasn't seen this firsthand. It's nothing personal."

The man threw his hands over his head and mumbled something about "royals" and "lost their minds."

"Seeing as we don't need your permission," said Lucian, pointedly looking at the two officials objecting the most loudly, "we're moving forward as Varojin and I planned. See to it that your teams hold their positions and expect us by midnight. Send someone to prepare an airship for us. Dismissed."

The Novarians began filing out of the room, a blend of emotions surrounding them: annoyance, approval, apprehension. Gritting her teeth, Astrea approached where Jin, Lucian, and Zephyrine spoke quietly among themselves.

"Jin?" Adi asked once the last of the Novarians filed out of the room and the door closed.

"We don't know if it's Nazarov up at the location Az's father told us about," Jin said, "but there's someone there."

"Maybe Theo?" Adi asked.

Jin shrugged.

"We'll go tonight and talk to the teams already in position," Lucian said. "Gather your things and meet at the garage in half an hour. We need to move." With a quick glance at Marko, Lucian headed for the door and disappeared into the hallway.

"What was that about?" Astrea asked.

"He's going to go talk to the grand duke," Marko said. How he'd gotten that from one fleeting look, Astrea wasn't sure. "But you heard him. Half hour. Go."

They dispersed, and Astrea jogged to catch up with Jin as he hurriedly explained the situation in more depth to Adi. A half hour was not enough time to do what needed to be done. Astrea needed to talk to Cressida and her parents. Eliana and Nicos. But where would they all be?

They started up the stairs that would take them to their wing of the palace. Astrea needed to get her gear. It would probably be in her room . . . she actually hadn't seen it since that awful day in the Badlands. Would the metal plates be with it, too? They couldn't go without those. And she needed—

"Az?"

Jin's voice made Astrea startle. He'd started to go into their small apartment. Adi was striding down the hall, the twins hot on his heels. She hurried after Jin.

"I need you to stay here, Az," Jin said as soon as she'd shut the door behind her.

Her throat tightened. "What?"

"I need you to stay here in Talmaris, where it's safe." As he turned toward her, his irises burned, like molten gold. "Please."

"You can't ask that of me." The words left her before she could even think to watch her tone. "What about Nazarov? And Theo? You just said the team would take care of it!"

"Adi and I will take care of it," he corrected, voice tight.

"You're going to make me stay here?"

He started for the bedroom. "You'll be with Ellie and Cress."

"No!" Astrea called as she ran after him. "No, I will not stay here. Why are you asking me to?"

"Because I never should've taken you on that skies forsaken mission to the Badlands," he said.

"But then you'd be dead!" She swallowed hard. "You'd be dead if I hadn't gone with you."

"And Saros would be alive and Cress wouldn't be going through what she's going through." Jin yanked the wardrobe doors open and reached for his black bag. "Time and again, I've made the mistake of taking civilians in with me. And you're my family, Az. My wife, my partner. I can't put you in harm's way. Not today."

Why was everyone trying to take choices away from her? Saros had for years, right until the bitter end. Nazarov wanted to, too. And now Jin? After all they'd been through together? They'd been getting on so well, moving past his need to protect everyone and everything. He'd been letting her stand on her own and fight for herself for months. And now he wanted to take it away?

"And you're *my* husband, *my* partner," she said, voice trembling. "I can't let you go into harm's way without me there. If you get hit with aetherium again, I *have* to be there. Even Lucian doesn't think he can heal that. You need me there. I have a right to be there! I'm part of this team!"

The words tumbled out in quick succession, so fast Jin couldn't counter her arguments. He stared at her with a pained expression, like he couldn't decide what to do or say next.

"I know you're part of this team," Jin said, "but knowing you're there—"

"Should be more of a comfort than a distraction! I saved your life!" Her eyes burned, heavy with unshed tears. "Skies, what more do I have to do to prove I can take care of myself? Of the team?"

"This isn't about that, Az."

"It sure looks like it from where I'm standing. It's the same fight we always have."

"This isn't a fight." His shoulders dropped. "I don't doubt for a second that you're an asset. I *know* you are. But Az, Nazarov's hurt you enough. Kaius has hurt you enough. Even your father . . ." He shook his head. "Please. Please, let me protect you this once. Stay here. Work with Noemi if you want to do something or help Cress. But please, no missions right now. Just this once, let me handle it alone. Take time to recover. I know you haven't—"

"No." Astrea shoved past Jin and grabbed her pack from the wardrobe floor. It was heavy. "I can recover when all of this is done."

She would take the time when they actually had the luxury of it. When aetherium was banished, when Nazarov was imprisoned, and when Aelius and Kaius were out of power in Helosia. Until then, she had to keep going. She had to stay focused. Busy. Involved.

Besides, Jin wasn't taking time to recover. He'd nearly died. Wasn't that just as bad as losing Saros? Was his physical stamina even recovered enough for this kind of mission?

His eyes fluttered shut, almost in defeat. Steel pain and midnight blue grief swirled around him.

"I need to go tell Cress what's happening." Metal clinked as Astrea tossed her bag over her shoulder. "I'll see you downstairs," she muttered, ignoring the weight of Jin's worry as it followed her out the door.

Chapter 12

Astrea sat in the corner of the small airship cabin, her knapsack next to her on the bench. Jin had barely looked her way the entire flight, instead focusing on discussing things in hushed tones with Zephyrine and Lucian. Some kind of intelligence, probably. Lennor and Civan had minded their own business and kept out of both Astrea's and Jin's ways, while Adi and Marko had taken over pilot duties.

Nothing was as it should be. Cressida wasn't there, Adi and Marko still seemed tense, and Jin . . . Why was he back to trying to take away her choices? Why was he so keen on leaving her out of this mission?

"And Saros would be alive and Cressida wouldn't be going through what she's going through." His words repeated in her mind as she thunked her head back against the wall. Did this all come back to guilt? Jin had to know none of that was his fault. No, he hadn't wanted to bring civilians into a war zone, but it had been the only way with the political nonsense the Novarian Council was pulling.

Astrea didn't think Jin wanted to control her, to take away her choices. Could he be that worried about her? But what right did he have to ask her to stay behind when she would be equally worried about him—and everyone else?

Or was it something he'd learned but hadn't shared? She suppressed a shiver. If so, why not tell her the real reason? Didn't she have a right to know if something was terribly, horribly wrong?

Her mind ran circles around the questions, taking a brief detour to a few nights before when they'd both woken up in the middle of the night, her from her nightmares and him whispering apologies about taking any of them into the Badlands. Astrea let her eyes close. Of course he felt that way, but why couldn't he see how *she* felt about this? That she needed to try to prevent anyone else from dying?

She'd changed into her armor a few minutes before, as they were already descending and preparing to land at the Novarian army's camp in the northwest of the country. With any luck, whatever information the Novarians had would let them either approach the Paragonian location within a few hours or by morning.

As the airship descended and finally touched down, Astrea gathered her bag and shook out the skirt of her armor. It was considerably lighter without the metal plates in it, and she far preferred this black version to the red one she'd had to wear down in Helosia. She didn't think she could ever look at that red armor again.

Nobody said anything as the ship powered down and the others began collecting their belongings. Soon, they were out in the fresh air. A few hundred feet away, low lights glowed near the edge of the forest clearing they'd landed in. There were some tents—no doubt the Novarian camp they were looking for—otherwise swallowed up by the dark night sky.

Taking the lead, Lucian started for that warm glow of the camp. Astrea stayed at the back of the group with Civan. Going up front to try to talk with Jin now seemed pointless. He obviously didn't want to speak with her. If he did, he would've tried during their flight, which had been several hours long. Astrea didn't blame him necessarily. After all, she hadn't been open to his request. She had barely even talked about it, had shut him down and decided she was going.

At the edge of the camp, a tall, plump woman halted Lucian's progress. They spoke quietly, so low Astrea couldn't begin to guess what they were talking about. But the woman's aura flared with red determination and teal approval just before she turned on her heel and headed into the small camp. When the others started after her, Astrea followed.

"I hope we don't have to sleep on the ground," Civan murmured.

"Yeah," Astrea said, a half-hearted response. She hated sleeping on the ground. She also hated sleeping without Jin. Would he be so frustrated with her that he wouldn't spend the night with her? Would they even sleep, or would they go straight for the Paragon's location?

They entered the largest tent in the middle of the camp, which would barely fit the whole of their group. Astrea squinted against the sudden brightness of the lamplight. A small round table sat in the middle of the tent, and laid out on top was a map of northern Novaria marked up with red and blue squiggles Astrea couldn't decipher.

"Everyone, this is Major Runa Haldane," Lucian said, then introduced the team to the woman.

She smoothed a pale, scarred hand over her blonde braid. "Unfortunate to meet you all, and more unfortunate is that we're still waiting on the last scouting team to make contact." She gestured to the map—specifically some of those squiggles—then said, "We're about ten miles out from the location the grand duke specified."

"Has there been any clear sign of the Paragon there?" Jin asked.

"Not sure if it's them, but it's someone. Coming and going mostly. A couple of our Lightbringers that I sent out have sensed this void magic."

Astrea's skin prickled, and it wasn't because of the cold night air. It shouldn't have been a surprise, but knowing they were so close to void mages set her nerves on edge.

"Should be hearing from the most recent scouts within the hour," Major Haldane said, "but I'll need you to hold in the meantime, Commander."

He inclined his head. "Whatever we need to do."

"Make yourselves comfortable, wherever you want. I can show you to a place where you can sleep if you want."

With Lucian's agreement, Major Haldane left the tent again and escorted them through the small camp. Several of the people stationed there were clearly not Novarian. Their uniforms were the colors of Tornama, the Taipoli Islands, and Delia. At least the alliance seemed to be pulling through despite the other countries' initial hesitations.

The tent the camp leader brought them to was small, maybe large enough for four people. Astrea opted to stay outside, finding a spot on the ground next to a nearby oak tree with a thick trunk while the others talked among themselves. With the lights from nearby tents, it wasn't *so* bad sitting alone at night.

Before long, Marko wandered over. It was still strange, seeing him in midnight blue fatigues instead of his old, more casual clothes. And yet it somehow suited him, like he was exactly where he was supposed to be.

"Why is it that I always find you sitting alone under trees?" Marko asked as he sat down next to her. He stretched one leg out before him and brought the other toward his chest, then leaned back on his elbows. Relaxed. He was so relaxed at a time like this.

"Why is it that you always bother me when I obviously want to be alone?"

He placed a hand over his heart. "You wound me."

"You haven't exactly been chatty the last few days," Astrea said quietly. "I was trying to give you space."

"And you want me to give you space now."

She shrugged. She didn't know what she wanted. All Astrea knew was that her heart hurt. Skies, it hurt so badly.

"Why are you here, Marko?" she asked, attention focused straight ahead. She tracked Jin as he moved around their corner of the camp. He didn't even look her way.

"Precisely because I haven't been very chatty lately. You're one of the few people I actually find pleasant to be around."

"Did something happen?" she dared ask. "Adi's been worried."

"Trying to play bridge between Lucian and Rami has its downsides," Marko drawled. "Lucian's been particularly rough around the edges lately. It's rubbing off on me."

"I don't know that you were ever smooth."

"Wounded again!"

One side of Astrea's mouth quirked up.

"What's bothering you and Jin?" he asked.

She sighed heavily. "Is it that obvious?"

"Considering you two are usually attached at the hip—him more than you—and now you two will barely look at each other, yes. And Adi may have asked me to intervene."

"Why didn't he do it himself?"

"He's going to talk to Jin."

Astrea rolled her eyes. "We don't need you to fix our problems."

"No, but sometimes talking to a friend can help," Marko offered.

"A couple of months ago you barely wanted to tell me your favorite color, and now you're going to offer me marriage advice?" Astrea asked, trying to infuse some energy and playfulness into her words. She was sure she failed.

"If I can help, I'd like to help."

Astrea shrugged one shoulder. "It's silly."

"It quite literally cannot be any worse than Lucian and Rami's arguing."

"He just . . . he told those military leaders off, told them the team had to go because of our experience, and then not five minutes later in private told me I needed to stay behind."

"Why would he want *you* to stay behind?" Marko asked. "You're the strongest skies damned healer I've ever seen."

"That was my argument." Astrea's cheeks heated despite the cold night wind. Up ahead, Adi touched Jin's elbow and motioned for him to follow. They disappeared around the corner of another tent. "He said he shouldn't have ever taken me or my uncle or any of the other civilians into Helosia like he did. He blames himself for Saros dying and Cress getting hurt."

"And he's worried the same will happen to you," Marko concluded.

"Yes, and he doesn't even seem to care that he'd be dead if I hadn't been there to save him."

That was the truly awful part of all of this. That he had brushed that off so quickly. Did he feel so guilty that he wasn't thinking about what it meant about his own life being forfeit? Or did he have some kind of death wish? She didn't think so . . .

"I just want to keep him safe," Astrea whispered. "All of you safe. If I can heal the effects of aetherium, then leaving me behind isn't an option."

Silence. All Astrea could hear was the blood roaring in her ears and the rustle of leaves in the wind.

"You're right," Marko said. "That we can't leave you behind. But I'm not surprised Jin asked that of you. I don't think I've seen a man more in love or more scared in my life. He doesn't want to put you in harm's way, and I can hardly fault him for that."

"You're getting soft," Astrea said.

Marko chuckled. "Well, while I don't wish bodily harm on you, the thought of Adi being here makes me feel sick to my stomach, especially after what happened in the south. And as much as I respect Jin's background and skills, he obviously doesn't always think straight when it comes to you."

"We're that easy to read?" Astrea quipped half-heartedly.

"Yes."

"Thanks."

"You can both be right and honor your needs," Marko said. "You need to be here for peace of mind and to save our sorry asses. And Jin needs to know you're safe so he can focus better."

Of course Astrea knew both things could be true, but Jin didn't seem to see it that way. And besides, how were they supposed to find that kind of balance? It seemed impossible.

"Figure out something together," Marko said. "It's the two of you against the problem, not against each other."

"And if he doesn't see it that way?" she asked.

"He'll come around. He sees how badly you're hurting, Az. We all do."

"I'm hardly the only one hurting."

"Maybe so, but . . ." As Marko shook his head, midnight blue grief fizzled around his body.

"But what?"

"I was there in Tornama, in the hall outside your room, when Lucian had to keep sedating you. The way you screamed. The way you screamed over and over again that you could feel it."

Astrea's eyes fluttered shut. She didn't remember much of that time, no doubt thanks to the commander's drugs. Maybe it was for the best.

"I felt Saros take his own life before the aetherium could," she whispered.

"I gathered as much," Marko said gently. "And that is not something any of us can ever understand. I know Jin sees that. He doesn't want you hurting anymore. It doesn't mean he can sideline you, but he's just trying to find a way to protect his partner. I'd want to protect Adi from that if it was something he could feel."

That awful, awful day.

Astrea still couldn't help but be a little angry at Saros, just as Sarsali said she was. Saros had taken Astrea's choice away. He had chosen his fate, to save her and disrupt that vision he'd had. And maybe that was his right. Maybe it *had* been the most merciful thing he could do for himself, for her, for Jin, even if she wished she could have saved them both.

And now, every night that she went to sleep, she had dreams of that awful day. That terrible feeling. She was never going to forget the feeling of that knife dragging across Saros's skin. She hadn't even considered that Jin and the others might have been haunted by her reaction to it all.

"You're quite wise," Astrea said. "And you never used to talk this much."

"Do you miss those days?"

Astrea liked having Marko as a real friend, someone who obviously had wisdom to impart. But she admittedly missed how much simpler everything seemed back then. How much simpler it actually was. "Not necessarily."

"I do." With a groan, Marko pushed to his feet, then extended his hand to Astrea. "So much less political nonsense to put up with."

She took it, letting him help her stand up.

"Come on," he said. "Let's go see if Lucian has any news about these scouts."

Slinging her pack over her shoulder, Astrea followed him. She didn't know where Jin and Adi had gone off to, but when they had time, she and Jin needed to talk. They couldn't be the team they usually were if they both refused to work through this issue together.

<h1 style="text-align:center">CHAPTER 13</h1>

Though the camp leader had promised they'd hear from the scouting party "shortly," the report had come in late, nearing three in the morning. Activity had been seen at the Paragonian site, so the rest of them had held off and stayed overnight at the coalition camp.

But finally, they'd received word that the location was clear again. And so now, they were loaded up into several trucks that were rumbling up the road deeper and deeper into the dense Novarian forest.

It was no wonder the Paragonian site here had been hidden for so long. Being this remote would prevent most people from ever finding it. Astrea's father had said the site was built into a cliff face and was difficult to access, so that added another layer of security for the Paragon.

Unfortunately, the scouts hadn't been able to determine who the void mages at the site might be loyal to. It could be Nazarov they were about to face, or it could be Theo's people. Either way, Astrea just wanted to get this over with. She rubbed her sweaty palms on her thick cotton leggings and tried to focus on anything other than the way the truck swayed beneath her.

"A few more minutes and we'll rendezvous with the team," said their driver, some Novarian soldier Lucian had introduced and whose name Astrea had already forgotten.

The truck rounded a particularly sharp bend. Astrea tried not to stare too hard at Jin. After her talk with Marko, she'd wanted to find Jin, but he'd insisted on taking the first watch while the others slept. It had been impossible for Astrea to get any real sleep between him not being there and having to sleep on a narrow cot. Had Adi not been able to get through to Jin? Or was he just going to continue avoiding her?

He hadn't gotten this stubborn about an issue in a while, at least not with her. She supposed she could force him to talk, but when had that ever gotten her anywhere with any of the people she loved?

The vehicle finally rolled to a stop, and the driver mentioned something about having arrived. Jin moved first, going straight to the doors and flinging them open. Astrea frowned. He wouldn't even look at her. She couldn't think about it too much. She had to focus. They all did.

The midmorning sun struggled to rise above the tree line, barely making the air any warmer. Astrea shivered and huddled next to Adi, Lennor, and Civan. They'd stopped off the side of the road, so close to the forest that Astrea would only have to take a few more steps forward to touch the trees. A few Novarians dressed in dark blue loitered in the shadows.

"Corporal Bakkar," Lucian said as he approached the bear of a man who stepped forward.

"Commander." The man's voice was deep and low, matching perfectly what Astrea expected from a man as tall as him. A few tattoos snaked up his exposed forearms, the colorful ink bright against his brown skin. A long gun was strapped to his back, and his thick, corded muscles flexed with every small movement. "Apologies again for the delay."

"Hardly your fault," Lucian said. "Is the site still clear?"

"Still clear as of ten minutes ago," said the corporal. "We're ready to go when you are."

"Lead the way," Lucian said.

The corporal started into the forest. "We'll approach from the southeast," he said, mostly to Lucian, it seemed. They walked side by side.

"The rest of the team is waiting there, and another group is at the northwestern edge of the location in case anyone tries to come back."

That made Astrea feel a little better, at least. The corporal only had two more people with him there. One was a short blonde woman with a tan complexion, and the other was a taller woman with sand-hued skin, small eyes, and dark, glossy hair. Neither was obviously a mage, though Astrea figured one of them had to be a Lightbringer if they were scouting for void mages.

"The corporal's a sharpshooter," Adi said, voice low. They were near the back of the pack, ahead of the twins and a half dozen paces behind Jin, Marko, and Zephyrine.

"You can tell that?"

"The only mages I know that carry guns, so . . . consider it an educated guess."

Astrea tried to glean anything she could from this Novarian team. The corporal's locs had been gathered into a long ponytail, which swung slightly with his steps. Nothing escaped his wall, not even a hint of what he might be feeling. Only the blonde let any emotions out freely, and even then, all Astrea could see was red determination.

They continued on, avoiding the thickest roots sticking up out of the ground. Astrea's breath came out in little clouds in front of her mouth. She attempted to keep both her footsteps soft and magic spread as far and wide as she could. At the edges of her senses, new energy blossomed, cool concern and prickly annoyance.

"Almost there," the corporal said over his shoulder.

A few hundred more feet, and they reached the edge of the forest. Waiting were two more Novarians in blue, a man who could've been the corporal's twin and another who looked somewhat like a younger version of Marko except for the narrower build and deep violet eyes.

And beyond them still was a tall graying cliff face rising above the forest. There didn't seem to be a fortress, but when Astrea squinted, she could make out what seemed to be subtle columns and narrow windows.

Finally.

And there was no void. She was close enough that she'd be able to feel *something* . . . assuming the inside of the building wasn't coated in aetherium.

"Commander, this is my brother Soren," said the corporal, jerking his chin at the taller of the men. Unlike the corporal, though, this man had limited tattoos. "And his partner, our Lightbringer, Elias," said the corporal, gesturing to the blond.

"Has anyone been inside?" Astrea asked none of them in particular, interrupting the introductions.

"We have," said Elias. "It was empty."

"You searched it thoroughly?" asked Lucian.

"Yes, Commander," said Elias. "Both me and the Lightbringer on the other squad. No hidden void mages, and none of that strange metal we were briefed on."

Astrea's shoulders dropped, and she swore Jin relaxed, too.

"Then let's get in there." The corporal tilted his head toward the clearing beyond the trees. "We're wasting daylight."

"It's barely even the eleventh morning hour," replied Elias dryly.

"And the sooner we get this over with, the better," said the corporal, already moving to the front of the group and starting for the cliffs. "Stick together, and keep up. I'm not waiting if you fall behind."

Astrea couldn't sense much from the corporal, but she had a feeling he was entirely serious. She hurried after the others, trying to keep up with Adi as he jogged.

But her legs struggled, tired after so much from the last few weeks. Adi slowed, and ahead of them, Jin slowed, too. They kept pace with her, and Astrea didn't know if that made her feel better or worse. Like she needed special treatment, or that maybe Jin had even been right all along, that she needed to stay behind. Or maybe, like her, they were exhausted from all that had happened and not getting much rest. Maybe they all should've stayed behind, as the rest of the Novarian government had suggested.

They pushed on, moving through the knee-high, mostly dead grass in the field between the forest and the cliff. Cold sea air slapped Astrea's cheeks and toyed with the hair coming loose from her braid.

The corporal and Lucian led them to the base of the cliff, then along its edge. The rock was rough, battered for a long time by the salty seaside air. Astrea stuck close to Adi, and Jin stayed right behind her. When his hand brushed the small of her back, butterflies flitted around her stomach. *I'm sorry*, the touch seemed to say. And when heavy regret and sunshine coated her skin, all Astrea wanted to do was throw herself into his arms and forget they'd argued at all.

Now was not the time. There were bigger things at play, and they could talk once they were finished here.

Up ahead, the corporal turned right, straight toward the cliff. With a quick wave of his hand, part of the wall opened, revealing a dark tunnel inside. Lucian ushered them all in. The ground underneath Astrea's boots was paved stones, not rough dirt. If this was some kind of hidden entrance, why make pieces of the fortress visible to the naked eye high above them?

Doesn't matter, Az. Complete the mission.

The tunnel continued up at an incline, bringing them higher up with each step they took. Jin's fire illuminated the space from behind, and Lucian's light cast an eerie pale glow up ahead. The walls were smooth gray and brown stone, nothing like the way the aetherium walls looked in the old tunnels in Talmaris.

"How far do we have to climb?" Zephyrine asked.

"A ways yet," said the corporal over his shoulder. "At least it's not stairs."

Translucent peach amusement circled Zephyrine's white hair for a moment, then disappeared. Astrea didn't really see the humor in the situation. This was the enemy's base, for skies sake. Or it seemed to be.

But Zephyrine always seemed to find the small moments of humor and joy, some incredible balance she managed to strike amid all this. She'd been the same on their mission to the Badlands, and she'd been the same for months. Astrea just couldn't grasp it. Maybe some other day, but not now. Not here, where the shadows seemed to stretch unnaturally and cold air stung her skin.

The higher they climbed, the more Astrea's heart thrummed in her chest. She hated this place, this darkness. It stretched on and on, seemingly forever above them.

Up ahead, Lucian's steps slowed. Ice prickled Astrea's scalp first, then spread down her neck, her arms, her entire body until every inch of her was covered in gooseflesh. And this wasn't the cold one might expect in late autumn in Novaria.

"Corporal, we've got a problem," Lucian said before Astrea could even take another step. "They're back."

"Well, fuck me," Corporal Bakkar muttered.

"Only six that I can feel," said Elias. "Only half are void mages."

Astrea shuddered. Only six, as if that would make this so much easier. Only three were void mages, as if *that* made anything better at all.

"Where?" asked the corporal.

"Seems like they're a ways above us," said Lucian. "Where does this tunnel lead?"

"Up into the main part of the keep, probably right to them. It's got some rooms but is basically a few big empty halls."

"Then they should be easy to find." Jin moved ahead of Astrea. His voice turned steely as he said, "Let's hope it's Nazarov."

Astrea hoped it was Theo, actually. Finding Nazarov was important, sure, but so was finding the antiquities dealer, their apparent ally. And she'd much, much rather find Theo Kadis today than deal with Nazarov at all.

"Tighten up," the corporal called over his shoulder. "We'll lead in."

With a nudge between her shoulders, Adi got Astrea to fall in line near the right-hand wall. She was once again sandwiched between him and Jin. Her pulse thundered so loudly in her ears she almost couldn't hear. Was this how so much of Jin and Adi's life had been, sneaking around to ambush enemies? She tried to soften her steps even though the void mages were still far away.

They climbed higher and higher through the tunnel, going for what felt like hours but was surely only minutes. Astrea focused on following Jin closely and on the energy around her. Aside from that cold void, she found whispers of annoyance and frustration, even boredom. No rage. Nothing volatile. She wasn't entirely sure what to make of it.

The floor began to flatten out, and soon, the faint outline of a door came into view up ahead. Light shone through the crack between the door and floor. Everyone dismissed their magic, leaving just that sliver of light to guide them the rest of the way.

The prickles of cold turned fierce, piercing Astrea to her very core. The void mages were close. Up ahead, Elias whispered something to the corporal.

Astrea grew dizzy. Ice blossomed in her shoulder joint, the very same spot she'd healed Jin. It unfurled in her gut, right where Saros had been hit by Kaius's aetherium blade. And worst of all, ghostly cold sliced across her throat.

Save him.

She nearly choked but managed to swallow the feeling.

How was she supposed to do this? Face the void again?

Jin had been right. She should've stayed behind.

Corporal Bakkar stopped in front of the door, a looming shadow. He signed several words, only a few of which Astrea caught in the low light. Something about Lucian. Then he made a few quick hand signals, which Astrea definitely did not know. Teal understanding blossomed around the others and lit up the tunnel for a moment.

With a nod, the corporal flung the door open. Lucian charged through first, followed by Elias, Zephyrine, and Marko. Wind howled, and pain exploded in Astrea's sternum. The very same pain when Lucian used his souleating. It couldn't be Theo if—

Jin sprinted ahead. The heat of his fire burning over his palms warmed Astrea's freezing cheeks. She went to chase him, but Adi pulled her back.

"What are you doing?" she hissed.

"Just wait," Adi said, arm wrapping around her shoulders and tugging her back again. "Wait."

Wait? Why the skies would she—

Pain sliced her arms, her cheeks. Her right knee nearly gave out as someone took a hit. She placed her hand flat against the wall next to her, steadying herself. Adi said something, and Lennor might've, too, but Astrea couldn't hear past the roar in her ears or the clash of elements and metal. *Save him*, her heartbeat seemed to say. *Save him, save him, save him.*

Wriggling out of Adi's grasp, Astrea scrambled ahead. Adi called for her, but she ignored him and burst through the doorway. *Look away.*

There. Jin caught in an intricate dance of flame and shadow with one of the void mages. Another fought with the other Lightbringer, and the third fought with Marko and Zephyrine, all while Lucian controlled the non-void Paragon members. None of them Nazarov. None of them Theo. Not Solana or Ninette or anyone Astrea recognized.

Skidding to a stop behind Lucian, Astrea threw her hands out in front of her. Cold burned her palms as she reached for the void mage fighting Jin. Annoyance and anger bled through the ice, a strange hot and cold burning that mimicked void fire. Astrea gritted her teeth and pulled hard. The mage stumbled. Jin grabbed their collar and kicked their legs out. Astrea locked her knees.

Still gripping that man's energy tightly in her left hand, Astrea reached for the mage fighting Marko and Zephyrine. Marko blasted the woman with wind just as Astrea pushed through the thick veil surrounding her. And there, for the taking, were annoyance and pain. She latched onto those and made the woman fall to her knees.

A shot rang out from behind Astrea. She flinched. The third void mage roared in pain and dropped to the ground.

She kept her grip tight on those void mages even as Lucian let the others go. Even as they were handcuffed and escorted to the middle of the room. She couldn't let them escape.

The void mage who had been shot writhed on the floor, clutching his leg and spitting curses as the corporal slowly approached him. He'd re-slung his gun over his shoulders.

"How do we keep you from jumping?" the corporal asked the injured man. He nudged the man's injury with the toe of his boot. Pain flared bright and hot right above Astrea's knee. When the man screamed, the corporal said, "Tell me and I won't have to do that again."

"We won't," the void man said. "I swear, we won't."

"Swearing isn't really a solution," the corporal mused before nudging the man's leg again.

His scream reverberated through Astrea's mind, bouncing around in her skull.

"Won't . . . we . . . swear," gritted out the woman in Astrea's control.

"One wrong move and she'll kill the three of you," said the corporal.

Astrea didn't think she could kill them even if she tried. But maybe they didn't know that, because they all nodded.

"Let them go," Lucian said to her.

Sucking in a deep breath, Astrea pushed away the annoyance, the pain, the anger, the mistrust, and that cold, cold void. They fell to their hands and knees, panting and gasping for air.

The brick floor broke apart, shooting up to bind their arms and legs to the ground. Adi muttered something Astrea couldn't quite hear past her own heavy breathing.

She sucked in another deep breath and closed her eyes as cold seemed to stick to her shoulder, her abdomen, her throat.

Save him, save him, save him.

Look away, look away, look away.

"Az?" Jin asked quietly.

When had he come over?

Jin stared down at her, a furrow between his eyebrows and concern bright in his eyes.

"I'm fine," she lied.

"Varojin!" called Lucian.

Jin's lips twitched, almost like he was about to say something. But he backed away, then went to where the commander stood near one of the void mages, leaving Astrea alone again.

Chapter 14

As Lucian and the corporal hauled the captured void mages farther into the fortress, Astrea took a small canteen of water Adi wordlessly offered her. Her hands trembled as she brought the cool metal to her lips.

"I can't believe this place," Adi said.

Screwing the canteen's lid back on, Astrea actually looked around them for the first time. The ceilings vaulted high above them, surprisingly detailed for being carved out of the worn stone. The same delicate features were carved into the pillars dotted throughout the room. Sunlight spilled in through the narrow windows to Astrea's right.

It was like someone had hollowed out the cliff itself to create this room. It was at least as big as the largest ballroom back in the Kalamian palace, and there were dark hallways to her left that Astrea couldn't see down.

"Yeah," she mumbled, passing the water back to Adi. Cressida would probably love this place, if only to see the way it had been made from the earth.

Pain blossomed in the side of her head just as Lucian's curse echoed through the cavernous room. They'd disappeared somewhere around one of the corners. But no panic came. No anger or rage or any other pain. Whatever it was, Lucian seemed to have it handled.

On leaden legs, Astrea started toward the hallway closest to her. Her boots made almost no sound on the thick stone floors. The farther she got from those windows, the less natural light there was. Starlight blossomed over her palm, casting a soft glow over the wide corridor. There were no paintings, no carvings, nothing. Just empty walls of mostly smooth stone. Stone, not aetherium.

"This place is creepy," Adi said from behind Astrea.

She jumped. "Skies, don't sneak up on me like that."

"Is it possible to sneak up on a Lightbringer?"

"Very much so." At least, it was when Astrea was so distracted, so untethered from her body. She shook her arms out and huffed. "What do you think used to be here?"

"I guess we'll find out," he said. "Let's wait for the others before we venture too far, though."

She followed Adi back out into the main room. The twins were pacing by the windows, looking outside. Marko and the other Lightbringer were talking to the non-mage captives in hushed voices. Marko's eyebrows furrowed, and Astrea was about to go see what was wrong when Lucian's voice echoed clearly through the room.

"Astrea!"

Confusion and annoyance scraped across her skin, rough like tree bark, but nothing to suggest anything was *wrong*. Still, she ran toward Lucian's voice as he called her name again. Adi followed her.

"What?" she asked as she turned the corner from around which Lucian's voice came. There on the floor were the three void mages, still bound and unmoving. The corporal had his gun pointed at them, while Jin and Zephyrine hung back near the opposite wall.

"It seems," Lucian said as he glanced up at her, "our new friends here don't want to say anything else until they can speak with The One."

"Nazarov's not here," Astrea said, as if that wasn't obvious. As if dread wasn't building in her bones as she said the words, because she knew exactly what these three wanted.

"Not him," said one void mage, a woman. Her pinkish skin was dotted with tiny scars, and her golden hair looked almost like honey aside from the streaks of gray near the roots. "He told us to meet him here, but he is nothing but a pretender, a false king. We have heard that *you* are our true leader." Her gaze flicked to Jin. "The sun and moon."

"Utter bullshit," Jin muttered.

Astrea fidgeted. It *was* bullshit, at least as far as she was concerned. But these people obviously didn't think so. Besides, what about her father? Clearly they didn't know he was alive, otherwise they would know Astrea was not the Paragon's leader. It was Valen, not her, if regular hereditary inheritance laws were used.

But did she tell them about him? Or did she play the role these people so desperately wanted her to fill? All three stared up at her with pleading eyes, the same way Ninette had looked that night in the Badlands.

If Theo was really leading some rebellious void mages and wanting to ally with her, could she get these people on their side, too? Find a way to use them to stop Nazarov?

Skies, she hated all of this.

Pushing her shoulders back, Astrea summoned the most courage she could and said, "You're right, Nazarov is a pretender and a mass murderer. Tell me, what do you really think the Paragon should do?"

"Nazarov must be stopped," said the woman. "Replaced by the rightful leader."

"Besides that?" Astrea prompted.

"Restore balance."

"In what way?"

"Through chaos and destruction, as the creed says."

Astrea held back a sigh. Of course, she would not be so lucky as to find rebels like Theo's, ones who thought Nazarov had taken that too literally and too far. How did she convince these people to not follow that path?

"Balance must be restored," she said carefully. Lucian's eyes widened, and Astrea felt Jin's attention glued to her face, but she didn't look away from the three void mages. Their cold auras pressed painfully against her skin. "But not in the way you propose."

"But—" started the woman.

"No," Astrea said with more force than she thought possible. "I am your One, am I not?" When the three nodded slowly, she said, "I do not believe chaos and destruction are the way forward."

The woman scoffed. "Of course someone born outside the Paragon would think that."

"You don't know anything about me," Astrea said coldly. "I was not born into your group, but I've seen what Nazarov's version of chaos and destruction does. The pain it brings. The loss. The agony."

Cold danced across her throat. *Save him.*

"Pain and violence only breed more pain and violence," she continued. "That's not the future I want for this continent."

"But chaos—"

"May be the natural order of the world," Astrea cut in, "but that does not mean you feed it with fear and torture and bombs. That does not mean you destroy innocent lives."

The woman studied her with curious bronze eyes. A small furrow formed between them. "Then what do you propose, Moon?"

Astrea actually had no idea what to tell this woman; she was no stateswoman, no diplomat. All Astrea knew was that this cycle of hatred, violence, and destruction the countries found themselves in had to stop. "If you tell me what it is you know about the pretender, especially anything that can help me locate him, I'll find a place for you in the future of the Paragon."

It was a promise she couldn't keep but one she would make anyway.

The woman pressed her lips together. She seemed to be the leader of the small trio, the only one who would speak.

"If you decide to take me up on my offer, tell the commander what you know," Astrea said, gesturing to Lucian.

She slipped past Adi, heading back toward the sunlight on the far side of the room. Astrea had made the only offer she could. If it was going to take Lucian more to get information out of those Paragon, then Astrea wouldn't stand in his way. She just also wouldn't stick around to find out how he might do that.

After the unproductive conversation Astrea had with the captured Paragon, she'd wandered off with Adi. The non-void mage Paragon were equally cautious to accept Astrea's offer.

The corporal's second team had arrived sometime after that with the news that they'd called in more reinforcements to secure the location, lest more Paragon show up. The Novarian military was arriving in a steady trickle, some coalition forces with them. The once-empty fortress was now crawling with mostly midnight blue uniforms.

And Astrea hadn't heard another word from the captured Paragon. Lucian and the corporal had taken them to a separate part of the building, one Astrea couldn't hear or see. And with the many soldiers now milling about, she could barely pick out the void mages' cold energy from the chilly afternoon air.

"It's too bad Noemi isn't here," Adi said as he walked behind Astrea, his fingers trailing the wall of the corridor they turned down.

"Why, would she like it?"

"Oh, no, she'd hate it," he said with a laugh. "But she'd probably love to try to figure out what might've once been here."

"Maybe Veiko will send some scholars out here to study it," Astrea said. She wasn't sure it would be a good idea for Noemi to join that expedition, though. She didn't need to be put in a potentially dangerous situation, not with even less experience than what Astrea had.

Adi murmured his agreement as he stooped to examine one of the walls. "Hey," he said, "bring your light over here."

Squatting down next to him, Astrea pushed faint starlight toward the wall. There, only about two feet above the floor, were carved letters. Void letters. It really was too bad Astrea hadn't thought to bring Noemi's cipher.

"We need to get someone to copy this down," she said to Adi. Though it surely wouldn't tell them much about Nazarov's whereabouts, at least it might give them more insight into the Paragon or maybe even Nazarov's plans.

"I'll go get someone." Adi hustled off, leaving Astrea alone.

The corridor walls rose high around her on each side, separating her from most of the energy in the main room. There were a few rooms they'd searched through, though they found nothing other than some rickety old beds, faded rugs, and empty bookcases. This place had been cleaned out, looking more abandoned than like a hideout Nazarov would use.

If he'd truly asked these six Paragon to meet him here, as that woman had claimed, why not show up? Was this actually some diversion? All an attempt to slow them down and get a head start? Or some kind of trap? If it was the latter, at least they had dozens of soldiers with them now. It seemed the entire camp, plus more, had come up to help safeguard the fortress.

Besides, where *was* Nazarov? The longer she went without hearing from him, the more nervous Astrea became. He'd ignored her for periods before, but after what happened in the Badlands, she'd expected him to become even more aggressive in his communication and tactics.

Astrea pushed up to her full height. Maybe they should've brought her father with them. Maybe seeing The One's brother would have gotten some stronger reaction from those Paragon members. Maybe they knew him or had known him once upon a time.

"Az?" Adi called as he strode back down the hallway. The flashlight in his hand bobbed up and down with each step. Behind him were two soldiers in Novarian uniforms, both with notebooks and pencils at the ready. "Lucian asked to see you. I'll handle this."

What could Lucian want now?

"Thanks," Astrea said.

She'd thought maybe she would need to ask someone to point her in the right direction of wherever the commander had been for the last few hours, but as soon as she stepped out into the main room, Lucian was at her side.

"We need to talk," he said, grabbing her arm and pulling her toward the tunnel they'd used to get into the fortress in the first place. With his free hand, he summoned his light. To the soldiers standing guard just inside, he said, "Excuse us."

The two saluted the commander, then went into the main room behind them. Astrea almost groaned. Somehow, talking with Lucian alone gave her the sense that something was wrong.

"What's going on?" she asked as Lucian half closed the door.

"It seems your . . . offer . . . to that void mage worked," Lucian said.

"What?"

"She finally gave us some information. She says Nazarov has been looking for a major source of aetherium. The Badlands didn't seem to pan out for him, so now he's searching elsewhere."

"Did she say how bad things went for him in Helosia?"

"Bad enough that many more are starting to question his leadership," said Lucian. "She says they aren't the only ones willing to listen to what you have to offer."

Based on what Theo had explained in the Badlands, about how Nazarov was trying to find ways to legitimize his rule, Astrea almost wasn't surprised by this new revelation.

"You think she's telling the truth?"

"She told me where she knew Nazarov was last headed." When Astrea gestured for him to continue, Lucian said, "He was going to Zaikud in search of reinforcements and supplies before beginning the rest of his search."

"Does she know where he's going to search?"

"Islands on the northern coast."

Astrea scrubbed at her face. "Alright, when did he go to Zaikud?"

"A few days ago, according to that woman."

"So, what, we go to these islands and hope we get there first?"

"That would be the next logical step, but there's one problem."

"Of course there's a problem," Astrea muttered.

"She can't tell us which islands."

Her eyes widened. "So we have to search them all?"

"We need to figure out how to split up the coalition forces to cover as much ground as safely as possible."

Unwelcome and unexpected tears slid down Astrea's cheeks. Now they had to go scout an untold number of islands in an attempt to find aetherium and Nazarov? How were they even supposed to do that? They didn't have many Stargazers at their disposal . . .

"Astrea?" Lucian asked gently.

Wiping at her cheeks, she muttered, "Sorry, I'm tired."

"I know it's not only that. I can see it."

"Of course you can."

"I don't mean to intrude or overstep . . . but Varojin was feeling just as badly earlier."

"You sensed this from him?" Astrea whispered. Jin had been so closed off from her. Not quite ignoring her but certainly not engaging. And yet he was open to Lucian?

"Only for a few seconds. You've both been off the last couple of days."

Lucian was the last person Astrea wanted to talk to about this, yet she found herself saying, "We had a disagreement about how much I should be involved right now. He thinks I should still be recovering."

"Could he be right?" In the glow of his starlight, Lucian's expression was almost soft. Almost. Almost like how Saros used to look at her.

"Shouldn't he be recovering too, then?" Astrea asked, wiping away more tears. "He nearly died."

"Perhaps you're both right."

As if Astrea didn't already know that.

"Have you talked about it?" Lucian asked.

"What's there to say?"

"Digging your heels in isn't going to get you anywhere."

No, it wouldn't, but since when was Commander Lucian Astor the epitome of compromise and flexibility?

Astrea huffed. Lucian may have been looking at her the same way Saros used to, but *she* was acting just like Saros. Avoiding a hard conversation, just as she had earlier in the year before they knew about the Paragon. Letting it hurt not just her relationship with Jin but letting it hurt herself. And Jin was falling back into his old ways, that role of protector he seemed desperate to play.

How easy it was to revisit old patterns. It was familiar, almost comforting in a strange way despite how much it also hurt. Comforting to fall back on the known instead of moving forward into the darkness stretching out before them.

If only they could go back to the summer, warn themselves about all that they would face. Set themselves up for success, avoid failure after failure after failure.

When Lucian set his hand on Astrea's forearm, she startled.

"You should both take some time," Lucian said. "Talk. Rest. You've barely had a chance to grieve."

"I'll grieve when this is done."

With a heavy sigh, Lucian said, "I know time is a luxury we don't have, but I'm ordering you to take a break while the general and I work some things out. Some things cannot wait, Astrea. Take it from me."

Astrea frowned. "What does that mean?"

"There are many people I've hurt and lost because I refused to take a step back and process what I'd—what we'd—been through. I either walked away or continued with blinders on. And despite my earlier concerns, you and Varojin are a good pair. Good people. I don't want to see you lose each other before you've even had a chance to get started."

Astrea didn't think she and Jin were losing each other because of one argument, but she took Lucian's point. If they started shutting each other out now, when things were this hard, then what? Where would that leave them?

"What about finding these islands and finding Theo?" she asked.

"You have dozens of people here to help you. People who, frankly, need to pull their own weight if we're going to move forward with this alliance. Let us do what we do best, and you can gather yourselves enough for what's to come."

Astrea hated the thought of taking a break at all. But the commander was right. She needed to really sit with what she'd lost, what her friends had lost. She couldn't ignore the wound festering deep within her. It may not ever go away, but trying to grit her teeth and bear the pain would only make the coming weeks and months that much harder.

"Alright," she said. "I will. But you might have to order Jin to do the same."

Lucian actually smiled, a real, genuine smile. "If it comes to that, I will."

CHAPTER 15

With twilight settling over the northern reaches of the country and the military leadership finally situated and ready to take over the fortress, it was time for Astrea and the rest of them to leave. Two airships were waiting down in the empty field near the cliffside, one which would be used to take the prisoners and the other which would take the team. The one with the prisoners was nearly loaded up and ready to depart, bound for Talmaris.

Astrea fiddled with the end of her braid as she stared down at that airship through one of the narrow windows. Lights glowed within, and after a few more moments, it lifted off the ground and ascended into the sky.

Despite Lucian's orders for her to take a break, Astrea had spent the rest of the afternoon searching the peculiar building for any more traces of the void language or something that might be remotely useful. She, Adi, and Civan had found a few words haphazardly carved into some of the columns and in doorways, but nothing that seemed important. Still, it would be worth bringing to Noemi and Tomas.

And now that the task was almost done, Astrea tried to make herself relax. Closing her eyes, she pushed her shoulders down and back. The air around her crackled with energy, everything from heady anticipation to prickling anxiety to grating frustration. She couldn't wait until they were up in the air and she could stop being on watch. Lucian had left with the prisoners, and despite the other Lightbringers around, Astrea couldn't bring herself to pull her barrier in.

"Az?" Lennor asked as she came up from behind.

Astrea glanced back. Lennor's shoulders were bunched up near her ears, almost like she was afraid. But nothing flared in her aura.

"Is it time to go?" Astrea asked.

"Yeah, Jin sent me to get you."

Jin really couldn't come over himself to tell her? To talk about this?

Falling into step with Lennor, the women wove their way through the small groups of soldiers until they found Adi, Civan, and Marko. Jin was still a ways off, speaking with Zephyrine and the corporal. He and his team would be staying to help keep watch for any stray Paragon that might show up.

"We should get down there and get settled," Adi said, nudging both Astrea and Lennor toward the door to the tunnel that would take them back outside.

Astrea moved without any protest. The most she did was summon her light over her palm despite Adi's flashlight helping guide their way through the pitch-dark tunnel. Even that small use of her magic made her temples pulse, like she'd overextended herself. And she probably had. The incident in the Badlands had only been a few weeks before. Was that enough time to truly recover from whatever the void magic had done to her body?

They'd been walking for what felt like forever when Civan asked, "Are Jin and Zephyrine coming?"

"Yeah," Adi said. "They wanted to make sure the corporal's got everything under control."

"This feels too easy," Civan said.

Lennor nudged him in the ribs. "Take the win for once, alright?"

"I'm just saying," he replied. "These void mages happen to believe Astrea is their true leader and easily turn information over to us?"

"I wouldn't call it easy," Marko said. "Lucian crossed some lines to get them to finally comply."

"He said my offer is what convinced them to eventually talk," Astrea said.

Marko shrugged. "Your offer . . . a little pressure from his souleating."

Cold horror prickled Astrea's scalp. She'd known they'd be questioned, but that? "No . . ."

"This is war," Marko said matter-of-factly. "It's hardly the worst thing he could've done."

Astrea hated this. Hated all of it.

There Lucian had been, just a couple of hours before, acting as if Astrea's words had made the difference. Acting so kindly toward her, understanding. Gentle. After he'd done the unthinkable to those mages.

Sure, those void mages weren't exactly their allies, but to do that to another person for information? Not out of self-defense or to preserve the lives of the team?

It didn't seem right. Not even when they desperately needed whatever information they would get. Maybe that was naive, but it still made Astrea's stomach churn.

"Was Jin in the room when he did it?" she managed to ask.

"He waited until Jin and Zephyrine were gone."

That almost made it worse, knowing that Lucian knew where Jin stood on the issue. That he waited until Jin was gone so that he could cross that line without any pressure to do otherwise.

To think that Marko was seemingly okay with it, too . . .

A few lights at the end of the tunnel grew brighter, Novarian soldiers with flashlights. As they passed by, Adi handed off his flashlight, and then they were out the door and back in the cold night air. Astrea shivered as a violent wind blew through the field. It howled through the nearby forest with such fierceness that it made the hairs on Astrea's neck stand on end.

Lennor stopped in her tracks and tilted her head slightly to one side. "That's not natural," she almost whispered. The ground rumbled a moment later.

"Someone should've radioed that in already . . ." Marko shook his head. "Get to that ship *now*," he snapped, shoving Astrea and Adi that way at the same time. "Len, with me."

"Wait—" Astrea started. Why hadn't the coalition forces radioed in about an attack? It had to be an attack, right?

Adi yanked on her arm and dragged her through the tall, dry grass. A thunderous boom exploded in the forest, quickly followed by a mix of flames and clouds. Civan sprinted after Lennor and Marko, who were nearing the edge of the forest.

Astrea tried to pull away from Adi with little success. "We have to help them!"

"They'll be fine." His footsteps never faltered, not even when Astrea stumbled. "My priority is getting you on that ship."

"*They* need to get on that ship!"

And what about Jin? Astrea tried turning around to look for him but saw no sign of her husband. It was just a lot of Novarian soldiers scrambling out of the tunnel, gray confusion flashing around most of their heads.

Adi ignored her continued protests as he practically dragged her to the waiting airship. The lights were on, and a shadowy figure moved around inside. Red rage and determination flared around them as they moved toward the airship's open door. Someone had to have broken through the coalition's line.

Astrea pulled back so hard against Adi's grip that they both stumbled, almost falling.

"What the skies is wrong with you?" Adi shouted at her.

"They're not on our side!" she screamed over the next howl of wind, so strong it nearly knocked her over.

The person running out of the airship threw something toward them. It glinted in the sun's last rays. Earth shot up out of the ground, blocking Astrea and Adi just as something hit the shield with a solid thunk.

"Get behind me," Adi hissed.

Astrea followed his orders.

She pivoted backward as he did, away from their assailant. Earth and metal clashed together, and as Astrea tried to get a better look, she caught flashes of dark green fabric amid the blue water and brown earth smashing into each other. The Zaikudi? Was that who was attacking them? Was Nazarov with them? She couldn't sense void mages, but that didn't mean he wasn't out of her range . . .

Astrea took a few steps back from Adi, closer and closer to the cliff face. Her back bumped against rock. There was no place else for her to go.

Adi blocked most of her line of sight with his wide frame. Red anger and rusty annoyance and green focus swirled in the air, visible even around her human shield. Throwing her hands out in front of her, Astrea snatched the colors. Pain rattled around in her sternum. Her muscles trembled, like she was already far past her limits. She yanked back hard, making their assailant stumble.

Adi closed the space between him and their attacker—definitely Zaikudi based on that dark green uniform. As Adi grabbed the Zaikudi soldier by their shirt and yanked them off the ground, Astrea pushed all those negative emotions back into them. Her veins burned hot and cold. Her lungs tightened. The Zaikudi soldier roared, thrashing about in Adi's grasp, but he didn't let them go.

Earth shot up, ensnaring the enemy soldier's legs first, then their arms. They roared again, straining against their new bindings.

Astrea's chest heaved. She could barely make out more green uniforms across the field, most of them melding into the darkness and swarm of Novarians. Still no sign of Jin or Zephyrine. Where were they?

Adi said something in broken Zaikudi. Astrea hesitated, watching as he glared at the man who had attacked them. She didn't speak Zaikudi, but even she knew the next words out of their enemy's mouth dripped with venom. Gray hate swirled around his head in a thick storm cloud, obscuring his bronze skin and dark brown hair.

"What's he saying?" Astrea asked Adi.

"I . . . don't know."

He didn't know? How could he not know? Even if his Zaikudi wasn't the best?

"What do you mean—"

Heat seared Astrea's skin. Flinching, she flung her hands out in front of her. Starlight sparked to life, knitting together into a tight, dense shield wide enough for her and Adi.

Up ahead and approaching fast was another green-clad Zaikudi. Fire danced over their hands, snaking through the grass and catching the field on fire.

Adi sidestepped Astrea's shield and sprinted ahead. The earth rumbled, then pieces of burning grass and earth shot back toward the Fireweaver.

Astrea froze. She couldn't do anything here. Nothing helpful. That Zaikudi had no emotions to pull from, no energy she could find. They were a heavy, steady wall amid the growing chaos.

Hot flames blasted through the air in a cone so wide that it not only caught on the grass but went over Astrea's head, too. Her shield protected her, and through its shimmering glow, she found Adi hiding behind a shield of his own. The front of it burned.

They needed Civan or Lennor, some kind of—

The fire morphed and moved, almost like water getting sucked back out to sea. Astrea's arms trembled with the effort of tightening her shield around herself like a cocoon, ready for the next blow that never came.

Jin sprinted past her, the enemy's fire twisting and twisting into a fiery rope as he ran. A gale gusted through the field, putting out the remnants of burning grass. Adi's shield dropped. He joined Jin, both advancing on the Zaikudi Fireweaver, forcing their retreat.

But they weren't fast enough, strong enough. Not with Jin there to keep ripping control of their flames away. Every time the Zaikudi tried to summon fire, it literally funneled toward Jin, only for him to throw it back at them.

Astrea managed to look away right before pain blossomed between her ribs and up into her heart. That Zaikudi's heavy wall faded away into nothingness. They were dead.

"Come on." Zephyrine's warm voice made Astrea startle. "Go with Jin and Adi. I'll get the others."

The white-haired general ran off before Astrea could even dismiss her shield. She looked tentatively at the man still trapped in Adi's earthen prison, then across the field. The Novarians seemed to have the situation under control and were rounding up the Zaikudi who hadn't fallen during battle. They could deal with this man, too.

Forcing herself forward, Astrea caught up to where Adi and Jin were waiting for her. They made a beeline for the waiting airship. As soon as they were inside, Adi and Jin started talking in quick half sentences, something about checking for any tampering on instruments and anything else that Zaikudi Tidebacker might've done.

Having Cressida there would've been nice. She was so quick to figure things out like that, but—

Pain stung Astrea's cheeks, her arms, her wrist, her ankle. Marko, Lennor, and Civan launched themselves into the ship, all of them covered in soot and scrapes.

"Come here," Astrea said, motioning for them all to sit on the uncomfortable benches near the cabin's rear windows.

Marko shook his head. "Gotta help Adi."

"Let me at least stop the bleeding," she said. The cuts on his face oozed blood, nothing deadly, but they didn't need him bleeding all over the instruments he might need to help fix.

With a sigh, Marko nodded. Astrea met him where he was still near the door, then gently set her hands on his face right near his ears.

"Your hands are freezing," he hissed, almost flinching away.

"Sorry." Astrea didn't really know what to do about that. Instead, she pulled on the stubborn trickle of magic right under her skin. It seemed to almost whine as it sparked to life, as if it were tired just like her. Her palms glowed, and then the dance of mirror healing and pain began on her cheeks. Marko's wounds healed over, freshly pink and smooth. "There. Go help."

He didn't even thank her as he hustled over to where Adi was checking all the controls in the cockpit.

Zephyrine swept into the ship, then wordlessly opened the floor hatch that would take her down to the engines. Astrea shook her head and approached the twins.

"What's hurt?" she asked.

"My ankle," Lennor said, "and all the cuts."

Astrea knelt on the metal floor, suddenly very grateful for the thin lining of padding Adi had thought to put into the knees of her leggings. "What happened out there?"

"The Zaikudi," Lennor said as she began unlacing her left boot. Astrea helped her pull it off, revealing a swollen ankle.

"You already heard Marko complain about my hands," Astrea said, and Lennor actually laughed.

"It's fine. Just do it." As Astrea set her hands on Lennor's ankle and pulled on her healing again, Lennor said, "It wasn't a big group of them, but they were armed with bombs. I think they were going to try to destroy the cliffside."

"That seems excessive," Astrea said through gritted teeth. As the pain in her ankle ebbed away, she forced herself onto the bench next to Lennor and began healing the small cuts all over her soot-covered face. "Were they there for us?"

"Not sure," said the Tempest.

By the time Astrea finished healing Lennor's cuts and Civan's wrist, which he'd twisted pretty badly, the other four had returned and seemed satisfied that the ship hadn't been tampered with in any meaningful way. Marko even got them up in the air and headed back for civilization. The ship's movement made Astrea's head swim, or maybe it was all the magic she'd used on very little sleep.

"Why would a Zaikudi squad that small try to attack us?" Adi asked, his attention fixed on Zephyrine. "It seems foolish."

"Maybe to try to figure out how strong our defenses are?" The general shrugged. "Or try to cause trouble on Nazarov's behalf."

Anything was possible, Astrea supposed, but it still seemed foolish. Like Adi said, such a small group of Zaikudi soldiers really didn't stand a chance against the group five times that size at the fortress.

The last glow of starlight faded as Astrea pulled her hand away from Civan's cheek. His skin was smooth again, slightly red compared to his otherwise tan complexion. That would settle shortly as the freshly healed area calmed down.

He gave her a small smile. "Thank you."

She nodded. All things considered, they were lucky there hadn't been more serious injuries. So very, very lucky.

And skies, was Astrea exhausted now. She slumped against the bench, then lay down on her side. Too much. She'd done too much. Used amounts of magic that wouldn't usually do this to her. Yet here she was, unable to sit upright.

The conversation continued, but Astrea couldn't focus. Jin said something about Talmaris, then Zephyrine replied. Their words were jumbled, static in Astrea's mind. Her vision blurred before she shut her eyes.

She just needed a moment . . .

Chapter 16

Low light pushed against Astrea's eyelids. She rolled over, burying her face in something soft. Warm. Comforting. It was all she wanted, to keep lying there, to keep her face turned away from those lights.

But nature called. With a groan, she pushed up. She was back in her bed in Talmaris. The lamp on the floor in the far corner was on. But Jin's side of the bed was empty.

Her heart sank.

Why wouldn't he just talk to her? Didn't he know she'd have a thousand questions when she woke up? Like how long they'd been back in the capital, how the team was faring, if Lucian had made it back alright, if they knew the status of the Novarian troops up north.

The clock on the bedside table said it was nearing three in the morning. They couldn't have been back for that long, then, unless she'd been sleeping for nearly a full day. The last thing she remembered was drifting off to sleep on the flight back.

She went to get up, but a small white rectangle caught her sleepy eyes. There, set neatly in one corner of the bedside table, was a small piece of paper.

Downstairs with Veiko and Ellie. Be back soon.

-J

Blinking a couple of times, Astrea reread Jin's neat handwriting. At least he'd left a note, even if she would've rather woken up with him there. It was the most he'd "said" to her since their ridiculous argument.

With a quiet groan, Astrea set the note back down and pushed out of bed. After using the facilities, she passed by the shower, finding its floor wet. Jin must have cleaned up.

She padded over to the sink and turned the water on. Her reflection looked exhausted, completely overwhelmed. Dark circles tinged the skin under her eyes. Her hair was a frizzy mess. And skies, how her muscles and bones ached. It was like she'd been run over by a streetcar.

She grabbed her hairbrush off the counter; Jin must have unpacked before he went to find Veiko and his sister. All of their things were set out neatly, as they always were. She wasn't even in her armor anymore but one of Jin's shirts.

After brushing her hair and securing it in a braid, she shed the shirt and started to draw a bath. Maybe a bath at three in the morning wasn't practical, but she didn't have the energy to heal herself, and she couldn't get back into bed when her body ached like this. Especially not when she could still feel dirt and sweat sticking to her skin.

When the bath was filled, she slipped into the tub, relishing the warm water as it cradled her exhausted body. Exhausted from so much. Her father. The search for Theo. Losing Saros. Cressida's pain. This strange situation with Jin.

She scrubbed herself clean with a washcloth and a brand-new bar of peppermint soap she'd found on the vanity. Some palace maid must have come by and set everything up during their absence. Peppermint wasn't usually Astrea's first choice, but it smelled nice.

Once clean, she sank lower in the tub and rested her head against the back edge. Would she ever get to go back home to Kalama? Would they really be able to figure out where Nazarov was searching for new aetherium sources? Would Cressida ever feel like herself again? Would Astrea?

"Az?"

Astrea startled so hard at the sound of Jin's voice that water sloshed over the sides of the tub. "Skies," she whispered, trying to reorient herself.

Jin stood right inside the doorway. Fatigue rolled off him in waves, threatening to knock Astrea over. She pulled her barrier back little by little, not so much that she felt like she would suffocate but enough to give her a reprieve. His golden eyes were tired, half-closed already, and his curly hair was damp and slightly mussed, as if he'd been running his hands through it again and again.

"Why are you in the bath?" he asked.

"My body hurts."

"Did you get hurt?" he asked, stepping closer. "During the fight?"

"No, I'm just tired."

He pressed his lips together, then went to the small closet tucked in one corner. After pulling out two large, clean blue towels, he returned and motioned with his head for her to climb out. The water had started getting cold anyway, so Astrea unplugged the drain and stood. Jin helped her out, then he wrapped one of the towels around her and draped the other over the edge of the tub.

And then he turned and walked back toward their bedroom door.

Astrea ground her teeth together. Maybe now wasn't the time, but was he ever going to talk to her? Really talk?

"Jin?" she asked, pulling her towel tighter around herself.

Pausing at the threshold, Jin set his hand on the door's trim and asked, "Yeah?"

"We need to talk. About our argument."

His shoulders rolled forward before he turned around. His mouth opened, then shut again.

"What?" she asked, voice cracking. There he was, just feet from her, and yet he felt miles away. Like he was on the other side of a chasm with no bridge. Why did this feel so impossibly hard? Why did every single thing have to weigh on her so heavily, when a month ago, she would've had little trouble working this out with him?

He ran a hand through his hair, messing the curls up even more. "I'm afraid that what I say is just going to make you even more angry."

"I won't get angry."

"You'd have every right to. I've been an ass. A complete and utter ass, and I'm still being one. I don't know why it's so hard for me right now."

"It's hard for me, too."

"Which is part of why I feel so bad. I'm your husband, your partner. I shouldn't be making things harder on you."

"We won't always get this perfectly right," she whispered. "I think we do a good job most days, not making each other's lives harder."

A hint of a smile tugged at his mouth. "I like to think so."

Astrea pulled her towel even tighter around herself. "I know these last few weeks have been really hard," she said. "I'm . . . I'm too much like Saros for my own good." Her voice cracked on her uncle's name, and unshed tears pricked at her eyes. "I get stubborn and avoid things, just like he always did. And you—"

"And I need to accept that I can't protect you from everything," Jin said quietly. "Adi's basically yelled at me twice now about it. As he should. I've been an ass."

"I don't think wanting to keep me safe makes you an ass."

"No, but not talking to you does."

She shrugged. "It certainly supports your case."

He chuckled, the first time she'd heard his laugh in . . . she didn't even know how long. And skies, was it like music to her ears.

But Jin sobered quickly, leaning against the doorway as he said, "We'd been doing so well, or I think so. Until this. And that's my fault."

"It's not like I exactly tried to listen to your perspective that day either," Astrea said. "We could have both handled it better."

"I just hate seeing you sad, Az," he said, face softening. "I hate it. I've always hated it, even when we were kids. I know I can't protect you from everything, but skies, it's like it's written into my soul that I have to try. Overriding that instinct is impossible some days. Leaving you be felt like the only way to give you any peace."

Fresh tears spilled down Astrea's cheeks. In a few long strides, Jin closed the distance between them, using his thumbs to wipe away her tears.

"Tell me how to make it up to you," he whispered, pressing his forehead against hers. Warm sunshine and cold regret warred on her skin. "Please, tell me how to make you stop hurting."

Pulling away, Astrea searched his tired face for one heartbeat, two. Then she pushed up on her toes, pulling his face down to meet her halfway. Her lips brushed his, then he pressed in, desperate, hungry. She opened her mouth to him, finding he tasted like malty tea.

Jin hoisted her up in his arms, only breaking their kiss as he started carrying her toward the door. Astrea kissed down his bearded cheeks, then his throat. His pulse hammered under her lips as she sucked on the skin there, and he let out a groan.

She needed him, needed all of him, but she was just so exhausted. And it seemed he was, too. Even though raspberry lust burned the air around him, he set her near the middle of the bed and walked over to the wardrobe. He pulled out fresh clothes for her.

"What, no makeup sex?" she asked half-heartedly.

Jin let out a tired laugh, those beautiful golden eyes of his filled with so much love. "If I wasn't dead on my feet," he said, "I'd have you all night."

As she fumbled with the bloomers and nightgown he'd passed to her, Jin took them back and helped her into them. Cool midnight air prickled her skin. He kicked off his shoes and trousers, then shucked off his shirt and abandoned them all on the floor as he climbed into bed with her.

Jin tugged her down and pulled her into a hug. "I'm sorry, Az," he murmured into her neck. "I'm sorry."

"Me too." She dragged her fingers through his hair as she repeated her words again and again. "I'm sorry, too."

And she was sorry. Sorry for not listening to him. For not trying to have a conversation with him sooner. For falling back into her old habits, for letting that lethal blend of hesitation and stubbornness get in the way. What if he'd died earlier that night, gotten seriously hurt by the Zaikudi? Then what? Or what if she had? They weren't promised tomorrow. They weren't promised anything. They needed to remember that, needed to live like every day might be their last together. Needed to make sure they said what they needed to say, that they came together to fight their problems instead of pushing against each other.

"I love you," he whispered. "I love you so much, Az."

"I love you, too." She barely choked out the words as tears built behind her eyes and in her throat. Her fingers brushed the faded shadowy mark where he'd been hit by aetherium. "I love you."

Astrea let her eyes drift shut as she curled up against Jin. His heart thumped steadily under her ear. He was *alive*.

They both were. And they were both there, talking—and more. And talking felt far, far better than drifting apart for even a few moments.

"I don't like fighting," Jin said as his fingers tangled in the hair at the nape of her neck. "I don't like it at all."

"Me either," Astrea said. "I know you want what's best for me . . . and I don't always know what that is. Lucian, of all people, proved that to me yesterday."

A hesitant laugh rumbled in Jin's chest. "Lucian?"

"He ordered me to take a couple of days off. Said he can see my pain very clearly, that I haven't begun to process it. And I think he's right. About that and that you need some time off, too."

"Lucian, of all people, giving good advice, and me, of all people, agreeing with him," Jin mused. "I know grieving probably feels impossible right now, but there's no right time for it. It just needs to happen."

"I know." She pressed closer to him. "You know Saros's death isn't your fault, right? That Cress's injury isn't your fault? We had to go with you to try to convince the council."

"I know. It doesn't feel that way, but I know you're right. I just can't help but think . . . well, was it a mistake? Should we have tried something else to convince them of my—our—loyalty?"

"What else could we even have done?"

"I'm not sure." Jin let out a long, heavy sigh. "Or should I have used my magic that day? Really used it, like Lucian wanted me to?"

"There was too much chaos," Astrea said. "I don't think it would have helped. It could have hurt the team, and we still would've had to carry you out of there."

He sighed again. "What's done is done."

"We have to move forward," Astrea said. "Together, like we always have."

"Together." He kissed her forehead. "Always."

Chapter 17

Curling up with Jin was everything Astrea had missed these last weeks. A soft bed, her warm husband, her barrier pulled in so she could feel only him.

It was exactly where she wanted—needed—to be even as some tiny voice in the back of her mind begged her to climb out of bed and get to work.

No, she would not. Not when Commander Lucian had everything under control. Not when he was right, that she and Jin needed time to breathe and process all that had happened. She hated admitting he was right in the first place, but ignoring his advice would only prove his point further, and she simply refused to do that.

Jin's chest rose and fell steadily under her cheek. One arm circled her, keeping her close. His hand rested on the curve of her hip. Astrea was practically on top of him, but he never minded that. With one finger, she traced the faint hint of shadow lingering on his shoulder. She hated it, that there was this reminder of what had happened.

He stirred. His hand drifted from her hip down to her ass, then up her back and to her hair. "What time is it?" he asked, voice heavy with sleep. His eyes didn't even open.

"Eight."

"How long have you been awake?"

"Only an hour." She'd only managed to sleep for a few hours after their talk.

With a gentle hand, Jin pushed her head down so he could kiss her temple. "Sleep."

She settled against him, willing her body to relax. His fingers explored her back, his touch so light it almost tickled.

"I missed you," she whispered.

"Let's agree to never fight again."

"Deal."

A quiet knock sounded out in the sitting room. Though they may have agreed that they needed a break from everything, it seemed the rest of the world wasn't willing to wait on them. Of course it wasn't.

Jin groaned. "Fuck me." He rolled over so Astrea was on her back. "Stay here."

As he left the bed, tugged on his pants, and headed for their door, Astrea sat up and pulled the blankets tighter around herself. Without Jin, she was freezing. Letting her barrier loosen, she was immediately rewarded with breezy surprise dancing over her skin. Just what she needed with the cold morning air.

"What are you doing here, Ellie?" came Jin's quiet voice.

Eliana replied, but her words were too muffled for Astrea to make out.

"I was trying to enjoy a quiet morning with—"

"Az!" Eliana called.

Astrea flopped back into the pillows and pulled the blankets over her head. Skies, she did not want to deal with whatever it was Eliana was about to bring to her. And bring it she was—literally. Eliana's quick footsteps stormed into the room, Jin's protests right behind.

"What are you still doing in bed at this hour?" Eliana asked.

Peeking out from under the blankets, Astrea found her best friend at the foot of the bed. Eliana was dressed in crimson, and her makeup was light but perfectly done. Her wavy hair now spilled down to her collarbone. She hadn't had it properly cut since before they left Kalama.

"The commander ordered me to stay away from work," Astrea said. "Me and Jin both."

Eliana set her hands on her wide hips. "He made no such comment to me."

"Well, he ordered me to before the Zaikudi ambush yesterday, and I'm just trying to do what I'm told."

"*Well*," Eliana replied, "while I can respect the commander's order, I want you to have breakfast with me."

"Why?" Jin asked, circling around his sister to get back in bed.

"*Why*?" Rust red annoyance flared around Eliana's head. "Do you even know what day it is?"

A little gasp left Astrea before she whispered, "Oh, skies." Her stomach dropped. "Oh, skies, it's your birthday and I completely forgot."

Tossing her hair over her shoulder, Eliana's expression softened. "With everything going on, I didn't expect you to remember, but I thought having breakfast together would be nice."

"I just need to get cleaned up," Astrea said.

"Sorry, Ellie," Jin said. "Of course we can have breakfast. Where are we eating?"

"The small dining room." She smiled pointedly at him, then turned. "We start in an hour, so don't be late." Her heels clicked across the wooden floor, and only once their door was shut again did Astrea loose a breath.

"I can't believe I forgot," she mumbled. After all Eliana had done for the two of them—the engagement party, helping with Astrea's wedding dress, the spouses-to-be party, the wedding itself—in recent months, and Astrea couldn't even remember her birthday? "Skies, I'm a bad friend."

Jin rubbed smooth, slow circles between her shoulders. "You're not a bad friend, Az. Ellie's right. So much has been going on lately . . ."

"Do you think she's going to miss her big party this year?" she asked. Eliana always had big birthday celebrations back in Kalama.

"Probably, not that she'll admit it."

Astrea nodded. She really couldn't forget Cressida's birthday in a few weeks either. Cressida especially deserved to have a nice day, whatever that might look like given their current circumstances.

With Jin's help, Astrea got her still-aching body out of bed and into the shower. He joined her, taking a few extra minutes to massage her scalp as he washed her hair for her. And by the time they were done, they still had a half hour on the clock. Astrea was all cleaned up—hair somewhat dry and braided—and wearing an emerald green dress with long sleeves.

"Here." Jin passed her both of her wedding bands before putting his on. He rolled up the sleeves of his black button-down shirt, then fiddled with the collar and top few buttons. "Am I presentable enough?"

"I don't think she'll care as long as we're there, but yes."

Stepping closer to her, Jin set his hands on Astrea's wide hips, then slid them around her waist. "And before we go, how are you feeling? Are we alright?"

Astrea had thought their conversation the night before had made that clear. She cupped his cheek. "Of course we're alright."

His smile was tired but genuine. "Good. Have I mentioned how sorry I am?"

"Only about a thousand times."

"Good."

"Come on." Astrea tugged on his hand, leading him toward the door. "Ellie's going to be even more disappointed if we're late."

The dining room Eliana had selected was teeming with energy by the time they made it downstairs. With a heavy sigh, Astrea pulled her barrier in tighter around herself.

"What's wrong?" Jin asked as they stopped outside the doors.

"Magic's wearing on me."

His eyebrows furrowed. "Do you need to see Ivy?"

"There's not much she can do for me."

It was magical exhaustion piling on top of normal fatigue and impossible grief. The only thing Astrea could really do was rest. Rest, as she'd been ordered. Ivy would probably tell her exactly what Lucian had. Another healer might be able to lessen some of the fatigue, but that wouldn't solve the real problem: the grief, the regret, the questions always pushing against her mind. It would just return and crush her under its weight.

She needed to find her balance again. A way forward, a way to keep busy, yet a way to rest and overcome.

Impossible. It felt impossible.

Squaring her shoulders, Astrea gestured to the doors. "Let's go inside."

Hesitantly, Jin pushed open the door on the right. It wasn't nearly as festive as Astrea had thought Eliana might pull off. There weren't any flowers on the table, not even a gramophone or radio playing music. No, it was like every other breakfast they'd had, only this time Veiko, his sister, and their wives were there. So were Marko and Lucian, as well as the rest of the Helosians.

Cressida had actually emerged from her room, even dressed in a bright blue sweater. Astrea's heart leaped. Her best friend was there, up and being social and smiling. Her aura burst with color, from steel pain to bright peach amusement. It didn't mean everything was suddenly better for Cressida—especially not with that cold steel—but this was good. Great, even, that she was feeling up to being out and about.

Astrea started for the side of the long table when Delfine called, "So good to see you, Prince Varojin and *Princess* Astrea."

Sugary amusement coated Astrea's tongue and danced across her skin, as if someone were tickling her with a feather. Though she knew the woman was just trying to get a rise out of her and entertain the others, Astrea forced herself to smile politely. She even relaxed a fraction as that same peach from before sparkled around Cressida. She'd take the brunt of whatever strange jokes Delfine had if it cheered Cressida up.

"Good morning," Jin said as he pulled out a chair for Astrea. "And happy birthday, Ellie."

"Thanks," Eliana drawled. "So kind of you to remember."

"Had we been home, I wouldn't have forgotten." Sitting down next to Astrea, Jin added, "Nor would your party be so small."

Eliana smiled tightly. "I know. I'm just giving you a hard time. Isn't that the younger sister's job?"

Nicos, seated next to her, held back a smirk.

"I'll say." Delfine reached for the white ceramic teapot in front of her. "Wouldn't you, brother?"

"You've certainly put in the effort over the years," Veiko replied as he leaned back in his chair. "And been successful for the most part."

"For the most part? I'm insulted."

"How about we get through breakfast without you harassing any of us?" Veiko said with a quiet chuckle. "Let Eliana enjoy her birthday."

Delfine huffed dramatically. "If you insist."

As everyone began chatting among themselves, Astrea settled in next to Cressida, helping herself to a scone and fresh raspberry jam. She wasn't in the mood to eat much, but Eliana would be worried if she didn't. Besides, it gave her something to focus on. It was a simple task, eating breakfast, but it helped her mind not stray too far into thinking about Saros.

"So, *princess*," Cressida said.

Astrea groaned. "Not you too."

"Don't I get a free pass?"

Astrea swiped some more jam onto her scone. "I suppose *you* can. No one else, though," she said with a pointed look around Cressida at Sarsali and Balthazar.

"Who, me?" Bringing his napkin to his mouth, Balthazar dabbed at the corners of his lips. "I resent the insinuation."

"It's hardly an insinuation when you've never let me live anything down, ever," Astrea said.

"She's right, darling," said Sarsali. "You always tease the girls."

"Only in good fun!"

"Maybe so," Astrea said, "but there's not much that's fun about being called princess." Not in her mind, anyway. Jin didn't like his title, and she didn't like being attached to his title. It made her feel . . . different. Other. She was just still Astrea Sovna.

"Fine, fine," he said, waving her off. "The 'p' word shall never leave my mouth again."

"Thank you." Astrea focused on Cressida then, really focused on her. Though her arm was still wrapped in bright white bandages, she wasn't using her sling. That was another good sign. "How are you feeling today?"

Cressida shrugged one slender shoulder. "Not bad, all things considered. Trying to come to terms with it."

"That's all you can do. One foot in front of the other and all that."

"And all that," Cressida mused, then nudged her plate toward Astrea. "Get me some more potatoes?"

As she went to reach for the serving dish, Jin reached it first and handed it over. She spooned two helpings onto Cressida's plate. Cressida dug in, devouring a healthy chunk in just a few moments.

It even got Astrea to eat a little more as she tried to listen to everyone's chatter. Delfine's mention of a delayed art exhibit at the university. Letizia describing something funny Helena did the night before. Adi and Zephyrine chiming in with a story about Jin's time at Fort Avalon, and Noemi scandalized by both Jin and Adi's antics over the years. Even Nicos shared a few anecdotes to tease Jin, who took it all in stride. Astrea *tried* to listen, but it all went in one ear and out the other. The potatoes were good at least, perfectly fried and only lightly salted.

They were still carrying on when the dining room doors opened. A brunette soldier dressed in Novarian blue slipped inside, a delicate white gift bag in one hand and an envelope in another.

"For you, Your Highness," the soldier said as she set the items down on the corner of the table where the grand duke sat.

"What's this?" Veiko asked as he took the envelope, running his fingers over the wax seal.

"From the Tornamian delegation, Your Highness."

Veiko's thick eyebrows furrowed. "Thank you."

With a small salute, the soldier hurried back out the door. As she did, Letizia stood and circled the table to take the gift bag.

"This one is *not* from the Tornamians," she said as she set it in front of Eliana. "A small token from us. Happy birthday, Eliana."

"Oh, you really didn't have to do that," Eliana replied. Her cheeks burned scarlet, almost the same color as her lipstick.

Astrea didn't think she'd ever seen Eliana get embarrassed about receiving a gift before. In fact, Eliana usually loved getting presents. There was a certain excitement it had always brought out in her, always clear in her aura. And now, only a hint of it surrounded her, replaced mostly by heavy uncertainty.

"Well, what is it?" Delfine asked, leaning forward across the table. "I was made aware of no such gift."

Eliana removed the peach tissue paper from the bag, then reached inside. She pulled out a stack of bars wrapped in gold foil.

"Is that chocolate?" Delfine asked before turning to her brother. "You got Eliana *chocolate* for her birthday?"

"We were told it's one of your favorites," Letizia said. "Milk chocolate with nougat pieces, from the finest chocolatier in Talmaris."

"I *do* love it," Eliana said with a smile. "Really, thank you both. Just what I was missing from back home, actually." Her gaze tracked straight to Nicos, who smiled softly at her.

"Surely a princess deserves more on her birthday," said Delfine. "Wouldn't you agree, Astrea?"

Astrea tipped her head back against her chair.

"Enough, Delfine," Veiko said, annoyed. He held the now-open envelope in one hand and a slip of paper in the other. "I'm sorry to cut this short, Eliana, but there's something I need to attend to. Please, stay here. Finish your breakfast. I'll see you at our meeting this afternoon."

Veiko stood, not giving anyone a moment to get a word in. Astrea frowned, watching as he and Letizia disappeared out into the hallway beyond.

"What was that about?" Jin asked once the door had shut behind Veiko.

Delfine waved a slender hand. "My brother sure does know how to make a dramatic exit. But please, don't worry too much about him. If it's important, he'll tell us later."

I should certainly hope so, Astrea thought ruefully.

"Let's do as he said and finish your breakfast, hm?" Delfine said to Eliana. "You can pick up whatever political games he has going on later. This morning's about celebrating, and we've *got* to make up for the lackluster gift."

"I actually really like it," Eliana said, adjusting the gold-wrapped chocolate bars where they sat on the table in front of her. "It was thoughtful and austere, which is especially important considering he's taking your country to war."

"Would it have killed him to get you something permanently gold at least?" Delfine asked.

Astrea had known Delfine was one to joke around and not take things too seriously, but this? This surprised her. She wasn't sure why, exactly. After all, Delfine had been raised in the palace, one of the most privileged upbringings she could've had. But Veiko didn't come across as caring too much about material goods, and while Eliana enjoyed receiving gifts, it was never about the monetary value with her. Some of Eliana's favorite birthday gifts over the years had been books and small trinkets, not the expensive jewelry often gifted to her at court.

"Tell you what," Eliana said with a sly smile, "I'll keep the wrapping after I'm done eating the chocolate. Is that permanent enough for you?"

Delfine rolled her eyes. "What was it you said about younger sisters earlier? Are they supposed to annoy each other?"

Eliana grinned. "You started it."

"I suppose I did."

Astrea shook her head, but everyone else around the table let out a collective laugh. And with that, they settled back into their breakfast. But Astrea couldn't help but look at the door every so often, as if Veiko might come back and reveal just what was in that letter he received. After all, if he was rushing off like that to attend to things, it couldn't be very good.

Astrea hoped she was wrong.

CHAPTER 18

By the time Delfine declared Eliana's birthday breakfast complete a half hour later, Astrea couldn't wait to get out of the dining room. There'd been enough clinking of spoons, smacking of lips, and general noise to last her the rest of the week.

Adi, Noemi, the twins, and the Nikaphoroses excused themselves first. Astrea was quick to get to her feet, eager to follow, but Delfine's voice rang out over the chatter.

"Varojin, Astrea, if you wouldn't mind?"

Astrea stopped pushing her chair in. She glanced up at Jin, who shrugged. Eliana's eyebrows furrowed.

"What's this about?" Jin asked.

"Stay for a moment, would you?" Delfine asked, voice relaxed. "You as well, Eliana and Nicos."

Zephyrine was the last one out the door, and she shot a questioning look over her shoulder. Jin made no move, nor did he answer. The general shook her head and closed the door behind her.

Still seated, Delfine folded her hands loosely over her abdomen. "My jokes from this morning aside," she said slowly, "we all have an image to uphold."

"I understand that," Eliana said. "I don't think I've done anything to warrant additional scrutiny, especially not with the other diplomats here."

Delfine eyed Nicos. "Perhaps not, but there have been whispers of . . . concern . . . among the delegates. Not just about your relationship with Mister Masalis, but Varojin and Astrea's as well."

Jin ran his hand over his face. "This again?"

"Not again," Delfine corrected. "It's a different concern. Courtly concerns. Concerns about what your relationships will mean for the stability of Helosia should we win this war."

"The *stability* of Helosia?" Eliana echoed.

"You act as if it's *my* concern," Delfine said, placing a hand over her heart and frowning dramatically in feigned offense. "I have no issues with the four of you. I know you all have good intentions, but some of the delegates are concerned that you both may make rash decisions for Helosia's future should Eliana be installed as empress."

"And we're going to make rash decisions because . . . our romantic partners are from normal families?" Eliana asked, rusty annoyance racing out from her in bright waves.

"You know how some of these people act," Delfine said, frowning. "As if the only ones able to lead are those born into privilege."

"So you don't agree with them," Nicos said.

"No, I don't." Finally, Delfine pushed out of her seat. "Of course I don't."

"That doesn't seem to be a given," Jin said. "Is Veiko concerned about this?"

"No, he's never been concerned with optics."

"Are you?" Astrea asked. Veiko may not have been, but Ysabel had been, and it seemed to Astrea that despite Delfine's protests, she may have been a bit concerned, too.

"What I'm trying to say . . ." Delfine pressed her lips together. "May I speak frankly?"

"You've hardly ever asked permission to do that before," Eliana said, earning her a glare.

"Even if I disagree with them," Delfine said, "it may be a good idea to play into your roles more. And perhaps Eliana needs to stop asking President Sikori about the structure of her country and whether or not she recommends democracy as a path for other nations."

Astrea and Jin turned to Eliana in tandem.

"What?" Eliana asked, hands perched on her hips. "I'm not allowed to ask questions?"

"I won't pretend I don't think about the very same policy changes," Delfine said. "But surely you can see what it suggests to the other leaders, that Helosia might be thrown into further chaos with a complete change in government structure. You know better than most that stability is going to be important for the period after the war."

"Stability doesn't have to mean autocracy," Eliana said. "I will not replace my father only to become him. You and Veiko have always known that. I made that clear to you both and the council months ago."

"Will you talk some sense into your sister?" Delfine asked Jin.

"What would you say if I told you I agree with her?" he asked.

Scoffing, Delfine threw her arms over her head. "Of course you do."

Astrea could take Delfine's point about possibly making the other continental leaders wary. If Eliana really did want to change Helosia's entire political structure, well, that was going to cause some problems even if it went as smoothly as possible. And problems in Helosia would cause hiccups for the other countries, likely economic. Still, Delfine's insistence was a little surprising. She'd never seemed quite so . . . serious.

"I wouldn't change anything immediately," Eliana said. "There would be a transitional period. Time for the aristocracy to get their affairs in order. For us to put a more robust electoral system in place."

"You speak as if you've already made these plans," Delfine said.

"No," Eliana said quickly. "I've merely been contemplating all of it. Jin inspired me, actually, quite a while ago."

"When?" Jin asked with a frown.

"When Novaria started taking Helosian defectors," Eliana said. "When Commander Tarkun was so disturbed by Helosians arriving, and you reminded me of exactly how our family has operated and built power over the centuries. I must do whatever it takes to prevent that from happening in Helosia's government again. That's my job."

Red pride swelled around Jin. "That's *our* job," he said. "You and me, trying to right Father's wrongs."

Astrea was sure her aura would reflect the same. It was sometimes easy to forget that Jin and Eliana were children of Emperor Aelius Auris, one of the most powerful monarchs to ever rule on the continent. They were so unlike him in what they valued and believed. It was nothing short of a miracle, in her opinion, that they hadn't turned out like him. Like Kaius.

"The delegates may not see it that way," Delfine said. "They don't doubt your desire to overthrow your father, but they want some guarantees. Information."

"I can talk to them at length," Eliana said, "but if I am to be installed as empress, then it's my decision that changes are made. My decision, with advice from those I trust most. Surely you can respect that, Delfine. Isn't that how we all do things in our monarchies?"

"It is," Delfine said. "But perhaps tone it down in public, at least until we've finalized our agreements? I respect your desire to create a better future, but we need allies in this fight."

Eliana nodded. "I understand that. I'll do my best."

"And they've been asking what we know of Prince Apelo," Delfine said. "Where his loyalties lie and what he thinks about all of this."

"We haven't had any contact with him," Jin said. "You know that."

Delfine shrugged. "It was possible something slipped by us."

"I can assure you, we haven't heard from him," Eliana said. "If we had, I would have asked to get my nieces out of Helosia. They aren't much older than Helena and Leo."

"As if your father would allow us to take in his grandchildren?" Delfine asked.

Eliana shrugged. "As if he'd allow you to take us in?"

Delfine's lips pursed. "If we could get in touch with Apelo, do you think the information we have about your father's plans would sway him to our side? It would look very good for the alliance if we could get three of the four Auris siblings to go against their father."

The elusive Prince Apelo. Astrea hadn't seen much of him when she was younger, and he'd moved away from Kalama shortly after getting married. He'd always seemed to fall between Kaius on one side and Eliana and Jin on the other, like he just wanted to agree with everyone and keep the peace. Jin had confirmed to her once that Apelo didn't really have a spine when it came down to it.

"I'm not so sure about that," Jin said quickly. "He knows how our father is, but he never seems keen on doing anything about it. I'm not sure that information about void magic and aetherium would change anything."

"Is it worth trying?" Delfine asked.

"It's worth considering," Eliana said. "Considering it very carefully, anyway. Reaching out to him might be a disaster."

"Then please, consider it," Delfine said.

"Is the alliance that weak?" Jin asked. "That our choice in romantic partners or Eliana's thought exercises on democracy could bring it all crashing down? That doesn't put us in a very good position to enter a war."

"I do not know for certain," Delfine said. "All I can tell you is what people are saying. I hear many things around the palace. For example," she continued, turning to Jin and Astrea, "several of the delegates have asked when you two are starting a family."

"What?" Astrea choked out. "What business of that is theirs?"

"What business?" Delfine asked with a laugh. "Astrea, my dear, you married into the Auris family. It's a natural question. Royals have heirs."

"That's none of their business, Delfine," Jin said, "nor is it yours."

She put her hands up in surrender. "I am simply the messenger."

A headache started to form behind Astrea's right eye. Oh, this was not how she'd imagined this morning going, not at all. No, she and Jin had discussed this. They wanted to grow their family, yes, but they wouldn't until things were safe, until it would be safe for a baby to be brought into this world. Until the Paragon weren't trying to force some role upon them both, let alone their child. Until Emperor Aelius was no more and their child could live in peace.

And even if that were somehow tomorrow, they still would wait until they were older, wiser, more settled. Then, and only then, would they take that next step. That was years away, if they won the war at all. And nobody's business, no matter what Jin's status was.

"Regardless," Delfine said, "consider this a warning that your movements are being watched, questioned, even if the delegates largely believe in your commitment to the cause."

"Let me get back to you about Apelo," Eliana said. "And in the meantime, I need to go speak with your brother. We have a meeting in an hour."

"Speak away," Delfine said. "Ask his opinion about these questions the delegates have. See what he has to say, too."

With a nod, Eliana said, "I will."

Astrea's chest tightened. These skies damned people and delegates and whatever political nonsense they were thinking of. How could they not see the bigger picture? That Eliana ruling Helosia would be better for the continent regardless of how much she loosened imperial control. That stopping Emperor Aelius and Victor Nazarov both would help bring peace. That Eliana and Jin's personal lives did not dictate their commitment to continental stability.

The dining room door closed with a thud as Delfine left the four of them on their own.

"So much for a nice morning," Eliana muttered.

"Chin up, Ellie," Jin said. "If the delegates' biggest concerns are now boiling down to our personal lives and political leanings, that's a much better spot than we had been in with them."

"Oh, you're an optimist now?" she asked.

"Just trying to look on the bright side for once in my skies damned life," he said with a small smile.

"I suppose." Eliana shook her head. "I'll catch up with you two later?"

"See you later," Jin said. "I want to hear about this meeting with Veiko."

As Eliana and Nicos left, Jin slid his arm around Astrea's shoulders. She wrapped her arm around his waist and leaned into him, savoring his warmth.

"What now?" he asked.

"I need to bring a few things to Noemi," Astrea said.

With a sigh, Jin said, "Back to the library we go."

By the time they got to the library, Adi was already there, talking excitedly with his sister as he described the attack the Zaikudi had launched on them just the day before.

"And then Jin came in and absolutely ripped the other Fireweaver a new one. Only way we would've gotten away, honestly," he said, leaning back in his chair.

"I hardly think that's the only way we would have survived that," Jin said dryly as he and Astrea circled the table.

Noemi's eyebrows furrowed, then she glared at her brother. "That sounds scary. I don't know why you're so excited by the whole thing, Adi."

"Nothing better than getting your adrenaline pumping sometimes," he said, though Astrea didn't miss the flash of orange anxiety above his head.

Why paint it so differently for Noemi? To try to get her to worry less, maybe? The same orange floated around the younger Kuwat sibling, complementing her raspberry pink blouse. Her spiral curls were extra glossy, like she'd put some kind of serum or treatment on them.

"You're obnoxious," Noemi said to her brother.

"Obnoxious I may be, but you love having me around," he said with a grin. Then Adi turned to Astrea and Jin. "What did Delfine want?"

Lowering his voice, Jin said, "To warn Ellie and me not to get too public about thinking Helosia's government needs some large changes and some nonsense about how our non-royal relationships look to some of the delegates."

"Classist nonsense," Noemi muttered. Magenta embarrassment flared bright around her. "I'm so sorry, Jin! I didn't—"

He laughed a deep belly laugh, cutting her off and sending warm amusement skittering over Astrea's limbs. "That's nothing to ever be sorry for," Jin said. "It *is* nonsense, which is why it doesn't really surprise me. We'll keep our heads down if we need to for the sake of the alliance, but it doesn't change what we're going to pursue."

"I'd expect nothing less from you two. But," Adi said, gesturing to the notebook Astrea had clutched to her chest, "I doubt that's why you're here."

As much as her mind was running circles around that strange and uncomfortable conversation with Delfine, and as much as she would've liked Adi's take on all of it, Astrea tried to pull herself out of that loop. She needed to get this part done, trust someone else with decoding this information for her so she could go back to bed.

"Something else for you to hopefully translate, Noemi." Astrea set her leather-bound journal on the table, opened to the right page, and slid it to the young scholar. "Copied from the fortress."

Pressing her full lips together, Noemi pulled the book closer and examined the looping letters Astrea had written down. She shook her head. "I recognize some of these words . . . something about an island?"

"That's where the Paragon informant told Lucian Nazarov might be heading," Jin said quietly. "So, what, was he pulling his information from old inscriptions as well?"

"Does it say anything more specific?" Adi asked.

"I'll need my cipher." The legs of Noemi's chair scraped across the wooden floor as she pushed away from the table. "I'll be right back."

She hurried toward the spiral staircase in the corner, her teal skirt swishing around her legs as she climbed. Noemi called Tomas's name as she strode down the mezzanine, all business.

"Maybe I can—" Astrea started, but Jin shook his head.

"What happened to rest?" he asked.

"Reading keeps my mind busy."

"And it's just more work."

Astrea tried not to pout. He was right, of course. Immediately throwing herself back into this conspiracy was not the way she would properly confront what had happened in the Badlands. It felt easier, though.

"I'll help Noemi with whatever it is she finds," Adi said. "And we'll bring it to Lucian if it seems like something that'll help him."

"You sure you're up to this?" Jin asked him. "You need to rest, too."

"I know, but I'm actually feeling alright the last few days," Adi said. "I don't mind, really."

Jin nodded. "Well, take a break if you feel you need it. Same goes for Noemi. Don't push yourselves too hard."

"Aye, aye, Captain," Adi said with a smirk and little salute.

Rolling his eyes, Jin took Astrea's hand in his. He tugged her toward the door just as Tomas and Noemi reappeared in the mezzanine, excitement vibrating around them both.

A pang of jealousy echoed in Astrea's limbs; she missed that kind of enthusiasm for research and knowledge. And she couldn't help but picture Saros there with them, eager to decode what messaging Nazarov might be following. That jealousy turned into a sadness that threatened to drown her.

Instead, she tried to focus on the good, on the way Noemi smiled and Adi started tossing jokes out as the trio got to work, on the way Jin's skin felt against hers and the sunshine pouring off him. His thumb drew tiny circles on the back of her palm, like he knew what she must be thinking.

With a shaky breath, Astrea left the library behind. If she was going to be useful to her team, she needed to take her break seriously and trust the others to get the work done. And trust them she did. She just didn't know if she trusted herself to withstand the rising tide of her grief.

Chapter 19

Astrea tugged her wool coat tighter around herself as she shivered and silently cursed the Novarian weather. Winter was right around the corner, and Astrea didn't see herself adjusting quickly. Kalamian winters had always been mild, rarely dipping so close to freezing.

In the two days since Eliana's birthday breakfast, Astrea had spent much of that time asleep or holed up in her rooms with Jin. He'd suggested a walk after breakfast for a change of scenery and some fresh air. The royal Greenkeepers were out in force, tending to the gardens and checking them for frost damage. Sarsali was with one group, carefully examining a section of rose bushes. It was good to see Sarsali back in her natural element, especially after the turmoil of the last month.

"What would you like to do today?" Jin asked, taking Astrea's gloved hand in his bare one. He didn't seem bothered by the weather in the least.

Astrea was just grateful that Veiko had supplied them with new wardrobes for the changing season. She barely even had any of these items back in Kalama, let alone thinking to bring them north when they'd fled in early summer.

"I don't know," she said.

Part of her wanted to go to the library to work, but what was the point? Noemi's examination of the texts taken from the old Paragon fortress hadn't yielded anything specific, as most of them were only parts of words or a few letters, as if the rest of the carvings had been lost to time.

But with the knowledge that the inscriptions mentioned islands, it had bolstered Lucian's determination to follow wherever Nazarov might be headed.

Another part of her wanted to crawl back into bed and nap all day. The more she actually leaned into Lucian's orders to take a break, the more Astrea's body seemed to be slowing her down. It was as if it had been deprived of sleep for weeks and weeks, and it now wanted her to catch up. She hadn't been sleeping well these last months, but the sheer exhaustion came as a surprise.

And another part still wanted to spend some more time with their friends, try to pass the day in a more cheerful way. Maybe Lennor and Civan would want to play cards. Maybe they could even get Cressida to join them.

"You don't know." Jin wrapped his arm around her shoulders and tugged her into his side as they walked. His body heat seeped under her skin. "I don't know either. Feels like we're just wasting time."

"Yeah."

They continued on, listening to the chatter of nearby soldiers and Greenkeepers alike. After a few more minutes—and after a particularly strong gust of wind made Astrea shiver violently—they turned around and started back toward the palace.

What did Astrea like to do in her free time? She'd always liked reading, but reading a novel at that moment seemed frivolous. Back in Kalama, when she and Cressida had all the freedom in the world, they'd spent so much time in museums, shops, cafés, parks. Astrea had passed many days in the Nikaphoros family kitchen, too, taste testing recipes for Cressida. Could they convince palace staff to let Balthazar into the kitchen? Maybe she could help him make lunch.

"Wow," Jin said with a laugh as they stepped back into the palace.

"What?" Astrea asked.

"Your face."

Astrea touched her cheeks. "My face?"

"I don't think I've ever seen it quite so red."

"Oh." Her skin was so cold to her touch that Astrea barely noticed.

"Let's get you warmed up."

"Oh?" she asked, trying to force playfulness she didn't feel into her voice.

"Not like that."

"Tease."

As Jin laughed again, sunshine and electric amusement flitted over her limbs. Astrea couldn't help but smile a little. His laugh always soothed something within her, even the torn-up pieces of her heart that didn't seem to want to be soothed.

"I'll start a fire when we get upstairs," he said, taking her hand, "and call for some tea."

"I'm going to need a lot of it if I'm to survive the winter."

"I'll personally ensure you do."

"I'm fairly certain that *is* a husband's job."

"One I take very seriously," he said.

As they rounded a corner to the stairs that would take them back to their apartments, they stopped short. Lucian, descending the wide, ornate staircase, stopped short as well.

"Oh," he said. "I was looking for you, Astrea."

"Why?" she asked. "Is everything alright?"

Lucian's thin lips pressed together, the only hint of his feelings. His wall was tight, as always. "I've brought Valen to the palace. To the guard-house. I thought it was only fair after his information actually got us somewhere."

Astrea stiffened. "He's here?"

She wasn't entirely sure why it bothered her so much. Her father *had* provided information that proved useful. It had gotten them closer to Nazarov.

"He is, and he wants to speak with you," Lucian said hesitantly. "I was trying to get him to give us something more about these islands, anything about them, but he's insisting that he needs to speak with you."

"Did he know about the attack at that old site he pointed us to?" Jin asked.

Lucian shook his head. "We're confident he didn't."

Jin frowned. "Does he seem to know about the islands Nazarov might be looking for?"

"Honestly?" Sighing, Lucian glanced at Astrea. "I can't tell . . ."

"But he gave us information last time when I spoke with him, so maybe he'll open up again if I visit him," she said, finishing what the commander was implying. It wasn't exactly how she wanted to spend her day, but if it would help . . . "I'll speak with him."

"You're sure?" Jin asked, peering down at her.

"I'm sure," she said.

"Both of you should come," Lucian said. "In case he wants to speak with you too, Varojin."

As they trailed the commander through the palace, Astrea's pulse quickened. What could her father possibly want to speak about with her now? Yes, she'd do what needed to be done to help the cause, but what could Valen possibly want with her? What could she even say to him?

After several turns down half-empty corridors, the halls became more plain. Soon, they were in the guardhouse, heading down a long passage Astrea hadn't seen before. Lucian unlocked a door to his left, then let Astrea and Jin inside. It reminded Astrea of the room at the police station, the one with the one-way glass into the cell. The only difference was this room was a bit larger and even more sparse. Stone walls, wooden floor, and nothing but the glass separating them from where Valen sat behind a table in the next room.

Dark circles had made their homes under his eyes, and he slouched in his seat. But otherwise, he seemed unharmed. His black hair was clean, his clothes were pressed, and he'd even shaved. At least they weren't treating him horribly.

"We'll be right out here," Lucian said to Astrea.

Just what she wanted, an audience.

Tentatively, Astrea opened the door to Valen's cell. As she stepped inside, he perked up. Green curiosity snapped around him for only a moment.

"Astrea," he said, almost sounding relieved. "I wasn't sure the commander would actually fetch you."

"He's a man of his word," Astrea said.

"He told me that my information was helpful, that you found something."

Astrea didn't know how much she could say to Valen, so she settled on a simple, "We did. Thank you for your help."

"Of course. I want to help."

"Then why wouldn't you answer the commander's questions about the islands he's looking for?" She crossed her arms over her chest. "That seems like a simple way to help."

Valen pressed his lips together.

"Well?" she all but shouted. "Why won't you tell him?"

"If I start giving him everything he wants—if I even have answers—he may not let me see you." Valen turned his attention toward the glass behind Astrea and asked, "Isn't that right, Commander?"

She was fairly certain that Lucian wouldn't have denied Valen the right to see her, not if Valen cooperated and provided them even more information about the Paragon. It was a weak argument at best. Backward, almost. Assisting them would earn him their trust, more privileges.

"You should sit," Valen said, motioning to the chair opposite him.

It was then that Astrea realized he wasn't in any kind of handcuffs or chains. The commander must have believed Valen wouldn't try anything.

"I'm fine, thank you," she said curtly. "What did you want to speak with me about?"

"I'd rather speak without an audience."

"And I'd rather not."

Valen let out a rough grumble. "They bring me from one prison to another, and now I can't even speak to my daughter alone?"

Oh, the things she could say. But Astrea swallowed her retort. Getting snippy with Valen hardly seemed like the way to get him to open up more. So, she called over her shoulder, "Commander, could you please go get us some coffee?"

Wariness drifted through the wall, then someone knocked on the glass. Only some of the wariness retreated, though. Either Jin or Lucian must have stayed. Probably Jin.

"He's leaving," Astrea said as she turned back toward her father.

"Thank you." If he suspected someone else had remained, he didn't say. Instead, Valen gestured to the empty chair again. "Please, sit."

Tentatively, Astrea pulled the chair out from the table and sat down. She shoved her hands in her jacket pockets. "The coffee probably won't take him long, so you might want to use this time wisely," she said, trying to keep her voice even.

"The commander mentioned a Zaikudi ambush out west, near the location I helped pinpoint." Valen's eyebrows furrowed. "Were you there?"

"I was."

"Were you hurt?"

"Not particularly."

"Then how are you?" he asked, his words almost desperate as he leaned forward. "You look exhausted."

"These last months haven't been easy." It was the truth, yet it barely scratched the surface. "It's all catching up to me now."

Valen shook his head. "This is my fault."

"The Zaikudi attack?" Astrea asked, her blood chilling more than when she'd been out in the gardens. Lucian had said—

"No, no, the rest," Valen said, blue sadness wavering in the air around him. "Had I not faked my death, maybe I could have convinced my brother not to go anywhere near you. Then you wouldn't be on this path. Maybe if I hadn't been a coward all these years . . ."

How was it that Astrea had been the one to go through everything, from the stalking to the abduction to the dreamwalking, the assassinations, Saros's death, the Zaikudi ambush, and yet here she was, in a position where one might expect her to comfort Valen?

"I don't think it's worth going down that path," she said, still trying to keep her voice even. "We'll never know. Self-pity isn't a good look."

"Perhaps not," her father said with a shake of his head. "No, it's not, but it's impossible for me to pretend I don't regret every decision I've made these last decades. Skies . . ." His ice blue eyes—almost colorless—met hers. "I asked to speak with you because I want to help, yes, but I want a relationship with you, Astrea. I want to make up for lost time. All the moments I haven't been there when I should have been."

Make up for lost time? That was what he wanted?

In what world was he entitled to that?

Every broken piece of her wanted to lash out at him, blame him for everything. And maybe in some ways he was responsible, but he wasn't responsible for all of it.

And they needed his help.

Astrea's voice trembled as she said, "No. The deal can't be that you'll only help us if you get to have a personal relationship with me. That's not actually helping us at all."

"But—"

"If you really mean it," she said, "if you really want to make up for not being there and not stopping your brother, then you should assist us without asking for anything in return. Help *me* without asking that. That would be the right thing to do."

"But—" he tried again.

"No," Astrea said. "You said once that we're family. Well, family doesn't offer help only in return for something selfish they want. Because that's what that is. You're being selfish, withholding possible aid just so you can make me sit in a room with you, just so you feel less alone or bad or whatever it is you're feeling." Tears burned her eyes. "My real family would never do that. And if you want me to even consider having some kind of relationship with you, I hope you learn to give just for the sake of it, to help because it's the right thing to do."

Valen stared at Astrea, mouth slightly open.

Good. She'd rendered him speechless.

Someone—Jin, a mix of warm pride and sunshine love—knocked on the glass.

Astrea shoved to her feet. "If you decide to actually help us again, Commander Lucian will take your statement."

She headed for the doors, hands balled tightly into fists in her coat pockets.

"Astrea, wait," Valen said. Chair legs scraped against the wooden floor. His voice cracked as he said, "Please."

Peeking over her shoulder, Astrea found her father standing behind the table, one hand flat against its surface and the other reaching under the neck of his shirt. He fished out a gold chain—the locket he'd shown her days ago—then slowly reached up with his other hand to unclasp it.

"You're right," he said. "Family doesn't help only when they get something in return."

"So you'll help us?"

"Whatever the commander wants to know, I'll do my best to answer, though I can't make any promises."

That was better than nothing, Astrea supposed.

"Here." He extended the locket to her. "I want you to have this, please."

Her eyebrows furrowed. "Why?"

"I loved your mother very much, Astrea. So very much. And you're exactly like her. I see it in you, that quiet fierceness." He held her gaze as Astrea willed herself not to cry. "Roxana always had a way of telling me when I was on the wrong side of a fight, even if that was because I'd picked no side at all."

"That doesn't explain why you want me to have that," Astrea managed to whisper as she gestured at the locket. "Don't you want to keep it if you loved her that much?"

"I've had it long enough," he said. "And I see in your eyes how badly you're hurting. Maybe it will bring you comfort, as it brought me comfort for so many years."

Astrea searched her father's face. Those cold eyes that were somehow warm around the edges. The subtle wrinkles forming around the corners of his mouth. The hints of gray in his hair. This man, whose blood she shared. Whom her mother had, by all accounts, loved. This man who tied her to the Paragon in ways she could never have fathomed, yet who also seemed to want to make things right.

She didn't know why, but Astrea closed the small distance between them and took the locket. It was cold between her fingers. She slipped it into her coat pocket, returning her father's small, sad smile before leaving the room.

It was only when the door was closed, separating her from Valen, and only when Astrea found herself in Jin's arms that she let her tears fall.

But the return of Lucian's heavy wall made Astrea pull away quickly. Not because Lucian couldn't see them like this but because there were more important things in that moment than her tears.

"Oh," he said as soon as he walked into the room. The soldier pushing a small coffee cart behind him paused, too. "Is everything alright?" Lucian asked.

"Fine," Astrea lied, wiping at her wet cheeks. "Valen's going to talk to you. He said he'll try his best to answer your questions, whatever you need to ask him."

"I see." Lucian glanced at Jin, then Astrea, then the second door again. "Then I'd best get to it. There's a lot I need to talk to him about." The commander motioned for the soldier to follow him into the next room, leaving Jin and Astrea alone again.

"Now what?" Jin asked.

"Let's get out of here," Astrea whispered, one hand clutching the locket. She didn't know where to go, but she knew she needed to get away from this room, from her grief, from her father.

Chapter 20

Astrea fumbled with her father's locket, turning it over and over again in her hands. The first time she'd seen this piece of jewelry, she hadn't even noticed the engraving on the front. It was a delicate image, two roses surrounded by leaves.

She traced the rounded edges, ignoring the way she trembled despite the fire Jin had lit in their room before he'd left to speak with Eliana. Astrea pried the locket open. There were her mother and father, so young. So happy.

Those grins. She couldn't get over those grins. It was like they didn't have a care in the world. She could almost see the pink and gold twining around them despite the colorless photo, despite the fact that her mother was dead and her father was imprisoned downstairs.

Would he actually give Lucian information?

Would he actually hold up his end of the bargain and cooperate without expecting anything from her in return?

Would this be another dead end? Could this be some grand manipulation by him to bring her that much closer to the Paragon?

Astrea stared down at her mother's round face—her own round face—wishing with every bone in her body that Roxana would somehow appear and tell her what she knew. What to do.

She wished Saros was there. He didn't always know what to say or do, but skies, she just wanted him there. Wanted him to hug her the way he had when she was a child, when they'd had to leave Irvina in the first place. Because that was how she felt now. Small. Alone. Scared.

But she wasn't alone. This wing of the palace was full of people who loved her.

And there were two people who loved her very much whom she hadn't spoken to often enough. Two people who loved her very much yet didn't know the full story of the last few months.

As much as Astrea hated to admit it, her father was right. She was hurting so badly. She never stopped hurting.

She'd always planned to tell Sarsali, Balthazar, and Saros together. That had always been the plan.

But now Saros was gone, and she couldn't wait.

She had to stop trying to bear this weight alone. Yes, Jin knew, and yes, Cressida knew. Eliana, Adi, Nicos, and the others knew. But Sarsali and Balthazar always had wise words to share. Had always been there to help her. And she needed help. She needed perspective.

Pushing to her feet, Astrea snapped the locket shut and kept it clutched in her closed hand as she headed for the door. She hurried past the guards—some of whom looked at her strangely—and stopped in front of the Nikaphoroses' door and knocked. Curiosity tickled the end of her nose, then Sarsali opened the door.

Her eyebrows furrowed. "Astrea? What're you doing here?"

"Can I come in?" Astrea asked.

Standing back, Sarsali opened the door wide enough for her to enter. Balthazar sat on the sofa in front of the fireplace in their parlor, one leg crossed over the other.

"Where's Cress?" Astrea asked.

"She's taking a walk with Lennor . . ." Sarsali circled around her and frowned, the bridge of her nose wrinkling. "You look like you saw a ghost, sweetheart. You're paler than usual."

A fraction of hope surged forth in Astrea's chest; hopefully Cressida was finding some peace with Lennor. And yet it did nothing to dull the ache in her bones.

She unfurled her fist, revealing the locket. She'd been clutching it so tightly the engravings had left a light imprint on her skin.

"What's this?" Sarsali asked.

"My father," Astrea said past the lump in her throat. "He gave it to me. He's been keeping it since before I was born."

With delicate fingers, Sarsali plucked the locket out of Astrea's palm and opened it. Her brows furrowed again, but then her expression softened. "Oh, look at Roxana," she all but whispered. "I know I tell you this all the time, but you look just like her, Astrea."

"Everyone keeps telling me that," Astrea choked out. Her father. Her mother's old friend, Kira, had said the same when Saros had taken Astrea to visit. Even Saros had told Astrea that not all that long ago.

"I take it that's not why you're here," Balthazar said. He moved over slightly on the sofa and patted the empty side. "Come sit."

Astrea made her way over and plopped down clumsily. Sarsali followed, then set the locket on the coffee table and sat in the chair opposite Astrea.

"Valen keeps asking to speak with me as his condition for giving the Novarians any information," Astrea said. "He keeps going on about how we're family and how he's missed me but . . . but he doesn't feel like family."

"Only by the barest of definitions is he family," Balthazar said. "You owe him nothing."

"I told him as much. I think it got through to him, because he said he'd cooperate with Commander Lucian's requests and leave me out of it."

"Good," said Sarsali with a nod. "Good for you."

"But I can't help but wonder if this is just him manipulating me somehow," Astrea said. "If this isn't somehow the Paragon's doing again, some complicated plan to get me onto their side."

"Would they really try something like that?" Balthazar asked.

Wiping her sweaty palms on her skirt, Astrea whispered, "Has Cress told you everything they've done? The Paragon, I mean."

"I would guess not since you're asking us that . . ." Balthazar frowned.

"I knew she was omitting details." Sarsali scooted to the edge of her seat. "What have they done?"

Air barely slid past the boulder crushing Astrea's lungs. Tears clouded her vision, and she hadn't even uttered a single word yet.

"Astrea, sweetheart?" Sarsali asked. "What's wrong?"

"I never got to tell Saros this before he died." Astrea wiped at her cheeks, but the tears kept coming. "He knew something had happened and that I was hiding it from him. He knew, just like he always had, but I couldn't bring myself to tell him."

Her next breath was shallow, barely enough air to keep her going. Still, Astrea said, "A few weeks after we got to Talmaris, Nazarov attacked the palace. He abducted me but failed to get Jin, and that was when I met my other uncle, the Paragonian leader called The One. He told me all about their creed and tried to recruit me, and when I refused, Nazarov . . ."

She swallowed a sob. "He tortured me. Wouldn't leave me alone. He would've killed me if I hadn't escaped. If Jin and Adi hadn't found me. He would've killed Cress, too, in that first attack on the palace, and I—" Another sob, but this one left her in a big hiccup. "And he snatched me while I was trying to heal her, and—"

The weight of the year slammed into Astrea so hard it was like someone punched her in the gut. Every inch of her body ached, as if covered in the bruises and beatings they'd all taken since the summer. Whispers of metal raced through her shoulder, her abdomen, her wrist, her throat.

The edges of her vision went dark, and her breathing turned rapid, shallow.

Astrea couldn't. She couldn't do it.

She couldn't tell them. She'd been wrong, this was too much—

Balthazar's strong arms wrapped around her in an instant. His familiar scent of leather and coffee enveloped her, snapping her back into her body. Astrea leaned into him, burying her face in his shoulder. He held her almost like she was a small child, the very same way Saros used to hold her when she was young. One large hand cradled the back of her head while the other rubbed smooth circles on her back.

"I'm sorry," Astrea wailed. "I'm sorry I didn't tell you and Saros."

Balthazar shushed her. Her tears soaked his shirt. Her face began to itch and burn red hot. Blood roared in her ears.

She needed to calm down. Astrea breathed in as deeply as she could, held it for a few seconds, then breathed it out slowly. A hiccup interrupted her, so she did it again and again until she finally felt the sofa cushion underneath her and the cold, heavy sadness coming from the Nikaphoroses. Her pulse still roared in her ears, and her breathing was uneven at best, but a fresh wave of exhaustion washed over her, threatening to drown her.

"My dear," Balthazar said as she pulled away and hiccuped again, "you don't have anything to apologize for. You know you can always come to us, but you must also know you don't have to. It's your story to tell, when and if you want to."

Astrea nodded. "I know, but I wanted to. I . . . I needed to tell you."

"Oh, sweetheart," Sarsali said from behind her. The three of them barely fit on the sofa, but Astrea still managed to turn toward her. Sarsali took her hand and squeezed it. "What do you need? What can we do?"

"I don't know." The thought of trying to tell them any more specifics was too much. Every fiber of Astrea's being buzzed, like she was a bomb ready to explode. "I don't know what to do. About Valen. About Saros. About any of it."

Balthazar took her other hand in his much larger one. "I don't know that there's anything to do," he said. "There's no changing what happened to Saros, and your father . . ." He sighed.

"What about him?"

"I don't know if this is just some grand scheme," Balthazar said. "I wish I could answer that for you. But you'll have to trust yourself and the commander's opinion."

"Has Jin seen anything in your father to suggest he might have ill intentions?" Sarsali asked.

"No, he thought he was being truthful enough last time they spoke, and Lucian said all the guards believe Valen's innocent in the Zaikudi attack."

"Maybe Jin could speak with him again," Sarsali said. "See what truths he can get out of the man."

Astrea reached across the coffee table and took the open locket, staring down at her parents' smiling faces again. "It's not fair," she said. "The Paragon stole my mother's life, and now they're trying to steal my future."

A future she had only just started to dream of. Would she and Jin ever get to take a photograph like this? Would she ever get to carefully choose a gift to give him when she told him they were having a child someday? Would she ever get to celebrate that with her family, among many other milestones they would all have?

"We won't let them," Balthazar said. "They've taken enough from our family. We won't let them take anything else."

Astrea looked up from the locket, first into Balthazar's deep brown eyes and then Sarsali's bright green ones. And as their warm love wrapped around her in a tight hug, Astrea knew it was true. They wouldn't let the Paragon take anymore, not while they lived on to fight.

CHAPTER 21

Even without any assignments from Lucian, Astrea had been trying to keep as busy as she could for the last week. Since that somewhat disastrous meeting with her father, Astrea had been spending her time in the precarious position of distracting herself and also letting herself feel her grief.

As if that were easy.

She'd been exercising with Adi and the twins, including sparring with them. She was still improving every day. Jin had overseen a lot of those matches, always offering her instruction when she needed it, which was often. The two of them had been spending time together, too: meals, long afternoon naps, Jin holding her as she cried. They'd spent time with the Nikaphoroses, the twins, Noemi, Marko, either playing card games or doing nothing important at all.

All the while, Lucian and Zephyrine had been focused on organizing the coalition expeditions that would head out to sea. Rami had reached out to her network to figure out where Magdi was, and Anjou Lazzaro was also going to use his ship to assist. Everything was being worked out without Astrea's help. Not that she was the right person to organize a navy, but laying low didn't sit right with her.

Not that it mattered. As Eliana had pointed out several times, some of the delegates were watching them, so staying out of the way but being openly supportive of the plans was the best thing they could do for a while.

Besides, Astrea was finding it a bit easier to sit with her grief now that she had slowed down. Talking to Sarsali and Balthazar had helped, both that first night and subsequent talks since. It didn't make her heart hurt less, but she didn't feel like she was barely treading water all the time.

And Astrea wasn't the only one working through all that had happened these last months. Jin was actually sleeping more, not as disturbed by nightmares. Cressida was steadily improving every day, too, and had finally finished making her metal prosthetic. Which was precisely why Astrea and Eliana were in her sitting room with her.

Eliana, perched on one of the armchairs and cradling a cup of coffee, was there for moral support. Astrea was, too, but she was also there in case Cressida's skin became too raw or irritated and needed healing.

Metal clinked on metal as Cressida tinkered with pieces of the hand a few feet from where Astrea sat on the floor next to her. It was finely made, a smooth silver color, though it was some stronger alloy Cressida had been chattering on about. Though she had only lost a small section of her forearm down, Cressida and her father had crafted the prosthetic to go up to her elbow, almost like a gauntlet on an ancient suit of armor.

The radio set up on the fireplace mantle changed songs, and Eliana stopped her humming long enough to ask Cressida, "Do you think you'll be ready to start using it soon? Have you tried it on?"

"I did earlier while I was with Ivy, but it didn't quite fit right," Cressida said. "Dad and I were adjusting it. I'm going to go back down to her tomorrow to see if it looks like it's fitted properly."

"You don't want to try it on now?" Eliana asked.

"Oh, I will, but Ivy's going to get final say about if it fits as it should."

"Then let's see it!" Eliana exclaimed.

"You're too excited about this." Sitting up straighter, Cressida slid the "gauntlet" on, wincing a little as she set it in place.

Astrea pushed up to her knees as a whisper of pain danced around her wrist. "What's wrong?"

"Just not used to how it feels," Cressida said with clenched teeth. She adjusted the gauntlet again, tugging it up so it stopped right under her elbow. The smooth metal shone in the lamp- and firelight.

"Seems like it hurts," Astrea said. More pain warred on her forearm and wrist, there and not. More ghostly than usual. Did Cressida still not have the fit right?

As she stared at her metal hand, Cressida's lips twitched. "Well . . . I'm not wearing everything I should be."

"Meaning?" Eliana asked.

"I'm supposed to wrap my forearm in gauze first."

"Then why didn't you do that?"

With a smirk, Cressida lifted her hand. The metal fingers moved with little sound, leaving the middle one up as Cressida flipped Eliana off.

"Hey!" Eliana cried, half laughing. "I was just asking a question."

Cressida grinned. "I know. I didn't think I'd need to bother just to try it on."

"Don't wear it long if it hurts," Astrea said. "We can get you the gauze."

"Yes, Mother." Flexing her new fingers again, Cressida said, "Alright, give me a task. I need to practice with this thing."

"Pick up your cup," Eliana said.

Slowly, Cressida reached for the delicate porcelain cup sitting near Astrea's. Both were empty, long since drained of their coffee. Cressida's metal fingers bent slowly as she grabbed the handle. Her brow furrowed as she lifted the cup.

"You look concerned," Eliana said.

"It's . . . strange." Cressida shook her head. "I can feel the metal, as I always can with my magic, but I expected to feel the cup in my fingers, and obviously I can't. I can't tell if I'm gripping too hard."

"You can't feel the cup at all?" Astrea asked.

Cressida frowned. "A little? The weight more than anything."

"It'll probably take some practice," Astrea said, though it felt like an entirely unhelpful comment. So obvious.

"I don't want to break it."

"I don't think Veiko's going to care if he loses a few teacups while you learn and adjust," Eliana said. "Though who knows, maybe the Tornamians will judge us for that, too."

"Meaning?" Cressida asked as she set the cup down, then picked it up again.

"Meaning that this morning, I was leaving Veiko's office and was cornered by Delegate Marosikis."

"What did she want?" Astrea asked as Cressida said, "Was Nicos with you?"

With a dramatic sigh, Eliana said, "Nicos *was* there. Marosikis was pressing me about some comments I made yesterday during a meeting."

"What did you say?" Astrea asked. Delfine's warning from the week before rang in her ears. Hopefully Eliana had actually listened and used caution.

"All I asked was how we're supposed to find Victor Nazarov's expedition team when it's a very vast ocean, many islands, and rough waters."

"I feel like that's reasonable enough to ask."

"One would think." With another hefty sigh, Eliana said, "Apparently not. She accused me—privately, at least—of not wanting to find Nazarov."

"What?" It was one of the most ridiculous things Astrea had ever heard, along with how, weeks ago, a couple members of the Novarian

Council had accused Jin of letting Nazarov go. It seemed like some of these politicians were just willfully misunderstanding Eliana and Jin at this point, damning them for the blood they shared with the Auris family instead of judging them for their months and months of actions.

Eliana nodded gravely. "And she implied that if I didn't fall in line with what she suggests, she'll start telling others on the council that I don't want to fix any of this."

"What is this woman's problem?" Astrea asked, trying to ignore the heat of Cressida's anger as it singed her skin. "Is she determined to make this harder than it needs to be?"

"Would any of them even believe her?" Cressida moved on from picking up and setting down her teacup to making the fingers of her prosthetic touch her palm one at a time, then ball into a fist. "She sounds like she's trying to make trouble."

"I hope they wouldn't believe her, but honestly? I don't know." Blue regret flashed around Eliana for a moment. "My father's council rarely listened to me, and Councillor Reis still isn't thrilled by any of this."

"Oh, Ellie," Astrea said. "Just because your father's council didn't doesn't automatically mean these new people won't. I know they've been giving you and Jin a hard time, but surely Veiko's support means something. He believes in you. We all do."

"I suppose." She fiddled with her coffee cup, twisting it between her palms. Her lips pressed together, as if trying to hold in what she was about to say.

"What is it, Ellie?" Cressida asked. "I promise I won't flip you off again no matter what you say."

With a small smirk, Eliana finally lifted her gaze from her lap. "I can't help but feel I've been naive about all of this. Thinking it would be simpler. I've got so much to learn before I can be a good leader."

"Isn't that one of the hallmarks of a great leader, though?" Cressida asked. "Someone who doesn't stop learning and trying to be better."

"That's part of why your father and Kaius are so terrible," Astrea said. "Because they believe they already know everything, already have the right opinion, and are the ones with the best plans. Even when it's clearly not true. And the people on his council? They're just pandering to whatever he wants to keep their power."

"A scathing review if I've ever heard one," Cressida said. "And a true one."

"I know that's true," Eliana said, "but I feel like I'm miles off the mark from where I need to be if I'm going to be successful at this. It all feels so, I don't know. Hastily thrown together."

"Ellie." Cressida shifted uneasily. "You were making plans for this months before we left Kalama."

"Thought exercises," Eliana corrected.

Pinning her with a look, Cressida said, "Regardless, it's not like you're unprepared."

"And you'll have smart people to help you," Astrea said. "Zephyrine, Jin, Nicos. We know there are others in Helosia who share your views; surely they have expertise you can lean on."

"I need to wrap my mind around the true scope of this." Eliana rubbed her forehead as if warding off a headache, but nothing was off as far as Astrea could feel. "I mean, we still haven't heard back from Apelo."

"Heard back?" Astrea asked as gray confusion swirled around Cressida.

"Anjou got him a message for us," Eliana said. "Like Delfine wanted. I don't know if he'll respond. I mean, I don't even know if he really got it."

So, not only was Astrea not helping the coalition in any way, but now she was behind on what Eliana was dealing with, too. *Great.*

The metal of Cressida's fingers clinked slightly as she flexed them. "You don't trust Anjou?"

"Oh, it's not about that," Eliana said. "But he can't personally take it to Apelo. His network—Zephyrine's network, or mine now, I guess—isn't guaranteed to get the message all the way to Apelo's estate."

"You think he'd help us?" Cressida asked.

"Skies if I know. I hope so." Groaning, Eliana rubbed her forehead again. "Enough about me. I need a distraction."

"Your turn," Cressida said, looking pointedly at Astrea.

"Me?" Astrea blanched. "Why me?"

"We've talked about my arm and Ellie's feelings, so now you have to tell us something."

"What if I don't have anything to share?" It wasn't that she didn't. Oh, no, she had plenty she could share with them. Astrea simply didn't think it was fair to be put on the spot.

"I've barely seen you, Az," Eliana said. "What's going on with you? Spending too much time in the bedroom with Jin? Ew, never mind." She made a face. "Bad joke. I don't want to know."

"And not true regardless," Astrea said, face heating. "I'm just..." She shook her head, the words almost stuck in her chest. "The commander gave me orders to step back from everything. And I needed it. I feel like I'm drowning."

"Saros?" Eliana asked gently.

"That, but my father, too."

As Astrea gave them more details about the specifics of her and her father's most recent interaction, she pulled out the locket and set it on the coffee table. She'd been keeping it close in the last week. She wasn't entirely sure why. Her father had suggested it might bring her comfort, and maybe it did in a way, since she could see her mother's face. But it also made her uneasy.

"I know he's started helping Lucian, but I still feel like he wants something else," Astrea said. "Maybe I'm just being too untrusting."

Cressida picked up the locket, holding it between her metal fingers as she used her other hand to pry it open. Her expression softened as she gazed down at the small photograph inside. "They looked so happy."

Swallowing hard, Astrea whispered, "Yeah, they did."

"Are you going to talk to him again?" Eliana took the locket when Cressida leaned across the table and offered it to her. Her lips pursed. "They really did seem happy."

"Why should I talk to him again?" Astrea asked, the words bitter on her tongue.

"You wouldn't want to try to get to know him?" Eliana asked. "Not at all?"

Astrea didn't know. It was like she didn't know anything anymore. Not about her father, about Saros, about military missions or politics or anything. Was this the feeling Eliana had been describing? That sense of naivety? Helplessness as the world continued spinning and she felt stuck?

"Don't talk to him if you don't want to," Cressida said. "But if you do want to . . . if you want to at least try, I wouldn't blame you."

Astrea shook her head. "Enough about me." Ignoring her friends' glares, she said, "Anything else we need to test out before we send you back to Ivy, Cress?"

Cressida pressed her lips together, then said, "I guess so."

As Eliana and Cressida began finding more items for Cressida to practice picking up that would test the fit and function of her new prosthetic, Astrea stayed sitting on the floor. Cressida's words ran circles in her mind.

Could she try talking to Valen again? Sure, she could try.

But would she? And would it even get her anywhere?

Although Astrea had insisted she could go with Cressida to see Ivy again, Cressida had declined and said she had to go on her own. Astrea didn't see why, but if that was Cressida's wish, she would honor it.

As she walked back toward her and Jin's room, Astrea fiddled with the locket's delicate chain. The guards lining the hall barely paid any attention to her, and soon, she was at her door.

Inside, Jin was walking around in only a pair of black pants. His broad shoulders and bare back glistened with sweat. Astrea tried not to look too hard at the collection of scars, the way they flexed as he moved.

"Did you and Adi have fun?" Astrea asked as she followed him into the bedroom.

"Don't know that I'd call getting my ass kicked fun," Jin said wryly as he headed for the bathroom.

"That bad?"

"I just feel like I'm not moving as fast as I used to," Jin said. "Like I'm half a second too slow." He leaned into the shower and turned the water on. "It's probably in my head. I'm distracted half the time lately anyway."

"I'm sorry."

He glanced over his shoulder, eyebrows furrowed. "What have you got to be sorry about?"

She shrugged. "That you're feeling like this. I feel like I haven't been attentive enough to what's going on with you."

"Not attentive enough?" A tight laugh left him. "Az, all we've done for the last week is be attentive. *I* had barely noticed I felt that way until now. Going up against Adi, Lennor, and Civan was what proved to be too much. I haven't done that in a while."

"Oh."

He rubbed the back of his neck. "I was going to clean up, then take a nap, if you want to join me." She nodded, and he said, "I won't be long."

Leaving the bathroom, Astrea went and locked their sitting room door, then returned to their bedroom. She took her time changing out of her dress and into a short nightgown. The silky fabric was cold against her skin, and the lace trim did little to keep her warm, but Jin would help with that. She took her time braiding her hair, too, before climbing into bed.

It was only halfway through the afternoon, and dinner wouldn't be for another couple of hours. Still, Astrea's body begged for her to lie down. She hadn't been taking care of herself. Not in a long time.

Before long, the shower turned off. Jin opened the bathroom door, letting out a puff of steam and the smell of eucalyptus. She tried not to close her eyes as she listened to him moving between the bedroom and bathroom, but she failed. His footsteps. The close of the wardrobe doors. Water splashing in the sink.

The mattress dipped, and Jin slid into bed with her. "Are you already asleep?" he whispered.

"No." She gave him a small smile. "Not yet."

"How's Cress?" he asked, rolling over to face her.

"Adjusting. I offered to go to Ivy with her, but she wanted to do it on her own."

"She always was one to try to figure things out on her own first."

Aside from the last couple of months, Cressida was usually open with her feelings. But when faced with a challenge of some sort—homework assignments, projects from her father, an issue with a recipe—she *did* prefer to take a crack at it on her own first.

And this situation, losing her hand like she did, was both an emotional one and a sort of puzzle. Maybe sorting some of it out by herself was what Cressida needed to do for her own comfort.

Jin smoothed some of her hair away from her cheek, letting his fingers linger on her skin. "What's on your mind, Az?"

"I hate that you know me so well."

"Liar."

A sheen of pink clung to his skin, warming her instantly. Astrea smiled at him again, but it disappeared quickly. "Do you think I should give Valen a chance?"

His eyebrows furrowed.

"You think it's a bad idea," she said.

"No. No, I'm just . . . surprised. You've been angry with him, rightfully so. I wasn't sure if you'd want to give him a chance."

"What if I don't know if I want to?"

"Honestly, I'm not sure I'm the best person to ask about this," Jin said. "Considering how I feel about my father."

"Please?" Astrea whispered. "Tell me what you think. You've met him. Would I be foolish to even give him a chance?"

Jin's features softened. "I don't think it's foolish to want to know him. I think it's natural."

"What if he's Paragon?"

"Then he's done a very good job of tricking us."

"You don't think he is?"

"I think Nazarov would already be on our front steps if Valen was actually on the Paragon's side. At worst, he's probably Theo's flavor of Paragon . . . a believer in their desire for balance but not the lengths Nazarov will go."

Astrea huffed. "I wish there was an easier way to find out for sure."

"Maybe when we find Theo, he can tell us more."

"Any news on that front?"

"Unfortunately, no. I'm beginning to fear Nazarov got to him. Maybe Nezrin was right after all . . ."

"I hope not." She hoped that not only because Theo had undoubtedly helped save them all in the Badlands, but also because Nazarov would certainly meet that kind of betrayal with the utmost cruelty. Theo didn't deserve that.

"Me too. Zephyrine has her people working on it," Jin said. "And as far as your father," he continued, pulling her closer, "if you want to talk to him on your own terms—not his—then I think you should. Go with what feels right."

"That's the problem," she whispered. "I don't know what feels right anymore."

"Then get some sleep and think about it later." Jin kissed her cheek. "I'll wake you up before dinner."

As Jin tugged her back against his chest and his breathing began to slow, Astrea tried to settle in, too. But she stared at the wall across from their bed. Would Saros want her to try to get to know Valen? Would he have at least suggested she hear the man out?

Knowing Saros, he probably wouldn't have wanted her to go within twenty yards of Valen. Wouldn't have trusted him.

And maybe Saros would've been right to think that way. But this was her decision, and it was hers alone.

If she was feeling brave the next day, she would go. She would go see Valen. At worst, like Jin said, he was hiding sympathies to the Paragon who believed like Theo did. But maybe, just maybe, she could get some closure if she talked to him and learned more about where she came from.

CHAPTER 22

The freezing water pouring out of the bathroom faucet was a relief against Astrea's hot face. She'd cut her exercises with Adi short, though Jin was still out there with him and Lennor. Even her shower hadn't cooled her down.

She turned the water off, then reached for the towel she'd set on the counter next to the sink. As she began to pat her face dry, a muffled knock came from the sitting room. Astrea let her awareness spread out, and a mix of worry and fatigue mingled in the hall.

Brow furrowing, Astrea headed for the apartment door. Noemi brushed some of her dark curls out of her face. Civan stood just behind her, unreadable.

"Hi, Astrea," Noemi said. "Can we come in?"

"Oh . . . sure." She stepped to one side to let the two of them enter. Noemi hurried in, her bright pink skirt swishing around her legs. Civan ducked his head and gave Astrea a small smile. "What's going on?" Astrea asked.

"I was hoping to ask you something," Noemi said, fiddling with a few loose papers clutched in one hand.

"Then let's hear it," Astrea said.

"How'd you narrow things down to find those obscure references to void magic in regular history books?"

Astrea frowned. "What? Why?"

"We thought there might be similar things to aetherium," Noemi said. "So we were reviewing the *Myths and Other Legends* book to start, but all that mentioned was the idea that Tytas Ramkas was chosen by the stars to receive aetherium."

"Which seems highly unlikely," Civan said. "Especially after seeing that fortress out west. We thought maybe we could find more specific information to lead us to the Paragon's original source."

Astrea supposed that made sense; if Nazarov really wanted to be the next Tytas Ramkas, that kind of history might give them more insight into his next moves. Or maybe it would give them nothing at all, since Nazarov seemed to be acting on a whim.

"And Tomas didn't give us much to go on before he left for some meetings," Noemi said. "I started pulling titles from the catalog—"

"Tomas doesn't like people touching his catalog," Astrea said.

Noemi smiled cheekily. "What he doesn't know won't hurt him." She extended her papers to Astrea. "There's too much for us to go through on our own easily, so I was hoping you might narrow it down for us, like if anything catches your eye."

Astrea scanned the pages, which were filled with dozens of titles written in small, neat letters. "Well," she said, "I can't tell you what to do based on titles, but I'd start with the first century preceding the Great Wars, then keep working backward. See how far you get before Tomas returns."

Noemi pressed her lips together and nodded gravely. "I thought you might suggest something like that."

"Sorry I couldn't be more helpful."

"No, no!" Noemi exclaimed. "I was just hoping for an easy win, I guess."

Astrea half laughed. "We're in short supply of those these days."

"Perhaps we'll get lucky soon," Noemi said.

"Luck has nothing to do with it," Civan murmured.

"What do you mean?"

"I don't believe in luck," he said.

"Oh, I do," Noemi replied. "Sometimes things just happen for no rhyme or reason. After all, not everything is in our hands."

Civan shrugged.

After seeing Noemi and Civan out the door, Astrea dropped onto the small sofa near the fireplace and pulled a blanket over herself. What would it mean if aetherium really had been out in the world for far longer than anyone else? Or had Tytas Ramkas stumbled upon the metal himself? Did it even matter anymore? All Astrea knew for certain was that they had to stop Nazarov from getting his hands on any more of it.

Wind roared in Astrea's ears. Rain pelted her skin, leaving stinging marks on her cheeks and hands. Hot and cold fire burned her from the inside out, her stomach, her wrist, her shoulder.

"Save him!" Saros cried from where he sprawled out on the ground, knife sticking from his gut.

Astrea couldn't save him. She couldn't save them both. Her hands were glued to Jin's chest, covered in his shadow-filled blood. No light glowed around her palms. No light, no light, no light.

"Save him!"

"I can't!" she tried to yell above the wind, but it stole her words and carried them away.

"Look away." Saros pulled the dagger from his abdomen. "Look away, look away."

Astrea tried to look away, but something froze her in place. She couldn't move, couldn't breathe.

"You will look, little Lightbringer," a familiar voice purred in her ear. Nazarov.

She tried to close her eyes, but cold fingers pried them open again.

Saros drew the blade across his throat. Astrea tried to scream, to look away. Nazarov held her head in place, forced her eyes open. She made no sound. Blood poured down the sides of Saros's neck before his body stilled.

"And so it goes, little Lightbringer," Nazarov whispered. His breath was hot on her cheek. "Tell me, when was the last time you visited his grave? Not since the funeral?"

"Why do you care?" she managed to ask. A scream built inside her lungs.

"Tragic, to lose one of the few people who loved you," he said. "But the Paragon love you, don't you see? They want you to help lead them."

"They don't know me."

"They don't need to know you to love you."

"Please," she whispered. "Please, leave me alone."

"I was wrong to say I didn't need you," Nazarov cooed. "I do need you, Miss Sovna. I cannot rule the Paragon with an iron fist for much longer, not while you run or live."

The hand gripping her neck loosened. The fingers forcing her eyes open let her go. And then Nazarov stepped in front of her, his bronze eyes flashing almost red in the raging storm.

"So it's your choice," he said. "Join me and continue the Ramkas line, or die just like your poor, useless uncle."

How many times did she have to refuse his offer?

Astrea spat in his face, but shadows swallowed her whole, pulling her deep down into the cold.

"Az, wake up." Jin shook Astrea's shoulder with one hand, the other cupping her cheek. "Az."

"He's back." Astrea rolled over on the sofa, right into Jin's waiting arms. "Nazarov's back."

"He was dreamwalking to you?"

"He made me watch Saros take his own life," she whispered through her tears. Astrea squeezed her eyes shut, but it didn't make that image go away. Her whole body trembled, burning with cold. "He says if I don't rule the Paragon with him, he'll kill me."

The same threats Theo had promised were on the table. The same threats Nazarov had implied for months.

But with things escalating across the continent, it seemed Nazarov might finally act on those words. He might finally try.

Jin pulled her into his lap on the floor, cradling the back of her head as she cried into the crook of his neck.

"Why won't he let me be? Why did he have to show me that?"

"I'm sorry," Jin whispered over and over again. "I'm sorry, Az."

She breathed in deeply, reveling in the smell of Jin's soap as it wrapped around her. He must've taken a shower after his training session.

"I think he's really going to do it," she whispered against Jin's neck. "I think he's really going to try to take me away or kill me. I think he's done playing his games."

"Hey." Pulling away from her, he cupped her cheeks. His rings were cool against her burning skin. "You know I won't ever let that happen."

She gripped his wrists, a tether to what was real. "I know."

"You are the love of my life. My wife, my partner. We'll make sure, together, that he doesn't get what he wants. He won't take you away from me. From any of us."

"I know," she whispered again as his words sank deep into her bones. Summer sunshine flitted across her skin and settled near her tired heart. He leaned in, placing a gentle kiss on her lips. It was chaste, sweet. How delicately he touched her now, like he was afraid she might break.

They sat like that, tangled in each other's arms, for so long Astrea couldn't be sure what time it was. She let all of Jin's love soak into the core of her being, trying to make it wash away the sight of Saros taking his own life. The feeling of Jin's blood on her hands.

And it was then, as she closed her eyes again and tried to will away those awful images, that she knew what she had to do.

She needed to talk to her father no matter what.

"And you're sure this is a good idea?" Marko asked as he walked with Astrea and Jin through the guardhouse.

"You said he's been cooperating with Lucian," Astrea said.

"I said *appeared* to be cooperating. That's very different."

"You think Valen's been withholding information?" Jin asked, his grip tightening on Astrea's hand.

Although she'd considered doing this alone, Astrea had decided that wasn't wise. Not because she thought Valen would harm her. No. She didn't know if Nazarov would dreamwalk again. Having backup was smart. And Jin *and* Marko being there? They would be great backup if she needed it.

"Not necessarily," Marko said as they turned a corner. "Just that it's possible. I prefer to be realistic, even if the commander is cautiously optimistic."

"Fair enough," Jin said.

Another few paces and Marko stopped near a door flanked by two guards. They weren't anywhere Astrea recognized; it wasn't the door to the small viewing room.

"This is where he's been staying," Marko said. "It's his quarters, I guess you could say."

Disentangling herself from Jin, Astrea shook out her arms and pushed her shoulders back. This wasn't exactly what she'd expected, but it didn't matter. Maybe Valen would even be more at ease if he wasn't in an interrogation room.

"I'm ready," she said.

Marko signaled to the two guards. They stepped aside, making room for the three of them to approach the door. Marko knocked twice, then opened the door.

It was a decently sized room, large enough for a full bed, small wardrobe, and narrow desk. A thick rug anchored the bed to the wooden floor. The overhead light was off, and only the lamp in the corner was on. It wasn't luxurious, but it was comfortable.

"Astrea?" Valen asked as he pushed off the bed. He was wearing simple slacks and a sweater. No shoes, just socks. He looked almost as if he'd been napping. Valen ran his hands through his hair. "Apologies, I wasn't expecting anyone."

"Sorry to intrude," Astrea said. "I need to speak with you."

He watched her for a moment, then gestured around vaguely. "Please, make yourself comfortable."

"We'll all be staying," she said.

"Yourselves," he corrected. "Please."

Astrea stayed rooted to her spot in the middle of the room. Her instinct told her to stay there, stand, ready to run. But would Valen sense her distrust? He still stood by the bed, his shoulders and expression tight. She needed him to be honest, and what better way to do that than try to get *him* to be comfortable?

Forcing her legs to move, Astrea went to the small desk and pulled out the chair. Jin followed her like a shadow and stayed standing a half step behind her. Marko, however, held his position near the door.

"Thank you," Astrea said as she smoothed out her dark blue skirt. "Have you been treated well while here?"

"Very well," Valen said, glancing at Marko before sitting back down on the edge of his bed. "Honestly, it's better than I've eaten in years. That alone is worth it. Please pass on my thanks to whoever's in charge of the menu."

Marko grunted.

"But I'm guessing you aren't here to speak of dinner," Valen continued cautiously.

"No, I'm not," Astrea said. "I wanted to check on you and thank you for cooperating with Commander Lucian. It's nice to know you took my words to heart."

"Well, it was easy when I realized how right you were," her father said with an uneasy laugh. "I was being terrible. I thought it was the only way I'd get to know you, but what right do I have to do so when it's my family that's dragged you into this?"

It wasn't that Astrea disagreed with that assessment. No, that seemed entirely fair. But rehashing the issue wasn't useful.

"I also came because I need your help," Astrea said. "It's more of a personal problem."

"A . . . personal problem?" Valen's eyebrows knitted together. "What kind? I'm not the best with interpersonal issues . . ."

"You remember the man I told you about, Victor Nazarov?" Astrea asked. When her father nodded, she continued, "He dreamwalks to me at unexpected times, sometimes when I'm awake and sometimes when I'm asleep. Is there a way to block out Dreamwalkers? Or put an end to their visions?"

"A terrible invasion, isn't it?" Valen muttered, then sighed. "I never was strong enough to shut them out. Both my mother and brother would use dreamwalking to speak to me."

"Your father?" Astrea asked.

"Died when I was a newborn."

"I'm sorry to hear that."

"Don't be," Valen said. "He was not a nice man, or so my mother told me." Gray hesitation swirled around him before he added, "Though she wasn't a very nice woman, so I'm not sure if it was a lie on her part or if he was worse."

"No way to find out now," Marko drawled.

Astrea almost glared at him. While true, pointing out the obvious was unhelpful.

"You don't know of any way to stop the dreamwalking?" she asked Valen instead.

"Other than sheer willpower? If I did, I'd tell you in a heartbeat." He smiled tightly. "I assume distance helps. My brother never tried to dreamwalk to me after my death, but I was . . ." He shook his head. "I was quite far away."

"He dreamwalked to me when I was in the Taipoli Islands and he claimed to be in Novaria," Astrea said. "I don't know that distance helps."

"He may have been lying to you," Marko said. "Or perhaps he got stronger over the years."

"You said willpower?" Jin asked Valen. "Like asserting your dominance in your own mind?"

"Like when The One and Nazarov fought in my mind," Astrea whispered. That day in the tunnels under Talmaris, it had felt like The One and Nazarov had been dueling for control. "How do I do that, though? How do I push him out?"

"It takes incredible strength," Valen said. "More than you realize. As I said, I was never strong enough."

That didn't answer Astrea's question. "Do you think about something in particular? Actually fight them? Is that even possible?"

"I once overheard others talking about it as though it was tug of war," Valen said, "only you're trapped knee-deep in thick, sticky mud, and the Dreamwalker is on solid, dry ground."

"Doesn't seem right considering it's your own mind," Jin said.

"No, but that's exactly it," Astrea said. Even when she'd tried to resist Nazarov earlier that afternoon by closing her eyes, that had seemed like a monumental task. And she'd failed. "I know what you're talking about. How do I get strong enough to force the Dreamwalker out?"

Valen shrugged. "I don't know, I'm sorry."

Tilting her head back, Astrea let out a long breath. Of course Valen didn't know. But this was a start. Why hadn't she thought of it sooner? Why was her mind still so slow?

"You're disappointed," her father said quietly.

"Frustrated with the situation," Astrea said. "I appreciate what you did tell me."

"If I think of anything that will help, I'll call for you," Valen said. "But of course, feel free to seek me out whenever you have more questions. I'll be here."

"Thank you," Astrea said, meaning it. At least now, she had something to focus on, a skill to build as she looked for ways to stop Nazarov from controlling her like that again.

Because she could not let Nazarov control her ever, ever again.

After a few more pleasantries and empty promises to return soon, Astrea left Valen's room. She meandered a few feet down the hall, then pivoted toward Marko.

"I need to talk to Lucian."

"Far be it from me to stop you," he drawled.

"I've barely seen him all week," Astrea said. "Where is he?"

"Likely in his office. It's where he practically lives now."

"Then let's go," Jin said, already ushering Astrea that way.

She picked up her pace, eager. Valen might not have known how to get power back from a Dreamwalker, but Commander Lucian or Vernie might know. They were both powerful Souleaters, just like her. Surely between the three of them, they could find a way to break through that control.

Marko knocked on the commander's office door. Before anyone opened it, angry heat burned Astrea's cheeks. Raised voices followed.

"You're always like this!" came Rami's muffled yell.

"Skies," Marko muttered. "Not again."

"They've been fighting?" Jin asked.

"Only like cats and dogs. And always about the same thing."

"Which is?" Jin prompted.

"They want the same outcome but disagree about the method to get there. Always. You'd think after all these years, they'd have figured out a way to make it work." Sucking in a deep breath, Marko knocked louder, then pushed the door open. "I can hear you two out in the hall."

Astrea peeked around Marko. Lucian was sitting behind his desk, arms crossed tightly over his chest. Rami mirrored his pose, though she was standing in the middle of the room. They glared at each other in a silent showdown, both entirely closed off from Astrea's magic.

"What is it, Marko?" Lucian said.

"Yes, Marko, what *is* it?" Rami asked.

Marko shoved his hands into his pockets. "Astrea wanted to see you because Nazarov reached out to her."

Lucian pushed out of his chair. "What? When?"

"An hour ago. I was asleep." Astrea recounted the tale for him, then explained her decision to go speak with Valen. "He said I'll need power and dominance to push Nazarov or any Dreamwalker out of my mind. He wasn't more specific than that, said he'd never been able to do it himself. I was hoping you had some ideas."

"Dominance?" Lucian murmured, his gaze fixed on one spot on the floor next to Rami's boots.

"Yes, you know, the thing you lack?" Rami quipped.

Lucian huffed, and rust red annoyance flared around him. It flared brighter when Marko said, "We don't need to know about your bedroom problems. We need a solution."

"Obviously," the commander said, his cheeks turning crimson.

"My father said it's very difficult," Astrea said. "He made it sound nearly impossible, but remember at the old Paragon house? When I told you it felt like The One and Nazarov had fought in my mind?"

"I remember," Lucian said quietly. "I'll need to have a think. Nothing jumps to mind about how to build or practice that kind of resistance."

"If only we had a void mage to help us," Rami said dramatically, hands on her hips. "Oh, I know! If only you would let me go out in search of Theo Kadis! Then I could find you a handful of void mages to practice with!"

Lucian's upper lip curled. "I will not have you going out there in search of him when we don't even have anywhere to look. It's a waste of resources."

"Not when you have resources like mine," Rami snapped. "Money. Connections. Those go a long way."

"As if greasing the right palms will find you a defector from an ancient and secretive cult." With a scoff, Lucian rolled his eyes. "Money can't get you everything, Rami. Don't you know that by now? Patience will help us in this situation."

Why was Lucian so against it if Rami would use her own resources? It wasn't like she was wasting Novaria's money.

"Still no lead on Theo?" Jin asked.

"Zephyrine might have something, but she won't tell me what yet," Lucian said. When Rami muttered something under her breath, he said, "No more complaints. This is my country, and you will do as I order."

Where Astrea expected anger or annoyance to arc out from Rami, peach amusement took their places. Sugar coated Astrea's tongue. What was this between Rami and the commander? Some kind of strange flirtation? Her nose almost wrinkled at the thought. Whatever it was, she certainly didn't understand it.

"I'll talk to Zephyrine, I guess," Jin said.

"And I'll get back to you as soon as I think of something, Astrea." Lucian waved at the papers on his desk. "If you'll excuse me, I'm behind on my paperwork, and the bureaucrats seem to really value it these days."

With a shake of his head and a heavy sigh, Marko headed for the door. Astrea and Jin followed, and after a moment, Rami did, too. When they were out in the hall, Rami turned to Marko.

"Don't even start," she warned before stomping away.

"Me? Never!" he called after her.

"Come on," Jin said, draping his arm around Astrea's shoulders. "We should be going, too. Let them sort this nonsense out on their own."

That, Astrea could do. She had enough of her own problems; she didn't need to take on Lucian and Rami's, too.

Chapter 23

Why was it that formal dining chairs were so uncomfortable? Astrea thought it was ridiculous. After all, they were often larger and more stuffed than normal dining chairs, but something about them was so . . . stiff.

She tried not to adjust her position again as Veiko and Lucian droned on about their scouting efforts so far. This dinner was important. But skies, her bottom hurt.

It had been a couple of days since Nazarov dreamwalked to her, and they still had no idea where he was. He hadn't returned to Astrea's mind, or anyone else's on the team, either. Just knowing he could show her that awful day again made it hard for her to sleep.

"We're getting reports that the seas to the northeast are too rough," said Veiko. "It's making it hard for our ships to pass."

Eliana spooned more vegetables onto her plate. "Storms?"

"So it seems."

"Natural?" she asked.

"We've no way to tell," said Lucian, "though at this time of year, it's not unusual for waters to get rough, especially around the Lost Isles."

"The what?" Nicos asked.

"Oh . . ." The right side of Veiko's mouth lifted in a small smile. "They're known by the rest of the continent as the Obsidian Isles."

"We call them the Lost Isles because they were once Novarian territory but are basically uninhabitable," Delfine said. "A terrible, desolate place, really."

Nicos's eyebrows furrowed. "Right . . ."

"Years ago, Rami and I visited several times as part of some joint Novarian-Tornamian military exercises," Lucian said. "There's not much out there, just a lot of empty land, dormant volcanoes, and snow, at least at this time of year."

"Sounds like a good place for Nazarov to be hiding," Jin said.

"Recent patrols haven't found any evidence of such," Lucian said. "But we'll be keeping a close eye on the area, as much as we can with the storms."

Astrea lost her battle with her chair. She tried not to wince as she adjusted. As she reached for her water glass, she found Delfine watching her.

The only good thing was that this dinner didn't include any delegates from the other countries. It was their original six from Helosia, plus Zephyrine, Marko, Lucian, Veiko, and Delfine. No meddling politicians. No distrusting councillors.

Delfine hadn't even cracked a joke about Astrea being a princess all night. Strange. No jabs at anyone else at the table, either. It was like something had changed in her. It wasn't malice or anger but a seriousness Astrea hadn't seen from her before. Not that Astrea knew Delfine well, but it was different. She didn't seem to be stuck in her grief about her aunt, so was it the war wearing down on her?

"Once the storms clear, we can finish scouting the area," Veiko said. "I'd prefer they go ashore to search for the aetherium—especially since your father has helped narrow down what they'd need to look for, Miss Nikaphoros—but we don't have the Stargazers. If there's no sign of Nazarov or the Zaikudi, we'll be forced to move on."

"What about Helosians?" Jin asked. "I doubt our father will give up on looking for alternate sources of aetherium."

"We haven't seen them either, but we'll keep searching," Veiko said. "With any luck, we'll beat them all to the source this time."

Cressida reached for her wine glass with her metal hand. Her fingers flexed slowly, closing around the stem. Carefully, she brought the glass to her lips and drank.

"It's amazing what you've created," said Delfine, nodding to Cressida's left arm. "Extraordinary that you have so much control."

"I'm not the first Metalli to do this," she said as she set her glass down again. "Nor will I be the last."

"Still, I cannot imagine," Delfine replied.

Cressida picked up her fork with her right hand and continued eating her dinner.

"We could use some Tidebackers on our ships trying to go east," said Veiko. "Would your man Civan be willing to go, Jin?"

Jin swallowed, then asked, "Civan?"

"He's a powerful Tidebacker, is he not?" the grand duke asked.

"He is."

"So? Would he be willing to go?"

"I'm sure Civan would like to help, but I'm not sure he'll want to go without his sister," Jin said. "Or the rest of us, quite frankly. I don't love the idea of sending him out there on his own, especially after what just happened in Helosia."

"And what would you do on a boat?" Delfine asked. "We need you here."

"Oh, the coalition suddenly wants me around?" Jin asked wryly.

"They'd certainly prefer it."

As Jin rolled his eyes, Veiko said, "I believe what my sister is trying to say is that you have a role to play here."

"Lennor and I could join Civan," Zephyrine said. "Two powerful Tempests aboard should help, no?"

"I'd still like to give the storm a couple of days to die down to avoid sailing into too dangerous of a situation, but if nothing's changed and we must press on, then it would be much appreciated," Veiko said.

The conversation continued on like that, points and counterpoints; Astrea didn't pay much attention to it. This boat problem wasn't exactly something she was to be involved in, nor was it something she was going to solve when the joint navies couldn't, either.

Cressida's fatigue pressed heavily against her bones. Echoes of pain were beginning to flare near Astrea's wrist, no doubt where Cressida's body was adjusting to the prosthetic. She'd have to offer to heal her after dinner, or try to get her to take one of the tonics Ivy had prescribed for bedtime. Getting Cressida to take any medication these days was nearly impossible.

"Then let's hope the storms pass soon enough," Zephyrine said eventually.

"At least Nazarov will be having a hard time if the seas are that bad," said Eliana.

"Indeed." Veiko dabbed at the corners of his mouth with his napkin.

"Or hope that his ship sank to the bottom of the ocean with him on it," Lucian muttered.

"Even better," said Delfine with a bright smile. "He has not contacted you again, Miss Sovna?"

"I'd tell you if he had," Astrea said, trying to even her tone. But why would Delfine bother asking? Of course Astrea would tell Lucian immediately if Nazarov reached out again.

In fact, if he did, Astrea would need to try forcing him out of her mind. She and Lucian hadn't come up with a specific plan for that, but she'd wondered if anger might help. Grief was strong, but it didn't carry the same heat that anger would. The same power. Maybe, if she could focus on her anger at the Paragon, it would be enough to disrupt Nazarov's dreamwalking. But she couldn't try until he returned.

As the meal dragged on, the echoes of pain coming from Cressida grew louder. At long last, dessert arrived. It was one of Eliana's favorites, a triple layer chocolate cake filled with raspberry jam. Astrea only picked at her slice, just as she'd barely picked at her meal. The food was fine; she just had no appetite.

"Thank you all for indulging me tonight," Veiko said as staff cleared their plates away. "It's good for our allies to see us as a united front."

All this for show? This couldn't have been a simple meeting to inform them of progress on the search for Nazarov?

"We should do this again, and soon," the grand duke continued. "Perhaps we can invite President Sikori to join us."

Astrea's eyes almost rolled into the back of her head. She had no issue with the Tornamian president, but skies, another dinner? Another pointless, stiff dinner? She'd let Eliana sort out the details; she needed to get Cressida upstairs.

As Eliana and Nicos stayed behind to speak with Veiko, Astrea ushered Cressida toward the door. Jin and Adi were a few steps behind, with Jin calling promises over his shoulder to meet up with Veiko, Eliana, and Zephyrine first thing in the morning.

"Do you still have tonics upstairs?" Astrea asked Cressida.

"Skies, not this," she mumbled. "Yes, Mother Hen. I'll take one before bed."

"Take one as soon as you're upstairs," Astrea said, "unless you'll let me heal you some."

"It's early; I'll live until I go to bed."

"Don't push yourself more than you need to," Astrea said. "I don't want you hurting yourself."

"I'm not hurting—"

"Liar."

"I'm not hurting *myself*," Cressida finished. "Does it hurt? Yes. But Ivy said that's normal."

Astrea grumbled her understanding. It wasn't that she expected Cressida's pain to be gone but rather that she hated knowing there wasn't all that much they could do, especially with Cressida refusing most pain management options.

"We need you all healed up, Cress," Jin said as they started into the palace's main atrium. The wide space was filled with guards and soldiers, who all stood at attention as soon as they saw Jin. "We're going to need you when we go back out to handle this aetherium."

"I never want to go within a mile of that stuff again."

"I trust no one more than you and Balthazar with it," Jin said. "But I won't push you if you aren't—"

Familiar cold prickled Astrea's skin. She flung her arm out, stopping Cressida from going any farther. Jin and Adi both stopped short.

"Az?" Jin asked. "What—"

Ice pierced Astrea's belly. Shadows snaked up from the floor, two figures following. Her legs begged her to run, to get away from that impossible cold now standing so close to her. Her mouth went dry. Jin took half a step forward, partially blocking Astrea's line of sight.

Shouts echoed through the atrium as Novarian guards surged forward, blocking the two figures from the rest of them. Colors exploded from the crowd of them: white fear, red anger, gray hate.

But through the throng of guards and past Jin's shoulders, Astrea finally got a clear look. One of the figures was taller and broader while the other was closer to Cressida's height.

Those brown and gray curls.

Those glasses.

Theo Kadis had just jumped into the Novarian royal palace.

The colors surging around the guards raged on, morphing and shifting until that gray hate overtook it all.

Hate for a man none of them even knew.

Hate because he was with a void mage. Because Theo had once been Paragon.

Not that Theo was innocent. No, he wasn't. But how could these guards hate someone they'd never even met?

"We come in peace!" Theo cried above the noise. "We mean no harm!"

"Skies damn it, Theo," Jin muttered. "That was the actual worst way he could've approached the palace."

It was bold, that was for sure. Foolish, too.

One of the guards reached for her belt, pulling a dagger from its sheath and brandishing it at Theo. The palace's front doors burst open, more guards running inside as they shouted warnings about the void and locking the palace down.

"He means no harm!" Jin yelled to the guards. "He's on our side! Stand down!"

The brunette guard with the knife lunged for Theo, slicing through his jacket and shirt. Pain danced along Astrea's skin, making her yelp. The void mage with him tried to put herself between Theo and the guard, only earning her a wound, too, and riling up the other guards even more.

"Listen to me!" Jin bellowed, stalking forward. "Stand down!"

The hate and fear pulsing heavily in the air lessened, and the guards actually listened. One by one, they lowered their weapons, their raised fists surrounded by swirling magic. Orange anxiety and white fear churned around the group as Jin pushed past them to approach Theo.

Leaning down, Jin whispered something to Theo that was too low for Astrea to hear. Teal understanding swirled around the shorter man, twining with his graying hair. Considering how he'd disappeared for weeks, Theo seemed fine. His cheeks and jaw were covered in a bit of scruff, and he'd just received that nasty cut from the Novarian guard, but otherwise, he looked as he always did: slacks, loose-cut shirt with the sleeves rolled partway up, slightly disheveled curls.

Jin stepped back, then ordered a couple of the guards to help escort Theo and the void mage. He ordered another to go get medical supplies. Then, taking Astrea's hand, he said, "We need to find Veiko." He ushered Adi and Cressida ahead, practically dragging Astrea after them. "Right now."

The back of Astrea's neck prickled, like someone was watching her. She peeked over her shoulder only to find Theo and the void mage both staring at her intently. The corners of Theo's mouth quirked up.

She didn't return the smile. Instead, she faced forward, trying to calm her thundering pulse. On the one hand, she was glad to see Theo was actually alive. They needed his help. But skies, the promise she'd made him.

The promise she'd made the Paragonian defectors.

The promise she couldn't keep.

The role she didn't want to play.

How was she supposed to lead them? She could barely get out of bed most days. Not that she wanted to lead them. But it still astonished her that they could see her as their leader simply because of her lineage.

Several of the palace guards rushed ahead, no doubt to find Veiko. And soon enough, the shouting began. Lucian calling for Jin, for the prince who was marching a void mage through the very heart of Novarian state power.

Talk about bad optics. Delfine would be having a fit if she knew this was going on.

"Skies," Lucian muttered as he rounded a corner at the same time as them. His gaze darted behind Jin and Astrea, then back to Jin. "You thought parading him around was a good idea?"

"We need to talk to him. He's no threat to us," Jin said.

Lucian's eyes narrowed.

"I would never hurt the sun and moon," Theo said from behind them. "Never."

"He helped us escape the Badlands," Jin whispered. "You told us that yourself. Is that not proof enough?"

"Fine," the commander said. "The grand duke's office, now."

"Adi, Cress," Jin said, "can you go tell the others?"

Adi glanced at Theo. Hesitation scraped over Astrea's skin. But Cressida tugged on his arm, muttering something about how they'd be "fine" without the extra help.

With them heading off to find the rest of their group, Astrea and Jin followed Lucian and more guards down the hall toward Veiko's office. It was formerly his aunt's office, and he hadn't changed it much aside from the new picture frames on the wide desk.

Zephyrine was seated in front of Veiko's desk, and the grand duke pushed out of his chair as soon as Lucian started barking orders at the guards to lock the doors and not let anyone else inside, save Marko.

"Jin?" Veiko asked.

"Grand Duke Veiko Volara, may I introduce you to Lord Theodore Kadis," Jin said almost sarcastically. "Theo, this is the new grand duke."

"A pleasure to make your acquaintance." Theo took a step forward, but one harsh look from Lucian made him stop in his tracks. "I apologize for our abrupt appearance, Your Highness."

"I should hope so," Veiko said, then gestured toward Theo's arm. "You're injured."

"Your guards are quick," Theo said. "It's a flesh wound. It's no matter."

Veiko grimaced.

"Where have you been, Theo?" Jin asked.

Pushing his glasses up the bridge of his nose, Theo said, "Elsewhere."

Veiko scoffed. "This is who I'm supposed to trust, Jin?"

"Please, if we could get comfortable, Your Highness, I'll tell you more."

Veiko's attention flicked to Lucian, who nodded once. With a heavy sigh, the grand duke waved for them all to sit, then plopped in his own chair, almost defeated.

While Jin pulled up an extra chair from the corner for Theo, Astrea took the seat next to Zephyrine. Still standing, Jin settled behind her. Lucian remained next to the grand duke, ever watchful. The void mage shifted their weight from foot to foot, and Astrea tried to ignore the cold swallowing the room.

Lucian had claimed Zephyrine had a lead on where Theo might be, and while that was surely true, and while it was probably a good thing that he had finally shown up, Astrea couldn't help but be a little suspicious about the timing. Nazarov *had* just dreamwalked to her two days prior, the first time in weeks.

"Now," Theo said thoughtfully, "where to begin . . ."

"Where you've been is a good place to start," Jin said. "You disappeared for *weeks*. I thought we were allies now."

"We are," Theo said with a curt nod. "Of course we are. Which is exactly why I've stayed away."

"Meaning?" Lucian asked. "You said you would be in touch soon after you left us in Tornama."

"*Meaning* I needed to stay away for Astrea's and Jin's safety, Commander." Theo rolled his eyes, as if that were the most obvious thing in the world. "Nazarov knows whose side I've chosen. I wanted to be sure he was not tracking me before I came anywhere near them. He's out for blood."

"You're so sure about that?" Veiko asked. "We thought he was focused on finding aetherium."

"He is a man of many interests," Theo replied. "Aetherium is most important to him now, I think. But either killing those two or taking Astrea alive is high on his priority list as well."

"He said as much to me," Astrea said. "When he dreamwalked to me. Implied he was out for blood, as you said." Nazarov's words echoed in her head, and she tried to force away the image of Saros dying. "He reiterated that if I don't help him rule the Paragon, he'll kill me, as me being around is making his job harder."

Gray confusion bubbled around Theo's head, his frown deepening the wrinkles around his mouth. At least that seemed like a genuine reaction. Maybe the timing really was a coincidence.

"When did he do this?" Theo asked.

"Two days ago."

"No instances before?"

"None."

"You're certain?"

"I think I'd remember if he was dreamwalking to me," Astrea said. Oh, yes, of that she was sure. Nazarov always let her know when he was around. It was all some big game to him, like a cat hunting a mouse.

"I ask only because he has the ability to be more subtle than he often is," Theo said. "I wasn't sure if he had begun trying to torment you in other ways, as he often has with Ninette."

Nazarov was targeting Ninette? What could he possibly get out of that, other than making her life miserable?

"Where is she now?" Jin asked. When Veiko shot him a questioning look, Jin said, "She's another defector."

"She's at a secure location with my other people," Theo said.

Jin shook his head. "That's not good enough. If we're to work together, you need to actually give us information."

"And if we're to work together, you must trust me a little, Jin."

"You've barely given me a reason to trust you."

"I got you and your people out of Helosia, didn't I?" Theo asked. "I got your wife out, even when turning her over to Nazarov would have granted me safe passage anywhere I wanted in the world. I could have done so and washed my hands of the situation, but I chose to save you because Nazarov needs to be stopped, and I can help you stop him."

Astrea's blood chilled. Nobody else moved a muscle as they all watched Theo, surely trying to evaluate if he was making some kind of threat now.

"And so you left us alone for weeks because that was helpful?" Jin finally asked.

"Yes, it was." Theo lifted his chin.

"I believe they've made camp at a remote location in the forests northeast of Talmaris," Zephyrine said.

Theo paled.

"Seems I'm right after all," Zephyrine mused. "Thanks for the confirmation, Lord Kadis."

He glared at her. "So you know our location. Does Nazarov?"

"I hope not," she said. "Is it someplace he visited with you?"

"No, I never told him about it. If you knew where I was, General, why didn't you come looking for me?"

"I *was* looking," she said, "but I didn't want to spook you. Would've gone up there tomorrow had you not shown up now. Which is awfully convenient given we just heard from your former boss."

"I had nothing to do with that, I swear." Cold fear pulsed out from Theo, making Astrea shiver. He shook his head. "If Nazarov has only come to you the one time, Astrea, then I'm certain he is focused on other things."

"We believe he's on his way to islands in search of more aetherium," Lucian said. "We visited the old Paragon base up in the northwest—"

"Magnificent place, isn't it?" Theo interrupted.

"You obviously know it," Zephyrine said.

"I've visited several times. But that's not why we're here. Yes, Nazarov wants more aetherium. Like Emperor Aelius, he wants to build weapons. With the right forges—ones the Zaikudi are very likely providing—it will only be a matter of time until Nazarov gets what he wants."

"Wonderful," Lucian muttered.

As Veiko leaned back in his chair, it creaked slightly. "Do you know which islands Nazarov will be heading for, Lord Kadis?"

"There are many rumored to have held aetherium if our old tales are anything to believe," Theo said. "But I can narrow it down for you."

Old tales of aetherium on islands? The *Myths and Other Legends* book hadn't mentioned that, nor had her father mentioned anything of the sort. Would Valen keep that from them? Would he even know? Surely he'd heard such "old tales" when he was still living with the Paragon. Noemi certainly hadn't found anything in her most recent round of research.

"I believe it's time we discuss our alliance, Miss Sovna," Theo said. "After all, if you're to be our new One, then there is much you must be educated on. We can get started as soon as you like."

"Oh . . ." This was certainly not the direction Astrea wanted things to go. "I'm very tired, Theo." A weak excuse but true nonetheless. "I think that's a conversation I need a clearer head for."

Theo gave a weak smile. "Tomorrow, then?"

"And where will you be tonight?" Jin asked.

As Theo pushed out of his chair, he said, "I know you're going to want proof of the things I tell you. I will gather what I can and return in the morning. Is that acceptable?"

"Before you go, Lord Kadis," Veiko said, "if Nazarov really is out looking for aetherium, what kind of forces does he have? What ships?"

"Forces? Plenty," Theo said. "But ships? I don't know. He's probably demanded the Zaikudi's help with that, too."

"What else can you tell us about the Zaikudi working with him?" Zephyrine asked.

"Just that they see Nazarov as a means to an end, just as he sees them, General," Theo said. "As I said, I'll gather what proof I have tonight and bring it all to you tomorrow. We need to get started quickly."

"Next time, Lord Kadis," Veiko said as he stood, "don't jump right into the middle of my palace. Use the front door like a civilized man."

Theo inclined his head. "Of course, Your Highness."

And then, as he joined hands with the void mage, shadows swallowed them whole. Cold spiked, and they were gone.

Chapter 24

Astrea collapsed back in her chair, accidentally bumping her head against Jin's midsection. "I can't be their leader," she said, mostly to Jin. "I only told him that so he'd help us when we were—"

"I know." Jin rested his hand on her shoulder, a heavy and comforting gesture. "We'll find a way to get you out of it."

Veiko heaved a sigh. "The council . . ."

"I think it's perfect, actually," Lucian said.

Lavender surprise flashed around Zephyrine.

"Lucian," the grand duke said, "you cannot be serious."

"I'm entirely serious." His midnight eyes met Astrea's. "These people seem desperate for a leader, even the ones we captured out west. They all seem to believe you are that person, Astrea. Their new One. So, we install you as their head of state, and we use it against them."

"That's far outside my ability!" Astrea cried. How could Lucian even be suggesting this? He knew that about her. "I'm no spy. I can't pretend to lead them. They'll see right through me."

"She *is* a bad liar," Jin said. "I don't think they'll believe it, Lucian. I take your point, but I don't think they'll believe her."

"Then what about you?" Lucian said to him. "You're her husband. They think you're this 'sun.' Be her consort, if that's what they'd even call it. Or insert Valen as their new leader, and we control him and tell him what to do."

"This seems like a terrible idea," Veiko said. "Are Astrea and Jin supposed to moonlight as their leaders forever to keep them in check? It's unsustainable."

"We only need them to do it for long enough that we can take down Nazarov and the emperor, then take down the rest of the Paragon," Lucian said. "It won't be forever."

"I don't know . . ." Astrea shook her head. "No, I think the longer we do it, the more they'll believe it, and the harder it will be to step away. And I don't think we can 'take them down.' There are too many of them."

"You want to let them continue on?" Lucian asked. "After all of this? This is a chance."

"No, but that prophecy . . ." Jin murmured.

"Yes?" Veiko prompted.

"The prophecy." Astrea pushed out of her seat, a dozen thoughts coursing through her mind. They moved too quickly for her to sort, but she could see what Jin was trying to say. "Of course. Skies, of course. Yes, that's it."

"I'm confused," Zephyrine said.

"The prophecy that Saros stole from the emperor's office. It said, 'The sun, moon, and earth must come together to restore balance.'" Astrea stared at Jin, trying to formulate some coherent thought to alleviate the confusion now pulsing around the rest of the room.

Back in the Taipoli Islands, right after escaping Kalama, Astrea and Jin had wondered if the prophecy might mean that all the elements had to work together to establish balance. It was what Saros always talked about, balance.

They hadn't looked at that prophecy in a while. It had seemed like a useless solution then, another dead end that really didn't solve their problems . . . but now . . .

"What about it?" Veiko asked.

"We"—Astrea motioned to Jin—"thought this version of the prophecy might have something to do with getting all the different magic users to work together, but we also didn't think that would be possible. We didn't think we'd find a way to get void mages to help us and assumed we'd have to figure out another way to take control back."

"And now you have some that seem willing to help," Veiko said slowly, teal understanding lighting up his aura.

"We bring the prophecy to them," Jin said, his eyes locked on Astrea's. "We show them it was never meant to just be you and me. We show them it has to be all of us working together if they want to stop Nazarov like they claim."

"If all six work together to restore balance . . ." Veiko murmured.

"Not just to restore it, to maintain it," Astrea said. "If we can integrate void magic back into society and all work together to keep aetherium out of war, isn't that helping to rebalance things?"

"A nice thought," Lucian said, "but why would they buy into that when their creed is chaos and destruction?"

"Has there not already been chaos and destruction?" Zephyrine asked. "The bombings, assassinations . . ."

"You wanted Jin and I to pretend to be their new leaders," Astrea said, mostly to Lucian, before she turned to Veiko. "Maybe we don't pretend to be their king and queen but rather show them a way out. A way to integrate into society at large. We can offer them a life where they don't have to hide."

Like she'd hidden for all those years.

"What makes you think that's even possible?" Veiko asked.

"I don't know if it's possible," Astrea admitted, "but I know that people can change."

Saros had changed, or he'd been trying to. And Astrea . . . well, she had changed, too. At the beginning of the year, she would never have imagined she would be in this position. Married. Speaking of war and alliances. Wielding her magic the way she did.

"I don't think everyone who has joined the Paragon is bad," Astrea said. "Not deep down. Misguided by people like The One and Nazarov, maybe, but not bad. Don't they deserve a chance to change?"

"I agree." Jin closed the distance between him and her. "People can change, Veiko. And if my time in the Helosian army taught me anything, it's that most of those people don't really want to be there or don't truly understand what they think they signed up for. People like Nazarov and his immediate circle may not deserve any chances at redemption, but the rest? The ones who were born into it or fed lies to bring them in? We should try to give them a chance at a normal life."

"One not spent in hiding," Astrea said again, almost a whisper.

Jin took her hand in his. It was warm, firm. He gave her hand a small squeeze, as if to say he agreed. *No more hiding.* Not from the Paragon, not from Nazarov, not from the emperor.

"A compelling speech," Veiko said as he gazed at them from the opposite side of his desk, "but we'll have to see what Lord Kadis can tell us. Locations, actual numbers, hierarchy. I'm willing to work with those who genuinely want to change, but the rest? That's a different conversation."

"I understand," Jin said. "Some things aren't forgivable."

Like whoever had bombed Talmaris. Whoever had taken out Grand Duchess Ysabel. That obviously had not been Nazarov's own hand, even though he'd orchestrated it all.

"Then tomorrow, we'll get started on all of this," Veiko said. "I'll figure out what to tell the coalition. And I suggest you two think about how you want to approach these people with your offer. This may be harder than you think."

Of that, Astrea had no doubt. Changing how you'd lived for a long time—hiding, fearing discovery, always trying to be small—was no easy feat. But she knew it was possible. She was proof. She was not the timid girl she'd been.

She was strong. Resilient. Capable.

And now she just had to find a way to convince the Paragon to see her side and take a step toward the light.

Astrea wrung her hands together as she paced back and forth in front of the roaring fireplace.

"You're going to wear a hole in the floor," Jin said.

"I don't care."

"Is this really helping you think?"

"No."

No, pacing like this was not helping Astrea think, but it was like she'd received a sudden jolt of electricity. Like she needed to move. Do something. And it was too cold and too dark to go out and train now.

There was too much on her mind. Cressida. The prophecy. Theo. Even the fact that Veiko had ordered a small contingent of soldiers to go spy on Theo's camp out in the forest.

"Please," Jin said, patting the spot on the sofa next to him, "come sit. Or we can sit in front of the fire, but you've got to stop with the pacing."

With a sigh, Astrea dropped onto the ground in front of the hearth. Jin sighed, too, and got up to join her. When he was sitting cross-legged in front of her, he took her hands in his.

"Now," he said, "tell me what you're thinking."

"Our version of balance," she said. "How on earth are we ever going to convince these people it's the right path forward?"

Yes, their plan seemed like the best option, but part of Astrea wondered if she even had any right to tell these people what they should be doing with their lives. But if it was this or what would surely be some kind of imprisonment by the continent's leadership, wasn't this the better option?

"It takes a lot to change minds about something like that," Jin said. "It's not all that different from the problem Ellie's going to have convincing half the country to support her being the sibling to take power."

Astrea chewed on her bottom lip. "Does she have any ideas?"

"Not that I'm aware of, other than presenting her case honestly and transparently."

"Well, that seems like the obvious solution."

Jin smirked. "Sometimes the simplest way is the best way. It's worth a try."

Worth a try? Sure. But it wasn't like presenting their argument was going to convince the Paragon members overnight. There had to be hundreds, maybe thousands, of people. She didn't actually know the full numbers. No one did, unless Theo had specifics he could share.

"Do you think Theo will help us with this part?" she asked.

"I sure hope so," Jin said.

"What about my father? Do you think he'd be any good with this?"

"Valen?" Jin played with Astrea's wedding band, twisting it around and around her finger. "Do we want to drag him into this situation? Wouldn't that be opening a can of worms?"

"Maybe we don't introduce him to the Paragon," Astrea said, "but he left. He got out. And he apparently knows other people who left, too. Or there's Nezrin, Theo's business associate. She left and moved to Talmaris. That has to mean something."

Hesitation scraped Astrea's skin. "I suppose it does. We could try talking to them."

"Now?" she asked.

"It's late."

"I'd like to have everything sorted before Theo shows up in the morning."

"We can talk to Nezrin with Theo," Jin said. "She'll want to know he's alive. As for Valen . . . I suppose we can see if he's awake."

Astrea would break down his damn door and wake him up if she had to. It wasn't quite the tenth evening bell yet, so it wouldn't be the worst inconvenience to him.

As she started to stand, Jin got up first and helped her to her feet. Then he tugged her closer to his body. "Come here."

He pulled her into a hug. Astrea wrapped her arms around his waist and buried her face in the crook of his neck. She breathed him in, his eucalyptus soap and freshly laundered shirt. He was so steady underneath her touch. Warm sunshine. Heavy determination mixed with a hint of fatigue.

"I can have Marko go with me if you want to stay here and get some sleep," she said. "I can feel you're tired."

"While I appreciate the offer," Jin said, pulling away and peering down at her, "I wouldn't mind talking to Valen myself."

"Something you need to ask him?"

"I want to see what else he can tell us about this One position you're supposed to fill," he said. "Maybe he'll be more open if it's just the two of us."

They headed out into the hall, letting one of the guards know they were going to find Marko. The palace corridors were quiet, no doubt due in part to the late hour. Only Novarian soldiers milled about now—no sign of any coalition members or their own guardspeople. It was almost peaceful, especially with the warm lights and occasional glimpse of the stars through glass domes high above.

As they entered the guardhouse, they moved past Lucian's empty office and toward a smaller one Astrea had recently learned was Marko's. It was almost more like a broom closet than anything, barely large enough for a small desk, chair, and a few shelves hanging on the wall. Marko was there, as was Adi.

"Good," Jin said, "I'm glad to see you both." He explained more in-depth what they had decided on with the grand duke, and then why they wanted to see Valen. "It won't take us long, or at least I hope not," Jin said. "I didn't know if I should clear it with you, Marko."

"Far be it from me to stop you from seeing any prisoners you want," Marko drawled. "You know where to find me if you need me."

"Do you want me to come?" Adi asked. "Backup?"

"I don't think we'll need it," Jin said.

"Well, I'll be here then, I guess."

They headed out again. Soon they were at Valen's door, the second time in two days. Jin waved the guards off, then knocked on the door. Confusion whispered over Astrea's skin.

A moment later, the door creaked open. Valen peered out through a small crack. Teal approval lit up his aura as he opened the door wider, the color blending with the thick sweater he wore.

"I wasn't expecting any visitors," he said with a smile. "Not even the commander stops by this late."

"I'm sorry to show up at this hour," Astrea said, "but I really need to speak with you."

"Nothing bad, I hope?" Valen asked, stepping aside to let them enter.

"Nothing that good, either," Jin said, "but not the worst reason we could be stopping by."

As he walked toward his bed, Valen's thick eyebrows drew together. "I don't follow."

"Well . . ." Where did Astrea even begin? She fidgeted with her wedding band. "I don't believe the rest of the Paragon know you're alive, and now they believe I'm the rightful next leader, not Victor Nazarov."

"You're not a Dreamwalker," Valen said.

"No, but I don't think that matters to them."

He frowned. "I don't like that."

"And . . . well, I may have sort of leaned into their expectations, only to get support from some of them," Astrea said, then explained a condensed version of the prophecy they'd found in Kalama, their mission to the Badlands, and how they'd needed Theo's help. She left out most of the details, though. "Anyway, now it looks like they're possibly willing to work with me and Jin as their leaders."

"You don't seem like you want to lead them," Valen said carefully. He'd been watching her the whole time so intently it was almost as if he were a Lightbringer.

"No, we don't," Jin said. "But we have an idea."

"Most of the continent's leaders want to imprison the remaining Paragon members after we take down Nazarov," Astrea said. "But with the prophecy, Jin and I were thinking that maybe it's about how void magic cannot be separate from the rest of magic and society. That we need to work together, all of us, to stop Nazarov and the emperor."

"And you want to . . . convince them of this interpretation of the prophecy?" Valen pursed his lips.

"I know the Paragon are taught about chaos and destruction as the means to restore balance," Astrea said, "but obviously you didn't believe in that. You said there are others like you who left, and there are these people who have broken off from Nazarov's leadership. Do you think there's a way to convince them to hear me out?"

"I'm not sure . . ."

"What convinced you to leave?" Jin asked. "Or the other defectors?"

Valen looked down at his lap. "Truthfully? Much of it was how my mother and brother treated me. But part of it was the knowledge that there was much more to the world than just the Paragon. I wanted to see it. I didn't believe it was that hostile of a place, as my mother always told me."

"And?" Jin asked. "Did you find it wasn't *that* hostile?"

"Of course it wasn't." Valen smiled sadly at Astrea. "I didn't find danger but love. Until my brother had to show up again."

"The world *will* be hostile to everyone if Nazarov or Emperor Aelius get their ways," Astrea said. "That's what we want to avoid."

"If I can have the night, I'll think on it," Valen said. "I'll try to come up with some arguments you can use to sway even the most hardline members. Enough of them have to be hesitant if what you've told me about Victor Nazarov is true."

"The night is all you have," Jin said. "Some of the defectors are meeting us here tomorrow to talk about next steps, and we want to present our ideas to the defectors' leader. I think he'll see our side, but the stronger the case we bring to him, the better our efforts will be."

"Give me until sunrise," Valen said. "I'll do what I can."

"Thank you," Astrea whispered to her father. "Really, thank you."

He flashed her that sad smile again. "I promised I'd help how I could, didn't I? I intend to keep that promise."

Although she didn't know her father well, something in her believed he meant it. She believed he would help. She believed that Valen Ramkas was there to be on their side, whatever that looked like. And she was grateful.

CHAPTER 25

Though she'd tried to sleep, rest had been the last thing Astrea's mind had wanted to do. All night, she'd been thinking about Theo, about Valen, about all of it. This huge, impossible task that now fell on her and Jin's shoulders.

But she would try.

Just an hour before, Marko had delivered a short note from Valen with his thoughts. And now, she, Jin, Eliana, and Nicos were nearing Veiko's office. Theo had arrived, as promised, and was already waiting for them.

"Do you think he's actually going to have something useful to say?" Eliana asked, keeping her voice low as they strode through the halls.

"He better," Jin muttered. "I'm not giving him more than this one chance. He's screwed around with me—with us—enough."

"Hm." Pressing her lips together, Eliana tucked a few strands of hair behind her ears.

Astrea didn't think Theo would be foolish enough to try to put up any more roadblocks, but she took Jin's point. He may have helped them, but his history with Jin was complicated, filled with deceit.

"Do you think the timing of all this—the dreamwalking and Theo's arrival, I mean—are connected?" Nicos asked. "Seems awfully convenient."

"Theo actually seemed scared when Zephyrine brought up the possibility of Nazarov knowing his location," Astrea said. "He seemed disturbed by the news of the dreamwalking, too."

"Could he have been lying?" Eliana asked. "Putting on a show?"

"It's always possible," Astrea said. "And though I don't exactly trust him, he did help us escape the Badlands. It's as he said, that handing Jin and I over would've been easier."

"I hate to say I agree," Jin muttered. "I don't usually believe in coincidences, but I actually don't think the timing is connected."

"Hm," Eliana said again.

After a few more minutes, they arrived at Veiko's office, and Marko opened one of the doors. The grand duke was inside, of course, as were Lucian and Zephyrine. Theo stood awkwardly in front of Veiko's desk, hands clasped behind his back.

"Theo," Jin said as Nicos shut the door, blocking out the guards waiting outside in the hallway. "You seem to have kept up your end of the bargain."

"I assure you that I have, Jin," Theo said. He stepped to one side, revealing a stack of slim notebooks and several tubes of paper on the grand duke's desk.

"And that is?" Eliana asked, voice tight.

Theo's brown plaid jacket wrinkled as he gave Eliana a quick bow. "All the evidence I've been able to pull together against Victor, Your Imperial Highness."

"That doesn't look like much," Eliana said.

Maybe it wasn't, but it was also more than they had. Well, it was if Theo was actually being truthful. If it was actually evidence or plans or *something*.

"Though Victor and I were partners for some time, there was much he hid from me," Theo said with a sigh. "An unequal partnership at best. I gathered items for him—books, artifacts, information—while he played to The One's old ideas and bided his time. I've brought you ledgers, notations, payments."

"What good is any of that?" Nicos asked. "We need to know where he's at, not what he's done. I don't think he's foolish enough to return to any of the places you would be aware of."

"It's proof of his plans," Theo said. "Proof of what he's been after. Notes from the Zaikudi government, contacts he had me reach out to there."

"Were you some kind of glorified secretary for him?" Marko muttered, drawing a glare from the grand duke.

"As Mister Masalis said," Lucian drawled, "that is not the most helpful thing. Where would Nazarov be going now?"

With a shrug, Theo said, "That is what I cannot tell you specifically."

"And yet it is that which would be most helpful." Veiko steepled his fingers in front of his mouth, his rough, rusty annoyance arcing out toward Astrea and grating against her skin. "Yesterday, you claimed you could narrow it down for us."

Theo pushed his glasses up. "I can tell you where the aetherium isn't, save you some time."

"Theo," Jin said, "stop playing games. Where would Nazarov be headed next? Surely you know. Something you helped coordinate with the Zaikudi, something slipped into one of those notes, something he dropped in conversation."

"There was much he didn't trust me with," Theo replied with a shake of his head. "As I said, it was an unequal partnership."

"And that I simply don't believe." Jin took a step toward him, towering over the much shorter antiquities dealer. "If *this* is to be a partnership, this is one of the many things you owe us."

Theo fidgeted with the buttons on his suit jacket. Hesitation scraped against Astrea's cheeks. He pressed his lips together.

"Well?" Jin asked.

"He's going east." Theo swallowed thickly. "He believes there is something there, or at least, that was the last I heard. I cannot be one-hundred-percent sure what his next move is. It's been weeks since I had contact with him."

Veiko's eyebrows drew together.

"He believed he found evidence of aetherium in the Veiled Peaks," Theo said. "Or the Lost Isles, as you may know them . . . A desolate place by the looks of it, though I've never visited."

Astrea frowned. They'd just been talking about those very islands, but Veiko and Lucian had said storms were making them hard to access. Based on the hesitation prickling her arms and neck, the others may have been thinking the same as her. Was the storm actually magically made, by Zaikudi and Paragonian mages trying to keep people away?

"Anyway, he seemed to believe that would be the place to find aetherium," said Theo. "And with how much is in the Badlands, especially near the Ring of Fire, I don't think it's unreasonable to believe there may be aetherium somewhere near these northern volcanoes, either."

"I thought aetherium came from the skies," said Eliana.

"Yes, Your Imperial Highness," Theo said, "but there are many forces—geological similarities, impact events, even magical interference—that could bring aetherium deposits to two similar spots. It's impossible to know exactly what may have led to this . . . if Victor is even correct."

Astrea pinched the bridge of her nose. Why was this only coming up now? How had they missed this? "Did The One know about this?" she asked.

"No, I don't believe he did."

"Does Nazarov know the tunnels under that house the Paragon used to operate from in the city are made of aetherium?" she asked.

"I believe so, yes."

"Then why did he never try to take it?" Veiko asked.

"Your military's presence at the site and Victor's desire to avoid a direct confrontation made it impossible, Your Highness," Theo said. "A smart tactic implemented by your aunt."

Veiko ran a hand through his chestnut curls. Midnight blue grief spiked above his head. "So that could very well be a target if he has Zaikudi backing now," he murmured.

"I don't know if even Victor is reckless enough to bring a war directly into Talmaris," Theo said. "I know the bombings were an attack, but I don't think he'd launch that kind of assault on that house. An increase in security wouldn't hurt, but his focus has shifted."

"To this potentially nonexistent aetherium on these remote islands," Lucian half stated, half asked.

"Yes, Commander."

"If we gave you a map, could you show us where Nazarov thought the aetherium might specifically be?" he asked.

"That . . ." Theo frowned. "I don't know if Victor even knows that."

"Could you at least try? See if you remember anything?" Lucian pushed. When Theo nodded, Lucian tilted his chin toward Marko, who left the room only briefly, presumably to pass the request on to one of the guards.

"Miss Sovna," Theo said, turning toward her, "have you considered what I said last night? About needing to further your education for your new position."

"Actually, I have," she said, "and I don't believe that's the right path forward for me or the Paragon."

Theo's eyebrows furrowed and his nose scrunched up. "What do you mean?"

"You believe balance must be restored," she said, "and so do I. But not balance in which the Paragon brings destruction or chaos. That cannot be our way forward together." She brushed her fingers over the note from her father in her dress pocket, then thought better of pulling it out. "I believe the way forward is us working together to stop Nazarov and to stop Emperor Aelius, then taking steps to create a world in which the Paragon can integrate into larger society if they wish."

"They will never go for that," Theo practically scoffed.

"I know it wouldn't be an easy transition," she said, "but how is living a life in hiding any better? You want out. Your friend Nezrin got—"

"How do you know about Nezrin?" he asked, yellow worry clinging to his skin.

"She's safe," Jin said. "She wasn't hard to find."

"And I know others have gotten out as well," Astrea said. "Though they have not had the same luck as Nezrin. They do not live openly."

Theo's eyes narrowed. "How can you know that?"

"Is that not something I should know as your leader?" she prompted, hating the question.

"It seems impossible for you to know unless you've spoken to someone besides Nezrin."

Astrea ignored that. "My point is that feeding into chaos and destruction will only breed more animosity, anger, hatred. Some of the guards here already hate you and they don't even know you, just as I can feel the hatred Nazarov has for me. That's no way for any of us to live."

"A lovely speech but an idealistic one," Theo said. "How are the Paragon ever to disperse into society at large? The ones born into it? It's all they've ever known."

"We can work with the other governments to create programs to help," Eliana said. "Give people jobs, enroll them in school. Let them choose where they'd even want to live to get started."

That was what Valen's idea had been. Offer the Paragon members a real way out, with structure and support. It wasn't fair to throw them into the deep end. No, they would need time and help. Things he'd found with his employer all those years ago. Astrea had brought the idea to Eliana right before this, and she'd agreed it might work. It was something Eliana wanted to do anyway, add more social programs when she took over Helosia.

Theo eyed them both, almost as if he didn't trust them.

"I think it's a good idea," Jin said. "Astrea and my sister are right."

"You believe I'm the moon," Astrea said when Theo still didn't say anything. "Ninette once told me that meant I am inquisitive and sensitive. I know what it's like to live in hiding and want more, Theo. I've lived that way my whole life. And your people . . . our people"—she swallowed hard—"should at least be given the option of a way out. Or resources to build their own community if they want to stay where they are."

Theo sucked in a deep breath and let it out slowly. "That was never, ever part of the plan. Not Victor's, not The One's."

"And how have their plans gone?" Astrea asked. "They've gotten plenty of people killed. But is the Paragon any closer to balance? Peace?"

Theo frowned.

"I'm not saying I have all the answers," she said, "but I'm very, very familiar with being backed into a corner with no way out. Let us offer them a way out, an option for a different life than what Nazarov can give them."

"It will not be an easy task," said Theo. "The Paragon are not a monolith."

"I never expected them to be, but I'd really like to give them options."

"Then I suggest we start small," he said. "Start with Ninette and the others, and we'll go from there."

The office door opened, and a blond guard passed a long, rolled-up tube of paper to Marko.

"It seems our map has arrived," said Veiko. "Shall we begin?"

As Lucian and Theo went to examine the map, Astrea let out a sigh. Maybe this plan would work, or at least partially work. Maybe she could convince Ninette and some of the others to take her up on this offer. Maybe she really could convince them she was their leader, if it meant saving people from the Paragon's destruction.

It had taken several hours—and several pots of coffee and tea—but Theo was sure the Lost Isles were the right next step in their search for Nazarov and the aetherium.

He'd ruled out other options, partially thanks to Noemi and Tomas's help. It was only with great reluctance that any of them had called on the two scholars, who had brought their ciphers and the book stolen from Kalama to serve as cross-references. Not that Theo needed the cipher. That hadn't stopped him from being impressed by it, though.

Astrea hadn't been so sure about letting Theo anywhere near the stolen book, but if they were going to trust him with this information—trust that he was being honest—then they had to trust him to at least look at the book. And with no void magic of his own, there was no way for him to escape easily.

They'd found no specific references to hidden aetherium in the texts, but with Theo's insistence on this being Nazarov's next target and the information they had from the captured Paragonian soldiers from out west, it was their best lead.

"These islands are far." As Zephyrine leaned over the map, her long white braid slipped over her shoulder. "Quite far."

"If there's even aetherium there," Lucian said.

"I doubt Nazarov would be wasting his time if he wasn't sure something was out there," Veiko said. "If we find him, we'll engage. Catch him that way. And if not, we can at least get to this aetherium first. It seems worth the energy and resources."

"As if it's that simple?" Eliana asked. "What about the coalition?"

Veiko steepled his fingers in front of his mouth. "No doubt we'll need to convince them, too. Will you testify in front of them, Lord Kadis? Tell them what you know? Be part of this effort to find Nazarov?"

Theo fidgeted with the buttons on his suit jacket, and one corner of his mouth twitched.

"If you do not," Veiko said, "it's likely they won't vote to go on this mission. And we need them to say yes."

"This won't be enough?" Theo asked.

"What could possibly be making you hesitate?" Jin asked as he leaned forward on the table. "You have the proof. You know Nazarov. You want to stop him as much as we do."

"Yes, but—"

"If you won't do it, then I have to assume you're lying," Jin said. "Just as you lied about so many other things over the years."

"Now that is not fair," Theo said. "I hardly lied."

"You never told me any of this. Never told me about my mother. Always let me come into your shop to talk about her."

"An omission is not a lie."

Jin scoffed. "Ever heard of the phrase 'lying by omission'?"

"As far as I'm concerned, Varojin is right," Lucian said.

Astrea fiddled with her engagement band. When Theo looked her way, she forced herself to hold his gaze.

"Fine," Theo said eventually. "Fine, I will tell them all of this."

Veiko shoved out of his seat. "Perfect. Let me assemble them in the war room. We'll see you in half an hour. Make sure you bring that void mage you came to the palace with. They'll want to meet you both."

As Veiko swept out of the room, Lucian hot on his heels—probably to collect the void mage from custody—Astrea slumped back in her chair.

Were they doing the right thing? Trusting Theo this much? Maybe Veiko was right, that even if the aetherium didn't exist, they could catch up with Nazarov and capture him. That would likely mean a full-blown battle with the Zaikudi, but this was a good opportunity. Well, as good as an opportunity they would get, anyway.

"Let's not keep them waiting," Eliana said, standing. Her heels clicked delicately on the floor as she headed toward the exit.

With tired legs and an even more exhausted heart, Astrea forced herself to follow Eliana to the door. They moved efficiently as a group, with Marko and Lucian herding them along through the busy corridors. A few of the Tornamian and Delian guards paid Theo extra attention, but none of them questioned who he was or why he was with Jin and Eliana.

The war room was still empty when they arrived, so Astrea settled in with her husband and friends, eagerly pulling her magic in before everyone else arrived and she'd need to open herself up again.

The other politicians trickled in slowly over the course of more than a half hour, and it wasn't until everyone was seated with refreshments that Veiko called the meeting to order. As soon as he introduced Theo and his void mage companion—a sickly pale woman named Dara—energy slammed into Astrea. Prickly distrust, hot anger, rough confusion, cold fear. She braced herself, trying to keep her eyes open even as colors swirled so quickly around the room that she grew dizzy.

"Excuse me!" Veiko shouted over the noise. "Settle down!"

Only when Lucian slammed his hand on the table did the room quiet. Everyone shrank back in their seats, Astrea included, as he glared at the crowd. "The grand duke has asked you to settle down, so settle down."

"Skies," Veiko said, pulling at the cuffs of his sleeves, "you'd think I'd have introduced a murderer with that kind of reaction. You all *knew* we needed to find Lord Kadis."

"And so we have," said President Sikori, eyeing Theo.

"Lord Kadis may as well be a murderer," sneered Delegate Marosikis. "You were still working with Victor Nazarov until recently, were you not? Were you not responsible for the bombings? The civilian deaths?"

"No," said Theo quickly. "No, as soon as he began to even whisper about that, I knew he'd gone too far. But you must understand, Madam—"

"Delegate Tei Marosikis," she said.

"You must understand, Delegate, that getting away from Nazarov is not simple," Theo said. "There are many Paragon members who do not live reclusive lives, most of whom would be able to find me should I have run away. That's why I disappeared for weeks. To give Astrea and Prince Varojin a buffer while Nazarov would be looking for me."

"A lame excuse," said Marosikis. "You worked for him for a long time, did you not, Lord Kadis?"

"I will take accountability for what I have helped him with," Theo said, "but there are lines you do not cross. Steps you do not take. He is far past that. I want to try to make things right. And I'm fairly certain I can start by leading you to where there may be more aetherium that he's after."

"Where there *may* be aetherium?" asked President Sikori. Her thin eyebrows drew together. "You aren't certain?"

Theo explained the situation with the Lost Isles, which only made the room erupt in confusion and anger once more. Astrea's eyes fluttered shut, blocking out most of the red and gray. Next to her, chair legs scraped.

"You all agreed we needed to find Theo and see what he had to offer!" Jin called over the noise. The others quieted. "This is what he has to offer. Are we taking him up on it, or are we going to argue among ourselves all day?"

"I vote to follow the intelligence and see where it takes us," Veiko said. "Who else is in favor?"

As the energy in the room slowed to a quiet, steady pulse, Astrea forced her eyes back open. Veiko stared all the delegates down. One by one, they began casting their votes, most in favor but a handful not. Among those not in favor? Councillor Reis of the Novarian Grand Council and Delegate Marosikis of Tornama.

"That settles it," said Veiko. "We will convene in two hours to begin planning the voyage. Dismissed."

Chapter 26

As the delegates dispersed into smaller groups around the war room, no doubt talking of their concerns and positions for the impending meeting, Theo approached where Astrea, Jin, Eliana, and Nicos stood in a tight circle.

"Astrea," he said.

Eliana sidestepped so that Theo could face Astrea head-on. Marko was right behind him.

"Ninette and the others are willing to hear you out," he said.

"How can you possibly know that?" Astrea asked. He hadn't had a chance to leave since she and Eliana had proposed their idea.

Theo gestured to Dara, who stood surrounded by multiple coalition guards. Their light blue, dark green, and midnight blue uniforms complemented each other in a strange sort of way.

"I asked her to reach out to them," he said. "They said yes."

"When?" Jin asked.

"Perhaps in the morning?" Theo pressed his lips into a thin line, then added, "I doubt we'll be done here anytime soon."

"You should bring them to the palace," Marko said. "I'll ensure Commander Lucian is aware of the meeting."

"How many will there be?" Marko asked.

"I'll bring a dozen," Theo said. "They can speak to the others."

"How many are there total?" Nicos asked.

"Enough that Nazarov won't have a full advantage over us in a fight," Theo replied. "Not all in one location, either, for their safety."

Goose bumps prickled Astrea's skin. Sure, that was a good thing, but the lack of specificity about it didn't sit right with her.

"If you'll come with me, Lord Kadis," Marko said. "I believe the commander wants to speak with you now." He tilted his head back to where Lucian stood across the room, staring at them.

Theo opened his mouth as if to say more, then offered the rest of them a tight smile before following Marko away.

With a sigh, Eliana turned her back on the room again and pinched the bridge of her nose. "How difficult do you think this will be to coordinate, Jin?"

"Honestly? I have no idea. I've never worked with a group this large. But I'd imagine it won't be *that* simple." Jin's large hand found the spot between Astrea's shoulders. "Would you—"

A throat cleared behind them. Jin shifted just enough so that Astrea could see Delegate Marosikis. Her brown eyes narrowed as she took in their group.

"Your Imperial Highnesses," she said with a sniff. "Interesting fellow you've brought into the mix."

"I don't see what's so interesting about this, Delegate," Jin said. "We all knew that if we found Theo Kadis alive, we'd try to work with him. Or were you not paying attention during those meetings?"

Rust red annoyance flickered around the woman. Astrea stiffened. What was Jin doing?

"All I'm saying is that he seems to be so *conveniently* helpful all of a sudden, Your Imperial Highness," Marosikis said. "Isn't that suspicious?"

"It may seem sudden to you, but he's helped us before," Jin said. "He was Nazarov's associate for a long time. If anyone would have information, wouldn't it be him?"

Marosikis shrugged. "All I'm trying to get at, Your Imperial Highness, is that some things are too good to be true. Best to watch our backs, is it not?" With a sharp turn on her heel, the delegate moved on and headed for one of the Novarian generals speaking with the Tornamian president.

"First she wants proof," Eliana said, "so we bring her proof, and then it's too good to be true."

"There's something off about her," Nicos all but whispered. "If she really wants more power in Tornama, Ellie, why would she be acting like this?"

"I don't know," she said, glancing back at where Delegate Marosikis stood. "I'd accuse her of working with Nazarov, but that doesn't seem right. Wouldn't she be trying to get you two"—she gestured at Jin and Astrea—"to him? Or Theo?"

"Let's keep an eye on her over the coming days," Jin said. "We can talk to Lucian and Veiko, too."

Astrea agreed with the delegate's point about watching their backs—it was best not to place unearned trust in Theo Kadis, and she wouldn't if he hadn't saved their lives in the Badlands—but what could they do at this point? Sit and wait to see if Nazarov really did uncover a huge cache of aetherium? No, that wouldn't do. Checking out this lead would be the smartest course of action.

"As I was saying before, Az," Jin said, "would you mind going to check in with Adi and the twins? Let them know what we're thinking? We might need to ship out sooner rather than later."

"You think Veiko will allow us to go?" Astrea asked.

"I don't really see a choice," Jin said. "I also want to talk to Cress and Balthazar about how we might destroy the aetherium completely."

She nodded. "I'll see what I can do."

Luck was on Astrea's side for once. After leaving the meeting with Marko, they'd gone to check on Cressida first, only to find Lennor, Civan, Adi, and Noemi already with her.

"Done already?" Cressida asked as soon as she opened the door.

"Not quite," Astrea said as she and Marko stepped into Cressida's room. "Jin wanted me to come speak with you all."

"Why does that sound like it's bad news?" Adi asked from where he lounged on the sofa. Orange anxiety clung to his skin, and he pushed himself up slightly.

"I wouldn't call it *bad*," Marko said.

As Marko explained the situation to the group—the deserted islands, the political nonsense—Astrea tried to gauge their reactions. Civan didn't move a muscle; he stayed rooted to his chair. Lennor's gaze darted between Astrea and Cressida, almost with some silent question. Noemi was, understandably, both anxious and confused.

"At least the islands are close," Adi said once Marko had finished, though he didn't seem convinced by any of it.

"I don't know that I'd call them close," Marko said. "It will take several days to get there with our best ships. It's no place most Novarians are sailing, that's for sure. There's hardly anything out there except freezing water and ice."

"Sounds dangerous," Noemi said. "But I'd love to see what's out there."

"You're not going," Adi said dryly.

"Of course I'm not going. But it would be fascinating to see and study. Maybe you can clear all these Paragon out and take me someday."

"*Maybe*," Adi said with a wry smile. "Maybe someday."

"Jin wants us to join the expedition?" Lennor asked.

"Yes, he thinks it's important we go," Astrea said. "He's not yet sure of the details, but he's insisting we go."

A slight furrow formed between Lennor's eyebrows, that same silent question. Would Cressida be ready? Astrea had no idea.

"He also wanted me to ask you something in particular," Astrea said to Cressida. "You and your dad, actually. About aetherium."

Bitterness coated Astrea's tongue as Cressida frowned. "What about it?" she asked.

"Any idea how we can destroy it?"

"I haven't really thought about it much." Cressida lifted her metallic arm up. "Been a little busy."

"I know," Astrea said. Of course she knew that. "Jin just figured you two are the experts. Should I go ask Balthazar?"

"Last I knew, he was working with Mariya on it," Cressida said. "He hasn't really been telling me much. Guess he assumed I don't want to know."

"Do you want to know?" Lennor hedged.

Cressida's metallic fingers flexed. "It is what it is, right? I don't see a reason to keep me in the dark."

Nothing swirled around her, no hints of grief or frustration or anger. Cressida was . . . calm, actually, if not vague.

"I'll go speak with Mariya, I guess," Astrea said. That seemed as good a use of her time as any.

Pushing to her feet, Cressida said, "I'll go, too."

Astrea hesitated. "Uh, sure, if you want, any of you are welcome."

"Oh good, a whole field trip," Marko murmured.

Lennor immediately agreed to join, and though Civan didn't say much, he seemed to be keen on going as well. Noemi, however, declared that she far preferred indoor temperatures and would be staying in her room. Adi, too, decided to stay behind, but only because he was going to speak with Jin.

After retrieving her coat from her room, Astrea met the others and headed out into the gardens with them. The day was blisteringly cold; the high winds did nothing to help. Astrea tucked her freezing hands into her jacket pockets, desperately wishing she had a hat and scarf. At least she'd braided her hair, so the wind didn't mess it up too much.

Up ahead, Cressida walked with Lennor. No colors danced in their auras. Astrea was just glad to see them both out and about together. She didn't really know what their relationship was—they were being intensely private—but after all they'd both been through, it was nice to see they still shared a connection.

"I'm beginning to think Kalama may be the much better place to live," Marko grumbled from behind Astrea. "I always forget how much I hate the cold."

"I like it," Civan said. Unlike the rest of them, he wasn't trying to curl up farther into his coat. He even turned his face up toward the clouds, as if he really did enjoy the biting air.

If what Theo said was true, Astrea supposed the next few weeks were going to be far colder. These temperatures were surely mild compared to the islands they would need to travel to.

The trees began to thicken, and soon, a gray brick tower rose among them. Smoke puffed out of the chimney on the far side. Although Marko knocked on the worn wood door, he let himself inside.

"Now who is it?" called Mariya. Her cane thumped against the floor, the first signal of her approach before she appeared in the archway across from the door. Her face fell when she saw Marko. "Oh, good. You've brought me an entire gaggle of visitors."

"Miss Sovna has an important question for you," Marko said.

"Of course she does." Mariya waved them farther inside. "I just put on tea for me and Balthazar. You might as well make yourselves comfortable."

"Dad's here?" Cressida asked right as Balthazar called, "Hi, girls!"

They followed Mariya through the archway into her office. It was messy as always, with books, papers, and leftover dishware strewn about. Just like Saros's office always had been. A lump lodged itself in Astrea's throat. Pain crashed into her like a powerful wave, so strong she nearly cried out.

"Astrea?" Marko prompted as she stopped dead in her tracks.

"Sorry," Astrea whispered, her face heating as she realized both Civan and Marko were looking at her. She forced herself to follow Cressida and Lennor.

While a workshop was to the right of Mariya's office, a small sitting room was to the left. It was hardly large enough for all of them, and Balthazar looked almost comical sitting on the tiny sofa.

Mariya leaned her cane against the credenza on the far wall, then began pouring tea from a porcelain kettle painted with stars. "What can I do for you, Miss Sovna?" she asked over her shoulder.

"To make a long story short, Jin wants to know more about how we might destroy aetherium," Astrea said.

"Exactly what we've been discussing lately," Balthazar said.

"And?" Marko asked.

"Balthazar told me all about your conundrum in the Badlands," Mariya said. "That Prince Varojin and Commander Lucian thought blowing it up might help."

"Would it?" Cressida asked.

Mariya winced as she turned to bring one of the tea cups over. Whispers of pain slithered into Astrea's joints and bones.

"I can do that," she said, joining Mariya and taking one of the star-painted cups. "Do you need healing?"

"Nothing you need to worry about," Mariya said. As Astrea began passing out the cups, Mariya took her cane again and moved toward the single armchair in the room. She sat down with a soft groan. "Cold always makes these old bones hurt more. They've been like this for many years. Nothing I'm not used to."

"Well, if you change your mind," Astrea said.

Mariya nodded. "As I was saying, Balthazar and I have conducted a few tests. Blowing the aetherium up doesn't seem to change the potential power it has."

"You're sure?" Marko asked as he took the second to last cup from Astrea with a grateful nod. His face was pink from the cold, making the scar on his cheek all the more prominent.

"As positive as I can be without seriously hurting someone in a test," Mariya said. "The shrapnel feels the same to me even after it's been 'destroyed.'"

"We need some way to destroy it," Lennor said. "It can't just exist out there for anyone to use to hurt people like that."

Cressida fidgeted with one of the pockets of her coat. "What about acid?" she asked. "What if we corrode it? Weaken it?"

"It's worth trying," Balthazar said. "I wouldn't have any other clue about how to change it. Would one of the Paragon know, Astrea?"

"They might, but I don't know that they'd tell me," she said. It seemed unlikely that Valen would know about that. Theo might, but his knowledge seemed spotty.

Mariya pushed out of her seat, her movements stiff. "Why don't we try it? It's easy enough to test. Come along."

Leaving the cramped sitting room—and their warm tea—behind, they followed Mariya over to her workshop. It was still dimly lit, and the tables that once housed all sorts of tools and equipment Astrea couldn't name were mostly empty. A few bars of dark metal—aetherium—sat on the far table.

"There's a cabinet behind my desk with glassware," Mariya said to Marko. "Get a wide, deep container, then grab the jar with the clear liquid marked 'c.' Meet us outside."

As Marko left and gathered the items, Mariya grabbed a bar of aetherium and said, "Now, things could get dicey."

"In what way?" Astrea asked, following the petite Stargazer back out into her office.

"Some metals react violently with acid," said Civan.

"I didn't know you knew that," Lennor said.

Civan shrugged, as if that answered everything.

"And because it could get explosive, it's best we test outside." Mariya pushed open the tower's front door, letting cold air blast into the room.

As they all shuffled outside, Astrea pulled her coat tighter around herself. Jin had better appreciate her braving the cold for this information for him. He owed her a warm bath later. And she really needed to talk to someone about clothes more suited for winter. Even her toes were freezing in her boots.

Once Marko joined them, Mariya and Balthazar began setting up their experiment. They set the glass jar on the ground some distance away from the building, then dropped a chunk of aetherium no bigger than Astrea's thumb inside.

"Who's the fastest runner?" Mariya asked.

"I'll do it," Marko said with a grumble.

"Just move quickly," Balthazar said.

With a lazy salute, Marko grabbed the bottle of acid and headed for the aetherium. Astrea and the others were back near the observatory's foundation, a good two dozen yards away. Rough hesitation scraped

Astrea's skin as Marko stared down at the glass container. With a shake of his head, he poured acid over the aetherium.

Bubbles formed as soon as the liquid hit the metal. Marko kept pouring until the aetherium was completely submerged, then jogged back to where they all stood. It was hard to see for sure from that distance, but it looked like the solution was almost boiling. Foam began to build at the top as the reaction raged on.

"How long do we give it?" Marko asked.

"Let it burn itself out," Balthazar said.

It kept going and going for what felt like forever but was probably a couple of minutes. Astrea's nose, ears, and fingertips all tingled with the cold. Jin owed her far more than a warm bath.

But soon, the bubbles slowed. The reaction stopped. Balthazar and Mariya both headed over to inspect the results, green curiosity bright around them—and Civan. But Cressida? She lingered near the observatory, as if frozen in place.

"Cress?" Astrea said, keeping her voice low.

"I can't believe that stuff was in me."

Astrea pulled her hand out of her pocket and set it on Cressida's shoulder. "I know."

"I can't believe I got it out of me."

What could Astrea even say? It was miraculous. "I wouldn't blame you if you chose to stay away from all this, you know. For a little while."

"I know. But I'd rather deal with all the feelings later and just figure out how to stop people from using aetherium in the first place. I need to make sure this doesn't happen to other people."

"Don't put off feeling everything for too long. You don't want it to fester."

"I won't let it, I promise," Cressida said. "But I need to ignore it all to get the work done."

Ignoring it never seemed to truly help, but if Cressida thought that was the best way forward for now, Astrea wouldn't push. "I'll be here when you want to talk about it."

With her metallic hand, Cressida took Astrea's and squeezed gently. "I know."

"This might work!" Balthazar called cheerfully.

Cressida's feet moved. Astrea followed her to join the others as they examined the now discolored aetherium. It had corroded, almost as if it had been left in the elements for far too long.

"It feels . . . different," Mariya said, waving her hand over the sample hovering above Balthazar's palm. "That emptiness is—" Her face scrunched up. "There? But not. Like it's far away. Weak."

"What does that mean about its properties?" Marko asked. "Will it still siphon the life force out of people?"

"I can't be sure," Mariya said, "but it does not feel quite the same."

Balthazar moved his hand as if waving, and the aetherium sample followed. Flakes fell off so quickly that it looked like a peculiar dirty snow. Underneath the white flakes was a dulled gray, not the same as regular aetherium.

"If we soak it in a stronger solution, we might be able to eat straight through the metal," Balthazar said. "Corrode it more deeply, make it basically unusable."

"What about dissolving large quantities of aetherium at once?" Marko asked. "Like if we find a mine shaft full of it."

"I don't know how we'd manage." Pursing his lips, Balthazar ran a hand over his bald head. "Extracting it first would probably be better. There'd be no easy way to transport that much acid."

"Could we make it on site?" Marko asked.

"That's still asking a lot."

"Well, we'd better figure something out," Marko said. "Because if we're right, and things pan out up north, we're going to need to destroy a significant amount of aetherium soon."

"Then we'd better get to it," Balthazar said.

"Tell Commander Lucian I'm going to need more time than he wants to give me," Mariya said to Marko. "I'll come find him when I have the specifics, but until then, you all need to be patient."

Chapter 27

Despite having been back inside for the last couple of hours, the chill wouldn't leave Astrea's bones.

Adi and Marko had decided to stand guard over her while Jin was gone, not wanting to take any chance with a void mage being on palace property. They'd lit a fire in Astrea and Jin's sitting room, then made themselves comfortable, even ordering a late lunch from the kitchen.

Laid out on the floor in front of the fire, wrapped up in a blanket, Astrea was almost cozy. The siren song of a nap called to her, but the men's quiet chatter kept her firmly planted in reality.

"All I'm saying is, I don't want to *only* ever live in Kalama if things go our way," Adi said quietly. "I don't find the weather here that bad. Fort Avalon got cold in the winters, too."

"Not cold like what's to come," Marko said.

"How bad can it be?"

"Bad."

"So you're saying you want to move all the way to the southern edge of the continent just because of some winter weather?"

"If you'll have me."

Warm embarrassment spread over Astrea's cheeks—not her own. So was it Adi or Marko? She didn't have it in herself to open her eyes and look over her shoulder to find out.

"Of course I'll have you," Adi said.

"Good," Marko said, "because I don't plan on staying in Talmaris."

"Have you always wanted to leave?"

"Not until recent years."

"I actually only ever lived in Kalama for a few months," Adi murmured. "I grew up west of there."

"I'd like to see it someday."

Embarrassment tickled the end of Astrea's nose as Adi exclaimed, "Really?"

Marko shushed him, and a heavy pause settled over the room. Did they think she was asleep? Maybe it was best to let them continue with that assumption. She didn't dare move a muscle.

"Of course," Marko eventually whispered. "Why wouldn't I?"

"I don't know, I—"

The door creaked open. Fabric rustled, then heavy footsteps crossed the room. Adi whispered Jin's name, then began speaking so quietly Astrea couldn't make out the details.

Oh, they most definitely thought she was asleep. Now Astrea really couldn't give herself away without appearing like she was eavesdropping. Which she absolutely was. She just hoped Marko really would move to Kalama; he and Adi were good together, and she liked having both of them around.

More footsteps, then sunshine settled on Astrea's skin. Jin's hand brushed her shoulder, then slid down her back. "Az, wake up."

She didn't actually have to fake the way her body resisted movement. Yawning, Astrea let Jin help her up. "How was the meeting?" she asked.

"Sorted out enough of the details that they're going to get started assembling a fleet and everything else we need." Leaning in closer, Jin brushed some of her unruly hair away from her face. "Lucian wants to speak with us."

"Why?"

"He didn't say. He asked us to meet him in his office."

With Jin's help, Astrea stood and started for their bedroom to clean up. As she passed Adi, he shot her a questioning look, almost as if asking if she'd been asleep. She smiled, then ducked her head as a slight flush crept across the bridge of his nose.

"I'll join you," Marko—still in the other room—said. "Mariya's asked me to pass on a message to the commander."

"A vision?" Jin asked.

Astrea fixed her hair in the bathroom mirror, then adjusted her sweater and opal necklace. Dark spots tinged the pale skin under her eyes. She hadn't exactly been sleeping enough. Maybe that would change now that the coalition had a plan. Maybe she could stop worrying about it all.

As she rejoined the men in the other room, Marko said, "And so that was our idea, but there are logistics to work out."

"Acid . . ." Jin shook his head. "A problem for the commander, I think. But good to know we're onto something."

When they entered the hallway, they parted ways, with Adi going to take a nap and Marko going with Astrea and Jin to see the commander. All the way to the guardhouse, Astrea kept trying to focus on anything other than what Lucian might want to talk with her about. Something about meeting with those defectors Theo wanted her to speak with? Maybe some kind of plan for what that would look like in the morning?

The closer they got to the commander's office, the louder voices echoed through the halls. Hot anger and equally hot desire surged across Astrea's skin. She blanched, then had to stop herself from cringing when she realized it was Rami and Lucian shouting.

Again.

"What is with them?" Jin asked Marko as they got closer. "What could they possibly be fighting about?"

"I wish I knew," Marko muttered. "Anything under the sun these days, it seems."

Words like "reckless" and "foolish" were thrown around by Lucian, and Rami responded in kind with "stubborn" and "has always been your problem." It was hard to hear anything else specific through the door.

"Skies," Astrea muttered as more anger and desire swirled around her, impossible to ignore. Was that part of the problem, how much they seemed to want each other? Because there was too much emotion coming from that room for it to only be Rami.

Marko crossed the distance to Lucian's office in a few long strides, then flung the door open. Rami and Lucian stood near the middle of the room, staring each other down. Tangled red and dark pink ribbons of energy swirled around them both, almost tying them together.

Lucian's eyes regained focus as he looked at Marko. He cleared his throat. "Were we too loud?"

"Half the hall probably heard you," Marko said. "Are you two ever going to work your shit out? Or do you need half an hour to go have an angry fuck and get it out of your systems?"

Lucian sputtered something about "no way to talk to your commander," but Rami let out a low, dark laugh.

"No, but thank you for the offer, Marko." Turning back to Lucian, Rami added, "Think about what I said. And pull that stick out of your ass. You know I'm right, and it's time you admit it."

As Rami stomped toward the door, Jin pulled Astrea to one side to avoid getting shoulder checked. Rami slammed the door on her way out. Tense silence settled over the four of them.

"What did you do this time?" Marko asked Lucian.

Lucian straightened the sleeves of his jacket and rounded his desk. "She doesn't want to listen to me. She never does."

"Have you ever thought about listening to her?" Jin asked, earning him a glare.

"Rami has proposed that she brings in some of her contacts to help with our search in the northern seas. As if their boats, perfect for the tropical waters of the south, will be suited for what's to come. As if civilians, smugglers, and general ne'er-do-wells need to be joining a military expedition." Lucian said each word as if he was speaking to a child.

"Maybe that's your problem," Astrea said. "Talking to her like she's a foolish child rather than a grown woman who obviously knows how to survive." Lucian glared at her, too, but Astrea said, "I'm serious. Rami helped get us into Kalama. Helped in the Badlands. Is this because you hate her brother that much?"

Back on their mission to the Badlands, Lucian had explained some more about his history with Rami, her brother's less-than-legal activities, and how breaches of trust ultimately caused the end of Rami and Lucian's marriage. It always circled back to Rami's brother, or so it seemed.

"What?" Lucian sputtered as he dropped into his chair. "What? No, that's not it at all."

"Then what?" Jin asked. "If Rami has people willing to help us, then I'd like them to join. The more we have against Nazarov, the better."

The commander let out a heavy sigh.

"Lucian," Marko drawled, "honestly, I know you miss her. Is that what this is about? Has seeing her again been too hard? Was I right about the hate fuck you two need to have?"

Lucian's jaw tightened. "No."

That was a lie, at least if the colors still swirling around the commander were telling the truth. And she was certain they were. When he dared look up from his lap, he caught Astrea's eye, then the colors receded.

While not always comfortable with the thought of other Lightbringers and Souleaters being able to read her, Astrea didn't see why he had bothered to hide it at all. It was clear. Even Marko could see it, and Marko was no celestial mage.

"Astrea, I had something I wanted to run by you," Lucian said, as if changing the subject would make them all forget what they'd just witnessed.

"What is it?" she asked.

"While Theo has been helpful in what he does know, I wanted to see if you would be open to me bringing Valen on the expedition to provide further guidance or possibly point us in the right direction."

Bring Valen? Astrea frowned. "What could he tell us?" she asked.

"He . . ." Lucian pressed his lips together.

"He what, Lucian?" she asked.

"He knows these islands," Lucian said. "Better than Rami or I do."

"How does Valen know these islands?" Jin asked.

Lucian tapped his fingers on his desk and cleared his throat. "He claims he lived there for a short while with a few other defectors decades ago."

"He did tell us he tried to get far away from the Paragon after faking his death," Marko said, glancing down at Astrea. "The Lost Isles would be very far away."

Skies . . .

Part of her couldn't believe her father had visited these islands, but the other part was disappointed he hadn't told her. Just when she'd thought he was sincere about trying to help them . . .

"Did he at least tell you willingly?" Astrea asked. "Or is he back to hiding things?"

"He was quick to offer the information up when I asked about them specifically," the commander said. "Not many details, but enough. He told me he lived there only for about half a year before moving back to the continent."

Half a year? That was a *long* time to live on abandoned islands.

"Did he know there's aetherium there, like Theo mentioned in the Paragon's old tales?" Jin asked.

"He said there were rumors, but he never went looking for it."

"Are there former Paragon still living out there?" Jin asked.

"He didn't seem to think so, but he said he doesn't know for sure."

With a huff, Jin asked, "When did he tell you this?"

"This morning, when I was asking him more questions."

"How easy would it be for someone like him to get out there?" Jin asked.

Lucian shrugged. "If he had help from a void mage, perhaps not all that hard. Or if they went by boat in the spring or summer. I never saw anyone out there on my few patrol missions back in my military days, and Rami couldn't remember seeing anything either, but that doesn't mean people don't make it out there at times."

"How often do your governments check the islands?" Jin asked.

"I reviewed reports from our Novarian and Tornamian patrols over the last six months, and they've not mentioned seeing any activity." The commander crossed his arms over his chest. "If Valen can tell us anything else, then it might just help us. We should see this as a gift from the stars."

Astrea fidgeted with her necklace, turning the pendant between her fingers again and again. "Couldn't we ask him for all of that now, without bringing him along?"

"I will," Lucian said, "but sometimes being in a place jogs one's memory."

"What happened to no civilians?" Marko drawled.

"You missed the part where Rami called me a hypocrite."

"At least you're aware of it," Marko said.

"You told her about wanting to bring Valen?" Jin asked.

"Despite the way things ended between Rami and me," Lucian began, "and despite the fact that I don't want her bringing all of her network on this expedition, Rami has a good head on her shoulders. That's part of why I always hated how she got dragged down by her brother's activities. But that's beside the point. I ran it by her without thinking, right after denying her offer of help."

"No wonder she yelled at you like that," Marko said.

Pinching the bridge of his nose, Lucian said, "I'll consider her offer. And Astrea, though I'd like your input, I'm going to bring Valen along so long as the grand duke consents. I just wanted to run it by you first."

And this was surely why Rami was so frustrated. Commander Lucian was, once again, being hypocritical and doing what he thought was best. Sure, many times, his leadership and ideas paid off, but what right did he have to unilaterally—or mostly unilaterally—make decisions like that?

"Only if you seriously consider Rami's offer," Astrea said. "And only if you talk to her about how you feel, because it's very clear to me that you two are on the same page, if you could just talk without all the yelling." Looping her arm through Jin's, Astrea added, "Marko has some information from Mariya. I'll see you in the morning before Theo's 'guests' arrive. Good night."

Lucian's eyebrows rose, and Marko gave Astrea a small, appreciative smile before she turned and dragged Jin out of the room with her. Her heart thundered a little louder in her ears, but she wasn't going to let Lucian get in another word.

"Wow," Jin said, taking her hand in his. "I don't know that I've ever seen the commander speechless."

"Yes, well, someone besides Rami needed to tell him he was wrong," Astrea said. "Maybe that'll get through to him."

"Maybe," Jin said.

Astrea yawned. She was too tired to deal with Lucian anymore, whether his hypocrisy or the revelations he had to share about her father. She didn't know what to think, but if Lucian thought it was credible, she would believe it.

"Let's get you up to bed," Jin said. "Sorry I had to wake you."

"Don't be. I wasn't even asleep."

"Really?"

"Marko and Adi seemed to need some time to talk so . . ." She shrugged.

With a chuckle, Jin shook his head. "Then let's actually get you to bed."

Chapter 28

Although Grand Duke Veiko had agreed to allow Theo to bring the dozen former Paragon members to the palace, they had not been allowed inside.

Not allowed inside, and not allowed to be on palace grounds without a large army presence.

Flanked by Lucian, Marko, Zephyrine, and Jin, Astrea felt at least somewhat secure. Lucian was there in place of the grand duke, and Zephyrine had joined as an extension of Eliana's would-be government. Theo was already waiting down the hill with his own people.

Astrea tried to tamp down the shiver dancing up her spine as she gazed out at the setup some ways down the garden path. Dozens of soldiers and guards—no doubt some of them Lightbringers and Souleaters. The twelve Paragon members Theo had said would show up, including Ninette. More than half were void mages, evidenced by the even greater cold Astrea sensed.

Was making these people stand outside in freezing temperatures with armed guards really the best way to convince them that Astrea and the others wanted to help? As she stopped walking, the gravel under her boots crunched extra loudly.

"Lucian," she said, "can we get these people some hot tea or something? Give them a little breathing room from the guards?"

"Why?" he asked.

"Because I don't want to appear hostile, and having them corralled like that?" Astrea huffed, making her breath fog up in front of her face. "It doesn't set the right tone."

"She's right," Jin said. "I'm not saying we break out the finest dishware and host a feast, but we've treated our other allies with respect. These people deserve the same."

"Do they?" Lucian asked, brows furrowed. "Some of them may be complicit in Nazarov's crimes."

"You're assuming their guilt without even speaking with them," Astrea said. "Please, can we just try to ease up?"

With an exaggerated roll of his eyes, Lucian said to Marko, "Could you arrange for this . . . tea party Astrea wants to host?"

The corners of Marko's lips twitched, but he remained stony faced as he headed back up the hill toward the palace. With that, Astrea continued on, trying to ignore the way energy buzzed underneath her skin. Her stomach twisted in knots. She reached for Jin's hand, which was somehow incredibly warm even with the cold morning. Frost glistened on the grass and nearby shrubs as the sun began its ascent.

Grand Duke Veiko had authorized Astrea to offer these former Paragon members exactly what she and Eliana had suggested: government assistance to establish themselves in Novarian society, with the promise that they would also try to get the other governments to consider opening programs of their own in case anyone wanted to move to another country. Would it be enough? Would they follow through with the idea because *she*, their so-called One, had suggested it?

At the bottom of the hill, the Novarian guards parted to make enough room for Astrea and Jin to enter the circle side by side. Theo had his back to them, and he was speaking to the Paragon in hushed tones.

They all looked so . . . *normal.*

Gone were their masks and the dark uniforms they'd once worn. They were all in street clothes: heavy jackets and sweaters, trousers and skirts, boots and wingtip shoes. There were all manner of hair colors, from red like Nicos to brown like Jin's to black like Cressida's. They were clearly descended from all parts of the continent, a mix of complexions, features, and even ages. Two had deep wrinkles and graying hair, while some were as young as Astrea.

These people, whose families had joined the Paragon at some point, who had been hiding all these years. Did they share that pain with her, that pain of hiding who they were?

Maybe Lucian was right, that some were complicit. Maybe they all were. Astrea didn't know.

But as she and Jin stopped a few yards away, Theo finally turned around. And as he did, the attention of all those mages slid to Astrea. To Jin.

"Ah!" Theo called cheerfully. "Your One has arrived."

It was a little too cheerful for Astrea's taste.

She cleared her throat. "Thank you all for coming," she said, entirely unsure where to begin. What did you say to people who wrongfully fit you into their prophecy? "I'm sorry it's so cold. I've asked for some hot drinks to be sent out." She glanced up at Jin. "Maybe we could get a fire, too?"

She was just stalling for time now, but Jin agreed. While he and a couple of Earthmover guards from the crowd got that set up, Astrea shoved her hands into her pockets to stop herself from fidgeting too much. The Paragon all watched her, not quite suspicious but certainly on edge. *Can't blame them for that*, she thought. She was on edge, too.

Once a decent bonfire had been built and Marko had returned with several palace staff and trays of tea, Theo rearranged the Paragon members in front of it. Some of them relaxed a fraction. Ninette, too, moved toward the front of the group. She smiled brightly at Astrea, as if the terrible things that had happened in that house never took place.

"Thank you all for coming," Astrea said again, then tried not to cringe. Why was she repeating herself? "Theo tells me that you're open to hearing my proposal for the future of Paragon members."

She was met with mostly blank stares aside from Ninette and Theo. Jin shifted slightly, angling his body more toward hers.

"Grand Duke Veiko and Princess Eliana of Helosia have agreed with me that it's not right to condemn all of the Paragon for the actions of your former One and Victor Nazarov." Astrea's stomach continued twisting in on itself. Her voice shook a little as she said, "I know firsthand of their cruelty, but I also know that people like Ninette and Theo have tried to right some of those wrongs.

"I don't know what right I have to be your leader other than being descended from your first One," she continued. "Honestly, I don't think I have much of a right at all."

"No, you don't!" called a large, surly man at the back of the group. His thick eyebrows furrowed as he returned Theo's glare.

"Hush!" Ninette said, rust red annoyance snapping around her. "She is speaking. Respect your One!"

"What I do know," Astrea said, "is that having to hide who you are and trying to get the world to ignore you is painful."

"What could you know about that?" asked the same man. "You're friends with royalty."

Astrea couldn't deny that. "I am, but . . . well, I don't know what Theo's told you about me, but your prophecy is not the only vision I've been part of. My late uncle had one of me dying in service of the Helosian military, and so we hid my magic away. It was exhausting, always living in fear of being found out and punished. And I don't want anyone else to have to hide."

Ninette nodded sagely, as if every single one of Astrea's words rang true in her soul. But was that actually the case, or was this Ninette's obsession with her as the moon? Astrea pressed her lips together.

"As I said before, although my heritage and the Paragon's traditions say I'm your next leader, I truly don't think I have a right to show up and start making demands," Astrea said. "I'm just one woman who, frankly, knows nothing about any of you. This idea might not suit what you think you need, but I hope you'll at least consider it. Especially considering the help you've shown me in the Badlands. And because I've spoken to other former Paragon members who have gotten out, and one of the things that helped them was having support."

"How do you know we need help?" asked one red-haired woman.

"Everyone needs help sometimes. There's no shame in that. We're not meant to go through life alone, whether that means we have an entire community or just our small families." Tears pricked Astrea's eyes. Her family had grown, but it had also gotten smaller. It would always be smaller without Saros.

"If you all want to accept our help, Novaria is prepared to offer it," Lucian said as he stepped up next to Astrea. "Grand Duke Veiko is also prepared to lobby other governments to secure you the same opportunities elsewhere."

Murmurs rippled through the tiny crowd.

"My sister is prepared to offer the same should she successfully take the Helosian throne," Jin said. "A place to start fresh and build whatever lives it is you might want. Financial assistance, schooling for your children, access to universities . . ."

"All we ask in return is your continued help," Astrea said. "We need to take down Victor Nazarov—"

"Down with the pretender!" shouted Ninette. Theo shushed her.

"We need to take him down," Astrea tried again, "and we need to stop Emperor Aelius from using his aetherium weapons. So . . . that's our deal. Help us win these wars, and Helosia and Novaria—and maybe others—will help you."

They all watched Astrea carefully, as if heavily considering her offer. She gripped Jin's hand, and he drew circles on the back of her palm with his thumb.

"I don't think they're going to take it," Lucian whispered. Gray confusion sparked in the air, and heavy disbelief leaked into Astrea's bones.

"What I think you all may be missing here," Jin said, drawing the Paragons' attention, "is that *this* is the prophecy. We have the original text to prove it."

He reached into his pocket and pulled out the scrap of paper Saros had stolen from Emperor Aelius's office. Theo approached him, mouth agape.

"Here," Jin said, showing him. "Read it."

Theo examined the paper, shaking his head in disbelief. "Where did you get this?"

"My father," Jin said, voice low. "Astrea's uncle stole it from him. He had it in his office."

"The sun, moon, and earth will restore balance," Theo read aloud. He turned it over in his hands, eyebrows furrowing as he read the back. It said the same in that void language. "This really is it," he said, then turned to the crowd. "The sun, moon, and earth will restore balance!"

"This is what we believe," Jin said. "That all elements—all mages, people—must work together to take down despots. To live together peacefully. *That* is the prophecy, not destruction and death. The continent would be a much better place without my father and without Victor Nazarov, if we could all coexist."

All eyes were glued to Jin.

He smiled down at Astrea as he said, "My wife is kind, empathetic, and thoughtful. She genuinely cares. She hates when people suffer. She knows how badly it feels." He looked back at the crowd. "I mean, she is a Lightbringer, after all."

Whatever words Astrea might've responded with stuck in her throat.

"She's always shown me great kindness, even when I probably didn't deserve it," Jin continued. "She believes in second chances. This is yours. Because if you don't continue working with us, well . . ." He shook his head. "The other countries may not take so kindly to that. I can't say what they'll do, but please. Talk to your people. Think on it."

The surly man in the back met Astrea's gaze, then said, "We will."

"Please," Theo said, "return to our spot. Discuss it with the others. I'll be back soon."

Some of the Paragon in the crowd linked hands, then disappeared in swirls of inky shadow. Theo approached Lucian, and Ninette wasn't far behind.

"Thank you again for meeting with us," Theo said to the commander. "I'll continue my work to convince them. I believe they'll fight, but getting them into larger social circles may require more time."

Lucian inclined his head. "I understand. It may be some time before we can commit to housing them and supporting them regardless. We need to finish things with Nazarov first. It should be easier when he's out of the picture."

"Astrea," Ninette said, pushing past Theo to move closer.

Astrea took half a step back. Jin's strong arms circled her shoulders, whether to comfort her or keep her from running away, Astrea wasn't entirely sure. The urge to run came out of nowhere, settling into her legs. Her muscles twitched, as if silently demanding they be allowed to work.

Why was it so hard to see Ninette this close up? Ninette had been the one person in that house to show Astrea any kindness or concern. She was also physically smaller than Astrea and was no mage. Astrea was safe here, with Jin at her back and Lucian, Marko, and Zephyrine around her.

"Hi, Ninette," Astrea said, trying to school her features and slow her heart. It didn't work.

Stopping short, Ninette frowned. "I approached too quickly."

"Oh, it's—"

"Theo said this might happen," Ninette muttered before taking a half step backward. Her delicate features pinched. "I am sorry."

"That's . . . alright," Astrea said. "Can I help you with something?"

"I wanted to tell you that no matter what the others may decide, I would like to accept the offer," Ninette said.

"Oh—"

"The One always told me you were a smart girl," Ninette said, her blue eyes wide. "And though I know he was a cruel man, he was right about that. Your idea . . ." She smiled. "It is a good one. I think many will want to walk outside the Paragon's borders if they have the chance."

"We're very glad to hear that, Ninette," said Jin.

Ninette smiled up at him as if he truly were the sun. "The prophecy was right," she whispered.

Goose bumps prickled Astrea's skin. She hated this prophecy, hated it, hated that it was *working*, even if that was a good thing.

"It's time we go," Theo said. "Thank you again."

Ninette nodded at him. "I will try to convince as many of them as I can of your kind and smart intentions, Astrea. Don't worry." And then she was off, taking a compatriot's hand and jumping away through the void.

Astrea slumped against Jin.

"Well," Lucian said, "that went about as well as I imagined. I suppose we should go tell the grand duke."

"You go on ahead," Jin said. "I'll stop by his office later."

When Lucian started ordering the mass of Novarian guards around, Jin tugged on Astrea's hand and started leading her up the hill toward the palace.

"Why didn't you want to go see Veiko now?" she asked.

"Lucian can handle it," Jin said. "Come on. I need a few minutes before we jump back into the fray."

Astrea wouldn't argue with that. Not just because Jin needed it but so did she. A few minutes, and then they could get back to work.

Chapter 29

"You're like a human version of those sweet shaved iced bowls we used to get in the summer," Jin said as he pulled Astrea into their room and locked the door behind him.

"I'm fine."

"Liar."

"So what if I am?"

"A liar or a human version of sweet shaved ice?" Jin asked as he headed for the fireplace. "I could top you with fruit, eat you."

"Be quiet," Astrea muttered despite the way the corners of her mouth twitched up.

"You'll have to make me."

Following him deeper into the sitting room, Astrea shucked off her coat and scarf and draped them over the arm of the nearby chair. Once Jin had the fire started, Astrea unlaced her boots, took them off, and sat near the hearth. She liked its warmth, but she also liked watching the way the flames danced. Almost a pattern but not quite. It gave her mind something to focus on and puzzle out, even if it was something she could never actually solve.

With a groan, Jin sat down next to her. He'd also removed his coat and boots. Something about his sweater suited him. The creamy color? The pattern in the thick knit? Astrea couldn't decide.

"I hated having to see all those people," she murmured. "What if they don't accept our offer?"

"Then it's likely one of the governments—maybe most—will begin trying to pursue legal action against those who want to remain with the Paragon."

"Wonderful."

"It's not that I'm in complete agreement with them," Jin said, "but anyone who still aligns with Nazarov should probably be removed from society. At least face trial."

Astrea traced swirls into the rug with the tip of her finger. "What if they don't agree with Nazarov's extreme ideas but still want to follow the Paragon's creed?"

"Then we'll deal with it."

"Just what we need."

"We will, I promise," Jin said. "But there will surely be plenty of defectors who want to take the offer. How could they not?"

"Change is hard," Astrea said. "Even when you want or need it to happen."

"It is, but that doesn't mean they'll all fail at changing. Plenty will embrace it with open arms."

"You're awfully confident."

Jin chuckled. "And you're awfully pessimistic."

"Sorry."

"Don't be. I just don't want you to get discouraged before we even have their answers."

"It's hard not to," Astrea whispered.

How had she lost Saros a little over a month ago? How had things changed so drastically in such a short time? Her life had changed forever, all thanks to that letter from the emperor and Nazarov finding her in the

Whiskey Dream. She hadn't even known it that night, who and what he was.

"You did well talking to them," Jin said. "And I meant everything I said. About you. They're fools if they can't see how good and true your intentions are."

"They don't know me."

"I do." Jin took her face in his hands, forcing her to look up at him. "You are that person, Az. Kind, empathetic. You gave me a second chance. You gave Saros one, too. You're giving Valen a chance in a way."

"Maybe that last one just makes me a fool."

"No," Jin said. "It's amazing to me that you even see the good in people. I don't think I would if I were in your place. Plenty of people let the world harden their hearts. You haven't."

"Maybe that's part of my problem. That I don't guard it enough. That I'm not hardened enough."

"How could that be a problem?" Jin asked, voice strained. "I love that about you."

"Maybe then it wouldn't hurt so much."

"Oh, Az," Jin whispered. "Believe me, it hurts even when you build a wall so thick that a cannon would have a hard time getting through. Trying to go through that alone is worse. It takes immense strength to share your pain."

"Talking about it doesn't make me feel strong. It makes me feel like I'm complaining. Like that man said, I'm friends with royalty. *Married* to royalty." She gestured to the room. "I live in a palace. I have everything I could want and need."

"Maybe that's true," Jin said, "that you live here and have powerful friends. But I don't think that negates what you've been through. Powerful and privileged people I served with in the military never would have held on as long as you have. They would have broken the second the Paragon took them.”

“I did break.”

“And yet you picked up the pieces, forged ahead.”

“I barely feel like I’ve put myself together again. How am I supposed to finish any of the work left to do?”

“With our help, and the backing of all these other countries. It’s not just the six of us anymore.” He delicately traced a tear trailing down her cheek, letting his fingers linger on her jaw.

Through watery eyes, Astrea gazed up at Jin. His warmth washed over her again and again, like summer sunshine desperately trying to break through thunderstorm clouds.

“And I know what you’re thinking,” he said.

Astrea swallowed hard. “What’s that?”

“That you don’t want to bother the others when they’re busy with their own issues and pain. So if you can’t, don’t. Lean on me. Whatever you need. I’ll always be here.”

Astrea smothered the sob building in her chest. “How can you give so much to me when you’ve been through the same? More, really.” All those years at war. Ilesouria. Posan. Corsyca. All the things he’d seen . . . how many times he’d escaped death . . .

“I don’t think you realize this, Az, but that sweet heart of yours?” One corner of his mouth quirked up. “Just being near you every day gives me solace, strength, peace. I know I can get through anything if you’re with me.”

“Really?” she whispered.

“Always.”

Astrea didn’t know who pressed in first, but their lips touched. Sour and sweet danced across her taste buds, and a fire lit in her belly. Wrapping her arms around Jin's neck, Astrea pulled him closer. She needed to be near him. With him.

With a growl, Jin pulled away long enough to haul her into his lap. He pushed her braid over her shoulder and went to work kissing her neck. One hand pressed in at the small of her back, holding her in place as he began trailing little bites toward her collarbone. Astrea curled her fingers into his hair; it seemed to spur him on.

"Off," he murmured against her neck, both of his hands tugging at the hem of her sweater.

As soon as they had it over her head, Jin tossed the garment away. Goose bumps covered Astrea's skin, the heat of the fire and the heat coming off Jin not enough to hold off the chill. His fingers quickly found the clasp on her brassiere. He had it off her in a second, his hands roaming her back, her waist, her chest.

"My smart, gentle, strong, beautiful wife," he whispered, placing kisses on her shoulders between each word. His fingers lingered between her shoulder blades, touching the raised scars there.

Deep purple reverence, raspberry lust, and pink love swirled around Jin in such a thick tangle Astrea could barely tell the colors apart. She cupped his face between her hands, bringing his mouth up to hers. As their lips crashed together, Astrea reached for Jin's sweater, trying to tug it up. She needed to feel his skin on hers. Desperately.

He broke away and pulled it off. His muscles rippled with each movement, almost catching the light of the crackling fire. Then he nudged her up, and only when she was standing did he begin pulling off her stockings and skirt. His hands traced her bare calves, his touch strong and appreciative.

"Tell me what you want," he said, the raspberry and pink growing brighter.

"You. Always you."

His belt, trousers, and underwear were off in another half a heartbeat, and then he was pulling her into his lap again. His erection pressed against her, almost begging to be let in. Astrea shifted, trying to line them up. Jin reached between them. As he slipped inside her, every inch of Astrea's body lit up. Jin pulled her flush against him. He buried his face in the crook of her neck as their hips rocked together lazily.

This was what she wanted. Not just him, but more moments like this. A chance to have a slow, quiet life, one where they weren't being bothered by generals and politicians and fanatics. Just the two of them, that house near the mountains she'd secretly been dreaming of.

She would fight for that future. Their future. Their friends' futures. One in which people weren't being forced to hide or serve, live in secret or die on the battlefield. One in which people could pursue whatever it was they loved, whoever they loved. One in which people *could* be soft and tender and not have to constantly watch their backs.

"I love you," Jin whispered against her throat. He nipped the skin, then chased it with a kiss.

Before Astrea could get a word in, his mouth traveled down to her breasts. Her head fell back as she swallowed another cry. Jin snaked a hand between their bodies, then pressed two fingers against her most sensitive spot. Pleasure sparked from her toes to the tips of her ears, and he soon had her unraveling. Her body shuddered, which made Jin kiss her harder.

"Good for more?" he asked.

"Yes." Astrea didn't want it to end. She didn't want to pull apart, face the real world again. She loved this bubble, this stolen moment.

Jin laid her down on her back right in front of the hearth. He hovered over her, golden firelight illuminating his skin and making his irises almost molten. A delicate pink mist clung to his skin. It seemed to thicken around the knot right below his collarbone, where she'd healed him. Where that hint of shadow remained.

"Beautiful," he whispered reverently as he pushed back into her. One arm bracketed the right side of her head. His other hand tangled with hers as he thrust into her again and again and again.

Astrea tightened her legs around his waist, reveling in the feeling of his skin on hers, the weight of his body above her. Her shield. Her partner, who saw her in such a different way than she saw herself. Maybe it was true. Maybe he really saw all those things in her. Maybe she *was* those things.

Her hands roamed his shoulders, his back, his hair. Her face warmed—from the fire, his love, the attention. And then Jin brought her to the edge again and followed her over. Bliss wrapped around her heart, settling there and thawing the permanent chill in her bones.

Jin rolled off her with a satisfied groan. He settled behind her, then wrapped his arms around her waist and tugged her toward him until her back was flush against him.

"I love you, too," Astrea said. "Since you cut me off before."

A deep, pleasant chuckle traveled from Jin's chest straight into hers. He kissed the back of her head. "I know."

She started to push up on her elbow. "I suppose we should—"

"No." Jin's voice was firm but gentle as he pulled her back down. "No, we're not getting up."

"But Veiko—"

"Az, if Veiko or anyone else in the alliance can't make a decision without me being in the room, then we're in grave danger of failing," he said. "They don't need me there all the time. Let me have this with my wife. They've had enough of the both of us for months."

"Maybe you're right."

"I *know* I'm right."

"Cocky," she whispered, which he answered with a wiggle of his hips. Astrea squealed. "Hey!"

Holding her tighter, Jin pressed another kiss to the back of her head, and sweet, fruity amusement filled her mouth. She relaxed against him, trying to find some pattern in the way his arm muscles flexed under her head. There wasn't one that she could find, though. So she settled on watching the fire through hooded eyes, on the way Jin's breathing slowed and hers mimicked his. And soon, the darkness of sleep obscured even the fire still burning brightly as they slept.

Chapter 30

Three days were not enough to prepare for a near-arctic expedition. In fact, Astrea found she was very much dreading what was to come: a short trip north to a navy base, then starting for the desolate islands in the morning. Earlier in the week, Grand Duke Veiko and his military leadership had authorized several small planes and airships to fly out to the Lost Isles despite the stormy weather. They'd returned successfully to their bases, reporting no signs of human activity.

Plenty of ships were waiting for them at the harbor: Novarian, Tornamian, Taipoli, Delian. Whatever awaited them on those islands, their extensive force would have to be enough.

Staff had stopped by earlier that day with new gear for everyone: heavy snow-proof coats and boots suitable for that environment. They'd also brought wool socks, hats, goggles, and even thick, fur-lined leggings for Astrea to put under her armor dress. How bad was this trip going to be?

And so now she sat in the back of a luxurious car, staring out the window as they approached their final destination by the sea.

Over the few days they'd spent preparing everything in Talmaris, Astrea hadn't had much interaction with the coalition council. Jin, Eliana, Nicos, and Zephyrine had handled it. She'd focused on helping Cressida and learning more from Ivy about how to help ease Cressida's pain, tonics to provide, and the like.

Astrea hadn't been so sure about Cressida joining them—not because she thought Cressida couldn't handle it but because she wasn't sure how the Isles' intense cold might affect her pain or her prosthetic. But Cressida had insisted, as had Balthazar. Mariya would even be joining them, though she would stay on the ships until they were confident they'd found aetherium.

The expedition team would be enormous. Their core group—barring Eliana and Nicos, who would remain in Talmaris—would be traveling on a Novarian Royal Navy ship. There were more Novarian ships, of course, as well as many from the other alliance countries. Rami would be there, and even Anjou Lazzaro was bringing his private ship and crew to help.

Jin's hand rested on Astrea's thigh. He drew smooth circles with his thumb, though whether to comfort her or himself, Astrea wasn't entirely sure. On the bench seat in front of them, Lennor, Civan, and Cressida sat together. Lennor had her head resting on Cressida's shoulder, and both seemed to be asleep. Civan stared out the window. Up front, Adi and Marko chatted quietly.

Soon, the thick forest surrounding the road thinned out. Just around the bend was a large metal gate, easily two stories high and blocking the whole road. A guardhouse sat on either side of the fence. The caravan in front of them began inching onto the base as soon as the guards opened the gate.

The base was full of nondescript buildings, a truly unremarkable place. A light dusting of snow covered the trees, grass, and rooftops. Gray clouds blocked out most of the midafternoon sun.

Before long, they'd stopped near a large, unmarked building. Several Novarians in dark blue uniforms trimmed with silver waited outside its doors, maybe a dozen feet from the drive.

Marko stopped the car. Astrea gently woke up Lennor and Cressida, then moved to climb out after Jin. He offered her his hand, and she took it. Cold wind blasted her immediately. She pulled her jacket around herself.

"Fuck," Cressida muttered sleepily as she got out of the car next. "Fuck, I can't wait to go home."

"It's not that bad," Civan said from behind her, making Cressida roll her eyes. "There were days in Corsyca that were colder."

"Hush," Lennor said.

"Just wait until you see how hot Kalamian summers get," Cressida muttered.

"Corsyca is actually known to have more humid—"

"Civ," Jin said, no doubt catching Cressida's irritated expression, "how about you go check in with Zephyrine? I see her waving us over. I'm going to help Adi get the bags."

Civan eyed Jin doubtfully, as if he didn't fully believe Jin's request was honest. But indeed, looking ahead at the other cars, Zephyrine *was* waving at them, trying to get their attention. With a small murmur of acknowledgment, Civan headed for the Helosian general.

"Sorry," Cressida said, pinching the bridge of her nose. "I'm too tired to deal with anything right now."

"Let's get everyone settled on the ship," Jin said, circling to the back of the car and opening the trunk.

With Adi and Marko's help, they got all the knapsacks out. Jin even took Astrea's despite her being perfectly capable of carrying it herself. He seemed to get some pleasure out of doing these small things for her, and who was she to deny him that?

As they merged back into the main group to speak with the Novarian officers waiting for them, Astrea hung back with Cressida and Lennor. A few words floated toward Astrea, something about "moderate visibility" and "slight seas" and how wind conditions might impact their timing. None of it seemed like something she could help with, so she tried not to worry about it too much.

Dark smoke puffed out from the smokestacks of the military vessels bobbing up and down in the water. They were varying sizes but all large, each easily able to carry hundreds to the Lost Isles. Their flags—the various blues, greens, yellows, and whites that made up the alliance—snapped in the wind.

"Have you ever been on a boat that size?" Cressida asked Lennor, jerking her chin toward the ships.

"Not like that."

Astrea certainly hoped that large of a vessel would be more comfortable to sail on than the small rum-running boat Captain Magdi had used to help them get into and out of Kalama all those months ago. She also hoped that by some miracle, it would be warm. The early winter wind seeped through her coat, sweater, and dress and right into her bones.

Though their group from Talmaris was comparatively small, the energy of many, many people lingered in the distance, coming from the direction of the ships all waiting on the ocean. Being able to keep them all at a distance was nice, if not still somewhat distracting.

After several more minutes standing out in the cold and wind, Lucian signaled for everyone to head for their waiting ship. As soon as Astrea's boots hit the deck, Jin guided her, Cressida, and Lennor toward the pilothouse. A roof extended from the actual structures, creating a kind of portico. On a summer day, it might have been the perfect place to stand and enjoy the view of the ocean. Now, though, nothing but gray skies and waters stretched out before them.

The heat inside the pilothouse made Astrea's cheeks tingle. She followed Jin and Lucian deeper inside. Warm lights glowed near the ceiling.

It was almost like one of those luxury cruise ships Balthazar's company had helped build in recent years.

"There are rooms on all three lower decks, but I'd recommend we stay on the highest," Lucian said as he strode down a hallway lined with blue wallpaper. At the end were stairs descending deeper into the ship. He started for them. "Dining room is up here on the main deck. Expect meals at regular hours. You can also go to the kitchen if you need something outside of normal hours . . ."

Astrea tuned most of Lucian's words out as she focused on descending the narrow staircase. He was going on about civilian protocols and more service provided by the crew, nothing that important for the mission. Mariya's cane thunked steadily on the carpeted floor.

Valen was surely somewhere on this ship; the grand duke had signed off on Lucian's plans to bring him along. Astrea still didn't know if it was a good idea or not, or if it was even just a waste of time. *I should probably try to find him at some point.* She wanted to ask him more about his connection to the Lost Isles herself, despite the commander already having done so.

"And here is where you'll be staying," Lucian said, stopping in the middle of the narrow corridor. It turned right up ahead. "This block of rooms. Mine's around the corner. They're small . . . not uncomfortable, but do be warned."

"Thanks, Lucian," Jin said.

"I'll mostly be upstairs coordinating with the captain, but please come find me if you need me," he said, then headed back the way they'd come.

With only minor discussion about who was taking what rooms, they all split off. Jin and Astrea took the one in between Cressida and Adi's; Balthazar was across the hall. As Lucian had promised, it was small. The bed tucked against the far wall was barely a double. The wardrobe and desk were barely large enough for a child. A small window near the ceiling let in a hint of cloudy light. All the furniture was built *into* the walls, so at least it was secure.

Jin flipped on the switch, lighting up a sconce placed over the desk. The warm lighting and wood-paneled walls helped a little; it wouldn't be so bad. They could make it work. Besides, basically anything would be better than sleeping in the storeroom of the Whiskey Dream's basement or on a small cot in the bottom of Magdi's ship.

"Let's settle in for now," Jin said as he set their bags down on the bed. The stiff blankets barely moved with the added weight. "We should be leaving port soon."

"Do you really think this is going to work?" Astrea asked as she plopped down onto the mattress. It was as stiff as the blankets. "Going to these islands, I mean."

He shrugged. "It's worth a try, right?"

"It feels like a wild-goose chase."

"This whole damn situation has felt that way," Jin said. "But I'm willing to take the chance if it means we get the upper hand on Nazarov for once."

Astrea nodded. It wasn't that she disagreed, but she just hoped they weren't wasting their time. After all, with Nazarov and the emperor both gunning for control of aetherium, they didn't have the luxury of wasting time.

Rolling onto her side to face the door, Astrea tugged the rough blankets up higher, cocooning herself inside. Even without Jin in bed, the space was hardly big—

One ship horn broke the silence with an angry wail. Others joined in, not quite as loud but enough to make Astrea jump out of her skin.

Jin chuckled, a warm, beautiful sound. "I should've warned you, I guess," he said.

Astrea glared at him. "Yes, you most certainly could have."

He leaned back in the small chair near the desk. He'd taken the last hour to go over some reports Veiko had given him that morning before they left the palace. Jin rubbed at his eyes with one hand and closed the folder with the other. "That's enough of that for now."

"Feeling sick?" Astrea asked as she pushed up and swung her legs over the side of the bed.

"I will soon."

"You don't get motion sick on airships," Astrea said. "Why boats?"

"Beats me. I've always been that way. I'll go see if the kitchen has any extra ginger or peppermint I can steal."

"Will it help? The herbs, I mean."

"Not as much as I wish they did. Are you hungry? Do you want me to get you anything?"

"I could use a hot drink, actually." As the ship lurched forward, Astrea's vision danced. Their room was so narrow that Jin could almost touch both walls if he stretched his arms out to his sides. The close quarters somehow made the ship's movement even worse. "And to stretch my legs."

"The dining room should have something. I'm going to speak with the captain after I visit the kitchen, if you don't mind."

"I can wait for you," Astrea said, taking Jin's hand as he offered to help her stand. His skin was warm, and his palms were a little rough.

"And leave my wife all alone?" Jin scoffed. "I could never."

Astrea's whole face heated as they stepped into the quiet hallway. It was such a silly, trivial thing, but she didn't think she'd ever get sick of Jin calling her that. *My wife.*

"Oh." Balthazar laughed just as Jin closed their bedroom door. With the tight corridor, Balthazar and Astrea were practically on top of each other. "Sorry."

"We were going to the dining hall, if you want to join us," Astrea offered. She glanced back at Jin. "Then you don't have to worry about me being alone."

"Perfect," Balthazar said, "because I'm feeling a bit peckish."

As the three of them headed back upstairs, Astrea tried to memorize their path. It was easier without Lucian droning on in the background, but she'd still get Balthazar or Jin to walk back to the cabin with her to be sure she didn't get lost.

They passed a few Novarian sailors on their way up to the top deck. Each one was dressed in a crisp, dark blue uniform trimmed with white. They all saluted Jin, too, and offered murmurs of his title as they passed. Thankfully, nobody mentioned anything to Astrea. She was sure that if Delfine were there, there'd be whispers of "princess" and "Your Highness" thrown in her direction, too.

After turning down a wider hall, Jin deposited Astrea and Balthazar outside two stately doors. "Here you go," he said. "I'll be back." Then he hurried off down the hall.

"Where's he going in such a rush?" Balthazar asked as he opened the door on the right.

"He needs to check on a few things," Astrea said as she slipped past him. "I'm going to wait for him here."

The dining room was much bigger than her cabin, obviously a space for the officers based on the detailing in the wood panels, pristine carpet, and the small chandeliers. It seemed silly to Astrea; why bother?

"And look who it is," Balthazar said with an easy smile.

There, at a round table in the corner by the windows, were Lennor, Cressida, and Civan. They had playing cards out and a pot of tea in the middle of the table. Balthazar headed their way, and Astrea followed him, trying to glean what she could off Cressida. But Cressida was closed off. What was she hiding? Pain? She was using her metallic arm to reach for new cards, so Astrea didn't think it was that.

"I hope we're not interrupting," Balthazar said as he approached the trio. "Astrea and I came up to get a snack."

"Pull up some chairs and sit, Mister Nikaphoros," Lennor said.

He chuckled. "Lennor, my dear, we've been over this. Just Balthazar, please."

Cheeks flushing, Lennor ducked her head and mumbled something that sounded an awful lot like "yes, sir."

Ignoring the heat of Lennor's embarrassment, Astrea helped Balthazar pull a couple of chairs over. She put hers between Cressida and Civan.

"Kitchen isn't serving much right now," Cressida said to her dad, then plucked a card from the center pile, the five of water. "Waiter should be over soon."

"I don't mind waiting," Balthazar said.

Astrea settled in, her attention drifting between the view outside and the card game as she tried to figure out the rules. A smaller ship sailed some distance away from theirs, keeping mostly the same speed. The graying waters and sky even looked cold despite the dining room actually being pleasantly warm. Astrea tucked her hands up into the sleeves of her sweater anyway and tried to focus on the game.

"I win again," Civan said with a smile as he laid out his hand.

Compared to the other cards, Astrea could make no sense of why he'd won, but Lennor and Cressida both made a show of swearing and sighing.

"I don't see why you're upset," Civan said as he collected the cards and began shuffling the deck. "I like this game."

"Because that's the fourth hand you've won in a row, not to mention all the other ones yesterday," Lennor whined.

"As I said, I like this game." Civan smiled again and continued mixing up the deck.

"It seems to me—" Balthazar cut himself off when a red-haired waiter in a navy uniform and apron strolled up to their table. "Hi, yes, what's your selection as far as tea goes?"

"Limited, sir," the sailor said. "Breakfast tea or peppermint tea are all we have."

"I'll take breakfast," Balthazar said. "What've you got to eat?"

"A selection of fruit and pastries until dinner."

"Just bring out a couple of pastries, then," Balthazar said.

The sailor nodded, then said, "And you, ma'am?"

Ma'am? That was almost worse than being called princess by Delfine and the coalition. Almost.

"Do you have hot chocolate?" Astrea asked.

"We do, ma'am."

Civan perked up.

"Could you bring a pot of it?" she asked. "And two mugs."

As the sailor headed toward the back of the dining room and through a small door, Astrea started to settle back in. But a tangle of uncertainty and curiosity moved closer to the dining room. She hesitated. It stopped, then started again.

Cressida shot Astrea a questioning look. As she began to explain, the dining room doors opened. Commander Lucian walked in, trailed by

. . .

Valen.

Astrea shoved out of her seat. She didn't know why; her body just moved.

Valen watched her curiously. Astrea still didn't know what to make of him. It seemed like he wanted to help, yet he held so much information close to his chest. Was he overly cautious after all his years on the run and in hiding? She wanted to believe that was it, but only part of her did.

"That's him?" Balthazar asked, voice low.

"Yeah." She swallowed thickly.

Balthazar made his way over to where Valen and Lucian stood. He was a big man with an imposing presence; if Astrea didn't know how sweet Balthazar was, she would certainly be intimidated by him. Next to him, Lucian and Valen both looked small.

"Balthazar Nikaphoros." He stuck his hand out to Valen. "I've known Astrea for many years. She's a wonderful young woman."

"From our few interactions, I've gathered as much," said Valen as he shook Balthazar's hand.

"A very wonderful young woman, just like her mother when I knew her," Balthazar said. "My wife and I have spent a lot of time with her over the years, helping Astrea as she grew up. She's basically my second daughter, actually," he added with a chuckle. "If *anything* happens to her—to either of my girls—well, I'll be a *very* angry man."

Cold fear worked its way up Astrea's spine as Valen cleared his throat. "And I have a feeling you're not the type of man any of us want to see angry, Mister Nikaphoros."

"No, I'd reckon I'm not." Balthazar smiled. "It was nice to meet you, Valen. If you don't mind, we have a game to get back to."

"Indeed," Valen murmured, taking a half step behind Lucian.

"The kitchen is this way, Mister Ramkas," Lucian said, nudging Valen toward the back of the room. "Vernie will meet us at your cabin."

As the two men disappeared out the back and Balthazar returned to the table with a satisfied smile, Astrea put her hands on her hips. "What was that?" she asked him.

"What was what?" he asked, feigning innocence.

"You just threatened him!"

"All I did was make it clear what'll happen if anyone messes with my daughters," Balthazar said. "What's wrong with that?"

"You're acting like he's going to murder us in our sleep or something, Dad," Cressida said.

"He may be helpful to us now, but I don't trust anyone much at the moment," Balthazar said. "Not with you two." He gestured toward Lennor and Civan. "Not with any of you, frankly, though I'm sure Civan and Lennor could do far more than me in a fight."

Lennor shot Astrea a questioning look, but all she could do was shrug. Balthazar had always been protective, sure, but this was new and rather unexpected.

The door at the back of the dining room swung open, and the sailor returned with a cart of pastries, tea, and hot chocolate. Balthazar relaxed into his chair as he enjoyed his snack and Civan began dealing cards.

Astrea started pouring hot chocolate for Civan when that small door opened again. Lucian and Valen reappeared, both of them carrying coffee cups. Valen trailed closely after him, only glancing over his shoulder at Astrea. He looked . . . sad.

Sad about what? That Balthazar had threatened him? That Astrea had grown up with three parents, none of whom were actually her mother and father? Was he jealous, thinking of all those missed years? Or was Balthazar right, that maybe they shouldn't be trusting Valen at all?

Chapter 31

A few days on a ship, even a large one, was miserable. Despite feeling sick, Jin had pushed on and helped Lucian and the Novarian military. Astrea had seemed to get her sea legs, but her head still felt slightly off ever since leaving port. The worst of the storms had cleared, but the waters hadn't been entirely smooth, either.

Much of the time had been spent watching Cressida, Lennor, Civan, and Adi play cards. Marko sometimes joined. Balthazar often did. Astrea had even started trying to learn one of the games whenever she felt she wouldn't get too motion sick.

It was the afternoon of the third day since leaving the northern Novarian port. The sun was low in the sky despite the ship's clocks pointing to nearly three in the afternoon. Thick gray clouds hung above the bleak scene as the ships dropped anchor. Even from inside the dining room on the ship, the Lost Isles were clearly desolate, just snow and ice and towering peaks.

"We'll be taking boats to the largest island in half an hour," Jin said as he strode into the room with Lucian. "Get changed. Bring your packs."

They all descended down to their cabins in tense, heavy silence. Anxiety choked the air, a cloud of orange that blocked Astrea's vision. She ducked into her room, and Jin followed right behind. He pulled their bags from where he'd stashed them in the tiny wardrobe, then began unpacking all their gear.

Astrea pulled on the thick, fur-lined leggings provided for her. The inside was incredibly soft, and the outside was covered by a thin layer of white leather. Her armor dress was constructed the same, lined with fur and wool and covered in much thicker, harder white leather.

"Here." Jin passed her a hood and mask combination, which would cover everything except her eyes.

It was made of dense, heavy cloth. Astrea frowned. "Is this really necessary?"

"Easier with the wind; your hood will get blown off," Jin said.

After tucking it into the pocket of her skirt, Astrea grabbed her gloves and stuck them in the other pocket, then reached for her bag.

Jin was dressed nearly the same as her, though his armor lacked the skirt hers had. All white, from his boots to his own head covering. His rings caught the room's low lights as he shouldered his bag.

"If you get too cold out there, let me know," Jin said.

"And do what about it, exactly?" Astrea asked. Besides, if they really were going to be running all around the island searching for aetherium, surely she wouldn't get *that* cold. Physical activity always warmed her blood.

"My fireweaving is good for many things."

A blush crept across Astrea's cheeks as memories of how Jin's hands warmed noticeably during their more intimate activities jumped to the front of her mind. Of course he could probably very well warm her up on a full-body scale, not just when they were in bed. "I see."

With a small smile, Jin tilted his head toward the door. "C'mon. Let's get out there."

As they reconvened with the rest of the group and headed out onto the main deck, cold wind bit Astrea's face. She squinted, keeping close to Jin and taking one of Cressida's gloved hands in hers.

The deck was crawling with soldiers. Half were dressed in heavy blue coats while others were in shades of white and gray. No doubt those were the ones who would be joining them on the island.

The thud of a cane on deck made Astrea peek over her shoulder. Mariya had followed them out. Her thick black coat stuck out amid the crowd, and she had a furry brown hat pulled down over her ears. A deep ache settled in Astrea's body.

"Damn cold makes these old bones hurt," Mariya said. She turned her small, broad nose up at Cressida. "You know what you're looking for?"

"Aetherium's pretty easy to spot, even without a Stargazer, though it'd be nice if I could actually feel the difference." Cressida's voice tightened as she said, "Color's all wrong, even in its natural state like what we saw down south."

Mariya gave a resolute nod. "Time to get rid of it."

"We'll try," Balthazar said as he came up behind his daughter. "We'll figure something out."

"Are we all ready to go?" called the commander from behind them.

Astrea turned. There was Lucian, dressed in white and gray. And behind him? Her father. What was he doing there?

Astrea hadn't seen him at all since that strange interaction in the dining room. She didn't even know what to say to him, what to ask. Yes, she'd wanted to ask him more about his time on the Lost Isles, but after the way Balthazar had approached him, she just felt awkward.

"Are we really bringing a civilian out there, Commander?" Zephyrine asked. "No offense, Mister Ramkas."

"None taken," Valen said with a tight laugh as he came to a stop behind Lucian. "It's a harsh, unforgiving place this time of year."

"You lived here during the winter?" Jin asked.

"No, no," Valen replied. "I left right before this time, and even that was bad."

Astrea studied her father's aura and body, watching for any sign of secrets or betrayals. But there was nothing. He was calm, a bit curious and nervous, but so was most everyone on the boat that Astrea could read.

"He'll remain on board for the time being with Vernie," Lucian said. "Until we need him."

Valen gave Astrea a small smile, as if he knew she was unsure about this entire situation. "I'm here to help how I can. I've promised the commander I'll stay out of the way." He hesitated, then said, "Do be careful out there, yes?"

Astrea turned away from Valen, staring out at their target and the small boats all speeding toward land. She needed to focus, and that would not happen when she was concerned about her father being around the mission.

"I think we're ready, Commander," Jin said, his gloved hand finding Astrea's. "Let's get out there before we lose too much light."

The boats that would take them to shore held twelve at a time, including whoever was controlling the motor. They were the perfect size for their party and their pilot.

The whole team sat around the edges of the boat. Astrea was squished between Jin and Cressida. Gray light and heavy wind beat down on them, and tiny droplets of freezing water licked Astrea's exposed cheeks. She didn't dare reach into her pocket for her head covering, though. Oh, no. She might just lose it. Besides, this boat was far worse than the large one they'd spent days on. This one was small, fast, and felt entirely unstable. Any extra movement would probably make her lose her lunch.

"I fucking hate the water," Cressida mumbled, so low Astrea almost didn't hear her.

"I hate *this* water," Astrea whispered back, holding onto both Cressida and Jin's hands.

Jin leaned down toward her. "Almost there."

Across from her, Adi shifted uncomfortably. But soon, as Jin promised, they approached the beach. The pilot brought them as close as he could, and the boat abruptly came to a stop as it hit the shore. Other boats were doing the same, with soldiers climbing out and heading to where a large camp was being set up.

With Jin's help, Astrea climbed out. Water splashed up to her ankles. But her boots were built for the water and snow and cold, and Astrea barely noticed if not for the sound. Jin helped Cressida out next, and Balthazar climbed out behind her.

"This is where we'll return for the night," Lucian explained as their group headed for the makeshift camp. Several white tents were already up, and groups of soldiers were assembling more. "It'll be our rendezvous point."

"No going back to the ship?" Cressida asked.

"Better that we stay here so we can head back out at first light. We may have numbers, but there's much ground to cover," the commander said.

"Lucian!" called a familiar Thasian voice. Rami headed up the beach, determination in every step. She was dressed in much darker gray than her former husband but still bundled up. She sized him up, then shook her head. "That looked better on you back in the old days."

With a sigh, Lucian said, "I'm here for a mission. I'm not taking your bait."

She grinned, a warm chuckle making her breath fog in front of her face. "Not in the mood for a few jabs?"

"Not when there's work to do," he said.

"So *serious*, Commander," Rami mused, and the corners of Lucian's mouth quirked up ever so slightly.

This was a far cry from their fight a few days before. Had Lucian actually taken Astrea's advice and listened to Rami? Could he even have apologized?

"Where's your crew?" Lucian asked Rami.

"Organizing with the rest of the Tornamians," she said. "I thought I'd spend the day with you lot, if you'll have me."

"If you think they're comfortable without you leading the way," he said.

She waved a dismissive hand. "They're adults; they don't need me babysitting. They'll be fine."

"Anjou should be ashore with the snowmobiles already," Zephyrine said. "Let's find him."

"Snowmobiles?" Adi asked, perking up a bit.

"You're not driving," Zephyrine said.

"Why not?"

"Because you crashed the last time I ever gave you keys to one," she said. "Come along."

Snowmobiles? Astrea thought. The rocky beach under Astrea's boots turned to hard, frozen ground as she hurried after the others. The snow here wasn't very thick, but beyond the camp and on the horizon, the white landscape gleamed.

Zephyrine led them through the throngs of soldiers and past the newly erected tents and fires, aiming for where a row of strange vehicles sat. They looked almost like bigger, thicker motorcycles, only with treads and not wheels. Even the handlebars and mechanical bits were an awful lot like the motorcycle Astrea had once shared with Jin.

Oh, how she longed for those days. An easy Kalamian summer day. Well, easy except for her void mage stalker. But still, that seemed like such a simple time.

"There you are!" called a man. With the fur-lined hood on his jacket pulled tight, Astrea could barely make out his face. "My wife finally decides to show up."

"Didn't want to waste my time waiting around for you if you weren't going to be ready, Anjou," Zephyrine said. "Are these good to go?"

Astrea hadn't seen Anjou Lazzaro since they parted ways all the way down in the Taipoli Islands. He still looked like most Kalamian men: average height and a sun-tanned complexion. But with the way he was bundled up and their one brief meeting months before, she wouldn't have recognized him if not for Zephyrine leading the way over to him.

Since arriving in the north, Anjou had been putzing around Novaria and along the Helosian border, collecting and disseminating information on behalf of their cause. He was the one who'd found out about the aetherium in the Badlands. Astrea had deduced that Anjou and Zephyrine ran some kind of information network throughout the continent.

"Just finishing gassing them up," he said coolly. His brown eyes settled on Zephyrine, then flicked over the group. "You're all going out?"

"And many others," Zephyrine said.

"I've only got ten for now. More will be unloaded soon."

"We can double up. Prioritize getting the other teams moving, too," Zephyrine said. "How long do you need?"

"Another fifteen minutes, then they'll be ready."

"Perfect, that's enough time for me to check in with the general and see where we're going first," Lucian said. "Thank you, Lord Lazzaro."

A quarter of an hour. A quarter of an hour, and then they'd be on the hunt for this supposed aetherium. Astrea just hoped they'd find it.

The meeting with the Novarian general had been smooth enough, providing Astrea with a better overview of the islands and what the plan actually was. While they were on the largest of the isles, the coalition forces had split up to cover as much ground as possible. Each island was being divided into a grid, with teams being assigned to different areas to keep this hunt organized.

The general had also been happy to report there was no sign of the Zaikudi and Nazarov in any of the nearby waters. There was, however, the issue of distance from the mainland and other ships, as well as ongoing weather issues. The general had warned them that radio communication with other fleets and bases would be limited at this distance, but the coalition would continue monitoring the situation at all hours of the day. It didn't make Astrea feel *great*, but given the circumstances, they'd have to do their best and stay vigilant.

And now they were on their way back out of the general's warm tent, into the frigid afternoon air. They had their assigned section of the island. They were to go northeast, toward a rocky and somewhat mountainous area. Balthazar had thought it would be the best place to begin looking for aetherium, as there were likely deposits in caves and tunnels much like the ones down in the Badlands.

"You know," Balthazar said as they approached Anjou's snowmobiles again, "Lodestar may have had a hand in building these, but I've never actually gotten to drive one."

"Because that makes me confident," Cressida said as she joined her father at one vehicle. "If you crash, Ma will kill you."

Balthazar grinned. "Don't I know it."

With a small shake of her head, Astrea followed Jin to the snowmobile next to the Nikaphoroses. Jin climbed on first, then Astrea climbed on behind him. It was significantly higher than that old motorcycle they'd ridden on in Kalama, like the rear was a perfectly raised seat so her line of sight wasn't entirely blocked by Jin's broad shoulders.

Much to Astrea's surprise, Lucian and Rami got on another vehicle. The twins shared, as did Adi and Marko, with Adi in front despite Zephyrine's earlier jab. Zephyrine took her own snowmobile for herself.

Anjou Lazzaro strolled around their six snowmobiles, passing out helmets. Astrea took one when offered. As she was about to put it on, Jin said, "Wait."

"What?" she asked.

"Put your hood and mask on first." When she gave him a confused look, he added, "You'll thank me."

Astrea removed the head covering out of her pocket, then pulled it over her head. It was a snug fit, and she really didn't love the feeling of the thick material on her face. But she would do as Jin suggested, discomfort be damned. It was only then, when she had her braid also tucked up under the fabric, that she slid the helmet on. It only added to her discomfort, but she tried to ignore it. She slid the small clear visor down over her eyes. Jin had done the same, as had everyone else.

"Ready?" Jin yelled over to Lucian, who was just two bikes down.

The commander signaled for them to move.

Jin revved their snowmobile's engine. Astrea slid her arms around his waist, holding on for dear life as the vehicle lurched forward and started across the desolate landscape.

<h1 style="text-align:center">CHAPTER 32</h1>

Bleak scenery raced by them as Jin navigated the snowy terrain. Astrea was immediately grateful for her hood, mask, and the helmet's visor. *Whoever had thought to add that was a genius,* she thought. She was miserable enough *with* them, let alone without.

The sun sank slowly in the sky as their group continued northeast. The sloping hills began to grow steeper, and in the distance, low mountains rose up on the horizon. Even taller ones peaked behind them, spreading farther north, east, and west. The island wasn't that large, at least to Astrea's knowledge, but the mountains seemed unnaturally tall. Maybe the work of some long-forgotten Earthmovers, if they had managed to ever get out to these islands.

They continued speeding that way, slowing only as the terrain became rougher. They went as far as they could on their snowmobiles, which brought them close to the bottoms of the mountains. By the time they stopped altogether, Astrea thought it might be a five minute walk to their destination. It wasn't terrible. In fact, the whole thing was rather impressive.

As Jin cut the engine and took his helmet off, Astrea finally let go of his waist and pulled her helmet off, too. The wind wasn't as bad around here, so she tugged off the hood and mask, replacing them with the earmuffs in her bag.

"We'll need to be closer if we're going to find that ore." Balthazar gestured at the sky, then asked, "We have enough time? That took longer than I thought."

They'd been away from the camp for maybe an hour, but the sky was beginning to darken with promises of snow and twilight.

"We'll make sure we do," Lucian said as he dismounted. "I don't want to waste even a single minute. Where do we begin?"

Balthazar shot Jin a questioning look, then shook his head. "Let's see if we can find any kind of cave. That'll be as good a place as any to start."

They headed for the base of the mountains. A few evergreen trees dotted the landscape—though they weren't nearly as tall as those Astrea had seen in the Antare Mountains—and what little vegetation there may have been on the ground was surely dormant and dead at this point in the season. Jin did what he could to melt the thickest banks of snow, which helped make their movements somewhat easier.

"This way," Balthazar said, heading north. "I can feel it."

"How far?" Lucian asked.

"Not too far."

They trekked on for some ways, until the snowmobiles were just a dark blob in the distance. It was only then that there was a break in the rockface, an entrance barely wide and tall enough for two people to fit through.

"We should move the snowmobiles closer," Zephyrine said.

As Jin, his team, and Marko split off to do so, Astrea stayed back with the others. A sudden gust of wind nipped at her cheeks and pulled at her braid, pulling some of the finer hairs out and whipping them around her face. Astrea tried to smooth them back, but her gloved hands weren't much help.

"Can you feel anything from here?" Lucian asked the Nikaphoroses. "Any metal?"

"I can always feel some," Balthazar said. "The real question is what's down there."

Lucian frowned. "Down?"

"Certainly doesn't feel like it's on the surface," Cressida said.

The commander huffed, though the sound was mostly drowned out by the roar of the snowmobile engines. The others came to a stop a couple dozen feet away, then turned the vehicles off and hopped back down to the ground. With that settled, Balthazar took the lead and started in through that opening.

Lucian pulled off his gloves and summoned light over his palm, and Jin summoned his fire. Combined, the starlight and flames cast a strange, white-red glow over the passageway. It continued up a ways, darkness swallowing up any traces of light. Besides the ice and snow, the stony walls were bare—but not metallic.

"We should go farther in," Balthazar said. "Something's this way."

With Balthazar and Lucian at the front, they headed deeper into the side of the mountain. Zephyrine followed, then Cressida and the twins. Astrea and Jin stayed near the back with Adi and Marko, and Astrea summoned her light, too.

The deeper they went, the thicker the darkness stretching out ahead of them became. The snow on the ground disappeared entirely, leaving dark gray rock underfoot. Pressure settled on Astrea's sternum, a hint of panic as the shadows around them surged. But it wasn't void magic, nor was it dreamwalking. It was just that intense darkness she still despised after all these months.

"You're sure something's here?" Zephyrine asked.

"Positive," Cressida said.

Astrea's left forearm had begun to ache, especially right below her elbow. She frowned. Up ahead, Cressida stretched her arms out to either side, then pushed her shoulders back.

"Ground's slanting down," Balthazar called over his shoulder. "Watch your steps."

Down, deeper into the earth and darkness. Balthazar *had* said whatever metal he sensed wasn't at the surface.

"Path is curving." Balthazar's next warning echoed more.

Glancing up, Astrea found the ceiling soaring higher, at least two men tall, maybe more.

"Seems only somewhat natural," Adi said as he took in the tunnel. "The bends are too perfect to be from nature, and yet the path isn't quite perfect enough to be made by magic."

Astrea tried to assess whatever it was Adi saw, but to her, it all looked the same. Dark stone lit by their magic, the occasional trail of ice covering what had to be cracks in the walls. Jagged rocks hung from the ceiling, now easily two stories tall.

They continued on like that until eventually, the ground began to flatten out. Ahead, an archway narrowed the tunnel. Balthazar and Lucian took tentative steps forward, their forms blocking whatever lay on the other side. Lavender surprise lit up Balthazar's aura.

"What is it?" Astrea called to him.

"Not aetherium," Balthazar said over his shoulder. Then he went deeper inside.

Not aetherium?

They all shuffled through the opening in a single-file line. It was a cavern—not a large one, but a cavern nonetheless. And instead of finding that near-black metallic stone she'd half-hoped to find, Astrea found . . .

"It's iron," Cressida said, her voice flat. Rusty annoyance spiked above her head. "We came all the way down here for iron?"

Of course they wouldn't find aetherium on their first try. That was just how things went for them, and surely there would be plenty of untapped resources on this island that Balthazar and other Metalli would have to sort through first. Still, Astrea couldn't help but be disappointed.

"All untouched, by the looks of it." Balthazar moved toward one of the walls, his gloved fingers trailing down a section of red-brown rock. "Your governments' patrols have never explored this?" he asked Lucian and Rami.

Lucian shrugged one shoulder. "That, I can't say."

"Surely some of the patrols, even if our specific one never did," Rami said to Lucian. "Surely someone. Why leave all this here?"

"It might've been too hard to excavate in the past," Balthazar mused. "Or your people are terrible explorers."

A bemused grin lit up Rami's face, but Lucian grimaced.

"Anyway," the commander said, "if this isn't what we're looking for, we need to keep going."

"There's still some ahead of us," Balthazar said. "I can feel it."

Adi was already moving that way, Lucian and Balthazar not far behind. Cressida started forward, but Astrea touched her shoulder, making her jump.

"Hey," Astrea said. "Your arm hurts?"

"It's just sore," Cressida replied. "The cold."

"Let me ease it. Keep you focused."

At Cressida's small nod, Astrea set her hand on her left forearm. Light glowed around her fingers, then seeped under Cressida's coat. They both sighed, Cressida in relief and Astrea in pain as her own body ached more.

"Thanks, Az."

"Let me know if you need more."

Jin set one hand between Astrea's shoulder blades, nudging her forward. "Let's go," he said. "Keep up with the others."

The next path, instead of going deeper into the earth, stayed flat. Divots and crevices in the wall revealed more iron deposits. Astrea's breath clouded in front of her face. They eventually came upon another room, this one filled with stalagmites and stalactites.

"No aetherium," Cressida said, turning around in a circle. "I don't see it."

"So we've wasted our time," Marko drawled from the back of the group. "Fantastic."

"Not a waste when we need to scour the island for the ore," Lucian said. "It's one spot we can mark off."

The commander removed his pack. After rummaging around in it, he pulled out a folded-up paper and pencil. A map, Astrea realized, as he set it up against the wall and began making careful marks on it.

One spot out of how many here? Hundreds? Thousands? Even with all the other teams out looking, there had to be a better way. There had to be a more efficient option. Could they somehow give Mariya better access to the island? Fly her around at low altitude to try to give her a sense of where the aetherium might be? No, surely someone had already thought of that and ruled it out.

Still, Astrea asked, "There's not a better way to do this?"

"None safe enough," said Lucian, folding the map up and putting it back into his knapsack.

"We should get going," Jin said. "We'll be losing light quickly."

Their trek back up to the cave's entrance was much quicker, but a thick blanket of darkness had settled over the world. Had it taken *that* long to get down there and look at everything? Astrea hadn't thought so.

"Skies damn it," Rami muttered.

"We should stay here, in the caves," Lucian said. "Wait until first light to head back to camp."

"With what supplies?" Jin asked. "No firewood, barely any rations, no sleeping bags or extra insulation."

"And risk going out in the dark? In the cold?" Lucian challenged. "That's the better idea?"

"Temperature hasn't dropped that much yet," Zephyrine said. "And the snowmobiles have lights."

"Weak ones," the commander replied.

"And we have a Fireweaver and two Lightbringers," said Rami with a huff. "Honestly, Lucian, we used to get into far worse situations with far fewer mages. The ride here wasn't rough. Even with just you and Astrea, and the existing lights, we'll be fine."

"Worst case, if we crash, we send up a flare," Adi said. "Someone can come dig us out."

Lucian narrowed his eyes. "Fine."

"Thank the skies," Cressida muttered. "Because either way, I was not staying out here."

After Astrea climbed onto the snowmobile behind Jin, she made quick work of changing from her earmuffs to that damn hood. Then she strapped her knapsack back on, took the helmet from Jin, and adjusted the visor. And with light building over one hand, she slid her other arm around Jin's waist.

As the vehicle surged forward into the cold night, Astrea let her light spread out before her, low on the ground but bright, far brighter than the weak headlights they were working with. Lucian did the same, creating a tapestry of white and blue on the snow. As they sped away into the night, Astrea glanced back over her shoulder at those mountains again. Surely, somewhere on this island, they'd find the aetherium. And hopefully they'd find it fast, before Nazarov and his people showed up.

Despite it barely being the seventh evening bell, night had fully settled over the island. Strong winds had slowed them down, and though they'd made it back to camp in one piece, they had found the camp itself not withstanding the weather very well. Despite the darkness, they'd been ferried back to their respective ships for the night, a safer and warmer option with the weather moving in.

Now, dressed in warm, dry clothes and seated in the officers' dining room, Astrea stared out at the window at the island. Well, what she could make out of it in the darkness, anyway. The moon and stars did little to show the landscape, just a faint outline beyond the other ships.

She'd asked Jin about how to make the search for aetherium more efficient. He hadn't had any ideas, either, and had suggested they be patient. He meant well, but how could they be patient when they were working against the clock? They had gotten to these isles first, and this was their opportunity to figure out how to get rid of the aetherium here.

Maybe if they couldn't find it, Nazarov wouldn't either. The emperor wouldn't. Maybe it was too difficult a task with so much ground to cover, or maybe the aetherium didn't even exist here at all. After all, Nazarov was going on old stories and hunches. Would ancient Paragonians really have found a way all the way out here?

Astrea yawned, trying to focus on Cressida, Adi, Lennor, and Jin's chatter. They'd finished dinner a while earlier, but sitting up here was better than their cramped cabins. Now, her friends spoke of nothing consequential, just shared interests like sports and cakes. Mundane, meaningless topics that at least seemed to offer them a distraction.

What was Theo doing back in Talmaris? Had he managed to convince the other Paragonian defectors to take their offer of assistance and, if people wanted it, assimilation into larger society?

Would any of those people want that? What if they didn't? Would they still demand Astrea become their next One? Would they buy into the facade she and Jin were trying to portray as benevolent outside leadership, even if it was a role they didn't want?

Who was Astrea to offer those people anything? Assistance, sure, but she was hardly the right person despite her lineage. She knew nothing about these people. This organization. Even with all she'd learned, she didn't *know* anything about them or their lives.

"Az?" Jin said quietly.

She blinked. "Yeah?"

"Did you not hear . . . ?"

His unanswered question hung heavy over their silent table. Astrea followed his gaze to where Valen stood awkwardly behind Cressida and Adi's chairs.

"I'm sorry," he said, "I don't mean to disturb you all . . . but Vernie has let me off my leash for a few moments while they speak with the commander." Valen gestured over to a table on the other side of the room, where Vernie, Lucian, Balthazar, and Zephyrine sat. Lucian's attention occasionally flicked their way.

"And?" Astrea asked, the word harsher than she meant for it to be.

"I was hoping to speak with you," Valen said. "You and your husband both. It's important. I promise not to keep you too long. Please?"

Astrea had no good reason to deny Valen a chance to speak with them. She pushed out of her seat, stepping around Jin when he motioned for her to do so. When they passed Lucian's table, Astrea gave him a small nod, as if to say, "It's fine." His brows knitted together anyway.

Valen led them out of the dining room, then a dozen feet down the hall to another door. He opened it, revealing a small room that looked like it was only used for storage. There were no windows, no people, and barely any furniture other than the handful of chairs and a fully stocked shelf in the corner.

"Again, I'm sorry to interrupt you," Valen said, tucking his hands awkwardly into the pockets of his black trousers, "but I've had much time to think today."

"About?" Jin asked.

"About our problem with the void mages your friend Theo is leading."

"I'd hardly call him my friend," Jin said. "Grudging ally, perhaps."

"Well, be that as it may, Vernie explained to me that last they heard, the defectors were still deciding whether or not they should take you up on your offer."

"That's what we heard, too," Astrea said.

"And you don't want to lead them," Valen said, more a statement than a question.

"Not really." Astrea crossed her arms over her chest. "Why?"

"They don't know I'm alive," Valen said. "But they could."

Understanding washed over Astrea. Valen wanted to step in. Be their leader.

But was that a good idea? Had this all been some long-planned ploy to get Astrea and the others to hand over control of the Paragon to him?

Part of her didn't think so. It was clear that he hadn't enjoyed his childhood in the Paragon, and he'd seemed so happy being outside the organization if that old picture proved anything. But what was one picture? What proof were stories from a man Astrea had never met?

"You want to lead the Paragon?" Jin asked.

"Skies, no," Valen said with a laugh. "No, that's the last thing I ever wanted, truth be told. But I am, technically, next in line by their laws. And you two don't want to do it. You don't have to."

"What if they accept the offer the grand duke and Princess Eliana have extended to them?" Astrea asked. "What if they want to leave the Paragon?"

"Then we all win," Valen said. "But if they do not, I thought this might be a better solution. If it's something you all and the grand duke would allow."

"As much as I can appreciate what that offer means, Valen," Jin said, "I don't know that it's something we can accept at present. There's an awful lot we don't know about you yet. Surely you can understand that with all we've witnessed, simply taking you up on your offer isn't an option."

"I understand." Teal understanding wavered around Valen's dark hair. "I certainly don't blame you for being cautious. But I thought it best I talk to you two first, let you think on it."

"We need time to talk to the others," Astrea said. "When we're back in Talmaris."

"Of course. I assumed that would be the case." Valen offered her a small smile. "I'd like to help. However I can. I know the commander brought me here because he thought I might be useful somehow, but I cannot fathom what *I* might do on that island. I have little survival training, no magic, and not all that much knowledge about the Paragon at present. Even my time spent here all those years ago is basically useless. This seemed like an obvious way for me to contribute."

A much more personal way to contribute, Astrea thought. One that would benefit her and Jin most, at least in what they personally wanted out of life. Not the responsibility of leading foreign people. At least Valen *was* one of them, even if he hadn't lived among them in many years. Would he be willing to take the grand duke's advice and suggestions?

Work with the Novarian government and other leadership to find some solution for the Paragonian defectors?

Was it even their place to step into such positions? Even if Valen was one of them, wouldn't it be better to have someone more familiar with their ways and ideas leading them? Someone not like Nazarov, and not even like Ninette or Theo necessarily, just someone who was reasonable, balanced, and more willing to open the Paragon up to change and opportunity.

"You look unsure," Valen said to Astrea.

She huffed. "It's a lot. I understand why we've offered them a choice of where to live and assistance, but is that the right choice? Should we be trying to help them stay together?"

"They can stay together if they wish," Valen said.

"Are we taking their choice away, though?" she pressed. "Don't they have a culture? Bonds? Ties to where they've lived? Who are we to demand they give that up or suffer the consequences?"

He gave her another of those small smiles. "You really are like your mother, worried about so many others," he said. "She would be proud of you, of all this you're working to achieve. I know . . ." He sucked in a shaky breath as blue sadness and mint relief tangled around him. "I know what Mister Nikaphoros said is true, about my role in your life. It's nice to . . . to know you did not inherit much from my side of the family."

A knot lodged itself in Astrea's throat.

"The Paragonian culture is not what you think it might be," he continued. "It's insulated, too insulated, no room to breathe. Steeped in fear and contempt for the outside world, blended with traditions members have brought in from their home cultures over centuries. Many have complained about this stagnation for decades while leadership does nothing."

She must not have looked convinced, because Valen said, "The Paragon are sick, Astrea. The continent is sick and has been for a long time. There needs to be some healing, and that can't happen with militaristic groups seething in their own isolation or with those in charge looking to dominate and destroy."

Maybe Valen would be a better leader than she thought.

"Even if you don't step in as The One," Jin said, "I'll talk to the grand duke about having you take on a more advisory role. It sounds like you still know your people well, even after all these years."

"It's hard to forget that type of environment," Valen said. "One that suffocates you so much."

Jin nodded. "That, I understand."

"Well, it's getting late," Valen said. "I'll let you two get on with your night. I'm sure Vernie will be searching for me."

When they returned to the hallway, they found Vernie leaning across the opposite wall. They smiled at Astrea, then said, "Mister Ramkas, the commander says it's time to retire for the evening."

"Very well," Valen said. "Good night, Astrea. Varojin."

As Astrea watched her father retreat down the corridor, she didn't know what to think, what to feel. He seemed sincere. He seemed to know what he was talking about. But her aching heart didn't know what to do anymore. She just wanted to see this through, make it out the other side in one piece. Stop Nazarov and Emperor Aelius, then figure out her family drama when the threat of aetherium wasn't hanging over the continent.

CHAPTER 33

Over the last several days, Astrea had spent more time in the snow and cold than she probably had in her entire life. They had little to show for it, other than more and more spots on the map marked off as not having any aetherium at all.

That was something.

Their ship had just sailed around to the northwestern side of the main island, where another group was setting up a secondary base camp. It was easier, the coalition agreed, to split each island up into quadrants and establish multiple bases. Groups would ultimately have to travel less and could thus spend more time searching each day.

The smallest of the islands—eight of them in total—had been completely cleared. That left the largest two to check. With so many more soldiers and mages, surely they would find the aetherium soon. If it was here at all.

Astrea shifted from foot to foot as she watched Balthazar, Jin, Adi, and Zephyrine gas up the snowmobiles. Towering mountains lay ahead of them; she didn't much see the point in bringing the vehicles, but Lucian insisted they ride as far as they could.

"When all this is done," Cressida said as she joined Astrea, "I'm going to demand my parents give me part of my inheritance so I can take a nice, long, and very luxurious vacation in the Taipoli Islands."

"That miserable?" Astrea asked with a small laugh. She'd been giving Cressida regular healing treatments in their time up here, enough to help stop the deep ache that always built up Jin her left arm.

"I'm cold. I somehow always end up wet despite what everyone here claims about this all being waterproof." Cressida gestured down at her all-white outfit. "My arm doesn't like it. Even my skin doesn't. I need to bathe in a tub of lotion."

"I don't know about giving you part of your inheritance for a vacation," Balthazar said as he strode over to them, peach amusement swirling around his wide form. "Seems like a waste."

"Doesn't a girl deserve the best when she's helped save the world?" Cressida retorted.

Balthazar laughed, a warm, deep sound. "Well, when you put it like that . . ."

Astrea couldn't help but smile, too. It was nice, seeing Cressida in better spirits again. She'd been joking around more the last couple of days, at least with Astrea, Balthazar, and Lennor. Maybe things wouldn't ever be the same, but to see Cressida coming back to life made the deep ache in Astrea's bones lessen just a little.

"All ready to go," Adi said as he and Jin approached.

Jin gazed up at the sky. Heavy gray clouds blocked out most of the early morning sun. "Looks like we're going to get snow."

Astrea tried to ignore the wind as it gusted, as if it was confirming that indeed, the weather was about to take a turn for the worse. "Where are Lucian and the others?"

"Here!" the commander called, right on cue. "We should get going."

"What took you so long?" Jin asked.

"Vernie brought some extra supplies to shore," Lucian said. "And Valen needed reassurance that we won't venture too far."

"Why?" Astrea asked.

"He seems worried about the terrain," Rami replied. "As if he's the one out here risking his life."

"Or maybe worried about Astrea," Balthazar said.

"Or that," Rami conceded. "At least Valen warned us about what he could, marked it off on the maps."

Since their talk in that storage closet a few nights before, Astrea's father had been trying to help where he could. He didn't remember the exact layouts of the islands, but he was helping flag what he could on maps for various teams, to try to give them some guidance. It had even saved one team from accidentally missing a cave, or so some of the coalition leaders had reported.

They mounted the snowmobiles, then took off one by one, Lucian and Rami in the lead. Astrea rested her head on the wide expanse of Jin's back as they rode, trying to take in the frozen scenery as they went. Aside from the much higher mountain peaks and evergreens growing in thick clusters, this part of the island looked much the same.

On and on they went, past the trees and closer to the mountains. Astrea wasn't so sure they'd find much. The whole thing was beginning to feel pointless. Maybe they'd been wrong to spend so much time here. Her only consolation was that, before they'd left Talmaris, Veiko had gotten confirmation of more coalition strikes against the Helosian army. They were hitting the Badlands especially hard—including targeting known aetherium caches—as much as they could while launching attacks from the Taipoli Islands and Tornama.

Part of Astrea wondered if they should go down there to help, where they knew aetherium actually was. Where she could be of use, healing soldiers and people trying to fight back against Emperor Aelius. Out here, in these snowy wastelands, it felt more like they were playing at hero rather than doing anything useful.

After an hour of riding, the terrain began to form small hills. It grew more uneven the farther north they went, until finally, they could take their snowmobiles no farther. Anywhere else they went would be on foot.

"Last night, I was speaking with one of the pilots who did an initial flyover of the island," Lucian said as they all began dismounting the vehicles. "She was telling me that these mountains were too foggy to see clearly, but she thought she saw dark spots. It may be worth going up."

"For what?" Rami asked. "Would aetherium really be at the top of a mountain?"

Lucian sighed, but it wasn't the usual annoyed huff he always made at his former spouse. No, it was a softer sound, and even the way he looked at Rami softened. "We can't leave until we know for certain."

"We won't have to scale all the way to the top for us to know if it's worth it," Cressida said. "Just far enough."

Rami waved a hand.

"I offered for you to stay behind today," Lucian said, almost gently. "Do you want me to take you back?"

"No," Rami said. "I'm just frustrated."

"Makes two of us," Astrea mumbled.

"See?" Rami said. "Astrea gets it."

"I am, too," Lucian said. "We'll be heading back to the capital in the next couple of days. Let's do our due diligence, alright?"

They started up the slope of the mountain. Jin melted the thickest areas of snow, and Adi, Balthazar, and Cressida used their magic to smooth out the roughest patches of rock. It reminded Astrea of the earthen elevator Adi had once made down near the Path of Ruin, though here, there was no need for such a display. The cliff faces weren't that steep.

By the time they were halfway up, snow flurries started to fall. Astrea may not have liked the way her hood and mask felt, but skies, if they didn't keep her face warm. Up this high, the wind was even worse. Whatever Lucian's pilot thought she saw, she better have been right.

It was another hour before they found somewhat flat earth again. It seemed almost like a path, like a ramp purposefully put there at some point. They followed it down a little ways, but it stopped at a dead end that turned into a sharp drop-off. So they headed back up, circling around the mountain.

"Have we gone high enough?" Rami asked when they stopped for a small break. "Can you feel anything?" she asked the Nikaphoroses.

"Something . . ." Balthazar murmured.

Orange anxiety spiked above Lennor's head.

"Something here . . . doesn't feel right," Adi said.

"In what way?" Lucian asked.

"Like . . ." Adi's eyebrows furrowed. "It's hollow."

"The way the aetherium feels hollow to Stargazers?" Jin asked.

"No, like the earth," Cressida said.

"Could it be a base again?" Zephyrine asked. "Like the one we found out west. Some old abandoned Paragon site?"

Rami's eyebrows furrowed. "Inside the mountain?"

Astrea fiddled with the buttons on her coat. It certainly seemed possible . . . but up here? How had any ancient Paragonians gotten here? The sailing trip alone would've taken some time, especially without steam boats. And during war? Or was this from before the Great Wars?

"We should look for an entrance," Lucian said. "Maybe that pilot was right. Maybe there's something here after all."

"Would there be an entrance up here?" Lennor asked.

"Only one way to find out." Lucian shouldered his knapsack, then headed higher up the slope.

Groaning, Astrea tugged her head covering back on and began to follow him. Cressida was surely right about that vacation.

The path spiraled up the back side of the mountain. Jin moved to the front of the line and began clearing snow again, as it was beginning to build quickly with the growing storm. As he did, dark stones appeared beneath their feet. The path turned sharply to the right, and there . . .

Dark pillars marked the sides of a hole.

A hole, in the top of a mountain.

Balthazar took a few tentative steps toward that opening, then shook his head. "Well, that explains why it feels like it does."

"Is it one of the volcanoes?" Astrea asked. "Is it dormant?" She really, truly did not want to be around if this thing was going to erupt.

"Doesn't look like it's erupted in a long time," Cressida said, toeing at the ground with her boot. "And I don't feel any tremors."

"I don't feel any heat, either," Jin said.

Yellow worry sparked in the air around some of the others as Balthazar said, "I don't think we were entirely wrong about it being a base. Come look."

They all moved closer to the edge. Jin held onto Astrea tightly as she leaned forward. Sure enough, there were stairs spiraling down into the darkness below.

"What the fuck," Marko muttered under his breath.

"Is it safe?" Lucian asked. "To go in, I mean."

Lennor whipped her head around to look at the commander. "Seriously? You want to go down a set of stairs into a *volcano*?"

"Just look at this," he said to her, motioning to the pillars. "They're not unlike the ones we found in the Antare Mountains."

"They're not metal, I can tell you that much. But"—Cressida gestured into the mouth of the volcano—"there's a ton of metal in there."

"This is no coincidence," Lucian said. "I would bet my entire fortune that this is an old Paragon site."

"Are you suddenly a rich man, Luce?" Rami asked. "I thought you weren't one who cared much about fortunes."

Astrea didn't miss the jab in Rami's tone. If the commander cared, he didn't let it show. Instead, he said, "No, I'm not, but still."

A volcano. A skies damned volcano, on these skies damned islands, with *metal* inside? If Victor Nazarov was hunting for any place on the islands, it would surely be this.

Which meant they had to go inside.

"We won't take those stairs," Balthazar said after a moment. "We'll make new ones."

He, Adi, and Cressida worked together, layering new steps made from the inside walls of the volcano. They were narrow, but the three managed to add a small railing on the inside spiral to prevent anyone from falling into that terrible darkness.

"I see the entrance," Balthazar called from where he was already heading down the stairs. "A large arch. It's not far. Come on."

Rami began her descent, and everyone else followed. Except for Astrea and Jin. Astrea's feet wouldn't move.

"You good?" Jin asked.

That darkness . . . Her chest tightened. She didn't need a nightlight every night anymore, but this was too dark, like those skies forsaken tunnels. She shook her arms out.

"Let's go," she said, taking Jin's gloved hand and leading the way. She had come too far to stop now. They needed to find this aetherium, and they needed to prevent anyone else from ever using it. To prevent it from hurting anyone else, like Cressida and Jin. Like Saros.

Lucian's light spread across the chasm, yet the shadows seeped in around Astrea. She pulled on her light, letting it flicker and dance as brightly as she could tolerate. They all stepped carefully, slowly, as they descended to where Balthazar waited for them on a platform near an archway.

Up ahead, Rami slipped and cried out. Astrea's heart skittered, her muscles tensing for her to run to Rami's aid even as her feet froze her in place. White panic flared around Lucian, his light disappearing. He lurched forward, grabbed Rami's forearm, and hauled her away from the precarious railing back toward the wall.

"Careful," he said, breathless as he stared down at her.

"I know," she said, but she held his gaze for a beat longer than necessary. She yanked her arm away. "I know."

"Shit." Marko rubbed his forehead. He was only a couple paces behind them. "Can we just get on with it?"

Clearing his throat, Lucian summoned his light again. Behind Astrea, Jin muttered a curse. She held her breath until she passed through the arch that led to more solid ground.

It was a narrow corridor, short enough that Jin, Adi, Balthazar, and Zephyrine all had to stoop slightly as they walked. Her light caught on the strange edges of the wall, on the jagged letters carved into the stone. Those void letters. Astrea had brought no cipher with her, but she could only imagine what stories these walls told. Stories of chaos and destruction, perhaps? Or maybe stories of a time before the Paragon's sickness, as Valen had called it?

"What the skies . . ." Lucian said as he took a few more steps forward.

Beyond her friends, Astrea could barely make out the way Lucian's light seemed to spread beyond the shape and size of the corridor.

"Well, fuck me," Cressida said.

They scrambled ahead, gaping and swearing as the passage opened to an enormous room with a rounded ceiling. It was bare bones, mostly rock and stone except for the large contraption in the middle. Astrea pulled off her head covering and took another step forward.

"It's a forge," Balthazar said, circling it. "It's a forge, Cress!"

"I can see that, Dad." Teal understanding twisted around Cressida, obscuring her white armor. "Oh, fuck me. A forge for aetherium weapons."

"How can you tell?" Rami asked.

Cressida turned, facing most of the group. "In that book we stole, it said that only powerful Sunreapers could help Metalli forge aetherium," she said. "We thought it might be possible to forgo the Sunreaper aspect if someone had a forge that generated enough heat. With modern tech, it's not that hard, but back then—"

"A volcano could generate that much heat for them," Jin finished for her.

Balthazar squatted down on the far side of the forge, examining something. Green curiosity sparkled around him, lighting up the whole room. Astrea swore that even a hint of golden joy crept into his aura, but it was gone too quickly to be sure. It wouldn't surprise her, though; Balthazar found old technology fascinating and enjoyed tinkering with things. If they had time, he probably would've loved to have stayed just to study how all this worked.

"Is that . . . even possible?" Civan asked, voice rough. "Wouldn't that be incredibly dangerous?"

"Dangerous, sure, but with the help of a Tephran?" Balthazar said as he finished circling the forge and stepped up next to Cressida. "Or with enough Tephran, I should say. They could hypothetically control the flow of the magma and harness it to activate the aetherium."

"So where's the aetherium?" Rami asked.

"There doesn't seem to be any here," Balthazar said. "Not in this room, anyway."

"What if Nazarov isn't coming here because he wants to *find* aetherium," Astrea said. "What if he's coming here for this forge?"

"Couldn't he access a more modern forge in a city?" Marko asked. "Why come all the way out here?"

"Maybe the site is important to him for some reason," Lennor said. "Like, historically. Did the books say anything about that?"

"What we have didn't even mention this place," Astrea said.

Noemi and Civan's expanded research hadn't suggested anything like this. But Lennor had a point. Maybe Nazarov was coming here for a specific purpose, one that ran deeper than just finding the aetherium. Maybe Tytas Ramkas even came to this place, and maybe that would somehow help Nazarov secure whatever power he needed to among his followers. Maybe it would be symbolic of something, crafting aetherium blades at this ancient forge.

"Do you feel anything?" Rami asked the Nikaphoroses.

"Nothing unusual about this forge, even if it's peculiar," Balthazar said. "And there's plenty of metal here, deep within this volcano. I don't know how we'd reach it."

"Could we get Mariya here somehow?" Zephyrine asked. "She could tell us specifically what it is, right? Then we won't waste our time."

"It will be difficult," Lucian said. "We could try flying here, but there's no good place to land."

"If she's willing to take a jump, Marko and I can get her down safely," Zephyrine said.

The commander nodded. "We'll have to try; I don't see another way."

Staring at the forge, Astrea twisted her head covering between her hands. They needed to get Mariya there quickly, and then they needed to destroy that forge and any aetherium one way or another.

"Excellent find, Commander," Mariya said as she settled into one of the soft dining room chairs.

Outside the ship, wind howled through the pitch darkness. By the time they'd descended the mountain and gotten back to the base camp, night had fallen. The weather had turned for the worse by the time they made it back to the boat to fill Mariya in on their excursion. Astrea shivered violently and clutched a mug of hot chocolate between her hands.

Most of the team had gone to restock their packs for the excursion they'd undertake the next morning. Only Cressida, Jin, and Lucian had remained behind.

"It wasn't *my* find," Lucian said. "But we need to get you up to that mountain first thing in the morning."

"Me?" Mariya chuckled, as if that was the funniest thing in the world. "I don't climb mountains, Lucian."

"No, but we'll fly you up, then have a couple of Tempests—"

"I'm not jumping out of a skies damn airship!"

"Mariya," Lucian grumbled, "we need you. We're running out of time. We *need* you, or are you forgetting that Stargazers are the only ones lucky enough to feel aetherium?"

"Right, lucky." Mariya rolled her eyes.

"C'mon, Mariya," Cressida said. She was seated on Astrea's left, just as cold and tired as Astrea herself. She rubbed absently at her left arm. "We really need you."

Something in Mariya's tight expression softened as she glanced at Cressida and Astrea. But then she glared at Lucian again. "Fine. But only because the situation is dire."

"Thank you," Lucian said. "Between you and Mister Ramkas, we should—"

"What?" Astrea choked out past the sip of hot chocolate she'd taken. "My father?"

"Yes," Lucian said, almost bored. "I told you I thought he might be helpful on this mission, and now he has a chance to pitch in. We need someone to read the inscriptions by the forge."

"He barely reads the language," Astrea said.

"Oh, he got at least half the words right last time we tried this," Lucian said. "It's better than us not being able to read any of it."

Astrea cursed herself for not thinking to bring Noemi's cipher with her, but an ancient forge hidden inside a volcano hadn't exactly been on her radar. She rubbed her forehead with one hand. "He told me the other day that he doesn't have many survival skills for such an environment—"

"He'll be fine surrounded by a group of very talented mages," the commander said. "It's only for a few hours at most."

"Are you sure?" Jin asked, keeping his voice low. "I know he's offered to step in for me and Az with the Paragon, but that's a lot different than bringing him out into the field. It's a risk."

"A risk I'm willing to take if it means we learn as much as we can," Lucian said. "If we're wrong about him and he tries to make a move, he'll have to contend with, as I said before, some very talented mages. We can handle one man."

Astrea wasn't so sure this was a good idea, but the commander had a point. None of them had thought to bring resources to help them translate anything they might find, so Valen was pretty much their only option.

She just hoped he was the right one.

Chapter 34

With the new day came the next step in the mission, and no one was keen on being at the mouth of a volcano a couple hours past daybreak, especially not after jumping out of an airship to get there. The only good thing about the new day was the distinct lack of snow flurries and dulled winds. It meant that, even with the cold, Astrea didn't have to wear her head covering unless they were moving fast.

Even her father didn't seem thrilled to be there. He loitered near the staircase that descended into the volcano's mouth, looking entirely ill at ease. Not that anyone could be expected to *enjoy* climbing down into such a dark, dangerous chasm, Astrea supposed. White terror, orange anxiety, and red determination snapped around him. Determination to what? See this for himself?

"Have you spoken to him much?" Rami asked, making Astrea flinch.

She glanced over to find the smuggler had practically materialized next to her. "Perhaps not as much as I should have."

"You do seem to be a woman of few words."

Astrea shrugged. She wouldn't say that about herself. She may not have been the most talkative of her friend group, but it wasn't like she was *silent*. "It's hard to know what to say to him."

"Lucian told me he wasn't around for you when you were a kid."

Now why would Lucian go around telling Astrea's personal story? She huffed.

"You didn't ask me, but I know what having a turbulent life feels like," Rami said. "Upheaval and loss, regrets and change. It's a lot. I don't blame you for keeping your distance." When Astrea frowned, Rami chuckled and said, "Take it easy on Lucian. He's just concerned. He didn't tell me your deepest, darkest secrets or anything."

"I have a feeling I wouldn't want you to know those," Astrea said, surprising herself.

Rami laughed again. "No, I'd reckon you wouldn't." She grinned, then tilted her head toward Valen. "Talk to him. Make sure the mission's a success."

Snow crunched as Rami wandered away again. Astrea shook her head. She was sure Lucian cared for her on some level, but confiding such concerns in Rami? She didn't have the energy to consider that too closely. Their relationship—Lucian and Rami's, that was—still confused her.

Instead, she pushed her shoulders back and approached Valen. "You sure you're up for this?" she asked him. The others lingered behind, explaining the situation to Mariya. "You can leave if you want."

Valen squared his shoulders. "Of course I'm not leaving," he said. "You need my help."

"We can always find another way," she lied. She hadn't been the one to propose this mission to him the night before, and she really wanted to see what he had to say for himself. Would he prove trustworthy and follow through, or would he make excuses at the last second?

Astrea and Jin had spent the last couple of nights trying to decide whether what Valen said about stepping in as hereditary leader of the Paragon was a good idea or not. If it would be necessary. If it was selfless, as he portrayed it to be, or some deeper plot.

Astrea wanted to trust her father. Skies, that did not seem like such a huge thing to ask for. But nowadays? There were very few people she actually, truly trusted.

Valen *seemed* truthful, but so had Professor Shalysko.

And then there was Raela, who Astrea had to take a gamble and trust enough to ask for the book instead of stealing it. That had paid off . . . to a degree. Astrea still woke up with nightmares about where Raela was now that Prince Kaius had her in custody.

So what was it to be with Valen? Was he, like Raela, ultimately trustworthy? Was the gamble to *fully* trust him worth it? Or would he be like the professor, who despite never fully earning their trust, easily betrayed them in the end?

That was what Astrea and Jin had spent time debating. Neither one had a good answer, other than that he had, so far, proven to be decently reliable. The commander had agreed with that assessment, as had Zephyrine, which only bolstered Astrea's confidence a little.

Valen pinned her with a look. "There is no other way, Astrea. The commander explained it to me."

"You don't *have* to help us."

"Perhaps not, but what kind of man would I be if I didn't help my daughter—and the whole continent to boot?" That determination spiked higher above his head, a harsh contrast to the low morning light. "There's a lot I regret about my life, and I won't add being scared of a volcano to the list."

Astrea averted her gaze from her father's hard expression back to the opening in the top of the mountain. Its darkness seemed even more oppressive somehow. "Did you ever run into aetherium when you still lived with the Paragon?"

"I don't think so," he said. "As I've told you, I only heard about it from old stories, and those always said all aetherium weapons had been hidden away. If my mother or brother had any, they didn't share such delicate information with me. They didn't respect me enough. I wish they had . . . I wish I could be of more use."

"Well, whatever you might be able to read when we get down there will be helpful," she said.

"I'll do my best." His voice softened as he added, "I promise. I know I haven't been there for you, Astrea, but I want you to be able to count on me now."

Astrea took in the worry lines that seemed permanently etched into his features, the subtle gray streaks in his dark hair, his icy eyes that almost reflected the blue sadness and regret swirling around him.

"It might take us a little while before we get to that point," she said slowly. "If you keep proving you're here to help, then . . . well, we'll see what the future holds. But I'm not making any promises."

"I understand completely," Valen said. "Frankly, I'd be worried if you threw all your trust into me, as much as I hope to have it soon."

Snow crunched behind them, and Jin's hand found its place between Astrea's shoulder blades. "We're ready to go down," he said.

Valen gave Astrea a tight smile. "Let's get to work, shall we?" he said before wandering over to where Lucian was instructing everyone to watch their steps.

"All good over here?" Jin asked as he and Astrea slowly moved to the back of the line.

"Fine," she said, voice low. "I think he's sincere about helping us."

"I do, too," Jin said, his voice near Astrea's ear as they started down the steps into the darkness. "We'll see how today goes. This'll be a good test."

Astrea really hoped her father passed, but she forced the thought away and focused instead on not tripping down the stairs. Her starlight flared over her left hand, and her right trailed the volcanic wall until she finally reached the safety of the landing.

As they all reached that room with the forge, Mariya mumbled something under her breath. Heavy wariness pulsed around the room, and electric excitement danced over Astrea's skin. The Stargazer moved toward the forge, her cane smacking against the stone floor with every step.

"I can't decide if whoever built this place was a genius or had a death wish." Mariya rested her cane against the side of the forge and stretched her hands out before her, almost like she was warming them in front of a fire.

"What are you—" Rami started, only for Mariya to shush her. Rami frowned.

They all waited. One heartbeat passed. Another, then another still.

"I feel it," Mariya said. "Deep within the volcano. Aetherium."

Astrea sucked in a sharp breath. It wasn't even a surprise, but still. Aetherium, here, somewhere beneath their feet. Anxiety and terror undulated around Cressida in a tangle of white and orange. Astrea took her hand and gave it a quick squeeze.

"How?" Adi asked. "Isn't it a space rock? How would it end up all the way down there?"

"The planet changes over millennia," Mariya said. "Surely an Earthmover should know that. It could have crashed here long ago and been lost to time."

"Sure, but how would anyone get it out?" he asked. "We didn't see any tunnels."

"There may be an alternate entrance somewhere closer to sea level," Balthazar said. "We'd have to check from every angle."

"Then we will," Lucian said. "We'll get more of the teams up here. We'll find it, and then we'll figure out how to destroy it. Valen, does anything jump out at you?"

Valen stood awkwardly with his hands clasped behind his back, almost like a child who was afraid to touch something and be scolded. He pressed his lips together as he studied the forge from a distance. "I've never seen anything like this, Commander."

"What about the inscriptions?" Lucian asked. "Can you read them?"

"If you give me some time, I should be able to at least get you a few phrases," Valen said, barely glancing in Astrea's direction.

"Then let's get on it," Lucian said. "We need to get moving soon."

Despite Astrea's reservations, Valen had come up with a handful of broken sentences. There were mentions of "The One's gift" and "chaos reigns," plus a few phrases that seemed connected to actually forging aetherium weapons, at least based on what Cressida and Balthazar said.

Nothing suggested the volcanic forge could do anything other than smelt metal, though the mention of "The One's gift" gave Astrea pause. The *Myths and Other Legends* book had talked about Tytas Ramkas's very first aetherium weapons being gifts from the heavens. Maybe he'd even forged them here, and that was why Nazarov was keen on coming. Maybe he thought that would secure his position as head of the Paragon.

She couldn't know for sure, so she tucked that information away for later as they waited for the small airship to land to take Mariya and Valen back to the boats. Astrea tilted her face up toward the weak sun. Even with better weather, thick clouds obscured most of the sky. All around her, warring energy surged and retreated: anxiety, relief, determination, frustration. Her skin tingled.

The airship landed on a flat patch of land beyond the base of the mountain, and as soon as the ramp unfolded and the door opened, Mariya started up into the ship. They would have to keep looking without her, as they had no adequate way to help her in the search for these tunnels. Her joints and bones hurt too much, and Lucian didn't want to risk his or Astrea's attention constantly being drawn to healing.

Valen had just headed for the ship when Lucian called, "Wait!"

Gray confusion spiked above Valen's head as he turned toward them.

"You're with us, Valen," Lucian said.

"I am?" Valen asked.

"We need the extra help," Lucian said. "This is no small task."

As Valen rejoined them a few dozen feet from the airship, he clasped his hands behind his back. "I'm not sure how much help I'll be, Commander," he said. "No magic and not much stamina . . . Won't I slow you down?"

Astrea agreed with her father. He *would* slow them down, and that was coming from her. She wasn't exactly the quickest one in the group.

"Any extra eyes will be helpful today," Lucian said. "This gives us an even number to split up, and besides, if we stumble upon any other strange encampments or forges, we'll probably need your knowledge, limited as it may be."

Maybe Lucian had a point, too.

"Well . . ." Valen squared his shoulders and lifted his chin. "It's as I told Astrea earlier, I'll help however I can. I promise to try to stay out of the way and keep up with you all."

"Good," Lucian said. "Varojin, Take Astrea, Adi, Marko, Cressida, and Valen around the northwestern side. The others and I will start from the southeast and work our way around to meet you."

After saying their goodbyes and making plans about when and where to meet if it got too dark out, Astrea and her group headed out. Cressida kept peeking over her shoulder, no doubt at Balthazar and Lennor. Orange anxiety vibrated around her head.

Astrea wished she had something comforting to say, but she didn't. They were heading out to investigate a dormant volcano in search of the void metal that had hurt them all so badly. It was ridiculous, unfathomable somehow despite seeing it all for herself.

Adjusting her knapsack, Astrea focused on Jin's broad shoulders in front of her and trudged forward. The sooner they finished this, the better.

The first few hours they were out yielded more of the same: snow and no good luck. Astrea was actually beginning to get used to this island and these hikes. Not that this would ever be her preferred way of living, but she was also capable of tolerating far more than she'd ever given herself credit for.

She swallowed a small sip of water from the canteen Jin had passed her, then offered it back to him. He drank more greedily, then shoved it back into his knapsack. It was the third such break they'd taken in as many hours. Valen seemed worse for the wear; his heavy fatigue pressed into Astrea's bones, and her muscles twinged with echoes of soreness.

"Are we good to go?" Jin asked the group.

Valen, in fact, was the only one sitting down. He'd found a decently flat, mostly dry rock to perch on a few feet from the rest of the group. When the others indicated they were ready, Valen stood with a soft groan.

"Couldn't we rip a hole in the side of this volcano and get in that way?" Marko asked. "Seems like the easier option."

"Could we?" Adi asked. "Sure. But have *you* ever tried tunneling into a mountain with no more than your magic?"

"You've tunneled underground," Marko said.

"Right, and that's soft earth, not layers and layers of heavy stone. Do you understand how much more energy that'll take?"

"Well, we need to get in there somehow," Marko said.

"Don't want to wear you two out unless necessary," Jin said, gesturing to Adi and Cressida. "Let's just get to our meeting point with Lucian before we make any decisions. I'm sure there'll be plenty of opportunities to take Marko up on his suggestion if needed."

They started up again, caught between the base of the volcano and smaller hills blocking the view of most of the northern ocean. Sharp air filled Astrea's lungs, leaving her nose and mouth in a cloud of white. Every time they'd stopped, Astrea had given Cressida a small boost with her healing to help stave off the building pain. She'd thought about offering Valen some for his aches, too, but Astrea wanted to save her strength for her best friend, who no doubt needed it more.

At the front of the group, Adi and Jin talked in hushed tones. Marko brought up the rear. Valen was sandwiched between him and where Astrea and Cressida walked side by side.

"So . . ." Valen trailed off awkwardly.

"Yes?" Cressida asked without sparing him a glance.

"Are your efforts always so silent?" he asked.

"Not much to say at the moment," Cressida replied. "I need to focus."

"Right, of course. Apologies," he said.

It was more than that, though. That orange anxiety had never left Cressida's aura. It choked the air around her, grating against Astrea's exposed skin.

"All of this is strange . . ." Valen shook his head. "My mother and brother were always bragging about our family's legacy. Stories they told focused on our ancestors' power, their ability to use the shadows and the void to their advantage against greater powers. But they never really spoke of aetherium aside old stories."

"Everyone likes the story of an underdog," Marko said. "Builds stronger bonds than some impossible and skies-given power. Gives them something to rally around and believe in, a story they can hold on to, one that validates their existing struggles and gives them hope of overcoming those very problems."

"You may have a point," Valen conceded. "Though hope is a fickle thing, isn't it? It's hard to hold onto. I've lost it many times over the years."

"Doesn't mean people shouldn't try," Marko said.

Astrea looked over her shoulder at them. They walked almost side by side, though Marko's posture remained stiff and immovable.

"Adi—" Cressida started just as Adi called her name back to her.

"Find something?" Jin asked.

Adi and Cressida both slowed. They paused, as if listening intently to the world around them. There was nothing other than the occasional gust of wind.

"There's an opening," Adi said, starting forward in quick, long strides.

"There's metal," Cressida said. "A lot of it."

Astrea hurried after them both, Jin, Valen, and Marko not far behind.

"Az, do you—" Jin started.

"No, I don't feel anyone," she said, "but if it's aetherium, I might not."

That thought was particularly disturbing to her, but she couldn't fixate on it. Even if it *was* aetherium they'd found, the chances of there being anyone else out here were low. There'd been no sign of anyone other than the coalition for nearly a whole week now. And if there *were* people, well, they'd just have to deal with it.

"Careful, Adi," Jin called as they approached a solid slab of rock, at least two heads higher than Jin.

Setting his palms on it, Adi began to trudge sideways. The rock moved with him, revealing itself to be almost like a door. A door one could only open with the help of an earth mage. Darkness waited beyond the threshold. Knapsacks rustled as Marko and Valen both dug around in theirs for flashlights. Valen's was tiny while Marko's was a small lantern.

"Stick together," Jin said as he headed through the opening. Fire ignited over his gloved palm, creating a smokeless flame that illuminated the corridor beyond the others' weak flashlights.

Astrea pulled on her light, too, its force much gentler than Jin's magical flames.

"Tell me as soon as you feel the metal," Jin said to Cressida. "Direct me as needed. We'll find it."

Find it and destroy it. That was all they needed to do. Find the aetherium in this dormant volcano, then figure out how to get rid of it forever.

Other than the occasional scuffle of boots, the corridor was eerily silent. Astrea's whole body tensed as she kept putting one foot in front of the other. They rounded one bend, then another. The deeper they went, the lower the ceiling became. Jin's and Adi's heads nearly reached it.

"Keep going," Cressida said. "I feel it, up ahead. It feels like the tunnel goes straight to it."

Jin broke into a light jog. Astrea's heart thundered in her chest, drowning out the sounds of their running. The light from Jin's fire showed the corridor widening and growing taller again, giving his head more clearance. They could almost run side by side now. Up ahead, pillars were carved into the rocky walls.

"It's in there," Cressida said, spurring Jin on.

A few dozen feet, and Jin sped past the pillars. Ahead of them lay a large cavern, its walls covered in colorful striations of brown, deep purple, and rusty red. And there, interspersed among the other hues, were chunks of dull black metal that gleamed in Jin's firelight.

Electric astonishment flickered behind Astrea as Valen said, "I've never seen anything like this before."

"This is it," Cressida said, breathless. "This is the aetherium Mariya felt."

CHAPTER 35

They'd done it. They'd found the aetherium.

Or some of it, anyway.

"Now what?" Marko asked as they moved to the middle of the cavern. "There has to be tons of this stuff here. Literally."

That was indeed the question. How were they going to destroy it here, now? They needed Balthazar and the others; maybe together, they could figure something out. They'd theorized acid would corrode the aetherium beyond usability, but how were they going to move this much to a lab where Mariya could treat it like that? Moving large vats of acid here to destroy it on-site seemed even more difficult.

"Hopefully Lucian and the others are nearby," Jin said. "It shouldn't take them much longer to get over here, unless they found their own place like this that they're dealing with."

Astrea wished more than anything that her magic could go farther and wider than her usual range, which was already painfully far beyond her body. But how nice that would be, to find Lucian that way. Or for him to find her that way.

"I can go outside and see if I can feel them," Astrea said. "Walk a little ways in their direction."

"I'll go with you," Jin said. "If you think your flashlights are enough, Marko?"

"Should you really be going on your own?" Marko asked. "What if Nazarov decides to show up now?"

"I know," Jin said. "We'll be quick, and we don't really have a choice."

"I've got another lantern in my pack," Adi said. "Go."

"I need my dad," Cressida said.

Needed him to help with that much aetherium or because of the anxiety and terror swirling around Cressida's body? Astrea wanted to go to her and wrap her in a tight hug, but she also didn't want to let on to anyone else that Cressida was upset. Because if not for those colors, Cressida looked confident. Head held high, shoulders back. So instead, Astrea flashed her a small smile.

"What should I do?" Valen asked.

"See if there are any more of these carvings like by the forge," Jin said, and Valen nodded. With that settled, Jin took Astrea's hand in his, tugging her along at a jog. "I don't want to leave them for too long. Let's be quick."

They hurried back through that winding tunnel with Jin's fire to light their way. Astrea's lungs burned with the effort. As soon as they were outside, he dismissed the flames, letting the midafternoon sun take over for him. A cold wind kicked up, biting into Astrea's exposed cheeks.

"Anything from them yet?" Jin asked as they continued east, the direction Lucian's group would be coming from.

"Nothing," Astrea said. All she felt was that wind, the fresh air, and Jin's heavy, familiar wall.

For nearly a quarter of an hour, they continued east, following the curve of the volcano's base. Ashy black rock and snow mixed under their boots. And the farther they got from that tunnel entrance, the more discomfort swirled in Astrea's belly.

"I think they must have found their own entrance," Astrea said as they came to a stop. "Or they got busy exploring other caves."

"Let's turn back," Jin said. "If they don't arrive within the hour, we'll all go look for them, together."

They started back the way they'd come, retracing their path in the thin layer of snow. Heavy silence settled over them, as if the world knew how important this next step in the mission was. Astrea really hoped Balthazar would have some idea about—

She yanked Jin back to a stop as an empty, icy cold pierced her sternum. "Void," she whispered. Was Marko a skies damned Stargazer or something?

"Here?" Jin asked.

"No, I'm lying. Yes, here!"

With a huff, Jin surveyed the area. There was nowhere for them to hide. No thick forest. No brush. Not even any particularly large boulders.

"We need to go," he said, as if that wasn't obvious.

"What about Lucian and the others? Could a void mage have them?"

"Let's hope Lucian felt it, too, if he's close enough," Jin said, already pulling Astrea into a run. "We need to get back to that cavern. Now."

They sprinted on. Astrea's pulse roared in her ears as the void moved closer, farther, closer, farther. Was it Nazarov? Had he finally shown? Was it his army, and that's what she was feeling?

"Wouldn't all the coalition forces know if the Zaikudi navy and Nazarov had—"

A rumbling boom in the distance cut her off.

"That'll be them," Jin said. "Ship cannon fire."

It came again, again, again. A steady, rhythmic chorus of explosions.

"And a lot of them, by the sound of it," he said between breaths.

Gritting her teeth, Astrea kept going, trying to ignore every new detonation and the way her thighs ached.

They had to be only a couple minutes out from those tunnels. They could get Cressida and the others, either to fight or run. Maybe together, all of them could go find Lucian and Balthazar—

Cold swallowed Astrea whole, from every angle, as red hot anger and electric excitement burned her skin. She slammed into Jin as he stopped short to avoid the shadows snaking up from the ground. Astrea pivoted to go back, only to find that inky darkness there, too. Surrounding them.

Four void mages appeared, dressed not in snowy white or Paragon black or even Zaikudi green. Their Helosian red uniforms were like fresh blood against the snow.

And there with them, two pairs of golden eyes.

Emperor Aelius and Prince Kaius, on the Lost Isles, dressed in Helosian red just the same as the void mages. Only their uniforms were trimmed in gold stitching, decorative more than practical. Astrea locked her knees as giddy anticipation slammed into her.

"My wayward son," sneered Emperor Aelius as he stepped forward. His breath came out in misty puffs. "And his wayward wife. I hear you've located some aetherium."

How could they know that?

Jin tugged Astrea into his side, half shielding her from his father and brother. Kaius and Aelius stared them down like hungry wolves, predatory and vicious even if their polished uniforms and carefully styled hair made them look more like they were getting ready to sit for an official portrait than fight in a war.

Kaius laughed. "Come now, Varojin. You think that you're going to stop us from getting what we want?" His focus settled on Astrea, making her skin crawl.

Four void mages. Two Sparkcasters, both with auras bright and full of energy. Could she do this? Take them all? Control them long enough for Jin to do something?

Astrea's fingers twitched at her side. Green curiosity and red anger flared around Kaius as he watched her. Jin still held her left hand; she moved her right. And Kaius pulled a pistol, aiming it right at her.

"Any attempts at magic from either of you and I'll shoot Miss Sovna with an aetherium bullet." Kaius smirked. "Crafted from the finest aetherium in the Badlands. Used to be part of my dagger, but I decided to repurpose it."

Astrea's blood sang.

Used to be part of my dagger.

The dagger he'd tried to kill Astrea with. The dagger that had killed Saros.

She sucked in a sharp breath. Jin squeezed her left hand as cold terror leaked out from behind his wall.

"Alright," Jin said. "No magic. No weapons. I swear."

"You do know how to listen after all," Kaius taunted. "Take us to the aetherium. I know it's around here somewhere." When Jin didn't move, Kaius motioned with his pistol. "Come on. You two in front."

With tentative steps, Jin and Astrea slipped past the Aurises and one of the void mages. Only when they were walking through the snow again did anyone follow. Astrea risked a glance back over her shoulder, finding Kaius still pointing the pistol directly at her. He sneered, though the emperor didn't spare her a second of attention.

I know it's around here somewhere. How did Kaius *know* it was around there? Was he bluffing? Had they been followed and somehow not realized it? No, she would have known if someone had been following them.

Jin still held her hand, squeezing it tight as they walked in silence. She squeezed his back, trying to convey everything in that silent, subtle motion. That she was sorry she hadn't sensed them sooner. That she was sorry they were in this situation at all. That he had to see his father, his brother, be faced with another aetherium bullet after barely surviving the first.

And when he squeezed her hand again, it seemed to say that *he* was sorry. That he knew how bad it must've been to have Kaius suggest the bullets in his pistol were made from the blade that killed Saros. That he couldn't believe they were in this situation, that he couldn't really do much of anything to get them out of it.

The team wouldn't even know who they were bringing back. Astrea *was* their Lightbringer, responsible for warning them of intruders. And now, she couldn't warn them at all.

As they returned to the narrow entrance to the tunnel, one of the void mages took the lead, flashlight in hand to light the way. Jin motioned for Astrea to follow.

"Scared I'll take her out the way I should have in the Badlands?" Kaius asked.

"Enough, Kaius," the emperor snapped. "Go ahead, Miss Sovna."

Jin nudged Astrea forward, blocking her from his father and brother with his body. She hated that he was doing that, hated that it made her feel safer at all.

The void mages behind them clicked on flashlights, too. Neither Kaius nor the emperor used their magic. That figured; they probably couldn't be bothered.

Down and down the dark corridor they went. Astrea wanted to shout out to warn the others but didn't dare. The group made no noise other than their light footsteps. Ahead, energy brushed against Astrea's magic, a blend of curiosity, worry, and boredom that barely drowned out the pulsing void surrounding her.

As they approached a familiar bend, Jin raised his voice and said, "Tell me, Kaius, how'd you know where we were?"

"Does it matter?" Kaius asked.

"I should think so. Are you having us watched? Buy someone off in the Novarian palace?" Jin kept each word raised, not to the point of shouting but to the point that maybe the others would hear.

Irritation scraped Astrea's skin as Kaius sniffed and said, "Please, I don't need to buy anyone off."

"Really? Because that's not how things ever went down in Kalama with those—"

"Enough, Varojin!" Kaius exclaimed.

"—women you paid to keep silent about their involvement with you and the—"

"Enough!" Kaius roared.

Oh, he was too easy to goad into that, and Astrea was grateful. The Auris temper could be exceedingly short. Up ahead, cold horror brushed up against Astrea's senses. They would arrive at that cavern in another minute at most.

As Jin started on again about Kaius's less-than-royally-appropriate activities involving gambling dens, drugs, and women, the emperor shouted, "Enough out of both of you!" His voice echoed off the walls, and that fear up ahead blended with cool understanding. "For skies sake, you're both grown men. Act like it and be quiet."

They knew. The team knew. Astrea sent a silent thank you to Jin, even if it wasn't wise to provoke Kaius when he was armed with aetherium and had it pointed right at the back of Jin's head.

What the team could do at this point, Astrea wasn't sure. But they had to try something. Maybe, if nothing else, the others would find a way to leave unnoticed and get Lucian and more reinforcements. Or maybe they could launch some kind of surprise attack.

"Now," Emperor Aelius said as they approached the cavern's entrance flanked by those two pillars, "if you would be cooperative for once in your life, Varojin, we can get on with this."

Astrea strained to pick out any colors or movement in the darkened cavern beyond. There was nothing. No light. No signs of life except for that steady wave of understanding and fear radiating from somewhere in the room.

"I don't know what you want me to say," Jin replied. The void guards' flashlights barely staved off the shadows. "This is it. Raw aetherium in a dormant volcano. You have mining crews ready to come in?"

"Offshore."

"And all that cannon fire?" Jin asked, turning to face his father and brother. "Your warships, I assume?"

"Fighting that pathetic alliance you cobbled together," Aelius drawled. But as he did, a faint sheen of orange clung to his body.

"Why are you so anxious, then?" Astrea asked before she could think better of it. Jin's shoulders stiffened slightly, but he didn't look back at her.

Kaius and the emperor both regarded her for a moment, whether in surprise or contempt, Astrea couldn't decide.

Emperor Aelius's upper lip curled. "Miss Sovna, that is no way for a young woman to speak to her father-in-law."

"As far as I'm concerned, you're not my family," she said despite the way her heart thrummed all the way up her throat.

"I finally understand why my son's taken such a liking to you," Aelius snapped. "You're just like him. I thought you understood respect and loyalty, Miss Sovna, but I was wrong about you, and I was wrong about your uncle."

"You're wrong about a lot of things, Father," Jin said.

Lightning flickered around Aelius's fingertips. "Tie them up."

One of the void mages moved to grab Astrea, but Kaius tucked his gun into the waistband of his pants and grabbed her first. "Go help your emperor inspect the aetherium," he instructed the guard. "I'll deal with the Lightbringer."

Kaius took something metallic from the guard, then wrenched Astrea's wrists forward and fastened on a set of handcuffs. Another guard was doing the same to Jin as Emperor Aelius and the three other void mages moved toward the wall near the door.

"Really?" Jin snapped, tugging at the cuffs and making the metal clink.

"Seems you need a time-out," Kaius cooed as he and the second guard forced Astrea and Jin toward the back of the cavern. Near the rear wall, Kaius and the guard shoved both of them to the ground. "Sit there and be quiet," he said, "or I'll gag you, too."

"Why not gag me now?"

"Because, brother, you led us to exactly where we needed to be. I'm feeling . . . generous." Kaius's gaze fixed on Astrea. "Very generous."

Disgust rolled through her. Why was Kaius always looking at her like she was a treat and he was a hungry, vicious dog?

With a smirk, Kaius started back toward where Emperor Aelius was now using his fire to examine the walls. The void mage followed him, not sparing a glance back at Astrea and Jin.

"Are you alright?" Jin whispered.

"Where the fuck did they come from?" Astrea asked. "How did they know we were here?"

"I don't know," Jin said. "I was serious about him buying information from someone. I don't see how else he'd know, unless my father has more source material than we thought. Where's everyone else?"

"They had been hiding, but . . ." But Astrea didn't feel them anymore. "They're gone. Maybe found an alternate exit?"

"Hopefully going to find Lucian," Jin said. "Do you think you could souleat this group? Stop Kaius from using his gun?"

"What if they all have aetherium weapons?" she asked, dread building in her bones.

"I don't see what else we can do, Az," Jin said, his attention fixed on his father and brother. They pointed to different sections of the walls, as if making plans for excavation. "I don't think my father's going to let me live this time if he gets me out of this cave. I'd rather we take our chances."

Astrea swallowed her fear and pushed away the horrible images of Jin and Saros covered in those aetherium shadows. "I can do it," she whispered. She *would* do it. She had to. "What now?"

"Now," Jin said, "we wait."

Chapter 36

Astrea had always hated waiting, but she especially hated it as she sat on a freezing stone floor, handcuffed, watching as Emperor Aelius and Prince Kaius made plans for their newly found aetherium.

Jin told her to be patient. To watch their movements, to find patterns in their emotions and reactions. The only thing Astrea saw, though, was the gray hate bleeding around Kaius any time he deigned to look in their direction. That and the rust red annoyance as Aelius argued with him about establishing some kind of base here.

Jin may have told her to be patient, but it had been over an hour. Over an hour with no sign of their friends. Either they'd been captured, too, or hadn't been able to find a way back yet.

Astrea and Jin needed a way out. Sitting there was not an option.

"Kaius," Aelius said after one of their disagreements ended, "I need you to return to our ship and check on how things are progressing. Ensure we've secured the waters before we commit to any plans in this mountain."

Kaius's eyebrows furrowed. "But Father, we—"

"But nothing," Aelius snapped. He pointed at the exit. "Go. Take two of the guards with you."

Glaring at Aelius, Kaius eventually signaled for two of the void mages to go with him. They trailed a few feet behind him, their shoulders exceedingly rigid. None of the void mages, it seemed, liked to be near the Helosian prince. The other two relaxed a fraction once Kaius left.

"Quiet at last," Aelius muttered, turning to examine the wall again. But then he raised his voice as he said, "Tell me, Varojin, who else knows about this deposit?"

"No one, as far as I know," Jin said. "Astrea and I lost our snowmobile and were going to try to get back to our base."

"Lost your snowmobile?" Aelius asked with a false chuckle. Annoyance scraped over Astrea's skin. "You never were that terrible at your job all those years you served me."

"Being forced into war is hardly serving *you*," Jin said.

Aelius glanced sidelong at him. "Watch your words, Varojin. Kaius may have taken that ridiculous weapon with him, but don't think I won't hurt you all the same if I must."

Astrea tried not to flinch. Would Aelius actually attack Jin? Probably; he'd once turned his magic on eighteen-year-old Jin as a punishment for speaking out of turn. It was just so . . . dishonorable. Abusive.

"May I ask you a question?" Jin asked.

"I know saying 'no' won't stop you," Aelius replied, a spark of red anger flickering above his head.

"If you think Kaius's weapon is ridiculous, then what's all of this for?" Jin asked. "Why do all of this with aetherium? We know you were testing the weapons down south."

Lips pursed, Aelius strode to where Jin and Astrea sat on the floor. "Why am I doing this?" he asked, crouching in front of Jin. "It is what Aurises are meant to do. We're meant to conquer. To persevere. To accomplish something to better Helosia, something our ancestors have been working toward for centuries. And what way to better Helosia than to take out all our enemies? What better way to secure our future?"

"Our future?" Jin scoffed. "What kind of future is built on bombs and murder and suffering?"

Aelius ignored him. "As for why I think Kaius's weapon is ridiculous, you should know by now, Varojin. Aurises don't need to rely on such silly things. We're gifted, our family. You especially."

Astrea's heart raced. Did Aelius know Jin was a Sunreaper?

"All those kills," Aelius said, leaning in toward Jin. More of that red rage circled the emperor, mixed with sweet, heavy satisfaction. "All those strides *you* made for our wars. For our country. Our family. It may have taken some work getting you out there, but I'm glad I sent you."

Steel pain and deep blue regret swirled around Jin in a thick cloud. His jaw tightened.

With a mean smile, Aelius said, "Didn't want your little wife to know about all that?"

"He already told me," Astrea said. Those four words brought more color around the emperor, more rust and red and gray. The void mages lingered behind him, hesitant.

"Then you know he's nothing more than a weapon I forged through trial and fire," Aelius said as he stood. "He could've been great, had he not gotten caught up in things he knows nothing about. Foolish as always, Varojin. You take after your mother that way."

Astrea's blood burned. She glared at Aelius as he walked away, warm satisfaction radiating off him.

"He's nothing like you!" she shouted, her voice bouncing off the walls.

"Az—" Jin whispered.

"He is not your weapon!"

Despite the anger circling him in varying shades of red, Aelius kept walking.

"He's not a monster like you!"

Aelius paused. Slowly, he turned and cocked his head to the side. "What did you say?"

"He's not a monster like you," Astrea repeated, breathing heavily. Her hands strained against her cuffs. "That's what you are. A monster."

"*I'm* a monster?" Aelius's eyes narrowed.

"All you do is hurt people," Astrea said, even as Jin whispered again for her to stop. "People die because of you and your selfish, hateful choices. You kill Zaikudi, Delians, Helosians—anyone who stands in your way. *You* are the monster, not your son. He's the best—"

Aelius stalked forward, grabbing Astrea by her coat and yanking her off the ground. "How would you like to join all those you accuse me of killing, Miss Sovna?" He shoved her back against the cavern wall. Red took over her vision, the emperor's anger. "Or should I teach you the same lesson I taught Varojin years ago, about what happens when you speak out of turn to your emperor?" Electricity flickered around his fingertips, its blue heat the only thing breaking up the red.

"Father—" Jin started, shoving to his feet.

"You're not *my* emperor," Astrea said. The red deepened. "You're just a pathetic, power-hungry man. That's all you'll ever be. Even if you manage to succeed in all this, the history books won't be kind to a wretched man like you."

"I never should've let you and your uncle into my palace all those years ago," Aelius hissed, pressing his forearm against the base of Astrea's throat. Nearby, white panic sprang up amid the sea of red. "Good for nothing liars, both of you."

"I'd rather be a liar than a monster," she spat.

Electricity flickered on her skin. Astrea clenched her fists, pulling on that anger and hate hemorrhaging out of the emperor. Someone crashed into Aelius—Jin. Astrea braced herself, flinging her hands out in front of her and grabbing hold of that hot anger again. She grabbed the freezing cold of the void mages, too, smashing through their veil and snapping up their fear and frustration. She yanked back, making all three Helosians cry out.

"Get them!" Aelius roared.

Astrea's palms burned from the energy coursing through her, and her wrists ached as the handcuffs pressed into her joints. She needed an out. Badly.

Burning hot hate slammed into her like a tidal wave. She stumbled back, crying out as that energy slipped away from her. Ghostly pain flared on her forearm, her thigh. Aelius threw Jin off him, a small dagger dripping blood onto the floor.

Jin shoved to his feet, no shadows showing up on his skin. Rage bled into his aura. Astrea wanted to heal him. *Needed* to heal him. But she needed to get those void mages under control.

She spun out of Aelius's reach just in time for Jin to barrel into him again. She pivoted, facing the void mage guards stalking toward her. Shadows flickered up their faces, so much like that night back in Kalama. The shadows at the edges of the cavern stretched and shifted, moving closer. She needed to—

The ginger-bearded guard charged. Astrea threw her hands out in front of her as best she could, bracing herself as her shield of starlight expanded. The void mage punched it. The shield shook, then began to disintegrate as his shadows spread along where his fist had hit it. He reached through, grabbed her by her coat collar, and yanked her forward. A blade sliced her arm at the elbow, cutting through a weak point in her armor.

Astrea coughed and sputtered as she fell to the ground, unable to catch her breath. Her skin felt like it was stretching to the point of drying, turning into nothing but ash. Darkness consumed the mage's face like a mask of pure void. Her muscles slackened, as if she were paralyzed. What was he—

Lifestealer.

He was a Lifestealer. He had to be.

Astrea couldn't reach her arm, not chained like this, to heal it. She couldn't—

Rock slammed into the ginger-haired void mage. The shadows consuming his face slithered back a few inches, revealing his copper eyes.

"Jin!" Adi shouted.

Wind howled, and a sickening crack echoed through the cavern. More wind and another crack, this one louder. Adi leaned over Astrea, extending his hand to her. She took it, letting him pull her up only to immediately double over, her breathing labored and painful. Marko was just a few steps away, and both void mages were in a heap on the ground. Dead.

Jin and his father circled each other, both covered in burns and cuts. Aelius brandished his blood-covered dagger at Jin again.

"I thought Aurises didn't need weapons," Jin goaded. "I thought that made us ridiculous."

"Whatever it takes to finally rid myself of you, Varojin," Aelius growled.

Marko started forward. The emperor lunged. Jin stumbled back. The tip of Aelius's blade sliced Jin's jacket, and Astrea screamed as—

Aelius stopped. His body froze, as if trapped in ice. White terror flared high around him, followed by red anger. He groaned and shivered as he bent forward.

Black hair and white armor popped up behind Aelius.

Lucian slid in behind the emperor, one fist clenched tight as the other came down on Emperor Aelius's back. Lucian's dagger glinted in the light of the lanterns discarded by the void mage guards.

He brought the blade down into Aelius's back, pushing straight through to the other side. Pain lanced Astrea's chest, not that of aetherium but that of cold, hard steel. She cried out, going limp in Adi's arms as her pulse roared in her ears.

Aelius coughed, then coughed again as his arm slackened. His knife clattered to the ground, right at Jin's feet.

With a thick, wet sound, Lucian pulled the dagger from the emperor's back. Blood leaked out of Aelius's chest, pooling on the ground as he dropped forward.

The pain stopped.

The emperor was dead.

The emperor was dead, and Lucian had killed him.

CHAPTER 37

"We need to get out of here. Now." Lucian wiped the bloody dagger on the emperor's back. Then he sheathed it on his belt. "There's a back way. Come quickly."

Jin stared down at his father's body. He didn't move. He didn't even seem to be breathing.

"Varojin," Lucian snapped.

"Jin," Adi said. "That mage did something to Az."

She sucked in quick, shallow breaths. It was like she'd run miles and miles, all the way from the Great Library back to the observatory, in Kalama's summer heat, with no place to stop and no water. Her mouth was dry. She could barely stand upright.

"Lifestealer," Astrea croaked past the stickiness in her mouth. "He cut me, and I—"

Jin was at her side in an instant. His wall was down, but it wasn't grief or sadness that brushed against her skin. No, it was minty cool relief. Relief that she was alive, or relief that his father was dead?

"We'll get her into the passage, then I'll heal her," Lucian said. "Come, quickly. Someone's on their way, but I can barely feel them."

Before Astrea could protest, Marko took her knapsack, and Adi hoisted her up in his arms. And it was probably good, too, because her hearing started to go, and her vision blurred as soon as they moved. Lucian led them away from the emperor's body to a small bump out in the wall.

There was a narrow opening, and Adi had to turn sideways to carefully move Astrea through.

Once inside, he set her down. Marko helped hold her upright as Adi rolled the stone slab shut after them, barely blocking out the sound of Kaius screaming and hot anger singing Astrea's skin. Heavy anxiety pulsed out from Adi as he picked her up again.

"This way," Lucian said, moving deeper into the shadows. Starlight swirled around his hand.

"You need to heal her," Jin said, his cuffs clinking with each step. "Now."

"We'll find the others up ahead," Lucian replied. "A couple more minutes."

"We'll move faster if we're both healed."

They rounded a bend, and the last of Kaius's flickering anger dissipated. Lucian peered at Adi, then nodded toward a narrow but tall rock. "Set her down here."

As soon as Adi set Astrea down, Lucian grabbed her arm. She cried out. Couldn't he be more gentle? His light seeped into her skin, and she groaned. It was like someone had jolted her back awake. Every part of her ached. Lucian grunted and shook his head, his new fatigue barreling into Astrea in a strange echo.

"Let me do yours, Jin," Astrea said. She didn't feel much better, but they didn't know exactly what healing lifestealing would do to the commander, and he couldn't get overtaxed.

As she sat up, Jin came to stand between her legs. Astrea focused on her breathing and on maneuvering her shackled hands properly as she healed the worst of Jin's wounds. He insisted they save the minor things for later, all the burns and scrapes he'd sustained.

"Hey," he murmured, tipping her chin up and forcing her to look at him.

"Hey," she whispered back, staring up into those beautiful golden eyes of his.

"You're alright?"

"Yes."

Perhaps "alright" wasn't the best way to describe how she felt. The mere implication that Emperor Aelius Auris was dead . . . the way Lucian had certainly committed an act of war . . .

"Are you?" she asked.

He smiled softly, earnestly, sadly, all in one. "There've been better days."

"I suppose there have," she whispered.

Lucian cleared his throat. "We need to move. Now."

"Can you feel them?" Adi asked. "The Helosians, I mean."

"No, and I don't trust that," the commander replied. "Come on. We'll get the Nikaphoroses to free you of those chains, and then we run."

With Adi's help, Astrea climbed down off the high rock, and then they were moving again. She still didn't feel good, but not knowing where Kaius or the void mages were was too risky. They couldn't sit around.

"How'd you find us, anyway?" Jin asked.

"To make a long story short," Marko said, voice low, "we found these tunnels shortly before we heard you and Kaius. Came in to hide, eventually ran into the others, and here we are now."

"A good thing, too," Lucian said. "Now we know where the aetherium is."

"Only in that other room?" Jin asked.

"As far as we can tell," Adi said.

Astrea didn't know whether to be grateful for that or not. That would make it easier, except for the fact that Kaius now arguably had control over that specific location.

Lucian navigated them through a series of narrow tunnels for what felt like hours, though it surely wasn't more than maybe half an hour at most. The going was slow, especially with the uneven floor. The walls here were gray and tan stone occasionally swirled with red or a deep violet. No aetherium. That was Astrea's only consolation. If Kaius and his void mages were somehow following them through the tunnels, she and Lucian would be able to feel them by now.

At last, the tunnel widened, and energy sped toward Astrea, almost as if it had been waiting for her to arrive. Worry and fear tangled together around her, wrapping her in a constrictive hug. More distance closed, and then voices came: Balthazar's deep tone, Cressida's higher one.

They entered a junction, which had several tunnels splitting off from it. The space was by no means large, but there was the rest of the team, all of them, huddled together. Cressida threw her arms around Astrea's neck, overwhelming her vision and tastebuds with minty relief.

"Hey, Cress," Astrea croaked. "Mind getting these off?"

Pulling away, Cressida examined Astrea's extended arms. With a flick of her fingers, the handcuffs pulled apart, falling off Astrea's wrists and floating in the air. Jin's did the same, his handcuffs shooting back toward Balthazar. Astrea rubbed at her wrists, trying to soothe her aching skin.

"What the fuck happened?" Zephyrine asked.

"My father and brother found us," Jin said. "They've got void mages."

"Emperor Aelius is dead," Lucian said.

Zephyrine stared, wide-eyed. They all did, even Valen where he stood awkwardly to one side.

"It was either him or Varojin," Lucian said, "and losing Varojin was not an option."

Zephyrine's chest heaved. "The emperor is dead."

"And Kaius found him," Jin said, then explained how everything went down. "Which means my brother is now the leader of the Helosian Empire."

"Skies help us all," Zephyrine muttered.

It most certainly had not been part of the plan. None of that had been, except for escaping, of course. Astrea rubbed at her forehead and let out a shaky breath.

Emperor Aelius Auris was dead.

Jin and Eliana's father was *dead*.

Kaius was now the emperor.

"We need to find a way back to camp," Lucian said, already moving toward another tunnel. He paused at its entrance, listening intently. "It's very likely the whole island is surrounded."

"Is there even a chance our navy isn't sunk?" Lennor asked. "That cannon fire we heard—"

"Was very well theirs *and* ours." Glancing back at Rami, Lucian said, "We cannot assume the worst."

"Never assume the worst," she said with a wry smile. "Until you can prove otherwise. Always assume you have a chance. We cannot go into this expecting defeat."

Lucian nodded at her, some tender look passing between them. Astrea would have to try to dissect that later, if they made it off this island in one piece.

"But you two are alright?" Valen asked, tilting his chin toward Astrea and Jin. "Are you hurt?"

"We . . . ran into a few issues, but we're mostly healed," Jin said. "Lucian's right, that we need to move. Kaius won't be far behind us once he brings in some Earthmovers and Metalli of his own."

"Fastest way out is down here," Lucian said, gesturing down the dark tunnel he stood near. "Haven't had a chance to explore much farther."

"How'd the Helosians find this place anyway?" Cressida asked as they hurried through the tunnel. Starlight flickered around them, casting eerie shadows along the walls and floors.

"Don't know," Jin said. "I think Kaius might've been paying someone off in the palace."

"Doesn't matter much at the moment," Rami called over her shoulder. She was near the front of the line with Lucian and the twins. "We can figure it out if we make it out of here alive."

As they walked, Astrea tried to calm her racing heart and focus on the air around her. No voids. No raging anger, no infernos of hatred. Nothing but the anxiety of their group, the heavy walls, the surprise and relief and confusion. She pulled at the rip in her jacket, trying to get a good look at the skin below. Lucian's healing was solid, as it always was. And up ahead, he didn't seem to be slowing down or too deeply affected by healing the effects of lifestealing. Doing so obviously wasn't as draining as healing an aetherium-inflicted wound.

Light trickled in at the end of the tunnel, growing brighter the closer they got to the end. Pausing, Lucian raised his fist. They all stopped.

"People," Astrea whispered. She couldn't see them, but she could feel them. If her friends' emotions had been like a steady breeze on her cheeks, this was a thunderstorm of rage and fear, forceful and unignorable, even in the distance.

"What faction?" Zephyrine asked.

"I doubt they're ours," Lucian said over his shoulder. "Rami, Marko, with me. The rest of you, wait for our signal."

The trio edged forward slowly. Jin and Adi moved to the front of the remaining group, Zephyrine and the twins at the back. Astrea held her breath.

The end of the tunnel was almost too bright to stare into, but the trio's silhouettes moved closer and closer to the end. They continued, and—

Fire blasted inside, its heat licking Astrea's cheeks. Jin sprinted into the flames. He barreled straight through, out into the daylight. Adi and Lucian followed him.

"It's Kaius!" Marko shouted before sprinting after them.

If they stayed inside those tunnels, they'd be trapped. The only way out was through. Just like Jin.

Astrea bolted. Outside, in the late afternoon sun, a small army fanned out before them, trapping them between the volcano and the sea. Cold void and myriad emotions swirled together, a nauseating mix. And the only thing separating their team—just eleven of them—from that army was a wall of Lucian's sparkling starlight, spread between two boulders and arcing high above their heads.

Kaius paced a short path in front of the wall like a caged animal.

"Varojin." The slight muffle didn't hide the hatred in his voice—or his aura. Gray and red surrounded him. "Father's dead."

"I know."

"You killed him."

Jin shook his head. "I did not."

"Oh, please." Kaius scoffed, and that hate and anger flared brighter. "You've always wanted him dead."

Jin didn't deny it.

"Surrender yourselves," Kaius said. "You're to be extradited to Kalama for trial."

"Trial for what?" Jin asked.

"Treason, patricide, desertion . . ." Kaius lifted a finger to go with each crime. "Need I go on?"

"There is no extradition from a place such as this, Your Imperial Majesty," Lucian said. "These isles are under the watch of Novaria and Tornama, and neither government will send Varojin with you."

"Your Imperial Majesty?" Kaius's head tilted slightly to one side.

"With the death of your father, you are emperor, are you not?" Lucian asked.

Kaius's rigid posture loosened. Something in his expression shifted, from rage to understanding. Vermilion pride swirled around him, and his smile turned nasty.

"It's what *you've* always wanted," Jin said. "Emperor Kaius Auris."

"Emperor Kaius Auris," Kaius mouthed, as if not believing it.

How had he not realized it?

Kaius's eyes narrowed. "Then by order of the emperor, you are to come back to Kalama for trial or face immediate death."

Adi and Marko widened their stances. Rami took several small steps back.

"Or will you hide behind this *Lightbringer* like the coward you are?" Kaius snarled. "Are you that scared of me, brother?"

"You've never scared me, Kaius," Jin said. "You're just a weaker, more pathetic version of our father."

Red rage exploded around Kaius. Lucian glanced over his shoulder—barely. But his gaze met Astrea's, and she knew what he wanted her to do.

"Weak?" Kaius seethed, and the crimson fog around him grew. "Pathetic?"

"Not even brave enough to join me in the army," Jin said. "All those years spent gambling, drinking, fucking, and what do you have to show for it?" He inched forward, closer to Lucian's shield wall. "No bills. No laws. No cabinet appointments or any real work. Not even a fucking war medal Father bestowed upon you out of pity. All you have to show is a crown you only earned because your father died, and that doesn't sound like much of an achievement to me."

Kaius's fists balled at his sides as he moved even closer to the starlight wall, a blur of red and gray. "I've—!"

Astrea flung her hands out, opening herself to all of that anger and hate. It burned right through her sternum and out her back, an agonizing pain. Astrea gritted her teeth. His energy surged toward her, weaving together into a tight rope that she pulled back on. Kaius stumbled, crying out as he slammed into Lucian's wall.

That hatred tripled with such force Astrea faltered. She stumbled back against Balthazar, and the connection with Kaius began to fray thread by thread.

"Get them!" he screamed. "Get the traitors! By order of your emperor!"

The Helosians attacked.

CHAPTER 38

Rock shot up behind Lucian's wall, arcing up to cover their heads and blocking out the sun. Adi, Balthazar, and Cressida all kept their arms raised. Outside, elements slammed against their earthen shield. Every hit made Astrea flinch.

"What do you want to do, Jin?" Lucian asked, chest heaving.

"Let me lead Kaius away," Jin said. "Separate him from the rest."

"You and me." Adi's voice shook, and his body strained as he maintained their shield wall. "I'll go with you."

"The rest of you, hold off the Helosians for as long as you can," Jin said, "even if it means holing up in these tunnels. Or try to get them to surrender."

"The tunnels go deep," Valen said. "I might be able to find us another way out."

"Stick together, whether you fight or flee. Stay alive." Jin's gaze flicked over the group. "Az and Zephyrine, with us."

Her? Jin wanted *her* to help him fight Kaius?

He'd once told her that Kaius knew she was Jin's weakness. But maybe today, she could be his strength. Kaius didn't know how strong she'd become. How strong Jin had always been.

"And if the Novarians come for you, go with them," Jin said. "Don't hesitate. Get out of here if you can." He glanced at Adi, then at where Zephyrine and Astrea stood. "On my mark."

Zephyrine and Astrea moved in close with Adi and Jin. Everyone else circled around Balthazar and Cressida.

Jin threw his gloves to the ground. His wedding and engagement rings glinted as fire blazed over his palms, and his voice was hard as stone as he said, "Now."

The earth shook. Their shield dropped. Kaius stood just on the other side, a line of soldiers at his back. Lightning crackled around his fingertips, his arms, his entire body, almost like a terrible thunderstorm come to life.

"Varojin," he sneered.

Zephyrine threw her hands forward and moved them from right to left. A gale swept in, blowing Kaius and his front line to the side. Jin sprinted through the opening, Astrea right behind and Adi and Zephyrine after. Kaius roared as cannon fire went off in the distance.

Jin hurtled across the open expanse of land between the sea and volcano. Snow melted with every step he took, clearing a path for the rest of them. Even several steps behind him, Astrea could feel the heat he radiated.

"Kaius is following," Astrea said between heavy breaths. She didn't dare look back for fear she would fall. "Or someone very angry is. Several people—"

"It's him," Zephyrine said, skidding to a stop.

Astrea dared to look. Zephyrine repeated the same hand movements as earlier, another unnaturally strong wind whipping across the barren land. Kaius and the handful following him stumbled, struggling to right themselves.

"Over here!" someone shouted. That voice . . .

Astrea dared look toward the base of the mountain. There, sticking out against the dark rock was a figure clad in white. A dark-haired figure.

Valen, her father. Waving at them from near an opening in the mountainside.

"What the fuck . . ." Jin muttered, already heading that way. "Get inside!" he yelled, but Valen ignored him and kept motioning for them, his eyes locked on Astrea.

Behind them, Kaius shrieked something to his small band of followers. It wouldn't be long before the Helosians caught up if Astrea and the rest of them stood there, caught between empty nothingness and the mountain.

"Circle back to see if you can get to Lucian," Jin said to Astrea as Valen began hurrying toward them. "Oh, for fuck's sake. Bring him with you. Zephyrine, go with them."

"What about—" she started.

Astrea grabbed Jin's forearm as cold pierced her skin and bones so fast she thought she might've actually been attacked. But no, it was that cold that only swept in when a particularly powerful void mage arrived. She'd know it anywhere. It was . . . different.

It was . . .

"Nazarov," she said.

Zephyrine sprinted forward, grabbing Valen and shoving him back toward the cavern.

"Go with—" Jin pushed Astrea to follow Zephyrine but yanked her back almost immediately.

Shadows swirled up from the ground between where they stood and where Kaius and the few Helosians had skidded to a stop. Gray confusion swirled around most of the soldiers, almost blending with the void magic seeping out of the snow.

"Finally," Nazarov said, almost bored, as he emerged from the inky darkness. His snow gear was nearly the same color as those shadows he controlled, a smudge against the snow and red Helosian uniforms behind him. "Commanding a navy with the Zaikudi is not the walk in the park I expected it to be." He smiled viciously at Astrea. "Little Lightbringer. Sunreaper. Earthmover. Your allies are stronger than I expected, but they won't last much longer."

Astrea's stomach twisted into knots. Cannon fire exploded in the distance, no doubt the three navies. The coalition, the Helosians, and now the Paragon and Zaikudi, all fighting each other.

They'd been so close. Come so close to controlling this aetherium, safeguarding it from those intent on using it for destruction. And now here they were.

Nazarov pivoted toward Kaius. "Your Imperial Highness."

"That's *majesty* now," Kaius barked.

Of course he would find time to make that distinction.

"Oh?" Nazarov sounded amused, condescending. "Is that so? Not just a princeling like your bastard brother anymore?"

Through gritted teeth, Kaius said, "Watch how you speak to me, Lord Nazarov."

"My sincerest apologies," Nazarov drawled, placing a hand over his chest. "So sorry to hear about the death of your dear old dad."

Jin leaned down toward Astrea, whispering for her to run.

Nazarov snapped his fingers without looking away from Kaius. Shadows snaked up from the ground, slithering up their legs. Astrea squirmed, but they didn't hurt. They were just . . . strong. Strong and alive, almost. A shiver tumbled down her spine.

"No one moves, Prince Varojin," Nazarov said, still focused on Kaius. "Now, *Your Imperial Majesty*, I believe you and I had a deal. Varojin for you, the Lightbringer for me."

Jin stilled. Cold confusion and panic warred on Astrea's skin, though whether it was Jin's or Adi's, she couldn't quite tell. Maybe both.

Kaius and Nazarov had made a *deal*? When? How? Had Emperor Aelius known?

"Jin," Adi whispered.

"I know." Jin tilted his head toward where Kaius and Nazarov were practically toe-to-toe. "Az—"

Could she souleat them? After all this?

She wasn't sure she had much to give, but she would have to try.

She nodded at Jin, not daring to make a sound.

"A deal's a deal," Kaius said, scrutinizing Nazarov. "Careful though, that bitch is obviously capable of more than she ever let on."

"Don't I know it," Nazarov snarled as he finally looked over his shoulder at them.

Astrea's fingers relaxed at her sides, and she sucked in a deep breath, focusing on Nazarov's ice and Kaius's fire. Their energy crackled through the air, an invisible lightning storm only she could feel.

Another deep breath.

Nazarov stalked forward, Kaius and his guards not far behind. Stopping a dozen feet away, Nazarov moved his pointer finger in a circle, and the shadows climbing up Astrea's legs began to recede as he said, "Play nice and I'll take them all away, little Lightbringer. I know how much you despise them."

Astrea willed herself to play the scared girl she was deep down inside as she stared down not just Victor Nazarov but Emperor Kaius. Her eyes widened and her jaw trembled as all the anxiety and fear pooling in her belly rose to the surface. Jin and Adi murmured their agreements to stay put if Nazarov dismissed the shadows.

Another twirl of his fingers and the inky darkness was gone. Astrea fixated on that hot rage and freezing cold, on the hate she knew she'd find once she pierced his veil. Her energy stretched toward them, eager.

"Finally learned to listen, hm?" Nazarov said as he stepped closer to Astrea. "After all this time?"

She clenched her fists. That mix of hot and cold that was so much like aetherium burned through her. She welcomed it, that surge of energy that made her muscles twitch. The cold crackling across her fingers as she broke through Nazarov's barrier and reached his deep, powerful hatred.

"I'll never listen to you," she snapped.

Nazarov and Kaius fell flat on their faces as Astrea twisted and twisted their energy together in her mind's eye. A swirl of dark shadow and gray hate and red rage began circling the two men. Her muscles seized, overloaded.

Adi sprang forward, meeting the Helosian soldiers moving in to attack. There were four of Kaius's guards, one clearly a void mage based on the way shadows snaked up her full cheeks. A wall of earth circled them, trapping them for at least a moment.

Grabbing Nazarov's collar, Jin hoisted him up with one hand, fire dagger burning in the other. Cold spiked as Solana appeared, her dark hair snapping wildly in the wind. She shoved Jin, then grabbed his arm and ported him away.

Astrea held back her scream, unable to let it escape her as she grappled with the energy all around her. An invisible force—Nazarov—pushed back and back against her.

In the distance, Jin elbowed Solana in the face, and Astrea's nose ached with the force of the blow. He spun, but Solana disappeared at the same time the Helosian void mage appeared, grabbed Kaius, and blinked away. Adi sprinted toward Jin and Solana, his curses drowned out by the howling wind.

Digging her boots into the ground, Astrea tried to brace herself. Oh, she tried. But that force pushed and pushed against her. Nazarov chuckled from where he was frozen, upright on his knees.

"You and me again, as always," he managed to say, the words strained. "My favorite kind of day."

"You're the worst person I've ever met," Astrea gritted out, equally taxed by this battle in energy, even if she was the one in control.

Up ahead, Jin was caught in a fiery dance with Kaius, slicing him on the cheek, the chest, the arm. Hot, burning pain seared her skin. Adi was nowhere in sight.

"I'm flattered." Nazarov managed a faltering smile. "But I can be so much worse, little Lightbringer."

Cold spiked, and a much smaller frame slammed into Astrea. Solana hissed something, but Astrea couldn't hear it past the ringing in her ears as her head hit the ground. The other woman wrestled with Astrea, trying to pin her down. But Astrea flailed and pushed, desperate, until Solana was off her.

"The fuck—" Solana started, scrambling off the ground.

No, it wasn't that Astrea had thrown her off. Valen stood a few feet away, breathing heavily. Solana scrambled upright and faced him, her head tilting to the side curiously.

Astrea shoved to her feet. What was Valen doing here? *How* was he here? He was supposed to be gone. He was supposed to be with Zephyrine, finding and helping the others.

Nazarov had gotten to his feet, too. He took one step forward, asking, "And who is this?"

"No one," Astrea muttered.

The two men were nearly equal in height, not extraordinarily large but slightly taller than average. Where Nazarov was leaner, Valen was bulkier, like he was built to survive a long winter. And where Nazarov had a light tan, Valen was as pale as the snow around them.

Astrea's muscles twitched and burned. Could the Lifestealer's earlier attack have weakened her that much? Her head pounded. Wind snapped around them, and fresh snow fell as the already cloudy sky grew darker. The sound of radio static filled her ears.

"I feel as though I've seen you before," Nazarov said, almost uncertain. His eyebrows furrowed. Nazarov was *never* uncertain.

"Maybe you knew my brother," Valen said.

"Your brother?"

"Cato," Valen replied. "Or as many knew him, The One."

A slow smile spread across Nazarov's face.

"Not a great leader, but a Ramkas nonetheless," Valen continued. "Just like me. I only hope I can do better for the Paragon, do *right* by its people. It's time for a change, but that change is not my daughter."

Solana's boots shifted on the packed snow.

"It's my understanding that you want to take this honor away from my family," Valen said to Nazarov. "It seems you and I need to have a talk, Lord Nazarov."

"What are you doing?" Astrea hissed.

Valen lifted his chin.

"Oh," Nazarov said with a low chuckle. "Oh, Mister Ramkas, what a pleasure it is to meet you at long last."

Cold spiked, and shadows swallowed Nazarov whole. Astrea scrambled toward her father but lost her footing on the wet ground. Her knees smacked into hard stone beneath the snow.

Nazarov reappeared behind Valen. He twisted, blocking Nazarov's punch with his forearm, but the force of the blow made him stumble.

"Run, Astrea!" Valen shouted. "Run!"

She tried to launch herself forward, but Solana caught her by her arm. Astrea hollered and thrashed but couldn't shake the woman.

Still cloaked in that undulating darkness, Nazarov grabbed Valen by the front of his coat and rammed a dagger right between his ribs. Hot and cold blistered Astrea's skin. Shadows snaked up Valen's neck, his cheeks, his eyes. He sputtered, then collapsed to the ground. One heartbeat, then another, of impossible pain.

And he was gone.

Astrea screamed. Solana dropped her arm. Astrea started forward, only for her vision to blur and darken. Something else tightened around her limbs—surely Nazarov's shadows, as her skin grew colder. She was frozen, stuck in limbo.

"Now," Nazarov purred in her ear, "only one Ramkas left standing in my way."

Solana snickered. "Finally."

Astrea's pulse quickened. She strained and strained against the shadows' hold. She imagined Nazarov's dreamwalking as a bubble, as a thing she could pop if she threw herself against it. She pictured her rage as a perfectly sharp, deadly dagger that would set her free. She pushed and stabbed, but it was useless.

Cold spiked and receded again in the distance. Nazarov and Solana still surrounded her.

"Your turn, Miss Sovna," Nazarov whispered in her ear.

"I thought you wanted to make me queen," Astrea managed to gasp out.

He tsked. "When I could have the end of the Ramkas line at long last? Replace them with my own dynasty?"

Metal brushed the base of Astrea's throat. She couldn't breathe. As Nazarov pressed the blade in harder, the darkness clouding her vision shimmered and shifted. An image took hold. The Badlands, the sand and storm and chaos of the fight. Saros, sprawled out on the ground, pressing Kaius's aetherium blade against his own neck.

"The end of the Sovna line, too," Nazarov hissed. "I told you not to cross me."

"Nazarov!" Jin's shout echoed through the emptiness.

Nazarov chuckled, making the hairs on the back of Astrea's neck stand on end. "Maybe it'll be your husband's turn first," he said. "And you get a front-row seat for the show. Lucky little Lightbringer."

He shoved Astrea to the ground. She coughed and sputtered. The shadows crowding Astrea's vision dissipated just in time for her to spot Nazarov and Solana jump away. When they landed again, Jin barreled toward them, his aura hot and red. Adi was behind him, swerving around their clash and going right to Astrea's side.

"We have to help Jin," Astrea said, panting as she staggered to her feet. "We have to—"

Fire singed her skin. Ghostly fire, burning flesh and muscle. Nazarov roared. Jin pulled back, a fiery blade in his right hand. Shadows snaked up from the ground, pulling Nazarov with them. Solana was gone. Jin sprinted through the open field, back toward Astrea and Adi.

Inky darkness swirled up, bringing Nazarov with it. He landed right between the three of them, angling his dagger at Astrea. He stalked forward, black spiking into his aura again and again.

Jin shouted incoherently. Heat coursed through Astrea's body, a mix of power and pain. Red and gray swirled around Jin as he ran, and fire ignited over his palms.

Adi tackled her to the ground, knocking all the breath out of her lungs. Rock encased them, creating a shallow dome. The ground shook. A loud boom ruptured the very core of Astrea's bones. She covered her ears and squeezed her eyes shut. Her entire body trembled and shook. Adi hugged her so tight she could feel his heart thundering out of his chest and into hers.

And as quickly as it started, it stopped. No more trembling earth. No more ghostly burns. No more ear-shattering explosions.

Adi tapped on her wrist, as if to tell her to stop covering her ears. Astrea pulled her hands away, only to hear the knocking on their shield.

"Is it Jin?" Adi asked.

"It's not Nazarov." All she sensed out there was bone-deep fatigue, hot anger, sharp disappointment.

The rock melted back into the ground. Adi helped Astrea to her feet just as Jin staggered forward. Adi caught him on one side.

"Did you get him?" Adi asked.

"He fucking jumped away," Jin muttered. "I did everything, and he still got away."

Everything. Cold horror prickled up Astrea's spine as she took in Jin's wilted form, the melted snow and burnt ground around them. The small crater where Jin had been standing right before Adi tackled her.

The explosion.

That had been him, the Sunreaper.

And it hadn't been enough.

"I think I hurt him, at least," Jin croaked. "He looked like he was bleeding pretty bad."

"Better than nothing," Adi said. "Should slow him down."

Astrea pulled on her light, letting its familiar, gentle warmth build around her hands. She set them both on Jin's broad chest, pushing her healing light deep within him. He sighed. Heat seared her muscles, almost like a fever. Astrea staggered back a step, and both Adi and Jin caught her before she fell. She was . . . exhausted. Utterly exhausted.

"We still need you in this fight, Az," Jin said gently. "I'll be fine."

Would he?

Would *she*? It was like the flu was ravaging her body, making her hot and sweaty but so cold, making her joints and bones ache to the point they felt like they'd disintegrate.

"He killed Valen," Astrea managed to say past the dryness in her mouth. "Nazarov killed him. With aetherium. One less Ramkas to stand in his way, Nazarov said. I don't even know where Valen came from, he was just *there*, and he was trying to help me, and . . ."

Astrea could not think about that now. She could not think about how her father had surely known exactly what he was doing. How he had just thrown himself in Nazarov's path, as feeble as an attempt that might have been to help her. How it seemed she was to lose everyone in her life who might be a parent to her. Everyone but the Nikaphoroses, the blessings that they were.

If she dared think about it now, the gaping hole left in her heart after Saros's death would split wide open again.

She wiped away the tears building in her eyes.

"Az?" Adi asked.

"I . . . can't right now," she said, staring up at Jin, her husband, and Adi, one of her best friends in the world. "We need to finish this."

"We'll come back for him," Adi said, gesturing to the small earthen dome nearby. Scorch marks marred its side and top. Valen. Adi had thrown a shield around Valen somehow, too.

"We'll finish this," Jin said, taking Astrea's hand, "and then we'll come back for him. I promise."

Chapter 39

Getting out of the snow and away from the destruction Jin's magic had caused proved a challenge, especially with his rapidly increasing fatigue. Adi should've been helping him, but Jin had refused. And besides, with Astrea's own exhaustion settling deep within her muscles and the way Adi's body sent echoes of pain out into the world, none of them were in good shape.

Still, they managed to find their way to the caves Valen had tried to point them to before, the way Zephyrine had run. It was a fairly straight shot through the dark rocks, no alternate routes splitting off from the singular tunnel. As they came around a bend, a new wall entered Astrea's awareness, almost like she was too slow to notice it earlier. Zephyrine nearly slammed into them, out of breath.

"Skies," she said, panting. "There you are. Where's Valen? He ran off while I was—"

"Nazarov got him," Jin said, then explained what happened. "Nazarov's gone. Kaius, too."

"Fuck," Zephyrine said, fisting her long white hair, which had sprung out of its usual braid. "Fuck, a few Helosians and one of those void mages jumped me, and he just *ran,*" she said, mostly to Astrea. "I'm so sorry."

"It's not your fault," Astrea said. "I think . . ." She huffed. "I think he meant for it to happen, in a way, but I need to focus right now."

Zephyrine's expression hardened. "I felt strong rumbles from the earth not long ago, back from where we left the others."

"Then let's get to them," Jin said.

They continued on through the caves, Astrea's weak starlight the only thing guiding their way. Zephyrine, at least, seemed to know where they were going, and led them down a too-narrow corridor branching off from the main one. They stumbled around the fallen Helosians the general had mentioned before. Soon, they were back in the cavern Lucian had taken them to after escaping Kaius.

Panic and terror swelled high above Astrea, crashing down like a tidal wave. "Something's wrong," she said.

The ground rumbled and shook as ear-shattering booms erupted outside. Astrea tumbled into Jin. As soon as the ground stopped rocking, they sprinted down the tunnel they'd first followed with the rest of the team, finding darkness at the end instead of daylight.

Darkness and auras alive with color: steel pain, orange anxiety, white terror, red determination. And then came a string of creative curses from Cressida.

"Cress!" Astrea shouted.

"Fucking skies," Cressida said, coughing.

Lucian's light exploded in the darkness, revealing a rocky barrier a few steps outside the tunnel entrance. Smoke and dust swirled around the group. Lucian was saying something about planes and bombs, but Astrea just threw her arms around Cressida's neck and hugged her tight.

"Are you alright?" she asked, her hands sliding to Cressida's narrow shoulders as she pulled away.

"Fine, if not for the fucking smoke," Cressida said, then coughed again. "I mean, shit."

"Novarian planes?" Jin asked Lucian.

"Definitely ours," he said. "The Zaikudi and Helosians are tearing each other apart out there."

"Good for us but not for them," Rami said from somewhere behind the rest of the group.

The muffled roar of engines came, and then more explosions. Astrea covered her ears, crouching on instinct. Jin moved with her, as if shielding her. As if he could, should a Novarian bomb miss its target and land on them instead.

"Deeper into the tunnels!" Lucian called. "Go!"

"Don't they know we're in here?" Zephyrine shouted over the next series of explosions.

"Possibly, but let's not take a chance!"

As they moved back inside the tunnel, Adi and Balthazar threw a rock wall up between them and the earlier sections. They all crouched in a group, waiting for the planes to stop their assault. Astrea leaned into Jin, still covering her ears as the noise never seemed to end. She squeezed her eyes shut, trying not to focus on the images dancing behind her eyelids. The shadows. Nazarov. Kaius. Valen.

Only after what felt like forever did the bombing cease. Pain drifted toward Astrea, not from her immediate vicinity but farther away. Enough to make nausea roll through her and her head spin. Lucian winced.

"There are survivors," he said. "It doesn't seem good, though."

That was an understatement.

They stood and dusted themselves off. Jin brushed a few stray pebbles and dust out of Astrea's hair, letting his hand slide down and linger on her jaw. She wanted to lean into him, into the safety his embrace promised, but she couldn't. She stood frozen.

Balthazar lowered the first barrier wall separating them from the outside world, orange anxiety swirling around him.

Lucian moved ahead to the second wall, still intact despite everything. He rubbed both hands over his face, like he was trying to clear his mind, then said, "I don't think we're in danger."

Astrea didn't think so, either. Not if the overwhelming waves of pain and terror were anything to go by. But she couldn't even voice the thought, too exhausted, too overrun by the deluge outside. Jin wrapped his arm around her shoulders, as if knowing exactly what she would be feeling. Lucian didn't look to be in much better shape than her, his posture wilted and back heaving with each breath.

Balthazar lowered the next wall, and Astrea wished he hadn't.

Dark clouds hung over the landscape. Snow and gray smoke filled the air. Moans and cries of pain came out from the mess—the utter destruction—laid out before them. The fallen soldiers in their red, black, and green uniforms. The ground pitted with holes and small craters. The red blood mixed with white snow and dark, volcanic pebbles. The smell

. . .

Whirling away from Jin, Astrea vomited onto the ground behind her, barely missing Civan's boots. Both Jin and Civan knelt down next to her, but she couldn't hear what they were saying past the roar in her ears.

All of this. All of *that* for what? The aetherium? How could it be worth *that* to any of these governments? Maybe she was naive, but how could anyone think that much suffering—only a fraction of what was surely happening on battlefields around the continent—was worth this terribly destructive resource? One that would only bring even more pain and suffering in its wake?

She sucked in one deep breath, then another. Civan handed her a canteen. She rinsed her mouth out, then managed to stand up with Jin's help. Her knees wobbled, not from how she felt about the situation but what all those soldiers behind her—the survivors—were feeling.

"Airships are landing," Rami said. "Novarian and Tornamian."

"Cannon fire has stopped, too," Zephyrine said. "I think it might be over."

Astrea didn't dare pull her barrier back in, lest Nazarov decide to make his grand re-entrance. It seemed like something he would do, wait until the fighting *appeared* to be over, only to come back with a vengeance. He would be so angry, not just because of Jin's attack but the fact that his coalition had clearly lost.

She walked in a daze, following Rami's instructions. Left and right, they zigzagged through the fallen bodies and debris as they headed for the airships. Soldiers and medics dressed in midnight blue and forest green—Novarians and Tornamians—exited the airships. Someone shouted commands to stabilize the survivors. A pair of Novarian soldiers approached Lucian, then began guiding their small team onto one of the waiting ships.

"Valen . . ." Astrea said, mostly to Jin. She fixed her bleary gaze on one of the soldiers, trying to find a way to explain where Valen was.

"There's a man we lost," Adi said from behind her, his voice tired but clear as he went on to explain where the army could find Valen. "Please bring him back to the lead ship."

The soldiers saluted him, then headed off.

"Thank you," Astrea said to Adi. He smiled at her, but it was tired. Sad.

They finished boarding the airship; Astrea barely took in the metallic gray interior before she collapsed on one of the benches against the far wall. Jin nearly fell down next to her, still somehow pulling her head into his lap. The last thing Astrea felt before the darkness took over was Cressida's metal hand in hers, squeezing tight.

Something cool and wet drifted over Astrea's skin, uncomfortable but reassuring. She squirmed, fighting against her heavy eyelids.

"Come now," said a gruff but not unkind voice. "No moving around when you're being healed."

Astrea managed to hold still, but the world around her bobbed up and down. Her head swam. She peeled her eyes open, only to find a bearded, red-haired man smiling down at her. His irises were the brightest sea green she'd ever seen.

"Ah, she's awake!" he exclaimed. "Welcome back."

"What's happening?" Astrea asked.

"You're back with the Novarian navy," the healer said. A Purifier, no doubt. "Just discharged your friends, but your husband's still asleep."

Some faraway part of Astrea's mind wondered how this man knew anything about her, as she had never seen him before. He wore the dark blue sailing outfit she'd seen all the Novarian navy wearing in the time they'd been away from Talmaris. Had Lucian explained?

She tried to ignore the rocking of the ship, instead listening to the room around her. Low murmurs, warring pain and relief on her skin and in her bones, stiff sheets on her cot. The infirmary. That had to be where she was. Astrea sank deeper into the mattress as the healer continued his work. She pulled her barrier back weakly, trying to block out the worst of the injuries and emotions in the room.

"Thank you," Astrea said as the man pulled his hands and water away from her arm.

"Best to take it easy the rest of the night if you can," he said. "The whole lot of you."

"Where's Commander Lucian?" Astrea asked, unable to lift her head. She glanced left, finding a wall. To her right, separated by a short distance between beds, was Jin, asleep.

"Told him he needed to stay here, but he left about ten minutes ago to talk to the captain," the healer said with a heavy sigh. "Not much one can do to stop a man like that, is there?"

"I suppose not."

"Let me get you some water, and I'll help you sit up," the man said. "I'm Finne, by the way."

As Finne walked off to a small metal cupboard anchored to the far wall, Astrea pushed up onto her elbows. The ship's infirmary was overrun, all beds full and being tended to by healers.

"How bad was it all?" Astrea asked Finne when he returned with a cup of water. She took small sips, wincing as the cold liquid burned her throat.

"Oh, bad," said Finne. "Helosians seemed to come out of nowhere, and the Zaikudi weren't far behind. Sank one of our ships, but the others mostly sustained damage. A good number of casualties, but theirs were worse. We've been pulling survivors out of the water all afternoon."

The way he said it so matter-of-factly didn't sit right with Astrea.

He must've seen something on her face, because Finne said, "But don't you worry. Your friends are all fine. Sent them back to their rooms."

"What about my husband?" she asked.

"He just needs some rest."

Jin's face, previously battered and burnt from his fight with his father and brother, was all smooth skin now, slightly pink from the healing.

He was alive. *She* was alive. All her friends had survived whatever that battle was.

Well, almost all. Valen may not have been a friend, exactly. She wasn't even sure how much she considered him family. Something deep within her ached, that familiar, awful dread strangling her heart.

"Miss?" asked Finne.

Astrea blinked, finding the healer watching her carefully. "Sorry," she whispered. "I'm just tired."

"Then let's get you and this husband of yours back to your cabin," said Finne. "I don't mean to kick you out, but we need the beds, and you two only need some sleep."

"Right . . ." Astrea didn't think she'd be able to walk. She doubted Jin would, either, if he was still unconscious after all that.

"We'll get everything taken care of for you," Finne said. "Lie down. You'll be back in your own bed in no time."

Astrea had no idea what that meant, but she decided to trust Finne. Surely they had some way to move an unconscious Jin back to their quarters. And so Astrea followed orders, lying back down on the hard cot. As soon as her head hit the pillow, her eyes closed, and she was out.

CHAPTER 40

Strong, familiar arms circled Astrea's waist. She sank deeper into the embrace, the warm but rough blankets, the familiar sunshine on her skin.

"Az," Jin rasped in her ear.

"Hm?" She tried to roll over but found there was no room.

"We should probably get up."

"What time is it?"

"I don't know. After sunset, at least."

Astrea forced her eyes open, finding only the dark outlines of furniture in their cabin. Finne the Purifier had said something about getting them back to their cabin, that they needed the infirmary beds. She couldn't remember how they got back. She didn't even know what day it was.

"We should find Lucian," Astrea said, trying to push up on her elbow.

"Hey." Jin held her still as he sat up behind her. "Hold on."

She thought something might be wrong, but Jin pulled her into his arms and lap, squeezing her tight against his body. She threaded her arms around his neck and relaxed against him, trying to memorize the steady *thunk thunk thunk* of his heart, the way he was warm and real and there with her, breathing. Trying to block out the images of Valen, Aelius, all those soldiers littering the ground outside that tunnel after the air raid.

Jin let out a shuddering breath, cradling the back of her head with his hand. His fingers tangled in her hair, almost like he couldn't believe she was right there with him.

"I'm here," she whispered.

"I know." He hugged her tighter.

They sat wrapped up like that for a while longer, their own private moment while the rest of the crew dealt with the casualties, the aetherium, the war. A whisper of guilt rolled around in the back of Astrea's mind.

When they finally pulled away from each other, Jin climbed out of bed first and flicked on one of the small wall sconces. Astrea squinted against the dim light. Her head ached. Their white jackets had long since been removed by someone else, but their armor was still on. They found the coats they'd worn on the drive from Talmaris to the sea, then ventured out beyond their cabin.

It was quiet. As Astrea opened her barrier wider and tried pushing it out, it was like someone was constricting her throat and lungs. But even without its normal reaches, hints of aches and pains and sorrows rolled through her, a mirror to her own.

"When I woke up in the infirmary, the healer tending to me said Lucian was speaking with the captain," Astrea said. "I don't know how long ago that was, though."

"Worth checking for him there," Jin said.

They made their way up to the next floor. The narrow corridors were mostly deserted. Jin turned down a few hallways Astrea didn't recognize, but they were soon nearing the exit to the open-air deck. Outside, stars twinkled in the sky. The ocean rolled gently under the ship, which was still anchored offshore of the island.

And there, outside, were Lucian and Rami. She had her arms wrapped around him, and he held her close, burying his face in the crook of her neck. Against the dark background of the night, the midnight blue grief wrapping around the two was almost impossible to make out.

"Let's go to the dining room," Jin said as he and Astrea quickly turned around.

They navigated deeper into the ship, eventually coming upon the dining room doors. Both were propped open, revealing a small crowd split up into different corners of the room. At one table? Adi, Lennor, Cressida, and Marko. Zephyrine, Balthazar, and Civan were noticeably absent.

Those present were barely holding themselves upright in their chairs. Astrea kept her barrier pulled in tight, lest she get overwhelmed by what the entirety of the crew was feeling.

"What's been going on?" Jin asked as he and Astrea sat in the last two empty seats at the round table. He flagged down a server, who agreed to bring out peppermint tea and hot chocolate.

"Haven't been up that long," Adi said.

"Nor have I," Cressida said, scrubbing at her face. "Shit."

"What the fuck happened out there?" Jin asked, attention fixed on Lennor, Cressida, and Marko.

"After you led Kaius off, it was just the Helosians for a bit," Lennor said. "Hard enough with their few void mages, but we were managing with the commander's help."

"Until the Zaikudi and Paragon showed up," Cressida said. "They were going at it with the Helosians. They didn't quite ignore us, but the Helosians certainly had their focus. I've . . . I've never seen anything like that, not even when the Paragon were fighting each other outside of Irvina."

"How bad were the casualties overall?" Jin asked.

"Didn't lose as many as we could've," Marko said. "Though the healers have been working nonstop."

Jin frowned. "And the aetherium in the volcano?"

"That's what Lucian is working out right now."

Jin scrubbed at his face. "My father?"

Marko looked at Adi. Lennor kept her gaze trained on her hands clasped on the tabletop. Cressida frowned.

"They weren't able to recover his body," Adi said quietly. "Sorry, Jin."

Jin's voice strained as he said, "Not your fault. I just worry what Kaius will do now."

"Nothing good, I'm sure," Cressida said.

"Never anything good with him." Jin sighed, a heavy, exasperated sound. "I can't believe my father's dead." Astrea slipped her hand into Jin's, squeezing tight as he said, "I can't believe I'm glad he's dead."

Pressing his lips together, Adi ran a hand down the back of his neck. "They did bring Valen back, Az. They'll bring him back to Talmaris for you."

Astrea nodded. She didn't know what to do about Valen, where to take him. Did she bury him with her mother, since they had apparently been so in love? Did she try to find out where he'd been living and bring him back there? Did she have a pyre for him, then let his ashes go to the wind?

She tried not to fixate too much on it, instead trying to listen to her friends chatter on as she drank her hot chocolate. Civan and Balthazar were apparently fine. Zephyrine was with the captain. Lucian and Rami were, well, indisposed.

"I'm surprised you're up at all, Jin," Adi said.

Jin shrugged. "Hard to sleep knowing there's so much to be done."

"And what about Nazarov?" Cressida asked. "Kaius?"

Jin shrugged again. "We'll have to find them."

"Or they'll find us," she replied, to which Jin agreed.

Astrea sank back into her chair, clutching her half-empty mug in her hands. Kaius, Nazarov, Solana, aetherium, Valen, Aelius. It was just too much. It was too much for her to parse through, a thousand thoughts circling her mind in a tornado she couldn't stop or untangle. It was all just noise.

"Commander," Marko said, drawing Astrea out of her trance.

"I hope you all haven't been waiting long," Lucian said. He stopped short of the table and tucked his hands in his pockets.

"Not really waiting . . . trying not to get cabin fever," Adi said. "How are you feeling? Any better?"

"Some," Lucian said, though the tightness in his voice made Astrea question if that were actually true. She still couldn't bring herself to open her magic again. "We'll be leaving in the morning."

"Leaving?" Cressida asked. "What about the aetherium?"

"Most of the rest of the forces will stay behind," he said. "We'll take any of the severe casualties with us to the capital, but forces fit to serve will stay here to guard the aetherium until we figure out how to destroy it on a large scale."

"Couldn't Nazarov just jump in with his army and wipe out everyone?" Lennor asked.

"Unlikely," Lucian said with a small shake of his head. "He and his Zaikudi allies were considerably weakened between us and the Helosians. It was bad. He'll need time to regroup. I hope to have a solution for the problem by then."

Astrea hoped so, too. Leaving didn't seem like the right choice, but they couldn't stay here for weeks trying to figure it out. They had to return to Talmaris and face whatever it was that would come next.

Chapter 41

Three days on a ship, weakened after magical overuse, was only made worse by the fact that Jin spent the entire time seasick. Astrea managed to spend most hours asleep, but his issues with sea travel made her head spin every time she awoke.

But finally, they were back on solid land. Ahead lay the Novarian palace's garages, dark shapes against the darker night. It had snowed while they were gone, and now the palace grounds glittered in what little moonlight there was. Marko pulled their car into one of the empty garage bays; several other trucks and cars followed behind, pulling into the other empty spots.

All Astrea could think about was going inside, giving Sarsali a long hug, then collapsing into that big soft bed waiting for her. Skies, she needed a good night's rest, not one tainted by choppy seas and night terrors about shadows, volcanoes, aetherium.

She nudged Jin's shoulder with hers. He'd fallen asleep about an hour earlier. So had Cressida and Lennor; Civan woke them both up. Adi groaned as he climbed out of the front passenger seat.

"We're back," Astrea whispered to Jin when he gazed down at her with bleary eyes.

"That was quick."

"You've been asleep."

Jin yawned, then opened the door on his side of the vehicle. He slid out, then helped Astrea. Her joints cracked. As they gathered their things, a heavy silence settled over the garage, made worse by the unending fatigue and thick orange waves of anxiety floating through the air. They were home, but there was so much to do and so much to untangle.

Astrea really needed to think about what to do with her father now that he was dead. And they'd have to break the news to Eliana that Emperor Aelius was dead, that Kaius was now the Helosian emperor—if someone hadn't radioed the palace and told her. Astrea already had a headache just thinking about it all.

As the rest of the group shuffled into the tunnel that would lead them under the gardens and into the palace, Astrea glanced over her shoulder. Lucian and Rami were still standing at one of the trucks—the truck they'd put several lost soldiers in. The truck they'd put Valen in. Lucian caught her eye and gave her a gentle nod, as if to say, "I've got him."

And so she let him. She would let Lucian do this for her, when she didn't think she could.

Their group was barely through the door from the tunnel to the palace when guards met them, saying something about escorting them to meet with the grand duke at once. Astrea paid them little mind, instead focusing on the feelings around her. Anxiety, terror, relief, and more, but no void.

Which meant Theo's void mages weren't around, nor were any others. That was good enough for her for the night.

The guards led them to a familiar part of the palace: the war room. Inside was warm; the fireplace had been lit, and the electric lights cast a soft glow over the space. Veiko, Delfine, Eliana, and Nicos were all waiting, none of them relaxed but instead surrounded by yellow worry. Eliana jumped out of her seat so quickly that she nearly knocked it over, but Nicos caught it before standing.

"Father's dead," Jin said.

"I know." Eliana's tan skin was less radiant than usual, and subtle dark circles had made their homes under her golden eyes. "I know. Kaius is blaming me."

"What?" Jin asked, throwing his knapsack on the ground by the door. "What do you mean Kaius is blaming you?"

"It's all over the radio broadcasts in Helosia," Delfine said.

"How'd news even get back to Helosia that quickly?" Jin asked. "Kaius didn't leave long before we did. It would take them far longer to get back to a Helosian port than it did us to get here."

"May have taken an airship from one of their vessels," Nicos said.

"Or sent Caliban back ahead of him," Astrea added. Void mages couldn't jump far in one fell swoop, but he still would've been able to get back to Helosia faster than Kaius would on a ship.

Jin scrubbed at his face and let out a heavy groan. "Fuck. Fuck, alright, what's Kaius saying?"

"That *I* killed Father myself," Eliana said, voice cracking as hot anger singed Astrea's skin. "I wasn't even there!"

"No, but he clearly sees it as an opportunity to weaken you politically," Veiko said. "Blame the runaway princess, secure his own power."

"Who killed him?" Eliana asked.

"Lucian," Jin said without hesitation. "Father was going to kill me. Lucian intervened."

Veiko blew out a heavy breath. "The commander left that out of his report when he checked in."

"He probably wanted to explain in person," Jin said. "It doesn't sound very good."

"Of course it doesn't sound good!" Veiko shouted and slammed his palm on the table. "Skies, he fucking killed the sitting Helosian emperor!

A member of the Novarian royal guard assassinated the most powerful man on the continent. It's a fucking act of war!"

"Assassinating is a strong word, Your Highness," Marko said. "The emperor was half a heartbeat from driving a dagger into Jin's chest. Lucian may have killed the emperor, but he saved not only a Helosian prince but a Novarian one if you want to talk politics. The emperor was going to kill one of the only heirs to the Volara house."

Cursing again, Veiko thunked his head back against his chair and stared up at the ceiling. Anger and frustration pulsed out from him in sharp red spikes. "If Jin hadn't abdicated all rights, maybe that would work."

"It doesn't matter if Jin abdicated," Eliana said, venom in her voice. "His own father was going to kill him. Of course Lucian had to do something."

Delfine bit her bottom lip. "People will hardly believe Emperor Aelius was going to kill his own son," she said, shifting uneasily in her chair. "And arguing the nuances of this isn't going to solve our problem. Kaius is already digging his claws into the media. This is bad for you, Eliana."

Astrea took a few wobbling steps forward. She pulled her barrier back toward herself, trying to ignore the energy in the room as everyone else joined her at the table. She settled into her seat with a small sigh.

"How'd Father even know to go to those islands?" Eliana asked.

"We think Nazarov's been in touch with Kaius," Jin said. "He said something about how Kaius promised him the Lightbringer, meaning Az."

"And Kaius basically abandoned Nazarov in our fight, so if Nazarov hasn't already double-crossed him, he probably will soon," Adi said.

"Why would Nazarov work with Kaius?" Delfine's eyebrows drew together. "I thought he wanted to take down the continental powers."

"Tytas Ramkas," Astrea said. When everyone stared at her, she said, "Tytas Ramkas used dreamwalking to torment the Sun King and convince him to abandon his Novarian allies. Nazarov wants to be the next Tytas Ramkas and take over the Paragon. He told me he wanted to create a new dynasty. He's probably been dreamwalking to Kaius, either sending him visions or otherwise communicating with him to manipulate him."

"Maybe that was his whole plan," Nicos said. "Get the Aurises there and try to take them out, but our coalition forces hindered some of his progress and so only Aelius died."

Astrea let her eyes fall closed. Could Nazarov have been trying to make such a big play on those islands? How many strings might he have been pulling? If he was already in bed with the Zaikudi, taking their leadership out would be easy. He had part of the Helosian ruling family dead now. Her father, too, another Ramkas gone.

"He'll probably try to strike at other governments once he recovers some of his forces and strength," Zephyrine said. "Anticipate something big. More attacks on civilians, assassinations, something of the sort. Perhaps even dreamwalking to other leaders to try to manipulate them if Astrea's right about the Tytas Ramkas angle."

"We'll get security increased as much as possible," Veiko said. "I'll convene the other leaders first thing in the morning and warn them about the dreamwalking. They'll be taking reports from their own people tonight. Give everyone some time to digest the news."

"Let's not take too much time," Jin said. "Now might be our chance to strike at both Kaius and Nazarov, while they're licking their wounds."

"We'll figure it out," Eliana said. "In the morning. We'll figure it out."

After their meeting finished, Astrea followed her friends upstairs. The twins disappeared into their own rooms, and Balthazar went to check in with Sarsali. But Zephyrine, Marko, and the rest of them headed into Eliana and Nicos's room, their anxiety a heavy orange cloud in the air. Astrea plopped onto the sofa next to Cressida, barely holding herself upright.

Nicos shut the door behind Jin with a definitive thunk, then locked it. He shoved several towels—already waiting by the door—between the door and floor, further sealing the room.

"Ellie?" Jin asked, eyebrows furrowing, as everyone else settled in. "What's this about?"

"We didn't tell you everything," Eliana said, voice tight.

"We aren't keeping secrets from Veiko, are we?" Jin asked. "I mean, skies, the way he's put his neck out for us—"

"No, no," his sister said quickly. A thick tangle of orange anxiety and mint relief swirled around her.

"What's going on, Ellie?" Astrea asked.

"Apelo's here," she whispered.

"What?" Jin asked. "Where?"

"He received our note," Eliana said. "I guess Kaius ascending has him spooked. He arrived at the border only a couple of hours ago. He's got Thana and the girls with him, and he warned us about how pervasive the rumors are about me killing Father. We'd caught some radio chatter near the border, but back down south . . ."

Skies. Prince Apelo was reclusive, prone to avoiding the imperial family when he could or trying to keep the peace. What could Kaius be up to if Apelo had fled Helosia?

Jin crossed his arms over his chest. "And why couldn't you tell me this downstairs?"

"I—*we*—think there's a mole," Eliana said, gesturing to Nicos. "Delfine and Veiko agree."

"What?" Cressida asked. "Like someone giving away information?"

"Exactly that." Eliana pressed her lips together. "I think there's someone in all the meetings we've been having who is giving information to Kaius."

"Why would you think that?" Adi asked. "I thought Nazarov was giving information to Kaius."

"Some of the things that are being reported in the Helosian press," Nicos said. "Some of that could only be known by someone in those meetings we've been having. One of them or their staff."

A headache pulsed behind Astrea's right eye. *A mole*? But who would want to give information to Kaius and the Helosians? Everyone in those rooms had agreed that Helosia having aetherium was bad news.

If anything, those ambassadors and politicians had been untrusting of their group *because* they were Helosian, *because* of their connection to the Auris family.

"And that's why I couldn't tell you about Apelo," Eliana said, voice barely above a whisper. "Veiko's going to send him to a safe house for the time being. Just until we figure out who the mole is. We don't know who they are or who might be listening."

That explained the towels under the door. Astrea pinched the bridge of her nose. Would Kaius really try to take Apelo out for some reason? Apelo had never been interested in Helosian politics. Was Kaius, like Nazarov, trying to take out *all* of his competition?

Yellow worry spiked high above Eliana's head as she said, "If Apelo really thinks his life is in danger in Helosia—"

"Then he can't come here, because the mole might tell Kaius," Jin finished for her. Fatigue rolled off him in heavy, oppressive waves. "Alright. We'll deal with Apelo later. Let's just think about this. If the mole has been feeding information to Kaius, and if Kaius has been working with Nazarov, could Nazarov have that information, too? Could he be trying to find a way to destabilize the alliance?"

"But why would someone be working with the coalition *and* Kaius?" asked Adi. "I mean, these people have all seen what he does. Don't they seem to dislike him, Az?"

"As far as I can tell," she said, "but just because someone is feeling something doesn't mean it's for the reason I assume. And not everyone is open to me or Lucian."

"Or maybe Nazarov's somehow manipulating both the mole and Kaius," Nicos said.

"Well, whoever is getting the information, they're trying to use it against us politically," Eliana muttered. "It's bad."

"We need to find the mole," Jin said.

"How?" Adi asked.

"Feed our different suspects different, mostly harmless lies," Eliana said. "Then see what pops up in the Helosian media. It'll take a little time, but it'll work."

"You've got someone in mind?" Cressida asked.

Eliana pursed her lips. "I'd like to meet with them all again to try to gauge their reaction to everything that's happened. That might tell us more."

Astrea's mind turned over the meetings with the coalition they'd had in the days prior to leaving for those islands. Nobody had seemed outright hostile, mostly just annoyed or frustrated. There was Councillor Reis, who remained somewhat obtuse about the whole situation. But to commit treason? Turn on his own country and the grand duke? Astrea could see him not trusting outsiders fully, especially after all that had happened, but he didn't seem like a traitor.

And then there was . . . "The Tornamian delegate," Astrea said. "The one you said wants to run for president, Ellie."

Eliana's eyebrows furrowed, but then teal understanding lit up the air around her. "Skies," she whispered, covering her mouth. "Oh, skies, that makes perfect sense. Marosikis. She's angling for the presidency, and Kaius was in Tornama, right after the equinox. She was probably looking for someone who would pay for information."

"And who better than someone who'll need to run a campaign very soon," Nicos said.

"Someone who doesn't have the deepest pockets to begin with," Eliana added, and Nicos nodded. How they knew that, Astrea wasn't sure.

"I'm sorry," Adi cut in. "Why would Kaius do that? I mean, couldn't he get the information another way? Like, doesn't Helosia have spies?"

"Yes, we do, but it's not the same," Eliana said, her words picking up speed as she paced over to the unlit fireplace. "If Kaius paid Marosikis, then Marosikis would have extra motive to tell the truth. And Kaius would have leverage over her, surely some kind of paper trail to incriminate her should the delegate ever try to cross him." She spun on her heel and met Astrea's gaze. "Yes, Az, that's exactly it. You're a genius."

"I don't know about genius," Astrea said, her whole face burning. "I just figured . . ."

"I have a feeling you figured right," Zephyrine said. "We need to trap her. Tomorrow?"

"Tomorrow," Eliana agreed with a determined nod. "After the meeting with Veiko and the others. I'll see if I can bait her into coming over to speak with us."

"How long will it take to confirm if she's the one?" Cressida asked. "I hate the thought of her being in meetings until we can prove it."

"I'll talk to Veiko—and President Sikori if he wants to bring her in on this," Eliana said. "But it'll take maybe a week."

Did they have a week to spare? Astrea blew out a harsh breath. She supposed they didn't have a choice. Hopefully Veiko would have some idea of how to prevent the ambassador from giving too much important information away to the Helosians if all this was true.

"What if it's not her?" Adi asked.

"We'll watch everyone at the next meeting to see if anyone else might seem suspect," Eliana said. "If they do, I'll figure out what to tell them as a test."

"And if it is Marosikis, if that's really how Kaius is getting some of this information, he might be giving it to Nazarov as well," Jin said. "But we still can't discount that Nazarov might be the one paying someone off. He and the Zaikudi have deep pockets, too."

"We'll investigate it all," Marko said. "I'll speak with the commander. We'll have a tight group working on this. Rami should be able to help; she's very good at figuring out where loyalties lie."

Astrea wasn't sure she liked the sound of that.

Hot water beat down on Astrea's back, each drop painfully wonderful. She hadn't had a real, proper shower in days. The one on the ship was too small and too cold to count.

She let her eyes close as she stood under the water, trying to get all of her hair wet. She hadn't had a good hair wash in days, either. It had been up too long in a braid. It may have been nearing midnight, but she simply couldn't wait.

The bathroom door creaked open, but that familiar sunshine spreading over her skin made her pulse slow. She didn't open her eyes, not even when fabric rustled and footsteps padded across the tile floor. Jin slid into the shower in front of her, tugging her close and tucking her head under his chin.

"Couldn't get to sleep?" he asked.

He'd stayed after their talk with Eliana to speak with both her and Zephyrine. There were implications about Kaius's ascension to the throne—and Apelo's reappearance—that they needed to think about. But Astrea had been too tired to be useful, and so she'd left them to it.

"No," she said.

Jin traced a short line up and down her skin, near her right shoulder blade. The pad of his thumb barely caught the beginning of one of the scars Nazarov had inflicted on her months ago.

They hadn't had much of a chance to talk on the journey back to Talmaris. They'd both been unconscious for most of it, and when they weren't, Jin was taking meetings with Lucian and Zephyrine. It had been a quiet few days, neither of them up for conversation even when they were awake.

"What're you thinking?" she whispered.

"That I can't believe Nazarov and Kaius got away. That my father's actually dead."

"Me either."

"For so long I've . . . I've wanted him gone, but knowing he's permanently gone is . . ."

"Still sad somehow?"

"That's the thing," Jin said. "I'm not sad at all. I just feel empty."

"Sometimes grief can feel that way."

"I know what that kind of grief feels like, and it's not that."

Astrea pulled away from his embrace enough to peer up at him. "Oh?"

"It's this . . . it's like I almost don't trust that he's not going to come back and make us pay. And I'm just so tired of death. I've seen too much of it in one lifetime, and I'm only twenty-six. I'm glad he's gone, because it means he can't hurt anyone anymore, but I still . . . I wish it had never come to this."

"I'm sorry you had to see it." Astrea cupped his cheek, and he leaned into her touch. "That's not easy, even if you hated him. Even if he was a bad man. Seeing death should never be easy, and I'd be more worried if you weren't feeling so conflicted."

He blew out another harsh breath, then gently took her wrist and brought it to his mouth. He kissed the vein running right up the center, blue against her pale skin.

"And then there's Apelo," she hedged.

"And then there's him." Jin pressed his lips together. "I'm glad he got the girls out, but I can't even begin to think what this means. I'll be curious to hear what he has to say once we can see him."

"You think he'll have something useful to share?"

"I'm holding out hope." Jin sighed. "How are you?"

"Empty, but in the grieving way." Astrea's voice cracked as she said, "I don't think I can take much more. I know I didn't know Valen well, but how many more people do I have to see die? How can my entire bloodline be dead?"

"It must feel awful," Jin said before pressing a kiss to her palm. "I can only imagine how bad that feels, so soon after Saros."

"I didn't even get a chance to know him." Tears poured down her cheeks, mixing with the spray from the shower still soaking her back. "I didn't give myself a chance to get to know him. I was stubborn, as always, and didn't give myself the chance."

"Hey." Jin pulled her in close again. She pressed her face against his chest, tears burning her eyes. "I know this hurts, but just hear what I have to say, alright?"

She nodded.

"I don't think Valen was ready for the chance to get to know you. That is a privilege, and he thought it was a right. I know he seemed to be changing his mind at the end, but Az, he wasn't a foolish man. He knew what Nazarov wanted. We told him. He knew the Paragon. He gave up his chance to know you so that you would have a chance to live."

Astrea choked down a sob. Jin was right, as usual. Valen had accepted that risk so that Astrea had a chance.

And it had paid off, at a hefty, hefty price.

"I can't take much more," she whispered again. "I can't. I'm so close to breaking. I can't lose anyone else."

Jin tilted her chin up, making her look at him. "Then we won't lose anyone else," he said. "We'll make sure of it."

"Alright."

"You don't sound convinced."

"I believe you believe it. I just don't see how we can guarantee anything of the sort."

"Maybe we can't," Jin said, "but we can try. We can fight for that, for our future. For our family's future, all of them."

Sunshine settled around Astrea's heart and in her bones. She would fight for her future. For her future with Jin. For her family's future, for all of these people who were putting everything on the line in this fight. She would keep going.

"We won't let them win," she said. "Nazarov or Kaius. They won't win."

"No," Jin said, angling his mouth toward hers, "they won't."

She pushed up on her toes and pulled him down to meet her lips. His mouth moved against hers slowly, like he was trying to memorize every inch of skin. Sour and sweet competed on her tongue right before Jin pulled away.

"Let's get washed up and go to bed," he said. "Turn around."

Astrea let her eyes fall closed as Jin worked shampoo into her hair. He continued in silence, and Astrea focused on the pitter-patter of the water and warmth of his love filling the bathroom.

Valen's death would probably always hurt in its own way, but it would get easier, just as her mother's had and as Saros's was. And though Nazarov may have dealt some heavy blows, so had the Novarian coalition. One way or another, Astrea was going to find a way to bring the Paragon—and Prince Kaius—to its knees. She had to if she wanted that future with Jin, with her family.

And there was nothing she wanted more.

CHAPTER 42

Another morning, another day since both Emperor Aelius and Valen Ramkas had died. Astrea couldn't help but stare out at the snowy gardens, wondering if the Helosians were preparing to bury the deceased emperor while she was here, trying to figure out what to do with her father.

What would he want? She had no idea. She'd barely known the man. She'd barely gotten a chance with him. Sure, there hadn't been enough time, but her own stubbornness had stopped her, as she'd told Jin the night before.

Did she have a pyre ceremony for Valen? Would he want that? Have his ashes buried near her mother's? Would *Saros* want Valen's remains there, perhaps tainting the spot?

"Astrea."

She startled, making the coffee in the mug clutched between her hands nearly spill over the rim. Peeking back over her shoulder, she found Delfine waiting at the dining table for her, looking all too formal and stiff with her black dress and hair pulled back into a tight bun.

"We should get started if we're going to get this done before the meeting," Delfine said, firm but not unkind. The princess had offered to help organize Valen's burial, mostly because nobody else had much time.

"Sorry," Astrea said. "I didn't even realize you'd come in."

The dining room door opened, and this time, Sarsali and Balthazar strode in, both surrounded by a thick tangle of blue sadness. She hadn't seen Sarsali the day before—had been too tired—but Astrea set her coffee on the table and stepped into her waiting arms. Sarsali smelled of cinnamon and cloves, and her thick sweater added another layer of softness to their embrace.

Sarsali squeezed her tight. "I'm sorry, sweetheart."

That emptiness threatening to swallow Astrea whole clawed its way to the surface, making her chest ache. "I'm just glad the rest of us came back safely."

"I know, but that doesn't make this easier."

Maybe it didn't, but Astrea didn't even know what this grief was, for the man she'd barely known. Grief because she'd been robbed of a future with him? Grief at being the last Sovna—and presumably Ramkas—alive now? Sadness at the lack of control she seemed to have over . . . anything? Maybe it was all three.

"We'll keep moving forward," Balthazar said, setting a hand on Astrea's shoulder. "All of us, together."

Astrea nodded. "Thank you for coming to help with this."

Sarsali smiled, the corners of her eyes crinkling. "You never have to thank me for that." She patted Astrea's cheek, then rounded the table and sat opposite Delfine. "Where shall we begin, Your Highness?"

Delfine blew out a half-defeated breath. "I suppose there's not much to consider. Pyre, if he'd want one? Burial location. We don't know where he was living, do we?"

"No, I don't know," Astrea said, grabbing her coffee and sitting on Sarsali's left. Balthazar settled on his wife's right and began pouring coffee for them both.

"Then we will give him something simple but respectful," Delfine said.

They made it through their meeting with no snide comments or witty remarks from Delfine. She was somber, her expression tight the entire time, as if she was truly sitting with the complexities of all that had happened near that volcano and all that might come of it yet.

They decided to have a pyre for Valen down near Irvina, though Astrea wasn't comfortable burying his ashes *with* her mother's. But, she decided, Valen probably would have liked to at least be near her. And if any of the old stories were true, that people's souls returned to the stars after their deaths, then Valen and Roxana would have to work out their own problems and tangled history now that he'd joined her up there. Astrea simply needed to put him to rest somewhere, and bringing him to Irvina somehow felt like the only right choice.

They would venture down at the end of the week, staying just long enough to complete the task, and then go wherever it was they were needed, whether that was back in Talmaris or somewhere else.

And there was, of course, Prince Apelo's arrival to think about, but there was no solid timeline for when they could talk to him face to face. Neither Jin nor Eliana had said anything else about their eldest brother's arrival in Novaria, and neither seemed keen on discussing it. All it did was make Astrea's head hurt. If Jin and Eliana didn't want to talk about it yet, Astrea would try not to think about it too much.

"Well," Delfine said, setting her pencil down on the notepad she'd been writing in, "I'll get started on the preparations after the coalition meeting. Are you joining us, Astrea?"

"Yes," Astrea said. "I'll catch up with you shortly."

Delfine tilted her head, then left the room.

Once the door had closed, Astrea glanced at Sarsali and Balthazar. "Do you have anything planned for Cress's birthday?"

Cressida's birthday was the next day. Astrea had only realized it when looking at the calendar Delfine had presented to select the day for

Valen's pyre. She felt terrible, not realizing it was so close to her best friend's—her sister's—birthday. She couldn't mess up Cressida's the same way she'd missed Eliana's. No, that couldn't happen.

Sarsali's eyebrows knitted together as Balthazar chuckled. "A little something," he said. "Why?"

"I want to make sure she has a nice day," Astrea said. "She deserves it, despite all this."

"No big bash like she'd usually have, but we've got it taken care of," Balthazar said with a gentle smile. "Don't worry, my dear. Just come to our room tomorrow morning, tenth bell sharp."

"I can do that." Astrea took the last sip of coffee in her cup. With a sigh, she stood, shook out her black skirt, and gave the Nikaphoroses a tight-lipped smile. "I suppose I can't be late for the meeting."

With them waving her off, Astrea followed Delfine's path out the door.

The coalition members were not happy.

Colors danced around the table, from red anger to rusty annoyance to white terror. Mistrust hung heavy in the room, like a thick fog clouding Astrea's mind and energy.

Mistrust of Nazarov? Of Kaius? Of Lucian, for killing the sitting Helosian emperor? Astrea couldn't quite tell. Maybe all three.

"Decorum, please!" Veiko shouted from the head of the table. "I will not tolerate such chaos today!"

The room quieted only somewhat. The colors remained, snapping out and twining with each other.

"Now," said Veiko, "we know Emperor Kaius and Lord Nazarov are foes we must contend with, but I'd like a status report from our generals."

Zephyrine tilted her head toward Veiko. "It seems our efforts are not in vain, Your Highness," she said. "We've made headway with targets near the Tornamian-Helosian border, as well as the Delian-Helosian border. And we successfully broke the blockade the Helosians were attempting near Katavena."

A blockade? Astrea had heard of no such thing, but they'd also been gone from Talmaris for quite some time.

The other military leaders spoke up, detailing outcomes of their recent military engagements. Skirmishes with the Zaikudi in the mountains out west, though there were few void mages involved. Bombings of military targets around the edges of Helosia, though they hadn't been able to fly too far into the empire due to Helosia's own air force. A few neutralized threats, too, attacks their coalition thwarted before Helosia was able to do too much damage.

From the sound of it, they were actually doing a decent job of preventing the Helosians—Kaius—from gaining too much control over the situation. Notwithstanding whatever aetherium he already had, but it didn't seem he was deploying it yet. That was a point of concern among the group, and they all agreed that it was likely forthcoming, especially now that Emperor Aelius was dead.

"And how is Helosian morale?" Veiko asked, directing the question mostly to Zephyrine. "Do we have any idea?"

"Informants suggest it is shaky at best," Zephyrine said. "No pay, attacks by foreign militaries, little word from their leadership about what's happening, and of course, more and more deserters."

"How many do we have now?" Veiko asked.

"Nearly five hundred have come up near Irvina," Zephyrine said.

"And another several hundred at both the Tornamian and Delian borders," said an ambassador from Delia. She jotted something down on the notepad in front of her. "That puts us at nearly a thousand."

"Not as many as I would have hoped," Veiko said. "But I suppose actually escaping Helosia would be a major obstacle here."

"Likely the reason we aren't seeing more," Zephyrine said. "Many will be stuck where they are regardless of their politics."

"And Corsyca?" Veiko asked. "The fighting is ongoing?"

"Indeed," said the Delian ambassador. "We are not able to pull our troops out, as I hope you can understand. Not when the Zaikudi and Helosians will see it as permission to push past our borders."

Astrea drummed her fingers on the table as the other leaders murmured their understanding, though not everyone seemed sincere in it.

"If nothing else, think of it this way," said the ambassador. "Helosian and Zaikudi attention are both split between that war and this new one. It will leave them divided, less focused."

Which also means Delia is divided and less focused, Astrea thought. But maybe that'd be alright with the rest of the coalition able to fill in the gaps. Nobody around the table protested the woman's suggestion.

"So now we must decide what to do about our situation," said Veiko. "Emperor Kaius and Lord Nazarov."

"We hit them where it hurts," said one woman, a Tornamian politician. "Return the favor on the blockades, hurt their economies."

"Increase the bombing runs," said another Delian. She flipped her blonde curls over one shoulder. "The more military targets we can hit, the faster we'll cripple both armies."

"What we need is a way to stop either army from using aetherium," said Eliana. "We all know that once that's on the battlefields in large quantities, the war will escalate to untold levels."

"Something we must figure out quickly," said Veiko. "A task I would like Mariya to continue working on. I'll speak with her after this meeting."

"Not my people?" Eliana asked, her voice mostly innocent and curious.

Veiko's gaze flicked to Eliana quickly. Teal understanding arced out from him as he said, "Your team hasn't exactly been the most successful on that front."

Eliana frowned. "We've been trying."

Delegate Marosikis shifted in her seat. She'd been quiet for most of the meeting, but now her attention was on Eliana and Veiko, then Jin. For his part, Jin tried to catch Veiko's eye, but the grand duke didn't look at him.

"And now it's time for them to focus their efforts elsewhere and let others have a crack at this," Veiko said. "Now, let us hope for another day of successful efforts on all fronts. I'll be in my office if any of you need me."

With the meeting adjourned, Eliana made a silent show of disappointment as she gathered her things and stood. Nicos joined her, whispering something in her ear and frowning deeply. Jin, Astrea, and Marko were quick to follow Eliana out into the corridor. She strode a ways down, then stepped into an alcove. The ornately framed painting behind her was of a long-dead grand duchess, who watched them with unnerving realness despite only being a portrait.

"Was I convincing enough?" Eliana whispered.

"I think so," Jin said quietly.

"She certainly noticed," Astrea said.

They continued on in hushed tones, talking of nothing important as Astrea watched the hallway. The politicians and military leaders spoke among themselves mostly, though several hurried off. After a few minutes, Delegate Marosikis stepped out of the small crowd and headed down the hallway, right toward where Astrea and her friends still stood.

"Your Imperial Highnesses," she said as she approached their alcove.

"Hello, Delegate Marosikis," Eliana said with a tight smile.

"Are you feeling alright, Princess Eliana?" she asked.

"Oh, I'm alright, thank you for asking."

"You left quite quickly. I'd been hoping to speak with you."

"Well . . ." As if on cue, Eliana's cheeks flushed pink. She lowered her voice and said, "Admittedly, I'm a bit frustrated with the grand duke."

"Indeed?" Marosikis asked, stepping in closer.

Got you, Astrea thought smugly. How easy was this woman to play? A few well-timed glances and frowns had her buying into Eliana's little plan?

Eliana, Jin, and Veiko had all thought that suggesting a disagreement between the Aurises and grand ducal family might serve as a good jumping-off point for the ruse. Some conflict was to be expected when working in such a large group, but it wouldn't be anything the other leaders would worry about. It was also an easy way to give Marosikis a fake issue to give to the Helosians; they'd briefly considered some kind of false military plan, but that would have taken too long and potentially created more problems.

"You haven't been able to see our long history with those in the palace," Eliana said, "but sometimes it seems as though Grand Duke Veiko writes me off."

"Why would he do that?" asked Marosikis. "You're clearly a smart young woman."

"He doesn't always see it that way," Eliana said. "You know how I've always been against the Corsycan War, right?" When the delegate nodded, she said, "I've been trying to offer avenues for a ceasefire or even peace talks for, well, *everything* that's happening, but the grand duke doesn't want to hear it."

"A ceasefire? The war has hardly begun," said Marosikis. A light mist of green curiosity and teal understanding clung to her.

"And yet I hate the thought of more death and pain. A few others agreed privately with me about seeking a more peaceful end to all of this, but the grand duke won't entertain us."

"I could put in a good word for you with President Sikori," Marosikis said slowly, voice hardly above a whisper. Warm satisfaction bloomed in Astrea's chest, a mirror of the woman's. "She might be open to such talks."

"If you wanted to run it by her, I certainly wouldn't be opposed," Eliana said with a small smile. "I know we haven't always seen eye to eye, Delegate, but it's nice to know we might be on the same page here."

"Well," she said, sucking in a deep breath, "it *is* hard to know your countryfolk are putting their lives at risk. A peaceful resolution should be the goal here. I'll run it by her today, if I can get a meeting with her."

"Much appreciated, ma'am," Eliana said.

Marosikis gave a small bow of her head to both Eliana and Jin, then left. It was only when her energy faded away that Astrea let her shoulders relax.

"I think she bought it," Astrea said. "She was satisfied with herself for proposing the idea of talking to her president."

"More like satisfied she has something to bring to the Helosians," Nicos said.

"And we're sure this was a good idea?" asked Marko. "Does Sikori know?"

"Sikori knows," Eliana said. "Rumors that some wanted peace talks in the coalition and others didn't is hardly the worst thing the Helosian press can report. Now we just have to wait and see how long it takes for the leak to spring."

"I give it a week, tops," Nicos said, staring down the mostly empty hallway. "We'll have our answers soon."

Chapter 43

The Nikaphoroses may have told Astrea not to worry about Cressida's birthday celebration, but Astrea wasn't going to let that stop her from trying to make the day special.

"You're sure Veiko won't mind?" Astrea asked Jin, watching in the mirror as he finished trimming his beard. She sat on the wide edge of the tub, twirling her wedding band around her finger. "There are a lot of bigger things to worry about."

"Veiko won't mind," Jin said with a laugh. He snipped another section of hair. "He'll be happy to help."

"Aren't you finished yet?" she asked. "You just did this yesterday."

"And yet here I am again," he said, inspecting his work in the mirror. "It's been driving me mad since we left for the last mission. It's nice to actually have a real bathroom to do this in."

Jin hadn't brought any shaving supplies on their expedition to the Lost Isles, and his beard had grown thicker and more unkempt in their time away. It must *really* have bothered him if he had to trim it twice in two days.

"There." He set the tiny scissors down on the counter, then started cleaning up the hair clippings. "It only took five minutes."

"Five minutes I could've been with Veiko," she prompted, making him grin.

"Well then, let's go find him."

Astrea jumped up, heading for the bathroom door. Jin followed her closely, reaching for her hand.

Her plan for Cressida's birthday gift was as simple as it could be: a stone or gem for Cressida to make herself jewelry with, as she *always* preferred to do. Back home, Astrea would usually go with Eliana or Sarsali to pick out a stone—or a set of them, like on Cressida's eighteenth birthday. But Astrea couldn't exactly go downtown to go shopping, not with the Paragon still crawling around. So she was going to ask Veiko to send someone on her behalf. She already knew what she wanted, too. A pink sapphire, something small but vibrant. Jin had assured her money wouldn't be an issue.

When she'd told Jin the plan, he'd made a comment about how he should've done the same to secure her a stone for her engagement ring, but she'd waved him off. Astrea loved her rings exactly as they were.

She'd just reached for her shoes when someone knocked on the door. Jin's eyebrows furrowed, then he went to answer it.

"Oh," he said, stepping to one side. "Hey, Noemi."

"Hi." Noemi smiled shyly. "Is now a bad time?"

"Not at all," Astrea said, abandoning her flats. "Come on in."

Outside in the hall, the staff were beginning to set up decorations for the end-of-year celebrations, though Astrea doubted there'd be much of a party. It wasn't for a few more weeks yet, but typically, parties happened all throughout the last month of the year. Back in Kalama, decorations included bright flowers and more tropical foliage, while here in the north, evergreen boughs, red flowers, and other winter foliage were brought in. At least it smelled good, like fresh pine.

Noemi stepped into their room almost cautiously. "It's so much cleaner than my room," she said as she spun, her silky green skirt swirling around her legs. "Not that I'm terribly messy! I'm simply not the best organizer when it comes to my personal space."

Astrea smirked. Eliana was the same way.

"Anyway," Noemi said quickly. It was then that Astrea realized she had an embroidery hoop, already fitted with fabric, in her hands. "I wanted to ask you something if you have a moment, Astrea."

"Ask away," Astrea said.

"Well, Adi told me it's Cressida's birthday tomorrow, and she's always wearing those pretty bandannas." Noemi held up the embroidery hoop, a veneer of magenta embarrassment sticking to her like a second skin. "And I thought I'd make her something, but I realized I don't really know what she likes, and you seem to know her better than my brother."

"She'd love that," Astrea said quickly.

The magenta disappeared, morphing into bright mint. "Really?" Noemi asked, and when Astrea nodded, she said, "Well then, what should I embroider?"

Astrea glanced over at where Jin still stood near the door, only to find him gazing at her with the gentlest of smiles.

"How about you two figure out what to do for Noemi's gift, and I'll go talk to Veiko about ours?" Jin said to her.

"Could you start a fire for us first?" Astrea asked. "It's freezing in here."

Jin meandered over to the fireplace, rearranging the logs and starting the fire. It wouldn't take long for the sitting room to get more comfortable. As he passed her to reach the door, Jin pressed a kiss to the top of Astrea's head. He called his goodbyes to both of them, and then he was gone.

"What's your gift going to be?" Noemi asked, taking the seat Astrea motioned to.

"A stone to put into a piece of jewelry," Astrea said. "Cress likes to make her own. But we need the grand duke to send someone to get it for us."

"Right . . . can't really go shopping, I suppose," Noemi said bashfully.

"Unfortunately not, because I think Cress and Ellie both would love a day out."

"Not you?" Noemi asked.

"I used to have fun going with them in Kalama," Astrea said. "I'm too anxious lately, after all that's happened."

"I understand that." She fiddled with the embroidery hoop in her hands, tracing invisible lines in the light wood. "Adi won't admit it, but I think he is, too."

"It's been a lot for all of us," Astrea said. "You seem to be settling in, though?"

Noemi gave her a weak smile. "Trying. Do you think we'll get to go home soon? I can't believe I've missed this entire semester."

"Now I see why Adi always said I reminded him of you," Astrea teased. "I'd be upset about the same thing if I was still in school."

At that, Noemi actually laughed, a light, tinkling sound. "School's important."

"Believe me, I know. Jin would probably disagree, but I get it," Astrea said, and Noemi laughed again. "School was always a happy place for me."

Any kind of studying had always been a happy place for Astrea, whether in her university courses or when Saros had taught her alongside the Auris children. Saros had always loved studying and learning, too. Her heart ached.

"Yeah," Noemi said with a half-sad, half-dreamy sigh. She looked down at the blank canvas of fabric. "So . . . what design would Cress like?"

Astrea forced herself to smile. She'd always miss Saros, but today, she wanted to focus on the good things she had in the present, not all the things she missed about the past. He wouldn't want her to dwell on that grief for too long.

"How about I call down to the kitchen for some tea and cakes first?" Astrea said, and Noemi perked up. "Then we can get started."

Keeping things a surprise from Cressida was easier than usual, maybe thanks to Lennor keeping her distracted. And now, Astrea fidgeted with the long ribbon holding her hair back in a half updo as she waited for Cressida to actually show up.

The Nikaphoroses really had gotten everything organized. Their friends, of course, but also breakfast, complete with a warm coffee cake covered in cinnamon and powdered sugar. It was one of Cressida's favorites. Astrea had no idea how Sarsali had pulled it off, but bright pink tulips—Cressida's favorite flower—were blooming in the vase in the center of the coffee table. It wasn't elaborate like years past, but Astrea was just glad they'd cobbled something together.

"Oh, she's coming," Astrea said as confusion, curiosity, and excitement floated toward her from the hallway. Lennor was in charge of bringing Cressida to the party at five minutes after the tenth morning bell, so that had to be them.

"Explain to me *why* you want to talk to my parents?" Cressida's muffled voice came from the hallway.

"It'd be nice to have a chat and some coffee!" Lennor said cheerfully. "Just go in."

"We need to kno—"

The knob turned, and Lennor threw the door open. Cressida leaned back, eyebrows furrowed.

"What's this?" she asked.

"Happy birthday!" Sarsali and Balthazar exclaimed, the rest of them quickly following suit.

Grinning from ear to ear, Lennor tugged Cressida forward by the forearm. Cressida's aura flared with magenta embarrassment and teal approval.

"You didn't have to do all this," she said, gaze flicking from her flowers to her parents, then to where Astrea, Eliana, and Jin stood nearby. A smile tugged at her mouth. "Seriously, you didn't."

"We didn't *have* to," Astrea said, "but we wanted to. You deserve to have a nice day, especially today."

"I guess I do, don't I?" Cressida asked as her smile grew into a full-blown grin.

Sarsali and Balthazar went about cutting cake and pouring coffee for everyone, then had Cressida sit to receive her presents. Cressida complained half-heartedly that it was awkward and unnecessary for them all to watch, but she did that every year, and every year, she loved receiving gifts. Not because she was materialistic, but Cressida genuinely enjoyed both nice gestures and nice things. She loved giving gifts just as much and always forced Astrea through the same ritual.

Civan gifted her a box of specialty chocolate truffles with raspberry cream. Adi gave her a new blouse made of bright pink silk that matched the tulips. Marko had opted for a novel, which only served to give Astrea a private laugh because Cressida was not prone to spending her free time reading. Sarsali and Balthazar had a family heirloom for her, a delicate gold chain that had belonged to Sarsali's mother; apparently Sarsali had thought to grab it before fleeing Kalama. Then there was Astrea and Jin's gift, the small pink sapphire, and Eliana and Nicos had added an emerald of the same size. Cressida adored the bandanna Noemi had embroidered for her with an intricate floral border.

And then there was Lennor. She fidgeted with the small white box in her lap. It was plain, barely bigger than the palm of Astrea's hand.

"Here," Lennor said, a furious blush creeping over her cheeks.

Cressida took it carefully, as if it were a delicate teacup and saucer. Her metal fingers flexed in time with her real ones, almost seamlessly. When she pulled the top off the box, she immediately looked back up at Lennor, wide-eyed. Lavender surprise flickered around her dark curls.

"Your own pocket stone," Lennor said, pulling hers out of her pocket and setting it in her palm. "I just thought . . . well, you know . . ."

Cressida lifted hers out of the box. It was nearly the same shape and size as the one she'd given Lennor back on that boat to Kalama. Only instead of the purple, green, and white swirls, this one was white and blue, almost the same shade as Lennor's eyes.

Hot embarrassment scorched Astrea's skin as Lennor began stammering on again, but Cressida threw her arms around her neck, pulling her in close. Astrea smiled; Cressida was *not* a hugger. But she clung to Lennor now, relief, embarrassment, and approval tangling in the air in a mix of mint, magenta, and teal.

"I love it," Cressida said. "I really love it."

Jin circled an arm around Astrea's shoulders and tugged her closer to his side. Cressida had been slow to move in this relationship with Lennor, and as far as Astrea knew, they still hadn't exactly worked out *what* it was. But whatever it was to them, the two women clearly appreciated and cared for each other. Cressida hadn't smiled like that in a long time, especially since coming back from the Badlands. And that was all Astrea hoped for Cressida, that she would smile like she used to, that she would find joy again.

And it seemed she had.

CHAPTER 44

As fun as Cressida's informal birthday party the day before had been, there was work to be done. Work that they couldn't be too obvious about given the lie they were trying to sell the delegate on with Veiko's help, that he didn't want them contributing any more to the hunt for information about aetherium.

That wasn't going to stop Astrea, though. It wouldn't stop any of them for that matter.

It had occurred to Astrea that they should recruit Theo Kadis for help with this, but she hadn't exactly wanted to reach out to him. She wasn't entirely sure if it was her father's death still hanging over her or the fact that Theo's followers were hesitant in all of this. Regardless, Theo hadn't reached out to her, either. Lucian and Zephyrine were keeping tabs on him.

And so Astrea had recruited Noemi, Cressida, Adi, and Jin to help her, though Jin didn't exactly find the prospect of reading enthralling.

"I thought we already sifted through all of this months ago," Cressida said as Astrea began passing out books.

"Some, yes, but not all," Astrea said. "And besides, we didn't know we would need to be looking for something like this. Something about destroying weapons or rendering them useless."

"I thought we were going to use acid to decay the aetherium," Cressida said.

"According to Lucian, that's proving difficult," Astrea said. "I thought looking into alternatives would be something useful to do while we wait on that and Eliana's . . . plans."

Cressida scrunched her nose. Noemi flipped her book to the table of contents. Her lips pursed, and her eyebrows remained furrowed, giving her an air of incredible seriousness Astrea could appreciate. It was better than Cressida's overly relaxed posture or already bored expression.

"Look at fables, illustrations, historical passages, anything about destroying weapons or something more metaphorical like vanquishing darkness or a powerful enemy," Astrea said. "Any questions?" she asked, finally taking her seat next to Jin.

"No, ma'am," he said, earning him a glare.

"Let's just get to work," she said. "The sooner we figure this out, the sooner you can do something other than read."

They'd been in the library for the better part of the afternoon, digging through old stories and trying to find any literal or figurative interpretation of the kind of destruction aetherium would bring. Tomas had even joined them at one point, though he'd since left for a meeting with the grand duke.

And now here it was, almost dinner time, with nothing to show for it. That figured.

Astrea walked back and forth in front of the fireplace, each step slow and deliberate. The thick rug muffled her steps. Cressida had long since sprawled out on the nearby sofa, though the other three had remained at the table.

What would be an effective way to render aetherium unusable? There was the acid test, of course. Astrea supposed they could try testing it on a volunteer since they knew she could heal the poison, but at that cost? It seemed like a risk. If a Metalli and Sunreaper were the ones to activate the metal, so to speak, what would deactivate it? Could they work together to somehow reverse the process? Would that even be a permanent change, though?

If a Sunreaper's intense heat activated the metal's properties, extreme cold might deactivate it. But they'd found that aetherium up in that volcano, which had been quite cold and surely got even colder at the height of winter. They didn't *know* that specific aetherium *wasn't* useless, but it seemed unlikely to Astrea since Mariya could still sense something was "wrong" with it.

Astrea pinched the bridge of her nose. What use was any of this? It felt like it had all those months ago, chasing leads that never seemed to actually pan out. Maybe she needed a break. She could come back to it later, when she wasn't so tired and frustrated. Maybe she just needed to eat something and take a walk.

Electric excitement danced over her skin, and a moment later, the library doors flew open. Eliana marched in, her crimson tea-length skirt flaring around her legs as she came to a stop. Nicos sauntered in behind her and shut the doors.

"We got her!" Eliana announced, her golden eyes practically burning in the firelight. "We did it. Delegate Marosikis leaked it to someone on Helosia's side."

Jin pushed out of his seat. "Already?"

"Zephyrine got word from Anjou; he had no idea this was planned and reached out to ask her if there really were cracks in the coalition," Eliana said smugly.

It had only been a few days since they'd fed that idea to the Tornamian ambassador. Astrea didn't know if she was impressed the woman worked so quickly or disturbed by the thought.

"Apparently there were several newspaper and radio reports that mentioned it," Nicos said. "Nothing too in-depth but mentioned during discussions of the ongoing conflict."

"Now we nail her ass," Eliana said with a malicious grin. "Veiko's called a meeting. We need to go."

"All of us?" Cressida asked.

"All of us," Eliana said. "Throne room. Veiko's got a plan."

When Astrea had meant a break from this line of research, she hadn't meant some kind of drama-filled meeting with the grand duke. *But,* Astrea reminded herself, *this is good.* They could get the delegate out of their hair and stop her from spoiling any other plans the coalition needed to make. Then they could actually speak with Apelo in person, too.

Jin snuffed out the fire as the rest of them abandoned their books. Astrea made a silent promise to return later when she was finished with this meeting and had gotten some dinner. She would figure this out somehow. She just had to.

The throne room buzzed with energy, a cacophony of gray confusion, green curiosity, and even rusty annoyance. Eliana and Nicos made their way through the growing crowd of politicians and diplomats, leading the rest of their group toward the front. More people were present than in the usual coalition meetings, from their entire Helosian group to whom Astrea assumed were additional staff members of the visiting leaders.

The dais and throne sat empty, but if Veiko "had a plan," Astrea could only assume that plan included some kind of grand entrance. There was no other reason to use the throne room.

They situated themselves in the front row, where the others from their group were already waiting.

Lucian, standing near the dais, moved toward them. "Eliana's told you what this is about?" he whispered to Jin and Astrea.

"Yes, why?" Jin asked.

"Keep an eye on her," Lucian murmured, barely tilting his head to his left.

Astrea glanced that way, finding the Tornamian delegation a couple of rows back on the opposite side of the aisle, and among them was Delegate Marosikis. Her flat expression suggested she was bored. She certainly wouldn't be for long.

"You think she'll try something?" Jin asked.

"Vernie's here, too, but if something goes south . . . I've been put under more intense scrutiny after what happened on the last mission." Lucian's attention fixed on Astrea. "I'm not asking you to hurt her, just help slow her down if she tries anything. Vernie's near the exit. Veiko's warned me not to appear as the aggressor."

Astrea wasn't sure *her* attacking a Tornamian politician, guilty or not, would be a good look in front of all these people. But she nodded. Hopefully Marosikis wouldn't be foolish enough to try to run away.

Lucian returned to his post as the door behind the throne opened. Veiko stepped out, and a hush fell over the room.

"Thank you all for coming," he said as he moved to the front of the dais. "Apologies for the short notice." He adjusted the cuffs of his black suit jacket, all business now. "But this could not wait."

As he spoke, his lavender eyes flicking over the small crowd, Astrea couldn't help but wonder what Grand Duchess Ysabel would have done in this situation had she still been alive. Perhaps it didn't matter, but dressed more formally and presiding over this room, Veiko looked so much like his late aunt.

"I like to think I'm a reasonable man," Veiko started. "I think I've mostly lived up to that word, reasonable. I try to see every situation for what it is, not what I want it to be. I do my best to accommodate everyone in this room, every member of the coalition doing the nearly impossible task of stopping not one but two very dangerous enemies. I like to think we've come a long way in a short time, working to trust each other even in such a dangerous situation."

The crowd murmured their agreement. Astrea took Jin's hand.

"But," the grand duke said, "it's come to my attention that we have a traitor in our midst."

Cold fear and heavy disbelief exploded from the crowd. Astrea braced herself against Jin's side, against the onslaught.

"A traitor?" called President Sikori. "Why are you only telling us this now, Your Highness?"

"It's a recent discovery, Madam President," he said solemnly. "And to bring more bad news, it's someone in your camp."

"My camp?" the president asked, voice rising an octave as more whispers spread through the crowd like wildfire. "Who?"

Oh, President Sikori was a much better actress than Astrea had anticipated.

Veiko's thin lips pulled into a weak, sad smile. "Delegate Marosikis," he said.

"This is an outrage!" the delegate cried, but her aura told a different story. White terror and orange anxiety tightened around her. "What proof do you have to throw around such a weighty accusation, Your Highness?"

"It's been reported by various outlets of the Helosian press that there are cracks in our alliance," Veiko said. "That ties are weakening, brought on by discord between myself and Princess Eliana. That she has suggested peace talks while I have declined them."

"How is that proof?" Marosikis asked from where she still stood amid the other Tornamians. They all shifted uneasily.

Eliana joined Lucian near the dais, all electric giddiness. "I have asked for no such peace talks," she said, facing the crowd. "Delegate Marosikis, there were many details the Helosian press had that seemed insignificant but would have been impossible for them to know without someone in our group's meetings revealing them. And so I lied to you. I've never once suggested to the grand duke that I want peace talks. You are the *only* person I suggested this to, so unless you've run around and told your colleagues, you're our leak."

"I told the president," Marosikis said quickly. "Maybe she's the one giving away information."

The Tornamians clamored to speak up, all of them denying ever hearing of such a thing. President Sikori rolled her chair up the aisle and joined Eliana.

"Here's the thing," Eliana said, "I also told the president, and I'm confident she wouldn't tell my brother or the Helosian press anything of the sort."

"Why not?" Marosikis snapped.

"Because she's had far more opportunities to spill far more information for a payday," Eliana replied coolly. "Our visits to Thasia, our plans to enter the Badlands, other more private conversations . . ."

"Delegate, is this true?" asked another Tornamian.

"Of course not!" Marosikis yelled, stepping away from her colleagues and into the center of the room. "Why would I betray our country?"

"Money," Eliana said. "You have your eye on the presidency. You need money to run a campaign. So tell me, how much has my brother offered you for this job?"

"That . . ." Red rage exploded in the delegate's aura. Astrea steeled herself. "You lied to me! You set me up!"

The crowd gasped.

Eliana rolled her eyes. "And *you're* trying to sell the rest of us out so you can gain a little more power back home."

"Did you even think about how there may not be a Tornama to preside over if we don't stop Emperor Kaius and Victor Nazarov?" President Sikori asked, voice tight. "You've endangered the very foundation of our nation because of what, money? Power?" She shook her head. "Are you that naive?"

The delegate opened her mouth as if to argue, then shut it, then opened it again. She spun on her heel and, as she tried to take off, stumbled. The dark blue carpet lining the center aisle bunched up under her feet, and Marosikis hit the floor with a sharp thud.

Eliana pressed her lips together, obviously trying to hide a laugh as Marosikis groaned. Even stoic Lucian had to suppress a smile.

Vernie and another guard were on Marosikis in a moment, hauling her to her feet and binding her wrists behind her back. Her aura burned with magenta embarrassment and gray hate.

At least Astrea hadn't had to go after her herself. She sent a silent thank you to Vernie and that carpet.

"Let this be a warning to you all," called Veiko, his voice bouncing off the walls. "Betray our trust and our alliance, and you will be punished not just in Novaria but by your respective governments as well. It's as President Sikori said: if we do not stop Emperor Kaius and Victor Nazarov, we won't have any countries to watch over anymore. We will be subjugated to their will and likely executed for daring to stand up to them in the first place."

Cold horror swept through the room.

"Think long and hard about any bribe you might accept to betray your people," Veiko warned. "Vernie, get the delegate out of here. The president and I will deal with her later."

Vernie murmured something to Marosikis, then yanked her toward the throne room doors.

"Madam President, if you'll meet me in my office within the hour?" Veiko asked, and the president agreed. "The rest of you, thank you for your time and dedication. Dismissed."

As Veiko disappeared through his private door once again, the crowd exploded into a fit of questions and comments. The Tornamians circled their president, yellow worry creating a fog around them.

"Well, that was exciting," Marko drawled as he joined them. Astrea didn't know where he'd come from; she hadn't spotted him in the crowd earlier.

"One more obstacle taken out," said Eliana, voice low, as she stepped into their tight circle. "Two left."

"Two much bigger ones," Jin said.

"Don't I know it," Eliana muttered. She sighed, then looked up at Nicos and Jin. "We should go speak with Veiko and the president. Ensure everything is smoothed over. I'm sure the other leaders will have questions, too. And then we'll figure out what to do about Apelo."

A flicker of annoyance passed over Jin's features, but he quickly schooled them and said, "I suppose so. We'll catch up with you all after dinner." He squeezed Astrea's hand, only letting go after another few heartbeats to follow his sister.

Astrea didn't envy him in the least. She was starving, and right on cue, her stomach rumbled. She'd told herself a break and a meal would be what she needed before getting back to work on the aetherium problem. And she'd had her break—including a show.

"Come on," she said to Cressida. "Let's go see what we're having tonight."

"Hopefully something halfway decent," Cressida replied as they started for the exit, "and not those terrible carrots again."

The rest of their group followed, sticking together as they wove through the crowds and made it out into the atrium outside the throne room. It was quieter and empty, save for the usual guards.

"Too bad you're not in charge of the menu," Astrea said.

"Believe me, when this is all over and I'm back in my own kitchen, we'll be eating better than we ever have," Cressida said. "I think we deserve it after all this shit."

"I think we deserve a lot more than a good meal if we manage to save the continent," Adi said from behind them. "Though food is the place to start. And then the longest vacation of my life."

Cressida laughed. "*The* longest and most expensive one I can take."

"No camping?" Adi teased.

"Skies, no."

As their banter continued, Astrea smiled, glad to see her friends in better spirits than they had been in a while. And as they passed the library on their way back to their quarters, she made a silent promise to herself. She'd be back to work soon.

Chapter 45

Jin and Eliana hadn't returned, even after dinner, so Astrea had gone back to the library, Marko in tow. Now, he snored softly where he stretched out on the sofa in front of the fireplace.

It was a little funny. After all, he'd joined as her guard and research companion, yet here he was, completely unconscious. He hadn't even had any good theories to help solve the aetherium problem.

The clock on the mantel above the fireplace said it was already an hour past midnight. Yawning, Astrea tucked her feet under herself and tilted her head against the back of the wide wingback chair she sat in. She needed to keep reading; there weren't many sources left to check. Then at least she could focus on something new first thing in the morning.

Her eyes closed. She still didn't feel quite right after the fight under that volcano. She hadn't told anyone about it. But whatever that Lifestealer had done to her had left her drained. That, or she was just pushing herself beyond her limits. Again. But right now, she couldn't afford to have limits. Not when there was so much yet to be done.

Skies, and she had to go back to Irvina for Valen's funeral. She almost wondered if she could skip it. But no, she was sure she'd regret missing Valen's funeral. There was already so much she regretted from this year, and she wouldn't add to that list if she could help it.

That hole in her heart, at least, wasn't threatening to grow bigger as she contemplated it all.

She really needed to wake up, get back to work. Her eyes didn't want to open. She didn't *need* to read to be productive . . . So what did she already know?

A Sunreaper and Metalli were needed to activate the aetherium.

If she went back to her earlier idea about extreme cold, maybe they could figure something out. Saros was always talking about balance, both in the world and within magic. Maybe there were mages out there with such intense control of ice that . . .

Or maybe . . .

That intense cold around void mages, their veil . . .

Maybe it wasn't about ice.

Maybe it was about the void.

A warm, gentle hand brushing hair away from her face made Astrea startle. Jin crouched in front of her, smiled, then tilted his head to Marko in a silent question. Astrea shrugged.

"I need to look at something else before we leave," she whispered. "I have an idea."

Jin pushed up to his full height, crossed the distance over to the sofa, and jostled Marko's shoulder. "Hey, Marko, wake up."

The Tempest jolted awake with a gasp. He pushed himself up, shaking his head and squeezing his eyes shut tight. "Sorry," he said, voice even raspier than usual. "Sorry."

"Go to bed," Jin said with a laugh. "I'll take over."

Marko looked first at Jin, then at Astrea. "Fine," he said. "Just please don't tell the commander. I can't deal with his attitude."

"Wouldn't dream of it," Jin said.

Pushing up off the sofa, Marko smoothed his blond hair back and tugged at his gray sweater. "Good night."

"Night, Marko," Astrea called after him.

The library door closed with a heavy thud. If Astrea spread her awareness out, she would no doubt find the guards stationed right across the hall. But she couldn't be bothered. She was exhausted.

Jin tapped her knee, motioning for her to stand. She did, and he took her spot, then pulled her down onto his lap. It was a good thing the chair was spacious, almost the width of a chair and a half. It let Astrea curl into Jin—her husband.

"What's this one more thing you want to look at?" Jin asked. One hand played with the ends of her hair, and the other splayed out on her thigh.

"I guess it's not something I can look at," she said. "But I had a thought."

"And what's that?"

"Saros always talked about balance," Astrea said. "And if a Sunreaper is needed to activate the aetherium, what if a void mage can render it inert?"

"You think they could?"

"Well, think about it." Yawning, Astrea rested her head on Jin's shoulder. "There's nothing colder than the empty spot between stars."

"True . . ."

"And I was thinking about how you can almost steal the fire of other Fireweavers, and how that Lifestealer almost got me in that volcano. What if a void mage could, I don't know, steal the void magic back out of aetherium?"

"Hm." Jin's thumb drew an invisible line along the side of her thigh, making a little shiver dance up her spine.

"You don't think so?"

"I think," he said, "there's only one way to find out. And that involves Theo."

"Which you don't like," she hedged.

"I don't think I'll ever like it, but you're right. It would make sense. It's as logical an assumption as any, at least. We should get in touch with him first thing in the morning."

"First thing," Astrea agreed.

If this idea didn't pan out, they'd pivot and try something else. Maybe the world really would just have to come to some kind of agreement about not using the material if they couldn't destroy it. But that wasn't something Astrea could solve at one in the morning. In fact, *she* couldn't solve that at all. It would take all the governments to work together.

"You were gone for a long time tonight," she murmured.

"Politicians never like to keep things short," Jin said wryly.

"Is everything smoothed over? About the delegate."

"It is," he said. "I don't think this will hurt the alliance. The president was more worried about the group no longer trusting her country, but that doesn't seem to be an issue. It's clear Marosikis was working alone."

"And what of Apelo? Will he get to leave the safe house soon?"

"Veiko's going to talk to Lucian about bringing Apelo, Thana, and the girls here. He wants to speak with them personally."

Astrea yawned again, making Jin chuckle quietly. His whole body relaxed, and he wrapped one arm around her waist, keeping her tucked safely against him. His fingers kept playing with the ends of her hair, and something about it was soothing.

"You know what this reminds me of?" he asked, voice low.

"What's that?"

"That night I brought you to my father's dinner party. Our first date."

Leaning back slightly, Astrea peered up at him. "That's not much of a first date."

"A party in the Palace of a Thousand Suns isn't much of a first date?" he teased. "Many people would disagree, you know."

"Hard to see it as a date when we were trying to spy on your father. I don't think a mission counts as a date."

"Alright," he said with a smug smile, "if that wasn't our first date, what was?"

"That night by the lake."

"Ah." He nodded sagely. "One of the best nights of my life."

"Only *one* of the best?" she asked.

His voice was all honey as he said, "The only two that top it are the night you accepted my proposal and the night you married me."

"The top three spots are all mine?"

"Every night with you is the best night of my life, Az."

"Wow," she mused, gaze flicking to his mouth. "You're smooth."

"Just being honest."

They shifted. Jin's hands skimmed her waist, and Astrea ran her hands through his hair. She loved those soft curls of his, the way the fire brought out all the subtle shades of brown.

She didn't know who moved first, but their lips met in a slow dance. He tasted faintly of whiskey and coffee, somehow the perfect combination even though she hated whiskey. He pulled her lower lip between his teeth, biting gently. She moaned, making him pull back with a satisfied smile.

"Should we go upstairs?" she whispered.

"Or I could have you right here." His hands drifted low again, caressing the small of her back.

"In the *library*?" Her words were barely audible. Heat filled Astrea's entire body, but she wasn't sure if it was the scandalous idea or the fact that she actually liked the thought. "We could get caught."

"It's very late," he said. Raspberry drifted in the air around him, so sheer she almost couldn't make it out. "Nobody's going to come around."

"Tomas would kill us both if he found out."

"Then we'll make sure he never knows."

Astrea didn't know what it was, but an uncontrollable fire burned in her belly. Every muscle in her body tightened. Her pulsed thundered in her ears. Her lungs filled with short, shallow breaths.

"Or we can go upstairs if you want," Jin said. "Your choice."

She swallowed. "Here."

Tangling one hand in her hair, Jin kissed her again. It was rough, demanding, like a man who'd been starving. Astrea focused on the way his mouth moved against hers. She squeaked as his hand slid up her thigh under her dress. His fingers slipped under her bloomers and met the evidence of her desire, making him growl.

"Would you believe I dreamed of having you like this in the library back home?" he whispered as his fingers explored her.

"You did?" she asked, breathless.

"I still don't think you understand what you do to me, Az. Stand up."

Face aflame, Astrea stood just long enough for Jin to yank her bloomers down and undo his belt buckle. He loosened the buttons on his trousers, then tugged her back down onto his lap, down against his growing hardness.

"There were nights I'd dream of finding you alone in the stacks," he murmured, placing a trail of kisses up her neck. "There you'd be, always in one of those beautiful dresses, hair braided but a little unkempt from all your hard work."

Astrea's pulse quickened as his fingers went back to work. She reached between them, pushed his clothes aside, and wrapped a hand around his erection. Jin sucked in a sharp breath, then nipped at the base of her throat.

"We'd always somehow end up kissing in these dreams," Jin said as she worked her hand up and down, "and you'd ask me to fuck you."

"Well, who are you to deny me that, even in a dream?"

He chuckled, a low, deep sound. "My thoughts exactly."

"And then what?" she asked, head buzzing as raspberry and pink swirled around them in a thick fog.

"Depended on the night. Sometimes I'd bend you over a table. Sometimes it was deep within the stacks, well hidden from sight. Others, it'd be just like this, where everyone could see us. I wanted you to be mine. I wanted to be yours. And I wanted everyone to know it."

Astrea lifted her hips, and Jin pulled his fingers out of her. She lined him up with her entrance, then sank down onto him, biting back a moan as Jin whispered a string of curses.

He held her there, hands tight around her waist, as he gazed into her eyes. "And now here we are."

"Here we are," Astrea said, barely choking out the words. "I'm yours."

"And I'm yours." His hands slid up to cup her face, his wedding and engagement bands cool against her hot cheeks. "Forever."

"Forever," she echoed, grinding her hips against his.

She buried her face in his neck and rode him. His energy wrapped around her in a tight hug, everything from that sunshine love to intense bliss to the heat of his desire. Astrea moaned into his neck, trying to stifle herself, aware of the fact that guards were right outside the library. She burned in the best way, growing brighter and brighter as he took control, as his fingers found that sensitive spot, as he thrust into her roughly, possessively.

She came undone with such suddenness it caught them both off guard. Jin swore as he followed her right over the edge.

Slumping back against the chair, Jin pulled Astrea even closer. He let out a shuddering breath as he traced lines up and down her back. He hadn't even pulled out of her, was still hard inside her. The long, loose skirt of her dress covered up anything inappropriate . . . other than her bloomers sitting on the floor.

"I can't believe we did that," Astrea said as she pulled away from him.

"It's hardly risky at this hour."

"It's risky enough."

"I think you're looking for the word 'exciting.'" He reached up, tucking her disheveled hair behind her ears.

"I can't believe you had that many dreams about this."

"I'm only human, Az. I've wanted the privilege of being yours for a long time."

"Not just to bend me over a table in the Great Library?" she teased.

"Skies, no, that's just a bonus."

She slapped his chest with the back of her hand. "Smart-ass."

He grinned up at her, and she couldn't help but giggle. "I love hearing you laugh," he said. "I could listen to that sound forever."

"It's hard to find much to laugh about these days," she said, focusing on the buttons of his shirt. It wasn't that she didn't want to laugh; she did. She missed it. She missed being happy, even if her old life had been hard in its own way.

"I know," he said. "But it won't be this way forever."

She peeked up at him. "Promise?"

"I swear it."

Astrea pressed a kiss to his cheek, then settled back on Jin's chest. His heart thumped steadily under her ear, reassuring and calm, like he always was.

Life had been hard lately—impossibly so these last months. But she was lucky. She had a wonderful family who had always loved her and who she loved back just as fiercely. She had new friends who already felt like something far more than that. And she had Jin as her partner, someone who complemented her in every way.

"Sorry we didn't get to reenact the rest of your dreams," she said. "You know, with the table and back in some dark corner."

He chuckled and kissed her temple. "Another day, then."

"Yeah," she whispered, her eyelids growing heavy the longer she listened to Jin's heartbeat.

"You're falling asleep," he said. "Let's get you to bed."

"Sure, now you offer me a bed."

"What was it you said before? Oh, that's right. *Smart-ass*," he teased. "Come on. I'll carry you if you don't want to walk."

Astrea eased herself off his lap, then took her bloomers from him after he picked them up. She managed to slip them back on, and after they both straightened up, Jin snuffed out the fire and they headed into the hall.

The guards barely paid them any attention other than a simple nod in their direction. Astrea didn't even have it in her to be embarrassed that they might've known what just happened. She focused on putting one foot in front of the other until finally, they made it back to their room.

And after cleaning up and changing into a nightgown, Astrea finally crawled into bed. Jin said something about it being a very long day, but Astrea was asleep before he could even finish the thought.

Chapter 46

The next morning, Astrea had woken far too early for her own liking, but it was like part of her mind knew exactly what she needed to do that day and simply couldn't wait to get started.

After an extra long shower with Jin to give the rest of the palace some time to wake up, Astrea found herself in the grand duke's office, taking a cup of coffee offered to her by a palace staffer, whose gray hair was pulled into a severely tight bun.

"Thank you," Astrea said to the older woman.

"Of course, Your Highness," the woman replied before toddling out the door.

Astrea's whole face surely turned red. *Your Highness.* She'd thought everyone was over that, but apparently she couldn't be so lucky.

"You wanted to speak with me about something?" Veiko asked as he settled in behind his desk. Papers were spread out before him, along with maps, books, and a coffee cup of his own. He was dressed as he seemed to prefer, in a thick sweater and simple trousers. Veiko certainly hadn't taken to his aunt's ritual of more formal wear. "Is this about Apelo? I'm sending Vernie out this morning to—"

"No, actually," Jin said. "Astrea had an idea last night about the aetherium, but it means we need to bring Theo back to the palace as soon as possible. Have we heard from him?"

"He's checked in and been tending to his own people." Green curiosity spiked over Veiko's head. "What do we need his help with now?"

"I thought it might be a void mage who needs to deactivate the aetherium," Astrea said. "You know, a Fireweaver turns it on, and a void mage turns it off." She went on to explain her theory in more depth, then added, "I don't know if Theo will have an ally powerful enough to give it a try, but I think it's important."

Veiko may not have observed a formal dress code like his aunt, but the way he steepled his fingers in front of his mouth and leaned back in his chair was like seeing the grand duchess all over again. "I agree," he said with a nod. "It's as good a shot as any. Let's give it a go. Today. Talk to the commander."

"We'll get right on it," Jin said.

"Let's keep this quiet for now, just in case it doesn't work. Don't want to unnecessarily get any hopes up," Veiko said. "And I'd like to be there for the experiment. Do let me know when Theo's arrived."

Astrea and Jin both went to set their coffee cups on Veiko's desk, but he waved them off. "Please, take it with you," he said. "Enjoy. I'll see you soon."

Dismissed, they both picked their drinks up and headed for the doors. Astrea sipped on her too-weak coffee as they went. The first thing she was going to do once they were able to go home was visit The White Lily, she decided. Well, maybe not the first thing, but one of the first.

They managed to dodge the council members and foreign politicians wandering the halls, making it to the guardhouse in record time. Lucian's office door was open, and he was inside at his desk, flipping through a folio. Jin knocked on the door anyway.

"Oh," Lucian said as he looked up. "Astrea. Varojin. Good morning."

"Have a favor to ask you," Jin said, making Lucian groan.

"That's all anyone wants out of me nowadays," he said. "Come in."

Once Jin shut the door behind them, Astrea explained to Lucian her idea about Lifestealers and how it might be able to render an aetherium weapon useless. "Which is why we need to get Theo here immediately," she said. "You can get in touch with him, right?"

"I can." Lucian scrubbed at his face. "I don't know that this is going to work."

"Neither do I, but what's the harm in trying?" Astrea asked.

"A fair point," the commander said. "I'll reach out to Theo now, see if he can get us a Lifestealer."

"His strongest one, or bring two if he has two," Jin said.

"I've got it covered, Varojin," Lucian said. "I'll come fetch you when we're ready."

By midmorning Marko arrived to collect them for "the test," as he'd called it. They'd grabbed Cressida and Balthazar, too, as Astrea thought it important for them to be there as metal experts.

Astrea had put on as many layers as she could—as suggested by Marko. The day was even colder than normal, apparently. She pulled at her scarf, adjusting it so it covered most of her mouth as soon as they stepped outside. Neither that, nor her hat, nor her gloves, thick stockings, coat, sweater, or dress were enough to keep her warm. She should've just worn the armor she'd worn on those frozen islands; that had done the trick.

The wind kicked up once they arrived down by the lake. Lucian and Veiko were there, as was Mariya. And so was Theo, though aside from his round spectacles, he was nearly unrecognizable. Like Astrea, he was bundled up to his eyes. With him were two people, one woman nearing Jin's height and the other much closer to Astrea's. The taller woman had a plump figure, snow white skin, and bright auburn curls. The shorter one was muscular and broad, and her brown skin was the same deep shade as Balthazar's. A tight wool cap covered her hair.

"Astrea, Jin," said Theo as they approached. "Cressida, hello."

"These are the Lifestealers?" Jin asked.

"Yes," Theo said. "Allow me to introduce Tania"—he motioned to the tall woman—"and Zola." The shorter woman gave a curt nod. "My two most powerful Lifestealers."

"I've already explained what we need to test," Lucian said.

"Let's get on with it," said Veiko. "Quickly."

"Here." Cressida pulled a sheathed dagger from her pocket, the one with lavender and sage green leather on its handle. The first aetherium dagger they'd made, entirely by accident. "Test this."

Jin took it from her, unsheathing it as he stepped forward. Tania met him and peered down at the weapon. She glanced at Theo, who nodded encouragingly.

"Here goes nothin', I guess," Tania muttered, her Delian accent thick.

She pulled her glove off, then set three fingers near the tip of the weapon. She sucked in a sharp breath, and her back went rigid. Shadows began to snake up her arms, into her eyes. But Astrea felt none of that hot and cold fire that would usually come from an aetherium wound. She felt nothing at all. Whatever Tania was doing, it didn't seem to be hurting her.

"Shit," Cressida said. "Look."

Astrea had been so focused on Tania that she hadn't realized the blade itself was changing. What had once been dark gray steel began to change, starting at the tip where Tania's fingers were. It had turned ashy gray—almost silver, though it wasn't metallic—and pockmarks had formed along the surface. It reminded Astrea of how charcoal changed after being burned.

But the shift only happened on half of the blade. Tania staggered away from it, blinking rapidly. Her eyes remained stained by shadow.

"Tania?" asked Theo.

"Fine," she said, voice rougher than it had been. "Skies, what the fuck was that?"

"It seems Astrea's idea works," Veiko said. "Zola, would you mind trying to repeat that on the rest of the sample?"

Zola's copper eyes flicked from Tania to Veiko, then to the weapon. She pursed her lips, then approached Jin. With a shallow breath, Zola set her short fingers on the untouched part of the blade. Shadows danced along her skin and up her eyes, too, and the rest of the dagger began to shift colors and creak. In a few breaths, the weapon had gone ashen all the way up to its hilt.

Zola flexed her hands. Unlike Tania, the shadows weren't lingering. She breathed in deeply and smiled back at Theo. "It feels good."

"Good how?" Lucian asked.

"Like my magic always feels," she said. "Like I'm stronger."

Astrea wasn't sure she liked the sound of that, but then again, if *their* void mage allies were increasing their strength, that was good. It wasn't like Kaius's would cannibalize their own weapons for only a short burst of power when aetherium was as strong as it was.

"Mariya?" asked Veiko. "How does it feel to you?"

Jin brought the dagger over to Mariya, whose palm glowed as she kept it just a few inches above the surface of the weapon. When she pulled away, she shook her head.

"I don't feel anything from it," she said. "Not that emptiness. It's as if it were any other piece of metal."

Cressida let out a sharp breath. "Really?"

"Really," Mariya said. "Something changed."

"Then we need to test it," Veiko said. "Ensure it's really changed."

"Oh, Your Highness—" Mariya started.

Veiko began unbuttoning his jacket. "I'll do it."

"Absolutely not," Lucian said. "I will."

"I will," Jin said. "We already know my body can handle it and that Az can heal it. This way, Lucian, if we do need backup, you're not the one incapacitated."

Astrea hated this. *Hated* the thought of what was about to happen. But they did need to test it.

She swallowed hard. She understood the logic behind Jin's suggestion, that they knew with absolute certainty *she* was strong enough to heal someone from the effects of aetherium.

But how could she? How could she do that again if she had to?

What if she had to and couldn't?

What if the test failed and she had to heal Jin from its effects, but she froze? What if it was like last time, when she couldn't save Saros? Would she feel the slice of this blade, too, over and over again, forever haunting her dreams?

What if she failed and Lucian wasn't quick enough to intervene?

Her chest tightened, and her vision swam. She couldn't breathe. That blade . . .

"Hey." Jin's gentle voice was muffled, like he was underwater. He stepped in front of her, blocking her line of sight to the rest of their group. His gloved hands settled on her shoulders. "Az?"

She forced herself to look up at him, trying to ignore the ghostly cold at the base of her throat.

"Deep breath," he whispered. "Just one. Hold it for as long as you can."

She did as instructed, sucking in a shallow breath. She held it until Jin hit the count of six, then let it out. She did it again, pulling in more air and holding until his ten count. The blurriness at the edges of her vision lessened. Her hearing sharpened a fraction.

"What if I can't do it?" she asked, the question barely audible

"I trust you, Az," Jin said fiercely. "I know you can do this, but hopefully you won't have to at all."

They didn't have much of a choice. Yes, Lucian could step in right that moment, but even shaken up, Astrea trusted herself with Jin's life. She had to be the one to do this.

"Alright," Astrea said, though her whole body was numb.

She could do this.

"Alright," Jin said, taking off his gloves and shoving them into his jacket pocket.

Snow crunched as Balthazar joined them and passed the ashen weapon back to Jin. Cressida was right behind her dad, watching cautiously as Jin took the dagger in one hand. He tilted his other palm toward the sky, then angled the point of the blade at it.

"I'll just make a small cut," Jin said. "On my mark."

Astrea took her gloves off, too, then set her trembling hands on his outstretched fingers and on his wrist. Energy pooled under her skin, warm and eager. "Ready."

"Look at me," Jin said gently.

She forced her gaze up to Jin's warm one.

"Lucian, you ready?" Jin asked without taking his eyes off Astrea. Behind him, orange anxiety and green curiosity snapped brightly in the cold winter air.

"Ready," the commander said, stepping closer.

"Me too," Jin said, then ghostly pain flared on Astrea's palm.

Her heart thundered so fast she thought it might explode. But where there was pain, there was . . . nothing else. No fiery hot and cold blending together. No impossible cold, except for the void mages behind Jin.

Nothing.

Astrea dared to look down. Blood pooled at the incision point, spreading into the lines of his palm. Red blood, no shadows. And mixed into that blood were crumbled, ashen flakes from the blade.

"Thank the fucking skies," Cressida whispered.

"Hold on," Balthazar said as Astrea's hands began to glow. "Let me get the metal out." He took Jin's hand, then waved the other a few inches above it. The little flecks of light gray shot up as if attracted to a magnet. Balthazar let go of Jin and nodded. "Got it."

Astrea pushed her healing light into Jin, and his wound closed. Then she threw her arms around him, pressing her face into the crook of his neck to hide her tears. He held her close, and for the first time, the full weight of his anxiety and relief washed over her, the combination threatening to drown her and pull her above water again in a violent tug of war. She didn't care about that or the biting winter wind.

"I'm fine," he whispered into her hair.

Pulling away, Astrea wiped at her eyes. "I know," she said, sniffling. Then she turned to Cressida and threw herself into her best friend's arms, too. "We did it, Cress."

"You did it, you fucking genius," Cressida said, squeezing her tight. Her cheeks were wet, too. "The end of fucking aetherium, brought to you by Astrea Sovna."

Astrea choked out a laugh. "Good riddance."

"Not to break up the party," Veiko said, "but practically speaking, we need to figure out what to do next. How many Lifestealers do we have, how to deploy them, and so forth."

"We should talk," Jin said to Theo. "All of us, if your people are ready."

"We are," Theo said. "We're ready."

There was always more work to be done, but just for a moment, Astrea relaxed. The knot around her heart loosened.

She'd been right.

They could finally fight back against aetherium.

Chapter 47

The day dragged on, and there wasn't much to do as they waited for Apelo and his family to arrive in Talmaris. Theo had returned to his followers to discuss next steps with them, and Zephyrine and Lucian had disappeared for a short while to concoct a plan to deploy whatever Lifestealers Theo could bring to them.

It was only knowing that people she trusted were working on the aetherium situation that Astrea allowed herself to try to relax. She'd gone to give Cressida some pain-relieving healing, then gotten roped into a card game with her, Lennor, Civan, and Noemi. It had seemed as good a way to pass the time as any.

"Try to beat this." Civan laid his cards out on Cressida's coffee table, smiling smugly. His cards were all in the fire and water suits, adding up to a total of forty-eight.

Astrea folded her cards, as did Lennor and Cressida.

Peach amusement swirled around Noemi, and her full cheeks rounded as she slapped her cards down. "No problem." They added up to fifty and were all in the celestial suit.

Civan swore under his breath. "How'd you win again?"

"I'm a woman of many talents," Noemi replied cheekily.

"This is mostly a game of luck," he said.

Noemi just shrugged, still smiling as she collected up everyone's cards and began shuffling the deck. "I played a lot with my grandmother growing up. And Adi."

"That explains why Adi almost always beat you back at Fort Avalon," Lennor said, nudging her brother in the ribs.

"He didn't tell you about his long history with card games?" Noemi asked.

"Not really," Lennor said. "Adi's good at talking about himself *without* talking about himself. Doesn't give too many specifics unless he finds it necessary."

"Really?" Noemi's wide nose wrinkled. "He never shuts up around me."

Cressida laughed. "Typical brothers."

"I don't do that," Civan protested.

"No, you could certainly stand to talk a little more," Cressida said.

"I do if it's worthwhile conversation."

Astrea shook her head. She agreed with Civan; sometimes sitting back and listening was best, like now. What could she add? She didn't have a brother, although Adi very much felt like one.

"Shall we go again?" Noemi asked, setting the freshly shuffled deck into the middle of the table.

The edge of Astrea's magic rippled as a heavy wall approached. She shifted on the floor; it felt like Jin was coming. Something about that desperate hold on the barrier between them . . .

A knock sounded on the door, and when Cressida called out, Jin stepped inside. His lips were pressed into a thin line.

"Apelo's here," he said.

Astrea pushed to her feet. "Sorry I can't stay for another game," she said.

"Hopefully this won't take too long." Jin nodded at the rest of them, then led the way back out into the hall.

He'd been gone for the last couple of hours to help Lucian and Zephyrine, as well as talk with Eliana about their brother's impending arrival. Astrea had promised she would be there, as Jin wanted her and Lucian to read Apelo and try to determine whether he was telling the truth.

Astrea fidgeted with her dress as they walked, smoothing out the aubergine fabric. Though she'd grown up around Prince Apelo, he was older than Jin by a handful of years, and he hadn't hung around the rest of them very much. Astrea barely knew him, and now he was her brother-in-law—besides also apparently being on the run from the Helosians. She could at least try to make a good impression.

When they reached the stairs, Jin took Astrea's hand in his. "We'll try to get Velia and Nina settled before we talk to Apelo and Thana," he said, voice low as they trudged downstairs together. "Letizia's going to take them."

"Alright," Astrea said. Velia and Nina Auris were Apelo's two young daughters, not much older than Helena and Leo, the grand duke's children. "What else?"

"I don't know. Haven't heard anything else except that they arrived and that we should go to the informal dining room to greet them."

As they approached the dining room, several new vortices of worry and fear crashed against Astrea, grating on her skin and making her overheat. Were Apelo and his family already inside? Two guards stood outside the door, but Astrea couldn't be sure.

She was about to ask Jin when a ball of anxiety approached from the opposite direction. Eliana appeared from around the corner at the far end of the hall, orange tangling around her limbs and nearly obscuring her garnet skirt and white blouse. Behind her, Nicos was calm, unreadable. Veiko and Letizia came along a moment later, as calm as Nicos. They were the picture of casual royals, with Veiko in a simple midnight blue suit and Letizia in a rich green dress.

"Are we ready?" Veiko asked, only sparing Jin and Astrea a cursory glance.

"Let's see what our brother has to say," Eliana said with a sigh.

Veiko signaled to the guards, and they pulled the dining room doors open. The grand duke and duchess strode in first, followed by Eliana and Nicos, and finally Jin and Astrea. She followed Jin's lead and moved to stand next to him in line with the others. Lucian and Vernie were on the far side of the room, presumably to give the Aurises some privacy where they huddled near the fireplace.

"Prince Apelo," said Veiko in Helosian. "Princesses Thana, Velia, Nina. Welcome to Novaria."

Prince Apelo Auris looked the same as his brothers: tall, brown hair, tan skin, golden eyes. Like Kaius, he was leaner than Jin, not quite so muscular, and his hair was a darker brown. Dark circles had made their homes under his eyes, and though he wore a finely tailored suit, it couldn't hide his wilted form. Fatigue mixed with the anxiety rolling off him in waves.

His wife, Thana, looked a little brighter. She shared the same sun-kissed skin and dark brown locks, and her eyes were a light brown. Their daughters, Velia and Nina, were the spitting images of their parents and had inherited the Auris golden eyes. Astrea hadn't seen much of the little girls, as Apelo tended to keep his family far away from the Kalamian court.

"We're just grateful you've welcomed us in, Your Highness," Apelo said, his voice deeper than Astrea remembered. It had a rougher quality to it, too, almost like he'd taken up smoking. Maybe he had.

"Yes, Your Highness, thank you," said Thana with a small curtsy.

Apelo's focus shifted. "Eliana," he said. "Jin. It's good to see you."

Eliana's posture was rigid, as if physically restraining herself. But she smiled—a warm, genuine smile—and said, "It's good to see you too, Apelo." Then her smile grew, and she squatted down. "And you, girls. You've gotten so big! I can't believe it!"

Velia and Nina threw themselves into Eliana's arms, giggling and squealing as she hugged them both tightly and kissed their cheeks. As soon as Jin crouched, too, Velia—the older of the daughters—flung herself at him.

"Uncle Jin!" she cried.

"Velia!" He hugged her tightly. "Aunt Ellie's right. You've grown so much!"

The situation may have been a terrible one for them all to be in, but Astrea couldn't help but smile. Her belly fluttered a little as Jin's wall relaxed and warm joy and mint relief leaked out.

"You should see my fireweaving," she said, beaming up at him.

"We'll have to find time for you to show me," Jin said as he pulled away from her. Nina padded over to him and threw her arms around his neck.

"If you'd like, Princess Thana, I can take you and the girls upstairs to get comfortable," said Letizia with a small, graceful smile. "My two little ones are with their nurse, playing. They're right around the girls' ages, if you think they'd like some time to run around before bed."

Thana glanced up at Apelo, who gave her a tired smile. "That would be lovely, thank you, Your Highness," she said to Letizia. "Girls, say goodbye to Uncle Jin and Aunt Ellie. We're going to go have a rest and a snack."

Velia and Nina pouted, but with extra promises from Jin and Eliana that they'd see the girls later that night, they finally went with their mother. Vernie led them and Letizia outside, and when the dining room doors thunked shut, Apelo wilted even more.

"I'm sorry we've shown up like this," he said, though Astrea couldn't decide specifically who he was speaking to.

"How'd you manage to get here, anyway?" Eliana asked, gesturing for them all to go and sit. "General Kanakos's network suggests movement around Helosia is difficult right now."

"It was," Apelo said, each step heavy as they made their way to the dining table. Astrea hadn't noticed before, but a tray of everything they'd need for tea was set out on one end. "Terribly difficult. Everything deteriorated so quickly the last month or so."

Jin pulled Astrea's chair out for her. Once everyone was seated, Nicos began pouring tea and passing out the delicate cups.

"What do you mean by terribly difficult?" Veiko asked.

Accepting a cup from Nicos, Apelo gripped it between his hands and stared down at the dark amber liquid. "Checkpoints everywhere, air raids, deserters—I wasn't convinced we'd be able to get to the border."

The grand duke frowned. "You would risk bringing your wife and children through that? Why leave at all?"

Apelo held Eliana's gaze as he said, "I know you didn't kill Father."

"I'm glad you can at least see through Kaius's lies," she muttered.

"Did Kaius do it himself?" asked Apelo, blue grief snapping out around him.

"What?" Eliana asked. "No."

"Father was going to kill *me*," Jin said, "and a Novarian commander saved my life." He didn't look at Lucian, and the commander didn't move.

Apelo frowned. "He was going to kill you?"

"Like he's been trying to kill me for years," Jin said, then took a sip of tea. "Remember what you said to me once? You know who he was, how he was. Father only ever wanted to control me or get rid of me. He would've killed me in the Badlands recently, too, if he'd had the chance."

"Jin, I'm sure—"

"No," Jin snapped. "You can't be sure of anything right now, least of all Father's intentions. You know how he was, Apelo. You always knew, and you never did anything to stop it."

Creases formed in Apelo's forehead as he frowned. "I was magicless, weaker than him. What was I supposed to do? I *tried*, Jin. In my own way. I tried to show you the path of least resistance."

"Great." Jin rolled his eyes. "And look where that's gotten us."

Heavy silence settled over the room. Relief, sadness, and acceptance twined around the table in strands of mint, blue, and silver. Veiko shifted in his seat.

"I came here and risked the travel," Apelo said quietly, "because Kaius is just like Father. Because as soon as I heard what he was trying to say about you, Ellie, I knew what was happening. A kind of coup, and it was only going to get more violent. Kaius was calling for you and Jin's capture, and it would only be a matter of time before he was calling for mine. You offered to talk in that letter you sent, and I knew I should come to you here."

"So you did this to save your own skin?" Nicos asked.

Apelo glared at him. "Mister Masalis, I resent the insinuation."

"He's not wrong," Eliana said. "Come on, Apelo. You see how this looks. You show up out of the blue, after months of no contact and years of minimal communication, and you ask for asylum? I'm glad you're all safe, and the thought of Kaius coming after all of us doesn't seem far-fetched in the least, but like Jin said, you never protected us."

"Did he hurt you, too?" Apelo asked his sister.

"Not physically." Eliana folded her arms across her chest. "But he did his damage."

Astrea's heart ached, and watching the midnight blue grief twining between the Auris siblings did nothing to help. Emperor Auris was an abusive man, but Astrea hadn't realized that even Eliana had been subjected to it. Not to that extent, anyway. Why had Eliana hidden that from her? Just like Jin had, all those years ago.

"Has your brother mentioned the Paragon?" Veiko asked. "Or anything about void magic?"

Blinking, Apelo shook his head, and the grief surrounding him receded until it was only a light mist around his body. "Kaius mentioned that name . . . I knew about Father going after that resource down in the Badlands, but he never mentioned that name . . ."

"They're an ancient cult of void mages who want to tear down the continental powers," Jin said, "and their new leader, Lord Victor Nazarov, is determined to bring all the countries under *his* control. Oh, and they previously wanted to use Astrea's and my magic to help them do that, but it seems now they'd rather just kill us."

Gray confusion filtered into the air around Apelo. "Lord Nazarov? As in—?"

"Yes," Eliana said. "The same one."

"Why?" he asked.

"The same as Father and Kaius?" Jin suggested with a shrug. "Power, dominance, greed . . . What I know for certain is that he wants to kill me and my wife, and he wants to destroy anyone who stands in his way."

Apelo frowned. "Your wife?" It was as if something switched in him, because Apelo finally looked at Jin's hands, then at Astrea. His jaw dropped. "Oh, skies, you actually married the Stargazer's girl."

Astrea shoved her annoyance deep down. "My name's Astrea," she said politely.

"Yes, of course, my apologies, Miss Sovna." Apelo cleared his throat and shook his head, then pulled at the collar of his shirt. "It's been a long few days. I just wasn't expecting to find Jin had gotten married, to you of all people. Not because you aren't a lovely person!" he added quickly. "I always thought his crush on you would go away."

Astrea's face burned as Jin said, "Well, it didn't, and it was always more than that. It'll have been two months since our marriage soon."

"Congratulations to you both," Apelo said. His small smile seemed sincere enough. "I'm sure the girls will be thrilled to hear they have a new aunt."

Pursing his lips, Veiko said, "Prince Apelo, I'm sure you can understand that while I'm willing to give you asylum, it will be on a temporary basis, and it will only be so long as what you tell us checks out. I have more questions for you, as does my commander of the guard, Lucian Astor." He nodded over at Lucian, who'd remained shockingly quiet the entire time. "Are you willing to work with us?"

"Kaius is unstable," said Apelo. "He shouldn't be allowed to rule Helosia. I haven't spoken to him in nearly a month, but he and Father requested I return to Kalama," he said. "I left Thana and the girls home and went by myself. Kaius was . . ." He shook his head. "He seemed to know things he shouldn't, and this look in his eye, well, I can't quite explain it. It almost seemed like he was raving to himself half the time."

Nicos glanced across the table at Astrea and Jin.

"What is it, Mister Masalis?" Apelo asked.

Nicos tapped his fingers on the table, then said, "Could that have been Nazarov dreamwalking to him?"

"Maybe?" Astrea half asked. "I never have to speak out loud when he dreamwalks to me."

"What's dreamwalking?" Apelo asked.

"Some void mages can communicate telepathically and send visions and dreams to others, Your Imperial Highness," Lucian said. "It's powerful and disturbing."

"We know Nazarov and Kaius have been working together," Jin said, "but it seems they've turned on each other. We think Nazarov was trying to manipulate Kaius the whole time but is likely now going to target him as well, as was always the plan."

Apelo cradled his head in his hands. "Skies," he muttered. "Skies, how did I not know any of this was going on? I mean, I knew something was wrong when you two fled, but *this* . . ."

"It's a lot to take in," Eliana said. "We've been dealing with it far longer than you have."

"Kaius is *not* well, Ellie. He was never the right choice, even before this spiral." Looking up, Apelo reached across the table and took one of Eliana's hands in his. "I've never wanted to rule Helosia. I was never brave enough, honestly. That job is too big for me. And besides that, I was hardly the best brother I could have been to either of you."

"Apelo—" Eliana started.

He shook his head. "You were always better than me, Eliana. Not just at the job we were born into but at knowing what to do. I'm good at staying out of the way." He swallowed hard. "But that's not what Helosia needs. It needs a change. It needs you."

The palace halls were quiet so late at night. Astrea padded down them carefully, silent even as Marko walked with her.

It had only been a few hours since their conversation with Apelo had ended, and he was now with his wife and daughters in another wing of the palace. The next day, Veiko would take on the role of introducing Apelo to the coalition leaders while Astrea and her family went down to Irvina to bury her father.

But first, Astrea had to return a book to Tomas. Jin had sworn it could wait until the morning, but Astrea couldn't sleep. There was too much on her mind. And so, while Jin was fast asleep in their bed, Astrea had convinced Marko to escort her downstairs.

They reached the library, and instead of finding a dark room, found the fireplace still burning. On the far end of the room, Eliana was seated in one of the large chairs near the hearth. Nicos was nowhere in sight.

Astrea frowned. "Can you wait outside?" she asked Marko.

"You drag me downstairs in the middle of the night only to abandon me in the hall?" he drawled.

"I won't be long."

They split up, and Astrea headed deeper into the library. She set the book she brought for Tomas on one of the large round tables, then approached the sitting area. "Ellie?" she asked.

Eliana flinched. "Shit, Az," she mumbled, shaking her head. "I didn't even realize you'd come in."

"You could clearly see the door, couldn't you?" Astrea asked. She was very grateful to realize Eliana was *not* sitting in the chair Astrea and Jin had shared on an earlier night. Astrea took that one for herself, her cheeks burning.

"Sorry, just thinking." Eliana plucked at her skirt.

"About what? Where's Nicos?"

"Sleeping upstairs."

"He's going to panic if he finds you aren't in bed."

"I do this often, actually."

"And he lets you?" Astrea asked. Nicos was nothing if not protective.

Eliana grinned. "He doesn't *let* me do anything."

"Fair enough."

Eliana's humor faded quickly, and she sighed. "I was thinking about Apelo and what he said earlier. About how he was never the right choice for Helosia."

"He wasn't," Astrea said. "A country needs a leader who can make decisions and take a stand. Apelo is kind enough, but he doesn't have the temperament."

"Listen to you," Eliana said, peach amusement flashing above her head. "That's as scathing a review as I'd expect from you, Az."

"Well, not everyone's meant to be a leader," Astrea said. "I think it's good that he can see that about himself. It'll probably mean a lot to Helosians if he publicly supports you."

"I suppose."

"Why don't you seem convinced?"

Eliana tilted her head back against her chair and sighed again. "I keep thinking about what that commander down at Fort Silverpine said, about Aurises and our violent dynasty." She closed her eyes. "I don't want to turn into my father or Kaius."

Astrea's eyebrows furrowed. How could Eliana even be questioning this? "You won't," she said. "I know you won't."

"But how do you know?"

"Because it's you, Ellie." Leaning her elbows on her knees, Astrea said, "Apelo was right that Helosia needs a change like you. You've got a good education, you've got experience with the council, and you already have plans to introduce so many positive changes. You think you'd just turn your back on all your values and ideas?"

"What if that kind of power corrupts?" Eliana forced her eyes open. "What if it changes me?"

"I don't think it will," Astrea said. "You've always been open-minded, Ellie, since the day I met you. Kind, even when you're frustrated."

"Unless it's Kaius I'm dealing with."

"Well, who can blame you there?" Astrea teased.

Eliana actually laughed, then wiped at her wet cheeks. Midnight blue grief and lighter blue sadness swirled around her in lazy loops.

"Would it be better to just . . . scrap it all?" Eliana asked. "Helosia's a mess. Maybe we need to start from scratch."

"I may not be the best person to ask about political systems," Astrea said.

"Please, Az? Tell me what you think."

Astrea pressed her lips together. "Well . . ."

"Yes?"

"Destruction . . . burning it all to the ground . . . seems easier, like a quick fix. But you still have to fix what's broken, and that's hard. Hope and change are hard."

"I suppose they are," Eliana murmured.

"But I have hope that we can fix it," Astrea said. "Scrapping everything doesn't mean the deeper issues in Helosian culture will work themselves out. There's still going to be more work you—everyone—has to do to improve things."

Eliana nodded. "I suppose you're right."

"I don't think it's unreasonable to think about those big changes, especially if they can help people," Astrea said. "You've always cared about Helosians. You were always kind to me, even when I was just a stranger encroaching into your house. You're a good person, Ellie. Something drastic would have to happen to change that about you, to make you like Kaius."

"Father always said those were weaknesses in me," Eliana whispered.

"And yet you held onto them, fought for the things you believed in," Astrea said. "You're strong, Ellie. You always have been."

"Then why do I feel so small?" she asked.

"Because Apelo's back, you lost your father, and the weight of the world is on your shoulders. I don't envy you and your position, but I know you'll do your very best for Helosia. I've always known that."

Eliana leaped up from her chair and threw herself into Astrea's arms. As they clung to each other, Astrea stroked the back of Eliana's hair.

"Thank you, Az," she whispered. "I'm lucky to have you as a friend."

"And I'm lucky to have you." Astrea squeezed her tightly. "Let's get you back to bed, Your Highness. Nicos is going to be worried if he wakes up and finds you coming back in the middle of the night, crying."

Eliana laughed and wiped her tears away again. "Skies," she said, sniffling. "Skies, you're right."

"I meant what I said, too," Astrea said, looping her arm through Eliana's as they started for the doors. "I believe in you. You're the right choice for Helosia."

"Thank you," Eliana whispered again. "I know you're right. It's just hard to hold onto my confidence all the time."

"Well, it's a good thing you have me and Cress around, then. We won't let you forget it."

"No," Eliana said with a smile. "I suppose you won't."

When they opened the door, Marko jumped back, looking skeptically at both of them. "Is everything alright?" he asked Astrea.

"I left my book where Tomas will find it," she said to him. "Let's call it a night."

"Finally," he murmured, though his voice lacked any edge.

As they followed Marko back through the palace, Astrea squeezed Eliana's hand. She didn't expect Eliana to be strong and confident all the time, but she hoped Eliana knew everything she said—everything Apelo said—was true. If they overthrew Kaius, Helosia would have many obstacles to overcome, but with someone smart, passionate, and kind leading the charge, Astrea was sure they could build a better future for the country.

Chapter 48

Astrea had been hiding from her grief, the complicated, uncertain thing that it was. Getting wrapped up in everything else—the aetherium and Lifestealers, Apelo's arrival, Eliana's worries—had been easy and somehow less painful.

Even letting Delfine organize Valen's funeral had been easy. In fact, she had joined them on the trip, as she was also going to Fort Silverpine on behalf of her brother to check on some of the Helosian defectors who had crossed the border in recent weeks.

Astrea stared out the truck window as it rumbled along the dirt road to the lake where Delfine had organized the pyre to take place. It wasn't the same location as where Saros's had been; Astrea didn't know if that was a coincidence or not, but she was grateful. She wasn't sure Saros and Valen would have gotten along, and she wasn't sure she could bear to go back to the spot where she'd so recently had to say goodbye to Saros.

Snow covered the ground, thicker in the forest than on the beach. Delfine was already there, along with several palace guards and soldiers. They stood in a loose circle in front of the small pyre, in front of the body covered in a black cloth.

Valen.

Astrea's hands shook as she opened the truck door, whether from the cold or not, she wasn't entirely sure. She managed to climb down to the ground without losing her balance. Jin hopped down behind her, his eternal warmth barely chasing away the frigid air. The rest of their friends were there, too, climbing out of other vehicles.

They were there for her, not Valen. And she appreciated it, especially with so much else to do back in Talmaris. But there was much to do at Fort Silverpine, too, and they'd be returning there shortly after they finished here at the beach.

Forcing her legs to move, Astrea started across the rocky sand, hands tucked into her pockets. She'd forgotten her gloves back at the fort. Of course she had.

"Shall we get started?" Delfine asked as the group approached. "Do you want to say a few words, Astrea?"

What was there to say? "No, that's alright," Astrea said. "We can continue."

Delfine went on to give a short speech anyway, one about sacrifice, family, and strength. Astrea didn't listen much. Her attention fixed on the pyre as everyone fanned out in a circle around it, on the body beneath that black cloth. Her lungs tightened. The snow flurries started again, coating the cloth in specks of white.

How was this possible? How was she supposed to bury Saros and her father in the same year? She'd had great privileges growing up at the Palace of a Thousand Suns back in Kalama, and Saros and the Nikaphoroses had been able to provide her with anything she ever needed. But this year . . . it was too much. Too much loss, pain, suffering. So much had been taken from her in such a short time.

So much had been taken from her in her life despite those privileges. Security in who she was. Opportunities to train and feel empowered in her magic. The ability to truly know her mother or her father.

Astrea's fingers dipped under the neckline of her coat, reaching for the locket Valen had given her. The one her mother had given him. The metal was cold against her skin.

It was a strange thing, growing up the way she did, with so much working for her and so much pain she had to endure along the way. She gazed around the circle, at all of her friends, her family, the people she loved most in the world. Where would she be without them? Astrea had gotten herself through so many tough days in the past, and she knew she could always count on herself to make it through. But it was so much easier to survive that darkness when surrounded by loved ones, the people who saw her—capabilities and flaws combined—and loved her fiercely anyway. People who had seen her at her best and her worst, who would fight by her side and lay their lives down with her. She would gladly do the same.

Jin had been right, all those nights ago, when he'd said that Valen had known what he was doing. Astrea hadn't gotten to know Valen well, but he'd loved her anyway. He'd loved her enough to step into the role neither of them wanted, and he'd loved her enough to pay with his life if it meant she would have a chance to survive.

Delfine finished her speech, then instructed two of the soldiers—Fireweavers—to light the pyre. They took aim, and then the pyre ignited. Astrea flinched.

It continued burning, the red and orange flames bright against the dark water and snow-covered trees.

Saros had saved Astrea, and so had Valen. She wouldn't let their sacrifices go to waste.

Valen's funeral had dampened the already sullen mood, but Eliana wasn't letting it show. No, in the new day, she was her vibrant self again, showing no sign of the doubts she'd expressed just the night before.

As she moved about Fort Silverpine's dining room, Eliana smiled and laughed, taking time to speak with each Helosian defector.

Astrea stayed put at the table she was sharing with Jin, Adi, and the Nikaphoroses, watching as Eliana worked the room. She'd opted not to go fully Auris with her outfit, instead accenting her black dress with hints of red and gold. Nicos mirrored her movements and outfit as he, too, spoke with some of the Helosians. They stayed half an arm's length apart, no doubt trying to avoid anything that might be deemed inappropriate.

Delfine was on the opposite side of the room, also speaking with defectors, in an equally somber outfit of dark blue. Her wife, Katerina, hadn't joined them, instead staying in Talmaris to assist Veiko however she could with the Apelo situation. The soldiers Delfine spoke with were animated, focused but amiable if their energy was anything to go on.

"I don't know how Ellie does it," Cressida said from Astrea's left. "How is she on all the time?"

"Many years of practice," Jin said. "You always had to be 'on' in our father's court."

"And Kaius's?" Cressida hedged.

He shrugged, barely looking up from the thick report on the table in front of him. "I'd expect no less," he said. "It's Kaius, after all."

The faintest hints of grief, relief, and worry warred in Jin's aura. Astrea squeezed his free hand, and he squeezed hers back. They hadn't talked much after the meeting with Apelo, but Jin did think his brother meant well and appreciated the warning about Kaius's mindset.

"Do you need to go help Ellie?" Astrea asked. "I can read for you."

"No, that's alright," Jin said. "Let her and Nicos do the talking for now. I'll step in when they need a break."

"Any good news in there?" Cressida asked. "You keep making quite the face."

"War is never good news," Jin said, his voice rough. "Air strikes are going as planned, focused on military targets, especially throughout the Badlands."

"Isn't 'as planned' a good thing?"

"Not when casualties are estimated to be high." Jin rubbed his eyes with his thumb and forefinger. "Moving in ground forces is going to be a nightmare."

"Do we have to go in on the ground?" Astrea asked. "Would these airstrikes be enough to weaken Helosia?"

Jin shrugged. "We have to go in eventually if we're going to take out Kaius. I'd rather arrest him, but I'm not so sure he's going to let that be the outcome," he said. That complicated dance of grief, worry, and relief continued around him. "I don't know that he'll surrender."

Astrea squeezed his forearm. It was so much to put on him, this burden of what to do with his family. Eliana may have shared some of that burden, but Jin was the one actually out on the battlefield, fighting. No doubt it felt a thousand times heavier.

"But I'd like to strike soon," Jin said, closing the report. His attention flicked up to where Eliana was approaching them, Nicos not far behind. "How are they doing, Ellie?"

Eliana gave them a tight smile. "It's been hard for them, hearing of Father's death, even if they disagreed with his politics," she said. "They understand things went wrong on those islands, though."

"You think you'll be able to correct the story with the rest of Helosia, too?" Cressida asked.

"I can try," Eliana said. "Delfine and Veiko have invited reporters to the palace. I'm doing interviews tomorrow to try to set the record straight."

"Will that work?" Astrea asked.

Eliana shrugged. "Don't know. It's the best option I've got, though. I have to try."

"Do you want me to sit in with you?" Jin asked.

Peach amusement swirled around Eliana. She smirked. "*You*, doing press?"

"I can talk to people," he said.

"Doing press is very different than talking to people, Jin," Eliana said.

"Wouldn't it help to hear it from me, though?" he asked. "I'm genuinely asking. Wouldn't it mean something, hearing the story from me?"

Eliana appraised him for a moment. "I suppose it doesn't hurt. But you can't get grumpy about it. We'll be talking to reporters for most of the day."

"Whatever it takes," Jin said. "Whatever we need to do, Ellie. Maybe we can even get Apelo and Thana in on it. Four against one, so to speak."

Astrea did not envy the two of them. It sounded like an awful way to spend the day, but like Eliana said, what choice did they have? They needed to try to correct Kaius's narrative, and they needed to do it soon if they had any hopes of bolstering the population's support for Eliana before she took the throne.

CHAPTER 49

The next week passed slowly. Snow blanketed Talmaris, and the temperatures dropped more. Astrea spent most of that time curled up inside. After Eliana, Jin, and Apelo's interviews with multiple journalists, they'd been busy discussing next steps with the other continental leaders and militaries. The Tornamian president had actually been glad to see Apelo, and the other politicians felt more comfortable moving forward after hearing his testimony.

That left Astrea largely to her own devices until Jin returned to their small apartment every night for dinner. She spent much of her time with Cressida, Lennor, and Civan—as long as the twins weren't helping Jin, Adi, and Zephyrine, anyway. She spent a good deal of time with Noemi, too, focused mostly on their shared interests and trying to keep them all distracted.

The end-of-the-year celebrations were only a few days away, but Letizia had told them all that the festivities would be small. Something for the palace staff and politicians to enjoy, but nothing lavish. No presents would be exchanged, and even the menu would be limited. Letizia had organized instead for extra food to be sent to the troops being sent into the Helosian Empire.

It seemed the time for air strikes and targeted missions was over. Jin didn't love the plan, but he had explained it to her nonetheless. The Helosian army had been amassing troops at strategic points along all its borders. The coalition wanted to strike first—and fast. Astrea didn't fully understand how it would all work in their favor, just that striking first would send the message the coalition wanted: Helosia's aggression would not go unchecked. There were surely details Jin wasn't telling her, and she was fine with that. What she had heard about the operation sounded like it was going as well as could be expected, and there had not been any encounters with aetherium weapons yet. Theo's small group of void mages, particularly the Lifestealers, were on standby.

Astrea was curled up in bed under a heavy set of blankets, exhausted after a sleepless night. Between reliving recent months in her dreams and waking up to find Jin equally disturbed, Astrea hadn't been getting much rest. The bedroom door was only closed over, and through its opening, she could hear Adi, Civan, and Noemi's low murmurs. She still wasn't supposed to be entirely alone, so she'd welcomed them in as long as they gave her the space to nap.

It was actually one of the few days she'd gotten to see Adi all week. He was perpetually busy helping Jin and the rest of the coalition. After sharing some hot chocolate, she'd gone to lie down.

Her eyelids grew heavy, but sleep wouldn't come. Not when she could feel the entire world pressing in against her: the worry, the exhaustion, the uncertainty. She pulled her barrier back inch by inch until it was just a cocoon around her and the bed. The blankets smelled like Jin, like the new soap he was using that smelled of evergreen trees. She inhaled deeply.

She yawned, then let out a weak cry as sharp pain pierced her spine and sternum. Shadows took over her vision inch by inch. Her body remained limp, impossible to move, as an unwelcome voice purred in her mind.

Miss Sovna.

What do you want, Nazarov? Astrea asked. He hadn't dreamwalked to her since that day on the island.

To remind you to stay out of my way, he said.

The image of ships took hold in Astrea's mind, four huge military vessels treading water quickly. They passed an unfamiliar coastline. Where was that? It didn't look like Novaria; it was too tropical. Tornama? Delia? Even the southwestern side of Zaikud? The ships flew the Zaikudi flag.

For a second, she thought about trying to force Nazarov out of her mind the way her father had said was possible. But no, Nazarov was showing her this for a reason . . .

That doesn't look like much of an army, she forced herself to think.

Nazarov clicked his tongue, and the image shifted into one of Kalama, covered in gleaming black stone and red blood and orange flames. *You're not a very good judge of all things military, now are you, Astrea?*

You don't know that.

I know that your little alliance misjudged Kaius's involvement in all this. I know there are those who would sell you out to Helosia in a moment. And I know that, despite this little act you put up, you're very, very tired. He practically cooed the last words, as if talking to a child.

How can you know any of that? she asked.

Because the prince told me, Nazarov said. *And I know this has all been so very hard on you, poor little Lightbringer. Now, leave the Paragon be and I'll take care of Kaius for you.*

And if I don't? Astrea forced herself to ask.

I already told you that you won't like what happens if you defy me again, Miss Sovna, Nazarov said. *I've told you that a thousand times, and I thought your father's death would've been proof enough.*

Her body wanted to shudder, but she couldn't move.

Either the Ramkas line ends or continues with you and me, he said. *Your choice how you want to play this.* The image changed again, this time to those snowy plains and a body on the ground.

She couldn't say anything. Couldn't breathe.

He clicked his tongue again. The image of the snow faded into the darkness. *Goodbye, little Lightbringer.*

Astrea jolted up. The light from the small lamp in the corner was as blinding as the sun.

"Adi!" she called, voice hoarse. She squeezed her eyes shut, trying to ignore the memories of all that pain, that horrible day in the snow and that horrible day in the Badlands.

Quick footsteps rushed into the room, and the bed dipped. Someone touched her shoulder. "Az?" Adi asked.

The pain threatened to swallow her up like a tsunami. She couldn't breathe. *"Either the Ramkas line ends or continues with you and me."* She shuddered. *"Your choice how you want to play this."* Bile crept up her throat.

"Breathe, Az." Adi's grip tightened on her shoulder. "As deep as you can, then hold it for five."

She sucked in a shallow breath, holding it as Adi counted, then blowing it out in a quick burst. She repeated it, counting silently in her head along with him.

"Nazarov," she croaked once her racing pulse settled. "Get Jin and Lucian. Zephyrine, too."

"Is he coming here?" Adi asked, forehead wrinkling as heavy concern threatened to topple Astrea over.

"I think he's going to Kalama, after Kaius."

"Fuck," Adi muttered. "Fuck, alright, let me go find them. Civ!"

The floor squeaked, and a moment later, Civan popped his head into the room. "What's going on?"

"It's Nazarov," Adi said. "I need to get Jin. Stay here."

As Adi stormed out on his mission, Civan shuffled into the room, hands tucked into his pockets. "Nazarov's back?"

"Seems that way," Astrea said, resisting the urge to pull the blankets over her head and disappear.

"Do you want to talk about it?" Civan asked slowly, as if the words were too heavy on his tongue.

"Not right now."

"Do you . . . want more hot chocolate?"

Astrea watched him for a moment, the way his narrow shoulders bunched up near his ears and he avoided looking directly at her. He fidgeted, as if he needed to do something. And so even though Astrea really didn't want anything to drink, she said, "Sure."

Forcing herself out of bed, she followed Civan into the sitting room. Noemi's gaze darted between them, yellow worry thick in the air around where she sat in one of the armchairs by the roaring fire. Astrea tucked herself into the corner of the sofa closest to the hearth, waiting as Civan went to the cart where all the hot chocolate supplies were. He came back with a delicate teacup full of the warm liquid and handed it to her.

"Thanks." Astrea made herself take one sip, then another.

She was going to be sick.

"This was Nazarov again?" Noemi asked hesitantly.

"I'll fill you in when Adi gets back," Astrea said before taking another drink. She couldn't bear the thought of discussing this more than once.

If Nazarov really needed more authority over the Paragon, killing her was the easiest way. So why was he still going on about making her bear child? What did he know that made him think that was a viable option? They needed to talk to Theo—and soon.

When a blanket circled her shoulders, Astrea startled. Her hot chocolate was mostly gone, so she managed not to spill any.

"Sorry," Civan said. "You were shaking."

"Oh . . . thanks, Civ," Astrea said, leaning forward to put her teacup on the table before nestling into the blanket.

Only a few more minutes passed before the air shifted. Intense hatred and anger burned Astrea's cheeks, and a moment later, the door burst open. Jin stormed in. He crossed the sitting room in a few long strides and squatted down in front of her. Steel pain floated around him as he gripped her hands.

"What did he say?" Jin asked, voice low.

She swallowed hard.

"What did he say, Az?" His voice was somehow both impossibly hard and soft, cold and warm. The pain in his eyes . . .

She couldn't lie to him, not even to spare him the awful truth.

"He said the Ramkas line either ends or continues with me and him," she whispered.

Noemi sucked in a sharp breath. Civan's fists clenched at his sides. Hot rage burned bright around Adi. But Astrea focused on Jin. The way his hands felt holding hers, the concern etched into his face, how he forced himself to swallow.

"He showed me an image of Zaikudi ships," she said. "I think they were heading south, based on the little geography I could see," she said, hoping that would somehow make it better.

It didn't.

"Shit," Jin muttered, pressing his forehead against her knees. His back heaved. "Shit. Alright."

"What does that mean?" Noemi asked. "If he's going south."

"We thought he was double-crossing Kaius," Jin said as he lifted his head. "That's probably his play. He's probably going to Kalama."

"But why would he tell you where he's going?" Noemi asked. "In what world does it make sense for him to reveal his location?"

"He wants us to go to him," Astrea said. It was the only thing that made sense. "He's baiting us."

"And it'll be the last time he does." Jin's voice tightened as he said, "This is it. We meet him where he wants, and we take him out. I'm done with the games. I've been done with them. And I'm done playing by the coalition's timetable."

"Jin, what about the plans?" Adi asked.

"Fuck the plans," Jin said, pushing to his feet and finally letting go of Astrea's hands. "We need a new one and fast if we're going to get to Nazarov first."

"We can't let Kaius take him out?" Adi asked.

"No," Jin said. "Kaius won't be able to."

"You think the entire Helosian army at his back can't take Nazarov out, but we can?" Adi asked. "Skies, Jin, I know we're good, but—"

"Kaius's ego is too big to let someone else take on Nazarov if he gets double-crossed," Jin said. "It'll be a matter of pride with him, and he's just not good enough. And Nazarov would never let Kaius, of all people, take him out. It's got to be me."

"He'll try to kill you," Civan said. "He's already tried."

"And he's failed every time," Jin said.

"It's clearly a trap," Civan retorted.

Turning back to where Astrea still sat stone-still on the sofa, Jin said, "I promised you he would never touch you again, Az. Every one of us swore he was going to pay for all he's done. Yes, he wants us to follow. Obviously he does. But if he's going straight for Kalama like I think he is, there is no better time to take him out. We cannot even risk him getting his hands on the Helosian military."

Despite the roaring fire, cold fear prickled Astrea's scalp and all the way down to her toes. White fear swirled around Noemi.

"I know I said I have to be the one to take him out," Jin said, "but remember what the prophecy said? It's going to take every single one of us to ensure that we don't fail again. We all have our roles to play."

✦

Veiko paced the same path in his office, back and forth in the space between his bookcases and desk. His expression was pinched, like he'd eaten a lemon.

"You want me to convince the other leaders to completely abandon all the plans we've made?" he asked as he faced Jin.

"I'm asking you to trust me," Jin said. "Nazarov *showed* Astrea. He doesn't do things without reason, even if he's hard to predict."

It was just Jin, Veiko, Zephyrine, and Lucian in the room. No politicians. No ambassadors. Not even Eliana and Nicos. No, Eliana was dining with some of those very same politicians, including Delfine. They'd managed to pull Veiko out of the dinner, but they wouldn't be able to keep him much longer.

Astrea fidgeted with the pleats in her skirt. Zephyrine caught her eye, then subtly tilted her head toward the grand duke.

"Veiko," Astrea said, "I know this isn't what was planned, but—"

"But it's necessary." With a groan, Veiko rubbed a hand over his face. His shoulders hunched as he blew out a heavy breath. "No. You're right. You're all right. We cannot take the risk of Nazarov gaining control of the Helosian military or its aetherium armaments now. Not right as we're starting to move in on the ground." Straightening, he looked toward Lucian, where he stood near the office doors. "You've been uncharacteristically silent, Commander."

"I'm not sure what to say," Lucian replied quietly.

Lucian, unsure of what to say? About something like this?

"Could you try anyway?" Veiko asked.

The commander pressed his thin lips together, then heaved a sigh. "I think we have no choice, but as Varojin said, Nazarov is hard to predict.

What awaits us if we catch up to him? A Zaikudi army with at least some aetherium? A Helosian army fully outfitted with aetherium gear? A team of Zaikudi and Paragonian assassins to take us out before we can even get close to Nazarov?"

"He wants me," Astrea said.

"Yes, dead or alive," Lucian drawled.

"No." At Lucian's furrowed brows, Astrea added, "Well, yes, but I think he'd prefer me alive."

"How could you possibly know that?" Lucian asked.

"I . . ." Swallowing hard, Astrea focused on her wedding band on her right ring finger, the way it gleamed in the lamplight. "I think Nazarov's losing control, or maybe already lost control, of the rest of the Paragon. The vision he showed me wasn't a large fleet. After what happened near those islands, I think the Zaikudi and Paragon are both losing faith in him."

"And so . . . he'd rather go back to his plan to try to make you their queen, sire your child, produce an heir to somehow get him back in their good graces?"

"Not their good graces," Astrea said. "To regain control. That's what he wants. He just wants control."

That was all men like Nazarov wanted. Men like Kaius and Emperor Aelius. They wanted control, and they wanted power, and they were willing to hurt whoever they had to in order to get it.

"Then how do we protect ourselves from whatever chaos he decides to throw in our path this time?" Lucian asked.

Astrea's heart thundered up her throat and into her ears as she said, "We offer me up—"

"Absolutely not," Jin snapped. "He's not getting within a hundred miles of you, Az."

"You said this would take all of us. I have to be within a hundred miles of him to complete the mission. To finally end this."

Jin let out a sharp huff.

"As I was trying to say," Astrea continued, "we offer me up as some kind of bait. You wanted to do that months ago, Lucian. Back when we first got to Talmaris. We organize something to lure Nazarov to us, and we take him out. How hard could it be?"

"Oh, Astrea, it's not going to be that easy," Zephyrine said gently.

She knew it wouldn't be easy, but still, she said, "Create a little chaos of our own. If he dreamwalks to me again, I'll tell him I've decided to take the easier option this time."

"And if he doesn't dreamwalk to you again?" Lucian asked. "He's been doing it far less lately."

"Then we get one of Theo's people to do it for us. Make contact. Invite Nazarov to speak with me, tell him I have an offer."

Jin stared down at her, still as a statue. It didn't even look like he was breathing.

"It's the only way," Astrea said. "We can trap him. Corner him in."

"You think he won't see the trap for what it is?" Veiko asked.

"I think he's desperate," Astrea said. "And desperate people make mistakes."

Veiko shook his head. "Astrea, I cannot allow you to put yourself in his path like that."

Rage burned somewhere deep inside Astrea, smoldering and growing so quickly she couldn't tell where it came from. "I'm sick of being told what I'm *allowed* to do," she said. "Nazarov tortured me—keeps torturing me." Her voice cracked on the last few words, on that admission she'd been keeping deep inside. But that was what all of this was. Torture. Nazarov didn't have to put his hands on her to make her suffer. "He murdered my father. Kaius killed my uncle. This whole thing centers around *me* in some twisted way. When am I going to get to control my own fate? I want to put an end to all of this. I need to end this."

Veiko glanced at the small clock on his desk. Yellow worry and steel pain surrounded him like a thick fog. "They're going to start wondering where I am," he said. "I need to think about this."

"It seems like we don't have much time," Zephyrine said.

"I know," Veiko replied. "I'll let you know before breakfast. I just need some time to think it over."

Before any of them could argue, Veiko stormed out of his office, leaving a trail of yellow and steel in his wake. Lucian gave a small shake of his head.

"We need to talk," Jin said to Astrea. "Alone."

Nervous energy buzzed under Astrea's skin as Jin practically hauled her back to their quarters. He'd shut her out, his wall tight around him. She hated this, feeling like she'd done something wrong.

No, maybe it wasn't the best plan in the entire world, but she was right. Nazarov was getting desperate. He may have been trying to lure her into a trap, but why couldn't they trap him first?

Jin pulled her into their sitting room, shutting the door behind them. And just when she thought they were finally going to stop, he kept leading her on, straight for their bedroom. When they were in there, he shut that door, too.

"What's going on with you?" she asked, wrenching her arm away. "Skies."

"I didn't want anyone to possibly overhear us." Jin's energy flooded out from him, relief and worry, love and respect, anger and anxiety. She took half a step back. "Sorry."

"What is it you have to say?" she asked, not entirely sure why she was so on edge with him. This was Jin. Her partner, her husband, whose sharp edges from minutes ago had already rounded out again.

"Are you serious about trying to trap Nazarov?" he asked.

"Of course I'm serious," she said.

"You really think you can sell him on whatever it is you want to tell him?"

"I didn't mention it before, but he . . ." She huffed. "He said he knew how tired I am of all this. And he's not wrong. I know I'm not a good liar, but—"

"But you think we can use that truth and his desperation against him."

"If I tell him I'm ready to talk and that he's right, that I *am* tired, I won't be lying."

"I hate the thought of even letting him be in the same country as you," Jin said, taking another step forward.

"Well, it's not like I love this, but it seems to be our best bet."

Closing the rest of the distance between them, he took her hands in his and twined their fingers together. "I agree. It's our best bet. Make him think you're giving him what he wants."

"But what if Veiko doesn't agree?"

"We don't need him to agree. We need Lucian and Zephyrine and the rest of the team to agree, and we need Theo's help."

"You really think we can pull it off?"

"We have to try." Yellow worry and white terror spiked high above Jin in quick, sharp pulses. "I'll be with you every step of the way."

"How?" Astrea whispered. "He'll expect you to be around."

"I don't know yet, but I'm not letting you face him without me." He smiled tightly. "We do this together."

"Together," Astrea whispered.

Jin pulled her to him, holding her tight against his body as he cradled the back of her head. Astrea leaned into him and wrapped her arms around his waist, breathing in that evergreen scent stuck to his shirt.

Somehow, they would pull this off.

They would end this just as they'd started: together.

Chapter 50

Jin had held Astrea closer than usual the night before—as if that were somehow possible. And now, they were back in Lucian's office, a united front as the others tried to dissuade them of their loose plan.

"This is the only way," Jin said, the third time he'd said as much in an hour.

"You can't put yourself in Nazarov's path!" Eliana cried. Hot anger and frigid anxiety pulsed out from her. "Skies, how can you both want to be so reckless?"

Astrea folded her arms across her abdomen. "Nazarov will be too tempted by my offer to pass it up," she said. "We need to figure out where we can trap him, especially if we're going to have to meet him in Kalama."

"And what do we do about the small problem that is Kaius?" Eliana asked. "How in the blazing skies are we ever going to somehow get around that?"

"A two-pronged approach," Lucian said, the first time he'd spoken in nearly a quarter of an hour. "We split up, as you did the last time you all went back to Kalama. Some of us go after Nazarov, and some of us go after Kaius."

"Like we're just supposed to manage that somehow?" Nicos asked.

"It will not be the team alone," Lucian said. "We'll have the help of Theo's people, and we'll have the backing of the rest of the coalition. If Nazarov and the Zaikudi are bringing in ships of people, so can we."

"Well, we're far behind their schedule," Jin said. "We'll never catch up."

"Not if we head down to Thasia," Lucian said. "Use that port to bring in Tornamians and Novarians, then the Delians can follow the Zaikudi east to Kalama, and the Taipoli can send ships up from the south. Blockade them in the harbor. It's near the palace, too, so it would force Kaius to engage with us."

Skies, Astrea was not built for all of that planning. "That's all well and good," she said, "but where do we meet Nazarov?"

"Where could we go that wouldn't endanger civilians?" Eliana asked. "Can we even avoid hurting them if we invade Kalama? I don't like the sound of this." Yellow worry sparkled around her head.

"We don't send in all of our forces," Jin said. "We warn civilians over the radio, and once we've got the blockade in place, we call on Kaius to surrender. While you work on that, Ellie, Az and I will trap Nazarov."

"Again, where?" Astrea asked. She didn't want innocent people getting hurt because of their plan.

"We need a map of Kalama," Jin said.

Lucian began rummaging through his drawers, then pulled out a rolled-up tube of paper. He spread it out on his desk, setting white marble paperweights on the edges to keep it flat. Jin joined him and began studying the map intensely.

"This is foolish," Eliana chided. "Nazarov's not going to buy it."

"He will if I sell it to him right," Astrea said.

Eliana ignored her.

"Where's someplace he would believe Az would suggest to meet?" Jin asked. "That's got to be a priority, otherwise we'll never get him to go. He'll be suspicious if we try to set it up someplace secluded."

"The library, maybe," Astrea said. "Or one of the museums? I could meet him there and then get him to follow me outside."

"What about someplace like the train station?" Adi asked. "It'll likely be shut down once the Helosians realize they're being invaded by the Zaikudi."

"The library has plenty of places to hide the team," Cressida said.

"What about at the palace?" Eliana asked. "There are plenty of secluded places there, it's a spot Astrea knows well, and we wouldn't have to split up so much if we're going after Kaius."

"The palace seems like a dangerous choice," Jin said. "For Astrea, I mean. Nazarov would see through it."

"What if I tell him I'm going to split off from the group?" she asked. "Tell him the plan, then ask him to meet me in the gardens. Do you think he'd buy that?"

Tilting his head back, Jin stared up at the ceiling. "I wish I knew. I don't. I don't know what he's going to buy."

"We have time to decide," Lucian said. "Let's think on it more today while we plot the rest with the generals and prepare everything we need. I promised to meet with them before the eleventh bell."

"I'll go with you," Nicos said.

"And we should talk to Theo," Jin said to Astrea.

She nodded. They couldn't do this next part without his help.

"Reconvene by the sixth bell this evening," Lucian said. "We'll get it all sorted by this time tomorrow so we can get on our way."

Just another day. Another day, and they'd be that much closer to making their final stand.

Theo had been coming and going from the palace to attend meetings with the coalition, the first real attempt by any of the governments to keep him in the loop and see what insight he had. But he hadn't been invited to the meeting Lucian and Nicos had gone to.

Perhaps the coalition leaders didn't trust him that much yet. Astrea and Jin had only found him thanks to the help of some of the palace guards. He'd been wandering around in the gardens, and Jin had invited him inside to talk.

"Well, this is a surprise," Theo said as he removed his checkered scarf and laid it on the table they'd commandeered in the library. The black, gray, and reddish brown colors complemented his long black coat well. He looked almost stylish.

"We need your help," Astrea said as she sat across from him.

Theo removed his jacket next, revealing a thick knit brown sweater underneath. "I've already told you I'm here to help."

"Good, and please remember you've just promised us that, because I don't think you're going to like what we're about to say," Jin said as he sat next to Astrea.

Frowning, Theo plopped into his chair. "What's going on?"

"Nazarov reached out to me again," Astrea said. When Theo's eyebrows furrowed, she explained the vision Nazarov had shown her. "He reiterated that my only options are to either die at his hand or bear him an heir," she said, and harsh disgust rolled out from Theo in waves. "I want to trap him so we can end this."

Jin went on to explain the plan in only the vaguest of details, that they were going to trap him in Kalama. "We'll need a Dreamwalker to help us set it up," Jin said. "If Nazarov doesn't reach out to Astrea first, anyway."

Theo's short fingers drummed against the dark wood table. Orange anxiety spiked high above his head.

"You don't think it's possible?" Astrea asked.

"I don't know with him anymore," Theo said. "You know how far gone he seems to be, but would he be desperate enough to believe you?"

"Well, even if he doesn't buy that Astrea's being sincere, wouldn't he at least agree to meet her?" Jin asked. "We could ambush him quickly."

"You can try," Theo said. "Victor's unpredictable these days. I don't know how he thinks assassinating Emperor Kaius will get him what he wants. He'll still have the army to wrangle into following him when he barely has the Paragon following suit."

"You don't have any idea what his plans might be?" Astrea asked.

Blowing out a long breath, Theo removed his glasses and rubbed the bridge of his nose. "Based on conversations we had . . . I'd assume he wants the aetherium weapons your father was working on, Jin," he said. "Maybe he figures he doesn't need control of the army, or maybe he figures enough will join him if promised money and glory. If he still has the Zaikudi backing him, it might be easy to start striking out at other countries."

"And if people refuse to comply?" Jin asked.

Theo's jaw tightened. "You saw what he did to Astrea all those months ago."

She swallowed hard. Of course. Of course Nazarov would do whatever it took to bend people to his will.

"Where would he believe I'd be willing to meet?" Astrea asked. "If we go to Kalama to do this, we need someplace accessible but not too public to confront him. Someplace I'd go and he'd buy into."

"Your usual haunts," Theo said. "He knows them."

"Was he following me for a long time?" Astrea asked.

"Not that long, but those few weeks in Kalama gave him a good idea of your patterns, or at least that's what he told me."

Astrea suppressed a shudder. How close had Nazarov been to her all this time? How had she and Jin not caught on to it sooner? She supposed that in a city of millions like Kalama, it would've been easy for Nazarov to blend in and keep an eye on her from a distance.

"Thanks, Theo," Jin said. "That'll help."

Theo's expression turned sad. "I'm sorry it's come to this. I'm sorry I ever bought into what the Paragon were selling."

"They've fooled a lot of people. It doesn't make it right, but I appreciate that you've come to your senses."

"Truly, I have. I know I have a lot to make up for."

"We'll deal with that when this is all over," Jin said. "We'll need you to coordinate the void mages helping us. We'll need Lifestealers with us to take out the aetherium weapons, as many as are willing to join the fight."

"Consider it done. They want to help, especially if it means stopping Victor. He's nothing in their eyes."

"Good," Jin said. "Coordinate it with Zephyrine once she's finished with the meeting."

Theo's eyebrows furrowed. "Where will you be?"

"I need to get my team ready before I join in the planning. They need to be prepared for what's coming."

Astrea didn't like the sound of that at all, and based on the orange anxiety flaring in Theo's aura, he didn't, either.

Still, he stuck his hand out to Jin for a shake. "Good luck," Theo said. "We're going to need it."

Leaving Theo to handle his own people, Astrea and Jin hurried back through the palace halls. Jin was eager to gather his team, and with each long stride he took, Astrea had to practically jog to keep up with him.

"We need to get everything ready quickly," Jin said, heading for the stairs that would take them to their wing of the palace.

"When can we leave?"

"Before sunrise, hopefully. We need to move quickly."

"What do you need me to do?" Astrea asked, already trying to craft a to-do list in her mind. They would need armor, supplies, maps, and—

"I'll need to go talk with the coalition leaders once we finish here," he said. "If you can get everyone else organized, then join me if there's time, that'd be perfect."

"Of course."

At the top of the stairs, Jin took a sharp left. He started knocking on the team's respective doors, drawing out whispers of confusion, especially from the guards lining the hall. As everyone began poking their heads out of their rooms and asking Jin what was going on, echoes of harsh words and rough annoyance came from behind Astrea, back near the stairs.

"Apelo!" Eliana called.

Prince Apelo stormed into the corridor, Eliana and Nicos right behind him. Rusty annoyance arced out from the princess and Nicos both, almost in sync with each other. Behind Astrea, confusion and curiosity reached out to her magic, and shoes shuffled and doors closed, no doubt the team coming to see what the commotion was.

"Jin," Apelo said as he closed the distance between them. "What is this about you going to Kalama?"

Jin faced his brother. "What do you mean, 'what is this about?'" he asked. "We're going to stop Nazarov and Kaius."

"You can't go back there," Apelo hissed, white fear radiating off him in harsh waves. "Not like this. I warned you about Kaius—"

"You warned us of something we already suspected," Jin said, folding his arms across his chest. "And while I appreciate the confirmation, it's nothing we aren't prepared for. This has to end now."

"What about the plan you all came up with earlier? The ground invasion—"

"Takes forever and costs many more lives."

"Apelo—" Eliana started.

"You two said I didn't protect you from Father," Apelo said, shifting so he could look between the two. "Let me protect you from Kaius. He's mad, I'm telling you—"

"What gives you the right?" Astrea asked. Apelo's eyebrows furrowed, the white surrounding him shifting to gray confusion. "You think you can just show up now and tell us—"

Jin set a hand on her shoulder. "Az—"

Astrea didn't look up at him, instead focusing on her brother-in-law, the man she hardly knew. "I'm glad you and your family are safe, and like Jin said, I'm glad you confirmed our suspicions. But what are you doing here if you're not going to help? Do you even want to help us? Help Kalama? Or are you still a pushover who'd rather let Kaius run amuck and let the world burn because you're scared?"

Apelo shook his head. "Miss Sovna—"

"We've been in this fight for months," she continued, voice low. "Sitting back and doing nothing will not save Kalama or the continent. It just gives Kaius and Nazarov an opening to do even more damage."

"But staying in Talmaris is safer," Apelo said. "You could all follow in on the ground as the troops clear the way, avoiding the—"

"I've lived over half my life on the sidelines, trying not to cause any trouble or draw any notice." Astrea straightened, pushing her shoulders back as warm pride flowed around the hall. "Our home is at risk. The world is at risk! Your father is dead, and your brother is unfit to rule. He's dangerous. Are you really going to try to convince us to hide?"

"It's not hiding—"

She ground her teeth together. "You said just the other night that Eliana is the right choice, the one to bring change to Helosia. She's a great leader. And Jin's a great leader, too. Do you even know what he's survived?"

Apelo ducked his head. "I've read some reports over the years."

"Then you know he's perfectly capable of taking care of himself and his people," Astrea said. "We have a team that will do whatever it takes to save Kalama, whether you agree or not."

Astrea understood Apelo's fears, his desire to keep his family safe. Saros had always made those choices, too. But in the end, he'd understood the magnitude of the threat. He'd made different choices. And Astrea would not let a cowardly but well-intentioned prince stand in her way. Not when all of them had sacrificed so much already.

"She's right, Apelo," Jin said. "You come to us at the very end, asking to work with us, when you've never wanted to do so before. I appreciate the sentiments, and I'm so glad you're all safe, but surely you can see the writing on the wall."

"Now is not the time for caution," Nicos said. "That's what Kaius and Nazarov want, for us to be cautious. Taking the fight to them is the only option."

Eliana sighed. "There may have been a time and place for caution in Father's court, Apelo, but here? Now?" She shook her head. "Too much is at stake. Kaius will destroy Kalama slowly, and Nazarov will destroy it now. We have to go. You can stay here with the girls."

Apelo looked between them, studying their faces. White fear mixed with red pride and midnight blue grief. "There's nothing I can do to change your minds?"

"No," Jin said, and the whole team responded with a chorus just the same.

"Alright." Apelo nodded. "Alright. How can I help?"

"Come with us to start drawing up plans for the invasion," Jin said. "Anything you know about the new situation in Kalama will be useful."

"Of course."

Jin turned back to the team and said, "Az will help catch the rest of you up. We need to be ready to leave by dawn if we're going to get to Kalama in time."

As the Auris siblings and Nicos left to go back to planning, Astrea faced the team. They all watched her carefully, almost as if afraid. Nothing in their auras suggested they were scared, though.

"What?" she asked.

The corners of Cressida's full lips curved up. "Never thought I'd see you dig into someone like that."

Astrea's body heated, all the way from her toes to the tips of her ears. "I don't think I dug into him, but he was being ridiculous, even if his heart is in the right place." She certainly didn't want to discuss that anymore, so she clapped her hands together and said, "Now, you heard Jin. Time to get to planning."

CHAPTER 51

After another late night, they had finally gotten a plan solidified with the coalition leadership, one all the countries felt they could agree to. Trying to get from Talmaris to Kalama in just a couple days' time would be difficult.

What Astrea didn't love about this plan was that both Sarsali and Balthazar were going. Noemi was en route to Thasia with them, but she wouldn't be joining them on the trip to Kalama. Apelo and his family were staying behind in Talmaris, which was surely for the best.

The airship was quiet as it began its descent. Nobody had talked much the last couple of days, instead focusing on sleeping or reviewing plans of what was to come.

They would set out for Kalama before first light, heading there in some of the massive Tornamian warships currently in port in the capital. It was as Lucian had originally suggested, that the Delians and Taipoli join with their own fleets, and the Novarian servicemembers and select Helosian defectors would be onboard the Tornamian ships. An entire fleet of airships had flown down, actually, to carry that many soldiers. They would fly to Kalama, as would units of the Tornamian and Delian air forces, trailing behind the warships so as not to give away their attack too soon. Even Vernie would be there. Rami. Some of the other Lightbringers Astrea had met and tried to train. Theo's people, too, though they were on a different aircraft.

Even Veiko was with them, as were some of the representatives from the other countries. They would work out of President Sikori's palace for this leg of the operation, while some of the forces stayed back in Novaria to deal with the Helosian troops near the border.

The sun was just beginning to set as their lead airship touched the ground. This routine was familiar now, the metallic thunk as the ship touched the airfield pavement, grabbing their bags, disembarking into the darkening night. Astrea was even accustomed to the heavy police presence, there to escort them to the presidential palace while military personnel took the rest of the new arrivals down to the docks and waiting vessels.

Astrea sat squished between Jin and Adi. Balthazar, Cressida, and Marko were in the row behind them. Though they remained quiet, the quick, steady pulse of electric anxiety against Astrea's cheeks told her everything she needed to know.

She stared out the windshield straight ahead, at the presidential palace gates and then the palace itself rising up before them against the nearly black sky. Only a hint of red remained on the horizon now.

This place . . . where she'd relived the horrible news of Saros's death. Where Cressida had lost her hand. Where so much bad had happened, so much pain.

Could they really do this? Could they really make it back to Kalama, dethrone Kaius, and destroy Nazarov and the aetherium?

Jin nudged her shoulder, startling Astrea. The car had stopped, and Adi was already outside, offering her his hand. She took it and scrambled out of the car.

Lucian began giving orders as President Sikori, Grand Duke Veiko, and the Delian and Taipoli ambassadors headed inside. Eliana followed, Nicos and Zephyrine right behind her. Astrea didn't pay much attention as she let Jin pull her inside, as leadership discussed a few things in hushed voices in the foyer.

This terrible, awful place. She swallowed hard. She hadn't been expecting it to be so painful to be back in these beautiful halls. *Complete the mission*. She had to do this. For Saros, for Helosia, for all the civilians now caught up in this mess.

It was difficult being back, yes, but Astrea had been through difficult things before. Surely more terrible things lay on the path ahead. But she'd survived. She'd been surviving for a long, long time, and she would survive this, too. She could endure another night in this presidential palace, and she could face Kaius and Nazarov again.

"Meet right back here at the fourth morning bell," Lucian said, the first of any of their words Astrea had managed to comprehend.

She blinked, trying to get rid of the fuzziness in her mind.

"You can return to your previous rooms," President Sikori said. "They've been prepared. The amenities are yours to use as you please."

Astrea followed her friends and family upstairs, the halls somehow both familiar and not. Those days after their failure in the Badlands were hazy at best, so consumed she'd been by grief and exhaustion. She tried to take them in now, but it was no use. She was seeing without seeing at all.

As the others started filtering into their rooms, Astrea found herself alone with Jin, Eliana, Nicos, Cressida, and Adi.

"Can we talk?" Eliana asked, tilting her head toward Astrea and Jin's door.

Jin let them all inside. It was the same as the rest of the palace, hazy memories poking at the back of Astrea's mind. Waking up in that bed, surrounded by those soft sheets and Jin's warmth. The horrible realization that Saros was gone.

Her throat tightened. She would not fall back into that spiral of grief. Not now. Maybe when all this was over, she could really, truly sit with the loss. All of the loss. But not tonight. Not when they needed to get to Kalama and put a quick end to the situation.

So Astrea took as deep of a breath as she could manage, holding it as she walked over to the bed and sat on the edge. She let it out slowly, then repeated the breathing exercise until she didn't feel like she was going to completely float away.

"What's going on, Ellie?" Jin asked as he sat next to Astrea. The others took up spots around the room, Adi by the wardrobe, Cressida in a chair by the hearth, Eliana and Nicos standing just before it.

Orange anxiety swirled around Eliana as she fidgeted with the delicate gold bracelet on her wrist. "I hope you know how much I appreciate you all. The entire team, yes, but . . . but this started with just us."

"I think that goes without saying, Ellie," Cressida said. "We know that."

"Yes, but . . ." Eliana's chest heaved. She pushed her shoulders back, all business despite the slight dark circles under her eyes. "Whatever happens over the next few days, I need you all to know how much I appreciate that you've always believed in me, even when I barely had time to be around."

"Skies, you're making it sound like something's going to happen," Adi said with a nervous laugh.

Eliana's expression was entirely serious. "Because it could."

"Of course it *could*," Adi said. "A hurricane could show up and knock us all off course and sink the ships."

"What a lovely thought," Cressida muttered.

"I just mean anything can happen," Adi said. "I prefer to hope for the best."

"I'm being realistic." Eliana's attention shifted to Jin. "If something happens, and Kaius takes me out—"

"He won't," Jin said.

"But *if* something happens," Eliana continued, and that anxiety spiked high above both her and Nicos, "I need you to promise me something."

Astrea's throat tightened again. She didn't like where this was going.

The room was so silent they could've heard a pin drop.

"I need you to promise me that you'll keep going, even if I'm not there to take power," Eliana said. "Give it to Apelo or one of the girls, or even transition the country into a new form of government, but do *not* let Kaius or any of his supporters hold power. Helosians deserve better than that."

"You think there's that high of a chance this could go wrong?" Cressida asked. Adi and Jin shifted. "What?" she asked them. "You think there is? Why'd none of you mention this before?"

"There's a lot we're dealing with," Jin said. "Adi might like to remain hopeful about missions, but the reality is anything could go wrong. *Anything.* There are a lot of people we're trying to coordinate, and this thing with Nazarov . . . You know how things went in the Badlands."

"I thought it might be easier with more support," she said.

Adi shrugged. "Not always."

"Kaius is going to want to take me out," Eliana said matter-of-factly. "There's still a strong amount of support for me. I'm an obstacle to him, nothing more. Please, promise me you'll keep going if—"

"I promise," Astrea said, the first. She didn't want to even contemplate a future without Eliana, but she understood too viscerally just how wrong things could go. "I promise, Ellie."

"I promise, even if I don't like it," Cressida said.

Adi nodded. "Me too."

Eliana raised an eyebrow at Jin. "Well?"

"I promise," he said. "But I hope you know you're strong enough to beat him. You know his weaknesses. How sloppy he gets."

"I know," Eliana said.

Jin glanced at Nicos. "You haven't promised her."

"I made him promise me already," Eliana said with a small smile.

"With both of us working together," Nicos said, "we should be able to get him."

"You should take Zephyrine with you," Jin said. "And Vernie."

"They're supposed to help you." Eliana's protest was weak at best.

"Yes, well, I'd feel better if they were with you," Jin said. "We can handle Nazarov."

"You're sure?" Eliana asked. "No offense. He's just slippery."

"He is, but we can handle him."

Eliana watched her brother for a moment, almost as if trying to read him the way a Lightbringer would. "Yes," she finally said. "You can."

Astrea hoped they were right.

Though she didn't get seasick like Jin, Astrea simply wasn't a fan of boats. Sure, the large military vessel they were on was a far smoother ride than Magdi's small rum-running ship, but she missed solid ground.

Civan snapped a piece of chocolate from the bar in his hand and passed it to Astrea. She took a bite, savoring the sweet, milky candy as she gazed out at the blood red sunset. Dark clouds loomed to their north, toward the Badlands. They would skirt by those storms, and they would be in Kalama sometime after midnight. It was taking longer than it had on Magdi's ship, thanks in part to how large the fleet was. Even with mages, they could only go so fast.

He snapped another piece off, then handed it to Lennor. She popped the whole thing in her mouth. Cressida politely refused the next piece Civan offered.

"How can you two be so calm?" Astrea asked, glancing sidelong at the twins. Nothing wavered in their auras, but they also weren't shutting her out. They were steady.

Civan shrugged. "A mission is a mission."

"Even one like this?" Astrea hedged. "One that, if we fail, spells doom for the continent?"

"A mission is a mission," Lennor repeated. "I try not to focus too hard on what'll happen if I fail."

"And that works?" Cressida asked.

Lennor shrugged one shoulder. "Mostly."

"Seems like a skill that'd be useful to learn," Astrea said before eating the second half of the chocolate piece still clutched between her fingers. The wind had kicked up in the last half hour, and now it tugged at Astrea's braid, trying to find strands of hair to pull loose. It was annoying, but she refused to go below deck, back to that dark cabin they'd been assigned.

"I had to in order to survive Corsyca," Lennor said. "Focus on the task at hand. Focus on the present moment. Think about all the what-ifs and other terrible things later. And make sure you do think about all that shit later, once you're safe."

"I don't think there's any way I could *not*," Astrea said. Her mind didn't work like that.

Civan cracked the last row of chocolates into thirds, giving Lennor and Astrea one each. He offered the third to Cressida, but she politely declined again.

"Don't have much of a stomach, if I'm honest," she said, staring down at her hands loosely folded in her lap. One made of flesh, the other gleaming metal.

What was she thinking of now? The way things had gone so poorly in the Badlands? All they still risked losing, especially knowing just how much aetherium Kaius might be controlling? Astrea took Cressida's closest hand, her metal one, and squeezed it gently. Cressida squeezed back.

Lennor's expression faltered, but she forced a grin. "Well, I'm surprised you're sharing, Civ."

He kept his attention fixed on the ocean, but Astrea didn't miss the tiniest of smiles pulling at one corner of his mouth. "Thought I'd be nice."

"I certainly appreciate it," Lennor said.

"Me too," Astrea added quickly. "Not just the chocolate but the company, too. I'm glad to have met you both, even with such sorry circumstances."

"Likewise, Az," Civan said.

It was Astrea's turn to smile.

They continued there, sitting on the deck and staring out at the final remnants of the sunset, until Marko's voice cut through the splash of waves and murmurs of the crew.

"Lennor! Civan! Cressida! Astrea!" he called. "One more team meeting. Let's go."

"I supposed we should get in there," Cressida said, "before your husband kills us for being late, Az."

"Oh, I don't think I have anything to worry about," Astrea said, trying to force playfulness she didn't feel into the words. "I can't say the same for you three."

"Captain Auris *does* appreciate punctuality," Lennor said wryly. She pushed up to her feet, then offered a hand to Cressida and helped her up.

And to Astrea's surprise, Civan did the same for her.

"Come on!" Marko called.

Astrea sighed. "Well, you heard the man. One more team meeting."

CHAPTER 52

The darkness of night threatened to swallow Astrea whole. She hated being below deck, even if she was safely wrapped in Jin's arms. The bed was too small, the room too cramped, the shadows too dark. And what light they did have was too bright to get any semblance of sleep.

But a knock on the cabin door signaled that it was time to go. Astrea and Jin climbed out of bed and found their gear. They dressed quickly, first in the clothes that would go under their armor. Jin had to help Astrea into her armor, into that particular battle dress Adi had made for her. Part of it was because they were using Astrea's summoned light to see, but the armor was also awkward with the thin metal plates Balthazar and Cressida had added. It was still too heavy for Astrea's liking, but she was going to try not to focus too much on that.

When Jin had finished tightening the laces and securing it on her, he took only the smallest step back. Those beautiful molten eyes of his wandered over her body, not appreciative but worried. The faintest sheen of white terror and orange anxiety swirled around him.

"This is it," he said.

"It is."

"We're really going to do this."

"We are."

His nostrils flared as he sucked in an audible breath. Then he reached for her, the silver and gold of his wedding and engagement bands catch-

519

ing her starlight. She dismissed it, the last remnants just a smattering of stars in the dark room. Jin's mouth found hers. She wrapped her arms around his neck, pulling him closer. He kissed her like he'd been starved of her touch for a thousand years, like it might be their last.

And maybe it would be.

This last, desperate play to stop Nazarov. If they failed, well . . . she would either be dead or his captive again.

Astrea fisted some of Jin's curls in her hand, trying to get closer to him still. She never wanted to leave the safety of his arms, of this cabin, this ship. But she had to.

As she barely pulled away, Jin pressed his forehead to hers. A few rogue tears slipped down her cheeks, and somehow, Jin knew to reach up and wipe them away.

"We're going to get through this," he whispered.

"I know."

"And I'm still fucking terrified."

"I can see it," she admitted, barely voicing the words. "And I am, too. I love you, Jin."

"I love you, too. I'm grateful for every single day we've had together." His voice was rough, strained. "And I'm already planning all the ones we still have ahead. We just need to get through today, alright?"

More tears burned Astrea's eyes. "I love you," she whispered again, hoping he could feel everything she couldn't voice, all the words building in her chest. Why did this have to be so hard?

Someone knocked on their door again. Jin pressed his lips to her forehead. His fear, his worry, his love—it all inched back from Astrea as he sealed himself behind his wall. Skies, all she wanted was to feel that sunshine instead of the cold air down here in this dark cabin below deck. But Astrea pushed her shoulders back and held her head high. She would feel it again. It was as he said; they had to get through today first.

On the main deck, a crowd of soldiers had gathered, all in Novarian blue or Tornamian green. Among them, the team, dressed in black. They couldn't wear the colors of another country—not with Eliana there to overthrow Kaius—nor could they wear Helosian red. It was still a strange sight.

A pair of Novarian and Tornamian commanders were shouting orders to the other soldiers, but Lucian, Zephyrine, and Jin pulled their team back around the pilothouse, where things were quieter. Besides the low light hanging from the structure, there was no light. Daybreak was still hours away, and the moon and stars were obscured by clouds. Beyond the ship was pitch darkness. They were still treading water fast, crossing the last stretch of water to reach Kalama's port.

"I assume Nazarov hasn't contacted you, Astrea?" Lucian asked.

She shook her head.

"Do we know where he is in the city?" Jin asked.

"We've heard from a few scouts that there's fighting all around the city . . . Helosians and Zaikudi," Zephyrine said.

Jin cursed. "I knew beating them here would be nearly impossible, but fuck."

"And we don't know where Nazarov is," the general said, making Jin curse again.

"What about Kaius?" Eliana asked, placing her hands on her hips.

"Either within the palace or gone." Zephyrine shrugged. "No one's sure."

"Fuck," she muttered.

"We should still split up as planned," Jin said. "Ellie, make your way to the palace if you can't get a hold of Kaius from the ship. The rest of us will go find Nazarov."

"Do we contact him?" Lucian asked. "Do we need to bring Theo over here?"

Jin glanced out at the dark sea, then back at the commander. "I don't think so," he said slowly. "If Nazarov realizes our forces have arrived, he'll probably try to contact Az, if not more of us. Let's give it a little while before we try anything else."

"If that's the case," Lucian said, "do you want to wait here or go ashore?"

"If Astrea's out there, we'll probably grab Nazarov's attention more easily," Jin said. "And if we can help take the port, I'd rather do that."

That had always been the plan: take control of Kalama's port as quickly as possible while the navies battled it out. A strong force on the ground, in the air, and in the sea was the only way they would gain control.

And besides, as Jin said, Astrea showing up would certainly get Nazarov's attention more quickly than if she remained hidden away on a ship. If she was out there, fighting and healing, someone would see and report it back to him. She was sure he'd have his people on the lookout for her and Jin both.

"Airships and planes should be here soon," Lucian said. "We'll have more support and reinforcements once they arrive."

"Ashore it is, then," Zephyrine said quietly.

The weight of it all settled on Astrea's shoulders, doubling as she looked at each and every one of them in their small circle. Eliana, somehow regal in her black armor and braided crown. Nicos, imposing in his matching gear. Cressida, her brow furrowed. Balthazar and Sarsali right behind her, surrounded by orange anxiety. Adi and Marko, standing close together but not touching. Lennor and Civan, of course, who were both steady despite it all. Zephyrine and Lucian, so different but equally important in all this. And then Jin, the unreadable Captain Auris.

This was her team, the people she trusted most in the world to accomplish their task. If they couldn't do it, she wasn't sure anyone could.

"Rami will meet us on the docks," Lucian said. "I need to radio her. Theo's people, too, to jump you into the port." He disappeared around the corner of the pilothouse.

"Sarsali, Balthazar," Jin said. "Can you stay at the docks with our people? Coordinate however you can to help the coalition forces? You know the city better than they do."

"Of course," Sarsali said, setting her hand on Balthazar's muscular forearm as he started to protest. "We'll help however we can."

"Good," Jin said. "Ellie, you know what to do."

"Stay on the boat for as long as I can while I try to talk Kaius into negotiations," Eliana said. "Move in only when unavoidable, and go straight to the palace."

"We'll return to the docks after we take out Nazarov," Jin said. "But we'll follow you to the palace if that's where you've gone."

Eliana nodded. "Good luck."

"You too."

Astrea pulled Eliana into a quick, tight embrace, then hugged Sarsali and Balthazar. This was it. They'd be separated for a few more hours, then this would be done.

"Things are going to be shaky while we fight the Zaikudi," Jin said to the group. "Be smart and be safe, especially those of you staying on board."

"We will," Nicos said.

Pushing his shoulders back, Jin tilted his head toward the pilothouse, then started around it. They would need to be ready to go as soon as they were close enough to jump with the void mages.

Astrea's palms began to sweat despite the cool, dry air. The breeze played with the hem of her skirt, not lifting it too far thanks to the weight of the leather. She walked beside Jin, trying to exude the same calm confidence he did, as if she'd also done this many times.

As the ship continued moving through the water, ever closer to Kalama, and as they began to move past the crowd of soldiers, Astrea's mouth went dry. Up ahead, against the backdrop of the darkened sky, was the hazy red outline of Kalama.

Red and hazy, as if smoke and flames were tearing through the city.

"Fuck," Jin said, fisting his hair.

"It's what Nazarov always showed me," Astrea whispered, cold horror racing through her body. "He often showed me Kalama on fire."

She had never taken that threat quite *so* literally. It had always seemed like part of his show, his attempts to control and manipulate her to do his bidding. Just as he'd shown her the palace made of dark stone—presumably aetherium, now that those images flashed in her mind again. It had all seemed dramatic, overstated, part of the terror he wanted to instill in her.

"What the fuck did he do to my city?" Eliana bit out, her rage singing Astrea's skin.

"Look," Nicos said, pointing overhead.

There, against that backdrop of red, orange, and black, were the outlines of small propeller planes. Something exploded in the distance.

"Those have to be Zaikudi," Zephyrine said. "I know they're not ours, and there's no way Kaius would turn the Helosian air force onto the city . . . right?" Her stormy gray eyes flicked to Jin.

"He might if the Zaikudi and Paragon have infiltrated," Jin said. "He might think it's the only way."

Astrea's whole body ached with the thought of what would be happening to Kalamians, regardless of who was attacking them from the sky.

No doubt they were terrified. Confused. Hurt. Anger bubbled beneath her skin, a mirror to Eliana's, Zephyrine's, Cressida's.

Bright orange lit up the darkness, illuminating the outline of ships up ahead. They were firing on the city, on the Helosian boats waiting in the port.

"We need to get ready," Jin said. "We'll need to jump on shore as soon as we're close enough. Where's Lucian?"

"I'll go find him," Marko said, already turning and pushing back through the crowd toward the pilothouse.

Astrea moved closer to the edge of the deck as their navy drew closer and closer to those ships. Dread spread to every inch of her body as one of their ships exploded with light. A missile whistled through the air, hitting what she assumed was its mark, a Zaikudi ship. Its hull and deck caught fire and lit up the dark.

Skies, they were attacking.

They were attacking the Zaikudi and Paragonian ships.

Astrea didn't know why it surprised her. Maybe it was just seeing it up close, actually happening instead of hypotheticals proposed by politicians sitting in safety on the other side of the continent.

"We're going to need to move fast." Lucian's voice cut through the noise in Astrea's mind, and she turned to find the whole team around and behind her, also watching as the two opposing navies moved into formation.

"What's the status on the Helosian ships?" Jin asked.

"Trapped, many disabled as far as we can tell from the skies," Lucian said.

Astrea hadn't realized it before, but if she listened closely, she could make out the roar of plane engines. The sky was still too dark to see much.

"So now's our time to make a dent in their forces," Jin said. "How fast can—"

The last of his question was cut off by surprised shouts from the nearby soldiers. They jumped back, away from the void mages popping into existence from seemingly nowhere, from the shadows spiraling up out of the deck.

Theo, among the void mages, pulled at the sleeves of his gray fatigues and shook his arms out. "There's one problem," he said before anyone could even get a greeting out. "My people say it's too far to jump. We need to get closer."

"Kalama's port wraps around both the southern and northern sides of the water," Jin said. "The palace is on the northern side, but if we can get close enough to the southern edge, they could jump us there as a start."

"How far is it?" Lucian asked.

He stared out across the water, illuminated now by the burning city and the ships exchanging gunfire. Every explosion and flash of light set Astrea further on edge.

"If we can go even another several thousand feet, we should get close enough," Jin said after a moment. "Right, Theo?"

"That should suffice," Theo said.

"Then let's get going," Lucian said. "Let me tell the captain." He ran back toward the pilothouse, yelling at soldiers to move out of his way.

"Zephyrine, will you go and—" Jin started, but she was already waving him off.

"Coordinating everything for you, Jin. Take that bastard out," Zephyrine said before jogging after the commander.

Nicos and Eliana gave them one last goodbye before they followed the general into the crowd. The rest of them watched in silence as the rest of the navy continued trading fire with the Zaikudi ships, hitting their mark more often than not. That was good, but were the Zaikudi even trying to avoid the damage? Did they have no powerful Metalli to help deflect missiles? Had they been—

"Oh, fuck me," Cressida muttered from beside Astrea.

She bolted forward, Sarsali calling her name, then swearing as Balthazar hurried after her. Someone shouted the warning of incoming enemy fire, but Cressida must've felt it first. Several more soldiers followed—Metalli, Astrea guessed—and spread out on the right side of the deck.

"Throw them back at those ships!" Jin yelled, pointing at the sea. "Take them out!"

Oh, Astrea hated this. Hated how every muscle in her body tensed, how it was just like that day when they'd escaped Kalama with the book. That was so long ago now.

The Metalli all shifted, lowering their bodies and hunkering down. Loud whistling filled Astrea's ears. The ship seemed to sway more under her feet, like they were gaining speed.

"We need some light!" Balthazar shouted.

Starlight burst to life around Astrea's hands. She pushed it beyond the edges of the ship. Her fingers trembled as she tried to keep it low, nothing to distract the Metalli. Nothing to distract them from the projectiles just feet from the—

Cressida took several sideways steps back, almost as if getting ready to hit the missile with a bat. She moved with fluid grace as the small projectile—no larger than Jin's forearm—moved closer. Cressida caught it in some invisible net, then sent it launching high in the air, above Astrea's light. Balthazar did the same, and the Metalli down the line all followed suit.

Astrea held her breath, jolting when several explosions lit up in the distance, all on the same ship.

"Don't think that took them out," Balthazar said. "Might slow 'em down."

"Good enough," Jin said. "Keep at it. Take out however many you can. Where's Lucian? We need to go."

"Here!" Lucian called, reappearing from within the crowd. "We're set. They're taking us as close as they can get us."

"Theo!" Jin yelled.

"They are yours to command, Jin," Theo said as he approached, void mages—and Rami—in tow. Their cold presence battered Astrea's every sense. "And yours, Astrea."

"No," she said, trying to meet every one of their gazes. "We're a team. Are you in?"

"Tell us where you need us to take you," said one, a young woman who couldn't have been much older than Astrea. Her blonde hair, pale skin, and copper eyes almost glowed red with the fires on the horizon.

"To that bluff," Jin said, turning and pointing. "And then from there, into the Kalamian port. Our team, then soldiers. As many as you can, as fast as you can."

The young woman nodded. "It'll be easier from the bow, Captain Auris."

The soldiers cleared a path as Lucian and Jin yelled at them. Astrea held Jin's hand in her left, Cressida's in her right, as they walked nearly single file up to the front of the ship. And there, as the crowd cleared, Astrea could see the outline of land.

"We'll need to take you in pairs," the young void mage said, mostly to Jin and Astrea. "That's the most we can each take."

The team split up. Adi and Marko. Civan and Rami. Lennor and Cressida. Lucian, by himself. And Astrea and Jin. Five void mages stepped up, the sixth and seventh staying back and organizing the soldiers Zephyrine escorted over.

"On your mark, Captain," said the blonde one as she grabbed Jin's forearm.

He gripped Astrea's hand tight, surveyed the team one more time, then said, "Ready."

Astrea steeled herself as the cold darkness swallowed them whole.

CHAPTER 53

The void seemed to consume them forever, pulling and pulling on every fiber of Astrea's being until her feet slammed into solid ground. She stumbled, and the world spun around her. Jin yanked her back toward him. The world was just darkness and cannon fire on the water below.

"Again!" the blonde called.

Shadows snaked up from the ground, wrapping around their limbs and pulling them back into the void. They jumped again and again and again, getting closer and closer to the port. And the closer they got, the more pain and panic met Astrea's senses.

They stopped again, right behind several tall warehouses and only a few dozen feet from the docks and the fighting. Smoke choked the air, and pain ripped through Astrea so quickly she thought she might've somehow gotten hurt. But no, it pinged around in her chest, ghostly and not hers.

"Farther?" the blonde asked Jin.

"No, thank you," he said. "Go back to the ship, quickly. Bring reinforcements. Ask General Kanakos, the woman with the white hair, to organize it all for you. Be as fast as you can."

"Got it," the woman said, then sent some silent message to her compatriots. They disappeared one by one, swallowed by inky darkness.

Jin rolled his shoulders back, then pulled his hood and mask down over his head. Only his eyes were visible. Everyone else did the same. Astrea hated hers, the way it pressed against her skin and mouth.

"Stay together," Jin said. "We take out Zaikudi and Paragon, try to get the Helosians to surrender. Cress can detain them. Are we clear?"

"Clear," they said in unison.

"We secure the port so the rest of the coalition forces can move in and use it as their base," Jin said. "And if we need to let one of the Paragon go so that they get a message back to Nazarov about us being here, so be it. Ready?"

"Ready," they again said in unison, though Astrea didn't feel ready at all.

They crept forward, Jin, Adi, and Astrea at the front, Lucian and Marko at the back, and everyone else in between.

They moved in the narrow space between two warehouses, shadowed by the tall buildings. Ahead, where the buildings ended and the port began to open up, and amid the smoke and glow of fire, a group fought furiously. Shadows and flames, water and wind and earth. Ghostly hit after ghostly hit smacked into Astrea—a punch, a sear of fire, the point of a knife. One figure in a red uniform went down.

Jin made the signal to move. He took three slow steps forward before he broke into a sprint, fire bursting to life over his hands. Astrea ran after him and Adi, trying to force her legs faster.

Jin engaged one of the Paragonian fighters, a mage clad in black and one of those terrible masks, its silver edges glinting in Jin's firelight. Void flames snaked up their palms and arms, pitch dark compared to Jin's bright orange. Adi raced past Jin, right for one of the other void mages.

Gritting her teeth and planting her feet shoulder width apart, Astrea flung her hands out, reaching for the freezing cold in front of her. She clawed her way through the void mage's thick, frozen veil, pushed harder as whispers of rage and confusion reached out to her. Her palms burned, like someone was holding them against ice.

But there. She broke through to the crimson and gray swirling together around the void mage. Astrea grabbed them and yanked back. The mage stumbled. Jin grabbed them by their collar, then shoved his dagger up into their torso. Pain bloomed under Astrea's ribs, and she was drowning, couldn't breathe. Jin pulled his dagger back out, and the Paragonian fighter fell to the ground in a heap. Blood pooled around them, but they didn't move.

"Gotta move, Az," Jin called to her, then started for where Adi and Lucian were doing exactly what she and Jin had just done.

She forced her legs to carry her past the fallen void mage and to follow her team.

With Lucian controlling two more void mages Jin and Adi were dealing with, Astrea focused on the final two locked in a battle with Lennor and Civan. She'd lost sight of Cressida, Marko, and Rami, but she couldn't think about that.

Astrea flung her hands out in front of her, searching for her way through that veil, for any cracks or weaknesses. Her lungs and muscles burned, and her fingertips ached, but crimson and gray, green and orange, all burst to life over the void mages like fireworks. She reached for those colors, pulling hard and then shoving back.

They stumbled. Crimson rage and orange anxiety spiked higher above their heads, and Astrea yanked again, so hard that pain began to swirl right under her sternum. Civan was on them in a moment, Lennor right behind, daggers drawn. All that pain bled away as those two Paragon fighters died. The twins were quick, efficient.

"Az!" Cressida's voice cut through the smoke and incessant ring in Astrea's ears. She was back near the open door of one of the warehouses, securing four Helosian fighters with metal bindings. Rami and Marko stood guard.

As Astrea ran up to them, Cressida said, "They've got aetherium weapons."

Marko held up four dark metal daggers.

"You're sure?" Astrea asked.

"Positive," Cressida said.

"Emperor Kaius told us we had to use 'em," said one Helosian man, voice rough. He was the biggest of the group, but their uniforms were all the same and gave no indication of rank. "Dropped off shipments a few days ago. Told us to arm ourselves. Just said not to cut ourselves with it."

"See this?" Marko asked in Helosian as he held up one of the daggers. "This is called aetherium. It's imbued with void magic and will suck the life force out of you if it breaks your skin. That's what your emperor is handing out to you."

"We didn't know—" the man tried.

"No?" Rami took a few steps around them and into the building, returning a moment later with a flier clutched in one hand. She held it up. "This didn't tell you anything?"

Astrea couldn't read it in the darkness, but the man said, "We were told those were propaganda by—"

"So you'll believe anything Emperor Kaius tells you?" Cressida asked.

"We're just doing our jobs," the man said, a weak argument. "You sound Kalamian . . . you know how the government is—"

Maybe not such a weak argument. Astrea *did* know.

"I do," Cressida said, voice hard. "And I know what that shit does." She held up her hand, the metal one. "Very bad things."

The man swallowed loudly. "Who are you, anyway?"

"Here to save your sorry asses from those guys." Marko jerked his thumb toward the dead Paragon soldiers on the ground. "Void mages and Zaikudi. They're the ones attacking the city."

"Why?" asked the soldier.

"Because there's a very bad man who wants to take out your emperor," Marko said. "And he'll be even worse than Kaius. Those aetherium weapons will only be the start."

"How long has Kalama been under attack?" Astrea asked.

"It started from the sky yesterday afternoon. The port siege started last night," the man said. "It's been nonstop."

"Shit," Cressida muttered.

If Nazarov's forces had been attacking Kalama for nearly a day . . .

"Is Kaius still alive?" Astrea asked.

"We haven't heard anything otherwise," said the man.

"Would Nazarov keep that quiet?" Rami asked Astrea. "If he'd killed Kaius, I mean."

"I don't think so," Astrea said.

No, if Nazarov had already gotten to Kaius, then he would've been gloating, probably dreamwalking to Astrea to tell her. Probably would've already had the rest of the Helosian forces killed or forced to submit to his will. Which meant they still had a chance to capture Kaius and transfer power to Eliana.

Sharp pain blossomed near Astrea's shoulder. She whipped around, finding Lucian downing a Zaikudi fighter clad in green. A tremble rolled through her; bile crept up her throat. Skies, it was too much. She turned back toward Cressida, who was watching her carefully.

"So, it's true then?" the Helosian man asked.

"What's true?" asked Cressida.

"That Princess Eliana is still alive and trying to return."

"Has someone said otherwise?" Cressida asked.

"The emperor said she killed her father, that—"

"She wasn't even at the battle," Astrea said. "If you don't want to be around any of this anymore"—she gestured vaguely to the skirmishes behind them—"you'll want to think long and hard about how you play the next few days."

The man pursed his lips, as if deep in thought. He sucked in a breath but cut off whatever it was he was about to say.

A large hand settled between Astrea's shoulders, and Jin walked up beside her. He pulled his mask off. "Who's this?" he asked.

"They're armed with aetherium," Marko said. "Whole port is, apparently."

"Fuck," Jin muttered.

"P-Prince Varojin," the man said, lavender surprise swirling up around him and his three compatriots. He stared up at Jin. "You're . . . you're here?"

"Of course I'm here," Jin said. "I'm not going to let my brother or some interloper destroy Helosia. What can you tell me?"

The soldier rushed to repeat everything he'd already told the rest of them.

"How many Helosian forces are here?" Jin asked.

"Many wounded," the man said. "Many transferred out. We're trying to keep them at bay until reinforcements arrive."

Cold exploded in the air, and then confusion and terror followed like a tidal wave. A fresh cohort of Tornamian and Novarian soldiers were a dozen feet away, void mages interspersed among them. The soldiers' eyes were huge, like they'd never been jumped through the void before. And they probably hadn't.

"Good," Jin said to the blonde void mage from before. "We need some of the Lifestealers immediately. We've got aetherium."

The blonde nodded. She and her team jumped away again, disappearing in flashes of shadow.

"How do they do that?" the Helosian man asked, his voice trembling.

"Doesn't matter," Jin said.

He barked orders at the newly arrived soldiers, who began cordoning off the area and taking the Helosian prisoners inside the warehouse. The rest arranged themselves into teams of three to four, growing their total number of fighters from nine to nineteen. It wasn't much, but it was better than it had been.

Astrea forced herself to suck in a deep breath. They'd claimed one tiny corner of the port, its southernmost edge, where there didn't seem to be any additional fighting anyway. It was all far up ahead, near the main gates and the docks closest to the northwestern edge—the side near the palace.

"Subdue the Helosians, terminate the Zaikudi and Paragon," Jin said to the new arrivals. "If a few Paragon escape, don't focus on that. It's fine. We'll get them all eventually. We move in squads, and we take this port inch by inch. Understood?"

"Yes, Captain!" the soldiers called.

"Novarians, with me!" Lucian yelled above the next explosion of cannon fire in the bay. Astrea flinched.

"Tornamians, with me!" Rami shouted.

The groups reorganized themselves, leaving Marko with the Helosians.

"Lennor, Civan, Cress," Jin said. "Stick together. Az, with me, Adi, and Marko."

Astrea hesitated. It wasn't that she didn't want to go with Jin, but she didn't like the idea of the other three not having a Lightbringer or a fourth to help.

"We'll be right near each other," Jin said, as if he could read her mind. "We're all going toward the gate."

Astrea forced her shoulders back. Jin may have said she was "with" him, but she wasn't going to just ignore the others. She was strong. She could watch over them all.

Jin tugged his hood and mask back down over his face as he said, "Let's go."

Chapter 54

Jin launched himself headfirst into the closest fight, a skirmish between two void mages and one Helosian.

Astrea flung her hands out, grasping at all three mages as they fought. Searing cold and blistering heat touched every part of her, but she held fast, straining as the others quickly disposed of the two void mages. She let go of the Helosian at Jin's command, but the woman attacked, fire flaring hot in the air.

Jin took control of it, sending it back toward the woman. The flames hit their mark, and the woman stumbled back, screaming as the fire ate through her armor and touched her skin.

"Stand down!" Jin yelled at her. "We'll let you live."

She seemed to be in too much pain to pay attention; Astrea could barely think with the way her own skin ached. Jin muttered something, then called for Astrea to heal the woman while he and Adi held her down.

Astrea gritted her teeth as she knelt on the soot-stained cobblestone and pulled on her light. It danced around her hands, a soft, warm glow. She set her palms on the woman's upper arm, and the wound began to heal, bloody and burnt flesh turning a slightly darker shade of brown than the rest of her skin.

"Who the fuck are you?" the woman seethed as she sat up, red anger clinging to her just like her red armor.

"Prince Varojin," Jin said. "We're here to get these people out of the city and out of Helosia. Are you standing down?"

Nearby, someone grunted, and pain flared in the back of Astrea's head. Lennor had another Helosian pinned to the ground, and Cressida and Civan were cornering a second.

Focus, Astrea told herself. If she could just focus, she could get through this.

The woman glared up at Jin from where she still sat, then spit on the ground in front of him. His jaw tightened. He didn't move as he called, "Another over here! Uncooperative!"

Two Novarians—a redhead and a blond Jin had assigned as guards for captured Helosians—arrived with handcuffs and dragged the woman away. Gray hate and crimson rage swirled around her the entire time, making Astrea nauseated.

On and on their teams pushed through the port, taking Helosians, Zaikudi, and Paragonian fighters down one by one. It was quick work, faster than Astrea expected given the circumstances. But the chaos of the port—far worse the deeper in they moved—mixed with the thick smoke and ongoing cannon fire seemed to be working in their favor.

And with each new round of soldiers their void mage allies brought in, the quicker the work became. Each team worked like a well-oiled machine, taking out more and more fighters. They pushed on, Astrea continuing to both subdue and heal Helosians. She was ready to retch out the meager contents of her stomach by the time they reached the very section of port where they'd snuck into Kalama months ago.

The palace loomed high above the docks. Its towers and spires were barely visible from Astrea's angle, obscured by the dark sky and smoke in the city. Surely Kaius was up there somewhere, holing himself up until the danger passed.

Or maybe he'd even fled the city. What then? Would they be able to take control of Kalama, force him to abdicate? Would he escape? But where could he even go?

Astrea's shoulders sagged. She was already tired, and the fight had barely begun. But focusing on only the fights in front of her, only on the pain and energy and not on everything else—the other soldiers and teams, the ongoing fight in the bay, the constant boom of explosives and roar of engines overhead—was taxing. Her mind kept trying to process it all anyway.

Another boom echoed through the port, vibrating into Astrea's very core. She ducked on nothing more than instinct, her hands covering her ears. Beyond that terrible vibration, she heard shouting, swearing. Ice cold terror and steely determination warred on her skin. Boots skidded to a stop in her line of sight.

Astrea forced herself to stand to her full height and pull her hands away from her ears. Cressida's whole body trembled as she held her arms up high, braced her legs, almost as if pushing back a boulder.

And there, midair, was a missile twice the size of Jin. Fire burned at its rear end, locked in a clash between its burning fuel and Cressida's power.

Jin shouted, but it didn't reach Astrea's ears.

Cressida's arms shook as she stood locked in this battle, her magic against a rocket that would easily destroy them all. It had to have come from the harbor. More explosions dotted the water, and several Zaikudi ships were on fire and sinking fast.

A strong hand grabbed Astrea's arm, but she shook it off. Jin, no doubt. Instead, she pressed her hands to Cressida's back, between her shoulder blades. Cressida's muscles spasmed under Astrea's touch. She braced Cressida, drawing on the light swirling underneath her skin and pushing it into her best friend.

Astrea cried out as new exhaustion tore through her like an angry storm. It was like she was trying to lift a thousand pounds. But she braced herself, braced Cressida and pushed more light into her.

And those strong hands returned to Astrea, this time on *her* back, as Jin helped keep them both upright.

"Throw it back at them, Cress!" he called.

"As if it's that easy, Auris!" Cressida shouted.

"It is for you!"

Peach amusement and rusty annoyance arced out from Cressida in a blinding flash. Her arms moved, inch by inch, until she launched herself forward. Astrea nearly tumbled after her, but Jin caught her by the waist and hauled her back. Cressida rested her hands on her knees, breathing heavily as the missile arced back toward one of the Zaikudi ships. It hit the ship's side, and the force of the explosion shook the air.

Cressida howled in victory. Astrea sank back against Jin as the full force of Cressida's fatigue mingled with her own.

"What were you doing?" Jin asked her, spinning her around. He frantically scanned her face.

"I'm fine; I had to help her."

"She wasn't injured, but you were healing her."

"Taking her fatigue," Astrea said. "Making her stronger." Giving Cressida's body back the energy it needed to force that missile away from all of them.

Dawning glinted in his eyes. "Shit, I never thought about that."

Astrea shrugged. She'd taken on fatigue before. From Adi, from Cressida. From Saros. Never in battle, though. "It seemed like the right time to do it," she said.

"I'll say."

Cressida practically tackled Astrea, her gratitude warm on Astrea's skin. "Skies, did you see that?"

"Told you," Jin said.

"Shut up, Auris."

He actually laughed, the suddenness of it disarming. "Come on," he said. "We're almost there."

To their north, the rest of their forces were gathering, rounding up the last of the Helosians. To their south, the coalition soldiers they'd already left behind were beginning to organize their prisoners. Jin led Astrea and Cressida north, meeting up with the rest of their team, who were gathered with Lucian.

"That's the last of it," Lucian said, gesturing back to the new prisoners.

"Fighting's slowed on the water, too," Rami said. "Look, some of the Tornamian ships are pushing in."

And sure enough, when Astrea looked east toward the bay, several ships flying the Tornamian flag were moving toward the port. Others were still far out, blockading the entrance.

"One of those is bound to be my sister," Jin said. "Let's get everything set and secure. Take a break before we keep pushing into the city."

Astrea's shoulders sagged as she followed Jin and the others toward where a group of Novarians was setting up a slew of supplies. Jin moved past them and toward a small, low building with crates stacked along its side. He ordered them all to sit.

"Don't you need us to do something?" Lennor asked as she tugged off her hood and mask. Her dark hair was frizzy, flyaways escaping her two braids.

"Sit while fresh healers come look at you," Jin said.

"We're not hurt," Lennor argued.

"I'm fine, Captain," Civan said.

Removing her face covering, Astrea sank down onto one of the low crates and rested her back against the side of the building. She wasn't hurt, but she was beyond exhausted. Her ears rang, and her head swam. It had been too much—too much noise, color, sound, energy.

"I need a minute," she said.

"Take it," Jin said. "All of you. I don't care if you're not hurt. I'll be right back."

Adi followed him, the two of them talking in low voices as they started for the docks. Lucian squatted down in front of Rami, starlight swirling around his fingers as he healed a large burn on her cheek.

"What did you do to me back there?" Cressida asked as she dropped onto the crate next to Astrea.

"Gave you your energy back." Astrea let her eyes close. She pulled her barrier in only somewhat, until it extended no more than three arm lengths away from her body. With so many other Lightbringers around now, she would give herself the reprieve. Her pulse stopped hammering so loudly in her ears.

"I didn't know you could do that mid-fight."

"Neither did I." Astrea had acted on instinct. It had felt like the right thing to do, the only option.

"Well, thanks," Cressida said.

Astrea laughed, a tired sound. "You're welcome. I couldn't very well let us be taken out like *that*."

"Oh, so you have some other way for us to die in mind?" Cressida teased.

"Nothing in particular, but that just can't be the way we go," Astrea said, half joking and half serious. Of course she didn't have anything in mind. Ideally, they'd both live for a very, very long time.

They lapsed into heavy silence, the sounds of the coalition forces drowning out Astrea's ability to think. She kept her eyes closed as she rested against the wall, trying to ignore the smell of smoke in the air and the shouts of soldiers and commanders alike as ships docked.

Jin and Adi eventually returned. They spoke with Lucian about rounding up the Helosians. And where Astrea expected to feel the commander's heavy wall moving away, it moved closer.

She cracked her eyes open. The rest of the team was still sitting, half asleep like Astrea. Lucian crouched in front of her.

"Varojin told me what you did for Cressida," Lucian said. "Let me take on some of that for you."

"We shouldn't both be tired," Astrea protested.

"Splitting it between us is more bearable," Lucian said. "Don't make me order you."

"Fine." She really didn't feel like fighting him on it; she just also didn't like the idea of him being down for the count. But she'd need to be at her full strength if she was going to deal with Nazarov anytime soon.

Lucian placed a hand on her knee. The glow of his healing light made Astrea squint. Warmth seeped under her skin, and it was like the impossible weight on her shoulders lifted. It wasn't gone, but it was less. She could breathe again, and if she had to, she could run and fight more. It was as if she'd gotten half a night's sleep.

"There," Lucian said with a heavy breath. "Now we can both rest for a bit longer."

"We don't need to go out now?" Cressida asked.

"We don't even know where we're going yet," Lucian said. "Zephyrine wants to send more scouts into the city before we make our next move. Airships are coming in soon, too. Let's regroup. Varojin went to get some food for us."

Astrea nodded. She'd let the experts figure out what to do next, instead focusing on pulling herself together for the next—and most crucial—part of the mission.

<h1 style="text-align:center">CHAPTER 55</h1>

Food and water helped clear some of the fog clinging to Astrea, as did letting one of the other Lightbringers from Novaria take on more of her fatigue. She actually felt like she could function again. The fact that the battle on the bay had stopped helped, too.

Between periodic breaks in the thick clouds, the moon and stars shone brightly in the sky. Astrea gazed out over the water, the last place she and Saros had been in Kalama together.

Skies, her heart hurt. She hadn't thought it would be this hard, being back. Standing in the same spots they once had while she fought off all those Helosians so they could escape on Magdi's boat.

A clamor near the gates—shouts and hot, pinging panic—forced her to look away from the water. A handful of coalition guards threw their hands up over their heads, obviously irritated. In a nearby tent the Novarians had set up, a radio crackled. Lucian signaled for Astrea to join him there. With a sigh, she climbed off the crate she'd been sitting on for the last hour and walked over.

"What's going on?" she asked him.

Like her, he'd accepted healing from another Lightbringer, and his shoulders weren't sagging quite as much now. "Void mage sighting at the gate," he said. "Jumped in and out."

"Nazarov's scouts?" she asked.

"Probably. Where's Varojin?"

"Overseeing the Lifestealers," she said. He'd wandered off about a half hour before with Zephyrine and Adi to ensure each and every aetherium weapon they'd confiscated was being rendered useless. They weren't far away; in fact, they were closer to the commotion at the gate.

"Then let's go find him." Lucian motioned for her to go first, and so Astrea did.

They didn't have an overwhelming force at the port, but it was enough that she felt somewhat secure walking around in the open. Yes, she *needed* to be out in the open, but having so many trained soldiers around at least helped her feel like Nazarov couldn't simply jump in and abduct her.

Jin met them halfway between his tent and the one they'd been in, his expression grave. "That was the Paragon, wasn't it?" he asked.

"So it seems," Lucian said. "Are we ready?"

No, Astrea wasn't ready, but she had to be. She pushed her shoulders back. "Sure."

"Don't sound so confident," Lucian said dryly.

"Just nervous." She had no reason to hide that fact, not when Lucian would be able to sense it and when Jin knew her so well.

"Me too," Jin said. "But we'll get through this. Do whatever you think you have to in order to set up a meeting."

"I will," Astrea said. "And until he reaches out?"

"Let's try to go about our business," Jin said. "I could really use some coffee, if you want some."

"You don't need to stay with the Lifestealers?" she asked.

"No, Zephyrine and Adi can handle it."

"I'll be waiting," Lucian called after them as Jin and Astrea headed for one of the other tents that had been erected closer to the water.

Soldiers there were brewing coffee and tea, passing them out to waiting coalition forces. Astrea and Jin got in line. She didn't actually feel much like coffee, but it seemed as good an option as any while they waited. Jin slid his arm around her shoulders, tugging her in close to his body.

"You did good," he said quietly.

"Thanks."

"I know none of that was easy."

She shrugged. "It needed to be done."

The line moved up, so they took a few steps forward.

"Can you believe how far you've come?" he asked.

Astrea could hardly believe it at all. Yet there she was, in heavy armor, waiting in line for a cup of coffee as their small army waited for the next steps in their plan to take back Kalama.

"Can you believe how far *we've* come?" she asked in return. "All of us?"

"Hard to believe it wasn't even a year ago we were running around this city and trying to figure out who was stalking you." Jin sighed. "Hard to believe a year ago I was still fighting in Corsyca."

"Maybe this is the last time you'll be fighting for a while."

They shuffled forward in line as Jin said, "Hopefully."

Astrea really couldn't believe how quickly all of this had unfolded, even if it had been months and months. How could such an objectively short period feel like a lifetime? She'd been a different person when all this started, though she liked to think she'd hung onto the better parts of who she was.

As they moved forward in line again, sharp pain erupted between her shoulder blades. Shadows encroached on her field of vision too quickly, faster than usual when being dreamwalked to. She cried out, nearly tumbling forward with the force of the invisible blow Nazarov dealt her, but Jin caught her.

My favorite little Lightbringer, Nazarov cooed. *What are you doing in Kalama?*

You told me you were coming here, Astrea said to the darkness. He showed her no visions, no images, nothing.

So you thought you'd pay me a visit?

I thought you wanted me to, Astrea said. *Why else would you tell me your plan? You kept telling me we needed to meet, and I thought it was finally time.*

Silence. It seemed to stretch on forever with those shadows.

But then Nazarov said, *Why now?*

Because they had no choice. Because Kalama was under attack, just as Nazarov and The One had always shown her in old bouts of dreamwalking. Because she couldn't let Nazarov or Kaius hurt anyone else.

But Astrea didn't say any of that.

I've been thinking a lot, she said slowly. *And you're right.*

I am? he asked. It almost sounded like he was smiling. *About what, little Lightbringer?*

That I'm tired, she said. And skies, was it true. Astrea was tired of so much. *I'm exhausted. I don't want to fight anymore.* That was the truth, too. She was tired of fighting, tired of pain, tired of it all.

Oh? he asked. *And what do you want me to do about that?*

Astrea's heart thundered so fast and so loud she was sure Nazarov would be able to tell. Jin surely could feel it, with their bodies pressed together as he held her tight. Whispers of panic and confusion brushed her cheeks.

This had to work.

She *hated* what she was about to say, even if it was for a very good reason.

You told me that my family line either ends or continues . . . with us, she forced herself to say. *You said it was my choice. I choose the latter.*

Why? Nazarov asked. He actually sounded unsure for once.

Because I'm tired.

That's your only reason, Miss Sovna? Because you're tired? Nazarov scoffed. *I find it hard to believe you'd abandon your entire cause and your . . . husband . . . because you're tired.*

Enough people have suffered, Astrea said. *Enough people have died. Ysabel, all those civilians, my father . . . my uncle.* She tried to swallow, but it was like her body didn't want to work. *If I do this, will you stop? Finally stop, like you promised?*

Silence. It dragged on and on, for so long that Astrea was only sure Nazarov was still there because her physical body was immobile and her mind was taken over by shadows. Back in the physical world, she could feel Jin moving, feel *herself* moving, like he was carrying her.

Where would he be taking her? Was something wrong? Had Nazarov somehow left Astrea stuck in this dreamwalking plane, rendered useless?

Jin set her down on something hard, but he still gripped her hand tightly. Everything around her was muffled, like trying to hear people talk underwater. Worry and confusion brushed her cheeks, delicate like butterfly wings.

Nazarov? she asked.

I'll stop if you agree to my terms.

Astrea doubted he would actually stop. In fact, she knew he wouldn't. Nazarov wouldn't stop until he got what he wanted. But she had to sell this.

She tried to infuse as much relief and pain into her voice as she could as she said, *What are your terms?*

You give yourself to the Paragon and continue the Ramkas line, he said, *and I will take out Kaius and halt my campaign, effective immediately. Eliana can have control of the country.*

Cracks formed in Astrea's heart as she said, *Agreed. Anything to make this stop.* She sucked in a deep breath, then added, *But you can't hurt them, alright? You can't hurt my people if I go with you.*

Silence.

Nazarov? she asked again. *That's the only way I'll do this.*

We have a deal, he said.

Where can I meet you? she asked. *To hold up my end of the bargain.*

I'll come get you.

No, Astrea said quickly. *No, the others wouldn't understand. They won't let me do this. I need to find a way to break away from them and come to you, someplace they can't track me.*

Jin squeezed her hand, as if to say he was with her, that he would track her, would be with her every step of the way.

A complication, Nazarov muttered.

Where are you? she asked. *I could come to you.*

Is Eliana with you?

Astrea hesitated, but apparently that was all the response he needed.

Good, he said. *I'm sure she'll be on her way to see Kaius soon. Go with her, but break off into the gardens. On the northern side of the palace, there is a small door to a cellar that will take you down a spiral staircase and into the dungeons. Meet me there.*

That's too hard, Astrea argued, though it sounded lame. *Someone will notice I'm gone before I can even find the door. I've never noticed one there before.*

Then what would you suggest? Nazarov asked sharply.

Astrea's chest felt like it was going to cave in, but still, she managed to reply, *There's a gazebo at the lake near the observatory. It's easy for me to reach, and it's secluded.*

Varojin won't think to follow you there?

He'll be distracted by Kaius for long enough for me to come meet you.

It was the only spot that made sense to Astrea. She knew the palace grounds like the back of her hand. That was the only place they could go where there would be ample room for the rest of the team to conceal themselves that was still easy enough to access. The other places she could think of were far removed, too far from the rest of the army.

And if he doesn't stay with Eliana? Nazarov asked.

I'll find a way to ditch him, Astrea said. *But you can't hurt him. I already told you that's part of the deal.*

Fine, Nazarov drawled. *I'll see you soon, little Lightbringer.*

The shadows receded. Little by little, the real world returned. Astrea stared up at the star-filled sky, visible through the break in the clouds. She was on her back on one of those long, low crates again.

"Az?" Jin asked.

"I'm to meet him at the gazebo by the observatory when Ellie goes to confront Kaius," she whispered.

"Shit," Jin muttered. "Shit, okay. Was that your suggestion?"

"He wanted to meet me in the dungeons, so I convinced him that was an easier place for me to meet him."

"No, that's good," Jin said. "That's good. You did really well. We can work with that."

Astrea's next breath caught her throat. She coughed, then forced herself to breathe through it.

This was it. There was no turning back now.

A different kind of fear had settled in her bones. This wasn't the same fear as when she'd been held under that house in Talmaris, when she'd barely understood what was happening to her. This wasn't the same fear as when she'd lost Saros and nearly lost Jin.

No, this was different.

She was about to willingly walk into what could very well be a trap set for her. Nazarov seemed to believe her, but she knew he could be setting her up the very same way she was trying to do to him.

She had to trust herself. She had to trust her husband, her team. She had to trust that whatever Nazarov had planned, they would be successful.

Astrea finally looked away from the stars and over at Jin, at those brilliant, beautiful, kind eyes. She gave him a weak smile. "So, when do we get started?"

Astrea had assumed they would have to fight their way through Kalama, past Zaikudi and Helosians alike, to get up to Nobleman's Hill and the palace, but they would not be doing that.

Jin, Eliana, Nicos, Lucian, and Zephyrine were hunched over a map at a table in one of the port's warehouses, carefully plotting a way to the beaches below the cliffs the palace sat on. From there, there were tunnels and pathways up to the royal grounds. There would be guards to fight, they said, but it was the quickest way to get to Kaius. All the while, the rest of the coalition forces would work to take back sections of Kalama and dispatch Nazarov's forces.

Astrea had always known about those tunnels—had traversed them with Jin and Eliana when they were kids—but hadn't even considered using them to get up to the palace now. She shook her head, grateful she wasn't the one in charge of this portion.

"That's it, then," Eliana said, straightening from where she was bent over the map of the city. The overhead lights caught on the gold laurel clips holding her braided crown in place. "That's how we get to Kaius."

"You're sure you want to do this?" Nicos asked.

"Well, it's a little late to go back, don't you think?" Eliana asked with a nervous laugh. "I don't want to be seen as a usurper, but he's not willing to negotiate, so what choice do I have?"

"With the city under attack like this, you might be seen as a liberator," Zephyrine said. "Kaius clearly doesn't have a handle on the situation."

Astrea had grown strangely accustomed to the explosions in the distance; another went off, as if on cue.

"Whatever the case, I'd like to get this over with," Eliana said. "Dawn will be here soon. We shouldn't drag this out longer than needed. Everything's in position, right?"

"We heard from some of the Delian squad leaders a while ago," Zephyrine said. "They're starting in from the western side of Kalama. We'll squeeze Kaius's and Nazarov's forces alike, force them to surrender or . . . not."

"Prioritize Helosian surrender," Eliana said.

"Already passed that on," Lucian replied. He'd been quiet for most of the planning, only chiming in when asked his thoughts.

Anxiety tied itself around Eliana in a bright orange knot. "Alright then," she said with a huff. "Let's get going."

"Wait," Jin said, stopping his sister in her tracks. "We still need to figure out what we're doing with Nazarov."

"Kill him," Eliana said bluntly.

"Besides that," Jin said. "How do we get Az *and* the team out to the gazebo without him noticing? What if he's waiting for her?"

"He probably won't go until he sees movement from our camp," Lucian said. "He'd be a fool to wait around for skies knows how long. We go up first, sending Astrea in only when Eliana goes."

"You think he won't be watching for the rest of us to be with Ellie?" Jin asked.

"We've already agreed to send a retinue of guards and soldiers in with Eliana," Lucian said. "There will be plenty of people they need to overcome in the gardens, so we send a decently large force in to the palace.

Amid all that fighting, you think Nazarov will really be able to ensure where you are? If most everyone's masked?"

Jin's mouth twitched, like he was fighting back some kind of argument.

"It's our best shot, Jin," Zephyrine said. "What choice do we have?"

"We don't have any choice," Lucian said. "That's our only option."

Jin's gaze flicked to where Astrea stood across the table from him. "Az? What do you think?"

"I think you're all much better at this than me," she said.

"Are you comfortable going all the way to the gazebo by yourself?" he asked, tracing the line from their entry point over to the observatory. "It's not a short walk."

"I know," she said, swallowing hard. "I'll be fine. Like Lucian said, we don't have many choices right now."

And that was it. That simple truth.

She would have to be fine.

"Alright." Jin sucked in a slow, deep breath. "Let's get going."

They all moved away from the table. The rest of the team was outside, wrapping up all the preparations Jin had asked them to finish. Astrea started for the warehouse door to go tell them, but Jin lightly grabbed her arm.

"Wait, Az," he said, watching as everyone else filed out. Only when they were gone did he look down at her. "You're sure about this?"

"Skies," Astrea said, trying to force a laugh. "The sooner this is over, the better. Can we get going?"

"If Nazarov comes after you sooner—"

"Lucian will know," Astrea said. Oh, she was very certain of that. Lucian or one of the other Lightbringers. She was already on edge. If Nazarov popped up when she was on her own, trying to reach the meeting point, she would surely be a beacon of panic in the dark morning. "I'll fight him off. You and Adi trained me well."

One side of Jin's mouth quirked up. "I know we did. I can't help but worry, though."

"That makes two of us."

He pulled her into a tight embrace. Astrea melted against him, trying to memorize the sound of his heart as it beat steadily under her ear. And when he didn't pull away, she forced herself to take half a step back.

"Go," she told him. "Get everyone in position."

Pain and pride warred in Jin's eyes. Taking her face in his hands, he leaned down and kissed her. "I love you," he whispered against her mouth. "Be safe. I'll see you soon."

And then he was gone before she could even tell him how much she loved him.

She just hoped he knew. And she hoped the team would be careful, that they really could pull this off.

It was time to take down Victor Nazarov.

Chapter 56

The small boat carrying Astrea, Eliana, Nicos, and Zephyrine toward the secluded beach beneath the palace rocked beneath them. Every rise and fall of the vessel on the waves made Astrea's stomach lurch. The only blessing was the first hints of rosy pink and lavender on the horizon.

Dawn.

Day was finally breaking.

Their small rowboat—one of several carrying more Novarian, Tornamian, and Taipoli troops—skirted close to the edge of the cliff they'd need to ascend. All Astrea could see from here was the shadowy cliff face, its brown and gray edges featureless in the near darkness.

Up ahead, the outlines of a beach and cavernous opening came into view. There should've been auras, ones filled with anger or frustration at so-called enemies breaching the compound. But there was just faint energy, as if everyone up ahead was asleep.

Astrea supposed they would be, given Jin's team had also come this way to get in place near the observatory. They'd left twenty minutes before Astrea and the rest of them. Jin, Adi, Cressida, Lennor, Civan, Marko, Lucian. All seven of them, somewhere high above, getting into position. Chills prickled Astrea's skin, but the air wasn't very cold.

"They're all unconscious," Astrea said to Zephyrine. "We should be good to land."

The rowboats pushed ashore, jolting Astrea as they collided with the sandy beach. Zephyrine and Nicos got out first, and as they gave the signal, Eliana and Astrea climbed out next. Astrea tried to ignore the way the wet sand squished underneath her boots and made the climb up into the cavern more difficult.

In one corner, several bodies lay slumped over. The torchlight on the walls provided enough light to show their red Helosian uniforms, their bound hands and ankles, even the cloth between their teeth to keep them from yelling. Their eyes were closed, their breathing steady. Alive, but Astrea doubted they'd wake up anytime soon. Even if they did, it wasn't like they could easily go anywhere.

"I haven't been here in years," Eliana murmured to Astrea as they watched more rowboats pull up to the beach.

"Me either," Astrea said.

"Funny . . . we used to come here to play and escape my governess, and now—" She shook her head. "Well, maybe not funny."

"This will be a happy spot again for us someday," Astrea said. She had to believe that. "We'll come back down here once you've taken over."

Eliana's smile was small. "Sure."

The entire stretch of beach was made up of boats now, ten in total, each carrying six soldiers, plus the rowers. It wasn't an army, no, but they had powerful mages and skilled soldiers on their side. Void mages, too, including some of the Lifestealers to destroy any aetherium they stumbled across at the palace. Balthazar and Sarsali had stayed behind, promising to work with the remaining military to keep the harbor in their control.

It would have to be enough, at least until reinforcements joined them.

Zephyrine quietly called out orders, organizing the soldiers into groups and telling them where to go and who to follow. Rami slipped out from among the crowd, dressed in black leather and armed to the teeth.

"You ready, Astrea?" Rami asked.

"Yes," she said.

"Good, because I'm going with you."

Astrea's eyebrows rose. "What? I thought you were supposed to go with the rest—"

"Apologies, Your Imperial Highness," Rami said to Eliana, "but I don't feel right leaving Astrea to get over to the others on her own. It's too dangerous."

"I can fend for myself," Astrea said.

"Oh, I have no doubt," Rami replied with a grin. "But Lucian, well, he'd never say this, but he sees you as more than his mentee, Astrea. You're probably the closest thing he'll ever have to a daughter. And he would never admit it, but he's very, very worried about this all working out."

"And so you want to help ensure it works out," Eliana said with a nod. "Good. Do it."

Lucian . . . thought of Astrea that way? Sure, their relationship had softened in recent months, had started going far smoother than when they'd first met, but she'd never gotten an inkling that he might think of her as anything more than a young colleague.

Her throat tightened, and tears threatened to spill down her cheeks. The emotion rolled through her, unbidden, as she thought of the commander high above, right across from the observatory where she'd grown up. Where she'd lived with Saros all those years. A place neither her mother nor father would ever see, and now a place Saros would never step foot in again.

Astrea forced all those regrets into a tiny box in the back of her mind. Now was not the time. She could cry when all this was over, when they'd deposed Kaius and permanently rid the world of Victor Nazarov.

"Alright!" Zephyrine called. She'd positioned herself slightly down-hill from where the other three women stood, and Nicos was right next to her. "Follow me and Masalis!" Nicos raised his hand. "Capture Helosians, kill Zaikudi and Paragon if we find any. Got it?"

The small army grunted their affirmation.

"We take the palace, and we arrest Kaius. Any other politicians you find, any palace staff, detain them," Zephyrine said. "There's a void mage guard inside, Caliban. The whitest skin, hair, and eyes you'll ever see. Kill on sight. Do not underestimate him."

Again, the soldiers gave an affirmative.

Zephyrine turned to look at Eliana. "Your Imperial Highness?"

Raising her chin, Eliana said, "Let's go."

Astrea pulled her hood and mask on as the rest of the soldiers did the same. Zephyrine, Nicos, and Eliana were the only ones to not do so—no doubt so the Helosian guards and soldiers would *know* who Eliana was. Even Rami obscured her face.

Eliana, Zephyrine, and Nicos took the lead, Astrea and Rami just a few steps behind. They crossed the last of the beach into the cavern, sand turning to stone beneath their boots. They began the ascent up the well-kept stone staircases, which led up to one level, then another.

The higher they climbed, the more Astrea could sense. Not just the entire group of soldiers behind them but more above. Boredom, caution, fatigue, anxiety, anger. It all reached out to Astrea, dancing across her skin and into her muscles.

Jin and the rest of the team had somehow managed to get by them. Things would feel different if they'd been caught. There'd be a frantic energy to the air, something not so expected given the attack on Kalama.

Besides, on the way over, Zephyrine had mentioned something about watching for Jin or Adi's signals, which had never seemed to come.

But there. Energy, blinking in and out, like in the Badlands.

Astrea tapped Nicos's shoulder and said, "There's aetherium." Then she turned to the soldiers closest behind her and warned them of the same. Whispers rippled through the group.

"When we get up to the gardens," Astrea said to Rami, "I need to cut left."

"You won't even notice I'm with you," the smuggler replied. "Well, *you* might. Nobody else will."

Astrea nodded and tugged on her armor. Everything was in place. All the metal plates were set. The laces were tied. She just had to make it over to the lake.

At the head of the group, Zephyrine paused and held her fist up. They all stopped on the stairs. They were so close to the top that Astrea could see the sky through the opening that led to the gardens. Thick trees and bushes obscured the path.

Zephyrine motioned again, this time moving her arm forward. She took off at a sprint, wind howling as she charged into the gardens and toward the palace. Nicos and Eliana ran after her, fire and lightning flickering over their hands.

Astrea scrambled up the last of the steps. Instead of going north and west like the rest of the soldiers, Astrea dipped to the left, toward where the observatory tower peeked above the trees in the distance.

Magic clashed behind her, leaving her skin tingling with energy and emotion. Pain and anguish, confusion, relief, focus. It all swirled back near where their army was fighting Helosian guards.

Gritting her teeth, Astrea tried to block it all out and focus on that tower. Rami was somewhere close behind her, but when Astrea glanced over her shoulder, she found nothing other than the thick gardens and flashes of magic and guns back near the palace.

Be careful, Ellie, Astrea thought.

She ducked under a low-hanging branch, one of its thick green leaves smacking her in the face. She muttered a curse and kept going. The veritable forest ahead was too thick for her to cut through on her own, so she'd have to go closer to the palace and get back to the observatory that way.

She swung to the right. Rami's energy remained focused and close by, though the distance between them grew the more Astrea ran out into the open. This probably wasn't her best choice, but without knowing where Jin and the others had cut a path to the observatory—if they'd done that at all—she wasn't going to risk slowing down and backtracking.

Well-manicured hedges covered in fragrant flowers flew by Astrea as she sprinted down gravel and grass-lined paths. She was able to stick to routes that kept her mostly obscured by the tall bushes, out of sight from prying—

She smacked into something dense and broad. Astrea stumbled back, light flaring over her hands. A Helosian woman stood before her, her red uniform covered in dirt and smeared with something dark. Crimson rage flared in her aura as she also took a step back from Astrea.

"Who the fuck are you?" the woman asked.

Astrea's light bled away from one palm as she reached out, snapping up that anger in a bright red rope only she could see. The woman cried out as she tumbled forward. Her chin collided with the gravel ground, and stinging pain erupted in Astrea's jaw. She ignored it, tugging again and again on that red rope. The woman groaned.

Rami's energy caught up to Astrea, curiosity and annoyance scraping over her skin. The smuggler slipped behind the woman, rope in hand.

"Sorry about this," Astrea whispered to the Helosian guard.

Rami bound her hands and ankles, and as she moved on to shoving cloth between the woman's teeth and tying it behind her head, Astrea dropped the connection. That burning hate faded away, shutting off completely as Rami cracked a punch across the woman's temple. Her head lolled to the side as she fell unconscious.

"Go," Rami whispered to Astrea. "I'll be right behind you."

Astrea forced her legs to carry her forward again, down the familiar paths of the hedge maze. She followed it: three rights, two lefts, and another right, finally coming upon the much wider path—nearly wide enough to fit two cars—that would take her to the observatory.

How many times had she walked this path before? Every day for fourteen years, she'd come home this way. Home to her cozy bedroom, that apartment she'd shared with Saros. Home to her uncle, his moods, his mess. What she wouldn't give to have some version of that back. What she wouldn't give to be on her way home now, on her way to visit Saros after a long day at work or spent with the Nikaphoroses. Some version of life that blended her old one with her new, her whole family instead of one with missing pieces.

But no, she was here for one thing.

The trees towering on both sides of the path waved in the breeze. Astrea forced herself to slow down as she neared the bend that would take her the final stretch to the observatory and the lake, the gazebo. Her heart thundered in her ears, drowning out the rustle of leaves and explosions in the city.

There, the observatory. Its weathered brick, its thick brown door. All the same, except for the shrubs being more unkempt than usual. There, all alone, without Saros or her to take care of it. Astrea's lungs squeezed.

And to her left, the lake. No ducks swam in its water this morning. In fact, no gulls cried overhead. They'd probably all been scared off by the invasion.

Astrea pulled her hood and mask off as she approached the water, the bridge that would carry her into the gazebo. The gazebo where she'd once sat with Cressida and lamented Emperor Aelius's skies forsaken project, where Jin had once promised to help her figure out who was hunting her. Its white marble facade was the same as always, unchanged even by the many months she'd been gone.

Shoving her hood into the deep pocket of her armored skirt, Astrea smoothed back some of the flyaways tickling her nose and eyelashes. That one steady presence behind her had grown into eight. Jin, Adi, Cressida, Marko, Lennor, Civan, and Lucian, no doubt. Even if Astrea looked over her shoulder, she knew she wouldn't find Rami there. Even staring at the landscape surrounding the gazebo, Astrea didn't see any of them. But she could feel them.

With surprisingly steady steps, Astrea crossed the bridge. She moved to the gazebo's farthest edge, putting her back to the water and the forest. The only specific energy she could pick out was anxiety, somewhere to her right.

Astrea braced herself against the railing. She barely breathed as she waited. And waited. And waited.

Nazarov had promised to meet her there, so where was he?

They'd thought perhaps this would be some kind of trap *he* was trying to set, but what if he was trying to distract them from some bigger plan or offensive? Had their gamble failed already?

She closed her eyes, trying to focus on the breeze on her face and that steady wall behind her. That had to be Jin. She didn't know how to explain it, even to herself, but it *had* to be. It felt like him, more than any of the others did.

Cold bled into the air, slowly at first but growing in strength. Astrea opened her eyes again. Tendrils of shadow swirled up from the ground just beyond the little footbridge. She gripped the edges of the railing.

Nazarov appeared in a blink, dressed in dark gray armor and armed with several daggers. His pale skin and dark hair almost glowed in the rays of dawn light creeping up behind the observatory and forest around them. He smiled that nasty predatory smile as he walked toward her, arms outstretched as if greeting an old friend.

"Little Lightbringer," he said. "I'm so glad you finally made it."

Chapter 57

"I promised I'd hold up my end of the bargain, didn't I?" Astrea asked as Nazarov strolled closer.

"This is just one piece of it," Nazarov said, dropping his hands back to his sides. "Only the beginning. We're going to have quite the partnership, you and I."

"As long as this all stops," Astrea said. "I want all of this to stop."

"I can see that." Nazarov's gaze roamed her body and settled on her face. "No offense, but you need to start taking care of yourself."

Her cheeks burned, whether from the insult or the strange mix of aggression and desire in his eyes, she wasn't sure. Potent hate burned within her. Astrea steadied her breathing.

"That's been a bit hard to do with"—she gestured vaguely—"all of this going on."

Nazarov appraised her again, sizing her up. He took half a step forward, then another. "It slows down after today," he said.

"I thought you promised it would stop, not slow down."

"Not until there's a new little Ramkas running around, until my place at the top of the Paragon is secure. Then it can stop."

"Always changing the terms," Astrea said weakly, an argument she'd had with him before. Hopefully he'd buy it again. "What is it that you mean, slowing down?"

"Think what you want, little Lightbringer," Nazarov whispered as he moved in closer, "but I'm still the one in charge here." He glanced down at her hands. "You won't be keeping those."

Her rings. He meant her rings.

"I didn't think I could get away with taking them off now," she said. "My friends would've gotten suspicious."

He sniffed. "Well, your friends aren't here now."

Skies, Astrea was not prepared for this. Not her rings, the ones Cressida had made her, that matched Jin's so well.

"I'm waiting," he whispered, holding out one hand.

Astrea pried her stiff hands from the cold stone railing. Every movement made her heart hurt, but she pulled off the ring on her left hand first. As she dropped it into Nazarov's open palm, she had to force herself not to cry.

His lips curved up in another vicious smile as he pushed in closer so they were toe-to-toe. Nazarov wasn't much taller than Cressida, but he leaned down toward Astrea's face, his breath hot on her cheek. "And the other one."

She pulled the ring off her right hand before she could think better of it. The silver and gold metal looked so wrong in his possession.

"Very good, little Lightbringer." Nazarov threw them into the pond without breaking her stare.

Astrea's heart broke a little more. He'd already stolen her necklace, the sapphire one Jin had gifted her all those months ago. She never took those rings off, not unless she was sleeping. And now here he was, tossing them away like they were garbage.

"You didn't answer my question," she said, squaring her shoulders. She would not let him see how much this hurt, and she needed to buy her friends more time, get them the perfect opportunity to attack. "About what comes next."

"What comes next?" His hands covered hers as he whispered, "We're going to go pay a visit to *Emperor* Kaius. Now, say goodbye to Varojin."

How did he—

Shadows snaked up Nazarov's hands and forearms, spreading around Astrea's body. Panic exploded behind her. He grabbed hold of both her wrists, holding her in place as she struggled to pull away. A shot pierced the morning, just one explosive crack that made Astrea jump out of her skin. Pain seared her upper arm, but she hadn't been hit.

Roaring, Nazarov dropped his hold on her. Light flared in front of Astrea, and she threw herself at him. Her shield bashed into him, propelled by the full force of her body, and sent him toppling. Nazarov crashed back, disappearing right before he hit the ground.

Jin sprinted around the edge of the lake, launching himself across the bridge and reaching for Astrea. He crashed into her so hard they nearly went sprawling on the ground. He righted them and backed Astrea up until it was only water behind them.

"Where'd he go?" Jin asked.

"I . . . don't know. I feel him." Astrea pushed her senses out wider and wider, every inch of her skin crawling as that cold appeared, then blinked away, appeared again, then disappeared. The rest of the team rounded the lake, Adi and Lucian joining them in the tiny gazebo. "He's trying to throw me off. He knew about you, and he said he was going to Kaius—"

"And Ellie," Jin said. "Lucian, the palace, we need to—"

"He's coming," Astrea said, bracing herself as the cold jumped closer and closer again.

Shadows snaked up from the ground, right between the four of them. As soon as Nazarov appeared, marble shot up around his legs, his arms. Adi yanked back, wrenching Nazarov's bleeding arm backward. He roared and winnowed away again, reappearing a moment later right next to Astrea.

Nazarov grabbed her wrist, and Jin still held onto her other side. Inky darkness swallowed them whole, sucking them into the void. They jumped again and again and again, around and around the gardens, until Astrea's head swam. The fighting was moving closer and closer to the palace, but Astrea couldn't figure out who was winning or where Eliana was. They were jumping too fast, too erratically. Everything was a blur of red and blue, black and green.

The shadows receded again, and Nazarov threw Astrea to the ground, sending Jin tumbling with her. She smacked into cool tile floors, and instead of morning twilight or even shadows, Astrea found red and gold amid white marble. Chandeliers, tapestries, and a disorienting mix of confusion, joy, and fear pulsing in the air.

The palace.

"What is the meaning of this?" Kaius shouted, his voice echoing around the room.

"Told you I'd deliver them, didn't I?" Nazarov drawled.

"You've attacked my city! My empire! We had a deal!"

Jin nudged Astrea. She rolled to her knees, then shoved to her feet.

Kaius was on the dais, dressed in red Helosian armor. Crimson rage and gray confusion danced in his aura. Caliban stood behind him, dressed nearly the same. Nazarov staggered forward as he tried to favor his injured arm.

"Your pesky brother's team *shot* me as I tried to make good on my promise to you," Nazarov said, "and you thank me by yelling at me?"

Caliban stalked forward, shadows snaking up his arms, but Kaius waved him off. The snowy-haired void mage glared at Nazarov.

"I'll yell at you all I want," Kaius snarled, lightning flickering around his fingertips. "Kalama's on fire because of you. Your forces have attacked *my* city."

"And yet I still bring you what you've been begging for," Nazarov said. "Your sister at your back door. Your brother and his wife in your throne room."

"That was only part of our agreement."

"Yes, I do often like to go back on those." Nazarov turned, smiling at Astrea. "Don't I, little Lightbringer?"

She tensed, caught between Nazarov's copper eyes and Kaius's golden ones, the way they both stared at where Astrea and Jin stood, like predators watching prey. Jin shifted his weight slightly.

"You bring them to me at the worst time," Kaius snapped. Gray hate and red anger swirled around him in such a thick fog that Astrea almost couldn't make out the details on his armor. "I was just about to go deal with my sister."

"And now you can knock this out of the way before you go," Nazarov said, pivoting to face him again. "Lucky you, three obstacles down in one day."

"More like four." Kaius hopped off the dais and took slow, measured steps toward Nazarov. The heels of his boots clicked on the marble floors. Caliban followed a few feet behind him. "Call off your army, Lord Nazarov, and I may let you live past sunrise."

"Let *me* live?"

Jin nudged Astrea with his shoulder—barely. She risked a glance at him, and he was focused on Kaius. Did Jin want to . . . work with Kaius to take down Nazarov? Try to get Kaius out of this room?

"Control them," Jin whispered.

"You heard me," Kaius snapped.

"And if I don't do what you want?" Nazarov asked with a chuckle. "You'll smite me with your lightning?" Black shadows spiked high above his head. "Here's the thing, Your Imperial Majesty. You don't scare me one bit."

"I don't?" Crimson rage pulsed around Kaius in bright, erratic spikes. Nazarov shrugged. "No."

"I should."

Cold swept through the room as inky darkness swirled up from the floor. Solana materialized by Nazarov's side, the edges of her mask sparkling in the chandelier lights.

Blue lightning flickered around Kaius's fingertips. Caliban stepped forward, shadows swirling around his hands.

Solana and Caliban lunged at each other, disappearing as the void pulled them both away. Roaring, Kaius sprinted to Nazarov.

Astrea threw her hands out in front of her, squeezing tight as Kaius's anger swirled into a tight rope that she pulled and pulled on. Choking, he stumbled forward, and his lightning skittered away into nothing.

Nazarov charged, but Astrea grasped at his icy veil, punching through until she found the gray hate that followed him like a shadow. She held onto it, feeding her own rage and hatred to both men.

Nazarov, for everything he'd done. Everything he'd put her—the continent—through.

Kaius, for murdering Saros. Because that's what he was. A murderer.

Her chest swelled, heat searing her skin as both Nazarov and Kaius strained against her. Jin rushed forward, fire daggers in both hands as he raced for Nazarov. Hatred, confusion, pain—it all crashed into Astrea like a tidal wave, swallowing her whole. She held onto both warmongers as desperately as she could.

"Jin!" she croaked. "More coming."

In the atrium behind her, and from somewhere deep within the palace behind Kaius, more were coming. More soldiers, more void mages. Whose side were they on? She didn't know. Couldn't tell. Not like this. Everything blended together, too much color and emotion as the doors behind the dais exploded open and the ones behind Astrea clattered against the walls.

Jin reached for Nazarov, to drive his blade home, but the sharp *rat-ta-tat-tat* of automatic gunfire made Astrea flinch and shy away. She lost control. Shadows swirled up around Nazarov, stealing him away into the void.

Swearing, Jin pivoted, searching the room. Pain seared Astrea's left forearm, her shoulder, her side. A familiar voice cried, "Nic!"

Oh, no. No, no, no.

Not Eliana. Not Nicos and Zephyrine and the rest of them here, now.

Kaius shoved to his feet, his rage flaring hotter.

Nicos hadn't been hit by aetherium. There was just pain, horrible pain, but not that telltale fire and ice echoing in Astrea's veins. Nicos was sprawled out on the floor. Zephyrine held Eliana back as Lucian kneeled and placed his hands on Nicos's arm.

"Sister!" Kaius shouted. "I see you finally decided to come home."

Electricity buzzed in the air, forcing Astrea to turn her back on her friends, her team. To focus on Jin, on Kaius, on where the shadows at the edges of the room stretched and morphed.

But she only felt one void mage. Just one, swirling around, impossible to pin down. Nazarov. It had to be him.

The pain in Astrea's arm died off to an ache, proof of Lucian's healing. Boots shuffled into the room behind Astrea, dozens of pairs. And behind Kaius, on the dais, were Helosian guards, several with guns pointed at the group.

"Stand down, Kaius!" Eliana's voice rang clear and true through the cavernous throne room. "Put an end to this *now*."

"Oh, I'll put an end to it," Kaius snarled, starting forward.

A fiery wall erupted between Jin, Kaius, and the dais. Anger and confusion exploded behind the flames, and Astrea grabbed that energy, holding on tight to those guards. Jin reached for Kaius, not with fire but his hand.

The shadows at the edges of the room stretched more, encroaching on where they stood in the middle, seemingly kept at bay by Jin's fire. Cold pulsed over Astrea's skin. Shadows swirled up from the floor. Nazarov reappeared. Metal glinted in the firelight. He slashed at Jin's arm, sending him reeling back a step.

He slashed again, spraying blood across the white floors, across himself, across Astrea and Jin. She cried out as the pain mirrored on her throat.

Look away, Astrea.

She didn't look away.

Kaius's hands went to his neck. He fell to the ground, spasming as blood ran in rivers across the floor.

Someone screamed. Color and emotion exploded in the air, a haze clouding Astrea's vision and mind. Her ears rang, and her head swam.

Kaius was dead.

Kaius was *dead*.

No shadows snaked up his skin. He simply bled out, killed by a vicious man.

Fire and lightning and wind and water raged through the room. Steel clashed with steel, and both sides locked in battle. Eliana shouted for the Helosians to stand down, and gray confusion and hesitation began to replace some of the red haze in the air.

Nazarov grinned like a madman as he sprinted for Astrea. She urged her tired legs to move, but she was too slow. He slammed into her, arms circling around her waist. But someone crashed into *him*, heat blistering Astrea's skin.

And then there was that cold again, sucking them in and tossing them into the darkness of the void.

Chapter 58

The shadows swirled and rushed around Astrea. Her back slammed into the ground, and her breath left her in a whoosh. The dawn sky hovered above her, creamy pinks and oranges and blues.

Nazarov peered down at her. Hot rage burned Astrea's skin, and then Nazarov's eyes went wide as someone yanked him off her.

Jin.

Astrea scrambled off the ground, nearly slipping on the soft dirt. They'd landed in one of the sparring circles near the barracks, a small crater in the landscape.

Nazarov slipped out of Jin's hold, pivoting back a few steps every time Jin advanced on him.

"Well!" Nazarov called out, grinning. "One more Auris down. You should be thanking me, Varojin. I just did you a huge favor."

Jin lunged, a fiery dagger in hand. Shadows snaked up from the dirt, swallowing Nazarov whole. That same darkness formed on the flat ground above the training ring. Jin sprinted up the training ring's wall, then ducked as void fire blasted at him from behind.

Astrea spun. There, opposite where Nazarov had landed, was Solana. Shadows snaked up her arms. Her dark gray armor matched Nazarov's, sleek like a second skin on her thin body. Daggers were strapped to her thighs, and she had another in her right hand, blood dripping from its tip.

"About time you fucking showed up!" Nazarov called to Solana, dodging the fire Jin focused on him. "What took you so long?"

"The snow-haired one was hard to kill!" Solana yelled back, her gaze fixating on Astrea.

Caliban was dead, too?

It was good, but—

Solana charged, racing down the slope into the training ring's bowl, right where Astrea stood. The void mage brandished her dagger at Astrea, slashing the air as Astrea pivoted back, farther and farther away from Solana—and from Jin, who was focused on Nazarov.

Solana reached for Astrea's arm, missing by a few inches. She swiped at her again, her hand slamming into the thick, impenetrable light of Astrea's shield.

Astrea dug her heels into the ground, shoving hard against Solana. The woman snarled and stumbled back.

"Stupid little Lightbringer," she hissed.

Echoes of fire burned Astrea's upper arm. She didn't dare look away from the woman before her, from the hate beaming out at her from behind that mask.

Lowering her legs, Astrea prepared for another blow. Solana charged, smashing into Astrea's shield with her shoulder. But Astrea pushed her back again, so hard that Solana tumbled back into the loose dirt with a thud.

Astrea sprinted forward, throwing herself onto Solana as she tried to stand. Solana screamed, and ghostly pain flared in Astrea's face, her shoulder. She fell on top of the woman, pinning her to the ground with her body.

She had to end this. She had to help Jin. He and Nazarov continued in a flurry around and around the training ring, a dance of flame and shadow.

Solana reached up toward Astrea, but she slammed the void mage's hand back into the ground. With her other, Astrea reached for Solana's icy veil, punching through as she fed her magic the rage and panic building in her bones. She hated this woman. She hated Nazarov. And she had to help Jin end this. This had to stop.

Her fingers brushed Solana's burning hatred and anger, the crimson and gray flaring to life above the woman's head in a thin band. Astrea yanked on them. Her sternum ached, making each breath painful. But she held tight, pulling harder and harder as Solana stared up at her, wide-eyed.

Solana struggled under her grasp, thrashing and tearing at Astrea as she tried to free herself. Astrea pushed down harder on this woman, hoping she would give up, pass out from the force of the energy Astrea pushed and pulled.

Something sharp pierced Astrea's right thigh. She screamed. Her magical hold faltered. Pain flooded her veins, hot and stinging. But *only* hot.

No aetherium.

Solana threw Astrea off her, sending her sprawling to her back. She shoved to her feet.

White panic pulsed in the air as someone shouted, "Astrea!"

Not Jin.

Solana cried out, crumpling to her knees. Her attention shifted to Astrea's right, toward the palace. Lucian skidded down the side of the training ring, one hand outstretched as he controlled Solana and the other gripping his weapon. Behind him came white hair and a gust of wind that knocked Solana to the ground.

Zephyrine and Lucian.

They'd come.

But where was everyone else?

Astrea winced as she tried to move. Blood coated her leg. She forced her hand to her thigh, closing her eyes as mirror healing and pain warred on her skin. It was too much. It was all too much.

Confident she'd stopped the worst of the bleeding, Astrea rolled over to her knees, then pushed up higher.

And there, above her, Jin tackled Nazarov to the ground. Wispy tendrils of shadow began circling them both.

Astrea ran. She ignored the pulsing in her freshly healed thigh. She ignored the sharp stab to her heart and the flicker of energy behind her that winked out as someone died.

She ignored it all.

Scrambling the last few paces up the training ring wall, Astrea threw herself on top of Jin just as the void sucked the three of them in again.

As they landed with a thunk, Jin rolled off Nazarov and shielded Astrea with his body. Nazarov jumped them again and again, a blur of shadow and trees taking over Astrea's vision, mixing with the pain and making her nauseated. When they stopped again, Nazarov shoved them both away hard.

Pain pulsed against every inch of Astrea's body. Crackling burns and sharp wounds, thudding aches and bruises. She took only a second to look Jin over; it was all they had. He wasn't untouched, his tan skin marred by burns and cuts. Exhaustion crashed into her, whether hers or his or both, she couldn't tell.

But Nazarov wasn't untouched either. He stalked toward them both, chest heaving. Blood trickled down both sides of his face, and his skin was blistered. His armor was torn in places, and blood leaked through, harsh red against the gray leather.

They were deep within the palace gardens, on soft grass and amid thick trees and shrubs. No one ever came back here. Not really. Jin and Astrea had always run this deep into the grounds as children when trying to get away from Kaius and the guards.

Jin pulled Astrea up with him and didn't let go. But his grip was weaker than it should've been. He drew in one ragged breath, then another. Heat built around his whole body, so much Astrea was afraid he might set them both on fire.

"You two have fucked with me for the last time," Nazarov snarled. "You will *not* take this from me. Helosia is *mine*! The continent is *mine*!"

"You're done, Nazarov," Jin said. "You've lost. Solana's dead. Kaius is dead. Half your fucking army is dead by now. You overplayed your hand."

"I did *not*!" Nazarov screamed, spit flying from his mouth. "I still have options."

Heat continued building around Jin as crimson rage and anger covered his body. "There is *nothing* left! You lost!"

Nazarov's eyes darkened. "We'll see about that."

He sprinted, closing the gap between them. He pulled his arm back, something metallic glinting in the rays of the rising sun.

Jin stepped in front of Astrea, the heat around him growing and growing until flames sparked in the air. "Az! Shield!"

Oh, skies. Oh, he was going to try to use his Sunreaper abilities, when he was so beaten—

She slammed her hands against his back. The muscles in his shoulders flexed and twitched as the heat surrounding him tripled, painful against her exposed skin. Astrea's hands began to glow, white starlight mixing with red and orange flames.

Her skin ached, and her muscles spasmed as magic coursed through her. She opened herself to it, nothing more than a guide as she poured more light into Jin. As his fatigue shrank, hers grew, but she held tight to him, unable to move. It was like they were bound together, linked by the energy flowing from her and into him.

That cold moved closer, closer, closer.

She braced herself, thinking of every good thing she could.

The Nikaphoroses and all the years they'd spent as one family, them and her and Saros. Tending to Sarsali's roses with her. Taste testing Balthazar's new recipes. Keeping Cressida company while she tinkered with her latest projects.

Eliana's fierce support over the years, her ability to always get a rise out of anyone nearby and make Astrea laugh. Nicos's steady and quiet friendship.

Adi's love for life, his constant curiosity. The way he cared about everyone, including stony Marko. And Marko's attempts to keep them all at arm's length, only to be broken down. His favorite color being green.

The cold moved, no longer in front of Astrea but behind. She shivered.

Lennor and Civan and Noemi, new friends. Lennor's energy, Civan's understanding, Noemi's determination. Zephyrine's wisdom and Lucian's steadfastness.

Jin's tender love. The way he always made her feel safe. How he had always accepted her as she was, never trying to change her or make her fit into what he thought was right. How he let her just *be* and tried to support her however he could. She could even feel it now, beneath the rage and panic and raw power. That sunshine, ever present on her skin.

The cold moved again, away from Astrea and toward Jin. It bounced around and around and around, so fast she couldn't keep track.

Astrea's light grew brighter and brighter, impossible to look at. Her eyes closed as red overtook the glowing starlight.

The world exploded. Jin *exploded*. The ground shook, and everything went dark.

CHAPTER 59

Chunks of earth and grass fell around them. Nearby trees and shrubs crackled and smoked as fire ate away at them. Black smoke swirled in the air, choking Astrea.

Pain flared in her shoulder, emanating down her back and around her ribs. She fell to her knees. The dirt beneath her crunched and crumbled, completely dry. Chunks of her armor cracked, dried out by all those flames. She pushed them away, trying to get a better look at the wound in her shoulder. With all the soot, she couldn't quite tell what had hit her. A rock, maybe?

Later, she promised herself.

They needed to finish this first.

Jin staggered forward, his breaths uneven. Nazarov was sprawled out on the ground, not fifty feet from where Jin had blown them all up. Even through the haze of smoke and dust, Astrea could make out Nazarov's burns, the blood covering him where his armor had been eaten away. Her entire body ached, like *she* had been set on fire.

Nazarov barely rolled onto his back, hacking and wheezing as he cursed.

"I told you," Jin said, stooping over him, "that you overplayed your hand." He grabbed Nazarov by the front of his armor and pulled him up. Nazarov screamed. "I told you that you lost."

A fiery dagger took shape in Jin's hand.

"Don't you want to show mercy?" Nazarov asked, coughing between each word. His cracked lips bled. "Your wife is . . . watching."

"This *is* merciful. You deserve far worse than this, Nazarov."

Nazarov opened his mouth to reply. His arm twitched.

"Look away, Az," Jin said. "Shield yourself."

Astrea had nothing left to give. Nothing. All she could feel was that pain radiating down her back, blood following its path. But she fumbled for her barrier, pulling it back and back until she felt nothing at all.

And she didn't look away. She would not. Not this time.

Nazarov's lips quirked up into a smile, and he threw his arm out toward Astrea. Something flew toward her as he said, "Say goodbye to the little Light—"

The tip of a small dagger pierced Astrea's skin, sliding through the opening between the metal plates covering her chest and shoulder. It burrowed right beneath her collarbone, burning her skin on contact. Hot and cold, warring fire and ice. Astrea yanked the metal free.

Jin shoved his fiery blade straight into Nazarov's heart. He screamed so loud it covered Astrea's cry, so loud she thought her ears would bleed. The smell of burning flesh carried on the breeze. Nazarov writhed, but Jin held him tight, forcing the dagger deeper and deeper.

And it was only when Nazarov stopped screaming—stopped moving—that Jin's dagger dissipated into tendrils of smoke, like blown-out birthday candles. He shoved Nazarov to the ground, lifeless.

Victor Nazarov was dead.

Kaius.

Caliban.

Solana.

Nazarov.

All dead.

The mission . . .

Astrea collapsed onto her side and closed her eyes as that terrible void magic ate her from the inside out.

"Az!" Jin drew closer, calling her name again. Panic exploded in the air, hot against Astrea's blazing cheeks.

"I'm alright," she whispered as he fell to the ground next to her.

"Hey, Az, look at me," Jin said, his breath hot on her skin. His hands pressed against her bleeding wound, and she cried out. "Az . . . Az!"

She forced her eyes open, finding his, the most brilliant gold flecked with amber made even more brilliant by the soot streaking his face. "He's dead," she said.

"He's dead," Jin said, taking her face in his hands. "He's dead, and you're dying."

"We completed the mission," she whispered, forcing her hand from the dry dirt to where his pressed painfully against her collarbone.

He barely smiled at her. "We need to go. I need to get you to a healer, Az."

"I'm a healer."

"Aetherium," Jin said, voice trembling. "You can't have anything left. You can't. I felt what you did for me. We need to get you to a healer."

Astrea had nothing left to give, but she had no time.

She'd given everything to take Nazarov down, and he'd still gotten her.

He couldn't win. Not like that.

Nazarov could not win.

She had fought too hard. Jin had fought too hard. She could not let Nazarov win, even in his death.

Her veins burned. Her muscles spasmed. Her light inched forward, brilliant and blinding.

"Tell me something good," she whispered. "Please."

"You," Jin said, the answer quick, sharp. He pressed her hand against her chest with his, his skin rough and warm. "You, Az." Sunshine

warmed her skin. "You're the best skies damned thing that's ever happened to me."

"That's . . . not specific," she groaned.

A tight, sad laugh left him. "Smart-ass."

One side of her mouth quirked up as she pushed her light deeper. "You
like it."

"I like *you*," he said. "I love you, Astrea Sovna, and you're not dying
on me today."

"No," she agreed, "I'm not."

He pressed her hand down harder. His palms warmed. Astrea sucked
in one breath, then another, as the cold eating her alive retreated.

Pink love and purple reverence swirled around Jin. They mixed with
the dawn sky, one of the most beautiful things Astrea had ever seen. And
she took them, letting them settle in her chest and make their home near
her heart.

"I love you," she whispered.

"Hold on, Az," Jin said. "Hold on."

But she was already floating.

*Warm sunshine skittered across Astrea's skin as she strolled through the
gardens with Saros.*

*They were unusually quiet, especially for the afternoon. No guards in
their crisp red uniforms. No aristocrats in their over-the-top outfits or
businesspeople in their stylish linen suits. No seagulls overhead, crying out
for attention. Not even the honk of cars in the city beyond.*

*"I'm going to miss this place," Saros said. His usual pensive expression
was different, too. His shoulders were relaxed. There were no dark circles
under his eyes. He even smiled, a real, broad smile.*

"What do you mean?" Astrea asked.

"I can't wait to see what it will become," he said. "But there's much to do before then. You and your friends have your work cut out for you."

"What do you mean?" she asked again. "Where will you be?"

"Oh, my dear," Saros said with a laugh, "it's time for you to go home now."

"Uncle?" Astrea asked as the image began to fade. "Uncle?"

Astrea gasped, her back and body arching off the ground. Someone pushed her down.

"Hold on, Az," Jin said.

More hands pressed against her, strong, unyielding hands. Light glowed so bright she had to tilt her head away and close her eyes.

Energy flowed through her limbs, from her head all the way down to her toes. It was both agonizing and comforting, a terrible pain and great relief. She cried out, and Jin pushed her down harder, trying to hold her still.

"Fuck," Lucian groaned as he pulled his hands away. The light died, and he fell back against the ground with a distinct thud.

"Lucian?" Astrea asked, voice rough as if someone had scratched her throat with sandpaper. "Jin?"

"It's alright, Az," Jin said, collapsing on top of her. "It's alright."

Tears pricked her eyes. She wasn't dead.

The aetherium hadn't gotten her.

No, this had to be real. The feeling of Jin's skin on hers, the morning sky, Lucian's muttered curses.

She was alive.

Nazarov was dead.

She was safe. *They* were safe.

"Where's everyone?" she asked.

"Dealing with the fallout," Lucian mumbled.

"Are they hurt? I saw Nicos get hurt."

"He's fine," Lucian said. "He'll survive."

Exhaustion weighed Astrea down more than Jin's embrace. It tugged at her eyelids, her mind, her body.

"You healed me," Astrea said to the commander.

"You did most of the work," Lucian replied with a wry smile. "I simply finished cleaning up the mess."

Astrea sucked in an agonizing, shuddering breath. "I'm so tired."

"Go to sleep," Jin said. "I'll get you back."

"No. Help me up."

"Az—"

"Help me up," she said again. "Nazarov can't win."

"He's dead," Jin said even as he helped her sit up. "He's really, really dead, Az."

"I know, but . . ." How did she explain this? Skies, her head hurt. Pain pinged around inside her skull—hers and Lucian's both, she was fairly certain. "Nazarov didn't want me to walk out of this fight. So I'm going to."

"Stubborn," Jin said, peach amusement flaring bright around him and coating Astrea's tongue in sugary sweetness.

Groaning again, Lucian sat up, too. He ran his hands through his hair, which hung loose around his shoulders and was covered in dirt and flecks of grass. He looked worse for the wear, all bloodied and beaten, skin sallow and shoulders slumped. He looked about as good as Astrea felt.

Still, with Jin's help, Astrea got to her feet. She steadied herself against him.

This had once been a beautiful, lush part of the Kalamian palace gardens. A perfect place to hide as children, now turned into a battlefield.

Obliterated, really.

The trees and foliage were just charred trunks and remnants of what they had once been. The thick green grass had been completely burned away, replaced by ash and the driest dirt.

All Jin's doing.

Well, Astrea had helped in her own way.

And there, fifty feet away, was Nazarov. A burnt, bloodied, beaten version of who he once was. He lay motionless. Astrea sensed nothing from him. No cold. No hate. Nothing but the quietness of death.

They had really won.

Astrea straightened, wincing as her thigh twinged and shoulder burned. They may have hurt, but that pain meant she was alive.

She looked first at Lucian, then Jin, and forced a smile. "Let's go."

Chapter 60

The three of them limped through the Kalamian palace gardens, away from that burnt, destroyed section and into the pristine part by the barracks. They passed the training ring where they'd just fought Nazarov, and a few guards dressed in Novarian blue and Helosian red were draping a sheet over Solana's body.

The morning sun crawled higher overhead, painting the sky a mix of lavender, pink, tangerine, and blue. The light almost gleamed off the marble palace, which was marked by splatters of dirt, blood, and gunpowder.

And there, sprinting down the steps of the veranda, was Adi. Cressida. Marko. Lennor. Civan. All were bloodied, bruised, and haggard—but alive and running toward them.

"Az!" Cressida cried, throwing herself past Adi and into Astrea.

Astrea and Jin barely caught her, holding her tight. "Hey, Cress," Astrea managed to say past the lump in her throat.

"What happened?" Adi asked, taking Lucian's place on Astrea's other side and helping hold her up.

"He's dead," Astrea said past the burning in her throat. "Nazarov's dead."

"But what happened?" Cressida asked. "It felt like the palace walls were going to come down."

"Let's get Az to a healer first, then I'll fill you in," Jin said. "And I need a fucking drink."

At that, Adi actually laughed, a deep, warm sound. Affection and pride rolled over Astrea's aching skin. Lucian may have helped ward off the worst of her injuries, but every step she took was agony.

Civan ran ahead of them, back into the palace, and yelled for medics. Despite Astrea's protests, Jin ended up scooping her into his arms, carrying her the rest of the way. Inside was a flurry of chaos. Coalition forces were dealing with whom Astrea could only assume were Kaius's stalwart supporters based on the way they were being arrested. She spotted Zephyrine speaking with more Helosians, all of whom radiated minty relief. Had they surrendered when they realized Eliana was there?

Jin carried her past soldiers from all their allied countries, past Helosians. Medics and healers worked on the injured. Astrea should have pulled her barrier back, but even breathing was hard. So she gritted her teeth against the onslaught of pain, relief, worry, pride. They went down corridors decorated with rich furniture, elaborate paintings and tapestries, and thick rugs. Astrea thought faintly that it was a shame the rugs would get so filthy with all of them trudging around the palace.

In the distance, police sirens. The occasional boom of an explosion.

"We haven't gotten them to stand down yet?" Jin asked.

"Reporting a holdout of Zaikudi on the northwestern outskirts," Adi said. "We're working on it."

"Fuck me," Jin muttered.

"We're working on it," Adi said again. "Just rest."

"I can hardly rest when my brother's dead and the city's still under attack," Jin said. "When my wife was hit with aetherium."

"What?" Cold horror bled into the air around Adi and Cressida.

"What?" echoed another voice—Eliana—as Jin strode through the two open double doors of the palace infirmary.

Astrea hadn't been here in years. It was deep within the first floor of the palace, a room that could fit a mere ten patients at a time. Astrea tried to push away from Jin's chest. Nicos lay in one of the beds, Rami in another.

"Nazarov's dead," Jin said to his sister. "How you doing, Nicos?"

"I don't think he's ever going to let it be forgotten that he took a bullet for me," Eliana said, voice tight and small. Her exhausted face was stained with mud, blood, and tears. Her hair was frizzy, her face filled with worry.

Jin set Astrea on one of the cots near Nicos and Rami. Nicos was shirtless, his left shoulder wrapped in bandages. A thin white blanket covered the rest of him, and he was propped up against a few pillows. Unlike Nicos, who began to protest Eliana's last statement, Rami was asleep. Bandages covered her forearm, and patches of skin on her face were newly healed.

Nicos took Eliana's hands in his. "I love you. You know that, right?"

"Skies . . ." Eliana sniffled. "Of course I know."

"Then you understand why I had to do my job."

"You scared me, Nic."

"A few little bullets can't get rid of me," he said, and Eliana actually laughed.

But she sniffled again. "That may be your job, but I need to go deal with . . ." The implication hung heavy in the infirmary, silent aside from the occasional rustle of fabric.

"Go," Nicos said. "Helosia needs you right now. I'll be fine."

Dropping Nicos's hand, Eliana stood and smoothed the front of her black armor, then wiped her eyes with the back of her hand. "Alright," she whispered. Mint relief, orange anxiety, white terror, and deep blue regret all swirled around her in a storm. "I'll be with Zephyrine. I need to go get a handle on things before word spreads about Kaius."

"I'll come find you," Nicos said. "I'll be there soon."

The corners of Eliana's lips quirked up into the smallest of smiles. "Alright." She gave Astrea the same pained expression, then Jin. "Heal up. We're not quite done yet."

"Should you—" Astrea started, but Jin sat on the side of her bed and touched her shoulder.

"I should," he said, "but I need a moment."

She nodded. Part of her thought to argue, to insist he go help Eliana deal with the fallout of everything, but Jin looked so exhausted. Exhausted, relieved, heartbroken.

It was only then that Astrea realized Cressida was gone. Adi was gone. The twins were both gone. Where had they disappeared to? Astrea almost asked, but she didn't have it in her. Wherever they were, they were safe. Maybe they'd gone to help Eliana.

"Nazarov's really dead?" Nicos asked.

"He's really dead," Jin said, head bowed low. "Him and Solana both."

Astrea's eyes grew heavy as the weight of that truth settled over her like another blanket. The biggest threat in the Paragon was gone forever.

"Good," Nicos said, voice hard. "Good."

It *was* good. And as darkness crept in around the edges of Astrea's vision, all she could focus on was the relief whispering over her skin.

They'd finally completed the mission.

The next few times Astrea woke up, she was tended to by familiar healers wearing midnight blue and deep green. Lucian had, at some point, crawled into the bed next to Rami. Nicos had left. And Jin had pushed a spare cot next to Astrea's and fallen asleep with her for what had to have been hours.

But when she awoke again, it wasn't Jin she found with her but Cressida. Cressida, Sarsali, and Balthazar, all three. Her family.

"Hi, sweetheart," Sarsali said.

Astrea launched herself out of bed, throwing herself into Sarsali's arms. Her whole body ached, like she'd come down with a terrible flu, but Astrea didn't care. The tears came unbidden as Sarsali held her close, as Balthazar joined and Cressida piled on from Astrea's other side.

Her family was safe, alive. There, with her.

"I'm sorry," Astrea choked out, finally pulling away to wipe at her tear-streaked face. "I don't know what's gotten into me."

Maybe that wasn't true. Knowing she was back in Kalama, safe with her family, alive after being hit with aetherium . . . after all they'd been working toward, all they'd—she'd—been through . . .

It was too much. The tears kept coming, months' and months' worth. It was her fear, her grief, her relief, all of it manifesting as this water cascading down her cheeks. The tears wouldn't stop, and Astrea didn't even try to control them. There was no point. It was everything she'd been holding back, all the terror coming into this day. She let her tears wash it away.

She didn't have to be scared anymore.

What had happened would always hurt. Stalking, abduction, torture. Ysabel's assassination. Knowing her father for only a short time. Saros's death. All of that would leave permanent scars on Astrea's heart.

But she'd come out on the other side, overcome Nazarov.

She'd grown stronger after every setback, survived every terrible day. She was still alive, and she would never take that for granted.

"I saw him," Astrea said as the tears began to slow.

"Who?" Balthazar asked. The cot across from Astrea's squeaked as he sat on it.

"Saros. Just before Lucian healed me, after Nazarov died." Astrea struggled to swallow past the dryness in her mouth. "Maybe it was my mind playing tricks on me, but he was here, with me. In the gardens. He said we had our work cut out for us to change this place."

"That we do," Sarsali said, stroking some of Astrea's hair back from her face. "Eliana especially."

"Is it bad out there?" Astrea asked. She'd somehow had the foresight to keep her barrier pulled in tight when she'd woken up, blocking out the rest of the world.

"Not everyone's pleased by the news of what happened," Cressida said slowly. "But we knew this would be a challenge. And there are plenty who are glad to see Ellie, too."

Astrea nodded. They'd never imagined that Eliana would simply waltz into Kalama, take over from Kaius, and Helosia and the continent would be at peace. No, Eliana had always known this would be a different kind of battle, one that would require a more delicate and steady hand.

But if anyone could do it, Eliana could. They all would, together. They'd complete this new mission, too.

Chapter 61

Two weeks passed by in a blur with so much to do.

Raela had been found alive in the palace's dungeons, neglected but mostly unharmed. Osin, the rebellious owner of the Whiskey Dream, was safe, as were Astrea's old coworkers. She hadn't been by to actually see any of them yet, but she would go once she had the chance.

The Nikaphoroses had been able to go into the city after a few days to check on Lodestar's offices and their home. Both had survived the invasion, though there'd been some exterior damage. Neither Balthazar nor Sarsali had been worried about that; they were relieved their staff and their home had survived. Cressida was glad that her parents' lives could return to normal.

Noemi had arrived, escorted to Kalama by a unit of Novarian and Tornamian soldiers. Adi, of course, was thrilled to be reunited with his sister and to be able to show her around the palace.

Lennor and Civan had no family to bring into Kalama, but they seemed content helping where they could—and relaxing when Jin gave them orders to take a break. Civan had even gotten nightly card games started, and he'd managed to find Astrea's wedding and engagement bands in the pond by the observatory for her.

Even Apelo and his family had arrived in Kalama a few days earlier, with plans to stay at least until he and Eliana felt the government and country were decently stable.

Astrea and Jin had both recovered from the fight with Nazarov, though Astrea didn't feel quite like herself yet. With time, she was sure she would. But grief and exhaustion were taking their heavy toll, the price to be paid after just trying to survive for so long.

Nicos and Eliana were stressed beyond their capacity, but Eliana insisted it was fine. She would rest when the city—and country—were stable again. With Zaikud the only country now opposing Eliana's ascendance and all that had taken place, the other continental leaders would need time to sort out what to do next. After all, the Zaikudi government had aligned with Nazarov. All the coalition's leaders insisted they had to face consequences, but nobody could agree on what.

The damage around Kalama was being repaired by Lodestar engineers and mages from around the continent. It was a massive project, and Balthazar and Cressida had been gone most of the week to oversee the work and get everything in order. Coalition healers were stationed around the city, still tending to wounded civilians and helping however else they could.

All that was really left was Eliana's coronation, a formality more than anything. They all needed to be there within the hour.

And then there was, of course, Theo and the rest of the former Paragon. Astrea had been dreading speaking with him all week, but Jin was with her, and they had Eliana's offer tucked away in the folder clasped in Jin's hand.

Astrea smoothed the front of her gown. It was a beautiful dress made of shimmering blue fabric that flowed around her legs like water. Jin was in a three-piece black suit. He'd complained about it the whole time he'd gotten dressed, but Astrea thought he looked good.

The whole fortnight had been strange, living in Jin's old rooms. The rooms she'd once visited him in when they were children, the rooms where he'd taken care of her after that fateful Solstice Night attack, the ones where they'd shared a bed for the first time and finally gotten over their past. None of it had seemed quite real. It was as if the last two weeks had been a hazy dream.

The main atrium of the palace was quiet except for the coalition forces standing guard. It would be some time before they all left. For peacekeeping purposes, Eliana said. To deter anyone who was keen on starting more conflict, which was especially important with the foreign governments in attendance for the ceremony later that afternoon.

"I asked Lucian to bring Theo to the smaller dining room," Jin said. "Figured that was as private as we'd get here."

"Sure," Astrea said. She hadn't really been paying attention to where they were going. These halls were both foreign and familiar, but they didn't seem as large as they used to.

They went down a few more corridors until Jin finally stopped at a closed door. Marko stood guard outside, looking entirely bored.

"You look nice, Marko," Astrea said. And he did. She'd thought he might end up wearing a Novarian uniform, but he was in a gray suit similar to Jin's. It matched his eyes. Even his wavy blond locks were pulled half up and secured into a bun.

"Not exactly how I prefer to spend my days," he drawled, but the smallest smile tugged at his lips.

"Me either," Jin said. "It'll be over soon."

"Thank the skies for that." Marko tilted his head toward the door. "Theo's inside. It's been quiet."

Jin turned the golden knob. The door clicked open, and Astrea followed him inside.

She couldn't remember the last time she'd ever been in this room, maybe at some point when she was young. The crimson wallpaper was emblazoned with small gold scallops, and the sturdy table in the center of the room could seat just twelve. The rest of the room was filled with the usual trappings, from gold-framed paintings of long-dead Aurises to expensive furniture and rugs.

"I always hated this room," Jin said as he closed the door behind Astrea.

"Your father never was one for subtlety," Theo said. His brown and gray suit matched his hair. A forest green pocket square was the only color in his outfit. "Why'd you want to see me?" he asked.

"This." Jin held up the folder. "My sister's offer to all former members of the Paragon, barring the ones who directly fought for Nazarov."

"I can't imagine there are many of those left," Theo said, pressing his lips together as Jin set the folder down on the table.

Most of the Zaikudi and Paragonian forces who had helped attack Kalama had died that day. Not all, but many. Those who had survived had been arrested to await trial. Eliana was unwilling to extradite them to Zaikud, and she had the backing of the other leaders on that.

Astrea wasn't really all that worried about the Zaikudi. No, she was worried about the Paragon who had followed Nazarov into battle. There were surely others out there who *would* have followed him.

"No, but we'll find the ones who are left," Jin said.

"With any luck, Victor's death will destabilize any movement they try to resurrect," Theo said.

Knowing with full certainty that no Paragon would ever come back to demand Astrea's leadership or downfall would have been nice. But there was no way she could ever guarantee that. No way any of them could guarantee Nazarov's destructive tendencies were gone forever. Many people in the world, Paragon or not, would harbor such ideals.

But there were plenty of former Paragon members who had never been keen on Nazarov's leadership, ones who no longer wanted to hide who they were and the magic they had.

"It's all outlined in there," Jin said, gesturing to the folder. Theo finally reached for it. "The aid the Helosian government can pledge to anyone willing to sign the treaty. Help with housing, schooling, integration. There are options for farmland if they want to live out where it's quieter."

"That's very generous," Theo said as he looked over the paperwork. "Especially considering how everything ended."

"We couldn't have done it without their help," Astrea said. All the aetherium in the capital had been destroyed, and the coalition forces were already working on plans to deploy Lifestealers and soldiers alike to find and destroy more aetherium. "Eliana wants to thank them for that."

"Yes, well." Theo offered them both a genuine smile. Warm pride and gratitude radiated off him. "I know I haven't exactly been the best to either of you, but thank you. Truly. I can't believe I ever thought to go along with Victor, all because I didn't like the ways of the world. I have much to atone for."

"You do," Jin said. "But if your recent actions have revealed anything, it's that you're on the right path." When he offered his hand to Theo for a shake, the antiquities dealer took it.

"I'll do my very best to continue what we've already started," Theo said, turning to Astrea, "especially as it relates to your . . . leadership, or lack thereof."

"Let me know how we can help," Astrea said, meaning it. There had been progress these last couple of months, especially among the void mages Astrea had worked with directly. She'd seen the shift in their behavior, their body language. Someday, they would stop seeing her as the moon, Jin as the sun. Someday soon.

"I will." Theo smiled again. "Well, I suppose I should go find my seat, then I'll start shopping Eliana's offer around."

"Expect one from Grand Duke Veiko and President Sikori soon," Jin said. "I spoke with them yesterday. They're both open to offering similar aid and just need to draw up the specifics."

Theo inclined his head, then scooted past them both and exited the dining room.

Astrea deflated. "Do you think this will actually work?" she asked.

"The aid? Yes," Jin said. "For most of them, anyway. It's a fresh start, an option to build the lives they want after being denied so much for so long."

Astrea stared at the dining room door, the path Theo had taken. Indeed, a fresh start. It sounded like the thing they all needed.

Eliana had opted to have the ceremony outside the palace, in the late afternoon sun to transition right into the customary banquet after.

Astrea hated standing in front of a crowd. But Eliana had insisted. All of them who had been so deeply tied to recent events were to be there with her in that moment. The only exceptions were Lucian, Marko, and Rami, as none of them thought the optics would be great when tensions were still high among certain sections of the population. Noemi had also begged Eliana not to make her stand with the group, and Eliana had agreed to let her sit with Marko. They were in the front row a few seats down from Apelo, Thana, and their daughters.

Eliana was not yet on the veranda overlooking the back gardens. Zephyrine stepped up to the edge and cleared her throat into the microphone. The crowd—a group of nearly two hundred coalition officials, Helosian aristocrats, and Kalamian businesspeople and journalists—hushed.

"Thank you for joining us today," Zephyrine said, "and on such short notice. Please, stand for your new empress."

The crowd pushed out of their seats. Anticipation was thick in the air, making it almost humid despite it being a mild winter day.

Two guards pulled the veranda doors open, and Eliana stepped out. Her gown shimmered in the late afternoon sun, a sunset in itself. The golden bodice bled into yellow, then orange, then crimson fabric, Helosia personified. Her dark waves had been styled perfectly, and no crown sat atop her head.

No, Zephyrine would be crowning Eliana. Nicos, off to one side, had the tiara ready. He was still as stone, but every color imaginable swirled around him. Purple reverence, pink love, crimson pride, and myriad others.

Eliana stepped up to the microphone and smiled at the crowd. "My fellow leaders and dear citizens," she began, voice steady and clear. "Today, I stand before you filled with both humility and resolve. Humility, for the weight of responsibility and collective recovery now rests upon my shoulders, and resolve, for the unwavering determination to lead our beloved Helosia toward a brighter future.

"In recent years, our nation has endured unimaginable hardship. We have witnessed the horrors of war and the introduction of aetherium. We have lost loved ones and grappled with the consequences of tyranny and conquest."

It was so silent Astrea wasn't sure anyone was breathing.

"My heart grieves," Eliana said, "for every family torn apart by not just these conflicts but the ones perpetrated by my father and his fathers before him. My brother planned to follow in their footsteps. I stand before you today not as a conqueror. I hope you can see me not as another Auris but as a beacon of change.

"My father and brother ruled with an iron fist, driven by misguided visions of power and dominance, values that were passed down by our forefathers. My father's reign in particular was marked by his relentless pursuit of expansion. I will not stand before you today and pretend Helosia does not have a troubled and bloody past. We cannot ignore that harsh truth.

"I always did my best to stand against their tyranny, but when I realized I couldn't make change within the system my father created, I knew I had to try something else," she said. "From the bottom of my heart, I wish none of these terrible things had come to pass. I never wanted to become your leader through war. I wish we could have made a difference without resorting to violence at all."

Eliana lifted her chin. "But I refuse to let all of this suffering be in vain. Let us honor the fallen by forging a new path. No longer shall Helosia measure its strength by the wars we win. Instead, let us measure it by the compassion we show, the justice we uphold, and the opportunities we create for everyone within our borders.

"The scars of war run deep within our people, but let them serve as a reminder of our resilience and our capacity for healing. Together, we shall rebuild what has been broken and emerge stronger, better. The road ahead will be fraught with challenges, but I am confident that together, we will overcome. Let us unite to build a better Helosia, not only for ourselves but for generations to come."

The gardens erupted into applause, teal approval and crimson pride exploding above the crowd and obscuring the sunset. The shock of it made Astrea take half a step back. Jin's arm circled her waist.

"Ellie sure knows how to give a speech," Jin whispered in her ear.

Astrea nodded. She'd heard Eliana's speeches before, often at parties or other social events, but those were always polite and professional, not about plans for the future.

Zephyrine stepped forward, calling on Eliana to kneel and Nicos to bring the tiara forward. It was an ornate golden crown, slim in profile but studded with diamonds and rubies. It was beautiful and perfect for this moment.

The crowd continued their cheering and applause as Zephyrine set the tiara among Eliana's dark hair. With Nicos's help, Eliana straightened.

"Long live Empress Eliana Auris!" Zephyrine shouted above the noise.

"Long live the empress!" the crowd called back. "Long live Helosia!"

There was one thing Astrea knew with absolute certainty: Kalamians knew how to throw a party.

It just wasn't her kind of party.

After Eliana's coronation, she'd taken time to give interviews with the journalists, then posed for photographs with the other continental leaders; she'd even roped Apelo and Jin into it. Astrea had, luckily, managed to avoid all that. But she couldn't very well skip Eliana's coronation banquet.

The sun had long set, and the festivities were now in full swing. There was music, dancing, and so much food. Eliana had sent food all over Helosia for the occasion, for towns and villages to celebrate with them. Down in Kalama, amid the repairs and rebuilding, the city was celebrating, too. Many of them, anyway.

"Hey, Az." Cressida plopped down in the empty seat next to Astrea at the nearly empty table. "How you holding up?"

"Oh, you know." Astrea waved vaguely at the populated gardens and the people enjoying the festivities. "It's better than that night you two dragged me to the club after work."

Cressida laughed. "You should be thanking us. You met your husband that night."

"And my worst enemy," Astrea added, though the words lacked any edge. "Besides, I already knew Jin."

"Yeah, but you didn't *know* him," Cressida said, bumping Astrea with her metal forearm. "Where is he, anyway?"

"Ellie wanted to talk to him before the night ended."

"Ah, back to business already?"

"You know her," Astrea said. "Always working."

"We'll get her to relax someday."

Astrea smirked. "Someday."

Comfortable silence settled between them as they watched the party continue on, the way Lennor and Noemi danced and Adi tried to pull Marko out onto the dance floor with them. Even Lucian and Rami had stuck around, though Astrea thought she had seen them sneak off a while before. She certainly wasn't going to go looking for them.

"Did your parents leave?" Astrea asked.

"Oh, yeah, they told me to tell you to visit them later this week for breakfast. Dad's promised to make cinnamon pancakes."

"I'd like that," Astrea said. "But I'll have to check my schedule."

"Your schedule?" Cressida asked with an incredulous laugh. "What could possibly be on your schedule?"

"Oh, this and that." Really, now that Astrea was mostly feeling back to her full strength, she wanted to talk to Eliana about setting up permanent healing stations—or maybe some kind of mobile healing service—around the city not just for those injured in all the recent fighting but all the people who had never been able to afford healing treatments in the past. But that would have to wait until morning. "Did you ever decide what you want to do?"

"What?" Cressida asked, pulling her attention from where Lennor was trying to dance amid a fit of giggles. "Decide what?"

"What you want to do now that we're home," Astrea said. "You weren't so sure about going back to Lodestar."

A sly smile pulled at Cressida's mouth. "I might've found the perfect spot for my bakery."

"Already? When did you have time to look?"

"It needs a lot of repairs, was hit pretty bad during the attacks," Cressida said. "It's right on the border of Nobleman's Hill and the Market District."

"Always a good spot," Astrea said.

"I told my parents I want to cut back at Lodestar and really look into this, and—"

"Let me guess," Astrea said, "they supported you, as I said they would."

"You're no fun when you gloat," Cressida retorted, but peach amusement swirled around her. Astrea laughed. With a heavy sigh, Cressida lifted her wine glass. "To new beginnings," she said. "And to best friends always being right."

Astrea lifted her glass, too, and clinked it against Cressida's. "To new beginnings," she echoed. Now she just had to figure out what hers was.

CHAPTER 62

Despite Astrea's erratic pulse and dreams of Kalama on fire lingering in her mind, waking up in Jin's arms was the best feeling in the world. She rolled over, burying her face in his bare chest and breathing in the smell of eucalyptus. She loved that smell. It was real, familiar, true.

"Morning," Jin said, voice raspy. One hand rubbed a large circle on her back.

They'd stayed up late the night before, well past the second morning bell. Kalamians—and Eliana—really loved to celebrate. Astrea normally would've been in bed much earlier, but her best friend would only be coronated once, right?

No morning light filtered through the curtains yet. Astrea didn't bother trying to look at the clock. It was still early, probably near sunrise.

"Can we go for a walk?" Astrea asked.

Groaning, Jin circled his arms tighter around her. He rolled over, pulling her back against him. "It's so early."

"I know, but I told Sarsali and Balthazar we'd be over for breakfast. They invited us."

That was actually *not* what Astrea had told Cressida, and she certainly hadn't told Sarsali and Balthazar that, but it seemed like a good morning to start a new tradition. Family breakfast, even if Saros couldn't be there to join them. He would want them to go and spend time together.

"And they're going to be making breakfast *now*?" Jin asked as he pressed a kiss to Astrea's jaw. He moved to the delicate skin of her throat.

"Stop," Astrea said, giggling and pushing off him. "You're going to make it very hard to leave this bed."

Sunshine love warmed Astrea's face, and Jin's amusement tickled the end of her nose. "That's the plan," he said, going in for another kiss. "Keep you here for the next few hours, and—"

"As much as that sounds perfect," she said, peering down at him, "I really need to get some fresh air." Those dreams still danced around the back of her mind, as they did almost every morning. "Please?"

"You never have to say please with me," Jin said softly, all that playfulness gone. "Let's get dressed."

They climbed out of bed, then got cleaned up for the day. It was a cool morning; winters in Kalama weren't terribly cold, but they still warranted an extra layer or two. Astrea put on a pleated midnight blue skirt, then grabbed her black sweater. She braided her hair, securing it with a bit of lavender ribbon, and slid on her wedding and engagement rings. Jin was just as casual, in black slacks and a black sweater of his own.

Together, they slipped out into the wide, quiet hallway. Only a few guards were around. Eliana's door down the hall was closed; she was still sleeping in her old rooms, the ones she'd grown up in. She'd said she couldn't bear the thought of moving into her father's apartment, and Astrea didn't blame her for that.

Outside, the sky was a mix of cotton candy pink, peach, and blue so deep it bordered on black. A smattering of stars still twinkled directly above their heads.

Hand in hand, they walked through the gardens. Astrea breathed in the morning sea air, letting the familiar cool saltiness clear her lungs and her mind.

Jin didn't ask her about it, just as he didn't ask her about it the other mornings they took these walks. The look in his eyes and the teal that sometimes flashed around him said it all. He understood, was haunted by the same things she was.

As they neared the eastern side of the palace, Astrea tugged on his hand and pulled him to a stop. "Let's turn around," she said.

Jin glanced back at her, then ahead again, toward the trees and the observatory tower peeking over the top. "Any reason you always want to turn back here?"

Astrea pressed her lips together and fidgeted with one of the pleats in her skirt. "I can't go back there."

"Can't or won't?"

"I *want* to. I really want to. But I'm scared of what I'll find."

"I'll go with you," he said. "We'll just walk up to it. We don't even have to go inside."

"Fine," Astrea said, reluctant but buzzing with energy. She'd wanted to come here so many times in the last fortnight, but there'd been so many good excuses to avoid it, excuses that had nothing to do with the pain threatening to bury her.

They walked familiar pathways—three rights, two lefts, and another right—to get through the maze and to the path that would take them to the observatory.

"Do you remember that night," Astrea asked as they walked, "when you drove a car back here to take me to break into Mattina's house?"

"Why are you thinking of that?" he asked with a laugh.

"I still don't think you were supposed to drive back here."

A deep laugh rumbled in Jin's chest. "There's no rule against it, I swear."

"Still."

His thumb drew circles on the back of her hand as they got closer and closer to the observatory. Astrea's heart thumped faster until it threatened to explode.

There it was, the place where she'd grown up. The place she'd called home for so many years, the life she'd built with Saros. It was all Astrea could do not to burst into tears the moment its weathered gray bricks and domed roof came into view.

Yes, she'd seen it on that terrible day when they'd managed to kill Nazarov, but this was . . . well, it was different.

She didn't know how long they stood there, staring at it. Jin didn't rush her. He never did.

Astrea squared her shoulders. "I want to go in."

"You're sure?" Jin asked. "I meant what I said. That we don't have to."

"I know. But . . ." She shook her head. "I want a fresh start. A new beginning. I need to see it again. Let it go."

"You don't have to let this go, Az. This was your home. Yours and Saros's."

Swallowing thickly, Astrea said, "I know."

They tried the front door, and it was unlocked. Saros probably hadn't had time to lock it up after he ran away with Jin and Adi that day months ago. The ground floor was dusty, and the stairs seemed to be in fine shape. The apartment door was ajar.

Inside was not the cozy and comforting space Astrea once knew. It had been ransacked. Her heart sank, but this shouldn't have been unexpected. After all, Emperor Aelius would've ordered the whole tower searched when he realized Saros had run away.

"We should've had someone clean it up," Jin said, his hand settling on her shoulder and squeezing once. "I'm sorry."

"No," she said. "No, it's fine."

It wasn't *that* bad. Just drawers turned inside out, books taken off shelves, pictures removed from the walls. It was the messy truth of what this place was, her and Saros's hiding spot for so long. Someplace they probably never should've been, but Astrea was grateful for all the memories nonetheless.

Jin followed her from room to room, helping her pick up the worst of the chaos. They tidied up old papers, reshelved books, and collected the picture frames on the kitchen table. It wasn't perfect, but it looked a little more like the home she'd once known.

The last room she had to venture into was her own. The floorboards creaked underneath her brogues as she walked down the hall and pushed the door open. It was surprisingly unscathed compared to the rest of the apartment. The drawers on her bedside table had been emptied, and her wardrobe had been sifted through, but there hadn't been many places to hide much in the small room.

Astrea ignored the mess. She crossed the space over to the window and opened it, welcoming the sound of waves crashing against the shore far below.

"I used to sit here and watch the moon and stars," Astrea said as Jin joined her. "I always dreamed of all the places in the world I hadn't gotten to see, of places where I didn't have to hide who I was. Saros never really entertained the ideas."

"Until last summer, when he wanted you to leave."

Astrea nodded. "Until last summer."

"Well," Jin said with a sigh, "now you've seen most of Novaria, more of Helosia, even Katavena and Thasia. Where else do you want to go?"

She turned away from the dawn sky. "Why?"

"Remember? We're supposed to take that vacation," he said, smiling. "And we never even got to have a proper honeymoon."

"There's still so much to do here. Ellie needs our help."

"I know," he said. "I don't mean we have to leave tomorrow. But I'm serious. We should go. I think we've earned it."

"I suppose we have."

"So what's one of the places you always dreamed of visiting?"

Astrea gazed out at the morning light, admiring the way its soft rays lit up Tinale Bay far below and chased away the night's shadows. "I don't think I really care where we go, as long as I go with you."

He slid one arm around her waist. She pushed up on her toes to kiss him. It was delicate, chaste, gentle. Jin's ever-present sunshine settled deep within her bones.

"Then let's figure it out," he whispered. "Together."

"Together," she echoed. "Our new beginning."

"Our new beginning," he said, smiling down at her. "I love you, Astrea Sovna."

"I love you, Varojin Auris."

As they stared out at Tinale Bay, Astrea knew they would figure it out together, just as they always had. This was it, what they had fought so hard for. Their new beginning. And she couldn't wait to see where it would take them.

The End

Epilogue

Six Years Later

There was a certain peace that came with the chaos of Astrea's family, with their colorful emotions and loud laughs. Now, if she could just bring a little order to her house, it would be the perfect day.

"Jin's almost ready, I'm sure of it," Astrea said, mostly to Sarsali.

The Nikaphoroses had arrived a half hour before to help set up the party. Cressida and Lennor were busy arranging cookies and tarts onto trays, Balthazar was trying to corral the rest of the family to get the back garden set up, and Sarsali was overseeing even the smallest details around the house.

"Then shoo!" Sarsali exclaimed, swatting Astrea's backside with a green and white striped kitchen towel.

"Hey!" Astrea cried, laughing as sweet amusement filled her mouth. "I don't think you get to kick me out when this is my kitchen."

"It's *my* kitchen today!" Cressida called over her shoulder.

"I hardly think Lodestar Bakery owns my house, Cress."

"Oh, just get out of here!"

Smiling despite herself, Astrea stopped fiddling with the vase of flowers Sarsali had given her and headed out into the hall. She wanted this day to be perfect, but she had to let Sarsali do her work. Sarsali knew how to put on a party, and she might've wanted it to be even more perfect than Astrea did.

Balthazar was ushering everyone else outside and into the early summer sunshine. The parlor and dining room were both empty now, and Adi's loud laugh grew distant and muffled. Astrea shook her head. There was nothing else for her to do except find Jin.

She took her time as she passed through the foyer. The stairs creaked under her feet, but Astrea didn't mind. She loved this home she and Jin had made, with its spacious layout and cozy bedrooms, its green and blue wallpapers and family pictures hanging on the wall. As she headed down the upstairs hallway, she straightened one particular portrait, a photo of their wedding day that included Saros. Her heart ached, but she knew he'd be so happy for them now.

"Jin?" Astrea called as she approached the room at the end of the hall. The door was cracked open.

The happiest giggle bounced off the walls, and Astrea couldn't help but laugh. She loved that sound.

"Are they ready?" Jin asked as she pushed the door open.

He had Penelope perched on his hip. She let out a delighted squeal and reached for Astrea. "Mama!"

Jin had been in charge of getting Penelope ready for her first birthday party. Eliana had sent over a delicate pink dress for Penelope to wear; the bottom hem was embroidered with white and purple flowers. It was possibly the cutest thing Astrea had ever seen, although she also thought just about everything Penelope did or wore was adorable.

"My sweet girl!" Taking their daughter, Astrea smoothed back some of Penelope's chestnut brown curls.

Penelope huffed and dropped her head to Astrea's shoulder. Warm excitement radiated off her, and Astrea hugged her a bit tighter.

Jin smiled warily. "I'm worried about her missing her nap."

"We'll let her sleep if she gets tired."

"*We* will," Jin said. "Will Sarsali? Or Adi?"

At the mention of her grandmother and uncle, Penelope perked up again. Her silver eyes widened.

"You want to go see your guests?" Jin asked her, and she babbled in return.

Taking that as an affirmative, Astrea started back toward the first floor. It hadn't been an easy road after the war ended six years earlier. Eliana had managed to calm most of Helosia's unrest within the first year, and things were even better now, but the reality of void magic still had civilians and governments on edge. There was always the possibility that someone would discover new aetherium deposits or that the Paragon would restructure themselves and start anew.

And yet, as Jin's hand brushed the small of Astrea's back and Penelope snuggled into her embrace, all those concerns faded away until they were just a distant memory. Astrea had never been so happy.

The last six years had brought so much change. Astrea and Jin had gotten to travel for fun. They'd bought this townhome in Nobleman's Hill, right down the street from where Sarsali and Balthazar still lived. Jin served as one of Eliana's advisors alongside Zephyrine, and Astrea split her time between helping Cressida at her bakery and volunteering at healing clinics in the city.

Besides opening Lodestar Bakery, Cressida and Lennor had gotten married. Though Lennor was still learning her way around the kitchen, she was a savvy manager. Eliana and Nicos had gotten married a year after she ascended the throne, and they were now expecting their first baby—of many, Eliana promised.

Marko had moved to Kalama the first chance he got, and he and Adi had already been married for four years. They'd even started working as mage trainers and hired Civan on to help. He was happy unpartnered and loved his new job.

They weren't the only ones making changes. Noemi had been working with Raela at the Great Library for years now, and though she swore at least once a month she'd leave if Raela didn't get more organized, Astrea saw the gleam in Noemi's eye every time she visited her old workplace. As for Lucian and Rami, Astrea never quite knew where they stood with each other. But they visited Kalama often, and it was clear they loved each other as much as they irritated each other.

They'd all lost things in the war, and they would always feel that pain. But Astrea loved how life had turned out. Even with the difficulties motherhood brought, she wouldn't trade it for the world. She loved her family—each and every one of the bunch—more than anything. And they all loved Penelope, the newest member.

"My Poppy!" Sarsali exclaimed as soon as they neared the kitchen. "Where's my Poppy?"

Penelope let out a series of squawks and babbles, her excitement and joy electric on Astrea's skin. As soon as Sarsali poked her head out into the hall, Penelope flailed her chubby little arms. All Astrea could do was laugh and pass her off. Sarsali adored being a grandmother and often strongarmed Astrea and Jin into letting her babysit for no reason other than to spend time with Penelope.

"My Poppy on her birthday!" Sarsali cooed.

"Hey!" Adi's voice came from the kitchen. "You don't get to hog her all day!"

Jin chuckled and rubbed Astrea's shoulders. "You do realize that's *our* daughter you two are fighting over, right?" he asked as Adi strolled out of the kitchen.

"And I'm her favorite uncle, right, Pops?" Adi asked. Penelope grinned up at him. "See?"

As they moved into the kitchen, Sarsali brought Penelope over to the counter to look at the pink flowers she'd finished arranging. Penelope reached out and touched one of them, heeding Sarsali's warning to be gentle.

"What'll you do if you're *not* her favorite uncle anymore, Adi?" Cressida asked. She opened the only white pastry box left on the kitchen island, unveiling a small three-tier cake decorated with red and pink frosting flowers. Poppies, specifically. "You want this outside, Az?"

"I think your dad set up a table for everything on the porch," Astrea said, starting for the window to check. Everyone was lounging around in the garden, regaled by whatever story Balthazar was telling them. "I think—"

"It's all set, sweetheart," Sarsali said. "You need to relax. Jin, make her relax."

"I just want everyone to have a nice time, especially since Lucian and Rami traveled—" Astrea tried, but Sarsali clicked her tongue.

"I told you we'd take care of it all," she said.

"I'll take the cake," Adi offered. As he waited for Cressida to set the cake on a glass stand, he leaned across the island and said, "And I'll have you know, Cress, that there's no way I'm *not* Poppy's favorite uncle. Wait until you see all the presents I got her."

"Adi," Jin warned. "We talked about this."

He frowned. "She only turns one once. Surely you can let me spoil her this one day."

"You say that all the time," Jin said. "She only does this or that for the first time *once*. You can't use that excuse forever!"

"Sure I can." Adi grinned, making his cheek dimple. "And Marko's not going to stop me, so get used to it."

Jin rolled his eyes.

"Enough talk," Sarsali said. "Let's bring you out to see Grandpa, Poppy. Do you want to go see him?"

Penelope was all smiles and giggles as they headed outside. Everyone was there, all smiles, too, as they cheered for the birthday girl. Balthazar made a big show of scooping Penelope out of Sarsali's arms, and nobody could agree on who got to hold her next. They eventually laid several large blankets in a shady area of grass so that Penelope could play with some of her new toys. Her favorite was a stuffed orange cat Civan had gifted her, and she made a game of throwing it and making Civan chase it down for her. Astrea wasn't sure she'd ever seen Penelope—or Civan—laugh so hard.

This was Penelope's first birthday, yes, but it was also the first time all of them had gotten together like this in months. Having everyone in one place meant so much to Astrea after all they'd been through together.

They spent the next few hours catching up, from Noemi's latest restoration project in special collections at the library to Astrea and Eliana's healing clinic project in the city to one of Adi and Civan's more troublesome magic students. They talked about Nicos and Eliana's impending foray into parenthood, Marko's attempts to get Cressida to offer more coffee blends at her bakery, and Sarsali's new gardening work. They even got Lucian to loosen up and have a drink, which Rami claimed he desperately needed.

And even when they had to move the party inside thanks to a late afternoon thunderstorm, Astrea didn't mind. In fact, Eliana had needed it, because as soon as she plopped onto the sofa in the parlor, she'd fallen asleep. Astrea didn't miss the fatigue that came with growing a child, but she was glad Eliana had a soft place to land.

By the time the seventh evening bell rolled around, their friends packed up their things and left for the night, promising to all get together again the next day before Lucian and Rami had to travel home. The Nikaphoroses stayed behind to help Astrea clean up while Jin got Penelope ready for bed.

Once they were gone, Astrea wearily climbed the stairs to the second floor. The hallway was dark, and only a low light came from Penelope's room. Astrea cracked the door open and found Jin rocking Penelope in his arms as he stared out the window.

"Is she asleep?" Astrea whispered as she joined them and set a hand on Jin's shoulder.

He glanced down at her, his smile both bright and gentle. Astrea knew that look. He'd worn it often since Penelope was born.

He was at peace, too.

Fatherhood suited him. He'd settled into it with more ease than Astrea could've imagined, and he doted on Penelope. The slower routines they had now as a family of three, days spent playing with Penelope in their garden or taking her to visit the Nikaphoroses. Days spent lazing around in the house while she napped, or even nights just the two of them when Sarsali practically forced them to let her babysit. Sometimes, Astrea would come home to find Jin and Penelope taking a nap together, or him reading stories to her, or cooking something new for her to try now that she'd started eating solids. He loved being a father, and Astrea loved watching him and their daughter.

"Bathed, changed, and asleep," he said, then moved to set her in her crib. He smoothed back some of her unruly curls and smiled again. "*Finally* asleep."

Jin turned off the lamp, took Astrea's hand in his, and led her down the hall to their bedroom. He helped her out of her dress, and only after they both showered off the long day did they climb into bed.

"It's a little early for this, don't you think?" Astrea half asked, half teased as they settled in. "You used to stay up far later than this."

"Chasing babies—and Adi—around all day wears a man out," Jin said.

"Do you miss it?" Astrea asked. "When it was just the two of us."

"Sometimes," he said. "And yet I can barely remember when it wasn't the three of us. It feels like she's always been with us somehow."

Astrea smiled up at him. She knew that feeling well. "Do you think everyone had fun today?"

"I'm sure of it. They love our girl."

"And she loves them."

Jin kissed the top of Astrea's head. "That she does. I'm glad she has such a big family to love her. Makes me worry a little less."

"Me too," Astrea whispered.

Life was fragile, but love built resilience. She knew, without a shadow of a doubt, that Penelope would grow up loved and able to overcome anything the stars might throw her way. Astrea and Jin would make sure of it, and so would her grandparents and all of her aunts and uncles.

"Thank you for giving us Poppy," Jin said.

"Well," she said wryly, "you played your role, too."

He laughed, warm and deep. "Smart-ass."

"You like it."

"I love it," he said. "I love you, always."

"Always," Astrea whispered, letting Jin's sunshine warmth and steady peace wash over her for the millionth time that day. With him, and with her family, she was sure that feeling would never end.

Books by H.E. Bauman

<u>The Darkened Skies Series</u>

Forged by Flames: A Darkened Skies Prequel

Under Darkened Skies: Darkened Skies Book One

Into Whispering Shadows: Darkened Skies Book Two

Amid Twisted Chaos: Darkened Skies Book Three

Beyond Veiled Destinies: Darkened Skies Book Four

Toward Dawning Light: Darkened Skies Book Five

ACKNOWLEDGMENTS

I can't believe this series is complete. I started dreaming it up in 2018, the first year Astrea Sovna showed up in my imagination. Six years these characters have been with me, and now their journey is complete. I'm happy to report, though, that my journey as an author is just beginning.

To my team—Sarah, Kayla, Michelle, Laura, and Jeanine—these books would not be where they are without your input, feedback, advice, and support. Seriously, it takes a village to get a book out there, and I'm so grateful you had my back.

To my husband, thank you for always cheering me on as I wrote this series, even when it meant long nights, early mornings, and many Sunday afternoons of me locked in my office. You believe in me even when I don't believe in myself, and you're just the best.

To my family and friends, thank you for everything as I've worked on these books. Buying copies, telling friends, and even not forcing me to talk about my books, because yes, I'm still so strangely shy about it!

To Hayley, at the risk of sounding so repetitive in this acknowledgments section, thank you for going from total internet stranger to one of my biggest supporters and best friends. I'm so glad we get to do this author thing together!

To my street team, thank you for not your your enthusiasm but your help in getting the word out about the Darkened Skies series. Your work for the author community doesn't go unnoticed, and I hope you know how much we all appreciate your effort!

And finally, to all my readers, thank you for finishing this journey with me, Astrea, and the whole Darkened Skies crew. Saying goodbye is never easy, but the love you've shown these characters makes it a little easier. I'll have new stories and new worlds for you soon.

About Author

H.E. Bauman is a fantasy author fascinated with all things magical. After spending her childhood writing stories, she went on to receive her bachelor's in English and has continued writing ever since. When she's not reading or writing, she enjoys playing tennis, immersing herself in video games, and spending time with her family.

If you want to get in touch, visit H.E.'s website or follow her on social media.